I AM NO ONE

To McKayla —

ENJOY RESPONSIBLY &
WITH LOVE,

[signature]

also by Benjamin Font

AT THE BOTTOM OF THE ORCHARD:
AN ILLUSTRATED FABLE

Screenplays
SEX/ABSURD (loosely based on the novella)

I AM NO ONE

OR

A Real-Time Portrait of the Life and Premature Death of the Artist's Career
as a Young Man due to Much Drinking, Absurd Romantic Notions, and an
Inability to Navigate the Modern Digital World

A COLLECTION BY

BENJAMIN FONT

Poor House, The
Los Angeles

Many portions of this book have previously been published as separate works, including limited handmade runs of *In Full Bloom* (125 Copies), *I Am No One* (100 Copies), and the Upper-Side of *The Good Life of A Holy Idiot* under the alternate title, "The Holy Idiot Visions" (40 Copies). The others were extraordinarily unsuccessful on a print on demand website that will not be named. This is the first time *Sons and Daughters of The Earth* and *Too Soon The Sun Sets, Old Man* will see the light of day.

Library of Congress Cataloging-in-Publication Data available upon request

ISBN 978-0-578-14411-5 (pbk.)
ISBN 978-0-578-14412-2 (e.)

Inquiries can be made to
Poor House, The
n/a Beverly Blvd.
Los Angeles, CA
4 2 4 . 2 4 4 . 0 7 4 9
poorhouse.the[at]gmail.com

Or under the Contact link at benjaminfont.com

Many a hand has helped in keeping me alive. To give a name to each of them would fill a book thicker than this one, and printing doesn't come cheap.

If I've done anything right at all, you'll find my love and gratitude rooted within these pages already, for without you they wouldn't exist.

Contents

Introduction

VOLUME I, The First Novel:

VOLUME II, The Shorts:

VOLUME III, The Second Novel:

VOLUME IV, The Epilogue:

Index of Sources

Although each of these books was originally composed separately, as wholly different works, they all share in the natural continuity of *autobiographical fiction*—which is a real thing—and come together here to form one big story that spans over six years.

Don't let that scare you. There's no need to read it all at once, or even from front to back for that matter. It should be read in a similar manner to which you might a tour guide to a strange, yet vaguely familiar destination. When all's said and done you're gonna see the whole goddamn place regardless, only this way you get to choose which parts you visit first.

As the decisions of all good tourists are informed ones, I'd like to give you a point of reference for each section of this collection:

The Good Life of A Holy Idiot – Lower-Side is a disgusting and unfortunate story of a young man with wild aspirations of becoming a *writer*. While visiting his hometown of Lincoln, NE for his mother's birthday, he runs into an alluring old acquaintance that unwittingly inspires him to take up residence there in hopes of developing a romantic relationship. The results are reckless, booze-soaked, and tragic.

In the *Upper-Side*, still suffering from the lingering psychological effects from his experience one year earlier, the same young man finds himself again in love, only now in the town of Monterey, California some fifty odd years after Steinbek's *Cannery Row*. "What remains of Monterey is an abomination, an orgy, a spectacle," with its own unique disgust, but observed with the intent of enjoying its inherent beauty and humor.

The Dogs Come When You're Gone chronicles a young man's awe-filled journey along the interstates of Western America, alone, while speaking aloud from "the dark space behind the brain" to a black and white picture of his Little Woman. By way of an electrical device either in the center console of the car, his shirtfront pocket, or in heaven, his sporadic dictation—"ridiculous, strange, scary, and sometimes just plain dumb"—was recorded in real time, then set down in type with the help of an angel.

Sex/Absurd is a multimedia play in three acts: the first is to be imagined as a play; the second is to be imagined as a movie being viewed in a giant auditorium—the same auditorium in which you have just viewed the play; the third is to be imagined as a living experience in the auditorium itself. The subject matter can be found in the title alone: Sex(i.e., coitus; males); Absurd(ridiculous, illogical).

Songs: I Can't Sing is the book on the back of your toilet or the one in your carry-on; it's the goofy smile that breaks the ice. A collection of poems and short stories that includes additional contributions by my brother, Brandon Font, this was written in the unpretentious spirit of amused observation, meditation, self-degradation, and just trying to get a brother to laugh.

In Full Bloom – a letter, a love story details the mental anguish of a man whom has always been told he looks like a certain celebrity, and the subsequent effects on his behavior and identity. After he inadvertently allows a young woman he's fallen for to believe he really *is* that celebrity, his aching desire, in conjunction with his ample knowledge of *Lolita,* incite him to go on the run. While in hiding, he writes a letter to his famous doppelganger with a desperate and quite unorthodox plea.

Sons and Daughters of The Earth follows the rise and fall of a modern Los Angeles based cult as recounted by its last surviving member from his deathbed, as well as it explores the beliefs and lifestyle that stood firmly at its foundation.

I Am No One – an imaginary memoir, from which this Collection takes its name, is an adventure love story concerning all of the different possible lives I could be leading with all of the women that I have ever met, seen, thought of, or dreamt up. In the various possible futures described, other possible futures continue to be explored through the writing of a book called, "The Imaginaries," whose purpose continually changes depending upon my current romantic situation.

Too Soon The Sun Sets, Old Man, quite frankly, is about being fat and washed up at the ripe old age of 25. It's a farewell to the profession, a resignation letter as a writer. And it's dead serious.

If any seemingly harsh words are to be found anywhere in this text, they should be taken either as casual observation or comic-artistic exaggeration. There is no one whom I wish to harm with the writing of This Book. If anyone is offended, I hope they'll find it in them to forgive me. More accurately though, dear friends and readers, I hope you'll find there's nothing to forgive me for. Should at any given moment you think you might recognize a face, a voice, a quirk, etc.— stop it at once. I'll remind you:

This is a complete work of fiction, I fucking swear.

I AM NO ONE

VOL

THE FIRST NOVEL

UME

I

THE GOOD LIFE OF A HOLY IDIOT
(2008)

For
l.w. and Mima

LOWER-SIDE;

Or, The Young Dead

1. THE SONG OF A BASTARD ANGEL

Once, I believed I was the dream of a king, a ghost, tugging at the reins of ghost horses across a deserted kingdom. I was the bringer of light who preached to The Dead: children of absorbed howling, stars fallen back from the heavens, lunatics wandering aimlessly through drunken crowds—and worse. God was forgotten. His saints were bastardized in rehearsed prayers and dissolved in a generation proclaiming, "Truth!" A generation of ugly, heartbreaking afterthoughts—beat by nothing but nostalgia and pride—which was destined to wash away before it had made any imprints. I was to kiss their dead lips, worn thin by vodka, and taste their absent love tremble away from and to nonexistence. Through my tongue they would know The Word, for there was nothing more my tongue could know.

My sole ambition then was to be a vessel of good. To act as the honey mortar of the Almighty Bricklayer, coating everything in His golden sugar so the starving children of America could feed upon it like hummingbirds, sticking their skinny beaks into the sweet nectar of life and drinking until filled. The Great Partitioner of spiritual rations, stuffing the emaciated souls of the new country with age-old doctrine they had forgotten how to digest. They would clutch their bellies as their entrails burned with It until the beast within them had finally devoured the ache. Then, in the suspended relief of absolution, they would take sight of the far off hills and obediently attempt to climb them. But that time is gone now.

We have settled elsewhere, deep below the calm light of the hillsides in the lowest part of a valley. The dream does not exist here. Only the terrible ghosts of the dream. Not the predictable, other-worldly ghosts that we are used to, but the real, living, breathing, and fucking ghosts of The Dead. The kind of lost figures of nightmares,

15

imagination, and memory.

From somewhere in this hollow arises a specific memory, the first memory, of my once skewed ambition. Papa Emilio had finished painting the house and left some of the dark grey paint from the shutters on the table inside, and in comes the tiny, supposed-Saint, K.B., with big head and googly, idiot-eyes to grab the still-wet paintbrush, just like daddy, to get to work. Finishing a long stroke above an electrical outlet on the white dining room wall, the poor fool is caught by Person Emilio who comes in now screaming at K.B. and forcing tears to well in those same idiot-eyes for a reason unknown to the boy.

The events to follow and those preceding occurred likewise, forming a long succession of good-willed failures and mistakes that begin with birth and the pain of its labor, wherein all saints are broken, or at least consistently break henceforth; the dream gradually evolving into the nightmare, and the ghost slowly being bound in the flesh and the sad way it fucks. With the very first breath itself, still crying and red, attached to dear mother, one must surely recall hearing the welcoming hymn—The Song of a Bastard Angel—in which the subliminal choir sings Damnation and the Christians praise Jesus. All in C Minor. It was that song which guided the doctor's hand to cut the umbilical cord as if it were a bone breaking in revelation at Golgotha—a suppressed orgasm: agony/ecstasy; an infinitesimal blink near sleep; a shudder upon a black sea, black hole. Another cancellation in the Cosmic Void.

Afterwards, yet aware of the grave circumstance that brought me into the world, I was raised under the pretense of "The Good Life" in the capitol city of this country's 37th state, Nebraska. The place where I grew up, was defiled, fucked, lost my innocence, hated, and loved. Where the perpetual swing of our household's temperament eventually uprooted any shred of tradition in our family and molded our imaginations to be an essential element of survival, as it must be everywhere —what martyr could truly bear the excruciating prick of the brass tacks and still be exalted by their suffering?

And we continue, to Nebraska! To the frontline of the dream charge of self-preservation. It was led by my two older brothers, Mitch(the oldest; a stoic, secretive genius) and Aden(a rambunctious, heartfelt life-force), who pressed us through the torrent of discouraging reality with such a perfected hallucination of stability and well-being that we became convinced we were the young stars of two movie dramas playing simultaneously on separate reels. Operating on a grand scale in the ether alongside the innumerable drama/comedy/horrors of humanity, Ours was a classic tale of dichotomy: dysfunction and fairy story. Each dependent upon the others' existence as joy is unsatisfied without sorrow. To some degree the belief still holds strong, though the number of films starred-in has grown exponentially, making it impossible to keep steady track of them in their intricate co-dependencies as the scenes all run together. The only discernable Fact in harboring such a perspective is the development of an affinity for the absurd—cyclists smoking cigarettes, dogs in wetsuits, marsh-mallows roasting indoors at gas fires, dandelion centerpieces at formal dinners. The main course being served is a roasted chicken inside of a duck inside of a turkey shoved into a hog's ass. Nothing could possibly taste better.

The landscape of the thirty-seventh state itself facilitated delusion. It became the liquid reflection of our inherent duality: cornfields were also the ocean, were also the pubic hair of the Seraphim, were also the offerings of a suitor, were also the shit keeping us alive; prairie skies were also the rivers leading to eternity, were also the Alaskan wilderness, were also the thin dress-fabric of the Whore of Babylon. One need only to have his eyes open for a moment in the phantasmagoria of this World, this dream and nightmare, before having to make a decision regarding his sanity, and quick—a moment longer and it may be too late. Write, or go mad. Being terrified of the latter, we are forced into This.

But where to begin in the grand contradiction?

This moment—this, now! Alone at a park in the flats above Monterey, California. My old wool coat laid out in the grass all woebegone beside me. Everything colored with the disillusionment of the young dream passed and the permanence of its broken promise. Peeling an orange with my thumbnail, its skin is as pale as if it were plucked out of a sandbox overflowing with cat shit. The grass and the trees are out of an old black and white photograph, penciled in green years later, Today, by the devil himself over a shadowy undercoat.

From out of these photographic trees, at the far end of the park, comes a flock of birds. We ascend with them. Should we fly North, two hours, maybe less in a straight shot from this height, we would land in San Francisco; South, 30 miles, Big Sur; or, just down the hill, Cannery Row, where Captain Steinbeck's face is in caricature everywhere, haunting the town with its intense curiosity. Past that are the tide pools at Asilomar. It is here that we make our landing.

A dead jellyfish floats like used dryer sheets just below surface against a rock. A little sea snail tugs at the jellyfish, eating his delicate protein bit by tiny bit. Microcosmic America. Certainly more real than in the Economics courses of distant universities where the boys sober up on their Fathers' dollar and make the skinny tramps next to them nauseous with the smell. The lesson, plainly: something has to die for something else to live. But what kind of death is it?

A seabird crawls up on the rocks behind me to spend the last moments of his own peculiar death. His right wing has almost fallen off. It's dangling at his side, limp. To wrap him up in my coat and rush him to the nearest vet could be cataclysmic. Any false move, any interjection, and the menagerie might come crashing down on me as it has before just for breathing in the direction of fate.

Moving up onto the beach, allowing the seabird to die in peace, toward the bench I usually sit on—(I am always sitting, walking, thinking, not-thinking, as if it were my profession to just be)—it's occupied by a mother and her three kids. She kneels in front of the bench digging through a bag for sandwiches. At her side, her littlest one is asking, "where's daddy?" In spite of the tender scene unfolding —you can see Daddy walking toward them, slowly revealing himself from further down the beach with a fourth child, a son—the words stick into me with the sound of Memory.

What I am remembering is the inability to bear the look of the two year old with bright blue eyes that sat beside me in the westbound truck with her mother, Maggie, as she rubbed her swollen eyes and whined, "where's daddy?" A bobble-headed figurine on a dashboard somewhere snaps at the spring neck and the hollow wooden skull cracks as it falls to the floor for a second time. The death is imagined at my feet. She was asking of my father, hers having impregnated her mother while on duty in the war, then disappeared none the wiser. To him she was just a good lay— convenient, at least—and a fine story to tell at a bar or in hell. Right after the one about the Blow job; right before the one about his friend's two fingers getting Blown off(both strangely similar in their sexual violence). But at two years old the girl knows nothing of that. What she knows is to eat, to laugh, to cry, to run, to scream, to sleep, to shit—(that not so well, going for days in a state of constipation, then finally letting out a little baseball of stool)— and how to show affection.

Driving through the majestic, pale landscapes of Wyoming with the tires kicking up yellow chalk-dust and snow, then the Great Salt Lake in Utah, the roadside messages laid out in rock in rural Nevada, and the brilliant mustard giants almost to the California border, she showed affection by rubbing my arm and saying "nice" and touching my face and tugging at my hair, giggling. She would grab my finger, kiss it, then squeal happily. "As long as she's happy," I thought— entertaining her now with a foolish spectacle of the faces and noises an elephant might make, and a frog, a bear, a rabbit, a sea lion, etc.— "anything to hold her attention and keep her spirits on this side of hysteria."

It was important for morale to be upheld because our every last worldly possession was bumping, shaking, and shifting along the interstate, being pulled behind us as a manifestation of the thoughts upsetting Maggie's stomach. They were homeless. To me there was nothing strange about it because I was always comfortably between places on fairy dust and the benevolence of my friends. To them it was new (though ending shortly thereafter). To Emiliana, *the two year old with bright blue eyes*, I should say—my step-sister if you will—everything was New. Everything was a startling discovery of excitement, and some things were discovered more than once with no less excitement. Her memory like an etch-a-sketch in the hands of an addict who draws over one image before the aluminum powder has settled on the last. Who can say which of the drawings were illusory? Or real? Or if it even matters at all?

Later on, I wonder, will she remember the three of us driving across the country toward the place she'll call home here in Monterey? And who will I be to her then? A be-mustached clown and her first great love? She must remember something, but when she recounts the journey—as we are inclined to do so throughout life—will it be in which it was told to her? with only the pauses filled by her own aluminum ash? Invariably, over time, the details are modified, deleted, exaggerated, and made-up, as if recalling them from a dream just woken from, book finished, or drunk worn off, but the effect itself remains indifferent to the flux. Rooted in the brain with such intimacy and importance, these pictures, these stories, however altered, will always arrive at the same indisputable Present Tense.

Back in the park above Monterey. Nighttime. Maggie is down at the house pruning the Christmas tree in the driveway while Emiliana sleeps upstairs with the TV on. Where's daddy? Don't know where your daddy is, but my father is in Hong Kong on business—he'll be back next week and, well, you can have him.

The pencil-colors of the day are washed out by night. The true shade of oil and charcoal is exposed. The demons are all at large. There's one in every doorway. Another is laughing in the winter clouds above Omaha, Nebraska. Since writing this he's killed eight people, and then his host. In the form of a 19 year old boy who just lost his job and broke up with his girlfriend, the demon left a suicide note at the boy's home and walked into a shopping mall with an assault rifle. From the third floor he shot those people down. The last bullet, saved for the boy, went straight into the brain.

It takes no courage to kill yourself in such a way, to give yourself up to the demon and rid yourself of this temporal hell in one easy pull of the trigger. It is nobler to be done over a lifetime, from the inside out, with a smile on your face and tears in your eyes the whole time. My own murder has already begun in this manner. Cause of death:

Specifics Unknown. But there is surely something killing me, a feeling. I am on my way out. Consider this my suicide note. Rather, consider this the beginning of a long letter that will explain my death, written without pretensions, from "the narrowness of my experience," etc, of sound body and mind, from the belly of a whale. Going mad is no longer an option. Thus, as a writer, as all writers must do, one consents to the warm, blubbery living arrangements of blubbering, usually jumping in genitals first with their hands behind their heads.

Looking forward through a periscope shoved out through the blowhole to the end of this letter, far ahead(I'm only in my young twenties yet!), there is nothing left of me to see. I will be dissected, divided, subtracted, pulled apart, scattered, and smeared throughout these pages over time. There will be no mess left behind to clean up. Only the black ink of every "I" will remain like ever-fading stars in the night sky, outlines of a long dead image, struggling to provide what little light they can in the vast darkness of their surroundings to form the varying constellations of a giant crucifix, a burning oak tree, a castrated pup.

Alone, on the way out of nowhere, if you look into this night sky, you will always find me here amongst the stars—once again as the dream, a ghost—with a smile on my face and tears in my eyes. And together in spirit, backward-facing, we will run, run, run...through the place where church organs play continually, slowly, and The Dead are arrested in the spectral flesh of a girl, an illness, a time—the Time of Death itself.

2. WARM MILK AND BRANDY

On the seventeenth day in October, about five years before the world is said to end, the first cold front blew into the Heartland of America as I arrived for my mother's first birthday since the recent divorce and my oncoming sickness took the shape of a girl. It was more a pathetic, Christian death of youth and drunkenness than anything else, but in the middle of that sort of thing, if you believe you've already found God, you search for a different way out—a person, this girl.

Returning to the plains from a small rented room in Rancho, Ca. with an arbitrary sense of grandeur, a bit older, a bit madder, heart heavier, hunger greater—a failure on the brink of another failure—the trees that had taken to their autumn dress now adorned the streets with the top layers of their wind-stripped garments. Magnolia blouses and burgundy stockings were strewn about as in a wife's bedroom that anticipates her husband's homecoming. The chimneys emitted perfume in The Haymarket—the historic district on the west end of downtown Lincoln, Ne. made up of restaurants, cafés and art galleries. We were going out to celebrate Mima's birthday over dinner at a place called Maslow's. It was while coming through the doors out of the cold, standing in the entryway to help Mima out of her coat, that I saw her— Lillian Jean.

She was wearing a dark grey wool skirt hemmed just below the knee with a long-sleeved black cotton shirt, black tights, and black flats. Her hair was cut from the long red-brown that I remembered, pulled into a short dyed-black ponytail at the top of her neck where a thin, silver necklace shone against invaluable white sand before disappearing beneath her shirt. It had been over two and a half years since we had last seen each other at the Arts and Humanities Program we attended, and we were only acquaintances then. All I really knew about her was that she was some kind of artist, or photographer, and now that she was maître d' of the restaurant I was standing in. The details were unclear, seeming to come like oxygen escaping from distressed lungs, bubbling from the bottom of a riverbed to the water's surface in a call for Help as someone or something drowned. I could've sworn it was Lillian calling out. And I was going to save her.

For a Tuesday night the restaurant was especially busy. Another girl was up front helping escort guests to their tables. We followed her to a table in back, and she was pretty enough—a brunette, slender hips moving with a European sort of confident swagger—but her features were only admired from behind for a moment, then were discarded as if she were a lascivious picture torn from the pages of a girly-magazine. My attention was on Lillian Jean. The image of her sticking in my thoughts like a line from a song that's moved you—the only part you can remember. Throughout dinner it was sung incessantly into the music box of my ear. The Irish melody made the blood heavy in my legs so that by time we had finished eating I could hardly stand. I had drunk too much water with dinner and became intoxicated by its purity. My pupils were dilated, the perfume still hung in my nose. I was a painter in perennial 5 o'clock light, a poet after an epiphany—my perceptions were heightened. The world spun on Benzedrine. Each movement was exaggerated in time, and my stride was the metronome to which it was dictated—seconds were marked by the varying depths of my muddy footprints in the riverbank, all leading towards the girl under water.

Dinner rush had let up some in the course of the meal, but there were still a few small groups waiting for a table to open up as we were leaving. The brunette girl must have been given other duties, I thought, or else had slipped away for a short cigarette, because Lillian was left alone with the patrons in the front of the restaurant. Mima waited outside for me—it would be just a minute I told her. Quietly love-drunk, with the exterior calm of one who need be in no hurry to get anywhere at all, content to just loaf about and be alive, I stood behind some aggravated Middle-western sap, listening to him complain to Lillian about the wait and try to get a free drink out of her. My bones vibrated within like tuning forks in tormenting sync with the pitch of her voice as she tried to pacify him. Finally coaxing him into stepping aside while she would see what she could do, the Corn-Johnny moved five feet over to a seat at the bar, displaying his empty glass on the counter, and stared at her as my patience was rewarded.

She said she had recognized me when I came in earlier, but hadn't said anything then because it had been such a long time and, besides, she was busy. We barely caught up: she told me she was a student at the University, but was thinking about taking some time off. She wanted to travel, maybe through Central and South America, she didn't know, but she didn't know why she should be wasting her money on an education that seemed to lack purpose for her either. She wanted more than that, though she couldn't be sure what that was. I told her I had moved away the summer after graduation, began traveling, moving up and down the west coast, and hadn't found anywhere to settle down yet. It was made clear that I was back in town for awhile to spend some time with my mother—still waiting outside—whose birthday it was tonight. Everything else was vague, by habit, not wanting or having the time to discuss the peculiarities of my life, nor to learn those of hers. All the while I felt my feet sinking in the bank completely—the mud reached my calves. Our conversation seemed to reverberate through a subterranean hollow as if heard in an honest to God fever. Something was coming on but the Ol' Johnny was now starting to get irritated again. His glass was still empty and the girl he was with looked bored as hell, which pissed him off more than anything. Lillian had to go act her part before he started yelling. It had been good to see me, as it was to see her. She looked at me once more, I was sure of it, then took off towards the back of the restaurant, out of sight.

The slender brunette, who had been nearby, returned from break with the yellow-smell of nicotine still on her clothes, and came over to fill Lillian's position. She must've been watching me like a prison guard watching an innocent man marked for death, heart filled with compassion, hand reluctantly at the holster, wishing she could only pull the trigger herself. End it now before the brain could create a struggle. There was nothing about the brunette that I could have noticed though, because I was searching for the dramatic, sad-looking piece of paper in my coat pocket, which I found with insane swiftness, and wrote my number on it in frighteningly neat hand. I asked the girl if she could please give it to Lillian, pulled my coat collar higher up my neck, and apologized to Mima outside for making her wait. It had only been a minute longer than I'd said.

Presently, then, my plans changed and I took a walkup studio apartment on the fourth floor of the Sullivan's building, above a vegetarian sandwich shop and a yoga room, overlooking the train depot in the Haymarket—coincidentally, curiously, just a few blocks down the street from Maslow's. At the time I told myself it was to be close to Mima, but with my current recovery, even if not complete, and the obviousness in which hindsight appears, it is impossible to put it down here. There was nothing then that I wouldn't believe in though—the things I thought I saw, and heard.

It was only about five miles south of the apartment, past the cemetery and penitentiary, where my mom and sister, Sydney(the family's true angel; the golden child and saint), due to the divorce, had moved into a smaller home in a middle-class suburban neighborhood. Her home was indistinguishable from any other on the block: tan-beige siding, white trim, a well-kept yard for our dog Bear to play in, an SUV parked in the driveway; her walls hung with impressionistic paintings (bad prints) of dull landscapes, and her shelves filled with framed pictures of her scattered children like still-lives from a yet-classic romance. None of it was tragic, but sentimental. They secluded themselves there, at the house—between there and the church, and Sydney to school—cutting themselves off from the prying community and its vulgar rumors, to cope with their lonesome change; that commonplace turmoil of so many modern households that have drawn their shades across the nation.

Behind the curtains of that nonexistent window I saw a collection plate being passed around church pews, filling with short-changed sympathies and alimony. The plate stopped in front of me. My offering of condolences and helplessness went unnoticed. The plate was passed along—was it to the right? was I in the right?—and I was left with nothing. Unable to see my mother, or my sister, I imagined them there, somewhere near the front, dressed in black with their veils covering their faces as if they were the very drapes of those countless broken homes that hid their true identities behind the gloom. Look, the two portraits developing in the dark room! Temporarily clinging to each other in the blood bath, they are peeled apart in a smear of emulsion, hanging up to dry—my mother, my sister!

The short distance between us was rarely crossed. Enough money was saved from working in the warehouse in California to afford three months rent of near-solitude in my single room, there on the fourth floor. A line should have been held taut from my apartment to my mother's place, stretched along the five miles of grass, concrete, playgrounds, midtown homes and apartments—*past the cemetery and penitentiary*—a tin can and a string, anything; but there was only

23

awkward, stale breath. The line had snapped from both ends before going up, weighed heavily with self-indulgence, or disregard, or fear—a telephone wire breaking at the touch of sagging branches from a great dying tree. The connection was lost and an umbilical cord was cut again. The fall-sky looked to be a womb in the belly of St. Frances' cave, no light, only shadows, bleeding from a crack in every stone, which were all in need of turning.

I could not see my mother, but she was all around me, having furnished the apartment with a few of the pieces that could no longer fit in her new home: a black leather couch and chair in the middle of the room, a rug, a small desk behind the couch, a bed and nightstand tucked into the corner, and a short bookshelf and chair set in the western-facing window. At the sight of it, the touch and smell, an un-convincing thought kept coming over me: "this is enough, this is enough." It may have been what made me sick. To think that my face, my presence just across town, across the world, would not cure her hurt with my petty empathy. I could feel her arms lifting from around me to wipe the mascara tears beneath her veil; I could feel her smile evaporate into a salty quiver; just as I could feel myself moving to the old worn desk against the wall and beginning to write.

I repeated to myself the promise I had made to Mima when I told her, "It's all going to be alright, some day, I'll have a little money and all these silly words here will be bound on shelves in homes and in libraries across America—and I'll buy you a nice house out East, or West—wherever you'd like—and I'll take care of you, really, and neither of us will have anything to worry about." As I told these words over and over to the tiny Mima in my head, my arm around Syd's shoulder, they both looked at me with those tiny in-the-head-eyes, so alive and happy as hell to see me, while the collection plate slowly continued making its rounds. With each diligent new page, my devot-ion was added to the offering; giving immortality to Her tenderness in every word that came from my hand, carving that strange silhouette into each black character scrawled across the pages of my legacy, I wrote blindly, idiotically, perfectly. The child was back again.

3. A SMALL BOAT, A SINKING SHIP

In the mornings, close to noon, waking up to the white-painted bricks of my studio—the blank walls of a mad man's residence that seemed to represent a child's purity—I was unaware of where it was I'd come, only knowing where it was I'd been, and still unsure if it were really me at all.

Heating the skillet atop the stove, burning butter and cracking an egg into the fat for breakfast, I flipped through the old beer and dirt stained notebooks from the westbound trip I made with Aden when leaving for the first time to California; then the mountaintop hideout, the story of the foreign prostitute, the drive up to the northwest, the holidays that followed—the peace, loss, and above all, the hope of each line. Through the poems, prayers, and songs, I revisited the faces, beds, floors, hotels, museums, galleries, bars, depressions, ecstasies, and thought back further still to where, or how, the dream had transpired—the ideal that moved me into the wild, through America and abroad, to seek out its imagined fruition. Was it on the country acreage as a child, naked outside of Lincoln? burning down that awful shed? Was it before my birth? Was it in the hospital as I sat over my high school sweetheart's sickbed? watching the chemotherapy terrorize her body? Or after she was well? Was it the moment my father took his mistress? The obscure conception was forgotten, or suppressed, and only the ending was left, detached, floating lightly through my already light head like a child's lost balloon:

There I am in a small boat, I can see it—sometimes beer-in-hand, sometimes just a fishing rod—staring at the white gurgle sea talk, the whispers, from the beginning of time about the end of time: subdued laughter over drowned sailors, gossip of madmen swimming through its frigid parts, and of fish leaping, the damning consequences of an upset tidal wave, and other things, terrifying things that have lost their edge. The sun starts to go down and leaves in a last brilliant flash of awe, reflected in the water and remembered by the soft surface. My boat is tied up for the night as I make my way back up to the house. The smell of food, the perfume of my wife's angel neck, and the sad joy of my gentle home greet me. My mother arrives, and through the door behind her the voices of children—

Even that vision would pop in a sudden burst of expanding helium and latex, too soon to have seen my children, the face of my wife, the cracked volumes on the shelf. It self-destructed in its own foolishness, its own sobering distance.

Although, later, the dream was reaffirmed in another vision that began in a car driving down a deserted prairie road. Everything dark, everything lonesome. Bumping over a hill, headlights suddenly coming at me, I jerked the wheel and spun the car into a roadside tree. A black spot; a jump in time. Crawling out of the wreck, I found myself amidst a group of hollering men and women. A house of lunatics that saw me and pulled me inside to heal my injuries over drinks. Hours passed, it felt, and everything became a beautiful magic trick; a big, laughing, screaming play about nothing. They led me into a room with a bed in its center—my childhood bed, which should have been back at my mother's. My suspicion grew towards my hosts and I began sweating

25

from all my folds, and joints. Nervous, cold, I lay down against my will and neared sleep. With a single blink a young girl stood over me, cigarette burning in her hand. She knew me for everything that's occurred since birth, and before then, and even those things just thought about in silent afternoons by myself. Her knowledge was invisible when looking at her, but I knew it was there. She was my guardian angel, and she said, with immeasurable compassion, "there is a plan for you." (Not all she said, but the only words necessary to share, and also the sounds that shot through my veins in a startling heat of truth.) It was then that she bent over, her one hand on my forehead, the other behind her back with cigarette still burning, to touch her lips to mine, parting them against me but altogether *for* me.

Gasping into the empty room, there was no one. The cross about my neck—a gift blessed by a priest at Medugorje, where the virgin is said to have visited and signed that the end is near—burned in my palm, clutching it, feeling Her warmth beating out a wonderfully simple Gospel of love and purity in my chest.

Before having that vision, thus renewing my good faith, I was so distraught over how fleeting the dream may be that I became obsessed with the faces of my wife and children, the cracked volumes whose titles evaded me. They were no nearer than the Pacific to the Atlantic, but I knew it was important that they were maintained by the same lunar tides, only touching different coasts. Each decision and event in my life was recalled so that I might ensure a safe arrival in my idyll. My past was dissected with deranged precision only to find my memory in utter clarity. The fever turned its eye on creation, coloring the walls with a chemical storm of those never-quite black, never-quite clearly seen images. Before they were covered over again, the story was copied into a notebook at the speed it revealed itself to me, with the same surgical precision my memory had undergone, in a neatly scripted hand of subtitles.

But who can say which of the stories were real? Or illusory? *Like an etch-a-sketch in the hands of an addict.* It didn't make a difference. The bricks would dry as they would, and, while they did, the story seized the opportunity for a short break.

Taking leave of the apartment on foot, the morning-story fell from my coat like dried mud and each step shook more of the words onto the pavement until they were completely forgotten and freed me upon the afternoon.

First heading over to Maslow's restaurant in my new freedom, I would see if Lilly were working. I hadn't heard from her since Mima's birthday and she never seemed to be on shift when I stopped by—it wouldn't be until the dead of winter that we would see each other again. Her absence, as it will in these cases, loomed in my thoughts, germinating there with the liberties of an ill mind, until she became the most beautiful symptom of my longing.

Disappointed to have missed such a girl of traits I had so carefully prescribed to her, I would walk another block up to Moon café where they had gotten to know me. They knew that on cold days it was coffee, and on a particularly mild day it might be an iced tea instead. Geoff, the owner, also knew that money was always short, so would offer me a sandwich or whatever else was on hand.

Usually in those months it was coffee; either at a table in the front window—where passersby comforted me with their distanced proximity through the glass—or in the courtyard at the back of the café. On a particular day in the courtyard, coffee untouched next to a red ashtray on the table, I indulged myself with an exercise of making simple observations about my surroundings without letting their details penetrate further than the surface of things. To myself, I thought:

I am in the courtyard, shielded from the wind. Three-story buildings surround me. One is a restaurant, one is the café, one is the barber, one is I don't know. Another used to be called "The Tub Factory." It is closed down now. Sexually Transmitted Diseases, maybe. Red brick—the buildings and the courtyard. The fountain is still on, though it's cold. Soon it will have to be turned off—hopefully before it freezes. A leaf falls from the tree next to me. Two. Three. A fourth. Wind sneaks in from the alleyway, and the smoke from my cigarette joins it. An American brand whose slogan reads, "Wherever Particular People Congregate." Four other people are in the courtyard: two 40-50 year old women, probably on a late lunch break; a mother with her child—a girl. The daughter wears a light blue puffy coat and red scarf. She's sitting on a bench in front of me, her legs dangling as she bounces to the rhythm of a chant she sings:

> *yr stuck in a ba-awx,*
> *yr stuck in a ba-awx,*
> *and yr gunnah get squ-ashed,*
> *yr gunnah get squ-ashed.*
> *yr stuck in a ba-awx...*

Were I not enraptured by the lyrical sights of my game, the implications of the little girl's song would have been frightening. I was in the box, and I was going to be squashed. She must have been singing their ominous meaning directly into my subconscious, though, because shortly thereafter the words came back to haunt me.

Before the girl haunted my brain she got at my body by other more obvious means. My short breaks sometimes extended into a few longer nights—maybe through the weekend. The condition these periods of

27

prolonged leisure left me in was nothing short of vulnerable, wrecked.

It was a Thursday when Jason showed up at the apartment and it was clear that it would lead into the following week. The bottle of wine he carried had no need to wait. My notebook was closed and two glasses were poured. He'd be getting married in the coming May; he didn't know when or if I would take off again. Had anyone other than him noticed, I would have been considered notorious for coming into town unannounced just to pick up a week later without goodbyes. This time the lease held me down, but the occasion was not wasted. The bottle was empty and Ainsley, Jason's fiancée, was getting off work. We hopped in the car, or sidestepped, and swung over to the south side of town to pick her up at the Chinese restaurant where she waited tables. It was a surprise to see me at first, and she seemed a little upset at the oncoming escapade she was sure to encounter as she had frequently on other occasions of my returns—I had apparently interrupted plans they had made to go on a date, which Jason himself had forgotten. A drink lightened her up from the bottle we'd bought en route, and she welcomed me cordially afterwards—soon enough you could even say she was amiable to the night's continuance.

Between the three of us, since the beginning, the dynamics of our intertwined relationship were strained by ambiguous loyalties, jealousies, and confidences. I was matchmaker, best friend, and confidante to both of them. Through me the two were introduced. Ainsley I had known since we were probably nine years old through the church our families attended; when she invited me to the party her parents were hosting early the previous summer, Jason, my closest friend of five years, came along with me. At the end of a long week spent staying up all night drinking, we showed up in her backyard smelling of whiskey, with purple under our eyes, asking for glasses to supply transport from bottle-in-pocket to mouth. That backyard was where they met and that was where they were to be married six-so months later with me as the best man. They both loved me in their own ways, and were grateful, but couples need their space.

At the time in consideration, everyone was hanging out at Ed's place. It was a three bedroom house in midtown Lincoln that his grandma owned and was renting to him for cheap. Ed was an old friend of mine that was constantly falling out of touch, but when we got together we picked up having not missed a thing. His hair was grown out and he had lost a significant amount of weight during the most recent apostasy of our friendship. It was part of the spiritual conquest he had begun through psychedelic medium, which would ease him into future drug abuses and sexual obsessions wholly physical in nature. Pieced together by abstracting passages from obscure books about time, adopting phrases from dead revolutionaries, and his own drug-induced experiences, Ed formed his own philosophies which he chose to divulge to the world through his music—no less a confused resurrection of the dead than the philosophies it represented. Aside from the bedroom he slept in upstairs, the other was turned into a studio—really it was a dim lit room with a piano, several guitars, a few bass guitars, and a drum set which came out as contrived semi-gonzo, half-folk nonsense, but it did give you a kick.

The third bedroom, in the partly unfinished basement, was rented out by Ethan Geitze, a dear friend. After a semester at an arts school in Denver, then dropping out, he came back to Lincoln in debt and Ed offered him the room at reasonable cost. Of the two I had known Ed longer, but Ethan was easier to get along with. He was the second oldest in an Italian-Catholic family of six boys, the youngest of whom was still only six. His mother was a saint. His father, who drank more than a father should, had worked on the railroad since before his first-born and had that quiet ruggedness about him that comes from being well-acquainted with the working class. Parts of that trait could be seen in Ethan, but he was also sensitive and optimistic, charming in a more delicate way, intuitive, good-looking, and well-dressed. He was a good musician, too, but too reserved to play in front of a crowd. Everyone respected him.

People were always coming and going at the house then in different stages of intoxication, hunger, lust, boredom, or loneliness. One might arrive with a gallon of wine for the long haul just as another would be leaving to go meet a friend—but not without having one last quick drink, of course. Coming in through the side door so the three of us—me and the couple with ruined plans that is—could go straight downstairs to see Ethan, it happened that no one was leaving. In fact, Micheal was just pulling up, and getting out of his car with him were two girls whose faces couldn't be made out in the dark. Their shrill voices, though, rushing out of the open car doors and cracking in the cold breeze, were enough to announce their presence. Waiting at the door for them, they came cheerfully up the driveway with arms around each other and, without introduction, hurried down the narrow staircase into the warm basement, calmly followed by my slightly intoxicated person.

Upstairs it sounded like there must have been people with Ed, too, because the walls and pipes were vibrating with off-tempo music while Ed's voice could be heard struggling through some sort of chorus, but Ethan put a stop on that misconception. Said it was just Ed and Mick, a musician friend of Ed's, and they'd been playing that same song for the past two hours. Each time it started over it was as if we, or the studio itself, were moved further away, and after a while it was merely a distant hum, like water circulating in an aquarium that everyone had

29

ceased looking at.

Micheal introduced the two girls to everyone as Natalie and Rosy—names that I thought fitted them. Rosy was a rough little Hispanic broad; Natalie was a Scandinavian prairie-girl, tall, thin, somewhat plain, but more feminine than Rosy. They sat on the couch next to Micheal, quietly talking to one another with drinks in their laps while the rest of us sat on the floor and Ethan coolly sitting off in the corner in a wooden chair. It was unclear how Micheal had met either of the girls. He had a habit of bringing around attractive(and sometimes hideous) acquaintances with little or no explanation, which could be entertaining at times, but also extremely dangerous for any drunk with a conscience. It was his eyes that sparked intrigue among the women—among anyone first encountering him, really—which were a wide grey-blue that expressed his entire character. Frantic, naive, and harmless, Micheal was like a young boy who had trouble getting through the day's lesson due to a hard-on he couldn't get rid of. The thing was carried around with him like a divining rod between his legs, constantly leading him to new shallow aquifers that he recklessly attempted to plunge into because he didn't know any better. He was fun to call up when one needed to hear the wolves howl, when there was nothing so important as getting drunk and allowing every whim to take hold of you, and toss you every which way like a sailor on his sinking ship.

The fact that Natalie and Rosy had come with Micheal was enough to make me behave in a manner of good-natured amusement toward them, more so than I would have if they had know Ethan or been girlfriends of Ainsley's. Then, it was the first night in weeks spent out of my apartment, so it may not have changed things so much. A round of whiskey was poured for everyone. The drink was taken to our well-being and the alcohol, indeed, made my hands still. The girls were put further at ease. Rosy claimed to recognize me from maybe six or seven years back. (Did she? I thought her face had been familiar.) We had mutual friends awhile back, but had never quite known one another. Natalie sat with her legs crossed, spinning her glass on her knee and watching us, as if she were waiting for something. She had grown up in a small town outside of Lincoln called Milford, and had only lived in the city for a few months, so this good friend of hers, Rosy, was introducing her to new people in the area. Still, it never came out how either one had been introduced to Micheal. Rosy was plainly drunk anyway. She had nothing better to talk about than how strange it was that she should run into me. "Yes," I thought, "what a strange and friendly little town we've found ourselves in...."

Though I sat facing the two girls, my surroundings were a mere backdrop to the sights that began to fall into my thoughts. Like water that had flooded the ship deck, and seeped through the cracked planks, they dripped down into the gulley where I sat at a table, drunk, responsible for nothing but my own impending drowning. Each drop that splashed upon the table, in the pots, in my hair, in my mouth, had a face, and a name. My mother fell upon my cheek, my father dripped from my nose, former bosses collected in rusty buckets that spilled over, women covered the floor with inopportunity—one fell into my whiskey glass. There, in the darkness, on the distorted surface of my poison, I saw back into the room in which I sat: vaguely there was Ethan, Jason, and Ainsley—someone else was sitting with them, then left. There was Micheal whispering something into Natalie's ear, who said nothing in return. Jason and Ainsley were leaving. When had the music stopped upstairs? Ethan was going to bed, Rosy was whispering now to Natalie. There was hate where Micheal's entire character showed, directed at me. Natalie grabbed my hand.

This is what she was waiting for: for me to be alone in the darkness of a room filling up with water, so high now that it could no longer be carelessly waded through, willing to take the hand of the nearest woman to pull me out. She led me up the stairs that seemed so innocent earlier by a hand that was far from it. Ascending from the dark basement into another dark room, we were gone. Then, black.

4. WALKING WITH THE DEAD

The affair with Natalie was short-lived. It was a relief for it to be over a week later. Had it lasted any longer it may have meant the death of me. The guilt and remorse, along with the fear of hurting her, had paralyzed my ability to ask her to leave, though still leaving me functional in other respects, provided there was plenty to drink. She was sweet to me, too; stopping by in the evenings to try and persuade me to leave my apartment, bringing me food that was so easily accepted. The meals were eaten, but it was awful to do so, as if I were ingesting her pitiful kindness incarnate which was being stolen from the rest of the world. My only penance was to throw them up later.

By me, the casual affair would have lasted that way indefinitely, so long as it didn't entail facing her with the unmusical and unbecoming truth. But, as luck would have it, she could not fake it forever.

She disappeared from my bed, my apartment, and my life without warning and without leaving any trace. 10am, opening my bleary eyes to the sight of her, this thin little blonde girl, the sunlight came through the apartment's single window with the color of Sunday's bathwater after the last poor kid steps out into the cold. The sound of the hellbound trains came and went from the yard outside. Hearing them pull

31

in and out of the station so horribly loud in my oncoming sobriety, but still drunk, they intensified the general disgust for myself, just lying there with the sound and the feeling while she scampered into the kitchen in heartbreaking bra and underwear to get me beer, then jumped back into the warm sheets. She wanted to tell stories from her childhood, strange reminiscences of her more recent past, and anecdotes about the different scars on her body. Big, thirsty, sad gulps of beer were taken as she recalled how she once ran away from her mother through a field, and got a deep gash along her spine while trying to crawl under a barbed wire fence. She had me graze my fingers over the raised pink scar. She told of how she used to drive around with her dad looking for her mother, usually drunk, in the bars and homes of the men around town—and her parents still together after years of these affairs, how? She said it was because her mom was too afraid to leave him, too afraid of what she might feel afterward—O, the regret! Growing heavier with each beer she retrieved for me, I listened to the stories with a sort of tacit smile on my lips because some day these same stories would be told to another man who would kiss her imperfections with such genuine adoration that she would feel OK. And, although she will have forgotten me altogether by then, and my love-sighs for her and every woman that's ever existed, my own specific role will have been played in her human drama.

How the smile of a comforted idiot turned into sleep is unknown. But she was gone when I woke up. She must have left with the smell of stale beer as her last memory and perhaps only that smell will she remember forever, because it's everywhere. Good riddance to her with that, and a sincere apology: I'm sorry. So fucking sorry....

Waking up alone then. Feeling *so fucking sorry* to have let everything go over the past week, my skin buzzed with the adrenaline of new sobriety. The evening room seemed sinister, as it were hiding in it a demon that would soon come out to slit my throat or rape me. The *manuscript* had still been writing itself from delusional memory—work was getting done—but this lurking spirit that drew me out of bed and to the window needed something else—something I recognized, and knew well in fact, but had long since put off. The only way to get rid of it was to get it out in Word, lend my hand to the ghost, to release it from the hounds in a longwinded requiem.[*] The "It" being poor Christopher Thomsen himself, the boy who had committed suicide when we were thirteen years old. He had haunted me ever since, in need of help. In the chair in the window I finally gave myself up to him, clenching my

---

* "Requiem for Christopher" is an unedited stream of prose for the deceased mentioned in the following line, which appears in full after the main text of the book
—BF

jaw for the duration, notebook and pencil right there in my lap, and told him, "Alright, go ahead now..."

What came was frightening beyond comprehension—a recurring nightmare that I couldn't quite shake, not till he had passed the plane and was in the good company of all those angels I would see, taking him into that room and closing the door without saying a word, just leading me out in the opposite direction. In the course of those sights, I became so inconceivably scared by *what came* that I had to get out—out of the window, out of the apartment, out of the building. For the first time I thought I was going out of my wits; that the sanity I treasured was at last being taken from me. Hearing the faucet crack, or the walls creak, my bones ached with the true isolation of my apartment. No more couches, floors, girls' poor beds. Just an ever-shrinking apartment that held me prisoner to my own inane absurdities and unfortunate bouts of despondency. The chant came back to me all at once—the light blue coat and red scarf rushing toward me from where it had been sung into my subconscious, blaring the words *yr stuck in a ba-awx, yr stuck in a ba-awx!*

They followed me out into the street, taking off in the numb direction of Nowhere, always looking behind me. The rest of the world had fallen off, crumbled under the sound of the scream—*yr stuck in a ba-awx, yr stuck in a ba-awx!* There was another sound—couldn't tell whether it was the ring of a shotgun going off or a bomb being dropped. It was making my ears bleed. The little girl had taken off her coat and scarf to reveal her naked grey body, with big ugly scar on her belly and blood coming down her thighs—she had mutated into a crazed midget whore with bad teeth, syphilis, and the flashbulb eyes of someone possessed. She didn't give a fuck about my money, just wanted me to contract *the disease.* Emerging from the gravel heaps of what was once the Haymarket, from under the bridge onto O Street, the whole town was a skeleton—O Street was its broken spine. Post Holy War America. The righteous had already been given their grace. The only inhabitants left stood around waiting for their orders, minions of the antichrist: this Girl.

She trailed me all the way up O Street, through neolithic downtown Lincoln where there was nothing but rundown bars situated on the bottom floors of fallen buildings. Inside, amongst the steel girders and rotten plaster, they were serving arsenic and bile—lines of crushed bone-dust were snorted off counters. The patrons, evil sycophants, were moving between the bars, desperately trying to get their fill—more arsenic, more bile, another line. In the confusion, they were unable to recall where they had come or gone; they did not even have the slightest sensation of déjà vu. Each was "a seedling in the wind, being swept every which way"—a tragedy in limbo, unaware of their own damnation, ever-returning to the cycle of the street.

Turned off at 17th Street to search for a way out of the city. Heading toward The University, The World of Academe was apparently deserted. Doors to the lecture halls were closed off by stiff bodies and burning books. Every last poet was dead. Only a single classroom was occupied by the hopeful glow of a reading lamp as I approached it on the outskirts of campus, peering over a few corpses to inspect its illumination: Old Gray Beard sat at the lowlight of his desk, pants at his ankles, jerking off with calloused hands—the scabs were peeling off and collecting at the base of his cock. His bottom lip had detached from his face and fallen to the ground—drool was pouring out of the hole. The scabs were floating in it. He was approaching release, the veins in his forehead threatening to burst, and my intestines unraveled at the sight—I collapsed against the wall of bodies, and began to get sick. Laying there spitting out the acids from my stomach onto the ground, he could be heard pounding his fist against the desk as he came, and, through the decomposing flesh of the deceased, he screamed with vengeance, *"yr gunnah get squ-uashed, yr gunnah get squ-uashed!"*

Somehow I found myself knocking on the door of an apartment—number 419 of a building on the north end of campus. Sal opened the door, his light brown hair unwashed, pencil behind his ear. I just stood there in a daze. With a distracted hello, though not unsympathetic, he let me in and I went straight to the couch for a seat—I absolutely had to sit. Sal had been like that with me since we met each other at fourteen—my arrivals never surprised him. Six months could have passed between the last time we'd seen one another and he would have been no less surprised by my appearance on his doorstep. I would still have been welcomed in the same casual manner, except maybe gotten a hug, and then be let in without a question.

Sal, who was a student of civil engineering at The University, had problems to calculate, texts to read, exams to study for, but seeing the state I was in, bless him, set them aside for the night and brought me over a beer while taking a seat next to me on the couch. Still a little frightened, the beer tasted good and helped my hands stop shaking. Sal's silent company was concrete, and much needed. He put a movie on, brought me another beer. We had both seen the movie before—a comedy about aspiring thieves who have to go on the run in Texas—and only watched halfheartedly, laughing as the images passed, but the movement and sound so soothed my nerve-racked body that I had forgotten my condition until it was over. With the movie ended, Sal turned out the lights and closed the door to his bedroom and left me sitting alone on the floor in his living room. It would have been too embarrassing to ask him to sit up with me until I could fall asleep because I was scared to be alone in the dark, and that the ghost of the devil was after me. Instead, in fear of the window-nightmare's return, the chant, the disease, I resorted to trying out the trick my brother taught me of doing stretching exercises and taking deep breaths. *In, out; in, out.* The prayer for serenity my dad had written down for me. *Lord, grant me this, or that, please lord.* Tapping various points on my body because it worked for Mima. The sequence of heart, or chest, palm, temple, whatever other points there might have been to tap, could not be remembered; I was distracted by the menacing presence of wall-shadows made by the light globes burning below the trees' barren branches. They turned those branches into Satan's fingers, they did, making them creep across the wall toward my limp body that now lay there on the floor in failed methods of relaxation, trying with difficulty to simply fall into a pleasant dream.

The pleasant dream never did come. Sleep, however, like a grey void between two black places, finally did.

5. THE FILM OF PARADISE

The holidays came and for a short while the delirium subsided. The neighborhood was transformed into a seasonal paradise. Carriage rides were given by big white Clydesdales that clomped around the corners, carolers sung on weekends, bells were rung by The Salvation Army folk in Santa hats, buildings were bejeweled with Christmas lights, hot food was served with drink, and everyone smiled a little bit more. It didn't matter if Hell still existed, because from my vantage point, in my studio in the middle of Holiday Island, all I could see was the December glow, the concentrated phosphorescence of children's dreams and impractical hope—the promise of better things.

From my current vantage point, a year away from Paradise, the December glow is diffused in the rain-clouded horizon, and drips from the gutters of the California homes like lit tips of fuses, inching inevitably toward their domestic explosives, ready to blow up the American ideal for good. Only the yearning will remain unaffected after the blast—the yearning for life to be set in order, your own home, your own family, your own books upon the shelf. The yearning for better things.

I am waiting for it here at One Reindeer Lane, the explosion, where I inhabit one of the two guest bedrooms. The other, to which a wall is shared, is occupied by my father and his once-mistress, now wife, and little Emiliana. No sound goes unheard. Across the hall, in the master suite, resides the owner of the house, a business associate of my father's named Rafik Suchry. He's a 37 year old bachelor, of mixed Egyptian-Armenian blood, who has made well for himself in produce and real estate since the age of nineteen. He's doing us all a favor in

35

letting us stay here temporarily, but my personal benefit far outweighs those of my father and his wife. There is nowhere else for me to go— I'm broke again and the novelty has worn off amongst my friends of good ol' Font coming through town, showing up in a van from the coast with bags in hand, beard grown and eyes wide as a child's, asking for a beer at noon. Those days are over.

A whole new saga has now begun at the house on Reindeer Lane where I am warm, fed, and encouraged. Its foundation is built upon a hangover of adultery, betrayal, and self-loathing. To live in it requires one to transcend any preconceptions of morals in a grueling intro- spection of Faith—at the core of its existence lay the half-answered questions of the ages. I recall them as a plate once held over my head, then dropped to the kitchen floor and shattered. The shards were sw- ept into a small pile that is yet understood, and the pieces still haven't been sifted, though we step over them every day. My last chance at life, or redemption, is to discover their truth by writing The Book.

Aside from the room and board, which is accepted with equal parts gratitude and humiliation, Raf introduces me around town as the writer he's putting up at his home and has offered to provide the funding for The Book. It is the first book of my generation, which the world will read tomorrow and forget the next day. I am writing it so that I can continue living, and so that the food will keep coming in— still not ridding myself of the image of my mother's home out East. The only instruction I have received to assist me in its completion has been in disjointed bits, learned from teachers who all died long before yesterday. Decades have passed since, nothing having changed for the better, and not a single artist was born in between. If M. Miller was, then, "the voice of the wise-ass street kid, who hangs out on the corner with his friends, who trades stories with them about his exploits," so said Louise D. in the introduction to Cancer, then I am, today, nothing but a country sap, on leave of my local alter for a joy ride across the universe, exclaiming, "*g a w d*, it's so bright, so wonder-full, so sad!" And The Book is the letter home from my sojourn abroad, written in a stupid tongue of bar-napkin illustrations. (Remember, "don't think of the words, just think of the picture better.") I am painting the picture for my fellow man, not concerning myself with the previous stroke, or if the brush is shedding, because in the end it'll all be looked at on the same continuous canvas, if looked at at all! And really the picture itself won't mean a damn, only the subtext will reveal the truth, and that truth will be Timeless.

Resuming the twilight, back on Holiday Island, the rotting meat of the thing that feeds me. A four-foot tall Christmas tree, pre-lit, was put up in the corner of my apartment near the kitchen and decorated with silver and red bulbs. I ate my solitary meals in front of it, on an old paint-smeared piano bench, with a glass of whichever cheap wine was on hand, and stared into the reflection on the distorted surface of the bulbs—the mirrored world was being filmed through the fisheye lens of each of these dangling ornaments, panning across the room from right to left: the frosted window panes, like empty glass pages awaiting melancholic fingertips; the half-finished canvas on the easel; the unmade bed; the well-organized desk, what, with dog-eared notebooks and my nearly finished manuscript; and then me, huddled on the couch with blanket over my shoulders, listening to Christmas music and thinking about all of the extravagant things that had yet been accomplished. Out of focus, with the edges blurred by possible misfortunes and previous failures, these appeared, too, in a succession of dream images from right to left, but with my big fat beat-up soul overlooking them with a silver and red gleam in my eyes, and sleigh bells ringing in my ears. To that soundtrack the future was traversed and I became the Prince of the Underground, The Great Poet of my Imagination, which, later, in the post-Holiday gloom, in its un-healthy grandiosity would declare, "I am everything, All at once!" with the sleigh bells having been trampled, and their sounds replaced by the voice of Vincent Gallo.

The door was kept unlocked during my dinners. The moment of my last swallow of the second glass of wine the door would open, just out of view through the kitchen, and call an ending to my digestive reveries. My beloved little Kira, barging in as expected, is saying, "h-e-l-l-o, Mister Font," before she can even see me, then coming into sight dressed in sleeping shorts that show off her cute chicken-legs and scarred knees. She moved in to her apartment upstairs at the same time I moved into mine, and made a habit of visiting me in the evenings, after she had washed off her make-up and tied up her clean blonde hair, with a friendly bottle of wine and a lap blanket to put over her skinny, bare legs. We had known each other long before we were neighbors, so there was nothing indecent about this, and I had in fact lived with her briefly once before in a big red house she shared with another young college girl. Mostly I slept on the couch downstairs by myself, or the floor, but sometimes I would find myself crawling into her bed with the boozy smell of lust and in the dark we moved just enough so that we knew we were alive. Since then we had given up each other's flesh for a deeper relationship of understanding and escape, though occasionally I still found myself falling in love with her on lonely hungover mornings when she'd come back down to my apartment to retrieve some trivial item forgotten the night before.

Those nights would start, as I had said, with Kira barging in with more wine for me, and behind her, trailing more discreetly, her best friend Carla with a quiet look of anything you might want to consider it—sadness, amusement, boredom, lovesickness, perplexity. She wore her dark hair, shy pale skin, and dancer figure with such a plain reservation that it allowed one to misconstrue into whatever desired, though I was able to distinguish between each quirk after spending endless days in her company talking happily—eventually, when I moved away again, for good this time, I think that was part of the inspiration of her hatred towards me. Neither one of the girls speak to me now. When I was still in their good graces, though, back during the nights they came giggling down the stairs to my apartment, Carla would sit next to me on the couch with her knees close together, slightly slouched over as if in mourning, and Kira would sit on the chair with the plaid blanket over her lap. Time passed in a dream. A dream that belonged to all of us. My interrupted reveries would be reconvened some five inches just below the shoulder of the bottle in John S.'s spiritual graduation, only we remained suspended there by the carols being hummed in the background even after the wine had been drunk to what should have amounted to "general and undirected sadness." In red-grape burps our personal thoughts were regurgitated from the deepest parts of our bellies in a cadence familiar to dumb-joy, almost unrecognizable when overheard from the muffled distance of vague memory, and nearly overlooked altogether when right there in the beauty of it, with the easy abandonment of the present to naïve optimism that always waits for *better things*. But, it's a closer, more careful ear now that hears those voices.

VOICE ONE: I'll have four kids, three boys and a girl, and eight cats and dogs—in a huge house—one room will be just for the animals, and

VOICE TWO: And your kids will smell like cat piss!

VOICE ONE: NO—I'll train the cats to go outside(hiccup), and I'll always keep the laundry clean...

VOICE TWO: You only have your two cats right now, little Gizmo kitty and whatever the hell the grey one is called, and I already choke on the smell when I open the door!

VOICE ONE: Is it really that bad? (biting bottom lip, nearly laughing; embarrassment is fleeting)

VOICE TWO: Your kids are going ta smell like cat piss.

(VOICE ONE now letting the laugh out, followed by a burp!)

Had we listened more carefully to ourselves we would have been able to decipher the hiccups and wine laughs, and heard them according to the rest of the melody—the saxophones pouting, the trumpets blaring nonsensical declarations, the accordion exhaling a smoker's wheeze, the bells chiming like perfect three-star tears. And, faintly, we would have heard the carousel rotating, loaded with negatives from The Film of Paradise, as the shots continued pouring in from every ornament and every corner of the room. All that could be heard then were the *red-grape burps from the deepest parts of our bellies*, and that the kids would smell like cat piss. Snowflakes had fallen into our ears and wet our drums with Youth. It was a wonderful sound.

Meanwhile, both of my older brothers had come back into town, along with our father, for what would pass as our first legally dysfunctional Christmas. We all said to make an attempt to salvage our togetherness for the occasion of the holiday, but deception is a favorite pastime of all Christian families—especially of good Christian families. We didn't see each other much. Aden and Mitch spent some nights at Mima's with Syd and Bear, and others at our Dad's nearly empty house somewhere in the same neighborhood—he not only refused to pass by Mima's house, but denied himself to even know where it was. He was living full time then in Shanghai, so it seemed practical that his house in Lincoln was furnished only with an air mattress, two bar stools, a leather chair, and a new, expensive, flat screen TV. If you slept there it was on the floor with your coat as a blanket. I remained in my own haunts, however, in my own apartment with my own bed, my own cheap wine, young women that would later despise me, and my own notebooks. I still had the manuscript to finish—the o b v i o u s "Next Great American Yaddaya." That seemed easier, much easier, to undertake than choosing sides in the ex-spousal wordless-debate going on across town—with hardly a paternal podium! What, with the orange juice and outdated milk in the fridge, with the long flight back to China awaiting him, with the slander of the Latter Day Saint-goers, with the well-known tragedies of his past called "Dad-Stories"—the farce we had all gotten used to. As if we all weren't dying!

No, I wanted Fiction. If rotten meat were being served, it would be on my own plate, taken by my own tree on the old paint-smeared piano bench in my own apartment! (I've just heard the child crying in the other room, only I was the child and the walls to my room are too close. Pardon the outrage, please, I'm sore today—the tree and lights were taken down, and January is the saddest month of the year.)

By the time Christmas had passed, none of us had forced ourselves into the formalities we had so promised each other, so longed for. It was too late to reclaim them. My fellow clansmen—(the clan does not exist!)—had returned to their new domiciles and, with irreparable regret, we found ourselves alone again in the saddest month of the New Year.

6. FLYING THROUGH A GREYSCALE

To be an artist is more than to assert a lofty sense of self-worth, or to carry the titles of classics around with you in a fancy leather bag, or in your brain. It is more than to just walk around with your hands shoved too-deeply into your pockets, to hold your head too-highly in the ether, or slouched too-encompassing towards death. It is more than cigarettes, drunkenness, drugs, or self-affliction. It is more than to mimic your predecessors, to retain images, or to have the skill to reproduce them. To be an artist, a true artist, is to *become*. The rest of those things are just common possible symptoms of the process, along with poverty, pretentiousness, promiscuity—and an over-emphasis of that, with a capital P, as in Prick.

Only once have I encountered a person that might have been an artist, and he died upon shaking my hand—the sincerity killed him. Myself? Let me tell you, *that*—

For a true artist a specific medium is superfluous—living is his medium. But, still, this isn't enough for the community. In order that they feed or house *the artist*, they need tangible evidence blown into their ears, spat into their eyes, or rubbed over their genitals. A masterpiece would be unnecessary, almost discouraged, so long as you have the *potential*—and very little is needed at that, so it's easily faked. Sometimes, often these days, it results in what we'll call these Artists producing unmemorable works of comparable pornography, which occasionally catches on! But the desire for immortality is overwhelming, that's what allows it. The community screams, "We're all gonnah be famous someday!" Because everyone wants to be etched into the legend of no-time, no matter how minute their role, they egg on whatever amount of artistic promise a person may have been endowed. They egged on my brother, Aden, in La Grande, Oregon, saying "Font, all you need is a little room with a typewriter and a bottle of whiskey!"—and his poems made them right. They egged me on in Lincoln by taking me out to chicken breast and steak lunches, and bringing me wine. But, in the end, all they ask you is, "Did you really think I was fat? I was never fat." (Like sweet Abbie Thomsen, talking about the short story I wrote about her called "Fine Things." She was always beautiful—and her sister.) Greedily, they ask for more. "If you write about me, someday—what will you write?"

Just give it to them. Tell them you drank too much and can't remember. Tell them you drank too much so you wouldn't remember. I'd rather like to lie in bed with the blinds drawn—I've given you enough already.

The manuscript I gave you a year ago—that was my proof. Do you not remember?

It ended with an image of a perfectly white butterfly, on a mountain outside of Denver, parting gently with his purple flower to crawl onto

40

my palm as I knelt beside him, and, in a manifestation of God's Will, returned him to the sky...watching him...as he fluttered up, and up, in an ascension to Heaven. No one noticed the flight.

It was the first week of the New Year. The slow old-age of winter, with its cracked and dry wisdom, had settled in with a disconcerting Russian cold—the manuscript was finished. Even then it was titled in jest, "Wayside Illuminations," to try and illustrate the stupid excitements of the travels it documented. It was as if King Beatnik himself had risen from the grave and had a half-drunk, rancid, deteriorating piss on a regular lined notebook; once it had dried, "Wayside Illuminations" appeared in full text, and stinking. But, as I said, it didn't matter because no one noticed. The only thing they did notice was that I reemerged into the night from my apartment, the shit-manuscript heavy and real in my bag, with a manic look that said, "Pour me a drink for every word that shall forever be in print! Fill my plate with more of your chicken breast and steak! Call Micheal—I think I'd like to hear the wolves howl!"

So it began like that, as a personal celebration of the accomplishment that validated my identity—supposedly. Jason picked me up from my apartment and as the first to see that manic look he took me straight over to Ed's where the lights were always burning and a bottle was always hiding in the cupboard. The company was sparse—it being another celebration on another Tuesday and all. Or was it a Thursday? Either way, only the regulars were present. Ethan and Jason congratulated me, though they weren't quite sure for what. Ainsley, who was busy putting sticky green leaves into a blown glass pipe, just raised her head for a momentary smile. Micheal stopped by, but was on his way to, of course, "see other friends"—he just wanted to say H e l l o, and have one, two drinks with me for the ride. The taste of whiskey haunted me afterwards, mixing with the sugary wine in my mouth. My tongue was all abloom, blossoming into drunkenness. I was growing sepulchral wings and my head was beginning to soar over the world of debauchery, and I wondered, had anyone noticed *me* take flight?

Around that same time, Ed had gotten into something he called The Green Monster—which were unmarked, not-so-small green pills of curious origin—that induced him to take naked quietude behind his locked bedroom door. At one point he came into the kitchen with an off-pink towel covering his cock, retrieved a bottle of Bud from the refrigerator, and returned to his bedroom. Not a word was said. It's doubtful that anyone noticed something so subtle as the invisible wings forming beneath my clothes when there were other things to watch:

Such as the effects of this Green Monster upon poor Ed, who had only wanted to understand a little bit better why he didn't belong, why his older brother was a football star of the Midwest and he was a failure, why his father didn't speak to him, or why he got an erection when Micheal would sometimes remove his shirt at the height of a drunken party—he had only wanted to know, Why? But, without giving an answer first, The Green Monster swallowed up his reasoning in one go, and left him naked in his locked bedroom, no less confused, off-pink towel hanging on the door knob, with balls in hand and now-empty bottle of Bud up his ass.

Such as, too, the effects of Casey Mayhan, Sal's cousin, who looks like something of a Mediterranean seductress, but more delicate, post heart operation, upon the unsuspecting Ethan Geitze. When she had come with me, platonically, to the New Year's Eve party at Ed's place, it hadn't taken long for them to become acquainted with one another and by midnight she was his. I was outside toasting the moon. Before, Ethan was optimistic. Now, he *exuded* optimism. They both did. With them in the room you didn't need the wine to become intoxicated— their presence should have been enough. Another long drink anyhow, for good measure, and my wings grew fuller, darker. From where I soared above this world, as my instinct carried me effortlessly along its due course, every detail of what was happening could not be seen, but it was a well known fact that far below the people were living.

After a week as such, coming back down from the clouds deject-edly with my wings battered and smelling of –aldehyde, I found myself arriving at a house on X Street on the north side of Lincoln. With me was Dunning, who had previously been the best painter in that part of the country, but was, at the time, retired at the age of nineteen. His decision to give it up came abruptly after finishing a greyscale portrait of a mother and her baby daughter in the hospital. The painting had been put on display in the old bottling plant where The Program was now located, and he had been approached by them about teaching classes on technique—he said the thought enraged him. His passion was Theology; painting had just been a hobby, one that he would no longer pursue because it was ruined.

Together we went through an unhinged screen door inside. From outside the house it appeared to be another slightly dysfunctional home of the American Dead, with sole porch light on illuminating a broken couch and an unused desk. From within it was positively dead and the devil lurked in the bustle of combating egos. The place was careening with Artists, hipsters, and the like—the walls had nearly split with their drunken talk of their latest works. Cigarette smoke made the inferno more believable. It was in the kitchen, in immediate search of glasses for a wine jug, that I saw Her—for the first time since my mot-her's birthday in mid-October I saw her. Lillian Jean.

Her back was turned toward me as she talked with another young girl, Dani, who I recognized from awhile back as her best friend. But there was an unmistakable, and unavoidable feminine grace about the girl with her back turned—the grace of a ballet full of cocaine pirouettes—which only Lilly possessed. There was a bottle of gin going between them, and a third party whose presence I dismissed.

In the near-three months since she was last seen, I had imagined having a thousand conversations with her—on any number of them could I start in. But, finishing with my second pour, thinking a few quick glasses would do me some good, loosen my tongue, Lilly beat me to it. Turning around, she said my name, in full, ending with her tongue up hard against the back of her front teeth on the "t" in Font. She was wearing rubber galoshes with her jeans rolled up to the tops of them. Outside, the rain continued down. Drops of it still hung in our hair, on the wool of our coats, on our boots, like wet pearls brought back in style for the purpose of this grand affair of our meeting again. She greeted me then with a hug, having to raise just enough on her toes to get her arms around my neck so that my self-confidence was restored—the past week had never happened. This was the true cause for celebration, the real beginning. I hated gin, but the smell of it on her made me want a drink for myself, made me want the whole bottle, and anything that might come after it. When she let go of my neck the wet pearls had been crushed by our bodies. Looking back, there's something sinister in the thought of those broken pearls, but then I imagined they were not unlike the smear of our emulsion after we had been peeled apart in the blood bath; our photos hanging to dry in heaven where the tragedy was already known.

The rest of the kitchen, the rest of the party, became the third wheel of our own private rendezvous whose presence I dismissed. The cigarette smoke became the mist of surf upon shore, and she became the inhabiting Siren of the island whose shore it had broke. She slurred a lullaby of an oncoming death from her desolation in sorrow into the imaginary sea as I steered in with wasted Salvation. At a distance, she app-eared—half-woman, half-bird, half-dead herself—just as the winter clouds during a January storm, falling apart in a ballad of six-point stars. What was once the kitchen was now Her sky dressed in romance crystals; those who were once whores were now dressed in Her virgin white. With a drink of her gin my approach resumed: once near enough for her face to take shape, near enough to touch the rocks which promised my Fate, her dark eyes came into focus as unfathomable drowning pools, each surface holding infinite reflections of Her Father's ghost—of her Self, ostracized, from which she continued to sing. And how low was her song that it still reverberates in the marrow of California!

In the midst of this lullaby I learned that she had, just two months before, split up with her boyfriend, John. She would've called me, but she no longer had my number. When I had given it to her she was still with John, and probably hadn't thought twice about where she misplaced it—even so, she said she was glad to have happened across me again. She wished she still had my number! The break up, she claimed, was to be the last of many that had occurred in the span of her relationship with John, which had lasted, until then, two and a half years. During those two and a half years they made love in a dingy midtown apartment building and lived out their young lives, doing everything together that cohabitation insisted upon: ate dinners, took showers, clipped their nails, fought over music choices, watched the storms, harbored jealousies, made acquaintances with neighbors, had friends over, drank until they got sick, went on trips to National Parks, to the Dakotas, maybe, to France and Germany, and they shared a cat. How she missed that cat! Aw, the kitty, she said she could just squish the damn thing out of fondness.

Learning these things, I quietly remembered John, and remembered even liking him, but, under the circumstance, the news of his absence overjoyed me in a selfish way that I could not help feeling slightly guilty for—his blood was still on the rocks, the surf still sprayed his cologne. Her belongings, some of them at least, were still with John at their old apartment, while in the meantime she was staying with Dani, who was housesitting for her sister. She asked me if I wanted to come with them to her house.

Dunning had been gone for an indeterminate amount of time. He left without me, knowing that I was waiting for this invitation, and knowing that it would come—he had more confidence in these things than I had in myself; for me it was just dumb-luck, (un?)fortunate happenstance. No one was making any choices, things were just happening. Did I want to go with them? Even if I hadn't wanted to, though it was all I wanted, I had no choice in the matter—as I said, things were just happening and I was all for letting them, even if it meant drowning in the undertow. Even if it meant never finding my way back home, and being doomed to wander through eternity in search of it, with only gin to subdue my unquenchable thirst. Even if it meant all of those things I would still go with them. In a moment, the three of us, together, polished off the gin; in the next, we tumbled that way from one dream into another.

The first night we spent alone together came only twelve hours after the night poisoned by the awful grain-taste of gin, which can hardly be recalled after leaving the party but for a few dimmed instances in the basement of unsuccessfully playing at the idea of making love, and the embarrassment that followed when Lillian dropped me off in front of my apartment at nine-am with the wintry rain still hanging in the grey

44

air like so many ink dots aligned to form the newspaper picture we were forging for The Future Obituaries. Not even Dunning could have given hope to this greyscale; not even he could have captured the perfect gloom, nor foreshadowed the calamity.

Back in the shadow of this time, again 9 o'clock, now evening, Lilly returned to my apartment in her same clothes, with the addition of an oversized Hemmingway-like sweater made of grey wool with big, brown leather buttons. Hanging from her tiny frame it gave the illusion of being her soul's distension. Everything, all of her sadness, had transcended her meek skeleton and pale flesh to be draped about her shoulders in its ash colored wool. She looked like an ominous angel who was visiting me in the night to make a revelation. I invited her in and waited for it to come. To touch her would have been too much, it would have made me a part of her, a part of something more than I yet deserved. I was content to just wait, sitting next to her on the couch with all the overhead lights burnt out, seeing only by candlelight and the indistinct red-torches of our cigarettes, and to listen for the ivory words of her disclosure to pass through the heavy wool of her sad soul.

Between drags of her cigarette, which were then Camels, it came in cloudbursts from an inner storm—her Father's suicide. The most natural thing coming out of her mouth, as if he had never been her father at all, just a man from a story. She skipped the sentimental insights about the man in this story—not a single detail about his character was given. The main thing was that he was dead, had killed himself. Another cloud burst: it had happened when she was fourteen, she said, somewhere in Missouri, I think. She moved around middle-America a lot at the time so the settings became unclear to me, though I listened hard, as best I could, and prayed for her. Her mom had remarried a big Motorcycle Viking with tattoos named Joseph Schmidt, and they moved to Lincoln for contracting work in the growing town—only a year had elapsed since her Father's suicide, but then he had been living alone at the time of his death, and been divorced for over another year already.

In those same early teen years, maybe thirteen?—she made the transition effortlessly, as I said, like it was the most natural thing—the doctors informed her that she would never be able to get pregnant. She told herself she had never wanted kids, and I prayed, "Lord, give me her burdens! Give me these things that lay restless inside her, that cause such awful weather. I can take it—give it to me! Give her peace! Heavenly Father," I prayed, "someday, give this dear girl of mine the joy of a child: a miracle." We ask for spectacular things out of love, fantastic things, miracles, but I wonder how many of us truly expect to receive them. The cloudburst dissipated. She took a drag of a newly lit cigarette.

She had her sketchbook with her, filled with drawings of old men she'd never met, of teachers she had had growing up, of malignant creatures and figures, and pasted-in photographs that she had taken of the simplest things—simple, but by her lens they were made more, made great, made beautiful. Fuck, I was in love, huh! I wanted to go with her to take pictures of the cows—something peaceful about a cow. But the cows meant nothing, so long as I could go with her; or, maybe she should just stay. With the most innocent intentions I asked her if she'd like that, to stay with me—it had gotten late somehow. Time was all cows. The night was all cloudbursts—I wanted to float on them forever. She said she would stay, but she wouldn't sleep with a man who wore his jeans to bed, she refused, made a big deal of a joke about it, so we took our clothes off and got into bed.

There was no need for sex—we didn't even fool around. We just laid there without our clothes on, me holding onto her, praying that her sorrows would pass through her skin into mine and looking up at the ceiling and the cold, noiseless heating pipes. There was an image hanging there that had escaped from the pages of her sketchbook—it was the anatomy of a young woman: it was in black ink, with the womb shrunken, the ovaries cancerous, and the fallopian tubes tied into dark knots. As we fell asleep, I imagined myself untying them...

7. THE FLOOD

The explosion came upon the ideal earlier than expected, and with impeccable stealth! Such that I hadn't realized it, at first, even though it was set off at the end of a count down from ten, which was heard clearly. Now it's inescapable, everything is falling apart: the nucleus of my existence has burst.

I didn't mention it before because the consequences were yet understood—I was tired and my whining was drowning out the sound of reality—but, in the thick of its adverse effects, the sordid event must be mentioned that spawned this evil storm—the reason this flood is rising.

I had just returned to Monterey from a short trip to Tacoma, Washington to see family. The week of Christmas had lasted too-long, with a too-rich diet, and too-cramped sleeping arrangements. A typical holiday, with my brother Aden there, my Aunt Susie and cousins, then Mima and Sydney arriving on Christmas Eve, just in time for a brief, heavy snow. It was the kind of snow that sticks only in your hair and on your coat, but which the ground soaks up before you can make angels. So typical, in fact, this holiday, that the four Fonts present—

unfortunately Mitch couldn't make it—went out for a walk in the pleasant display and stepping inside at the corner store where I used to get my candy fix in my five or six year old youth, I bought everyone orange-cream sodas and a lottery ticket as a joke. Drinking our sodas, we continued on walking and saying the damnedest things: Aden declaring exemption from "the blue-flash and false capturing of the digital generation of fabricated memorabilia," or something like that; Me gloating over something my aunt had said the day before: "Boy, you're only twenty-one years old, what wrongs could you have done? You're not a bad person—unless maybe you've killed someone!" This last part was laughed at, I felt great, inspired even, but then Mom and Syd chimed in with, "or if you've gotten someone pregnant." Aden said the comment was aimed at all of the men in our family, and that the only two women we had were embittered by our abandonment. The subject set me off. Too-much had been said.

Anyhow, returning from this little vacation, depressed, New Year's Eve, I resolved to not act pitiful and wallow at the house alone. Instead, I would go down to the bar alone, act pitiful and wallow there. At least there would be the idle drinking and open purses, maybe a few free drinks. THREE-TWO-ONE. When the ball dropped a woman I had just met, named Anelle, whose friends had been paying for my drinks just as I'd hoped for, turned around and kissed me. With what vigor! Only a 35 year old divorcée with two kids(a five year old son and a two year old daughter, who were staying with their dad for the night), could have had such a sexual appetite—nearly overwhelming—and expressed it so easily in just a few slips of the tongue and her hand pressed against my stomach. What vitality! I reciprocated, rather, didn't object to this action, by settling one hand on the side of her square, mature jaw, and holding my drink at arms length away with the other to keep it from being spilled in the transaction.

This seemingly insignificant kiss feigned as a dud, and the dinner date the following night, but on further inspection the heavens would have been noted as mulling over the clouds, collecting the dust of unfulfilled dreams and conjuring a nasty forecast that would read: UNFORGIVING RAIN, with a chance of rubbers needed. High: Temporary. Low: Eternal. Details, See Below.

The whole of Monterey Peninsula is going under, being enveloped by broken vows. The violence is spinning wildly in perfect control, growing exponentially. Spermy rain is covering everything. Trash is pasted to the pavement by the sticky stuff. Rivers are overflowing; new ones are forming. Waves have reached the roads—seaweed, sand, and rocks are blocking Ocean View Blvd. More jellyfish are dying. Branches are falling over neighboring small town Pacific Grove. Gates are unhinging. The power is out. Shelter is being sought in a dark café with a paper-and-permanent-marker OPEN sign in the window.

From my seat in this dark café we will have to carry on for now. My clothes are wet, my hair dripping, and my fingertips purple. Three older gentlemen sit nearby, talking out the storm—could care less about trying to listen to their conversation. Doesn't concern me. Everything is falling apart, as I said, and the idea has taken over. It's all I can think about. And with the walls of my residential niche disintegrating the whole time!

Dead-deer Lane has changed; the quirks are being renovated. My father and his wife have moved out, and little Emiliana, into their own house in Pacific Grove where the pedestrians walk out in front of cars, which in turn, at 15miles per hour, have to stop. The gardens there are eaten by deer. Raf's bachelor lifestyle is back in full swing. A different guest stops over every night, pokes her head in to introduce herself to me then retires to the master suite—I can never remember their names. The reintroduction of this persistent "snatch," as they call it, this casual necessity of ego-petting, which is all it amounts to, has left me on the out. No more pats on the back and no more canoodling with newscasters for me. The Book? Even a paperback won't bend the way he wants it to—forget about it! Here on the out with me, though slightly further out still, is Anelle, whose name can't help but be remembered because it was only a moment ago that I left her company. She asked me to come to her apartment where she was waiting for me with the door to her children's room shut, candles lit, and music playing—a cold bottle of champagne on the table next to two glasses. Naked beneath her thin black dress, she was just waiting for me like that! I had no intention of going, but the only bone in my body that dared move sought out the opportunity without a second thought and went on ahead of me. By the time I caught up, the deed had been done and her postcoital snores were cuing the thunder. The thought of it disgusts me. My joints are all locked up. I'm paralyzed by devastation.

Being immobilized such, stuck here in the dark of this café at a table near the window, I can do nothing more than watch as the chaos continues to unfold. A morbid sense of well-being comes over me, makes me want to casually slide my teacup off the table to hear it break. Makes me want to burst out laughing. It's wonderful. It's as if the world is being purged by this storm. Its molecules are being separated with the utmost care, of a gentleman with two prying fingers that works over The Collective Tramp, and then pours bleach down the open *snatch*! What a fantastic sensation. In my temporary blindness, as my eyes undergo the process of this sanitization, the images through the window can just barely be made out—they're still coming down alongside the rain, and, likewise, are rising again with the flood waters, collecting in dismal gutter-streams that mix with memory and work through the grey antimatter of my brain's alchemy:

At once everything becomes white. A clean, radiant white without distinction. Somewhere the sound of marbles dropped on cardboard. Each *plop* is a quake through the white, a writhing current of motion sickness like a light breath over a bowl of milk, or gasoline fumes on a summer day. Try to concentrate on the folds. Unravel the compressed aeons that make up their ethereal yarn. Somewhere the marbles continue to drop like a mantra, more intricately weaving their muted rhythm into the white, kneading it into varying densities—semen collapsed upon cotton, sugar pressed into silk, heavy cream curdling. One of the marbles, a single particle of the debris, hardly bigger than a quark, penetrates the white-cardboard of my dome, and comes under the microscope of delirium: cascading through the abyss it begins to tremble, transform—the transmutation is occurring before my mind's eye! Right here in my glass head It is an alligator, jaws opened to reveal a gob of spit in his teeth, that clamps down, *snap!*, on the ass of a soldier —a glint in the soldier's eye, ignoring the pain, looking down-barrel of an M16, he pulls the trigger and the recoil breaks his clavicle; a diadem of blood hanging in the corner of a dark-skinned mouth, agape against the soil of an unknown country—an iridescent spill, running in a crude river that flows through me as truly as my own patriotic blood, pumping red Indian paint brush, blue Wyoming sky, and the white Thread of a fabric once sewn into Stars. Through my veins shoot these celestial strings, tethered to the vaults of my heart, where they shorten, wind, and twist in curlicues that spiral into the double helix of life itself, like the highways, interstates, railroads, and rivers that are interwoven into the DNA of America. If only I could take hold of this thing within me—this life-force! Run with it along each of these arterials, like a traveling musician on a penniless tour, singing until my engine died! Blow it out through America from a foghorn that sounds like Sigur Rós. If they tried to detain me for disturbing the peace, I would laugh in their faces and tell them, honestly, I didn't know there was any. They'd have no ground to hold me on.

If only I could take hold of this thing within me, indeed! I am running with It already, but parallel to It and with a half-inch between, just out of reach—the space there is occupied by a monster, a glutton, a sadist, a bitch; it's greed topped with envy topped with deceit, gobs of infidelity, and a whole lot of other shit besides. Human in every aspect. My own skin covers the rigid skeleton and it's thicker than all of the fat in the Arctic. A shameful coat of misdeeds and vice. But within is the seed, the chemical compound of Idea and Action: *the double helix of life itself.* It may be cold here, but it is not dead yet! There is a pulse, it just has to be searched for. Dig through the layers of luxurious fat and you'll find the varicose lifelines of America, long pressed against the

49

gelatinous skin underneath, and they're ready to burst—Search every crevice, flap, nook, and fold of this gargantuan whore and you'll find it: that one faint beat, that single thump that is the sound of life. The trouble is in cutting it open—sticking the knife into yourself and sacrificing the past, killing off all your demons, forgiving yourself. I'll chew through it if I have to, all this high-caloric sin I've stored up, the fat of my transgressions. I am a desperate man. I will do anything to pierce the amniotic sac that encloses this Idea, take any anti-coagulant Action that might let the blood gush forth, to free the life within.

Therein lies the trouble, I say, because aside from the big Talk there is a large part of us, the human part, that doesn't want to close the half-inch gap and start anew. That dirty fat may not warm us, but it's all we know and there's something comfortable about the way we wear it. Besides, what would we do with ourselves if we could truly live without a care? How would we divert the hours we once spent in self-loathing? in feeling sorry for ourselves? in reliving our heinous pasts? I tell myself that I would get a boat, take up painting more often, learn to play an instrument, to speak another language, read all the classics for pure enjoyment, but even while I tell myself this I am remembering another storm, one far removed from what is currently precipitating, but just the same is a part of it—one leading directly to the other: the Monterey rain pounding on the glass falls far deeper through the abyss, ten degrees below freezing, where it becomes snow over Lincoln, which then drifts, more specifically, into a puffed up memory. Soft white stars are coming out of the sky, spectral white daisies and baby's breath, like salt shaken in slow motion over a paper-mâché setting.

It had only been a week since Lillian and I had started spending our nights together and, as usual, she called on me late in the evening. We were at the apartment on a bottle of wine and she was still riled up about a fight she had had with John earlier. He was threatening to put her belongings to the curb because they were just sitting at his place, haunting him, and he wanted them gone. A few picture frames had already been smashed. Before he could do any more damage to her stuff, she said, she wanted to pick them up—not another moment could pass with them in his possession. She wanted me to come with her.

Maybe 20 blocks southeast, around 16th and D, was the old apartment. The drive took only a few minutes. John was waiting out front when we arrived, his skinny figure dark with the building lights behind him, a black trash bag at his feet. Having parked on the side of the building, Lilly got out of the car and left me there to wait. The flower petals flaked off the cloud-heads like dandruff, and the residue was building up in the streets—big orange plow trucks were just starting their blinking routes. One came down 16th street where I was standing, pushing the snow into oily heaps onto the sides of the street. Couldn't tell if it had made a noise. I was in a daze, half-watching the truck get smaller down the street, half-picturing the argument going on inside. I was still watching the truck when Lilly was suddenly back outside, a few steps away from me, with two black trash bags in hand. "That bastard, he's breaking all of my shit—do you hear that?" She shook one of the bags, apparently the sound proved her claim, but my hearing must have still been off. She said there was more.

I wondered what I was doing there. My presence felt, if I felt anything at all, wrong. John came around the corner with two more bags and a mouthful ready to come out—I stopped him where he was and the look he gave me was gut wrenching. I was the last person he wanted to see; this *was* wrong, and there I was standing in front of him with two and half years in trash bags in his hands. He set the bags down in the snow. "Come help me grab some more of this."

There were eight or so bags at the top of the stairs in the darkest hallway ever stood in by young men—the sight of them made my guts ball-up a little more and I wanted to cry for Poor John getting the worst of all this. "Sorry about all this, John," was the only thing that came out.

"I don't know what's going on between you and Lilly, but I wonder if you know what you're getting into," said Poor John. "Good luck." I knew all too well, and that knowing made me want to hug him—had a little wine in me, too. There was no sense in this scene, and I wished I could just sit him down to have a drink. There was something about him, the way he had said "good luck" to me, and meant it. Gut wrenching, as I said, the whole damned thing. He set his bags down in the same spot of snow he had the last while I took mine all the way over to the car. Lilly was sitting at the wheel ready to go and told me to get in, we were leaving—she'd get the rest of it later. I didn't ask any questions, there weren't any answers that I would have cared for—I just got in the car, silent, and she pulled out onto the road. As we started back toward my apartment I watched the front door of the building with as much interest as I took in the big orange plow truck, and I saw John come out with another set of bags—he yelled something after the car, threw the bags on the ground, and stood there, a skinny dark figure, as Lilly kept driving. John evaporated completely into the dark.

The image of him standing there losing ground, becoming the night, scared the hell out of me. Someday Lillian Jean would be leaving me in the same way. Never would I tell her I loved her after witnessing that sight, for fear it would accelerate the process of my own elimination. In the reality of the sickness, it must have also been exhilarating, the prospect of such genuine sadness. Not only did the human part of me want to love and be loved, but the sick part wanted to be left in a flurry, in a blaze—it wanted to be hurt. It didn't just want these things, it needed them. One couldn't be without the other. There was to be a beginning and an end, and each part was to be enjoyed equally and wholeheartedly, in its own natural course, while cataloguing the seconds in between to memory. Henceforth, moments were to be savored as if they had already passed, and I were recalling them by some trivial item freshly plucked from the trash bag history of our own doomed love. The effect was elating.

8. SO LONG LOVE, SO LONG LONESOME

Being nostalgic at every waking hour of the day, for the very hours you are pissing away, a strange thing happens to your elated consciousness. You begin to live in something close to a dream, but detached slightly from it. The forms become nearly *too* lucid. You are the narrator to the greatest film ever made, playing your role from somewhere in outer space while simultaneously watching, and the only angles being shot are hi-def close-ups.

Perhaps that is all love really consists of: being situated squarely in time and having the ability to look upon it as if from a distance, like you are holed up in a dark room in the center of your own universe, and by way of a single pinpoint of light you are surrounded by images that are enlarged to grand proportions. They are put through the filter of sentiment, and, though they are right in front of you, you can't quite grasp the exact emotion that was tailored to the event, but the very intangibility of it transcends any *known* emotion and it takes on a myth-ical quality, which is then deemed *Love*. Everything becomes of extr-eme importance after that.

For the first time in my adult life I became fully aware of my surroundings. I remembered what it felt like to be wide awake, and what it felt like to have just awoken from a particularly satisfying dream while no longer having the desire to fall back asleep to try and recapt-ure the dream just departed. There was only the desire to look around and take it all in. My lips were swollen with song. The sole intelligible phrase that sputtered out, which sputtered out all day long, was *Lillian Jean*.

In hindsight, the authenticity of these heightened perceptions is questionable. That they should have been inspired under the name of a woman is surely suspect, but even this skepticism cannot completely strip me of what I felt then. The sensations derived from a simple walk through the town I had known all of my life, but was then experienc-ing again for what felt like the first time; the morning rituals that preceded the walk.

Anywhere between eight and ten in the morning the alarm went off at the apartment—depending on what time Lilly had to be at work. If any part of our bodies were uncovered overnight they were frozen at this point and the blood had to be shaken back into them. A half-inch of ice covered the window, top to bottom, and wouldn't completely melt until near enough to sundown that it would instantaneously begin to freeze over again. Our breath was visible and our spines were icicles.

Lilly got out of bed first, leaving me to take on the last bit of warmth in the sheets that remained from her body—they still smelled like nicotine, old coffee, flowery sweat, unwashed hair. Watching her dress, I would recall the way I had held her the night before—sometimes stupidly, sometimes gently—and recall the prayers I had said for her, the miracles requested. The thought of her body mixed with mine, the tangle of our tongues and limbs, the tingle. "Lilly, it's so goddam cold!" I'd say, not wanting to desert the bed we'd made love in, as she pulled on her argyle long johns over her thin white underwear up to, but just below, the tattoo on her side. The meaning of it, this tattoo inked into the soft skin of her right side, was never quite understood: just circles; small, big, interlinked, and side-by-side. Maybe some sort of metaphor for life, maybe just inane lines that served no greater purpose than to draw my attention to that sensuous area of her skin— that torturous area just above the protruding bones in the hip that made you want, and gave you, something to hang on to. "It's so cold," I'd complain again, though not really caring, not while I was striving to memorize each dainty curve of her body. So turn the heat on, a simple thing. I avoided telling Lilly that the money had nearly run out and heat couldn't be afforded.

In my head we were still making love. She was slipping into the layers of her winter clothes: a cotton tank top over her bra, a long-sleeved shirt over that, her Hemmingway sweater, a pair of jeans over the aforementioned long johns(over the underwear), two pairs of socks, the top pair made of thick wool, then a long, blue wool coat with brown toggles; then finishing everything up by smoothing her hair down into that short ponytail at the nape of her neck. This was all performed to the soundtrack of the screeching morning trains which very well could have been headed to Seattle, where only a few months later, after all the money was gone, I would find myself unloading their freight and waiting for Lilly's letters. Sometimes accompanying the sound of the trains was the music we had forgotten to turn off the night before, barely audible, or a neighbor making breakfast, and the echo of doors opening-closing in the hallway. Once Lilly was ready I hurried to hop out of bed into last night's clothes and brush my teeth in order to head out the door by her side.

53

She hated Moon café, where I frequented, but there was a place right next door to it, called Mill, where some friends of hers worked. On the occasion they were on shift we saved the cumulative three dollars that two small cups of coffee would cost us; always a short cup with Lilly—never any time for more than that. Two snow and slush blocks to get to Mill, the short cups of coffee were taken onto the veranda—priding it on being the last of its kind—where we sat down five feet above street level for stiff-fingered cigarettes with the wind tightening our faces. In the deadening prairie cold there were faint odors of Naan baking at the Indian restaurant, wood-fired ovens just warming up at Maslow's, where Lilly was still working at the time, and something sweet and creamy that could never be pinned down to a certain location. Also there were onions sautéing at the hotel's restaurant up the block, and french-fries. It was the smells that made everything real. Only real people needed food to eat, and the Haymarket was full of the smells of this food—all at once they succeeded in only smelling greasy, but still that smell made you hungry for whatever was producing that grease. Then the smell of her Camels—the last whiff as it was exhaled down the length of the veranda, putting out the butt into the ashtray and telling me she had to get to work, half of her coffee still unfinished.

When she said goodbye it was with a feathery hug like the cold wind, no more or less personal. With just the hug lingering, nothing else, I sat back down to finish my cup and watched her turn the one corner it took to get to Maslow's. As she turned the corner, I remember always thinking that our last kiss had been missed, or skipped; that she had deprived me of the last touch of her lips, the one concrete thing that should be held perfectly in memory. In all of the mornings spent in that manner, I never got that kiss. Only a small cup, half a cup!, of coffee and a hug. Then there was time to kill.

Lillian was working double shifts then, so it wasn't until after 11pm the call would come from her. Sometimes, if she went out after work to drink at some offhand party I wasn't invited to, it wasn't until three or four in the morning. And, that is, if she was ever heard from again at all.

For a short time, the bottom half of my coffee, this was reflected on. Lilly was imagined to have just walked away from me for good, without even a kiss! Then, regretfully, standing up from the table, the last cold sip was downed while taking one last glance at the particular angle her cigarette had been smashed into the ashtray. The specific bend of her discarded filter was the final piece of evidence of her existence.

Determined to not go back to the apartment—having just been left by the woman who I loved, and who slept there with me the night before—I began walking with collar up, hands in pockets, on the snow-covered sidewalks west of downtown. With a few straggling flurries in the sky, The Narrator took on a grave tone. He mentioned, in utmost seriousness, the names of the places passing along P Street, now on the way into downtown, or the services they offered, but only on the side of the street which I walked, the north side: Vince's Italian Ristorante, Moon Café, Duff's Tattoo and Piercing in the space above Moon—a small break here came at the gated opening that leads to the courtyard behind the café—then The Chocolate Accents store, Old Chicagoff, The Gas Station, Lincoln Journal Star, and so on. And he mentioned some miniscule detail, in unwavering tone, that was witnessed through the windows to each of these establishments: spilled cream on the café counter, colored hearts printed on a chocolate lollipop, smeared butter on the edge of a plate, the green six-ball missing the side pocket in a game of pool, etc.—from here the details were extrapolated, backstories evolved, idiosyncrasies fabricated, nuances refined, until eventually I found myself, exhausted, in the heart of downtown Lincoln, filled up with this humdrum and wondering about my own existence. I reconsidered the ashtray. Were there two butts, or one? Luckily, there was always someone downtown to run into that knew you some-how, from some-where, or through some-one. It was like a quick pinch, if you played it right—it brought you right back down into things. There was nothing interesting about the dialogue— "no, I am, uh, actually...I'm over at The University," they said; or they might be "just working, j u s t - w o r k i n g(blows into hands)—saving up money to move away this summer." It was never asked what you, or they, were studying, what the place of work was, or where the plan was to move. Often, the fact was that neither one knew the other's name, and it was too ridiculous to ask after the initial "what are you up to?" Not to mention giving a shit less about the answer. *If you played it right*, and did get off with just a quick pinch, rather than a coarse rub on the arm, it was only because you happened to look up first, and at the first hint of recognition you shot an alarmingly big smile, in combination with a nod, picked up the pace, and kept moving.

Then there was a stop at the library or bookstore. Either provided warmth for awhile even if you weren't in the mood to sit down with a book. Usually, the library was opted for because it was bigger and had public restrooms. Whatever it may be inside of you that needs to come out, to not be able to relieve yourself of it is to take the joy out of living—the only thing you can think about is when you'll be able to *go*. Just knowing the restrooms were there made the library a much more comfortable environment—you could rest easy with all the other bum inhabitants. So I did, strolling leisurely about the stacks, taking a seat here and there, getting up, picking out books at random. After reading the first few pages of a dozen or so books like that, losing track of time and making two trips to the toilet, I was shaking with ideas. Circular ideas, stolen, that altogether went nowhere. An uproar of images and words that put me not only in my next move, but also with Lilly, in an old dream, twenty years older, and in the library in each of those dozen books to boot. To keep from passing out I had to get out of there.

Back on the street, by pure habit, suddenly on the same route but in the opposite direction than taken to the library earlier—what time was it now? Along P Street, again on the north side, inevitably heading toward Moon café in the Haymarket. An absurd amount of money was squandered then on coffee, and now and again a bag of pistachios. Aside from my meager diet of eggs, potatoes, and onions, which came cheap, coffee was the only thing regularly purchased—well, cigarettes too; rent was paid far enough in advance that it was no longer considered an expense, the heat, as I said, was done without, and I didn't own a car. If I wanted to travel longer distances there was a bike on hand, or I need only call up Jason or Dunning—my friends were good to me, and I yet felt as if I were imposing a burden. Not back then.

It happened that a phone call to Dunning became unnecessary, especially when my plans were to stay in. He started showing up at the apartment unannounced after his Theology course ended at around nine o'clock. Having long since left the café, maybe taken a hot bath, read a little, wrote a few nonsensical poems just to pass the time, then finished my dinner, the door opened—never any knock—and Dunning came in through the kitchen. "KawrlFont!" He threw his bag onto the counter. This was his way of greeting me, always the last name with the first, bastardized, slurred without a pause between them, as if they were just one word, followed by a hug and a kiss on the cheek. "I love you—how have you been KawrlFont?"

Dunning had a way about him that was questionably effeminate and promptly ignored. If it weren't for his religion he might have tried sitting in my lap. But he was innocent enough and was good company besides. I liked it when he came over and even expected the visits—had he not showed up one night, his absence probably would have inspired worry. Disregarding the kiss on the cheek, Dunning was told to sit down, that he was out of his mind, ironically, and that it was freezing. "Lillian left me again today."

Instead of sitting down, Dunning paced about the kitchen and checked the cupboards, telling me she hadn't left. It wasn't uncommon for him to take this time to stuff a few items in there from his bag: a box of pasta, some cans of soup, potato chips, crackers; he would end up eating most of it anyway, storing it invisibly somewhere in his 6'1" 135lb frame after a few glasses of wine. And, speaking of, after he clo-

56

sed the cabinets and finally sat down, he would blatantly ask, "where are those girls with the wine? I thought they said they'd be down here fifteen minutes ago."

Kira and Carla, who had not been deterred by the addition of Dunning to the scene, rather welcomed him cheerfully, gave answer to this question by stomping down the back stairwell, then blasting into the apartment as usual—they actually *pushed* the door open with the wine jug, I think, judging by the sound they made. It was miraculous that they never failed to bring that promised-wine! And another glass for Dunning? That was no problem, of course. It should be mentioned here, because it gave way to the conversation for the rest of the night, that there was no reason Dunning's presence wouldn't have been acc- epted by the girls; he and Kira had known each other for most of their lives, having attended the same schools up until high school. There were plenty of old stories to tell and, in later nights, even more judg- ments to be made. But, in the first nights, there were just the few gla- sses that were poured and downed, and the talk that became their rem- iniscences. Carla and I listened without a word. In our quiet way, we learned and relearned to what extent Kira had been a tomboy and a troublemaker growing up. Dunning recalled times when she had pissed on this person, flung shit on such and such doorstep, gave a handjob to so and so, but there were so many bizarre occurrences, which Kira willingly laughed at and added her own spin to that I lost interest in even pretending to listen.

When they got into this vein, which was apparently necessary for them to become reacquainted as adults, my glass was topped off and, leaning back on the couch, I might even close my eyes and wander off to more relevant places where I was at the center of everything and things spun around me at my command. Shit and piss didn't strike my fancy. Love is what had me and in the dark room to which I wandered it absorbed itself in my melancholy, going over the time spent in it with Lillian. Her cigarette in the Mill ashtray was brought into the picture and I was glad to have made the effort to remember the sight. In the span of maybe twelve hours it had come to signify our entire relat- ionship. The clarity of it nearly brought me to tears. Getting worked up like that, with tears in an unnoticeably thin membrane over the iris, and a cathartic smile so lazy you could only see it in the corners of the eyes—it felt great. I was at home in my own sentimentality. None of the night's shit or piss could snap me out of it—only the woman that put me in was capable of bringing me out, and that's what event-ually happened.

On the counter the phone was going off. Lillian Jean calling, hour unknown. She was downstairs. Was anyone there? Should she come up, she wanted to know, or did I want to leave with her? On varying nights the answers might change, some, according to the amount of wine left in the bottle, or what the weather was like, or what time she had to work in the morning, but the end result was the same—we were together. That was the only thing that mattered.

Once you've lost someone, no matter how abstract their loss may be, to have them come back is the most unexpected and gratifying thing in the world. They can truly be appreciated because you know what it's like to be without them. It's an ancient wisdom, but to rediscover it for yourself is invigorating. When Lillian called, whether it was at eight pm or four o'clock in the morning, I was elated to receive her. However short the time allowed was, it was accepted graciously, as a gift, and everything within it was done to prove my love.

9. DANCING IN THE GOD-DAMNED

In the hours before Lilly called, true or not, *we became* the artists at 8th and Q Street, the new American Impressionists—or at least I did. Everyone else was just there for the entertainment. Dunning had moved in to help me with rent—his clean clothes were kept in various kitchen cupboards, his dirty clothes in the Lazy Susan, and his sleeping bag and pillow were laid out in the closet. If he got too drunk on a given night he might not make it to his neat, private bed in the closet, though, instead taking to the tiled bathroom floor, or, if he really tied one on, save us, while I was still sitting up with guests he would get into my bed—just five feet away from where we were sitting—and call out to me, "KawrlFont, when are you coming to bed!?" then mumbling for a while longer before falling asleep. Nights like that the piano bench was moved and I slept on the rug, or headed off with Lilly to whichever couch or guest bedroom she was staying for the night—it would still be another month before she had her own place. The morning after there would be a note from Dunning apologizing: *sorry about last night...see you after class. love, Dunning.* Or, once, returning to the apartment around 10am, there was a different note taped to the door: *out of food...will pick some up after work. see you then. sleep with me already would you!* The notes were never mentioned to Dunning. There was no need—we both knew what they meant. I just tossed them and chose not to press the matter, though it was preferred for him to find his way back into the closet.

The way Dunning got drunk—drunk enough to sleep in the bathroom or to invite me into my own bed—was by complete accident. Beforehand, he would be holding the most dazzling conversations, with not a drop that showed, until, at some ambiguous moment, he stood up, stumble-danced his scarecrow frame over to the bathroom, then came back without a single inhibition like he'd just pissed them away, and he would say something so lewd as, "Yes, all of the Buddhists are going to hell." He was a sober zealot, but with wine it was incomprehensible. Then, what was I? The Brazilian girl that was there the night the Buddhists were condemned was a good friend of Dunning's and cried when she heard that all those peaceful people were doomed such! I just laughed at its absurdity and pictured their robes being set afire, not because I thought that's what hell was, but because I wanted to further amuse my unhealthy self. I reassured the Brazilian girl that the Buddhists weren't going to hell and told her that, lucky for them, Buddhists didn't believe in hell.

As for the dazzling conversation, there was never a starting point, nor an ending. Everything, as it does in the head of a lush, picked up where it had been left the night before with only slight alterations in the company. And the company! Kira and Carla were still coming around with Kira's new boyfriend along with them, called Adrian Stavas by name. He was a jazz musician from an affluent Southern family, North Carolinians to be precise, that had dropped out of college to pursue a career in music while his brother was flip-flopping in decision of whether to be a Jesuit Priest or a Medical Doctor. All of his life Adrian had had maids cleaning up after him and it turned him into a slob. The mess after he had been over was almost intolerable—finding gum stuck on mirrors, on light bulbs, in cabinets, and other places. Playing the saxophone well was no excuse. But how could I tell him to get out of the apartment when it was his girlfriend who was supplying the wine? There were priorities to be considered. I gritted my teeth while scraping the gum out of the sink.

On top of that, no one was going to Ed's anymore, so the spillover of guests arrived as well. Ed had gone off, no, say *gotten off* on the deep-end by then: eight-balls of coke, whole boxes of mailorder whip-its, all-day-long drunks; the blinds were never opened and tinfoil was put over the glass windows on the doors. Micheal still ventured over there occasionally, but even he was scared off after showing up one night more than half-drunk, wherein Ed answered the door naked, cock in hand, and invited him in. Porn was going on two screens in the living room and Ed recommenced jerking off to it the second his ass touched the couch cushion. "Micheal, what do you like? Tell me what you like." Micheal, who had sat down the couch opposite Ed, watched this happening out of one open eye, and could hardly utter what it was that he liked—"black women... big...black...women, with...asses." Then Ed started searching through computer files and googling those words: *big black women, asses.* Soon enough he had a video going on the smaller of the two screens, just for Micheal—a scene from the wild African desert of a bright pink flower backing right up into the middle of the shot. As

59

it inched closer and closer, Ed turned to Micheal, who recounted this whole story to everyone without cracking a smile, and said, "Micheal, let me suck your dick, just to see how it feels," after he had come once already onto a nearby towel, which Micheal had also watched out of that one eye. "Just watch the screen and don't think about anything." Micheal went on to say that he played like he was asleep, and that Ed had given up—really anything would have been possible at that point, though. It wasn't worth thinking about.

This is just *part* of the periphery, which I have related because it correlated to the influx of people coming over to my place; the other part, in turn, was carried on right there at the studio. Anything could happen, but nothing did—not of importance anyway. There were no expectations, no prerequisites, no exemptions. Bring the whole sour lot was the motto and everyone took it to heart. It made for quite the display. Decadence could be intriguing, for a time. Everyone was drunk on wine bawling about *their* suffering, performing science experiments in open flies that yielded no results, taking handfuls of pills and spooning nonsense out of their asses—if only to make room for another bottle! After the show's completion the dance macabre repeated itself, but with all the steps memorized there was no longer any reason to stick around. Surely not to wait for someone else to trip, because the tripping itself was a part of the dance—those falls had been memorized too and even the blood you saw was fake. For God's sake, it's been going on for so long like that, the participants are now all certified acrobats: professionals. Protocol? The worse the better, the quicker you get your papers signed. The train wrecks even come with instructions and safety nets—ten feet below everything they hang in giant stretches of twine spun from middle-class boredom, dead literati, sad pop songs, and megalomania. It's pathetic.

That we should finally come back to the very center of all this futility and find that this is where the conversations were happening is no less tragic than it is adherent to an historic societal principle—it is, in fact, the fundamental inspiration for philosophers and holy men alike. After the bread has been got, then what? And why? Join the dance, recount the steps, repeat—put your arms around whatever hips may be situated in front of you and carry on? More bread—Then what? Dance until the heart gives out, find yourself still kicking and dipping your flesh into the fleshy retreat of another all the way into the ground? No more bread then—so? What? Dunning and I were the only ones at the center asking *now what* as we sat out the dance, though there was usually an interchangeable accompaniment, sometimes two, that served more as a wall with ears—something to bounce our voices against. Whether or not the sounds heard bouncing back were heard correctly is of no consequence because, either way, what was heard became the foundation of the life that then did grow from and about me: All things were Holy.

Without any distinct starting point, as I said, there was a reaffirmation of this Holy Faith in our conversation.

"Exactly," Dunning said, "it's beyond us, all of us, to truly comprehend the meaning of it all—but, in the absence of that knowledge our faith is made perfect!" And, what, with modern doctrine, I likely said—in two thousand years only a fraction of the impurities could be imagined; the adaptations of the initial Truths to suit the needs of this war, that ruler, what have you. Which wasn't to say those Truths had been destroyed, or completely covered up, but they had been disguised in self-soothing parable and partly omitted besides. "That perfect faith is the only thing we have—if we can obtain it," Dunning continued, "which is what I struggle with, about going to Church I mean—see, because they preach this doctrine, the hypocrites, and they preach it from an altar they place even *above* The Throne."

The Throne of Modern Christianity, of The New Believers! Another swig of wine and I began, drunkenly, idiotically. "Their acts of praising—they literally *look* like they are *acting*. You went to one of the New Churches for a bit, right? Well, then you know the innocuous music, the closed eyes and raised hands, the crosses on street corners. It's all so irreverent to me. And they call God their *friend*, yeh know? As if their personal relationship with Him is a nonchalant affair in which He lies in their bed, strokes their hair, listens to music with them— plays with them, they say. They're running through a field together and they're the only one that sees Him, that's the way they think. You're damned if you're not running through that field with them! Maybe it's just beyond me, maybe my heart has been *so hardened*—though I doubt it—that I'm incapable of such a relationship—and do I really want a relationship like *that*? To me it seems degrading. Where's the majesty? Where's the *incomprehensible greatness*? The *Holiness*? Remember, I say this knowing I'm no better—I talk a big one, but, so? Maybe this talk makes me worse; *of course* this talk makes me worse. I am even more so responsible for the perversion of God than any of those other people." No, that couldn't be; at least I was trying, searching—Dunning added in my defense. At least I had a pure heart. "Pure!" I laughed, "Pure? If you only knew, Dunning, some of the things I've done. I'm the ugliest person in this room...(look around)...my good intentions are a joke—I don't mean them to be, they *are* honest—but, look! What good have I done, really?" This was preposterous to Dunning, who could never think such a thing about me, not with his limitless affection, though I don't know why—he had clear evidence otherwise. He even used my own words to exemplify how *humble* I was, which were laughed at. "Did I say ugliest? I was joking, I meant *proudest*. Even in my self-loathing I refuse to believe that any of these people are closer to anything than I am."

"You're laughing!" he said. "You can't even take yourself seriously talking like this—don't joke now." One of the ears on the wall was grinning, grinning so big and indiscriminately that I suspected he hadn't heard a thing, rather was close to passing out while sitting up. Dunning held for a moment per my request—we had to watch as his head made the last bob into sleep. There was something so great in that, our man, how he took the high road; how he just fell sound asleep like that, still smiling.

Around then it broke off. Right before Dunning could finish his thought, which undoubtedly would have been too gracious for my likes, and he did his stumble-dance to the bathroom thereby returning with eyes crossed and zipper left undone. For just one last second he might hold it together, just long enough to say, "Kawrl-Font, the thing about you, is, you don't judge anybody—you don't care one way or the other what the person next to you is doing, because it doesn't affect the state of your soul. Maybe it's just that you don't give a shit, but I think it's actually that you care so much, that you're willing to overlook a person's shortcomings and love them indiscriminately." Then his eyes, still crossed, rolled back into his head, his pants came off, and another glass of wine was poured.

Next day. After reading whatever note Dunning had left me before leaving for class or work, I sat down in the window and tried to recapture the night before. It never came out quite right. Even just now I've put it down falsely, but the specifics could go one way or the other, because, as it was, the talk itself was as old as time—it was the same conversation had ages ago and still no concrete answers: just speculation and renewed faith; young men endeavoring to understand themselves through lots of wine. After seeing how mundane the first few lines appeared, all attempts at transcribing the conversations were scrapped and I began writing down a stream of whatever sat before me— thought or object—starting with the most obtuse:

"Again it has become the thoughtful dark," I wrote with a heart full of belief, "and on the floor I have neatly laid sheets for my bed. In this absence of light it is easier to commune with the deceased, having departed gracefully and dignified and without pride and quietly and with a ruckus and peacefully and with fear and with remorse, through murders, drug abuses, age, weak hearts, war, childbirth, suicides, carelessness, malnourishment. The countless natural causes, the countless wrong doings. Hate, Sorrow, Loss, Delusion, Sin. A sinner awaits his death in prison—perhaps he grieves over his damnation, perhaps he grins over the memories of the young girls he'd raped. 'Let him who is without sin caste the first stone.' Be it just for petty evils? Does the culmination of our wrongs amount to any less of a disregard for God? 'But the Old Testament!' they yell. Is this but the practice of our supposed rights as men? Religion & faith are not opposites, but not near the same, though both have been diluted. Are we wayward saints, misled thru aeons of these impurities?

"While in limbo of the question: A needle penetrates the skin of the sinner as he lies strapped down to his chair; a gloved hand guides it, pushing a clear liquid down through the syringe, through the needle, and into his bloodstream. Say, 'what is *that* solution?' A firing squad of the brain, terrorists of neurotransmitters, warriors in the belly of a Trojan horse. No matter, the rapist is dead(I've hardly noticed, though his victims remain scarred). The traitor, the politician, the zealot, and the wrongly accused have also been killed off. I have not surpassed their chest facades to witness them truly and judge their hearts—have you? Silence. Death is glorification, and Christ rose from the dead. It must be so! The earth is cursed with ignorance so that greatness can only be achieved in hindsight—the proverbial perfect, of which nothing is, but the singular God, whom we have removed from his ethereal throne with cheap visions, and exploitations. My God is your God. We speak in secular tongues that are inconsequential. Our temples and synagogues are great earth-distances apart, but are neighbors, too, and colleagues, and our prayers become united in _____. They are heard, unbiased, and unseen, as our inaudible songs of hope—repentances, psalms, whispers to our beloved dead, covenants—traverse through the thought-muddled dark in our aspirations of righteousness we know to be vain until Salvation... Amen."

Laughable as it is, I have provided this reproduction, verbatim, straight out of the notebook in which it was written, in order to ascertain that *we were* spinning our own adaptations of doctrine, but we were overtly conscious of it—we took any and all chances we could get to admit to it, which may have been the charm about us. We were helplessly deranged with spiritual ideas and procured an odd sense of hope by announcing them. All we could do was try to spread our Hope. We found that the people who overheard us *trying*, as few as they were, were attracted to us and were willing to listen to a hell of a lot more. So we gave it to them—why not? At Moon Café, where they held weekly poetry readings on Tuesday nights, the ramblings came to a zenith.

Tuesdays, Dunning and I walked down to the café as an excuse to get out of the apartment. Around eight o'clock the microphone turned on but the place was still deserted, aside from a woman in her late twent-ies that looked like a school teacher(the one everyone dreamed of screwing), the couple of baristas on shift, and Geoff, the owner. *Why not*, I thought, with a whiskey burp and a cough, going up to the microphone and shouting off some short monologue that had people off the streets peeking in. Having been impressed by this, I guess, Goeff, the poor guy—who had once offered me free sandwiches and coffee—was now asking if I would be the featured reader the following week, bring in a crowd. He'd give me some free drinks and an hour in front of the microphone to do as I pleased, if that sounded alright. Can you imagine that, with the shit that was falling out of me then? Free drink, huh, I laughed—serious?—sure, I would do it, but couldn't promise a crowd.

The first reading was a let down. Only about ten people came, but Geoff, for whatever sad reasons, couldn't get enough of it for himself —he asked me to come back again for another featured reading. The second reading was the real show; the one where I died and had to watch from a distance.

Beforehand there was the usual congregation at the apartment, and afterward we reconvened in a similar manner—between, though, happened something unforgettable.

Ten minutes late, with a handful of friends in tow, I showed up at the café to find another 30-so people gathered in the brick courtyard behind the building. For mid-February it was unusually warm, but cold nonetheless—we were still in for one last snowstorm. With your coat on and the warm drinks you could hardly feel a thing. *I* was barely there to feel anything, reading under the ridiculous alias, *Elijah DuPont*, whom was introduced to Geoff some months back. That was the person who was asked to appear, and did so with notebook in pocket, setting down a drink on the chair next to him in front of the crowd— he was someone else, but still a part of me; perhaps more of *me* than Kyle or Karl Benjamin Font had ever been.

When he first spoke, bees came forth from his mouth, tiny buzzing bees that stung the audience a thousand times then died on the spot. Died next to the man his friend's had come to watch. The audience shuddered a tad, and their arms grew expectant goose-pimples. They couldn't look away because they might miss the spectacle they now knew was coming.

He introduced himself by way of a poem—no, not a poem, he said—a song: a terrible, but necessary song, without any musical tune. And the audience? He introduced them as well, to themselves, and asked that they please not take him too seriously, but he was a degenerate more than anything, and a little bit of a drunk. And to prove that he should not be taken too seriously he read a *love song*—the lowest of the low, this love song—and when he finished he *apologized*, but they could move on now, change the narrative pace, if anyone was listening. Was there anyone still with him? Everyone kept their eyes to the front, waiting. Himself, he had given up listening right after the bees. Apropos of the love song, as to seamlessly relate one work to another, he would read a short story, he announced, one that would surely make the audience fall in love with him if they hadn't already. He was absolutely broke and depended on their love; he was about to ask them for a favor. And he did ask for it, too, this bastard, by sending around a tip jar and telling everyone to give what they could—anything would help! Twenty-five dollars came back up to the front, which wasn't bad for a poetry crowd filled mostly with students. Although *I* was moved by this, and went over several small purchases to make with the money, *Eli* just lit up a cigarette, emptied the jar into his pockets, and passed it around again.

By this time there was a three-piece set playing behind him. They had showed up for their own slot, but jumped in to back him after listening patiently for ten minutes and granting his request. The upright bass, the guitar, and drums scored out a rhythmic depression that he nearly started to sing to. He exhaled between songs and let the music fill his silence—he looked through the smoke at all of the faces still settled on *him*, and they caused a change in him. An inexplicable sadness rose out of everything. The music drifted in sad waltzes, reverberated off the sad buildings, dissolved the sad crowd's whispers, and the cigarette in his hand burned ever sadly, slowly. Eli had forgotten the cigarette until just then when he looked down at it in his hand, and he remembered another cigarette—*she wasn't there*; No One was there. He was alone on a pedestal in a garden full of dolls with their heads put on crooked and their backs turned on him. The fingerling tree branches poked his shoulders and pointed to one doll after the other, which then stood up and sat back down in a plastic wave around the garden. The plants were all dead, except in the pots with cigarette butts where the grey stems grew like cancer and the petals were molten tar. Still looking down at the ember glow of his love's eye, Mr. DuPont noticed that there was a cancerous flower growing in its ash. He put it out with his heel into the red brick, then looked up and took in the things around him: they were in the courtyard he thought he knew, the music continued from behind him, the drink sitting on the chair was gone, and the crowd waited for him to speak. He admitted to them that he was a bit tired now, but, he'd end with something befitting the evening. One last song to bid them good-night:

"We talk," said the man, "as if we were preaching over rooftops, or shouting into microphones(he shouted): *I am me, hear me sing!* The holy men of the drunken night, we *talk*...and talk, and talk...devouring the words like messy fruits, spitting the seeds across the room—religious rants drooling from our hungry mouths. We are fed by conversation—discussions removed from time, plucked relentlessly from the ages—ever-repeating the half-answers of the cosmos. We talk until the wine is gone, and past that—until everything has been pulled apart and spilled, then dried up and exhausted. It all lay out there in the open, in silence...and shapeless...stinking of indecision, of curiosity, of yearning —stinking of the odorless Void. Incomprehensibly on the brink of our tongues, at an unobtainable distance, is that expectant twinge, that taste with no description. It leaves us quiet, and still—*in*action—slowly evaporating into Hell, helping no one in our withdrawn static. We are but holy songs of the drunken night, hardly men. So, thank you, for everything, and Good-Night."

10. COCAINE AND IRISH THIGHS

In the excitement of believing in the Becoming—somewhere, somewhere, *somewhere* in the excitement—Lillian stopped coming over. At what point, exactly, remains unknown. Looking back, her inconsistencies certainly were clear enough. If she weren't going to see me she called and told me she was busy with a friend that had come into town, or made some other promises, some excuses; or she didn't bother calling at all for a few nights.

There was one day, when she was moving into her new apartment at 13th and C Streets in the building next to the Everett schoolyard (just two blocks away from her old place with John, her ex-boyfriend), she called me to ask if I could help her move in some of her furniture. Then, a few hours later, she called back to tell me that John, conveniently nearby, had already helped her out and all there was left to do she could do by herself. She said she didn't need my help anymore; what she meant was that she didn't need *me*.

Lilly had quit her job at Maslow's and took a different position at a café downtown, called Sohemian, where the hipsters frequented for their café au laits, espressos, and their big town pompousness. Please, I knew of the people that went there and had nothing to say to any of them. The baristas, who were all friends from that same vein—which John belonged to—drank beer all day at work, then, after closing down shop, they'd get roaring drunk in the back lounge together until four or so in the morning and clean up the mess just before reopening at six.

One of the last nights Lillian came to visit the apartment, around 2am, after drinking with John and the like for several hours at the café, she showed up in a goofy drunk that inspired her to put music on and use anything around the apartment, including the air, to act like she were playing the instruments. My legs were the keys, being tapped on beat as we sat on the edge of the bed. It had been one of my quieter nights, with Dunning off playing poker at the weekly Christian game, and the rest of my friends—that's what they were called then—were doing whatever the hell they could get their hands on. No thought was given to what they were doing—I actually wasn't concerned, contrary to what Dunning thought.

With it having been a quiet night(spent reading, bathing, listening to music at a nearly inaudible volume, and limiting myself to one short glass of wine much earlier on), it frightened me to have Lillian there in the state she was in. It seemed that her goofing might mutate at any moment into a crazed hysteria that would lead to my furniture being turned over and screaming. The bag of cocaine sticking out of her pocket especially terrified me, and I was careful as to how I went about handling her. Choosing to lean back on the bed with my hands folded over my belly, I casually asked her how her night was—good? Lilly was too enthralled by the concert Lilly was putting on to give any more than, "Yeah, work was alright—James brought in a case of Old Style." But, had I heard this song before, she wanted to know, more importantly, forgetting the details about her night and that the music was coming from my machine. I thought about the little bag of coke in her pocket and said nothing.

Still leaning back on the bed as the musical performance continued, I began to think about how I had arrived in that moment—about what had happened to leave me lying on the bed with the woman I claimed to be in love with, while she tapped about like an anxious child with that filthy powder in her bloodstream, oblivious to whose hand it was that now rubbed the small of her back. As far back as could be remembered I had always been a "romantic"—even in the fourth grade I went as far as to steal a bottle of my mother's perfume for my young Valentine. In none of my reveries had I foreseen Lillian Jean. She was the reason I had yet settled, the reason I had always lost interest and kept on searching, but had never before given a face to or a name. And now that her face had fully formed, with a tiny square jaw and sharp chin, almost sinking in in the middle, and been accosted with so much pining and devotion, I was helpless to it.

While lying there like that, with an occasional remark from Lilly about a new song that had just started playing, my thoughts took their course and the other women in my life came into view. My first love, Mary Bilson, who I courted at fifteen and dated for the following two years. She got sick in that time with a rare kidney disease, which her dad, by chance a kidney doctor, caught early enough to treat. Once a month she had to spend a few nights in the hospital for her chemotherapy treatments, where I slept in a bedside chair for the duration. When she was released from the hospital after these treatments she was nauseous for another week after, with anxiety attacks and heart palpitations, too. Her dad had to lay with her then and rub her back, just like I was doing for Lilly, so that she would relax and be able to sleep. Mary took prednisone to help with her recovery, her cheeks swelled from it, and she got sick intermittently throughout the process, but, eventually, she recovered to full health. Afterwards, though she was well, the quality of our relationship that had once made it perfect was flawed. Not to mention, during the same time period, I had watched as cancer took her grandmother away from her. She couldn't look at me anymore without a maturing sadness, filled with the permanence of death and near-death—I had become the physical representation of those things to her. The only thing I could do then was to excuse myself quietly with a kiss on one of her puffy cheeks.

After Mary there were a number of girls I chased. With my expectations inflated by the inopportune emotional trauma of Mary I was consistently let down. Perhaps in a single instance, regarding one Betsy Plum, my indefinite disappointment can be illustrated. It was Christmas Eve just after my seventeenth birthday, and for the few weeks leading up to the day frequent attempts were made at winning the affection of this wide-eyed, curly blonde haired, fair skinned, inherently Middlewestern girl, named Betsy. A particular night before Christmas Eve, standing at the edge of a mostly dried-up lake, with the mud carved out by innumerable overlapping fissures, my efforts warranted a long kiss and embrace that was fashioned from moonbeams and shot through me with an unruly certitude—"*that* is romance," I thought! And that was the thought with me on Christmas Eve, waiting with her kiss-taste at the same dried-up lake, where she was said to meet me, with a dozen gerber daisies in hand and a neatly wrapped gift box that hid inside it a matching set of cashmere gloves and a scarf—light pink with speckles of kelly green, her favorite colors. For three hours I waited there with the flowers frozen into my hands until finally admitting to myself that she wasn't coming—maybe she just couldn't make it, there was something unavoidable that kept her from meeting me. It was inconceivable, what I was saying, that *she couldn't make it*; I knew that she never intended to make it and that I just wasn't worth the trouble. In a dejected stupor, deciding to confirm my predictions, I drove over to her parent's house where she was found dressed and healthy. I gave her the package and the flowers, and as she took them from me she apologized, but I was just too much—we were only seventeen...

Sitting up in bed, the parallels couldn't help but be entertained. There I had waited for Lillian Jean with all of the flowers that could be afforded, blood money and all, only when she didn't come and I then showed up in a dejected stupor on *her* doorstep, she was found to be a little feverish and was naked as the day she came. Not knowing what else to do, she invited me in and even pulled me by the shirt for a quick fuck. After it was over she felt nothing, just a temporary silence in the afterglow and a warm body that could've belonged to anyone. As for this *fucking*, I've had my contentions. Since the first time I lost my virginity, back at seventeen—when Annie Locke crawled through the basement window of my mother's house with the void-like smell of winter and, without knowing I was drunk, got on top of me like a dutiful free-love agent of the world—I resolved to abstain from sex until marriage. This resolution abided to the moral fiber that was carried with me up to that point anyway, so was happily returned to after that slip in judgment, that terrible mistake that left me staring into the paint of my bedroom walls the following day, asking the Great Lord in Heaven Above to forgive me of my sins, and, likewise, repenting that way for another month after.

Therefore, when only a few days had passed after the desired baptismal effect was felt on my conscience, and my soul was fresh as a newborn babe's, it came as a mortifying surprise to find myself losing my virginity for the second time. On this occasion it was to my good friend Hunter's ex-girlfriend, Ali Hideaway, on an unfamiliar bed, which probably belonged to someone's older brother, at the end of a party thrown at a vacationing parents' household. Whiskey-limber, again, only part of me was functioning, and that part was functioning sloppily, like the last leg of a piece of machinery near breakdown. The way I remember it, the act went on for an unreasonable amount of time, and by the end of it, which was a breakdown that preceded the full success of this machinery, I was so close to tears that I had to excuse myself to the bathroom to get a look at the person in the mirror who was responsible for this abominable act. Returning to the room, Ali was sitting on the bed, fully dressed, inspecting her nails. We were both thankful it was over.

Perhaps if the approach to these matters had been more practical, I would have saved myself the guilt, humiliation, heartbreak, paranoia of 12 pregnancy scares, 9 abortions, 5 successful births of bastard children, and countless suicide attempts—these figures are obvious lies, but where is the differentiation between the reality of them, and what has happened in my heart? Are the abstractions of any less value? Either way, I was an idealist, and was determined to reform myself of this natural broken condition and atone for its repugnance on my own terms through a series of starts and desertions of varying Paths to Enlightenment.

Paradoxically, it was these impractical tendencies that brought me to my present disposition, which is more practical, coherent, logical, sane than any I have encountered. I am in a fragile state of perfect equilibrium, in line with the cosmos. Floating forward, the indiscretions are of the past. The light of my being is now rectified in an infinitely intricate prism. Everything is the spiritual part of The Holy Triptych. It is a piece of Art that I am producing by way of Spanish Fly-filled-darts that are shot out through a McDonald's straw concealed in my coat pocket, matched with an equal part of disciplinary serum—of which a side-effect is phallic paralyzation. However, the result is not most notably in the bone, but in the eyes, which become depraved with the physical necessity of sex, so that even the ugliest aspects are trimmed down, sucked in, and tucked away until they too become attractive. It's a Fuckfest Holiday with a lacking interest in intercourse. The beauty, then, is in the defilement itself. *Even the ugliest aspects*, I say, but, more directly, I mean that *especially* the ugliest aspects become attractive: they are constant reminders of the broken condition and proof that I am now existing slightly parallel to it, broken in a narrowly separate way. The difference in this existence, I should mention, is so nominal that it constantly overlooks the other like a glance over the shoulder of a gentleman at an adjacent urinal—always just to size things up. Although I am a quarter-inch bigger, or fuller, and nth degrees more satisfied, I am still malcontented. Because, in the blink of this glance—whether it be into memory, or into surroundings—there is enough sadness, loneliness, disillusionment that provides more than ample fodder for the arc of time between tangents, which is necessary to continue the current trajectory.

Without the touching points of these co-existences, you run the risk of falling into your own orbit with the cosmos, rather than simply being perfectly aligned. A dangerous thing, to become your own sun and moon of indifference—detrimental, and likely irreparable. So, the experiences are savored, brooding over their contents like a dead man in search of his own killer: Himself.

A moment ago in the café, without a sign of the storm's surrender, my glance moved from the window to over the shoulder of an unsuspecting lambikin, a beautiful, young female with mixed blonde and brown curly hair like my mother's, that muttered the words: "I don't want to be any-thing, to any-one." The words sent me hurtling back into my own realm, and here I remain utterly disturbed.

Scrambling the sounds, redistributing their pitches, and playing them over at different frequencies, it becomes clear to me why they sent me hurtling back: Lillian Jean muttered that exact phrase to me. Hearing it again has brought me full circle, back into bed with Her, lying with one hand over my belly, the other moving absently on her back, wondering over those fatalistic words.

The drugs had worn off some, and there was a break in the music that allowed her a moment to recall the immediacies: bed, lamp, heartbeat, breathing, train, *slam*, rug, couch, bed, bed, heartbeat, breathing...breathing...breathing...body, hand. And she then became aware again of where she was, that there was someone lying on the bed behind her, and then who that person was: Me.

My eyes were situated on something so distant from where we were at the time that I didn't notice she had made it past the possibility of shattering until she rose from the bed and turned out the light. With my head still struggling through the last parts of reminiscence to return to the present, I was vulnerable to dementia. Had she spoken, my faculties may have been restored enough to draw clearer distinctions between thought and thing, idea and action. But, in the dark, there was only Her, two heartbeats, and breathing...breathing...breathing that led backwards into the vast emptiness of sexual cognition.

Sex, then, was going to be the gateway into universal exploration, the grand entrance into permanent spirituality—I thought that in the act I could lead Her, the perennial *Her*, through the existential landscapes of the masterpiece I have only now started to dream of. Though this objective failed, to call it *fucking* would still be blasphemy—it was so much more than that. And, in that respect, I have never fucked anyone. I have only given myself, parts of myself, in an attempt to bond with the humanity that one day will be left for good, with all of my goodbyes left between the Irish-colored thighs of these pages.

The next time I can remember seeing her came on another quiet night some two weeks after she appeared at the apartment in her goofy drunk with the baggy of hell sugar in her pocket. That is when everything collapsed.

In between there had been warning signs of the end, and a profound sense of doom, most prominent in that the last of my money was spent. The foreboding was mostly dismissed after March's rent was somehow scrounged together by working for three days as a clerk at a law firm, then calling in sick on the fourth day—the entirety of which was spent in bed thinking that I was going to die, without even fully comprehending what was soon coming—and afterwards refraining from going altogether, without any further efforts of calling in with ill-excuses. Thank God for the timing though. It may have given false hope, but I could afford to quit because I was paid back the last two-hundred dollars owed to me by a former warehouse coworker in Rancho, Ca., who I had lent the money to for hospital bills he had accumulated from an abscessed tooth that poisoned his body in early August. He wired me the money just a few days before rent was due and everything was settled. With one fiasco avoided, the chance of another more serious catastrophe was not considered.

Beforehand, on the night that it happened, Dunning, who had recently taken up painting again, and accredited me with the inspiration, was at work on his first canvas since quitting the year before. It was a reproduction of a photograph that had been taken in the first year of his life, of his father holding him on his shoulder and looking out of an overexposed window. He had undertaken the piece with a passionless calculative technique, of first outlining the figures in delicate pencil on the two-foot by four-foot stretch, then, with the original picture clipped onto the upper left corner, began with layers upon layers of white, greys, black that would later amount to perfect black-white skin tones, depth, meaning, but at the time was still mostly just graphite marks of a sadly laborious work. While he dabbed on one of the first layers—a lighter shade, hardly distinguishable from the white of the canvas—I sat in the window chair with a notebook that not a single word had been written in since talking to Lilly—after two full weeks I say—and was told that she would meet me that night at the apartment. No idea when to expect her, or if she would actually end up coming. And nothing to do but sit there in the window, waiting.

It's the waiting that sends one climbing up the walls—and I was always waiting then. To be alone is not a terrible thing so long as you know ahead of time. Some of my most contented moments have been spent by my lonesome. Like when I rented a room for the night in a cheap hotel in Bordeaux after being lost and hungry all day in the city on foot, wandering about with my duffel bag, and not speaking a word of French!, and sat down on the bed with my dinner of cheese and lettuce sandwiches, red wine, water, and a chocolate bar laid out beside me, opening the window with my shoes off to cool my sweaty feet in the blowing breath of Mother Mary's month. Another person might have spoiled it. But to be promised a bit of company only to be denied it, or to have no clue as to when this company will arrive, and be destined to simply wait—then that is torture. I wonder, how many hours have been whiled away such, in these hours of Wait? Where within them you become incapable of thought, your head is a blank, you mean nothing. *You are no-thing to no-one.* The only thought you have is *when*, and the only feeling is relegated to neither anticipation nor defeat.

I was less than nothing, living in a nonexistence. Dunning, too, speechless at his work, a semitransparent changing screen separating us, seemed like a ghost to me, hovering in the void like a leak of gas in a giant womb where a cashew shaped embryo was attaching itself to the uterine walls: a ghost that had never had the luxury of losing its flesh; a stillborn idea whose only Salvation would come in being expelled into a bowl of piss-water that gets flushed out into the drainage pipes of America. But *when*? By the quality of night, had it been judged by the few couples that walked under the Haymarket lamps with dinner leftovers in styrofoam boxes, and the few doors that echoed in the hallway, and that the midnight passenger train had not yet pulled in to the station, it would have been said to be around ten or eleven o'clock. However, those details weren't registered until much later on. At the time all that was noticed was that it was cold enough to freeze the puddles of the day's extended winter rain, and that it was dark—and that Lilly was somewhere in that darkness.

When she emerged from the darkness it was with a spark, a buzz, an electrical current that revitalized the life within me, then grew rapidly outward in a sudden awareness of my bones, organs, muscles, flesh. Everything that was jolted back into place trembled in the wake. The sound is what sent the initial shock through me—the phone going off. Although she had been given the door code on several occasions, Lilly called up from the street to be let in. By the time she climbed to the fourth floor, the waves that were shooting through my veins had churned the blood into clay. My limbs were doughy, a labor to move. Like in a dream where you must run!, but can't make the first step toward safety. Adrenaline knocked about me erratically without an outlet. My nerves were frazzled.

Answering the door like that, trying to recover from the extremes of wait/arrival—the instantaneous jump from nonsexistence to supersensitive existence, where vertigo takes a strong hold on you—the sight of her put me over, standing there with no discernible change. It was too much to see her in the same outfit, with the same smell, and the same indifferent disposition, cool as if she had only seen me earlier that morning and were stopping by because she was in the neighbor-hood. I was visibly afflicted: a noticeable quake in my hands, slightly paler, the occasional shudder overtaking my body to release an accumulated mass of adrenaline. But with Lilly there was no sign of a struggle, as I said, cool as ever she came in, set her things down, and sat next to Dunning on the couch—miraculously, while my back was turned to open the door for her, he had put away his paint brushes and made himself a drink which he then sipped on the couch with his legs crossed. The candidness, that's what put me over; the way she was convinced of the normality of it all. Refusing to casually sit down with them and stare into the vacuity of *small talk*, I poured myself a drink to soothe my nerve endings and subdue the jerks, then told her we were going for a walk.

Had I not done this, but maybe poured another drink and reduced myself to stirring quietly in my seat, it never would have come out.

Down on the frozen street with the trainghosts while walking Lilly back to her apartment, she felt a previously unrealized obligation to tell me something—she was pregnant. She hadn't intended to inform me of her missed period, of getting sick, of her trip to the doctor, but there was something about the walk, the lamps, the cold—something about being near me and suddenly feeling desperate and frightened that made her reveal those things to me. There was a shred of weakness, a break in her exterior calm that was so apparent it could not be

73

disregarded even by my common illness, or absorption. She needed my advice because she was alone and I was the father. The *father*, to think of it—she was pregnant!

Immediately, sitting down together on a bench to exchange silences, two worlds opened up before me—two glorious worlds, each revolving around this divine conception. Presently there was a magnification, a clarity—we seemed to sit within a bejeweled chrysalis where the beautiful history of all living things was exposing itself. Brought to the forefront of their ever-changing facades, made up of stone, brick, skin, bone, metal, illuminations like tiny suns covered by soot emanated from the surface of everything. Noticed a screech from a train, a crack in the sidewalk—but they were more than a sound, and a fault. They were the brakemen and laborers of all time; they were the travelers and family men; they were history itself, and, sitting there with dear Lillian Jean, we were a part of it.

In the other we were more than just a part of it, we were *It.* I was the brakeman and the laborer, she was the homemaker and the mother —under different facades, of course, but the timeless sentiments were definitely at the center of things where we lived in a small apartment together with our child. Where we made conjugal sacrifices and compromises, and indulged in aspects of the futile traditions of normalcy so that we could provide for the greater meaning that we found in one another and in our child. *The Father!* Suddenly the vision with the boat and the perfume, which had once broken before the faces therein could be distinguished, was interwoven with the features of Lillian Jean and myself. From the mouth of each delicate apparition extolled the words, *"there is a plan for you."*

A whole different world was opening up for Lilly, which spun on the same axis as my own, but in an entirely separate direction. Regretfully, there is not a single detail of this world that exists for me— except maybe a vacant sound—because, after a time of silences conjoined by naive utterances, she rose from the cold bench where we sat, and walked into it alone.

11. LIGHTNING IN THE SNOW

No one knew She was carrying within her the seed of a child conceived on faith, growing patiently against the curved dome of her angelic reproductive cathedral. In her practical and worried thinking, Lilly had no intention of keeping the child and asked me not to speak of it to anyone. Unable to do anything else for her since she had departed into the mysterious folds of this miracle alone, I kept that wish; I kept my mouth shut up with the taste of her sanctified womb, and watched as

74

tears lulled on the pulpits of the prying eyes of the guests that didn't cease coming to the apartment. They were there, looking, but they saw nothing—I was like a vacuum. The entire town was taken in by me and became the dried up lake of my disappointment. Each street, alley, empty lot, yard, and basement was a quagmire, a corridor in the innumerable overlapping fissures of this lake, and within them I was lost.

Out of the labyrinthine walls came Lilly's voice like a tape-recorder, skipping a bit. A phone call: she was drunk, the sounds couldn't all be made out, a skip, a scream—*abandonment, abortion.* The walls were sweating like the cool underside of dead flesh, a cough, a skip, a cry! She was crying to me—*abandonment, abortion.* My mouth was still shut up with the taste, my responses were limited. Her accusations flew violently through the underground shadows of my head and filled it up with their oils and impurities. Morosely, the resulting abdominal cramps that doubled me over were cherished. The sweat from the walls soaked through my clothes, my hair was pushed back from covering my eyes. I was on my knees in the middle of a street. The street had no name, and no signs, the buildings had no windows— I had no voice. Opened my mouth to scream: Nothing. From each surrounding surface still echoed her voice—*abandonment, abortion.* The words streamed over my face, leaked into my mouth, plugged my ears—the taste cobbled my throat. Another cramp came in my gut—I hoped that it would burst, or bust, or spill, or gush out something. Nothing. A pit was inside me, mud in my mouth, couldn't move—like an itch, I wanted to shove my claw-finger through my bellybutton to scratch, scratch, scratch until the pit crumbled, the soft shell decomposed into the mud, and there was nothing left but the source of the thing, which would continue to be clawed at, probing through the hole where once my mother fed me—*scratch* until the blood came! Until from the thing itself, no bigger than a taste bud scab, no less human; *until the blood came* forth and flooded the labyrinth, where it mixed with the sweat and drowned out the thought at its foundation—Me.

If I were ever a bird, my wings were then stripped to the bone-structure and stuck out of the mud, and my feathers stuck out of my nose. Still in the middle of an anonymous street, disappearing beneath it, further down yet, the weight was even greater—my chest was near collapse. Would I ever fly again? Above me, tell me, was there a tombstone to mark my death? Tell me, was there a giant crucifix? No answers, no movement—just the troubling awareness of sinking and a horrible slurping sound of the suction, of the body going in standing straight up. I let it take me. A skip, a beat, the voice at the other end of the line, a wail: *you are nothing.* Only the sinking, and the cavernous wall —which one? There was only one, all enveloping—it burped, farted, spat out a fresh voice: "Come back inside. Get out of the rain!" ("Kira?

Don't grab my hand like that—don't you see that sound? Leave me where I am!") Just step to either side, where it's warm—you'll be fine.

A step aside in a safe room filled with light: the morning twilight; hours noon to five. Lying in bed post blackout, contemplating the slew of bourbon shaded images decorating the wine stained rug, and the first stages of the masterful fresco that would never be finished.

Mornings were for digesting the atrocities and poking at their related ulcers. What that meant was that I couldn't leave the bed until my belly was taught with my own corruption—until I was pregnant with self-hatred, -loathing, -degradation. More than once, stubborn in this practice, the knock at the door went unanswered. Maybe it was Kira to check in on me, or maybe it was the landlord, which then meant there would be a note slid under the door:

Noise Complaints. People coming and going at ALL hours.
This is unacceptable. Call As Soon As Possible.
—Management

Eventually, getting out of bed at the switch-on of the downtown lamps, the note was read. The landlord was called with a disinterested tone later, and told that I was unaware of the activity. He speculated about my sanity. He asked Kira, knowing we were friends, if I didn't have a screw loose, or maybe more than that? It didn't matter. Hanging up with him, there was only another warning, another eviction threat, or something about the police, and then the afternoon began. First with a long, hot bath taken without any of the lights on, then a quick rummage through the remaining bottles to finish off their bottoms; then, with breakfast had in those few drops, I dressed and went out for a walk.

The walks began around six and were actually more of a staggering waddle—what, with all the shit in my belly and a little liquor to start it boiling. Crossing streets, traffic was held up by my load as they watched me to make sure I made it safely to the other side. There was a bomb beneath my coat and the time was wearing down. Huddling in doorways for the occasional light, the other pedestrians froze to see the spark, then hurriedly moved on once the smoke was exhaled. They were unsure as to what was avoided, but as they passed me there was an uneasy relief, then I moved on as well and the time shimmied further down. Meandering about that way with a wild glare until midnight, I found myself back at the apartment, the crystalline countdown starting to flash dashes, and a crowd gathered before my arrival; if I had been lucky enough to gather enough various leftovers to form a pint, instead I'd be settled somewhere along the walk—the sculpture garden, usually, or a dark inlet near the train tracks. Mostly, the walk itself was a last act of Will around the perimeter of the convoluted passages of my drunkenness, where I peered into the cracked surfaces

76

from the dry shores, hoping to gain some sort of knowledge that might save me in my later navigation. But, the gates always opened before getting a good enough look, the dirt was doused and stirred up again, and I stumbled into the corn-maze no less bewildered than before, thinking how I should have stayed in bed.

The last, very late snow of the season inspired me to continue walking along the perimeter of the abyss even though no bottle-remains were procured. In a sickening sobriety, I walked until the snow had gathered five inches about me—there was a nauseating lucidness about it that enchanted me. Already near University, taking shelter where I could at my friend's dorm in room 806, Sandoz, Lincoln, Nebraska, America, Earth, Hell—she let me in and returned to her studying, ignoring me as I sat down in the window to watch the snow. A million or so Angels in the middle of a great big pillow fight in Heaven, I thought, and all of their spilled feathers floating down over the plains like sad-beautiful reminders of the ugly heartbreaking path to Salvation. The snow was heavy, wet, fat, so it was easy to pick a single flake out and follow its soft destiny of the ground—occasionally, one of the snowjewels rebelled, desperately struggling to remain in freefall, and hovered at the window for just a few short heroic moments before succumbing to its silent death. On the eleventh floor of the building to the northwest, third window from the top, on the far left(far west), someone was taking photos. The flash went off toward the last winter scene and got lost in the weather, then the room went dark again, and lifeless. Below there was a group of three brothers, friends, lovers, that happily ran about and threw snowballs at each other, then re-aimed them at a massive low standing billboard instead, which made strange hollow pang-thud sounds when it was hit. But it was all disinterested and shallow, I thought further, like used condoms floating in a whore's toilet. Through the screen of the open window I yelled, "tell me something n e w!" The flash went off again, got lost again, and the poor window died again. The billboard made its strange hollow pang-thud again. The snow continued its morbid descent. I closed my eyes to it because it would always be there, as there was no old world and absolutely no hope for a new one. "There is only here," I said, "which is nowhere." Now and forever...

More, it was a still life of dissolution. The composition was wrong, the faces and shapes oblong—their meaning was abstract. There was suggestion of movement, but it led only here, *which is nowhere.* We were the statuettes whose jaws hardly opened. We were idle, all of us, just watching. For then it was not my hand that glided across the page, it belonged to a microscopic transcriptionist that wrote on an endless scrawl in a hidden side-room of my head as I dictated—magnified, he would have looked similar to cupid, with the silly round face, grapefruit cheeks—and he sweated over the scrawl, hardly keeping up with the fish-neurons as they swam in. Incessantly, he returned to the dark speck at the front of my brain, over and over, writing:

A small girl, quite petite, but with intimidating eyes—no, not eyes. But something in her makes me withdraw, as if protecting myself from her. She has short dark hair and pale skin. Her smile spans the length of her face, but is not equally happy—it's tortured. She is thin, her stomach flat and enticing, but slightly transparent: through the window of her skin it is clear that she's pregnant. She's drinking, apparently from a flask in her back pocket. She's very drunk already, and the more she drinks the bigger her smile gets—it's wrapped almost completely around her head. The baby's yet to develop, yet, somehow, is still squirming in there, drowning in toxins—she's killing it, purposefully. A forced miscarriage. It's unbearable.

The scrawl was wet and tearing from his nervous sweat—the ink ran together and became illegible. For a brief, excruciating moment the pen openly bled in a mess of unutterable sorrow. I was forced to open my eyes to the obnoxious sight of everything, which didn't console me. The horizon offered nothing. Stability offered nothing. Love nothing. Travel nothing. Either coast nothing. The still life had been white-washed over and then, too, was nothing. Each of my separate lives passed without moving—nothing was moving, because there was nothing anymore. I yelled again, "I have heard that song before, and it sounds similar to the one *before it*—sing so *my* untrained ear can understand!"

The angels went silent, and still. The pillows dropped to Heaven's translucent floor. Invisible vases, holding bouquets for Saints, dropped also—and shattered. Champagne glasses broke, marriages ended, chalkboards scratched, babies were kept inside of their mothers' wombs for a split-second more, prolonging their pain. The weighted branches of trees, bent over in snow agony, finally snapped and fell to the base of their trunks. But, my eyes, so self-absorbed, only caught the reflections of those things. I hardly noticed the significance of the lightning that struck through the snow, cursing me.

12. THE LADYBUG'S PROMISE

Over a thousand miles away, and a few states, in a small Eastern Oregon town, Aden was enduring his own breakdown. It coincided perfectly with my own, owing to a sort of esoteric fraternal empathy. It happened that after he returned to La Grande from a two month job on a Washington Fish Trap, having wrecked his car while he was out there, and shattered a dream, he moved about the couches at some friends' places, drank too much, then stopped, then wanted to die. He returned to Lincoln in mid-March to see a doctor, and, hopefully, to restore his well-being during his short stay at Mima's.

Usually when we are together we are an inspiration, a light, a poem —a *koan*. There is a competition of witticisms, obscenities, obscurities, where one of us tries to top the other, expand the paradox, coax a laugh—and always about serious matters like our deaths, our existence. It's all a joke somehow when we are together—usually. If you're not laughing then there's a chance, an inevitability really, of crying. So you keep the tears in your eyes all stopped up glistening, and the big damned smile on your face and sigh, "oh well."

The most recent word received from Aden—who sends word often: stories, poems, essays, how yeh doins and such; he is a writer, too, my brother, and a better one at that(later I'll publish him, I swear, if no one else does)—*the most recent word from Aden* came on the brink of the flood. It was addressed to the made-up affectionate name he had given me:

Neil,

Just wondering if you had crossed paths with that sad soul of a creature, Dartanyan. Yeh know, the brown abused poodle, Dartanyan? He is your neighbor—Ya, he exists too, buddy. He is out there suffering his demons, too, Dartanyan, he is. God, he could hardly look at me, Dartanyan, poor fucking dog, the day that I met him. His eyes were sad as hell, man. (just cause it's hard to tell the tone in here, I'll come out with it—I'm laughing as I'm writing this—Dartanyan—say it a couple of times!!)

I'm all packed and ready to leave Tacoma. I'm a little sad actually—not everybody has kind, caring family, boy, these days, huh, yeh know. I enjoyed reading your stories all winter—it helped me get through it, dear boy. Tell dad I said Hi.

What! I was laughing too when I read it. You're still carrying me, your baby brother, you son of a bitch, so calm down! The thought of him sitting up in Tacoma, Washington, ready for another few months out on The Trap, which he tends to now without illusion, and actually writing down those words just for me. He was probably sitting on the same blue couch at our aunt's that I've spent many a night on while bumming around that rainy state, just finished with his own six week stint working on the train docks in Seattle, a thirty mile commute at the ungodly hours of morning—the same way I did when in need of money last year, badly, and needing to get the hell out of Lincoln for awhile, at least until Jason and Ainsley's spiritual union, if that is the right terminology, at the end of May. Funny, all these stories happening at different times, but chalk-full of the same things, names, feelings, reactions, and me and Aden at the center of them all—which is to say, everyone at the center of it all. Sad, too, like my brother said; sometimes it's too much for us and we can't find it in us to laugh any more, though we do try. It's a cycle of reawakening: you start down, way at the bottom of everything, with all of the shit—you tread carefully, learn how to ease up a bit, discover new ideas; then you're alright for awhile—and in a moment unknown, without thinking about it, there's an epiphany. You are neither alpha nor omega—but you are within them, and of them. You are a brilliant emptiness, a strange sound within the light. The key isn't to prolong the euphoria, it's to elevate the cycle on a whole. You will crash down again, but maybe not as far, and you'll see how beautiful everything is even on the descent.

But, last mid-March, right at the center of it all, we both found ourselves beginning all over again.

Way at the bottom of everything, with all of the shit, the sight of one another was enough to express what we had known before we saw each other—that it was too much, for now, we said(but without actually saying it). Aden's thin face—native-looking cheekbones, shark fin jaw line, arctic puppy-eyes—had trouble with masking the insanity, the peeling apart of the innards by way of mental slaughtering, like cutting the skin slowly off your living body—at any moment the blade could slip and send you screaming. Just too much. At the apartment, where he stopped by in Mima's borrowed car, there was no mask at all—not on me. Everything was said plainly enough in the pathetic bottles, dishes, blankets, candles, clothes; Dunning's overly large canvas with hardly any progress made. It was a caricature of something—something Russian, but younger, like America; something artistic, *idiotic*. The bed looked so fucked-out and the window wouldn't close all the way. One look around at that, and one look for me at his face, and we decided it was best to go out, anywhere—a drive into the country, a walk.

The thaw had come to most parts of Lincoln, leaving the spongy ground behind it and burying the streets in leftover gravel and salt. On harder ground, snow still hung around in patches, and in dark melting heaps, porous. One of these wintry come-shots temporarily housed a ladybug like a pinprick of blood atop the snow. She was promising me spring there, but I didn't hear. Coming off that much drink everything is muted by the sound of your heart ravaging the backs of your ribs—*thump thump da dump thump!*—and the stinking smear of rotting earth that covers your soft brain, nearly ruining it; your hands are as weak as little ducklings that follow Mother clumsily, barely able to move from their folded position in your lap. My wasted hands, they fumbled with the seatbelt as we got into Mima's car. Without her there driving we felt delinquent, but we were too tired to joke about the feeling. Aden drove in silence, straight forward, out into the western flats outside of town.

Willa Cather haunts those parts: she is the space and the imagin-

80

ation, the color. It was sunny, the light shining on her stockings' grass, a few dry gusts from her singing mouth, a blue ribbon tied against her neck-less sky. Traversing her bird watch belly was a clear vein, a narrow path through an open field—walking on it, your coat picks up and flutters from the brush of her fingers against your vitals. It was cold enough, our coats *did* flutter, we blew the occasional breath into our hands—she was there.

Walking over that soft skin of her prairie flesh, we stared over everything in search of her eyes. Where were her eyes and how did they see us? Our own eyes: Mine were hidden behind a pair of glasses, too-big, that were found lying around the apartment that morning—they made me feel more like a junky than I would have otherwise. I fought the feeling by eating a giant green apple, as if the thing could save me. In Aden's the dog had died, and there was an absent awareness, a detachment, that ran on the course of the river he had left in Oregon. It was the small things, he told me from somewhere on the riverbank; the minute details were the things that killed him, the dog. He was driving back out to the trap after a trip to the grocery store in town, curving along the gravel road that followed the river—he wasn't going too fast, he didn't think so at least, but there was a skid and a bump, and the car veered into the ditch where it hit the far slant and turned over. The first car he had bought with his own money, two-thousand-dollars: a manual Toyota Corolla, worn-out blue. He crawled out of it and looked at it upside down in the wet sand some ten feet or less from the river. He could have gone in—a mile per hour faster is all it would've taken. He wasn't hurt, thankfully, standing there next to the wreck, but he didn't notice that, nor did he think about the money—*it was the small things, the minute details* that he went back to: the groceries. A few bananas were flung into the front seat, a loaf of bread was flattened, a broken can of chili oozed its sad brown juices. It was too much, he said, the broken can of chili. And why? Maybe it was a tangibility of the fact that he couldn't be happy, not completely, out there on the trap—not in the way he used to imagine himself, as the pleasant bodhisattva hanging onto Nature's breast, teaching contentment, sighing at all the mountains, and saying, "I am a mountain, too." He had yet taught himself how to be a mountain, or how to change back, but the idea and the truth was there within him, illusive, heartbreaking.

There were nights on the trap that he found himself wanting to go into the city to get drunk, if only on the lights. He hated that fuckin' urge, which signified that he was still far off, stacking stones at the base of the mountain; he still had a lot to learn about being that mountain. "But, oh well," he said. "You look like shit, bah, did I tell yeh? You're scaring the hell out of me, you are." It must've been the glasses, I thought—his own reflection. A dry fart of a cold song swept through

81

and our coats fluttered. Somehow, we had walked deep into the middle of the field. My apple was down to the core so I dropkicked it into the grass. Aden knew I was going to do that, I'm sure of it. The self-proclaimed ignoramus, as Aden was, he seemed to know everything and laughed about it as often as he could.

"Well," I said, "I feel like shit—and I scare the hell out of myself to be honest. You saw the apartment, huh"—(Yeah, he did; it looked like shit, too.)—"That's how everything looks; for now, at least—what?" (a look he was giving me) "Don't ask how it happened—I have no idea." There were only vague shapes, muddled hues—first looks with no depth perception. It was a watercolor, not a sonnet, see!, and I was using my hands—clasped together in prayer, I used my hands, because I didn't know the words then. What I did know was that the money was gone, Lilly was gone, and, soon enough, I would be gone. "I borrowed some money from Mima, and Dunning," I continued aloud. "How much? Eh, well, enough for a month's rent—and the landlord, the bastard, is going to keep the deposit on top of it, though he's making me move out early. The money doesn't bother me, you know, but the debt does. J.B.(a cousin on my mother's side, the son of my aunt Susie, whose blue couch had once been made my bed) said he could get me work up there for a bit at the dock he manages in Seattle—just long enough to pay my debts and have a little in pocket when I come back for the wedding."

The wedding, how bizarre. It gave a break in our monologues, and a laugh. "Jason," Aden said, "that guy is getting married?"

"Oh, yes, he is"—Papa Muff, with his curly blonde hair all tucked away for the ceremony—"can you imagine? Everyone's going to be there. You remember Ed, don't you?" (Aden makes a gesture with his hand as if he were holding a condom between his two fingers, saying *lets do this*, just like the proposition Ed made, and then told us about, to a young Hawaiian girl in a bathroom.) "You should see him! You should see it all. Something bad is happening all over town, if it's not just to me. We are all dead. Well, maybe we're not dead, but we are all dying and will probably get there soon. Oh well, I guess, huh."

For a moment my heart stopped against my ribs, rested there between beats, and I heard the hint of the song—it was a lark! She sang of springtime, and the rebirth. This I heard, like a call upon Golgotha, yes—thinking back it becomes much clearer, much louder; then it was below a whisper, hidden in my coattails. Then it was the air that caught my apple kicked into the sky, that dropped it in the long grass to be lost in Ms. Cather's knee-highs. *Oh well*, I'll say it again, indeed, because nothing is ever the same once it passes. Each month is the saddest, and each love is the last, only while you're in them. The memory of them is what remains, and in time it becomes clearer than the moment it came. That is how they are carried with you forever, right there beside you in its mythical boat along the river where the fluid emotion ever-changes for the better. The watercolor is in a delicate frame...

The date of the procedure was learned by way of the tinbox voice at the other end of the drunken line, when I was also asked to please not inquire about any further details. "You've done enough," Lilly told me, "Dear God."

When it came, Aden was still in town. We had ascended, slightly, the curve of wellness, which is measured in the depth of your step and the slime on the back of your tongue, by making habit of our walks together, and having a midday coffee afterward. Our throats were raw, our gums bled a bit, but we were getting better. Sometimes on our walks, the gauze shoved between our cheeks and teeth, we said nothing; sometimes we said even less—it depended on something out of our control. On those days we just rode silently along in our own private boats on our parallel rivers: the colors streamed in pinwheels, reflections faded, then shimmered in different parts of the stone bed, and without a current we drifted freely on nonexistent axes with the river on all sides of us, in all directions.

When it came, as I was saying, we were walking together in that fashion as the river formed into two lakes just outside of downtown Lincoln, near The University football stadium. One was within the other, or above—I couldn't tell, my equilibrium was on a tilt, and I was nauseous. They were called by one name: Branch, or Briar. Names meant that much to me then, by which I mean nothing. Everything lost its name once you were out on the water. I pushed off in my boat from a little rock on the muddy shore, aiming toward the middle of each lake where they met at a tiny island, upon which an oak tree was burning. Like the embers falling, my hand dipped into the water with a sudden flash of orange and went numb—with all the snow having melted, the temperature had dropped and the water-levels had risen. A sense of frigid youth, and a young identity melted there, too—the water inched up more. Closer to the island, the smoke smelled like sterilization, and skin—bleach and bone, tissue singed by hot copper wire—after a cough there was no smell. The shore was still just behind me, its buildings no shorter or taller—the lakes could be crossed in one jump, or not at all. My head tilted further toward the other side, the pinwheels streamed, spun backward, popped out of the water, and zipped by the burning tree. At last, I was on the island, under the tree. The shore and the buildings were no longer visible. Near the base of the trunk, ash was falling onto a plate-glass window in the ground. Through the oak-dust, from a safe distance, I observed the waiting room of an office as if it was a private viewing of an art collection and a single piece were illumined behind protective museum glass:

Six chairs against one wall, a door—the letters on the door had been removed. Six chairs against another wall; six chairs against yet another. Behind a screened-in desk sat a receptionist with her back turned. Charcoal lined the folds in her white uniform. Against the wall with the door, which crimson paint leaked from under, sitting in the second chair closest to the door, was the girl who had once been Lillian Jean. That name had been aborted at the first push into the water, excreted into non-gravity in a sanctimonious arabesque along-side another name: ___. Her name was now Memory, now Fiction, and it was written on a placard in the subterranean galleries of my consc-iousness. It was immersed in its own essence and fragility in the conun-drum of preserving its ephemeral nature. Hung on the walls, the reve-lation of her features bares no surprises—she is your sister, your aunt, your first love, your heartbreak, your dream. She is the trait you recollect fondly, and the annoyance you later adored. She could have been your mother. Either/or: you knew her, you loved her.

From out of this decorated frame she looks directly into the eyes of the audience—the crying onlookers, head over heels in desperation —and communes her holy despair.

On the island, under the tree, blowing away the ash in hopes that she could feel me watching her. Her stare was fixed above me, though, on the embers of the burning oak tree—the leaves that ignited, the twigs that caught fire, and the grey-flakes that fell into my hair. "I am with you," I told her, "right there beside you. Don't worry." My cond-olences were the pinprick of her blood on a come-shot, like the promise of the ladybug. She didn't hear. She just heard the sound of her heart ravaging the backs of her ribs, and a name she hardly recogn-ized being called by the receptionist, whose back still remained turned. As she stood up, and the door opened, I pushed against the island's slope to begin a wan float into the open lake. Leaning back in the boat, limp, letting my arms over the sides to rinse my hands in the water, the clouds received the word repeated skywards: "Sorry, sorry, sorry..."

13. KANSAS INTERLUDE

When executed flawlessly in front of the curtains, a set-change is a spe-ctacle in itself, wholly aside from the acts it conjoins. The actors exit stage right, stage left, and the lights go down to call an ending to the aquatic scene, wherein the cellophane rippled in feigned breezes, the candles burned tissue behind drilled holes in a plywood tree, and the cardboard boat rolled smoothly on urethane wheels. The stagehand

84

phantoms, the imaginative gnats, like so many waterbugs in the night, splice the velvety dark—sit up on your seats now, squint—displacing the props, almost unseen, in a revolving motion whose sounds are covered by the impatient coughs of the theatre-goers and the squeaking of their chairs. This is happening—can you see it? We are on the move...

With a last look toward the young girl with the diamond in her tooth, having dodged the scooted chairs and unread papers just to see her, and found her back was to me—something about the hair though! my mother's—I leave the café, absurdly high-spirited, for no reason at all. Into the luminescent near-green streets, a sort of pallid reflection of the weather parted, I begin walking like a ghost, revolving, too, behind and through the several transparencies of past and present, the multi-layered stages of now and then. Coming and going in-between the sets, the storm is a memory, a damp sock, a downed power line, an uprooted tree here and there. We are like the storm ourselves, passing freely among the acts, making both entrance and exit at times obscure with solemn evasiveness, trying to arrive at what—being? ourselves?

Arrested in the transient theatre, one layer within another, on the convoluted stages of this dreary comedy we are propelled by the fugitive belief—that unsupported, unchallenged belief that beyond the bend, across the ocean, over the hill, down the tracks, etc.—through one hole or the other—is the sparkling fountain of the New Eden: The Good Life. As with past decades of our ancestral romantics, this destination is pursued with an ill-harnessed conviction, some vague sentiment of serendipity, a borrowed nostalgia, which amounts to excitement and insanity, denial. There is no precise identification of its whereabouts, but a mad dash is commenced in the forward direction of its fleeting borders. Ever-arriving in the supposed location of its previously formed picture, made in boyish delight while lying in bed, or reading the lines of your own variable classics, you discover its experience is muted—a faint familiarity, a recognizable line, or face, composes a spectral rendition of the place, the real one I mean, which has never existed outside of your perfect imagination in the unrestrained possibility of your personal literature. If we could see rightly though, as in hindsight, by distortion in the rearview mirror, once we had made our escape, mid-arrival, would we see that the picture was the place? That we were the shapes in the great landscape? Maybe, but we still paint more in the new segment in space which we've come—where are we? We continue this awkward tango...

Oh, I am laughing as I say this—nonsense, no—because I have returned to Reindeer Lane and learned the locks are being changed and my things are to be moved out. I've been looking at a map all the while! Nearby is a note from Raf, who I haven't seen in over a week, that says, guess what? It's time for me to go. Immediately. Wonder if he's angry because I forgot to feed the fish, which was the one favor asked of me while he was in Las Vegas for the weekend, doing whatever it is he does. It's not that the task was forgotten, I just didn't have the money to buy more fish-food and it was only one day that he, the fish, went unfed. This is of no importance. The map is arranged flat on the desk and deserves my full attention. Each city name emerges from it sets of buildings and streets, some person met, a specific neighborhood, a strange couch, a free meal. Likewise, the names produce a scene from a movie, or an excerpt from a book, a line from a song—Yes, I am humming. I am humming the tune of a Christmas song, long past. Forget the map for now. The notes are like the ornaments hanging on the trees before they were taken down and set to curb. The reflective greens, the shimmering reds, champagnes, and burned breads. How sad that this rhythm arose, I hum, but how sweet—(because this is the way you think when you're alone)—how sweet the rivers and roads that pass through the so many places I'll never go. A stop in the song, a smile. Dancing between rooms on the central coast, if I were so much as to look at a dandelion all the yellow would rub off on me. The prevalence of the pedigree, ah, the yellow under the chin!

On a whim, passing through the entryway of the house, I open the door and run outside—instantly I realize the roots of a tree, defying gravity, sticking straight up from the earth in the yard. They stretch toward the firmament, and their blossoms stretch through the dirt where the sun must shine below it, creating pale glares against The Gate, and the birds, all doves, must be suspended upside down. Their call and response is a chestnut! A tweet! A shimmy in the grass: a shake, shake, shake; repeat. A continuation of the song, a languid smile. Lying above the underground tree, lighting my terribly rolled cigarette, there is nothing in particular that worries me but this calm itself, of being everywhere and nowhere, and simply watching as the lights fade in-out, in-out.

Fading in, we enter upon a morning when once the fugitive belief took hold of Dunning. Against his better judgment, understandingly in the post dawn of springtime, with as much reason as that of my present high-spirits(no reason at all, like a certain narrator's decision to take tea, when usually it was declined), Dunning decided to drive to Lawrence, Kansas. The night preceding the departure was spent at the studio with Aden playing the guitar on the floor and the three of us carefully drinking beers. Carefully, I say, meaning that with each sip we were cautious to not have too much, in that it might result in an infernal backslide of recovered nerves. A few beers were enough. And, thus, waking early without the typical hindrance of hangovers, Aden and I agreed to accompany Dunning for his trip and unquestioningly got into his off-blue Honda Civic.

A good drive, wavering at 75 to 90 miles-per-hour, with sparse construction on the over 200 miles of southbound interstate, will get you from Lincoln to Lawrence in about three hours. We made it in two and a half hours of a sunny streak that blended the cornfield blondes with the soybean green bikinis that were freckled by cows and farmhouses. Nothing was said of this beautiful Middlewestern lady whose body we trampled, as if arriving in Lawrence we would find ourselves on the soft skin of her shaved muff and talking about her ahead of time might spoil the fun. On the map Lawrence, Kansas is hardly the lascivious woman described, but is an arbitrary speck just west of Kansas City, and when you get there the speck comes alive, like a single viral cell that suddenly encases its own fastidious petri dish, and develops into a town which then reveals its mostly contented, half-hip inhabitants in their pretension: the local eccentrics, the art students, the loafing hobos that smell like body odor and incense. Everyone smells the same there, like a dirty asshole. The attraction in going then was that the stench differed, though not by much, from that of Lincoln. None of us could've appointed a disparity, nor did we care to. The only thing was that we were on the move.

Off the interstate, you are deposited directly into the bottom of the main digestive tract of town, called Massachusetts St., which will take you through the too-quaint shopping district if you follow it straight in, below the tree-lined shade and green hills of The University; if you trail off just to the left, it will put you into a gravel parking lot behind an office building on The Riverfront. Without any money to buy even a cup of coffee from any of the cafés in that wool and leather district of hipsters, it was suggested we perform the latter. We could park the car there and climb down under the bridge, through the beer bottle mattresses of day-wandering bums, to sit by the river(which took its name from the natives, and then gave it back upon the entire state) for an hour or two of sunlit reading or napping while waiting for our dear friend Wendy, who we had made arrangements to stay with, to finish the last of her day's classes.

The water was high with spring, dirty, moving faster than I cared to let my heart beat, but pleasantly enough carrying an occasional piece of litter that would get caught in the water-dipped brush along the bank which we sat—Dunning with a book I once loved by the mad scientist-painter-writer, V., and Aden tuning his guitar strings to match the pitch of the venerable folk songs he was surely singing in his head. I rolled my coat into a pillow, being that it was unneeded for warmth on such a day, and laid myself in the grass, first drifting and snagging in the mental confluence of river and litter, then dispersing my thoughts laterally, to a night three years prior, when I last found myself visiting the town on those same auspicious banks.

It was around the time that I had started living out of my car—a rusted, dented shitbox of a Cavalier, color of a rotten plum. In the early Lincoln winter, with the ground already frozen, I began desperately maneuvering myself in search of an outlet to combat my susceptibility to inertia, which had become a type of mental anguish and restlessness. Restlessness, the word itself is as cheap as its misrepresented ideals, which surround the word with picturesque images of grand rapids and coastal forests and fishing villages and speed trains and Eurasian jet planes—its an ophthalmic trick, a miscalculation between the eye and the brain. These images, they'll torture you, and before you have the opportunity to chase after their mythic exhalations, if ever you do, their symptoms will find way to surface in peculiar forms. In the old, if I can pretend to have this knowledge, when the images have been suppressed, there is softness toward the pastimes, copious hobbies, or a blind attachment to their salvaged religion, or a hopeful look toward the young. In the young there is usually destruction—self or otherwise—and a confusion of its counterpart, creation. When I was living out of my car, by choice mind you, it was with a grotesque excitement and satisfaction that I fell asleep, tucked into my sleeping bag, breath clouding the windows with the images thought to be obtainable. And, with the same feeling, I fed myself by sneaking sandwiches into my coat sleeve at the grocery store, drank by sneaking a bottle of liquor into the other. Happily, I admit, the behavior was absurd, and, likewise, I admit that not the volume of a single laugh during that period need be changed, because every one was enjoyed. However, laughing aside, travel offers a more reputable, more constructive path to the same cathartic means—any chance you get, take it, and run! (The map is burning in my pocket.)

Around that time, as I was saying, the chance, the trip, occurred in the same spontaneous fashion that it had with Dunning, as more of an amused suggestion on Jason's part. This was before the engagement, before Ainsley. We had been doing some yard work at his mother's house for a little money, digging holes into the frosty clay, when the urge came out in cold exasperation. "We should take a drive, get out of here for the night," he said. The sleeping bags were already in the car, and the twenty dollars a piece we were given for the work would go towards gas. Lawrence seemed the closest place, if it mattered, and around nine o'clock, a few hours past dark, we took off in its direction. Gathering momentum, the white serpentine dashes of the road slithered into one continuous line. Each tree, or silhouette of a tree, trimmed by the straightedge of a headlight, was further away than the last from the town we had left—this is what mattered. Little was said as we drove, as there was an understanding, something, of the significance within one another, whose essence was not to be disrupted. Silent men on the road, we are so serious—ha! When we do talk, me and Jason, it is a sardonic game of leap frog, one of us jumping over the other in a verbose sacrilege of ourselves, for the hell of it, until all that remains at the conversation's end is that stuff untouched, underneath, that bonds us together—the essence, which has its own place in Heaven, my boy.

Midnight, when the old angels come out to seat you in holy oblivion, we came into dead midweek Massachusetts St. where there was only one live-spot running—a jazz bar on the second level of a narrow rustic-type brick building. All of the buildings were different colors of painted brick, vertically exaggerated and close-set, which took the sad ping-pongs of the jazz and its hungry bellies beneath them, internally farting, and the pencil tap drums, and mashed them together against every surface of Mass. St., then recoiled them in sparkplug refractions that sounded as if the band were performing a ventriloquy. We sat for awhile on the sidewalk, distractedly looking at the closed storefronts while listening to the strings being pulled and the crowd spilling their beers upstairs, until deciding to pick up something to drink ourselves and set up to sleep for the night. Eventually, finding our way back to the parking lot of a hotel we had come across on our way into town, we cracked the windows and parked the car beneath an inconspicuous tree. Wrapped in our coats and sleeping bags, we drank cheap screwdrivers out of paper cups, quietly, until we both fell asleep. If we had found nothing, or done nothing, we still felt great—in the morning we walked through the hotel lobby and took a long swim at the indoor pool to prove it, wearing thrift store trunks we bought for a dollar, then leaving them poolside when we changed to go kick about town-and-park all day before driving back to Lincoln.

Back then our options of where to stay were limited to those of a transient countenance because we knew no one that lived there. Three years later, waiting for Wendy at river's edge, there were a handful of places open to us. I called Wendy—who just sent a care package to Monterey last week with chocolates, bless her—because she was kind-hearted, generous, a dork with a sweet neck that betrayed her dorki-ness, tan legs, and long blonde hair, whose company made you feel slightly childish, in only the good ways, yet still cutely disciplined and self-assured. And because she seemed like she didn't belong there, not to the place that I knew. She put you at ease to be around, always, with her genuine affections. In fact, when we met her out front of the theatre on Mass. St. later—her Cherokee blood, of what little there was, somehow more distinguished in her early tan and matching brown eyes—it should have been embarrassing, because it was her dad who had given me the law firm job, which I botched. But, all she said about this was, "My dad told me he hasn't seen you in awhile because you were sick(how long was it; three weeks? a month?)—we were worried about you..." She hugged us all hello, having not met my brother before, and held on a bit longer to me. "Are you okay?"

Considered the question: Was I okay? Not at the time, no. I was actually dying, if I remember right. I told her I was fine, I supposed. I was OK. Without reason for disbelief, she accepted the answer, and said, "aw, B-e-n-n..." drawing out the 'n' like that. I no longer considered the question, just let the tip of her tongue stay pressed against the roof of her mouth, tickling her palate, rumbling the consonant of my middle, proper name.

The vibrato of this 14th letter as we are led on the Kansas stage, from left to right, toward the cardboard box restaurant where Wendy would buy us all dinner, causes a quake in the floor that moves into the rafters—the lights, attached to these beams, then flickers in-out, in-out like a nervous twitch in the corner of an eye. The strobe effect shows our feet, time lapsing in slow-motion, inching toward the thin-framed eatery...in-out, in-out...until the glass finally breaks, and the sound, the last part of my name, stops. The lights are now off, but we are all OK. Exit.

14. THE CAT IN THE CLEARING

Five weeks before the lease would have been up at the end of April, the apartment was empty. Another week and there was nothing that committed me. It was an opportunity for me to reinstate my freedom, which I was convinced I had had until signing my name to the document and securing the semi-permanent residence some months back.

I was unsure of the length of my stay upon returning to Lincoln for Mima's birthday. Things like that were never certain. A few weeks might have been better. But, driving with Mima through the midtown neighborhoods, looking at old houses, old wives, walking dogs, when she asked if I had considered moving back, even for a little while, the irresolute idea of renting my own place came into my head. 'Just for a little while,' I thought, 'for her.' (Lilly in the very back of my mind, just behind Mima.) It was to be a surprise.

Mima knew nothing of the apartment until I directed her in the car on a different drive, a different day, to The Haymarket on the pretense of going to the café where she might order a cup of hot chocolate— first I wanted to show her something. The expression of astonishment, exceeded expectations, gratitude, and love, often kept me company in my lowest; standing at the bottom of the building, looking up from the outside at the windows of the fourth floor, the way she laughed and hugged me, putting her childish hand to her mouth in that unabashed gesture of shock—tears distilled the hazel sadness of her eyes into joy. But what happened to that look? Where was Mima now? (And Lillian?)

Now it was empty, the apartment, except for the mattress, which was moved to the floor beneath the window. The walls remained persistently white, and the pipes overly exposed against the ceiling, but the light had been changed—it was more faded. Vast and empty, it contained a vacuous quality which can only be instilled when an object is extracted from space, naked, like the eyes of a man who usually wears glasses when he removes them for a moment to his right hand. Even if you have never seen the man before, his face appears to lack something—there is an absent feeling, a depressed shade somehow. Something is not right.

It was my mother's furniture that was gone, not mine, sure—yet nothing was right. Five months of my own Season where the weather never changed. And now it was ending.

A U-Haul truck was rented for a day to move the furniture out: the couch, the chair, the bookshelf, the desk, the nightstand. Dunning was already living elsewhere—his clothes out of the cupboards, his sleeping bag out of the closet. Aden had flown back to La Grande. Just like that. It was Jason who helped me, guiding me into the alley, conducting with waves of his hands, pointing his fingers as the disproportionate truck reversed into the eight-so feet between wall and fence. He appeared to be an angel. His tufts of curly blonde hair were ringed by the sunshine and his forearms, swollen by celestial labors, bore a tattoo of the bleeding, praying hands of the crucified Lord Almighty that twisted with each turn of his wrist. An angel!

As we ascended—as did all things holy, remember—to the floor level of the apartment in the grinding shaft of the freight elevator, which would fit all of my mother's things in one go, he spoke, this angel, with a voice that carried an iron ring—"Now what?"

We were only able to be straightforward when there was a task to be performed. The methodic lifting, turning, rug rolling, and instructional interjections—(got it, lift, turn this way, that, upright, bring it in)—allowed us the uncommonly terse manner of speaking. "Now what?" he asked me, and the elevator came to a stop.

I explained the offer J.B. gave me at the train docks where he supervised. "I'll have to borrow the money for the plane ticket to Seattle, but I've talked to Kira about it, and she said she could lend me the amount."

"And then you'll be back in time for the wedding?" Our voices knocked about the hallway with the sound of someone having trouble climbing the stairs. ("Hold on, let me get a better hold.")

"Yeh, of course. It's going to be a short trip—just there and back

91

with hopefully a little bit of money in between. Six weeks. Besides, I'm the best man: do I have a choice?"

"No—absolutely not," he said with feigned seriousness, a facetious smile. ("Set it down, right here.") The smile became bigger for a moment, then there was a zen-like snort. We moved from the elevator back into the apartment mechanically and a door slammed on the floor below us. The smile infected me. We were like The Ancients, moving stones.

Two small barefoot men are at work relocating a pile of bright amber rocks in an open green field. No one is around to hear them speak, but their words are recorded in Heaven.

MAN ONE: *"But, how does the boat get into the bottle?"*

MAN TWO: *"Well, you simply believe."*

MAN ONE: *"And how does one simply believe?"*

MAN TWO *"Like this."* He stops at his work, then stands on his head.

MAN ONE: *"Well, now I see!"*

"Are you ready for it?" I asked, meaning the wedding, but he knew that. The smile remained; another, louder laugh came out.

"No—absolutely not." The smile slackened with a sense of satisfaction. He was pleased with himself. The curt honesty of his answer, though, was somehow a contradiction of itself—he was ready; he was there all-ready. Our work continued at steady pace and the elevator was filled. It started downward.

The two small barefoot men stand over their completed task. They are proud of themselves. Still, no one is around to see the work they've done.

MAN ONE: *"All of the stones have been moved. Now what?"*

MAN TWO: *"Now we break them."*

MAN ONE: *"Break them...how?"*

MAN TWO: *"With the heels of our feet."*

MAN ONE: *"But why?"*

MAN TWO: *"Because the sun is shining."*

MAN ONE: *"And then do we move the broken pieces back?"*

MAN TWO: *"Only if our heels are bruised."*

MAN ONE: *"Well...Now I see."*

After these words were repeated for the second time, a gunshot of hysterical laughter breaks out between them. They both begin to jump up and down.

Pressing down on the accelerator in the truck, the weight of my foot slowly took us through the alley into the street. Only a few people were walking. Only one chair was filled on the café terrace. Sun, shade, and pavement—everything moved. Through midtown Lincoln we passed the same parks and yards that were there in October separating me from Mima. The inmates scattered the prison yard. In clusters they played pickup games of baseball, some walked along the perimeters, some sat and smoked, and talked, presumably, like violent monks about their captivated religions. We drove by, free, and the familiar things in the back of the truck shook. The cemetery contained no mourners. As signs of their last visitations, bundles of satin flowers that sunlight had begun to strip the color from rested against headstones. The inert shame of stationery objects was a memory. Everything moved like a prayer candle exploding. The sun shone over it, and it moved, it flickered—behind the clouds, too bright to see, something new was opening up. Film reels were singed, disintegrating into blinding light and particles of dust. Once it simmered, then we would be able to see....

Standing in the sun in the driveway of her new home, Mima watched us coming down the street with one hand shielding her eyes. Her mouth showed more teeth with each consecutive house we passed on the block. Pulling alongside the curb in front of her own house, Mima's smile broke in full. Bear pranced about in the yard, jumping over bushes, dodging imaginary obstacles, body wriggling tail to snout. She stopped, pissed, then shot forward again and ran towards me and Jason as we got out of the truck. Mima gave us both hugs. She loved seeing my friends; when I was gone they were my reflection for her—a living picture of something about me she could always remember. She looked well, as she always did, but there was nothing about the way she looked that fooled me. Although the skin around her eyes and mouth was unwrinkled, and she still looked healthy and young like the beautiful twenty-one year old she had been when she met my father—just older than her own little girl—I knew she felt that she was being left again. By her baby boy this time, for the second time. Probably by her husband, too, the way she saw things. She was always being abandoned.

Moving her things back into the garage, where they would have to be stored due to the lack of space inside her little home, she looked at the reality of the objects as we fixed them into a puzzling formation among old boxes of photographs, our childhood clothing, and the golf clubs she had purchased when their had still been a chance at salvaging her marriage with Dad. Not a wrinkle showed in her face, but within her were the gaps between the formations, the cracks, the misalignments, the absences. Everything was being moved, shifted, and shaken within her. To her, I was already gone.

Bruised bare feet in hand, sweating, sitting atop the pile of gravel just crushed from the rocks, the two small men are silent. They gingerly let their feet drop back to the ground then stand. The sun is going down. They begin to stuff handfuls of the gravel into their pockets, as much as they can hold. Heavy with the weight of their work, pockets bulging, they take their last handfuls of gravel, still silent, and clench their fists around it at their sides as they take off in the direction they had come.

Out of a clearing in the middle of a cloud, no color, an emptiness, the dust particles collided and clasped together—a raindrop sprouted from the air, fell briefly through the thickening atmosphere, then evaporated into blue. Lillian called.

It was the last night in the apartment when she called. The mattress was out already, but I planned to sleep on the floor under the window with blanket and pillow after performing my nightly routine that was to prepare my body for the docks: a number of stretches to loosen the limbs, clear the head, in addition to several pushups and crunches. The plane for Seattle was leaving the following evening. Lilly wanted to see me beforehand.

One a.m., finished with my floor exercises, I looked around the place one last time. I stood up and blew out the candle in the window. The blanket and pillow could stay. So could the bag of potatoes in the cupboard and the two eggs in the fridge. She wanted to see me. Her voice had brought up a dream within me—I saw her face with clarity and the wretched smile was wiped off. Her mouth was smooth and complacent, injured slightly, but set in a magnanimous straight line. I was on foot outside of the apartment without thinking, dropping the key in the mailbox on the way out, forgetting to look back.

Ahead of me my eyes were fixed the however many blocks to Lilly's apartment, past the neighborhood's captivity of lingering scenery —the bench where we had sat when she confessed she was pregnant, the upside down chairs on the closed terrace where we had our morning coffees, the restaurant where she worked when I first saw her after returning. Set to the sound of my steps, in a dream, there was a birthday party—our child's birthday party—wherein I sat at a table with my father and Mitch, waiting for Lillian Jean to arrive with child. My brother's vivid blue eyes, intimidatingly smart and intense, stared at me as my father spoke. "You," he said, "you and your artist friends—you get drunk, you abandon your responsibilities, you get your kicks, for nothing. And you justify this, what, by writing it down? You don't write quite well enough for that, son." All of these things fell into space, as if they were minute distractions alongside a path in a midnight park. After passing them they became nothing. They were the dark themselves, and only the way ahead of me was illumined by the iron post lamps. Only ahead of me: Lilly's apartment.

As the virga confirmed its name, evaporating before reaching the firm ground of reality, I arrived. Inside the apartment she waited for me on the couch with a beer. Opening on the first knock, Lilly let me in and grabbed me a bottle from the fridge. I looked around at the decorations on the wall. The first time inside. Pictures she had taken were hung of her ex-boyfriend, trees around a lake outside of town, bedposts, lamps. Noticed there weren't any pictures of cows—eventually, maybe. A snow globe with figurines of The Beatles at their instruments inside was on the counter, broken. She told me it was knocked onto the floor recently by some young drunk when she had people over. Her father had given it to her. I looked at it again and the crack was a little bit bigger, and thicker, and continued expanding. Sitting down beside each other on the couch, the only seating option available, my gaze moved from the snow globe. The tapestry on the wall next to the door opposite of us was of oriental design, but was colored in the light hues of the psychedelic sixties. It covered a large piece of plywood that was nailed over a hole in the wall. Everything at one time had belonged to someone else—the tapestry was her mother's. The couch that sunk in the middle she had found on the street, and the coffee table she was given by a friend. Empty packages of cigarettes littered the surface—she had started smoking American Spirits. She offered me one and tossed the matchbook into my lap.

There was a time when any of the transmutable phrases stuck floating around my head for her could've been taken at random—any of them might have expressed my grief, and regret, and love for this girl I said I knew so well. The girl that I had prayed for. None of them came out though, because it was a different girl, and neither of them, sadly, did I ever really know. Nothing was known about this Lillian Jean, *this girl!* Smoking, taking sips of my beer, looking about her apartment—I desperately looked for the picture of a cow. Nothing.

"You've got a nice place," I said, fittingly. Her cat came out of the bedroom where the only other light was on, a lamp, and jumped onto Lilly's back. Aw, kitty...*squish.*

"It's alright, but the other tenants are crazy. The woman across the hall is a crack addict, I swear—the other night she was screaming in the hallway, crying, and knocking on her door because she had locked herself out. I was watching her through my peephole—I didn't know what to do. The cops ended up coming and cuffed her right there in the hallway and the woman kept on screaming. And then they took her away. It was pretty sad." She lit a new cigarette and threw her empty pack on the coffee table with the rest. "She has cats, too. You could hear them meowing in there for a few days after she was gone." On cue, the cat, which had moved into her lap, arched its purring back and jumped to the floor, then went into the kitchen for water.

Getting up from the couch and walking to the window, I imagined the lost details of the woman's story, wondered if she had kids somewhere, or if I had seen her somewhere around town. How had she gotten there? Overlooking the playground from the window, its desertion made me want another beer. Without asking, I went to the fridge and got each of us a cold bottle. "Is she back now?" I asked.

"I don't know. I never saw her come back. The cats aren't making noise, though." Lilly, too, thought about the details lost, then added,

"Maybe they're dead in there, the cats."

"Maybe they escaped through a window and they're getting fat with the other downtown cats, huh."

"Y-o-u...are optimistic, *huh*."

"I am a child." The word made us quiet and we finished our beers. If she resented me, it was because she had to. She didn't let it show, however.

"Are you staying tonight?" It was past three in the morning and the key to my apartment was in the bottom of an otherwise empty mailbox. The sound it had made going in came into my ears. I was leaving the next day, but that night I would be staying. Going into the bathroom as she took the bottles to the sink, my face in the mirror was pale as the inside of the clouds, so I ran the water over my hands, splashed the color into my skin, and let the stream fall over my mouth and through it. The water made my tongue cold and freed it of the smoke and beer taste.

Lilly was in the bedroom pulling the sheets down on the right side of the bed where she had always slept when staying over at my place. She was wearing white cotton underwear and a thin t-shirt that exposed faint lines of the tattoo on her side. She jumped beneath the sheets. "Are you coming?"

She didn't make me take my pants off as she once would have. The light turned out and, still wearing my jeans, I laid down on top of the sheets on the left side of the bed. Within minutes Lilly was asleep, innocently snoring away her few beers in a pleasant and girly cadence as the cat tip-toed along the window ledges. The cooling vents struggled to huff their stale air into the night. While listening to those noises, letting my eyes adjust to the light, I tried to make out the pulsating grey images. At last they slipped gently into focus, and, just as suddenly, they swayed further against themselves, advanced into the darkness and I was asleep, too, with Lillian mysteriously at my side.

15. ON THE NORTHERN BUS

Noise at the airport is a vibrant jumble of steaming milk and engines, cell phones rumbling and producing impersonal sing-songs for their owners, suitcase wheels rolling over tiles, children crying, and escalators choking on the weight of chubby businessmen in sweaty suits. Then noise ceases, your ears pop, ensues again with the sound of traffic, and you are somewhere else, standing on terra firma with bags in hand, wondering how you got there and thanking God you got there safely.

Seattle looks the same year round: wet, grey screens of perpetual drizzle with a leftover smell of the day's catch, and an expectant smell of tomorrow's. It was getting dark and J.B. was waiting for me in his car out front, flashing his headlights at me. He hadn't shaved in a few days so the light brown stubble was soft over his flushed cheeks, and the hair below his lip, right in the center, was a little longer yet, and darker. He was smiling energetically even though it was a Thursday night and he had been working all week. His enthusiasm amazed me. We had been close over the prior two years since much of that time for me was spent living between his place and the couch at his mom's. Besides me and Aden, who didn't come around freeloading quite as much as I did, J.B. only had his two sisters by way of siblings—another male companion gave him a rise. He loved seeing me and my brother. And there I was again, showing up for my spot on the floor with work not starting until Monday.

J.B. lived with two other young guys, both of whom I'd met several times before during my prolonged visits. My presence hardly disturbed them. When we got to their duplex, situated in a reserved, working class community southwest of the Tacoma Metropolitan area—about 35 miles away from the more northern Seattle where the docks were—they welcomed me without looking away from the TV by saying, "A-y-e, Bloom." They liked thinking that I looked like an English movie star and called me by his last name as a joke. Still, they didn't get up.

My suitcase was put behind one of the recliners in the over-furnished room where the TV was playing either reality shows or softcore porn—I didn't pay it much attention. They were mesmerized by it, though, laughing in their seats with blankets laid over their laps. J.B. had already gone up to bed. His girlfriend, who he'd been dating for six months, was up there waiting for him. She had come down for only a rushed introduction before going back up. She was a short, dark haired girl, with lean, tanning salon legs, finger to thumb wrists, and a seven day a week ass, which I say half-jokingly because it seemed as though she were always up there waiting for him. Quickly, she was put out of mind.

With them upstairs and the TV yet turned off, I made my bed with the spare blankets in the corner of the room and went outside. The rain helped my eyes, tired from traveling, and the cigarette made them worse. Laughing could be heard coming through the doors to the patio. The trees there were a darker green than I reme-mbered, richer, and the grass was even softer. The moon was almost unnaturally clear. The backyard was small, enclosed by the dark green trees and a high wooden fence. There was a grill on the patio filled with ash, empty beer cans, and cigarette butts. I put my half-gone cigarette out in it and nearly laughed—*How did I get here*, I thought, then thanked God again that I had gotten there safely, and told myself it would only be for about a month and a half. Just six weeks or so. Forty-five days to be exact. A short blast of idiotic laughter broke into the yard.

Routine was the keystone of my existence. At the end of each day's monotony, the calendar dates were slashed off in my head. Only so long to go.

The morning commute was forty-five minutes to an hour's drive on the 5 North, which was slept through as J.B. sped, probably half-awake, through the light traffic of 4.30 in the morning. By six, the laborers had to be fully alive on the docks, fighting through the third cup of shit coffee and ready to start unloading the first railcar. The drunks and the fuckups were there, the temp. workers with papers in hand to be signed off for the day's labor that barely got them by— there was something unattainable and beatific about them all as they tied their boots and poured their now fourth cup of coffee.

The veterans of twenty or thirty years, a group of four teamsters, rushed around on forklifts with cigarettes dangling from their mouths, pushing the car doors open with their forks and muttering unintellig-ible shit as they sped by to prep the area for the first Push.

Each push was a neat stack of fifty 60lb. boxes of frozen meat— chicken or pork usually, occasionally chicken's feet—that had to be thrown into line individually from the refrigerated railcars, and were then taken to the opposite end of the dock to be put into large containers that would be put onto the backs of semi-trucks at the end of the day to be driven throughout the country. In a full day, rotating in pairs until around noon, you ended up throwing something like a thousand boxes. By the three hundredth you forgot yourself. The wor-kers were ex-marines, or bums, or fathers of three, or miscreants fresh out of prison with badly inked tattoos—they all looked the same on the dock. There was only the innate ability to survive amongst every-one, and it had to be proved over and over again in *the next push*.

We were all hands and brute, uncoordinated, yet successful, strength. Amidst the work, in the frigid air inside the railcar, the men blew out cold smoke, farts, and jabs at each other just to pass time. Old Chawlie, one of the veterans steering around on his forklift, drove into the railcar with an iron crash as the pair waited to start the next throw, speaking through his dangling smoke, saying, "Gottahm rile yeh up boys, eh—get that shit in there, how yeh do! Hurry up, what's that? Naw, naw—not like that," Old Chawlie would say, and then have to get his big haunches on down off the forks with cigarette still in mouth to straighten out the boxes for you, come on, huh, chuckling to him-self as he hoisted those haunches back on up to the seat where, inevit-ably, he would carry out the rest of his days.

Once the work was done, the selfless entity that performed the morning's tasks was dissembled and separated into its various destinies. Last cigarettes were smoked, one more free cup of coffee was had. Some of the men, the temps, got their papers validated and headed off to the bus stop, or walked down the street to the liquor store. Some of them stayed outside of Seattle in a tent community they had formed together—before heading back out there it was customary to stop by the nearest bar, a discreet door a few alleys down. The old veterans cleaned up and shut everything down, then went home to whatever they had—some had families, some didn't. The guy usually paired with me to throw, Carlos, a thirty year old Hispanic invalid that lied about being from Los Angeles, stuck around with nothing better to do than crack jokes and taunt J.B., who was sitting around with all his paperwork done, waiting for the truck drivers to pick up the day's loads. More than a few times, they found Carlos asleep under the railcars in the mornings. A month after I left he was fired for failing a piss test.

There were about four hours of downtime like that for J.B. in the office, shooting the shit with Carlos until closing down at five. Instead of waiting there with him, I walked into downtown Seattle to kill time wandering the streets, skipping into bookstores, eating bananas, and inspecting bums—anything that would keep my thoughts occupied, clear of the mailbox back at the duplex, which couldn't be checked until six and might contain a letter addressed in my name.

Lillian and I decided to write back and forth, and talk on the phone once a week. No one wrote letters anymore, we said the morning I left, waking up at her apartment and going to the café for our last fatalistic dialogue. The letters would be our special world—exclusively ours—that were only mentioned on the phone as much as, "Did you get it?" It became a new form of torture and anxiety, the letters. But to find one of those small envelopes waiting for me in the mailbox with her CAPITALLY SCRAWLED hand was complete vindication. My letters to her were intimate descriptions of dreams, an intense feeling, living flower petals, and apple orchards. I took her hand-in-hand with me on long walks on the train tracks, along the Puget Sound, through zen gardens, through playgrounds, and to dinner at my aunt's on Sundays. She even knew all the names they gave me on the docks (matchbox, Kansas, Iowa, any Middle-western state really, etc.). Lilly came with me everywhere in every detail given to her on paper; wishing she were actually there with me, I proclaimed all of my sincerities to her, signing my name with remarkable or immense love. The letters were so ludicrous and verbose because failing health, mental or otherwise, allowed me to see them as reparations for our previous tragedy. They were the last sob to set us free.

However, Lilly's replies were plain and forced. She wrote about weather, someone we both knew, a car accident she had seen. She did include pictures, though, quotes, and drawings of anything she pleased: a bug, a tree, sailor pants. Things that were there to make me laugh. The only candid phrase that ever came was between mention of the sky and well wishes—she wrote that she had walked by my old apartment and looked up at the window I had once sat behind. She said to have missed me then, but was unsure if it was really me she missed or if it was the idea of me. And that was it—we were clambering around in ideas, searching between the longing of window and street for something that was situated beyond the threshold of death. Our love was the lament for everything unborn; irreparable maladies of the soul that we tried to grasp in our abstract affection for each other.

I read the line over a few times at the table after work. The television was on again, but no one was laughing. I read over that line until it got dark, then put it away in a brown paper sack that was folded into my suitcase. It was a lost cause that couldn't quite be given up. To find her again in the sordid unnamed mourning, and reclaim her face before my blemish, where we could begin last mid-October when the eternal ache was but a seething feeling, high on the brink of expansion. It could have become anything else then.

There wasn't any work on the docks sometimes and I needed something concrete, something spiritual. With what was left of my paycheck after paying my debts, I boarded the North/South Bus toward Portland or Vancouver for no good reason. Tucked into my coat pocket next to my bible, Lilly's letter was carried close to my heart, trembling.

Like in a dream the landscapes passed, a sad childish dream, just beyond the suffocating pane of dirt covered glass: dusty baseball diamonds waiting for summer, a shallow winding creek, birds taking to flight over a field—we followed them together, me and Lilly—a tractor deserted in its long grass, roadside gardens hiding their vegetables in the ground, the cracked paint of an abandoned build-ing, the tips of trees moving feverishly away from the glare of the sun and the single big grey cloud that promised Salvation, the grazing horses clomping through old mud puddles, the innocent face of an awkward young girl.

The landscapes receded quickly into a tired nowhere of waking, unsettling the new silence like the memory of a dream at dawn, having left the imprints of their boyhood enchantment with vivid emotion upon my heart and intestines. They overwhelmed me in their absence with the desire to continue along, to witness each face, song, breath of the green-humped countryside, to find solace in their illusive wonderment.

A rushing current, northbound from Seattle, the seasons were changing, passing. The sleeping-ghost allurements of the unknown outstretched beside my desperation in their subtle majesties. The Greyhound Bus was like a drunken boat on the red wine highway crossing into Canada. In the seat at the far back, my body ached, and my hands were cracked and sore from unloading freight with the other invalids on the docks. The docks had all been paid that day, and were lonesome for the weekend. Their hobos were now off littering rural campsites with empty bottles, rolling cigarettes with one already smoking between their lips; or they were pouring water over grease fires in their apartments and evacuating the buildings with the smoke. A few seats up from me there were two children playing—a pleasant little hand clapped another pleasant little hand. Refuge was taken in their chants and in the simple perfume of a young harlot passenger asleep across two seats. The green earth spoke through my window, but I was lost, alone. The rain translation sprouted flowers. I prayed that the children not pluck them all, and to leave a few for me, to better understand the sentiments. *In the seat at the far back*, my palms were sweating with anticipation and were wiped on the empty seat next to me, too-aware of its unfilled space. I turned back to the lull of the dreamscape, awaiting the approaching destination.

Vancouver, British Columbia. From the station it came upon me. Like an addict's shameful need, trembling and sick, it enveloped me. The vast emptiness of a new alone, with the appetite of a self-proclaimed god and the face of a girl—Lillian Jean. The letters were hot coals in the starch bag, warming their place against my mad heart. Quickly, I found a cheap hostel just west of Chinatown above a small grocer. My bag was hidden in the pillowcase of an open bottom bunk. I rearranged the sheets to disguise it, then hurried out of the room past the smell of young travelers, pot, and dirty laundry onto the street. *The face of a girl.* Led by the eyes, the nose, the mouth of my unfed Angel, I came to the south shores of the English Bay at dusk where the turning sands were searched, the lapping tides, and all of the scattered beach faces. Two young men bumped lines of cocaine off newspaper spread over a log. They snorted and lifted their heads, searched the faces, the dark waters, then went back for more. A few Hispanic girls sat on blankets with an FM radio tuned to a Latin trance as they shared laughs that were drank from a bottle. Two middle-aged women walked their dogs on an offset path. Everyone was in couples, paired up, except for the old bottle collector who hunched over his heavily clinking bag.

The faces, all of them, leading from the south shore to the east, were wrong and unwelcoming. Lilly was in a bed somewhere in the middle of a different country. Vanity hurried me on.

Turning back onto the streets, heading in the direction of the city

centre where they eventually narrowed into Gastown, the bars and restaurants were still well lit, and the crowds moved from place to place
with their backs turned to shield their cigarettes from the coastal wind.
Down a short flight of stairs in a rustic-looking pub, taking a seat at the
bar, the husky old man drinking his dark pint of beer was reading the
paper, so didn't see me.

"What can I get yeh?" The woman at the bar leaned over to ask
me the question. I ordered a whiskey. It wasn't *Her* face, but it was
warmer, and kinder. I decided to stay for a bit and resume my search
outwardly into the bar: the patrons' affection moved no further than
the flushed faces of their local circles and was diffused at the edge of
their tables. It reached me in subtle impatient gurgles of 'why are you
here?' and 'what are you looking for?' The woman at the bar offered
me a fourth drink. She closed the tab for me. These faces weren't ugly,
but they were lacking something spiritual, something concrete. The
Angel remained unsatisfied. The bar was abandoned.

The secluding crowds of smokers had dissipated. Easily moving
along to Hastings St., the shop fronts were shut down or boarded up. I
was lost, alone. Half-drunk, I stared into the stars so long that they disappeared.

Ten dollar rock! E. Hastings: couples huddled beneath blankets in
doorways, men moaning crack-sales cross the street, fiends coming
down from terrifying highs. The moon reproached the night it had lit
and left suddenly—a shuddering black fear, the junkies' fear, of themselves. *Ten dollar rock!* An empty stomach gnawed at its lining, and broke
holes into the unceasing longing for a warm bed, a bus headed OUT,
the face of a girl. She crossed the street toward me, approaching with an
external glint in her eye—I was reflected in them. "How are yeh tonight, sweetheart?"

"I'm fine, thanks—how are you?" She was walking beside me now,
her face contorted in a scared look at a man standing ahead of us in the
middle of the sidewalk.

"Oh, you know(she sniffed), things have been better." The man,
short and thin, his white skin gone grey, motioned at her with his shirt;
he held it in his hand, exposing his bare chest, sunken and sweating.

"How come you haven't been returning my calls?" He ignored me,
looking directly at the woman and speaking the words with harsh
spittle flying. (She spoke: "Quit botherin' me!") "Ah, com'on! Don't
do this!" He waved his shirt angrily at her as we continued walking past
him. The features of his face shrunk into one another. He stood in the
same spot on the sidewalk, still talking, but we were too far off to hear.

"I'm really glad you're with me. That guy's been bothering me for
days," she whispered. ("No problem.")

"You look like a nice guy—you're a nice guy, right?" ("Around

102

here maybe.") "Well, what are you doing *here* then?" In her face I remembered the words *why are you here, what are you looking for?* There was a hint of dull orange-red cautiously spinning its thread into the tearing sky, like a fire reawakening at dawn to soothe the pain of last night's freeze. "Sweetheart? You wouldn't happen to be looking for a date, would yeh?" ("No. Sorry.")

"Oh it's fine. I didn't think so." She didn't leave my side immediately after the polite refusal. With the dead intersection right ahead, she waited until we came to it, then smiled at me and turned the corner—lost, alone.

In the shut-up sky above the clouds the tears were crusting over the morning's bad dream as I found my way back through China-town and up the hostel stairs. Some of the travelers stood around on last beers, eyes red as mine—the blood vessels swelling, soon to burst with remorse. The others, *still* dreaming, groaned into the blue rain-haze of their bunks at the fumbling disturbance of retrieving my bag from its pillowcase hiding. The bed was left unmade. Checking out, letting out my breath behind me, the night's loss, the streaming vision of dark hope, evaporated with the evil ghosts and all those damned souls fabricated in loneliness—*the face of a girl!* Lillian Jean, my aunt, my mother, my sister—those dear faces of unconditional love! Along the street toward the station they fell into the rain now lining the sidewalk like a spilled bedpan on a kitchen floor, joining the surface waters of a river bending, whose fragile arc I followed, never quite breaking as it led me back into the early bus.

Southbound, coming back into the States, the bus left in the same rushing current of seasons changing, dying. The half-woken stream of humbled hillsides and glory faded with nicotine turned and tossed in their bed of leaves. The images were displaced by the worried midafternoon, spent on the verge of sleep, trying to forge a different dream to conceal the end of a cigarette, the prostitute, the piss on the kitchen floor—the face of a girl. Only so long to go.

16. A CELEBRATION OF ALL THINGS

The wedding was set for the 25th of May, but it was necessary to come back into town a week in advance to attend the rehearsal, the bachelor/bachelorette party, and to watch as the wedding itself was called off and put back on a handful of times. It was both depressing and exciting. The week was conflicted by the madness and confusion that surrounds any young marriage.

Lillian was supposed to pick me up from the airport, as per arranged over the phone. But she didn't show. None of my calls were ans-

103

wered.

Carla ended up getting me at the airport in her raspberry red two-door Cavalier—it was in better condition than the one I drove in high school, but its body still evoked the memories made in my own. Carla was on time, waiting for me out front of the municipal airport when I came out. The six weeks had gone by for me in Washington in a rush that wore me out. My body was sore and my bank account had little to show for it—managing finances has never been a strong suit of mine. It gave me pleasure to find that time stood still in Lincoln. Everything was in preparation for the ceremony. Nothing could change until the groom kissed the bride. All was unsettled, awaiting the marriage's consummation. The sheets were turned down but both parties were in a fright to hop in. Just do it, we should have said, *genitals first with your hands behind your heads!* But we hardly would have believed in it ourselves. We all had our reservations about them then.

Ainsley came to see me the first night back in the basement at Carla's where I was sleeping on the couch. She came in through the door from the backyard in a frazzle, her eyes puffy, and she wanted to stay there with me so we could talk. It was like the summer she and Jason first started dating, when she would take off from the parties we were at, running down the block in hysterical tears with me chasing after her. Catching up with her as she had settled in the grass, dress absorbing the August dew, sobbing and pulling out clumps of grass in her angst, she'd say, "Why does he treat me this way? He treats me like shit. It's okay that he gets drunk with his friends, but when I have one drink he goes ballistic!" She seemed scared of him sometimes, but they stayed together and at the end of summer were engaged. Maybe a month separated it from her last break up, with the other two months of summer acting as a layover of her two relationships.

Throughout high school Ainsley had been with the same fuck up that was now strung out with the friends she'd left behind. There had always been someone; she didn't know anything outside of the support of a man. She was nineteen and had never left the influence of her parents. It wasn't so much Jason that she was scared of as it was the big, big world—making it on her own. Her attachment to Jason was more than a fear of him then, it was the fear of life itself. For Jason, she was the first serious interest after an adolescence of celibacy and religious condemnation. He was spiritual, though—giving his virginity to her had only been a part of it, and not near the most important part.

"Ainsley, he does love you, yeh know, but, well, maybe he has trouble conveying it through the filter of his norms. What I mean is...he's used to being alone, and showing affection—he wants to, I know he does, but it's a contradiction to the behavior he's accustomed to, see. Things will change."

"But, why does he have to treat me like that? He screams at me in front of you guys—for what?"

Backwards as it was, the engagement became the stability of their relationship—the planning only prolonged the issues. With the date now within real distance, a week away, I felt like she was asking the questions again. Why? For what? The problems were still the same. What could I say? She didn't want my biased counsel anyhow, she wanted me to hold her hand and tell her it would be okay. Sitting up with her on the couch, listening as she repeated herself, I said the words she wanted to hear. "It'll all be OK," I said, and, as the sound of her crying was stifled on my shoulder, I tried my best to believe it.

Once you have left a place, even if your body was never set in motion —but in your head you escaped—it never looks the same. As many times as the area changed for me in moving back and away, I knew that this was the last time Lincoln would be seen that way, as mine. The town itself seemed like a memory that could've been someone else's, and the name of the town was interchangeable with the different people I had been growing up there.

In a thunder storm, a prairie boomer as they call it, I walked into the park near Carla's, which surrounds Holmes Lake, and sat under one of the large wooden awnings. The rain had soaked my clothes on the walk and each drop against the wood created a tiny, cold prick on my skin. I saw the place where a little boy had once kissed a little girl— neither one of them was recognized. They were childish phantoms that would forever be left to the Great Plains, kissing in the dark, and in the same instance their lips would be parting. The cracks on my lips had bled out their color—the rose shade was barely an imprint on the envelope addressed home. The rain washed off the scent of any perfume. Falling from the edge of the awning, the water was like a silk sheet with silver runs that mended themselves, then ripped again miraculously, and enclosed me in the safe-haven of its canopy. Ostracized from the green-blue immediacies of the bright storm, thunder toppled over me like a young bride's cry in her wedding chambers—*why?* Ainsley could still be heard.

The ground was still wet the next afternoon when Jason and Ethan showed up to go camping for the night. There was a big bottle of whiskey, some beer, onions, potatoes, and hamburger to cook on the iron skillet, an axe, and three little-pinky sized joints. It was the first time I had seen either of them since I'd been back, and noticed Jason had lost some weight. The wedding was on at this point. Although the parents of each side continued to detest the marriage, and actively tried to prevent it, Ainsley and Jason had made up the morning after she stayed with me. He knew where she had been—he quite nearly thanked me.

We used to talk about living together, the three of us, the way we got on so well. Ainsley's parents owned a place in Breckenridge, CO that we could've moved into—a grand cabin with seven bedrooms up in the mountains of beautiful Colorado. We could have gotten jobs at a resort, Ainsley could have made her jewelry and sold it at a shop in town. Jason was going to cook, gain some experience in the kitchen; eventually we would open up our own place. The details were all planned out. The menu was all but written. Around the fire we still talked about it, distantly though, in the way one talks about the deceased and the outrageous memories from adolescence—we were eighteen when we first dreamed of opening a restaurant.

With reverence, the tent was set up on the same campsite we used two summers before. The conversation moved accordingly. Everything coincided on a twisted curlicue timeline, spasmodically moving back and forth upon it, gaining momentum.

Around the constant yellow quiver and orange lapping of an open fire, shadowy faces changing expression rhythmically upon the surface of straight mouths and fixed eyes, anything said is a cosmic vibration— ultimately indistinguishable, yet utterly irreplaceable. In a painting the conversation might be captured in a group of close-set oil splotches that border a touch of light that resembles an areola. An axe is a shimmering dot of grey. Without breaking the cycle, we took turns with the axe, chopping off two foot segments of a giant branch that was dragged out of the long grass into the clearing next to our site. Each of us had blisters on our hands, but we worked through them regardless —Oh, but the fire must roar! The sun was gone, the skillet was heating, and we were hungry. Jason took care of the food. He chopped the onions and potatoes directly into the hot oil in the skillet and a new stream of savory smoke went into the night with each starchy disk. Rag over handle, he shook the pan and regulated the heat, letting the juices marinate, simmer, seasoning to taste, and served it to us steaming with thick hamburger patties thrown on top of it all. We refused to drink until after the meal.

Trampled in the grass along a small lake nearby was a footpath made by decades of fathers and sons with fishing rods, and young men just like us carrying a lot in their heads and a little something to drink. The three of us took the path in single file and settled on the partly exposed roots of a tree as old as the path whose branches hung over the water with caught fishing wire and moth dust. It was the last outing Jason would have as a single man, at twenty-one, without having to first ask his wife if she minded—something more extravagant should have been planned. He showed no sort of remorse about it, only a quiet urgency and a reserved happiness—he was wearing the ring already. He handed one of the tiny joints to me, close to laughter. "Just for me," he said, "aye?"

Ethan was already smoking his own, standing next to the water and rustling the surface with the toe of his shoe. I didn't like pot because it stimulated my anxiety—I was always on the brink of several miniature heart attacks. But, it was Jason's last night out with us, and nothing else was planned. For months we discussed one last trip together, hopping trains, or visiting Lawrence, KS again, or going further, but time had dwindled somehow and there we were a mere hour and a half outside of Lincoln, sitting by the water. I took the joint from him, inhaled, and held it—all night I would sit there smoking with him if I had to, I thought, talking about the other shit we could have done, or said we would still do one day. My heart could explode if it pleased. The night signified only the deliverance of a new day.

By morning the lake appeared to be smoldering, steam hovering over it in a slight teeter. The fire had gone out during the couple of hours we slept. Smoke was stuck in our hair and clothes. For an hour or so we sat around the ashes and warmed our bare feet. Ethan lit my cigarette and returned to his own. There was some whiskey left, but we thought better than to drink it—the big party was that night and we couldn't show up drunk.

My duties as best man should have included organizing the party—which was ambiguously decided to be a joint one—but all I could manage was to show up with the groom in tow, and Ethan, who remained unusually quiet thus far, which I paid to his strong disapproval of the wedding. Somehow, the number of a stripper was procured as well. The other details were cleared in my absence.

At six o'clock the three of us got to the house after a quick rinse to subdue the smell of whiskey and fire on us. We were the first there. The party was being thrown at the same place I ran into Lillian Jean when we drank gin in the kitchen together and watched the rest of the crowd disappear. The owner of the house, a quiet, estranged acquaintance of ours—though a better friend to Ainsley— excused himself into a side room on our arrival. Everything in the house had been cleaned for the party and we were free to make ourselves comfortable. The way things can happen sometimes, and connect almost too-perfectly—it's laughable. Cheerfully, my first drink was poured at the kitchen counter where I recalled meeting Lillian: the sight of her rubber galoshes, the gestures she had made to her friend were still there. In my heart, I was still drinking gin, though my throat burned with something less volatile. The whiskey was sweet.

Kat, the stripper, wouldn't be there till eight, which meant there were two hours to raise the money. None of us could afford it. Even after working the docks, there were only two hundred dollars in pocket, which was all that was needed to leave town with. I put fifty down anyway and poured us all drinks as guests started to arrive. At the door we touched each one for five, ten bucks toward the stripper—enough was collected by seven o'clock. Groups of people were coming in that I hadn't seen for years. People whose names I never cared to get right because their faces were enough. They were there to see Ainsley, I guess, or the stripper, though none of them were sure who she was marrying, until both women showed up to the party and eventually Jason was drawn alongside Ainsley into the spectacle at the center of the room.

Because Ainsley came through the door first, looking like an obscene pink cartoon, having been dressed and embarrassed by her bridesmaids before the party, Kat slipped by inconspicuously. After she was given the money the music started within minuets—then everyone saw her. She was a slender, fair skinned redhead that could've been mistaken as Ainsley's sister. Her eyes were green, but you barely saw them in the dim light, and her dress was off by the fifth dance move— you had a better shot at counting the freckles on her tits than you did at seeing those eyes. Her hair swung over her face, she touched her elbows to her knees, she undid belts around the circle. As her performance carried on, dollar bills were wedged into the string over her hip and spaces shrunk between the onlookers' shoulders. I saw Ainsley and Jason through the lusty-faced crowd: they were standing together in the doorway to the kitchen, laughing. Jason reached behind someone's back to a table set with bottles and glasses and poured his bride a drink. Handing her the glass, he leaned forward, just at the neck, and gently kissed her on the forehead. Everyone yelped as Kat pulled some little bastard's face into the crack of her ass—more freckles from the right cheek were added to the count.

Kat glanced up into the crowd, scanning it for the couple that was pointed out to her just before beginning. She had been dancing for over half an hour, and it was time for the closing act. She saw Jason and Ainsley the way that we left them, the latter receiving a kiss on the forehead from the former, and she grabbed each of them by the hand, pulling them into the center of everybody's attention. Two guys in front were made to give up their chairs for the couple as Kat seated them each with their backs together. It was now clear who the groom was. No one cared. The crowd wanted the act to continue. There was no protest from the couple to what Kat The Stripper was doing, but their expressions were clearly of alarm. Instead, they kissed one last time, turned their heads, and put their hands behind their backs where they could hold onto each other. As it was her grand finale, Kat gave it her all. Sweat broke into beads near ten freckles on the back of her neck—she had tied her hair up for this last part—as she encircled the bride and groom with her fragrant sex, which by then the whole room smelled faintly of, along with cheap liquor, tobacco, incense. She grabbed hold of a wooden beam that crossed the width of the room, lifting herself into the air above them, bringing the flesh of her heels together like a move in an Irish fuck-jig. The two pairs of hands tightened together at the chair backs. Kat twisted her body around and repeated the same move in the opposite direction, then dropped down to the floor again in front of Ainsley. She could have done anything to them and been cheered on all the same for it—they would have endured it, too, however degrading, because when they stood up from those chairs they would stand at the same time and go home having shared the experience. They laughed as Kat finished the act with a final slither of the midsection, bringing her face into Ainsley's where she then raised her lips and kissed her forehead in the same way she had seen Jason doing. Then the music went off and Kat slipped back into her dress just as inconspicuously as she had come in. It was over.

Seventy-five white chairs were arranged on the southeastern outskirts of Lincoln, on the acre lot that makes up the backyard of Ainsley's parents' house—the location the couple was introduced.

An aisle formed on the steps where they met and led up the steps to a humble altar, which was also the origin of a small stone waterfall trickling down the one side of the steps, then recycling back to the top. Soft water blue sky, velvet green grass, lethargic wind—the intimate texture of a still-life. The groomsmen were put in seclusion in the basement to tie their ties, lace and relace their cognac leather shoes, and tighten the belts around their brown slacks while listening to the frantic high-heels on the wood floors overhead. Watching out of the basement window, the seats filled. My date, Carla, in her navy blue dress and turquoise necklace, sat with Kira near the back on the right side of the main aisle; Dunning was talking with them, underdressed perhaps in his jeans, but with a demeanor elegant enough to offset his dress—he crossed the aisle and politely engaged my mother where she stood with Sydney and two other women from church. He hugged her, and my sister, then exchanged a few words before he excused himself. Seeing Mima in her white heels and matching earrings reminded me of going to church with her growing up, sitting through sacrament and Sunday school so desperately hungry, then coming home to the great big meal that Dad had fixed for us. The last time I went to church with her I nearly cried in the pew while admiring her—she was speaking for the first time in public, baring her testimony of The Church, staring directly at me. There is a natural sense of beauty in my mother and she decorates her frame simply to justify it. She is a smart woman. And my sister, Sydney, is every bit my mother. Standing next to each other, hand on one hip with the other at their mouths or jaw lines, they looked like two quaint women in society that are genuinely interested to listen, and to watch.

From behind them, through the gates, walked Sal into the backyard with his cousin, Casey, holding onto his arm. She let go of Sal as he headed toward Dunning to shake hands, and she came straight to the door of the basement. Ethan opened it for her, whispered something in her ear, and they kissed. He closed the door and she, laughing, caught up with Sal where he was sitting in the row ahead of Carla. They were all there. Even Ed had come. His long coarse hair was parted to one side and slicked behind his ears; his tie loosened slightly where his top button was undone. He stood off to the side of the chairs next to Micheal, neither talking, with his hands in his pockets. We were all there, and the ceremony was about to begin.

The sound of high-heels descended one flight of stairs, traversed over our heads through what would have been the dining room, and clomped down another flight of stairs into the basement. It was Ainsley's sister. "These are for Jason," she said, tossing me a palm-sized box. Inside was a pair of cufflinks Ainsley had made for him, like two dark pupils cut from a sheer black stone and ringed by silver. We formed a line at the door, ready to walk down the aisle, and I gave the box to Jason. "Congratulations," was all I could say to him, and I gave him a hug. He put the cufflinks on and took his place alone at the altar as the rest of the bridesmaids clicked and stumbled down the stairs in line next to us. Everyone was seated, our arms were linked, and the music started.

Slowly, we exited the basement door into the light and climbed the steps, one by one, meeting Jason on the altar platform at the top where he stood with his left hand clasped on his right wrist at the small of his back, waiting for his bride.

Flower petals adorned the aisle steps which the bride was to walk after emerging from the door we had come. Ainsley's father walked her to the bottom of the steps and kissed her on the cheek. She was the only point in focus, rising in all white against the dulled colors of blurred dresses and sky and pool. From my position next to Jason, a step below him, I observed her approaching the altar: her complexion was a mosaic of images—of her crying, laughing, bawling, screaming, shouting, singing, whispering—each one writhing beneath her skin in myriad emotions that were encompassed in her radiance. Everything was concentrated in the glow of her absolute happiness. Joining her hands with Jason's, the needlepoints of her eyes deadlocked on his, she absorbed the light around them as the minister began speaking. His voice came as if it were from downhall at the very end of the corridor; Ainsley was in the main room. Her light overtook the voice, and nothing could be heard until their mouths were seen colliding in a kiss.

The formal reception was held in a large tent next to the house. For awhile I remained on a bench swing off to the side of the tent in the company of a three year old boy wearing a clip-on tie and chocolate around his mouth. He looked like I did at his age.

"You know," I said, picking him up and sitting him down next to me on the swing, "it's a wonderfully sad day today." His eyes were huge and round, like everything surprised him, though I suspected that nothing did. "You already knew that, huh? And you have your whole life ahead of you to live with it. You shouldn't be wasting it over here with me, though. I bet you any of those nice people in that tent over there would get you some more cake if you wanted it." The boy's sister, a seven year old girl in a floral print dress, came up to us on the bench and took him by the hand. She looked at me, perplexed, then skipped off with her brother. Carla came walking towards me from the tent. She had been watching.

"What're you doing over here, boy?" She had a sweet way of talking to me like that. I think that Carla was in love with me, though I was undeserving of anything like that. She sat down.

"Just trying to get a little bit older over here."

"Who was that little boy?" I wasn't sure, but it very well could have been me. "Well, you looked adorable over here with him. I bet you're going to make a great dad some day."

"You think so?" Under the tent I could see Jason and Ainsley making the rounds to everyone's table—shaking hands, thanking everyone for coming, suggesting they have more to eat from the buffet. The cordiality made their marriage seem more coherent, as if they had been together for years past, and were still happy somehow.

"I do—and your kids will be adorable too." Carla stood up from the bench and turned in front of me. With her hands on the knees of her dress she bent forward and pecked my cheek, then offered both hands to me to help me from my seat. There was still the second part of the reception to attend. No one had toasted the couple yet...

Later in the evening, changing venues for the informal reception at The Apothecary building downtown. More food was set up, a full bar, several tables, and a dance floor. The room had finely decorated paneling, like you'd expect in a wealthy manor's library, gold and chrome fixtures on doors and lamps, green marble slabs in the bar and bathroom. At the front of the room was an iron landing that could be reached by a ladder that silently tracked against the wall on two sets of hard plastic wheels. Once everyone had arrived, I climbed up it and asked that the music be turned off—just for a minute. The necks tilted backward in the crowd, their heads held in juxtaposition with their square, half-turned shoulders. Just below me, Jason and Ainsley were standing one in front of the other, Jason's hands wrapped around her waist, waiting to hear what would be said. Whether or not the toast was to be given at all was speculated about for the entirety of the preceding week, because the couple, and their parents, were perturbed at the countless things I could possibly say. I stared at my dear friends without a word in my head; I stared at them, set my drink down, and began to speak.

"It was the end of a long week when Jason and I walked into the backyard at Ainsley's parents' home and the two of them met for the first time," I said. "Since then I have been beside them through the persistent ups and downs that followed, and watched as they became inseparable parts of each other's lives. For awhile you question it, you have your doubts—because you wish well for both of them. But, over the past week, watching them, I no longer have those questions. I know that they are going to make it. Now, at the end of a long, turbulent two years, and the beginning of many more in their new life together, I ask that you all lift your glasses with me: to the happy couple."

Without breaking the contact of my stare, my beer was raised to Jason and Ainsley, and the rest was swallowed in one go. Climbing down, the music started playing again and people pushed by me to get to the dance floor. Through the swaying hips, and hop steps, and shoves, came the bride and groom holding hands as they approached. Finally standing face to face, the three of us, they said thanks discreetly —they knew what I had been trying to say. As the dancers continued gathering around, they embraced me, together.

17. PASSING THROUGH A WAKE

After a celebration, when the balloons are deflated, the confetti is ground into the carpet, the dishes are scattered on end tables and piled in the sink, and the last guest parts at the onset of a hangover, there is a declined exhilaration leftover, a nostalgia, a feeling of disappointment, a relief, a calm. After the wedding there was no reason for me to be in Lincoln, but I decided to wait a week before leaving anyhow— the atmosphere of a wake seemed attractive.

I was asked to housesit for Mima, seeing how I was still in town, as she and Sydney were going out of state for a church conference. It was just me and Bear the whole week until Lillian called. She was sorry she hadn't seen me, or called earlier, but she'd had to work so much lately, she said, and it was her first day off. She was the perfect company for a solemn goodbye. The next day I was leaving for California.

Sunny and pushing toward summer, it was humid out and our first plan—to go on a walk on the country trails south of town—was put aside to go for ice cream instead. Her hair had grown some since we first started seeing each other, but she still wore it in the same low hanging ponytail that now reached two inches below her neckline. At a local shop just north of my mom's—(had to walk to get there)—we both ordered a small ice cream cone with peanuts and stuck them up-side down into paper cups. We sat out front on a bench in the shade, eating the ice cream with spoons. Neither of us knew what to say, but she had been the reason I stayed—for a chance at one last look at the girl immortalized in my head. She told me she had gained ten pounds, but you couldn't see it—her exposed arms were thin as ever. She was dressed for the coming summer in a tank top she found in her car and threw on, a thin skirt below the knee, and a pair of loosely tied tennis shoes. It was the closest I would ever get to seeing her naked again, but I remembered how she felt, and that I had once held her was enough for me—just sitting there. She said she was going to Costa Rica soon. She'd been working so much to save for the trip, just like she had talked about. She was going to move out of her apartment and store her things with her mom—go for a month or two. It was good to hear she was going to be able to go. I could imagine her there on the beaches and in the cities, I could see the pictures she would take. With some regret, I knew that whatever I came up with in my head would be all I'd ever see of her trip—this was our last goodbye. Later in the night she would leave me.

By chance, we were both going to The Theatre that night for a musical performance. She said we could meet there; she had dinner plans with John in the meantime, but she promised she would see me. On that, she left in a hurry, her ice cream unfinished, and I remained seated on the bench after she'd gone. I didn't wonder if she would show that night, I knew she would be there, and held onto that thought, knowing, too, that it would never be true again.

She was with her friends outside The Theatre, having a cigarette in the sultry downtown air under the marquee. Her friends all hated me, and protested her even talking to me. I respected their devotion to her. Still, when she saw me she put out her cigarette and walked over to where I was standing.

"Sorry, but, I can't really talk with you right now—my friends." I knew already. "After the show—alright?"

Music is a continuous artistic moment that has the ability to overc-ome the boundaries of time. One minute can be an entire season, while another might be only half a breath. From my seat in the balcony on the left side of the stage, being provided an aerial position which gave me an eerie detachment, the audience looked like actors backstage that revealed their quirks prematurely. Some laughed too loudly, or were already drunk; some cast open gazes over everyone, lonely, as an invitation; some pushed through to their seats and got their cameras ready, or pushed through from their seats to get to the bathrooms. Drinks were ordered from waiters with flashlights that came through the booths of the lower level. A couple of faces were recognizable from around the small town. I could see Lilly at her table. Her friends looked like the ones that were drunk already—out of their purses you could see them sneaking tiny bottles and pouring them into glasses of ice under the table. Each note that night was drawn out longer than it had been before; each moment watching over the crowd, with Lilly in the middle of it, taking up two years in hell.

When the last falsetto broke, Lilly met me at my mother's house where I sat on the front steps with a cold, tall can of beer and watched Bear chase fairybugs until she tuckered out. Bear followed Lilly up the stairs and sat down at our feet. "Want one?" She nodded her head and handed me a cigarette in return, not bothering to ask. She looked tiny on the stairs next to me with her knees bent in one against the other, her elbow resting on the right knee with the cigarette jutting out of her limp hand. A southern part of the same train tracks that led behind the old apartment were visible from Mima's place—they were deserted that night but we both seemed to be staring in their direction, waiting for the distant whistle and screeching steel to come along and cut our silence, or bring back a lost feeling. For three beers we watched for one, but it never came. Bear was asleep on the steps, her breathing bringing her chest against our legs.

It had gotten late, and Lilly had to get going—she had work early the next morning. I held her hand as we got up, careful not to wake Bear, and walked her to her car at the curb. Opening the door, she turned around and kissed me, her hand dropping from mine and moving to my shoulder as I pulled our bodies together for the last time. With the silence still intact we separated and instead of saying goodbye she smiled and got into her car—I closed the door behind her. As she drove away, the reflection of the street lights became smaller and smaller on the top of her car, then became nothing, and she was gone. With tears in my eyes, smiling, I searched the stars for any of the constellations that might harbor a recognizable vapor of myself. I couldn't make out a single one, and almost laughed. Lilly had left me for good this time, but remembered to kiss me goodbye.

I am living under the same sky, just a moment before the present, a half-step behind with only a hair in between. The follicle is deep set in my reflective dome where I am riding on a black bicycle atop a green hill above Monterey Bay, scattering flocks of loafing geese and circling a memorial to Father Junipero Serra—the first man of The Church to settle here. The sea lions are barking. What are you barking about you ugly bastards? Don't tell me, I bark back at them. There's not a care in the damned world! *w-h-o-o-o*...

Taking off in front of me, down the hill toward Cannery Row, on a gold spray painted cruiser with a basket on the handlebars, is the girl from the café where I sat out the storm. Her name, remarkably, is a name I thought was behind me—Lillian. Her curly hair is blowing backwards toward me with the smell of chlorine and coffee grounds. Neither of us are sure how we got here. But, we are here, just up the beach from where my dad sat at twenty-three when he had come to Monterey from his abusive, alcoholic childhood in New York to attend the Defense Language Institute—when he had first dreamed of calling it home. Now living out that dream at forty-nine. Poor guy.

On the path, with this new Lilly leading, we pass a woman on roller skates, two men and a woman, Hispanics, with a small dog to each of them, and a late twenties chap without his shirt on—a white guy, tanned meticulously. He says hello. Lilly tells me he's a notorious gay porn star in the area, and even on the cloudiest days he can be seen roaming the peninsula without a shirt on. I guess he *is* in good shape. *w-h-o-o-o!*

Just before the tourist shops of Cannery Row is an abandoned building, right on the water, tagged with graffiti and boarded up with water-logged plywood. They call it The Castle. We have to duck through a hole in the fence to get to it, and climb over, around, then down exposed foundations to get on the side of the water, out of sight from passersby, where the surf breaks on broken bottles. We sit down six-so feet above water level on one of the shitty cement walls of The Castle with a paper bag full of wine bottles and try to decipher the colorful mess of cryptic messages. President W's face has been stenciled in a corner of one of the walls—he looks suspiciously like a primate. The water stuck within parts of the ripped up foundations, left over from the storm's swell and other high tides, has the strong smell of piss. Torn up mattresses are shoved into The Castle's nooks. Sea otters are playing in the water, slapping their tails against the surface as they barrel roll, then dive under. We can no longer see them, so we forget them. The moment is passing. The hairs are all falling out. Church organs no longer play.

Six or seven waves come in present succession against the rocks at Asilomar, where I have come, alone, to consider the next move. Lilly waits for me at her house on Spaghetti Hill. The sky could be stretching anywhere. High tide has cleared the beach of its carcasses, and the death is lost at sea. Only the comedy remains in the rain-dimpled, smiling white teeth of each wave. A different set of sea otters is playing. The sky is a blank slate of countless tears, like the transparent body of an ethereal ghost—the clouds become electric. Allowing my eyes to dilate, in order to lose focus of the foreground, strings of star-like lights begin to materialize—spinning clockwise and end over end, bulbs sparking and sliding freely between the static-charged stems. The horizon is an ambiguous division of water and sky. There is no struggle for form. There is nothing to run from. Everything is interwoven, and free: a carbon flower of incomprehensible botany, growing incessantly in the fecund gardens of an obstinate dream.

In the concurrent existences of history and destiny, the next move is a finite electrical bead on a grapevine eternity. There is nothing to become that has not been already. I am content to float wildly through the atomic hierarchy of this dream as an effervescent gas, a collision of particles, a spontaneous flash. Within me the waves persist in a hundred couplets that stir the ancient sea foam of my vitals. There is no decision left to be made. I am living.

UPPER-SIDE;
Or, Visions of Spaghetti Hill

1. WALTON ST.

There is a faded light, an off-key tone, a bad habit, a memory, a nightmare, called Monterey, California. The town is full of ghosts. The Man is dead here and the delicate flatworms have all been collected and cased perfectly in glass jars. What remains of Monterey is an abomination, an orgy, a spectacle—the uncomfortable feeling of a dull blade being shoved in through the ass.

In a corroding Victorian home on Spaghetti Hill on Walton St., not far from Tortilla Flats—between San Francisco and San Luis Obispo, along the coastal line where men of the railroad earth have worked the early morning tracks just to send their wages home to their mothers(who were saints just like mine)—I am living together with my girlfriend, Lillian. There are twelve of us living here, not including the cokeheads staying intermittently(between binges) on the couches, the dogs, the cats, the cockroaches, the raccoons. No one knows how they got here, to hell, but we are all stuck. *"De infierno a infierno, qué hay?"* ("From one hell to another, what difference?")

The difference for me is love. By mistake I ended up here, and for Lillian I remained. The most intolerable of things can be withstood for love. It's the sixth month now of our long night's stand—the best night of my young life. Don't run. This is not a tragic love poem, a bowl of oranges and chocolates, a verbose masturbatory fuck, or even a parlor trick. It is a clarification, a delousing, a cry of distress, a lament for the dead—expired literary figures, working girls, little grocers, carnivores, fidelity—which I am only able to put down because she is with me, asking for more.

The past three months Lilly has been putting me up here rent-free because she likes to take care of me. She encourages me not to work, only to keep writing. She goes to work all day at the café to support us while I sit at the desk she has set up for me in the window of our bright sea-blue room. The desk is actually a small table with cracking red paint that we found at the dump; as a chair I am using a trunk with rusting hinges discovered on the same trip. Framed on the desk is a picture of Lilly's mother for no other reason than she is the Mother of Hope itself; next to it is a sparse bouquet of yellow and crimson flowers in a beer bottle filled with water. I think that they might be daisies, but really I don't give a damn. The only thing that I care about is that I am alive, I am happy, and I am free.

When once I asked myself, "where to begin in the grand contradiction?" I knew nothing. I was frightened to admit that there was no beginning or end, that the starting point was an arbitrary occurrence within me. I am the contradiction. Women know. To begin with the mistake—first of being born, then everything that follows—is of no consequence, so long as there is hope in Something. Not a naive one, but a fatalistic one that knows better of its outcome and goes on hoping regardless. I am a man of hope, of Faith, of passivity—*divine deliberation*. Everything will make its way back to where it belongs.

For now my place is secured here on Walton St. as the sweet natured failure. Still young enough that it's thought charming to find me with beard grown, in need of a haircut, sitting midday on the front steps with a book by a dead author at my feet, asking for a cigarette that is quietly smoked while thinking of my father's words, "the only thing any of you kids could do to break my heart is to start smoking." Then thinking of him, too, however many years ago in his own youth, when he had come from his broken New York home to this very town and dreamed the very same things I am right here and now. But you can't live in the refrain of not breaking your father's heart, or your mother's, especially when their hearts are broken already, so you smoke the rest of that idiotic cigarette and go on thinking that you are still young and people are still willing to help you out because some day your talent will be recognized and you'll remember them in your prayers and that's all that counts in the end.

The idea of youth is having the belief that it's eternal. The meantime is an endless period that can be filled with anything or nothing—drinking beer, smoking cigarettes, watching TV, jerking off, going for bike rides, eating french fries dipped in mayonnaise, breaking things, or any other listless habits and pastimes. But some of us can never truly be young in this way. Instead we live out our youth in portions, in five-minute tidbits, as if we were recollecting in old age what we thought being young might have felt like. At twenty-one years old I feel much older. The activity of life has an impossible nostalgia. I am watching from a distance.

118

If Truth tends the soil of this country, as they say, then the garden will grow itself accordingly and there is no part left to be played by me but observer, watching from up above the world in the vantage point of this laughable old soul of mine. And for you, my dear girl—Lilly with the dark blonde curly hair like my mother's once was, Lilly with the diamond in your tooth, Lilly with the unimaginably green eyes of a woman and the tiny amber heart in the iris—For you this Truth is recorded. If some of it sounds a bit off, as it should, then my faculties have not failed me. Truth is the greatest absurdity.

The same stars visible in a cool, clear, night sky anywhere on earth hang over Monterey like guests at a party in heaven. Down below hang the fallen stars, the dead, the hopeless guests of a different party that is carrying on simultaneously. Neechie, the overseer of the house, is drunk and sitting in his oversized armchair in the middle of the kitchen wearing a bathrobe that's too short and slippers like some sort of gay modern day apostle. 'Daddy's Puppy' is asleep on his lap. The dog, called Beamer, is Neechie's greatest source of pride after himself. He's always singsonging to it, "who loves you? Daddy loves you! Jesus loves you! I'm Jesus!"

There is a rumor that this self-proclaimed prophet and Jesus-freak, which I believe Neechie to have started himself, once left the house in his same homo-ascetic terrycloth garb and was enveloped by a black cloud of birds—a shroud of assumed crows—that followed him down the hill for wine as an ominous sign from God, his Father. All things are now a revelation! He sees crosses in window frames and in the shadows that are caused by them, in his dirty pubies caught in the shower drain, in the last noodles at the bottom of his stew. After the revelation he turned his dead mother into a saint like the rest of us desperate Christians. Her picture is pe-rpetually illuminated by a divinity candle in the foyer that all entrants must pass. It was the diab-etes that killed her—too much chicken, too much sweet drink.

Sitting a-cross from Neechie and puppy, seen over top of the sixteenth glass of cheap, sugary wine that the spiritual lunatic has consumed today, is a tiny lumberjack buddha with thick, dark rimmed glasses and a thin mustache that curls at each end. "Everything that exists has already existed and exists in the same way that it exists now and therefore we know everything already of our existence and all things are the same." The little buddha, in his red-black-checked fla-nnel, flails his arms in front of his face after this proclamation, encircl-ing his head to emphasize that he has surely just blown our minds.

Neechie, whose stuttering has actually been *improved* with drink, says "oh, uh...o-oh, *yeah*. I'm...so...in-tune...with... you..."

Next to this little buddha is the skinny bitch that earlier looked into our room as I was laid out on the bed resting my eyes, trying to ease my nerves while waiting for Lilly to get off work, and had somehow forgotten to close the door. Standing in the open doorway, addressing her little man, she said, "I will *never* be like that. You will *never* see me just lying around *like that*—I will always be with the people, *living*." And she put her arm around his small, plump waist and walked off. But she's alright, I guess, because really she doesn't know any better and now she just sits there quietly listening, beaming at her little buddha's smooth, round face as he continues.

"This kitchen is God, this table is God, this beer bottle is God(holds up his tall brown bottle and inspects it)—I don't need the stuff inside it, I could easily quit; but that is God, too, and Every-thing—" and he abruptly stops here to swing his arms again in wide, all-encompassing circles, then twist the ends of his mustache *because his mustache is God*....

With God all around us in this big old house the demons are equal-ly pervasive, showing their evil faces in every way and another. For nearly fourteen years the inhabitants of the house have been the sordid duplicates of a singular peephole: prostitutes, run-aways, fuck-ups, sch-izophrenics, drug addicts. Neechie is the only consistent resident here on Walton St. and has lived here for all of those fourteen years. At one time or another he has occupied each of the five bedrooms on the first floor—the paint schemes correspond with whichever drug he was on during that period. The calm, sea-blue of our room represents his varying lengths of sobriety. As a result of Neechie's prolonged res-idence, most of the shit crammed into the house belongs to him, Beamer's piss covers everything, and every picture on the refrigerator contains his face. A grotesque, wide-smiled, dark-skinned face pock-marked by old acne and perversity.

The insane vanity of this horrible face with crossed-drunk eyes, after his eighteenth glass now, bombards its visitors in fashion of a mother whose sole affection is her child—again, himself. Both guests are quieted by the man, *so in-tune with them*, as he produces various objects, yearbooks, videos, that he thinks might glorify his existence. Personally, I have already seen his big purple dick three times, his high school yearbook in which he was voted 'most unique' too many times to count, his leather jacket with James Dean's face stenciled in glow ink, and a twenty minute VHS compilation of commercials, 5 o'clock news interviews, and taped modeling performances in Podunk Colo-rado from when he was young and skinny, but still sickening. Even a music video in which someone that simply *looks* like him is played repeatedly.

The guests are polite—the little buddha smiles his big unaffected smile because he has already seen these things, and he giggles occasionally like it's the first time—but the sheer loneliness of it all is more than a person can handle. Neechie, honestly and gleefully, chimes, "I'm really not this vain, you guys, usually," and displays yet another article from his endless memorabilia. In the foyer the divinity candle continues to burn clearly over the dead saint.

The sun is atop the morning fog making it so bright grey outside it hurts the eyes. Neechie is alone in the kitchen eating leftover baby chickens in his usual armchair with the TV on at full volume broadcasting talk show after talk show that can be heard from any room in the house. After watching intently over his big plate of greasy chick and 40 oz. of King Cobra—or is that two liters of Chardonnay? —while daddy's puppy sits at his feet lapping up the same slop but of a smaller portion, he hoists himself out of the overstuffed chair to knock on door 303. He's knocking on our door, but we don't let him in and don't say anything. We don't want any wine yet—it's 9.15 in the goddam—and we don't want any of his food even though we're hungry. He makes the stew in his bathroom sink. Sometimes you have to just play like you're asleep and let the rest of the world carry on without you...

Life within the confines of our aquatic colored privacy is a good one, a quiet one. Under the high ceilings of our bedroom with two tall windows that open onto the street we have a bed, a bookcase, a nightstand, an empty grocery store basket for food, and a record player that doesn't work. The old plain white of the walls is visible through the badly painted vibrant brushstrokes on the door, in the corner, and in a few spots on the baseboards where a dog, Beamer presumably, has clawed and scratched while his owner once suffered the terrors of a withdrawal. In bed we look into the imperfections to break eye contact as we try to make up for the night before.

Last night we were in a sleeper cabin on a boat going nowhere and Lilly, high on something, tried hiding herself from me in the corner of the cabin just a few feet away, terrified for reasons unknown as I tried consoling her by saying, "babe, I'll never hurt you like anyone has before and I'll never leave you." Through the slats in the door comes the voice of some cocksucking, longhaired Frenchman that's knocking to be let in—maybe not a voice, but somehow I know he's there and his intentions are clear that he wants to take Lilly away from me and adopt her as his daughter, so she *does* let him in and he goes over to her in the corner where he puts his arms around her and starts kissing her neck as she peers over his shoulder at me with a gut wrenching, vacant look and I turn the guy around by his ponytail and with one quick swing I break his big mother-fucking skinny French nose then wake up.

Certain details I am apprehensive about recording. It is unclear if they are in fact the memory of a dream, or the memory of a semi-suppressed drunken reality. They appear to me so vividly that I am convinced they are somehow partly true. I am not out of my mind, but I cannot be positive about anything. In order to completely retain the integrity of these inconsistent realities, I am obligated to include all things. Fact and Fiction are a convergence of the same Truth in these visions, and, as the Holy Idiot, it is impossible to tell the difference between them.

We are never as cruel to each other as we are in our dreams. Things have changed though, since the first night that we really met at the café. Upon leaving the cantina across the street, after a few drinks by myself, I walked past the café window. They were closing up and she was dutifully sweeping in the front with her cute swimmer's arms. We had exchanged only a few words before, but I had noticed her alright, and when I saw her there in the window decided to try for one last glass of wine before she went home. The manager served me and I sat there at a table as she continued to sweep up around the shop. It was her friend who talked to me this time, some snooty little brunette girl who had it out for God knows what, but had been told by Lilly that I was off limits(she had noticed me as well), so started conversation on those grounds. She invited me to the bar with them where we all had a short drink and I didn't get a word out of Lilly who was pissed off she hadn't been the one to invite me—but I didn't know that then.

Somehow we ended up at their apartment having beers on the balcony overlooking the pool. Still not talking much, Lilly walked down to the pool in her little two-piece number alone and dived in. Gliding through the night water's reflections of the other balconies' lights, one cupped hand after the other, she pulled her small figure in feminine strides from one end of the pool to the other with a trail of subtle waves following. She got out with cold, wet hair that covered the top of the Dalí elephant tattoo on her left shoulder blade, then came back inside where her friend had seen me watching her and decided to give up on me and go to bed, finally leaving just me and Lilly.

Till 4am Lilly stayed up with me in the living room, a movie on and two glasses of warm bourbon poured into coffee mugs. We drank, but she still told me little about herself; I told her even less about myself. I did learn that she was alone like I was, but for her it was the first time since she had left her home in Austin, TX eight months before and she wasn't looking for anything—she wanted to be nothing to no one. All I wanted was to be a nondescript and a hero. She went upstairs to bed and I laid out a nice set-up for myself on the living room carpet—a blanket folded in half with a pillow at one end and two neatly placed blankets to cover myself with. But I couldn't sleep there easily until ten minutes after she had gone upstairs I went there myself, knocked on her door, and asked politely if it would be alright to kiss her goodnight. With the lights off we kissed and in the morning she woke up wanting to feed me. She made me a nice bowl of bunny-shaped pasta with cheese just like a kid might eat, which I ate on the couch feeling just like a kid myself, but happily aware of it and completely in love.

She no longer allows me that illusion. That the two of us will last forever like the innocent little child wants to believe. She asks me if after we're separated, someday, I'll write awful things about her, or if I'll try to look her up somewhere when we're old. She doesn't mean much by it, just wants to be reassured that I *am* still in love with her and don't resent her for anything, but the way she talks it's as if it is a certainty that the day will come when we aren't together. She doesn't understand that I'm fragile and need the illusion that that day will never come; otherwise what's the point? And while laying there in bed with my hand on her cheek she sees the sad, distant change in my face and asks, "what's wrong?" Thinking to myself, 'it's all so big and painful and *what is the point*, but try to be sweet to everyone, be generous, don't think about money, don't think about food, forgive everyone(hardest of all yourself); accept the sweetness of others, accept their generosity, and accept their forgiveness(though you don't deserve it)—and think about existence itself so you can appreciate it better.' But I just kiss the soft skin above her green eyes, smile at her, and say, "Nothing."

Fog clears for a mild early-spring sky that's not so blue as the paint in our room, but still a beautiful blue that carries the sea lion's barks of 'what we do today?' all the way up Spaghetti Hill. Having made up twice, we both feel alright and are walking down the hill towards the café, past all of the rented homes, apartment complexes, and flowers. I've never studied the names of the flowers so I name them myself as we go: there's the Angel's Horn(big, soft, floppy white, like a velvet conch shell), the Jelly Flower(small bunches of purple bead-ish flowers growing conically as if they were grapes still on the vine), the Clown Flower(thin stemmed, yellow-petaled flowers that are so perfectly shaped that they seem like fakes and could squirt water at you at any moment), and so many others that I probably just don't see. Lilly picks me a Clown Flower that I stick to my trusty, old wool coat by putting the stem through a button hole in my lapel, just like every other day, as a reminder that she'll be getting off work around ten and to behave myself until then.

123

* * *

Everyone eye-fucking each other, or eye-fucking themselves at the café. And everyone eye-fucking my dear, sweet Lilly while she serves them their food and drink, the bastards. Men around town have heard about the miracle green-glass of her eyes and their whiskey-red constellations in the right light—some visit the café just to see them. The others, the regulars, are mostly recovering drunks from the rehabilitation center across the street(next to the cantina), failed and aspiring poets, quiet old novel readers, and students from the Defense Language Institute; all harmless. Then there's the man in spectacles and wool johnny-appleseed cap that orders a pot of tea and an orange sliced in half, the cocksucking, longhaired Frenchman from the dream, and the drunks that have yet to recover, or perhaps never will. Making it harder yet on this particular group is that beer is available at any time, open to close. These guys will appear at random with their crumpled mass, small mass, of onedollar bills that are flimsy from the sweat of their pockets—their foreheads sunburned, their eyes wrinkled from squinting, their speech difficult and loud. "Here—come sit down!" They call out the words as bait to attract any one that will listen, or even pretend to.

With the cup of coffee Lilly gives me for free I sit down next to the chubby, Filipino bum in a tan jacket and Hawaiian shirt, not necessarily having to say anything, but just to give him a fixed object in which to direct his lonely rants. "What's my name?" he says, "Well, I don't think I know your name." He laughs at this trick of his, of pretending to have been engaged by me first. Inexplicably, he is drinking very expensive beer and has somehow wrangled up enough money for a second one—the first bottle empty on the table. "Ah, ma name's Frank." A fat, dry hand is shoved at me. I shake it and introduce myself as Joe, then feel bad for lying. He's watching another bum in a brand new red bandana out the window who I saw just a few days ago at the library where he'd been napping, then woke up and asked me for the time. The library was closing, ten till six, so he walked with me for a few blocks, sang, and complained that his bandana had been stolen. Before he turned the corner, though, and I remember this clearly, in the middle of bitching because his bandana was stolen, he said, "but, ah well, at least I'm alive and my dick hasn't fallen off. That's all yeh can ask for, to be able to wake up in the morning and shake that thing a bit." Now here he is again strutting along the sidewalk, dick intact and red bandana back on his head.

"You know that guy, Frank?"

"Yeh. Timmy. Yeh, I know him. He's headed to the party at Del Monte, same place where I'm goin', too, right after this." He has his full bottle of beer in hand, and looks perplexed by its presence there.

"Wanna come? (then to himself) *Ah, I left it up at the counter!*" The look on his face changes as he gets up for the glass he left at the counter. I get up, too, and go outside.

It's impossible to be alone in a small town—only in the city and in nature can you get lost. Everywhere you go someone recognizes you, and they are all in need of company. One of the aspiring poets—a heavy set, round-bellied, goatee and leather jacket, ex-military poet, named Pablo—approaches me from his table outside the café where he's been watching the busses at the Transit Plaza come and go between Salinas, Carmel, and Pacific Grove. He shakes my hand with a deep and cordial, "hello, sir." Pablo is the only one of the café bunch with any talent and the only one that likes me. The rest of the Wednesday-Night Poets hate me because I stood at their microphone half-drunk to read some little thought I had put down in my notebook one brilliant afternoon, and before reading it told them that three minutes, the time restraint, wasn't long enough for a blow job—not a good one at least, especially when you're giving it to yourself—hahaha—which is all it amounts to up there...and I went on harmlessly, but no one laughed. The joke was directed just as much at myself as it was the desperate, contrived-cadenced slam poets, and the big bear of an army soldier from the evangelical south that read his poems in a dialect that doesn't exist anymore. Still—you've got to be able to laugh at yourself, because we're all full of shit and I'm laughing right now as Pablo and I have already taken off in the direction of the wharf, absurdly walking side by side. He's the chubby thirty-three year old, white-skinned Hispanic that's spent time in the military, and working in the fields with the migrant workers, learning to speak Spanish and to take shit from all of the hardworking men; I'm the goodhearted kid from the middle of America with nothing else to do but look at all the different landscapes and listen to the stories that inhabit them.

Pablo, like all writers, wants to talk to me about *writing*—not just writing, but his own writing. "What I know about poetry I've learned from poetry itself and the life of a poet. Once, only once, have I taken a course in writing, and the whole thing was shit—I would launch my professor, who I liked, into these discussions by letting him know what I thought of it. He used to tell me, 'there is nothing to be learned truly about poetry in the classroom for a true poet; for him his place is in the world. It is the unsuccessful poets who find themselves in the position of the teacher, where teaching then envelops all of the time they should be spending writing.' And that's so true—you want a cigarette?"

"Yeah, thanks." With some amount of guilt and gratitude I let him light it for me as we're coming onto Fisherman's Wharf where a few European tourists walk in and out of the souvenir shops and restaurants. They seem disappointed that up here in California it's not as warm as they thought it would have been. Even with the sun out the water brings in a chill that leaves you wearing jeans and a coat and wishing you could afford to buy one of those big bowls of hot chowder that are stinking up the wharf with their clams and potatoes. At the end of the wharf the docked and anchored boats are chiming, bonging their loose mast lines and creaking in the water the saddest *ooo-errwahh, eee-aawws* like yea-old puppies tied up for the night—red-eye lights blinking 'lets...go...lets...go' while looking past the bay into the open waters beyond that hold all possibilities. None of them move. Pablo turns his square head from the water back to me.

"You know, take or leave that little bit of advice—but I have been around some." (motions to start moving back toward the café) "This older broad I've been seeing, she's got a place, a huge place, right on the water in Pebble Beach. Her bedroom has full windows on all sides, with the bed in the middle of the room, so when you're on it you can look in any direction and see a different beautiful site—out one wall you see the shore and the water and the rocks, out another you see trees; nothing but great, big, green trees. And a stocked kitchen— anything you want. She used to let me stay there over the weekends... we don't really see each other too much right now, but that's how it is with her—she's been busy." ("Yeah, they come and go.") He lights me another of his cigarettes, then continues as if I don't believe that he *has* 'been around some.' "The great thing about older women, though— and this one is a cougar, a real cougar—is that they know exactly what they want, and they're up front about it. She said to me, 'Pablo, we don't really share the same position in society'—she's got a nice job, banking or something; kids from the divorce, a family—'and my friends, family, and colleagues wouldn't really approve of us—you are quite a bit younger than I am...what I'm saying is, in public I won't acknowledge you if we happen to run into each other, but I do like you, and I love having you on the weekends when I can.' God, can you imagine? You can't get upset with a woman when she's that up front about things—and to me, that's it! Shit, as long as I can stay at a pad like that and have all of the great sex I want—ah, she's amazing. What's it like where you're from? The women I mean..."

"Well, believe me, it's a lot younger. Every fall there's an influx of good-looking girls coming into Lincoln to start at The University. The ones that didn't grow up in Lincoln are mostly small town farm girls from around Nebraska—the town almost seems like the big city to them. It's their first adventure away from home."

"Is it anything like Iowa City? I've never been to Lincoln, but I've been to Iowa City—the girls there are crazy." (me: "Never been there myself.") "Yeah, well, I was passing through there one night and stopped at some reading I had heard about. After it was over I was asking the MC about places to stay for cheap, and yeh know, he said he'd call a place for me, pay the difference of my room on his credit card—cos I had made forty bucks in the poetry reading, so really he only paid about ten or twenty dollars—but while he's on the phone there are these three girls, and they're young, they're checking me out, and I sort of smile back at them—but they don't say anything. The guy's on the phone, though, and they hear him book me the hotel room—he tells me the hotel and the room number, and I know they hear him too. So when I get there I have a bottle and I figure I'll have a few drinks, watch TV, go to bed—but half hour later there's a few soft knocks on the door and I hear giggling...I know it's them...so I open it up thinking this is crazy and of course there's a few awkward introductions—'we saw you at the reading,' whatever—but I invite them in and see that they brought beer with them. And after they have a few drinks they start talking sexually, out of nowhere—saying like, 'her breasts are misshapen,' or saying one is bigger than the other. I was trying to play it cool, kind of mess with them, so I said to one of them, 'well, why don't you show me yours, they don't look too bad.' And the other one says, 'no, it's *mine* that aren't the same size,' and she shows them to me, no questions, just took off her shirt and kept talking. Soon enough *both* of them had their shirts off and were letting me feel their tits, just talking normally the whole time, and after a few more drinks they were in just their panties—fuck, Iowa City is *crazy*!"

Out front of the café again, the story comes to what can only be called the climax. "In the morning," he says, "I ended up having sex with one of them—but I came after a minute and her mom showed up at the hotel a little while after, pissed off, and she made the girl go home with her. It was bizarre..." Then he says he's got to get going so he takes off to his car to leave.

All I can say is, "jesus." Not the real Jesus like my Poet Brother says, but the lowercase one that doesn't mean anything, just expresses a sort of amazement, or shock.

Lilly says that I am like the Uncarved Block. Like the glassy petrified wood so wave-beaten by the ageless tides of careening oceans that *thlump, shlump, shlwup* over my impenetrable surface only to make me shinier, sturdier, and more beautiful. But she's wrong. This stuff really does get to me. It gets in me. Sex is everywhere. The Bay serves as the vaginal inlet of California and the town of Monterey seems to be the G-Spot. If there was ever a Bear Flag Inn, a real one I mean, which coincided in perhaps a less real existence than that fictionalized pre-war Inn that sold beer and women alike, then it has long since been out of business. The services are being given away for free here, indiscriminately.

Consequently, I have vicariously contracted all of the local diseases —syphilis, gonorrhea, scabies, anonymous rashes, ringworm, warts, etc. Only a few weeks ago I saw a case of the worst.

She was staying in the meth-and-acid room in the front of the house, painted purple and black like a bruise on the brain, meticulously streaked with silver. This girl, Trish, this small-time whore and addict, never had any need for money—she was staying on a simple series of exchanges: sex for drugs, drugs for rent. Two other people were living with her—a stripper and her ex-fiancée's younger brother from Arizona whose brother, the fiancé, was stabbed to death a few months before. He introduced himself by mentioning the deceased and claiming he had 'died in his arms.' We were supposed to be awed, I guess— or pay some sort of tribute. Most likely that's how he interpreted the resulting silences.

Now these three were holding a number of little orgies in their bedroom. The Arizona boy would take on Trish while the stripper had it out on the couch with some nameless date; then the date would make his way over to Trish, and quickly inside of her with a baggy of cocaine. All the while people leisurely playing a game of cards as they waited their turn. With the card game as a decoy, the stripper was allowed to sneak away to our bedroom door some nights to peak her frightening head in and ask, "can I just watch?" Dear God, the coke would then migrate across the hall into Neechie's bedroom to be snorted maddeningly behind the dark blankets hung over the windows, and, in turn, rent was covered for the next week. From there the exchanges continued. Everyone got a little closer to death.

Other men were coming at all hours, puking in the bathroom, drinking whatever they could find, doing whatever they could find— whomever—when the Arizona boy had someone's wine-stained sister pushed onto the edge of the bed pumping it in and out and holding a pillow over her face, choking her. When he pulled out she became the link to the disjointed orgy that coursed throughout the other rooms of the house...

The sister is actually a troubled young girl from Seaside that worked at the café with Lilly, who we both liked sober, but was a violent and perverted drunk. She would drink up all the cheap wine she could handle, then disappear into a mysterious depravity—taking swings at us, cursing us, telling us to fuck off—and then she usually fucked off herself, taking off into the night where we couldn't find her till morning. When we did find her it was with some sad story of her hooking up with one of the sailor-boys that hung around the café—the same sailor-boy who was visiting the gay couple inhabiting the other front room of Walton St. where he would let one of the guys suck him off, then turn him around for the other end until he came. Afterwards saying, "Look, if you give me fifty dollars we can do this once a week." That tortured sailor, he had to put it that way because he couldn't admit to anyone that what was right there in front of him is what he really wanted; that tortured sailor, he still can't admit it to himself.

Meanwhile we learned that Trish, at the center of all this, was HIV positive. How exactly we learned this I don't know. There were no solemn confrontations, there was just a quiet, morbid rumor that consciously circulated to all the involved parties and resulted in a big trip to the doctor. They all lined up together in the physician's office for the test. After the results came back negative they began a celebration that had them drunk within the hour. They were all fucking again in the next.

As I relate this wretched affair the trumpets begin to blare their ten o'clock lights-out up at DLI, near the statue of Father Junipero Serra, the first man to bring The Church to Monterey. The Bible says that the sound of the trumpet will signify the end. To me it marks the beginning. It is the first horrible note in this off-pitch tune, these memories within the nightmare. Any note could follow.

2. BEAUTIFUL DISGUST

In The Mysticism of Sound and Music, a Sufi teaching by Hazrat Inayat Khan, he says the further you look into life, the more it expands, and opens up to you, and every moment "becomes full of wonders and full of splendors." Life on Walton St. is formed by these wonders and splendors—they are filling up my head with a beautiful disgust and I can't sleep well.

No sleep at all last night. The blonde headed Iowa kid upstairs brought home a girl from the bar, stumbling drunk into his room. He serenaded her for an hour on his guitar before getting around to the twenty minutes of creaking bed and floor which we presumed to be Sex. Lilly and I jumped on the bed the whole time, hitting the ceiling with our palms, throwing shoes at it, screaming shut-the-fuckup. Then it stopped.

Just drifting into the sweet, expectant void, 4am, we hear the horrifying cheek-slaps of Neechie on the opposite side of the walls playing the sickening tune of his own instrument. His dick, he says, when it becomes erect in his sleep and knocks against his chin to wake him, informs him when to pray. Sometimes he must forget— twice at those ungodly hours is inhuman. It scares me to think of what the beast is capable of. No one is safe.

129

To avoid the hazards of seeing anyone in the house I don't leave the room. Right here in the middle of the day I have just pissed into an empty bottle, then gladly dumped it into the bushes growing beneath our window. No risk of confrontation in that. Bacon and chicken smoke and stale wine creep under the door from the kitchen like the smell of excess itself while the voice of the Iowa kid booms over the squeak of some talk show host. It's unavoidable even though there's work to be done. I'm on the last chapter of a book about Everything, as you have to tell anyone who asks. Really it's about growing up drunk in Lincoln, NE and the consequences thereof and it's a bad book. Still don't know why I'm writing it other than to clear the shit out of me and feel a bit better after it's done. Thank God I'm not a drunk anymore, although I do like me a drinky here and again, huh there, bahh...

But, as I say, the confrontation is unavoidable because the Iowa kid is bringing me in a glass of wine in good faith to apologize. He's sorry about last night, he says, hungover. "But I'm proud of myself for not doing anything I regret." ("Not doing anything you regret—what was all that noise then?") "I didn't have sex with the girl; just ended up kicking her ass and sending her home this morning with a few bruises ...it's no big deal."

So we were wrong about what we heard, and it's worse. It is a big deal, I think, and get the hell out of my room but leave the wine with me because I have more work to do—"Okay?"

When I arrived in Monterey in November by accident—somehow finding myself broke in Lincoln after returning for my mother's birthday, which I have never missed, and having agreed to drive my dad's eight year mistress-now wife to the far west coast where he awaited her to live out his dream in Pacific Grove—I started The Book in the home of a man named Rafik Suchry, a wealthy bachelor that looks like The Prince of Egypt. He let me live there for free while working on it and promised to publish it upon completion. Then I nearly killed his fish by forgetting to feed it when he was out of town one weekend. Subsequently, I had to find somewhere else to live. Now I just don't know. What I do know is that anything can work with enough money behind it, even a bad book. And that it was a strange hell in that house, fast-paced.

Mornings Raf was gone by six. Evenings he was back by six. Always moving in a confusing rush of make-money. He owns a produce company and several pieces of real estate, but his hands are in everywhere. He's notorious about Monterey. High on a green hurry he would come flying into the house with some woman, turn the music on, and pour drinks. They would come into the office with one for me

130

and he would introduce me as 'his writer.' The women, usually young about my age, would look me over with what I assumed to be either disbelief or contempt, but Raf always took it as a sign of interest. "He looks just like that guy from—ah, what's that movie?" She always knew what movie he meant and it was always different than the one before it. For the bottom half of the drink they marveled over the likeness of my appearance to whichever actor it was that night, then their empty glasses were put in the sink and they were back out the door. Four months like that, being reminded of what you look like.

"The soul will always desire to return to its original state of independence, imposing a crushing sadness upon it for its lifespan in the body." It's not the physiognomy of my person that upsets me, it's the identity it lacks. Not a single line on the face, nor a single curve of the bone, belongs to me. Their symmetry and plainness are simply a tragic idea that allow a starting point for free association of the flesh— the body. It could belong to an actor, a former lover, or a dead bro- ther. It could belong to anyone.

For my Christmastime birthday, which I share with millions of other people besides little baby Jesus, my Poet Brother came down to visit from his job on the Oregon fish traps and he saw it too, this hell, right there in the winter solstice anti-spring under the winter moon of the eccentric.

It frightened him in the Alvarado St. night at the bars when we were crisscrossing the local haunts with Raf—the playboy-saint of all maritime doom, he called him, not The Prince of Egypt. Barging into any old place like the pack of wolves we were, Raf was buying drinks to celebrate the day *his writer*(me; unpublished) was hatched from the ether. Drinking itself, I should mention, is no good for thinking, but just one drink, even after the first sip, will relax your nerves so you *can* think. A period of calm takes place between that first sip, then, and that one that sends you over the edge into hollering shit-talk about the weird faces of others whom you'll never know and never love—or that silent, cocked-eyebrow drunk when it slants upward and is raised so terrifyingly high like it's about to go shooting right off your forehead and change your whole appearance into the demon that is inside just waiting for the golden drunken opportunity to run wild on the night that forgets all the calm, beautiful thoughts that it started on. It was neither or both in that scene of that night and I don't know how it happened but it doesn't matter, because in the best moment of the glittery, whiskey-seachange night Raf said, "you hear those sealions barking down at the bay?" Still wondering 'what we do? what we doooo...?'

After leaving, my brother wrote to me:

131

Neil(always with his affectionate name for me),

Advice is probably the last thing you want to hear when the eyes go sour and the mind plays tricks with self-worth and confidence, so I will not give you any. In fact, I have none to offer. As your fellow citizen in exile and because of my unique sea-creature like awareness of echoes and glowing nerves, I am able to imagine a dreadful Catalonian suffering with a little Irish and it hurts like hell. Remember that 'Font' is a deep and lonely well-spring, lonely as hell at times, but a source of cool life-giving water at the bottom of dark nothingness and slippery cobblestone.

Now he's a few hundred miles north in the fog writing poems and prayers on the backs of his eyelids for me and I wish he knew the depth of my gratitude.

A little wine deep down in the well of my tummy, soothing. Feeling like an old paisano warming my toes in the light on the porch and thinking of nothing in particular.

George, the twenty-three year old love of Neechie's forty year old life, stops by looking for him. Neechie is down at the beach with Puppy and the three hippies that have been sleeping on the couches. The house is quiet. "Can you tell him I came by?"

Usually when George shows up it is in a frenzy, high on cocaine or meth or ecstasy, which includes a few of his teenage friends. Odd to see him in the day, almost sober. Neechie is convinced that one of these days when his honey arrives it'll be with boxes in tow to *come back home*, but George has confided in the rest of the household that it's only when he wants a blowjob that he's around. He says he's not interested in 'that gorilla.' "Yeah, I'll let him know," I say, though I have no intention to do so.

Trish was thrown out of the house now that Neechie is kicking his habit again, and hopefully kicking George, too. A new girl already occupies the front room with her cat, Kitten. She's painted it a pale yellow and taken the old, sick mattress to be burned at the dump. The house continues to revolve interchangeably, hardly noticeable.

I have yet to meet the man in the back of the house. He never comes out of his coffin shaped room, whose dimensions I have figured to be eight feet by ten. We can hear him in there like a full grown mouse, skittering, shuffling, grunting—a combination of paranoia and chronic masturbation. His jerking off is the most heinous and persistent noise in the house alongside the TV in the kitchen. All day he sits in there moaning as if it were killing him to touch himself—awful. Graden, his name, has apparently been sitting back there for the past four years since he was asked to leave the police force for something drug related, or possibly tampering with evidence; perhaps it was his bi-polar disorder, or his schizophrenia. And maybe Graden is dying back there in that big coffin, or at least one of him is, and none of us are doing anything about it.

To concern yourself with the abstract deaths of other people is a waste of time and energy though, because, "oh my god, we're all gunnah die!"—just like the thought of everyone in the world that wakes up notoriously unhappy because they're working some lousy job to pay bills they don't understand and might get run over or blown up before they get home at night anyhow. Not me though because I'm an angel in my imagination and angels never die we just go back to where we came from, see???

In the same sunny mood of a paisano comes Ron lopping up the front steps into the broken cement courtyard. Off work on the whale-watching boats for the day, he heaves his dense Scottish frame from side to side as if he were still on the water and smiles behind his scraggly red beard. "How's it going, sir?"—("Going well, sir.")—the formalities, I suppose, are just for fun because he knows to just sit down, hand me a cigarette(without asking), and to watch the street: flat, white petals blowing ever-slightly in the seabreeze and busted down hammock mimicking their movement like in heaven or in a horror movie. Just watching, smoke blowing, ash lengthening. I have always liked men of few words, me and my Poet Brother both. That he can just sit here with me silently makes me truly like him, Ron, even though he's in love with Lilly.

My Genius Brother—the oldest; a PHD at Duke—has a difference in opinion. It enrages him when I don't say much; he thinks I'm being pretentious. If I am being pretentious I don't mean to be. I like him and how much he talks, and I could listen to him for days though he makes me feel shitty about myself sometimes—but, hell, I like most people.

"Want some wine?" Ron is already standing up at the bottom of the stairs. He knows the answer. The Book can wait. Any time is good for a break so long as it's to sit in the sunlight of a park, drinking wine, and being happy.

Incredibly great weather and two bottles of wine. A bench in Friendly Plaza. Wind spraying mist off the fountain onto the tiles encircling it. A homeless man sitting on a nearby bench with his pack on the seat next to him, staring at the fountain and enjoying the shade. I walk over to him with one of the bottles to offer him some—"Nah, I'm alright," he says.

Baffled, I return to the bench where Ron is sitting. "He said no. He doesn't want any." (Just as confused, "he doesn't want any?") "No —that's the strangest thing; as a bum I don't think I could ever turn

133

down free wine, or anything, but Oh Well."

For some of the bottle we don't talk, but further on down it comes. Ron tells me he never graduated from high school. He got made fun of for being fat, for being a dork, and eventually got fed up and dropped out. A funny and sad thought to think of cool, bearded Ron that way, who can tell me the name of any bird in the sky and most of the creatures under water. And who is now dating a good-looking, dirty-hip, tattooed girl from the Mojave Desert—normally she'd be hanging around with him, jobless and homeless(both living out of the backs of their trucks), but she's back home right now patching things up with her dad and sister who she just abandoned one day, unannounced, when she took off on a drive that somehow led her to Monterey.

Ron's love for nature and all of the sweet inhabitants therein began when he was a child, about ten, and moved onto a ten acre plot of the great outdoors in Carmel Valley with his family. He explored the seeming wilderness all by himself, catching frogs and fish, swimming in the river, learning to navigate trails and build practical contraptions out of scraps found lying around. His dad, with the temperament of an artist himself, encouraged him only through example in his own handiwork. "My dad," he is telling me, "used to be rich; well, maybe not rich, but he was pretty damn wealthy. He had a contracting company in Southern California where we used to live—they developed entire neighborhoods down there just north of San Diego. One day, after we moved here, it hit me that we didn't have money anymore when he went from leaving in his truck in the morning with all his tools in back, to leaving on a bike pulling his tools behind him in a wagon. And it's not like he was going anywhere—he didn't have any work—he would just leave, then come back and start taking things apart, like TVs, radios, and he would work on them for awhile then get bored and leave all this junk lying around. It really pissed my mom off, that's for sure." They ended up separating, though they both still live on the same property, only his dad stays in a guesthouse somewhere further back on the lot. "Yeah, we should all go out there sometime—it's a beautiful place."

Strange how sometimes couples will stay together long after it makes sense. They are willing to comfort themselves with their own inane miseries because it is what they know. Usually they don't though; usually it is the opposite. The slightest human error will lay the foundation of a greater calamity—the two are instantaneously doomed. There are few people that are truly happy together, and I think it is because neither one of them were happy to begin with, and neither one of them knew what could truly make them so. Their expectations of love were so unrealistic that they could never be met, and they remained unhappy. The solution then is what, low expectations? Don't ask for anything and you'll be pleased with everything you get? No wonder the Filipinos sing, in Thailand they smile, and the drunken Danes are so damned content...

There may not be any validity in that but those are the dumb thoughts I have as the two of us are walking down the twilight hill toward the beach, not drunk, but with that precious, lofty air that comes with just enough drink. Like an Irishman, or a Filipino, Ron begins to sing a ridiculous verse that goes, "gah-gah-gahgahgah,"—then I realize it's actually one of those seabirds laughing overhead and think, 'whoa, boy, better be careful now—don't drink the hard stuff.' We go into the corner shop near Del Monte and buy four tall boys with two dollar bills and a handful of quarters, and drink the first one the rest of the way to the water.

Walking through the sand in the dark the waves come up to our feet, then feel as if they are going to pull us in with them as they roll back out. My head gets light watching the water, watching the stars, so we sit down in dry sand to take it easy and open our second tall boy. Out of the blue: "You know, you're a lucky guy to have Lilly."

In my head: ("I like you Ron, so don't talk about my Lilly.") Aloud: "Yeah, no kidding." The fact that he is undoubtedly in love with Lilly is partially why he likes me, because she does, and probably why I'll end up hating him. For now though I ignore it because we both have our love affair with the ocean to concentrate on—*plsh-ploosh-pfwhooooo*—and the giant lady earth, the residence of our existence. Because it is incomprehensible to us we look at it in terms of a woman. She'll take care of us as long as we're sweet and respectful, and are conscious of all Her other lovers and our siblings. Her Ovarian Moon rests magnificently high over the mirror-water as a sign for all us children of the night, reminding us to look up from whence we came and let out stupid, quiet sighs for Her and the things she does that we'll never be able to understand.

The bum's fire is burning low, almost out, further up the beach, looking not unlike a reflection of the moon itself. They are likely too drunk, or asleep already, to do anything about it. Imagine Frank there with orange fire-colored skin thirsting for clean water in his unknowing sleep; Timmy there with red bandana pulled down over sun-exhausted eyes. Nothing in them to keep them awake listening to the sounds of the ocean, to give unnecessary praise to each slopwash of salt and sand. They are just simply there, taken care of, and will wake up tomorrow morning no happier, no sadder, but will have the sounds of a gently whispering Mother to soothe them, and maybe some splashing dogs and blissfully yelping kids building sandcastles and they will be OK.

Unaware of time lapsed, I repeat myself: "You're right, Ron," I say. "I AM LUCKY."

3. A SUNDAY SHOWING

Sabbath. The day of rest. Someone's birthday, someone's funeral, someone's anniversary. Holy peace. Sunday—the only day of the week the behavior on Walton St. changes.

Talk shows are replaced by Television Evangelists roaring halle-lujahs in the empty kitchen. Neechie attends first services at The New Hope Church. The hippies sleep till noon in their new room—the gay couple moved out on a whim to God knows where. Wonder in the Holy Peace of morning...

A large house of too many rooms to count—Mima and Sister, Syd, there with me; I am watching the old maid affectionately prepare dinner to be eaten later on. The house inexplicably recedes with my mom and sister into a bright summer cornfield like back in Nebraska, surrounded by dirt roads with fresh tractorwheel marks leading no-where. On all fours I take off into the rows of corn that hide me from—

I am running like a beast, an animal, a creature of the wild sex world that creates its own monsters first in the imagination—the self; I am running low to the ground from a primitive intangibility. The cornstalks cut my face and the dirt my hand-paws kick up sticks on my tongue...I am dying of thirst like the drunk bums of the beach and a lake materializes. In front of it is a sign: MESS WATER. (huh?) On a massive tricycle adapted for use in the water rides a young boy with a mohawk—the pedals splash the surface of the mess water. A plywood box is attached to the handlebars. 'This water clean enough to drink?' The question is directed through the mind to the back of a dirty blue bonnet being worn by someone standing on the pier I have walked out onto—she turns around and it is the old cook from the house! Somehow, without her saying anything, I know she has a child some-where in the lake's vicinity, missing. No help. Moves; a drinking fount-ain in her place whose plumbing blatantly dips down into the lake for its source of water—the fountain is otherwise freestanding at the end of the pier. The water falls through my mouth while attempting to wash out the dirt—none of it goes down; can't drink the water...falls through my mouth—dirt remains—no fucking water going....

Awake in the holy early morning of peace—hungover, thirsty. Can't drink the water in the house because the pipes are rusted and the water's brown. Graden drinks the water, so I've heard, but he's crazy. No way I'll spoil the quiet by moaning that my belly hurts and it needs water. Lilly is waking up the way she gradually does with sleepy green eyes holding sleep-boogers that I wipe out for her. We're at our best in the mornings. *Hallelujah!* No spoiling that with aches you gave to yourself.

Empty wine bottle propping the window open, beer bottle-vase knocked over in the night with flowers—water on the floor is no worry. A conscientious wind belonging to the inherent laziness of Sunday cools us in the sheets. Nothing like the Sundays of childhood when I would be forced out of bed to attend Sacrament at The Church of Jesus Christ and the Latter Day Saints(Mormon) with Mima, having to listen to four year olds bare their testimonies from the whispered words of their own mothers into their ears while my Catholic raised father prepared that big feast for us back at the house. No food for us here. No mother or sister. Just me and Lilly in bed letting the afternoon come as slowly and deliberately as anything else. Wind blowing the truest gospel I've ever heard.

The matinee is crowded with elderly couples and the only seats open are the bad ones in front that cramp your neck. No matter to me though, I don't have to pay to get in and have little interest in the film. It's about building happiness upon other peoples' unhappiness in the conjugal life. Only reason I came is there's nothing else on my schedule and I'm attracted to the Hollywood starlet playing the main role. Lilly's on the short shift at the café.

Working the theatre doors is a friend of Lilly's named Sasha—she gets us into all the shows for free. Sasha is the petite, large-chested daughter of The Town Printer, Lean Basho. She's not Jewish but every bit of her looks it, or Russian. Dark hair, light skin, koala bear face with rings around the eyes. She fancies herself in the likes of a Dostoevskian character, which I laughed about to myself while lending her a copy of Notes From Underground a few weeks back—she would undoubtedly identify herself as the prostitute. There's no way she'd make a decent prostitute if there is such a thing, having just let me into the matinee at no charge, though she does have all the loneliness of one.

Neck hurting and eyes sore from having to focus on the screen so close. Slouched deep down in my chair with my coat over me as a blanket, occasionally allowing myself to sleep. Not a single character is likeable or interesting. All of them lie, all of them cheat. By the end of the movie I am so frustrated that I walk right past Sasha at the door as she's saying, "well, I'll see you guys later then?" and continue aimlessly around town trying to feel better, thinking of all the lusty looks Lilly has ever given me and of all the scratches she has put into my back. She's given them to other people before me, and she'll give them to other people after. It's terrible that even the good things can hurt.

Especially the good things when you think of them for all those other people. Nothing makes me special or deserving of them anyway, so why all the complaining?

Pacing in front of the café, waiting for Lilly to get off work, I imagine everyone she's been with and going to be with. Women will make you crazy about nothing. And everything. Once they've got you you're haunted by the smell and the taste and the look and the feel of that damned thing they've got between their thighs—the root of all sorrow, desperation, tragedy, life—and you lose yourself in it. Before Lilly there was no sex. There were honest mistakes. There was an abortion. There was loneliness. There was consolation. There was purity. There was Self. There was God. Now there is instinct and long-ing. I am a beast, an animal, a creature of the wild sex world. She created the monster within me through the wonder of her sex—it's ugly and jealous. The faces form of the people she sees in my absence. A skinny, pock-faced regular wearing a dark ball cap stands nearby in the spot he's been standing all day. 'Is it you, buddy? You meet her here when I leave?' Feeling not angry, just sorry for myself I ask him for a cigarette and he tells me, "Sorry—quit smoking about a year ago when I quit the booze, too." A damned lie because I've seen him smoking only days ago and why he would need to lie to me about it makes me extremely suspicious. "Does Lilly smoke?"

Sure of it now that he's rubbing it in my face, talking about her— "No, she doesn't," I say. But you knew that already, didn't you?

The pathetic question and his ravaged face make me feel sorrier for myself somehow, and for Lilly, and think of the sense of horror and pity that face must induce as it hovers in the sweaty dark. "Well, I'm on my way," he says, and he extends his hand to me in an odd way like he's trying to maintain the twitch in his muscles.

Ten minutes later I'm still in front of the café as a white van pulls up to the curb. The guy in the ball cap is in the driver's seat with the engine idling, gesturing to me with one predatory hand to come over there. Standing curiously at his window his face looks so accused and pitiful to me, as if he were cursed with it to atone for some previous act of disgust in his life, that all the hideousness suddenly goes out of me—I forgive this man for the things he may or may not have done. "Here." He hands me a pack of cigarettes that, I guess, he just bought at the convenient store a few blocks away. I laugh in his face—not laughing at him, but at my own confusion and ridiculous accusations.

Genuinely: "Thanks—you know, you actually made my day."

He shines a damaged smile at me that creases his cheeks twice on each side. "No problem. Enjoy the bad habit."

As he drives away I light up feeling guilty now for different reasons. And pretty fucking silly, wow. You are here right now, okay?

Sweet little Lilly girl is right inside about to get off work and when she does she's going to come up and hug you because she's happy to see you and you're both doing alright.

Telling myself this, Lilly comes out of the door with work shirt in hand and hair still up and she comes up to me just as I thought for a hug and a kiss on the mouth. "Hey, babe," she says, "lets get out of here."

Out of Monterey, out of California, out of America? I put my cigarette out, which, yeah I enjoyed, and like yea-old puppies tied up with each other—*'lets...go...lets...go'*—we take off together back up the hill, or back up to hell.

Although it's Sunday there's a commotion at the house. Apparently George came by earlier with the prostitute he's been living with and was trying to convince people to sleep with her. The little sixteen year old runaway, Joe, came in with them too. George and the prostitute are gone, but Joe is still here. Too high to speak, little Joe is now drinking orange juice straight from the jug in the kitchen. Everyone is in an uproar.

Each of the three hippies has an instrument out—bongo drum, guitar, mandolin—playing and singing nonstop as Joe watches with young, mad eyes in silent terror and ecstasy. Neechie is gyrating his hips as he pulls a baking tray of chicken legs out of the oven and fries more chicken legs on the stovetop. Heavy smoke—chicken and cigarettes. Wine is going round in a massive jug only a quarter gone. Graden is actually out of his room, drunk, smoking a joint, licking his old white man lips while shouting unintelligibly—his jeans rolled up to mid pasty-calf and the ass torn out. The Television Evangelists are preaching on mute.

Poor molested Joe doesn't know what to make of any of it, but is asking, barely getting the words out, if I have a cigarette for him. Neechie is asking if we want any of his nasty chicken. Ron—who I hadn't realized was here, but has just come out of the bathroom—is clapping me on the back hello. The wine jug is reeling around the circle and we take some even though it's not the happy, good kind of daytime parks. Everyone is talking, dancing, scooting around the floor on milk crates, shouting, laughing. I don't know what to make of it either, Joe—somehow we ended up here too and I'm sorry you've got to see this. Just take this pitiful smoke I'm offering you to the front porch and close your eyes for awhile.

As a courtesy we sit down for a song and the movement and sound becomes a type of seasickness, earthsickness, that the wine amplifies in burgundy streaks, stained teeth, spilled drops on the floor, sticky footprints ohmygod—it reminds me of all the small town kitchens

139

growing up where everyone is trying to forget the shit they saw in the daytime, or thought they saw, and live out big night dreams of crotch-grabbing in the bathroom and conversations of incredibly brilliant drunken infamies. Really it's just getting fucked up—futile attempts at abandonment, oblivion; inflated Egotism that by morning is a base vulgarity and a terrible headache so that you never want to wake up and face the facts. No one wants to see Tomorrow.

In the Great Southwest I remember understanding this for the first time when I drove into the thirdworld-town of Socorro, NM—where both of my brothers were living for the summer—and saw the strange melancholy of drunk natives in front of liquor stores, men asleep under trees, junkies strung out in corroding adobes, stolen bikes, drugs exch-anged on sagging stoops, glowing arroyos, Government Checks, and waiting forever to see Tomorrow.

"Mañana, mañana, mañana," they said in the 11o'clock sun that had turned the whole town into a giant stucco and chrome mirror, blinding the midmorning sleepers just getting out of bed and forcing the weathered old men to take shade under the plaza trees where they held their tall cans of beer so gently. Tomorrow they would sober up, tie their shoes, shave their faces, wipe their asses—until then they would just sit in the dark spots of the bright-hot town and drink and play chess and nap. At eighteen the philosophy of do-nothing charmed me as it would any young man, unemployed, seeing different parts of the world with all that Go-literature stuffed into their heads—it was so calm and harmless. Just drink beer in the sunshine and don't harm any living creature. For the hottest part of the days we would sit in front of the fan that scanned back and forth in pleasant gusts across the room as we read, juggled soccer balls, drank beer, and stared out the windows to the west where the brown peaks of Mother Magdalena silently prayed for the inhabitants' salvation.

It was fine for a few weeks, but after that you blow yourself out with too much drink one night and it all gets ruined. The Lady Ghost of the Rio Grande no longer takes pity on you and she stops protecting you from the river demons that sneak up the banks just after the sun sets and it's cool enough for everyone to come back outside. That's how it happened—one night I walked down to the well-watered soccer fields with Aden(The Poet Brother) and a bottle of whiskey. Dark yellow desert splotched with pale mint surrounding the unbelievably green, by contrast, soccer fields. We watched some of the locals play a pick-up game, drinking from our bottle on the sidelines smiling our idiot grins and thinking, "Don't harm any living creature." Calm, harmless. But once the bottle was gone something else took over and I'm not completely sure what happened. Someone who looked like Aden disappeared into the locals' bar, and someone who looked like

140

me stole the car from my brother's driveway. I can hardly remember the drive to Las Cruces, except for screaming along the two and a half hours of road, and meeting an adorable little Mexican girl the following morning by a water fountain outside of a restaurant, then kissing her in the park well into afternoon.

When Tomorrow came—as it has to at some point, two days later in this instance—I was groaning on a flight to Rancho, California where a job had been lined up for me in a warehouse. None of us brothers felt very good about what had happened. Though I did have that girl's number and it seemed strange to me that we were born on the same day—only she came three years after I did...

But, back in the kitchen comes George, without the prostitute, now with two drugged-out looking guys that don't say a damned thing. One of them looks like he's just been in a fight with a bump over his right eye and the other looks oblivious, standing there with red t-shirt slumped over his potbelly and mustache twitching over his lips as he wholeheartedly concentrates on counting the pills in his hand—he keeps dropping them to the ground and having to crouch down with some trouble to pick them up. No one mentions anything as the music continues and the pills continue to be counted and dropped. George smiles at Neechie as he grabs two chicken legs off the stove and leans against the counter to eat them. Neechie slides over to where George is standing, still gyrating, and presses up against him—"ah, get the fuck off me, huh!"—but Neechie keeps grinding and the boy keeps smiling with bits of chicken covering his teeth and tongue.

"Oh, no, n-o-o—y'all just hear that? My honey ain't gettin' 'way from me this time!" Neechie is beyond drunk and there's no stutter left in his voice.

Lilly is sitting with one leg over the other in a chair as I stand behind her in the doorway—Ron, as he sometimes does, has slipped out without anyone noticing to go sleep in his car for the night. Good for you, Ron. Nowhere near drunk enough for this I squeeze Lilly on the shoulder and she gets up mid-song and we back into the bedroom then slide the chain over the door behind us. It's early still and they'll be playing in the kitchen for a few more hours, but we just want to be alone and forget those things that make us all sssick come morning.

The drums play, the beats change, the chords hum, the voices raise, lower, raise like heaving crescendos of rain, and with all of that sound it is impossible to hear us as we quietly make love in the middle of everything. And as we lay here afterwards it is with a magnificent sense of detachment that we eventually hear Graden go back into his room, George and Neechie argue in theirs, and the instruments finally put down for the night. Monterey, California, America, Earth, Hell—Tomorrow we'll leave them all...

4. PERVERTED HEROES

Someone once said that when you meet your heroes you either find that they're not the person you thought they were, or you find that they are exactly like you. For better or worse, the only real hero a man has is himself. Certain kinds of men attract certain kinds of people, and in remaining true to himself there are a number of acquaintances and mishaps unavoidably similar—but in the end there is only Him and His experience.

The imagination, as it records reality, dreams, drunkenness, and visions will integrate each of these disjointed stimuli into a single entity of man's creative existence—His Experience. If He chooses to believe entirely in whatever is revealed to him, then He will find the result to be supreme happiness. I have chosen to believe in my Self. For worse I am my own hero, and for better I have the others like me.

Perusing the second floor of the library I am overwhelmed by the hundreds of thousands different stages of my own heroism—I haven't lifted a single title. All of my myriad names left heartbreakingly on their shelves. Whether it exists or not, there seems to be a collective consciousness amongst the writers of present and past; a genuine sort of empathy is evoked by the struggling sight of old manuscripts and love letters because, as a writer, you wrote them yourself once and none of it made complete sense until you died, then were born again to look back from afar. They are all a part of me, and therefore held in the same affection/contempt that I hold myself. It's almost a sacred place, the library—it's a place you feel real comfortable taking a shit in.

Having just cleared my bowels and feeling deeply at peace with myself it offends me personally to find a man in an aisle near the back of the second floor, sitting there on the carpet with the screen of his laptop turned so I can see it. From a ways down it was a blur, now closer the screen has become a clear image of an overweight woman bent over on all fours with the camera focused on the dark, sweaty folds of her ass and the hangdown of an uninviting bush. Three feet away he notices my steps and snaps the screen closed onto the keyboard and looks up at me so utterly frightened that my pity temporarily outweighs my disgust.

One aisle over, under the shadows of dead bugs, my temper flares again as he recommences his internet smut-search. Scrolling through images, finger on the touchpad rectangle, he sounds like a rodent rummaging through a cereal box in the cupboard, that desperate and greedy bastard. His laptop now resting on the windowsill, I realize that the figures through the glass are those of children, thirteen to fifteen year olds, hanging around the open balcony with afterschool backpacks scattered across tables, chatting up the breaking innocence of adolescence.

They're right outside the window laughing, throwing things at each other, crushes are making handjob-eyes across the patio area, and this son of a bitch stands here with a hardon poking through the pocket of his jeans! Instead of busting his computer, stomping it in with my heel, breaking off his hardon, I casually return to scanning the shelves, which have be-come a jumble of unfocused words undulating across their covers and spines.

As I go down the stairs to leave he is still there with his computer open, so I stop in at the front office to interrupt the three cackling older women—"There's a pervert in your fiction section." The woman I've addressed has tears in her eyes from laughing. ("What?") "There's a pervert in your fiction section. He's not bothering anyone—yet—but I thought you should know he's there, looking at porn(black movies!!), and anyone that might venture into, say, H through R, could potentially be disturbed by him. He's not being at all discreet."

Her face is more annoyed at me than it is perturbed by the incident itself, as if it has happened hundreds of times already—"The fiction section you say?"—("Yeah. Just thought you should know.")—"Okay, well, thanks," she says, and leisurely heads toward the reference desk.

Regaining my appetite while walking through the farmer's market, inhaling the smoky odors of various foods, with only a vague question lingering about whether the pervert would become hungry for these things as well. Hungry for Indian dishes, kebabs, sweet breads, french fries, deep fried clams, honey and cinnamon almonds. The fresh earthiness of produce in damp cardboard boxes. Surely he wouldn't.

Hurrying between couples carrying bags of groceries, eating chicken kebabs and hot pretzels, with two dollars in my pocket that wouldn't afford me even a root beer float, I feel like an athlete or a thief—slender, agile, working through the unsuspecting crowd of market shoppers thinking, "Never in Monterey," as I run off with their rice bowl. The thought helps ease my stomachache from too much coffee this morning on an empty belly as I turn up the hill to go for a nap.

Not fifteen minutes into coursing through images of in-the-head on the big, soft bed that still smells like Lilly there's a knock at the front door. No one else—maybe Graden—is in the house so it's my job to answer. Sasha is standing on the front porch in knee-high, leather riding boots and a dark brown, wool top coat, black hair straight down at her shoulders. With her back to the door, staring toward the street, distraught, she looks just like the Dosteivskian character she wants to be, and she's come here to tell me that someone I love has just been murdered or that she's pregnant with someone's bastard child. Not today, I'm thinking, not while I'm hungry. It's too perfectly ludicrous. But when I open the door she turns around and says, "I know Lilly's not here, but I'm really lonely." She says it very sadly and seriously in a way meant to imply nothing—just that she's Lonely. "Are you doing anything?"

As much as I was looking forward to a nap, I know that just last month she was in an institution for depression, eating applesauce for a week on suicide watch. For whatever reason it makes me think of my mother all alone in her home far away in Lincoln, NE where the men of my family have left her with Sydney, the baby girl, in her last semester of high school courses. "No, I'm not doing anything." I am overcome with the urge to hug her because it might be just what she and my mother need right now.

When I pull away she asks, "are you drunk?" Awful that's her first reaction, but for all she knows I could be—there's enough to drink here to be out of my mind. However, I'm not drunk at all, I just happen to think that sometimes people need to feel the touch of another human being to remind them that they're not the only one in this big world feeling a bit off—we all know how to sing the

bbbbbbbbbbblllllllllluuuuuues.

Sasha's house is a block up and a block over from Walton St.— contrary to the image she wants to exude of herself as the impoverished narcissist with incestual issues, her little one bedroom house is clean, well-decorated, and paid for directly from a trust fund. On her front porch, where you can almost see the bay between the renovated Italian fishermen's houses, she hands me a cigarette from one of the three open packs in her purse.

Though she grew up only fifteen minutes away on a ranch in Salinas, she likes to tell people that she's from Portland. She lived there for two years before she was forced to come back to California. The circumstances aren't completely clear, but it had something to do with the apartment she was living in—downtown Portland—where there were a number of sex fiends, sadists, drug addicts, street trash, and perverts. She coolly tells me about it while taking horrifyingly deep drags on the porch suspended above the bay. "When I first met my roommates they were sitting in their new apartment watching videos from the eviction party they had thrown at their last apartment. They were all drunk at this party and they were sticking things up each other's asses while everyone sat in a circle cheering. God, they were depraved. They even went as far as to steal the leftover stale bread from this sandwich shop close by and stuck the crumbs into their asses. Then someone would ask, 'do you want that toasted?' and they would light it on fire." (Part of me detests everything she says; part of me laughs, cringes, asks to hear more.) "This guy, Glitch"—she interjects here to mention that he had legally changed his name to 'Glitch' when the person that bore his birth name had kicked his heroin habit—"He let his girlfriend at the time give him an enema in front of everyone. Agh, they were all sadomasochistic, too. I'm so glad I don't live there anymore. It's just that the journalist part of me was so interested in the phenomenon of these people; I wanted to learn more about them so I could write their stories." She says she's glad she doesn't live there anymore, but it's obvious that she's proud of the fact that she at one point did.

She enjoys telling me all of this. It's almost as if she's boasting of the exploits like they were her own. She tells me more about Glitch, and about Ines, her lesbian roommate that was in love with her. She even claims to be a 'pseudo-lesbian' herself. Then there's the three-some that involved Glitch, Ines, and a second roommate—a gay kid named, Derek. The details were recounted to her in the elevator the morning after, now she recounts them to me a year later. It involved, simultaneously, blow jobs, sodomy, tongues, and cashew flavored pussy. She is persistent in the description with the cashew—somehow that smell and that taste had been so real to her that it stuck.

Inside she rations out a little wine for me. The spotless sink catches the sound of the faucet dripping—my suspicion is that she has purposely not tightened it completely. Self-consciously I read her some of my book, which she listens to with her legs crossed and hand on jaw to signify that she's interested. After I finish she tells me that only men can write that way. Honestly, vividly. A woman just sounds like a whore. She puts a bag of low-fat popcorn in the microwave and asks if I could read part of a story she's writing. It's about her Portland friends. She pours a tad more wine and I read it silently, thinking to myself that it's funny, almost over intelligent, unnecessarily wordy. Before I can say anything she blurts out, even more self-consciously than me, "I just don't know how to write any of it down—can you help me with it?" She wants my *literary* advice. I remember that she leant me a copy of Anaïs Nin's *Diary* awhile back, and then quoted her—though on the subject of June—saying: "She is the woman I want to be." I manage not to laugh, but what a load of shit! That she should want to mimic the relationship of Anaïs and old Mr. Henry. What, with her pseudo-lesbianism and this goddam literary talk. You want me to be your Henry? and Lilly to be our June? Fuck you. Not today. Not while I'm hungry. It's too perfectly ludicrous.

The power goes out. This gets her off, I'm sure.

The microwave was the problem and the popcorn is burnt. She sends me out to the side of the house to squeeze in the foot and a half of space between the neighbor's wooden fence and the wall of her home where the fuse box is located. With the rosebushes scratching my arms as I reset the fuses I'm thinking, "I am not an asshole. I do not paint cunt-portraits. I do not want to break my own nose in the afterlife." Going over in my head how easy everyone wants the labels laid out for them; to simply adopt the archetype—no adaptations, no personality. Even Lilly that day as I sat in the salon waiting room, drinking free coffee and eating free cookies, flipping through a book of hers I'd found by an old drunk(Kerouac), as she got her hair done all pretty and perfect by some young hairdresser. On the opposite side of the waiting room screen I heard her voice amongst the blow dryers and chemical spray as the hairdresser asked her about me. Lilly: "He wants to be a writer." Predictably, as everyone asks, the girl wants to know what I write. Lilly says, "well—he likes Kerouac...his stuff is all kind of like Kerouac's I guess." Hearing this I became so embarrassed with that stupid-great book in my hands—even more for her, though, than for myself. What do you know? Thankfully, the hairdresser didn't know who he was. But, my God—for better or worse, let a man be Himself. A greater man can teach you technique, discipline, order, but it is your own philosophies that create your own peculiar way of living. His Experience, invariably narrow, is the only thing absolutely unique about a man. To take that from him is to leave him a genetic shell, a faceless offspring, a Bastard of the Earth. It is to leave him dry, defiled.

In spite of everything, I put aside my temporary bitterness and go back in to the house. The power is restored. I suggest to Sasha that she start in the elevator. Have them describe their own affairs as candidly as they were described to her. Let everyone tell their own damn stories and put them down with nothing else in mind but "be genuine, be honest, be kind, be gentle." Let things happen and accept them tearfully, happily, peaceably.

5. A CELEBRATION OF NOTHING

I can see everything in the sky, the air—the grey sparkle and glitter of Bay water spray, atomic seams of the chaotic order—the electric fabric of the world, dazzling—majestic flight of pelicans' gentle swoop, seabirds falling in with the ocean wind, falling out with the flap of the wings—No birds or distinction between anything; Only tiny beads of silver daytime stars of eternity that fly like worms... buzzing particles of grey matter; buzzing particles of the underlying existence of everything—They've been described as fairies, I believe—sunlight ghostflies of the shit of the world, and the shit of heaven, delicately unmasked in every degree of my Vision—the twirling make-up of the obstinate dream, incomprehensible—Dear Botanist of the Great Garden of carbon beings—

Sitting on this damned old bench on a rock wall of the Bay, anywhere—maybe Irish shore, maybe Venetian port; American blue blood of all Idea, Action, Consequence—manifest! manifest!—the seal tail *shwap* is no more than a trail of dust created in the firmament...end over end these glowing strings, with silver water droplets running down their tendril veins—what do you mean? In the awful confusion of perpetual struggle, I still know Nothing but mystery. The fairies beat their phosphorescent orb-wings—see? see?—light and movement; the sky, the air—Everything—skewed Vision of the great morning, great fog, great ocean—the perfect light of Harmony's grey-glowing fairies as if seen by dizziness, or vertigo—all things set in stone; also, all things Go—the great world, incomprehensible; the obstinate dream of the existence of everything—I CAN SEE IT, sitting on this Bay bench of the damned morning, careening on the edge of the rock wall with truth sickness of the soul and the possibility of toppling over into the sorry and glad waves that could both swallow me easily as they swallow all time itself—Nothing I can do to change what the great sea-god does—chew up rocks on any shore, chew them up into dust like the harbor seal *shwaps* of the tail...then Nothing.

Like the immutable cries of 'waahhhh' said the ancient sailors, said the innocents, says me—unchanged since the first sound of all perfect time—cried with the idiot disgust of death, of Holy Life...Dear God, to have somehow seen the peaceful grey blood of all things—the interconnected lines of unspeakable truths left wide open, protected in a glorious fervor of the fairy guardian angels—easing that thing called *perpetual struggle*, to allow a truly holy existence of simplicity. In the name of The Father, The Son, and The Holy Ghost, Amen.

With gusto I finished The Book in one last quick, excited sweep of the hand, moving it automatically as my baffled head orchestrated the thoughts from this Holy Vision. If I don't burn it then maybe I'll wipe my ass with it. Either way it's done and forgotten.

Lilly, the sweet girl, brought me home gifts in a brown paper sack to congratulate me—four bottles of wine and two packs of cigarettes. A sweet melody of burgundy and smoke. With her it is always described as music. She is the music herself, and all of the time it plays. Sometimes the music is described at full volume that you can dance to in any fashion and any step could strike a beat; sometimes it is described as being real low, barely audible, barely moving—not like a flower caught by breeze, but like an entire field in a vast prairie that when you look at it you don't know exactly if it sways, all you know is it's beautiful and you can't explain why and you don't need to anyway. And sometimes it's like those little gifts brought home in a paper sack. *A sweet melody*. Or like when she's asleep, and all there is is an occasional light snore or sigh, and she closes the inch gap between the back of her body and the front of mine by scooting her little ass right up against me because the space separating us was just too much. You can't explain exactly what it is that makes it so beautiful, and there's no need to.

Her day off. We take two of the bottles around town on bikes like the first day we spent together. Riding down to the tourist wharf for free samples of hot, savory clam chowder that taste so damn good served in their tiny plastic cups. We lock up the bikes to the rack and start on foot with our hands clasped in one another's as children do. Climbing up the fire escape of The Golden State Theatre, then hopping over to the connecting rooftops of the downtown eateries, we look down onto Alvarado St. in the sad, aging daytime. Our wine is almost too sweet, peering over the building's edge, giggling, spilling a little onto the sidewalk below then ducking out of sight—the tops of a hundred small buildings as if from a painting in a different world. "HEY!" A skinny, bald man with a well-trimmed grey goatee shouts at us from the fire escape. "WHAT THE HELL ARE YOU DOING ON MY ROOF?!"—("We're just looking!")—"IF YOU DON'T GET THE FUCK OFF MY ROOF I'M GOING TO CALL THE COPS!" In our childish joy we look at each other and try not to laugh; we don't want him to call the cops on us and ruin our day, so we get the fuck off his roof, quickly scale the chain link fence back to the fire escape, and rush by him down the stairs back onto the street as he's screaming, "DON'T LET ME EVER FIND YOU TWO UP HERE AGAIN OR I'LL KICK YOUR ASS!"

We're already gone though, laughing inside one of those shops filled with unnecessary knick knacks that attract mothers with young children and tourists covered in unneeded sunscreen. The sun is never bright enough here. We try on different styles of pirate hats with big brims and big feathers, and decorate ourselves with rings, necklaces, swords—forget the sun, it's a beautiful day taken straight from *Breakfast At Tiffany's*, strung together and relocated in the reality of small town Monterey where good fiction comes to die attractive deaths. The clouds in the sky are bright white, puffy sons of bitches that are everywhere in the shape of a fish, a raccoon, a boat, a clown, a human heart. Lilly pockets a lighter for me with a wooden case that has a pirate ship etched into it so I don't have to use my shitty cardboard matches.

Lighting up on the move—spinning or fading from one place to another like in the movie—and blowing out the last ice cream cone cloud of smoke as we enter the lobby of a giant hotel that stretches up into the sky-menagerie as the only inanimate object. We each grab a green apple from the fruit bowl on the front desk. I swipe a set of wine glasses from a table in the adjoining restaurant. Chomping into the green-skinned sweet-sour meat, riding UP in the elevator, we kiss off the stickiness from our lips. All the way to the top floor, the fourteenth floor, where a banquet for the beautification of the peninsula is just ending—the old faces dressed up for so much effect, with money spent for boutonnieres, are getting on the DOWN elevator, confused by our frantic youth spilling past them with apple cores and wine glasses clinking in hand. We pick up a few crumbs of bread off the white linen tablecloths and take them to the balcony. Both glasses are filled with our very own cheap wine. Sweet girl of my Monterey—this is to you!

In the softness above the town we down our glasses like children of pleasant grape juice, smacking our lips, *ahh*. I pluck some of the roses that line the planters of the private balcony and stuff them into my empty glass. "Are you going to throw that?" She asks with wide-eyes that dare me to explode the red-petaled blood lust onto the fourteen-story-below sidewalk where the timing would have to be perfect as to not crash onto someone's head. She knocks her glass onto the landing two floors down—it smashes; no one on the street notices. "Am I going to throw it? No—hahaha—absolutely not." The green light switches to yellow, switches to red, and I hurl the glass like a grenade toward the stopped intersection—petals fall from the glass, trailing it as it floats so far down onto the street, shattering in a flurry of red-petals and glass shards that scatter and settle onto the pavement without hurting anyone. We bump into each other, sprint toward the exit, and burst into laughter that hits every sharp note of Her scale, rising in harmonizing tones. Her melodic identity reflecting itself in my own, which creates a sound so wild, ecstatic, primal, cerebral, reverent; continuously changing in a multitude of forms to express the greater character at hand—my god, the divine liquidity of sound! that echoes through the elevator shaft all the way BACK DOWN.

From outside the elevator doors in the lobby, where a camera would be positioned in a film, we see the reflective chrome doors slide to each side from the tiny separating space in the middle—a young couple appears utterly composed, straight faced(look closely though and you can see the littlest smile in the eyes), exiting the elevator arm in arm and walking calmly out of the shot.

The inclination to celebrate early is depressing and unavoidable. Not a week after resolving to wipe myself with The Book—having strengthened this conviction when a freelance editor took me out to a bar in Pacific Grove and bought me several margaritas only to tell me that she was having trouble getting through it—I run into Pablo outside of the nighttime café. He's wearing shined loafers, nice slacks, and a clean, heavily starched, white dress shirt—the shirt is tucked in and his hair is slicked back with oil. "What're you all dressed up for, sir? Yeh look good."

"Well, they're gunnah publish my book." Shaking hands, offering me a cigarette. Slight smell of wine on his breath, slipping between his teeth, which are all shown to me in the most confident smile a man could give—white as his shirt.

Meekly, surprised: "No shit—congratulations. Who's the publish-sher?"

"This small press in Arizona. They read some of my poems awhile back. They got a hold of me yesterday and said they wanted to publish the entire book of poems." ("god, that's great.") Ron and Sasha congratulate Pablo as well—they've both been sitting with me, helping to finish the last of our wine from our now deteriorated paper cups. "I don't think I've ever met you before," Pablo says to Sasha, not surprisingly, quick to initiate her into the conversation and probably picturing her bent over in some anonymous hotel room.

He introduces himself, then Sasha: "So you're getting your book published?" By no chance attracted to him, being that he would crush her, she most likely prods at this success to annoy me.

"Yeah—look...I'm about to go across the street to have a few drinks to celebrate; you guys want to come with me?" (Knowing I don't have money, he continues) "I can't spot all of you, but, Font, I'll get you a round and Sasha—do you drink?"

Sasha drinks, we all do, but she can't hold her liquor. That slight frame—starved, anemic—she's completely drunk by the third, pass out drunk by the sixth. Even better, I'm sure he's thinking, with her second glass of wine just emptied and all of us already stepping inside the cantina.

A one story, defunct chalk rock building with a warning sign on its heavy oak door that shamelessly proclaims to be a safety hazard in the event of an earthquake. The local haunt for the real drunks. Daytime you can find Joe serving coffee 'with a twig'(brandy) with a mustached grin to seventy-six year old men. The old Johns drinking their spiked coffees are so stoned and lonely that they'll buy you drinks just for talking to them—especially if there's a girl with you, and they'll buy doubles for her to try and make her smile, and eventually try to grope her because they deserve a little feel they've been so nice. Nighttime the street fog persists indoors with bad breath and the leftover cigarettes they let the regulars smoke against state law during the day. Beer from bottles, a fireplace that's never lit, and a jukebox—two television sets on mute.

At a table next to the dark fireplace the four of us sit while Lilly is hard at work just across the street being harassed by half-drunk gremlins telling her bad jokes—nothing I can do because they're customers, and I'm invisible to her from within the old-timey dinginess of the low raftered bar. Red candles are lit in the center of the occupied tables, which are sparse. The dim red light from the candle on our table illuminates ten or so empty glasses and three full ones. Ron is in a pissy mood because Pablo is buying all of my drinks, and it kills him that Pablo repeatedly announces to everyone that I am a *poet*, like himself, and we must look out for one another. I egg him on by drinking whatever he puts in front of me—misunderstood 'whiskey-sodas' that are actually 'whiskey-sours' and taste like shit—but it really makes no difference one way or the other because I'm not paying.

Sasha is sipping rum and coke through a skinny red straw stuck into Pablo's glass. Her eyelids aren't heavy quite yet but I am careful to watch her and to watch Pablo so that his pudgy hands don't go anywhere but right there on the table where I can see them. No piddling ditties, or coochie rubbing, or ass grabbing. Pablo, not out of place to be so terribly flushed in the face, is breathing his horrible alcoholic breath onto the side of Sasha's slightly drowsy face, telling her again that she should be proud to sit here with us, the poets. Ron quietly drinks his scotch, neat, with no expression. Sasha agrees.

The space between the fog is narrowing. The voice of Pablo and the sound of the jukebox is distancing and losing its division. Not drunkenness—detachment. In my head there clears a space where I am looking down over a wide, brown field that covers all the ground between each horizon—a giant circle of men and women wearing all white hold the ends of a massive white sheet that they puff up and pull down in unison, which shoots several people into the air that then fall back down to be caught softly in the linen—once, twice—until one last raise of ALL ARMS AT ONCE sends them flying through the air over the field, toppling head over heels, airborne, with legs flailing—inaudible screams, heartrending—they fall to the ground in various spots...

Walking on the ground now, through the scattered bodies strewn over the brown, dead grass of a vast farm; the hard, tortured soil underfoot—I can't feel my toes; I must be hovering like a ghost— Broken legs, blood from mouths mixed with spittle; a little girl in a patterned dress has been impaled by a wooden post and her bloody panties are disgracefully showing—another body is suspended limply further down the line of posts, but I don't go that direction...I walk toward the farmhouse for help where a beaproned woman is walking out the door to approach the mass of people in white that are silently praising O Lord of Hullabaloo, the creationist, who, like a magician, waves his hand over anything and says his magic word, *Dada*, and it becomes—the husband sees me coming and bolts out of the door with shotgun loaded, pointing it at me whatthehell as I run behind a tree that has just appeared—shot fired...reloads; another shot fired...with the barrel bent to reload again I run on him and grab the gun between my right arm and side while pushing him over—

151

And on the TV just inside I see a video playing of people marching through a sandy street as it miraculously begins to rain on them, but it is not on TV, it is right here I am in the rain and Lilly is with me and all the sand has washed away—I've misplaced something, but I know it's just right over there in my mother's driveway, so the anxiety doesn't come—the rain turns to sleet, warm somehow, and near a wooden bench set against a dreary grey-shaded background is a man in a long, wool coat fussing over a brown box secured by two rubber bands that form a cross on the bottom of the box—he's trying to tweak one last word on the manuscript within as Irwin Garden, the famed poet, comes along from nowhere with those thick glasses of his, with the one big and one bigger eye, crooked, and that black, bushy, crazy-patriarch beard of his, a cigarette comically poking out from below his mustache hairs and he is smiling so goddamned big though you can't see his mouth as he subliminally narrates, 'and here old ___ is with his box full of *po-ems* all packed up and ready for the *publisher*,' while snapping the rubber bands against the box with thumb and forefinger, wherein I find myself looking down again, now at the butt end of his joke—the sad brown box with neatly prepared, stressed over manu-script—and it is my long brown-wool coat blowing in the wind, whipping the sagging brown box that has lost all importance, remembering the words *absurd* and *pathetic*, which are followed by a healthy realization: "I am proud of the fact that I made such a miserable failure of it; had I succeeded I would have been a monster." Then ecstasy.

6. THE BAKER'S CONSCIENCE AND THE BUM'S

A clear conscience. No remorse or resentment. Absolutely no bitterness. The inimitable relief of submission. A lightness. I am a regular no-body—proud, hungry, in need of money.

Walton St. has become an indicator of my well-being. It measures in the direct inverse. The only sign of life within the house is a noise through the walls, a varying volume of the TV, and the changing app-earance of the mess in the kitchen. Someone has started a compost pile in a paper bag. Maggots are born in the eggshells. I am inspired. Daily life invigorates me.

Decide to give up my mornings lying in bed, ostracized from the mess of the rest of the house, to go looking for a job. A real one. No more ridiculous literary aspirations. This is nothing. It is merely a seq-uence of blurred photographs. There is no camera. There are only my eyes, a notepad, and a will. The main thing is to survive, and to laugh. No more crying over spilled booze and spoiled plans. Go along with it and join the work force.

The owner of the café offers me a job on the spot to work in her bakery. I accept it with an image of myself kissing Lilly goodbye in the mornings, still more than half asleep, and riding down the hill in a cold fog that awakens the senses. Putting on my white apron in the small, hot bakery—smiling wanly—forming croissants, strudels, éclairs, and cinnamon rolls. The sugary scents permeating my skin and hair; my sweat smelling like the icing on an ordinary cake. Returning home I am tired, but my energy is restored when I find Lilly off work—having cut her shifts in half now that I'm helping with the rent. She is so proud of me, her working man, that she pulls me into the bedroom, sets the lock, and seats me on the edge of the bed. She undresses standing up. Exposing first her bare stomach, then her breasts(no bra). She lets me unbutton her jeans and slide them down to her ankles, then she steps out of them completely nude(never any panties). She could be anyone —the imagination is an amazing thing—but all I see is Her. Leaning over to kiss me, already hard in my pants, she begins to remove my clothes one flour dusted article at a time. My fingers run along the curves of her ass, one stray finger finding the soft madness of her inner thighs, warm—higher up, wet. She eases herself down onto me by the inch, settling into position like a thick needle being secured into a pincushion. We sew up all the loose ends. Untie all the knots in the intestines.

But none of this happens.

The first day, as imagined, I take off into the fog on bicycle, dreams pleasantly slipping into the damp grey awareness of a beautiful morning. Reminds me of the City of Destiny where the real American heroes still exist in the precious moments when the moon lingers in the grey washed sky, casting hazy-wet yellowy-silver light over AM streets in a timeless mysticism. The featureless working class faces of the predawn heroes; the providers anxiously awaiting their next paycheck; the offspring of the unbound pilgrims that sought the fortune of their limitless imaginations and found contentment only in death. They are the comrades of the past, and of the present, who deny the inevitability of their futures to share in their ancestral visions of a forgotten West. I have never been of their divine blood. I have been in their laundry rooms, in their breakfast diners, on their docks, only in stints—amidst them temporarily to observe, to pry, to mimic, to love; not, as they presumed, to exploit. With the grey baker's morning happily bayside, and the evening's promise of lovemaking serenity, I wonder —Can the blood change? For it is not tangible blood that bleeds red when the skin is pricked by hardship or labor. It is spirit. Without conceit or pretension, it is hopeful and persistent and brilliant.

My father contains this spirit—once hurrying along through predawn himself, driving doughnut trucks with bloodshot eyes, then rushing over to Pacific Rim Exports, then to haul boxes for a moving company. All just to pay the bills and try to raise his children honestly. Unfortunately, spirit is not passed through genetics. It lies nowhere within the spermy dna swimming through my father's loins, nor anyone's father's loins. I am not my father. *We* are not *our* fathers. My work ethic has proved to be easily distracted, erratic, and short-lived. Not dissimilar to a jazz quartet in which I am playing every instrument and the tempo is changing as frequently as the ideas and moods—all without warning. Though I tire quickly, the tip jar always fills just above poverty and I am warm and fed at day's end. For this I owe thanks to my friends—But I am carrying on...

Even if the blood does change, the world does not. Personal preferences aren't considered. Fates are coordinated in celestial schemes. The brain-body dreams on a tether.

At work my idyll is shattered. Martino the baker turns out the pastries by himself. Sara the crazy Italian woman curses and makes sandwiches from his bread. They have me washing dishes and scrambling eggs. The white apron is a consolation.

On a whole it is tolerable. The real trouble then with having the job—as it is with any job—is the change that occurs in the head. Time passes in monetary increments. This year in Calif. it is, at minimum wage, eight dollars an hour. I consistently arrive twenty minutes late and lose two dollars. This is made up for by periodic short breaks. A restroom break is three minutes—three a day makes thirty-nine cents. Smoke break is seven minutes—two a day makes a dollar eighty-two. Other miscellaneous breaks account for an additional dollar sixty-two—an extra two minutes to retrieve eggs from the fridge(twenty-six cents); another three minutes looking for the proper label to put on a chicken pesto sandwich(thirty-nine cents); tying and retying my apron a grand total of fifteen times, at thirty seconds each(ninety-seven cents). In all I weasel out something like four dollars for doing absolutely nothing—that's two bottles of wine.

The rest of my wages are hard earned. They've turned me into their labor bitch. The overworked asshole grinding out the mandatory details just under the radar. Moving, counting, sliding, cleaning, lifting, frying, watching. My tasks are underappreciated. It wasn't the owner that hired me out—to him the dishes may as well be cleaning themselves, and the eggs may as well be laid pre-scrambled. I discover this thing about the owner some eight dollars into my first day, struggling to keep the sink spotless with one yellow-gloved hand, stirring the eggs in a giant vat with the other, and pushing the stocking cap back on my head with yet another. The real owner, who is actually a man, comes into the shop wearing expensive jeans and a button down shirt three buttons loose at the collar. He is having a conversation through a tiny device set in his ear that blinks a tiny blue alien light to signify reception. He sticks his bare hands into trays of pastries, fingers the eggs, molests a bowl of pan-fried potatoes, and shovels the food in his mouth. Stray bits inevitably fall to the floor, which, later, will be my job to sweep. My presence doesn't alarm him. I'm not sure he even notices me as he continues his seemingly imaginary conversation and closes the door to his tucked away office in the back of the bakery. So long as he signs my checks.

"Sean"—Sara says as she and Martino cease working to direct obscene gestures at the closed office door, slashing fingers across their throats—"the sonumabitch!" When I look back at her she laughs, slaps her knee red in the face, and says something in an unintelligible Italian-Japanese. "Ah-mygod! Gabriel!"

Sara is in love with me even though she calls me by the wrong name. I remind her of someone else she's in love with who, though I don't tell her this, is a good friend of mine—Gabriel, her Archangel. She says we could be brothers. Martino, sweating as if he were still back in his Mexican desert, rolls his eyes while inspecting his chocolate covered croissants. "Mygod, Sara! You're gunnah scare him away!"

"Shutup!" She screams back, "Shutup, shutup! He's amyboy, Martino! Fuckayou!" They go back and forth bantering. Just like that all the time. He tells her that she's old and disgusting. She tells him that she named her cat after him and that the cat is a bastard; he's always whining to be fed and he's fat already. He says he'll kill her by throwing her into the oven, but she's wielding a knife and she will cut-a-his-fuckingthroat. I've stopped washing dishes to listen. Another dollar-thirty goes straight into my pocket.

The days are long, violent, and filling. Sara incessantly feeds me. She puts into my mouth flatbreads, raised breads, quiche, cookies, muffins. As she holds the food up to me in her peasant-like fingers I think that I am getting fat, but probably I am just gathering my strength and will soon be at a healthy weight. Lilly says that I have been too thin lately and could be mistaken for one of the many homeless men about town, an anorexic, or a vegetarian. I love my meat, though. The thought of lamb makes my mouth water. I welcome the new feeling of a comfortably taut stomach. A potbelly would overjoy me.

Despite Sara's malicious rebukes, she is a kindhearted woman. She has the birds on the same diet she has me. They come all the way inside the bakery for her to feed them. Although it's unsanitary, it's sweet. Martino, unwittingly baking the manna, shoos them away and immediately starts another fight with Sara, "the dirty animal-whore." She keeps our bellies warm here, though, so I have to take her side. Martino's belly, she says, is warm enough already with tamales and beans and rice and beer. She chastises him when he attempts to sample her quiche. The quiche is the baby of the whole operation. Her special treat. It's for the angels.

Sara knows my little time-tricks. She assists in indulging them. After devouring some of the fluffy egg pie, with the buttery crust, she gives me the best part of my day—an errand to the café for clean rags and aprons. It takes only three minutes to get there because I'm excited. Lilly is working the counter with another girl whose face never quite comes into focus. The morning customers have all been assholes. One was a cunt. One claimed to be Swedish royalty. Another is refusing to let her make his drink. (As it turns out, the squatty, bald, Italian man who harbors the unprecedented hatred for Lilly is Sara's ex-husband. Sara has repeatedly cursed the man herself, and has gone as far as to offer Martino a sum of money to ensure that he be put into the oven. An ugly, ugly man.) He stands at the end of the bar awaiting his shot of espresso, which was pulled too early and probably tastes like shit. When the no-faced girl serves it to him he takes a theatrical sip and starts shouting, "Ah! Ah! Now thisa is how you make an espresso!" Lilly looks livid, as if she's going to choke him to death with garlic cloves. At least the garlic might counterbalance the smell of his burning flesh.

When Lilly sees me there's a sea change. Her face turns bright and the bitterness washes away. She comes around the counter and jumps on me, then hangs there for a moment. She tells me she's sick of her job and sick of Monterey. Not the owner, but the café manager, interrupts us to ask me how the job she got me at the bakery is going. I lie from habit to avoid being rude. She knows that I'm lying but doesn't mention it, then goes to retrieve my fresh linens. Lilly and I stand together briefly in the early, early afternoon; both of us disillusioned, both of us sick of Monterey.

The rags and aprons are stuffed into a bag that's slung over my shoulder. I have what I was sent for—Lilly just a bonus—and have to get back to the bakery. She slides her tongue between my lips, discreetly, and against my tongue. A quick oxytocin high comes with our saliva merging. Then I'm on my way.

The ride back is slow. Hardly pedaling. When I see Lilly later we'll both be tired and it will seem later than it really is. We'll take off our clothes and lie in bed—just talking. The best hours of our day will have been spent and the people will have worn on us. There will be noise elsewhere in the house, but it won't interest or amuse us. We'll sleep through it easily, perhaps without any dreams. In eight hours I'll have earned sixty-four dollars. About fifty-eight after taxes. Not nearly enough for a ticket out of this place. Really, in the end, it's not enough for anything.

156

Back on the bum. At the end of two weeks they either stopped scheduling me at the bakery or I quit going. One paycheck in the bank. Signed and dated by the delicate and chubby hand of Sean The Owner himself. All the time in the world.

Leisure is the muse of genius. I may be faking the genius—or the possibility thereof—but the idle hours remain in my affection. All hours retain the light of morning, wherein the most pure of thoughts come. The lamp is perpetually lit.

It's a dangerous position I've gotten myself into—of trust, hope, reliance. The world is fooled. It believes in me. Its people are desperate. Happenstance helps feed the notion of grandiosity. I'm only a quarter Irish, but it seems I have all their luck. Had I been born business savvy, or without a conscience, I would have exploited my good fortune. For one, I would have taken painting more seriously. Indulged in the trends of body modification—cut my tongue out, had my eardrums burst, sewed my eyes shut. Anything I produced would be considered a masterpiece. I could get away with murder in the name of Art, with my condition and all—deaf, mute, and blind...forget that it was self-inflicted. No—remember. It would be so much better yet! *"Impeccable recreations of pure human emotion,"* they would say. *"A true pioneer in understanding the role of sacrifice in the modern-American psyche."* Of course, I wouldn't be able to hear these praises, but I imagine that I would get one of those big, stupid grins on my face as if I'd been drinking, and they would sign them into my hands. Guide them straight down to my crotch, I would—*Pure Human Emotion*, straight from the source. A massacre might follow and my innocence would be preserved. Try to charge me with something. With hardly a faculty about me, what—my good judgment must have slipped with my hands. A great laughter bursts from within me—ahhahahahaharrgg. One finger rises in sign, right in the middle. The other hand mirrors. If the point is not gotten to soon—as, most likely, it won't be here—then I will politely, still through sign, ask them to begin again from the top by a bit of bodily pressure squeezing right down onto those two hitching posts. But that's a-whole-nother incident, I suppose.

And if not painting, then my creative vocation would be employed musically. Sing lyrics so hip they don't make sense. Any venerable tune behind it, slightly altered or sped up. An unquestionable hit.

While each of these possesses the stroke of genius, they both require a certain amount of ambition. Which, being a man of leisure, is a particularly difficult trait to harness. My interests are reserved. My action minimal. Getting out of bed is as pleasant to me as staying there all day. I have a fondness for keeping my eyes open in the dark, locking myself in the horrors of daytime closets, barricading the crack under the door. The things you see there...

Your eyes adjust to the shadow shapes of the shadow abyss. The skin tingles. There is a phantom weight between the shoulder blades. Like in the memory of an Irish Chapel, the Joyful Mysteries reverberate through the dark as if they are rising through the floorboards. The angel's declaration resounds with imminence from the bottom of the well...*the Lord is with thee*...while each bead passes between thumb and forefinger like a single grain of salt crashing against the hull of a transatlantic ship—a star at dawn, an ever-fading landmark that guides one back home. Forehead wet with holy water and sweat, like the outside of a glass in sunlight, filled to the brim with guilt and yearning. The Sorrowful Mysteries now tremble through to the surface, vibrating in submission...*Father, into thy hands do I commend my spirit*...from the mouth of the glass, beads spill like tears down its sides, slowly filling the void with truth. Waves of darkness wash over my eyes as I clutch my precious parts—the cross that hangs from my neck, given to me by an Irish Mother, blessed by a priest at Medugorje. Like black tides pulling in and out the walls erode until I am floating in a murky sea of dense sleep, or near sleep. My eyes are both open and shut. Each faint image, each shadow within the shadow, contains a tangible clarity. The tides continue in deep inhalations and exhalations of furthering darkness like the heaving chest of a monster—I am pulled into the depth by a growing presence. She stands behind me, a dull phosphorescence with the great gravity of everything, piercing my back like an electrical current and pulsing into the rhythm of my heart like the buzz of a TV set. Through short flares in my heartbeat she speaks...*do not be afraid*...and reaches out for my hand. In the touch of fingertips passes a fleeting vision: grey drops of polluted rain fall into holy water through the corroding roof of the chapel, like the modern gospels preached in irreverent churches. The candles are blown out by choir-boy lips, their red lights lost to the devil's hymn. The priest has tied his robe around his head and stands naked at the altar. The hand leads me into what I know is the confession booth—the smell of mold and decay. It's not been used for some time and the walls sink in as if they were hard of hearing, listening intently for absent repentances. The dark is overwhelmed by the putrid silence. Then I am alone again. In a terrified film on my tongue is the sour taste of salt and vinegar.

Leisure is the muse of both God and Devil. As the axis of Love intersects that of Hate. Passion is a variable coordinate. Marriage and murder are plotted in juxtaposition. Atheists see the unfortunate circumstance of themselves; Men of Faith see the same. With one thing there is always the other.

When I am out of bed I remain in paradox. The dreams persist. This is not an issue of Faith—it is one of Free Will. A decision is made to slaughter or nurture. Though behavior marks a definitive action, the brain makes infinite alternative impressions. "The 'as if' is so much a part of our life that it really isn't artificial." The coexistence creates the ultimate reality. Some men, as to abstain from daily pleasures, will devote themselves to the behavioral patterns of sweeping the porch, or mopping the floor, thinking that their diligence will set them free. But a wandering mind is capable of committing tremendous spiritual atrocities. No one is exempt from their own dual nature.

This being said, it should also be noted that blabbering is quite probably among the deadliest of sins. But I find myself unable to stop. There is a desperation that possesses me.

A terrifying strike in conscience. An arbitrary remorse. A heaviness in being. Still, no bitterness.

Accomplishing the feat of rising from bed, I spend the true morning in a significant dream about nothing. The feeling is as if I have just jerked off thinking about a woman I know and have the need to go to her to ask for so much forgiveness. She is nowhere to be found. It is 8.30 in the morning and the tears are about to start absently.

This early in the morning the abstract sadness brought on by this nothingness succeeds in shrinking, or expanding the size of the world to that of your own existence—sticking it within that tragic space of your flip-flopping dome. When it hits before you're fully awake you feel hopeless, like your best years have come and gone and you haven't the strength to recall them. You feel dead. You are cast into the Unseen and the others all seem to be sleepwalking. The somnambulists are carrying guns—they fire aimlessly at your ghost. But there are worse things than being killed by a man in his sleep. Much worse. Besides, the second time around is probably nothing.

The fog has broke cold and grey. Summer nears without a sign. The magic period of the central coast town is extended. From the rocks emerges the Chinaman, and behind him comes a long line of exact reproductions of himself. He has never had the option to die, being that he *is* death, so he carries on, duplicates himself, and lives in quiet cohabitation with his replicas. The Chinaman is actually Irish. A small man resembling a hobgoblin with tough skin and a crooked grin. He wears his old blue jeans, a newsy cap, and a corduroy jacket. He travels by foot and bicycle and by supernatural powers. We have been diligently tracking and recording his whereabouts as to solve his mystery. He is everywhere.

There are documented sightings of him headed up the hill and down, crossing streets and recrossing them, walking at one end of town and on the other. He is always on the move. Only moments ago, at the café, he tipped his cap to me—I waited thirty-seconds, to avoid being detected, turned around, and he was gone. Five minutes later he reappears from the opposite side of the building. Where did he go—what?

Simultaneously, he has also been spotted inside a local bar and perusing the aisles of an antique shop. The employees, recognizing him, were extremely suspicious of his presence and began communicating through walkie-talkies in an attempt to trail him—several of them walked briskly among the aisles, trying to keep him in sight. He evaded them for twenty minutes, allowing himself to be seen occasionally to keep up the excitement of his mockery. They never saw him leave. In the bar he was becoming very drunk.

Only one person has had the gall to confront him—Gabriel, The Archangel. He has somehow befriended him and the two frequent the bars together. He refuses to divulge any of the drunkenly revealed secrets—maybe because he has forgotten them. In any case, he finds our behavior to be lewd.

After the second disappearance of the Irishman at the café a bird flies through the door and flutters ineffectively at the window. Wondering if it is a hobgoblin trick, I use a newspaper and gently grasp the bird in it, whispering to him that I know what he's up to. Outside I set him free, but he immediately flies back to my feet and hops slowly, dejectedly, with holes in his tail feathers and shit on his beak. I toss a few crumbs at him. He doesn't go for them. He causes an acute sense of loss and pity within me. It convinces me to go for a stroll.

The afternoon-morning I am walking off the contemptible sins I encounter in my idleness. They are great sins. In action and consequence, they are tremendous. They trouble the brain and the heart. Cholesterol rises, blood pressure sky rockets. It is combated with rhythmic steps, nicotine, a nip of booze. Moveable idleness.

As I say, meandering about town, walking off these things with a little practical exercise that clears up the brain, I happen across Gabriel The Archangel and The Hobgoblin. They are sitting together in what Ron calls, 'Wino Park.' The mention of Ron reminds me that I haven't seen him in awhile. Jessie's back in town and it's his busy schedule on the whale watching boats. They give him two strong weeks on, then two slow ones. We see him during the dry spells.

The bench my two dear friends are sitting is secluded along a tree-lined path. Gabriel looks more like a samurai than an angel. A worn out samurai that's been drinking beer all morning and has plans to do so well into the evening. His black, hip length hair is pulled into a bun at the back of his head; his dark Asian-Pacific skin is slightly puffy. His eyes wide and tinted with a yellow-grey shade. He claims that Bob, the alleged name of the Irish Mystic, has been with him all morning. By the beer look in Bob's averted eyes I believe what Gabriel says, that he's been with him all morning. I also believe what I saw with my own eyes.

From a backpack Gabe withdraws a beer and invites me to sit down. "So, Love, how've you been?" He calls me 'Love' because he thinks that I'm a woman stealer. His girlfriend, Zadï, supposedly has a thing for me.

"Things—Gabriel—have been...all-right..." My attention is paid to Bobgoblin, who quietly sits next to Gabe on the bench with a complacent smile that probably knows more than I ever will. The beer feels fine, just fine—a bit warm. My anxiety fades in its consumption as I ponder the mystery within feet of me. He looks so plain, sturdy, tangible. But so do I. It becomes clear to me that my own behavior is a mystery. Life has carried me on a strange path and it almost seems as if I had nothing to do with it. I—this oddity of human flesh, this spiritual flash of light condemned to a short period of being called 'Man.' I have no intention of holding out to live a long life. Death runs the show. It should suit me to live barely past a hundred. A fraction of that of The Bobgoblin.

"Just all-right, Love? You look pale, man—have you eaten today?" It is always a question of the appetite with Gabe, just like with the Chinese. It is a sort of extended greeting. Gabe loves to feed, and to provide. It's in his blood. At heart, his musical, glad, Filipino heart, he is mainly two things: a host and a storyteller. Many times I've filled myself at his table with lasagnas, pestos, curries, lamb chops, steaks, potatoes, vegetables, salads, eggs, beer, good whiskey, martinis. Many more times I have listened to the mania of the youth he is losing. At twenty-four he's an old man, retelling all his same stories from the east coast and Pacific Islands—his father's, too. His father is a veteran of the Vietnam War and has killed an unknown (high)number of tunnel-crawling enemies. The fact comes up often when Gabe's been drinking. But there is too much to go into for now—it would be better to dismiss it, move on, and let him tell you these things himself.

The whole of the Gaelic Mystery, however, can be described thus: _____. This is retracted in the next moment. It is the vast, ever-changing landscape of loneliness. I have not yet eaten today...

The Crown and Anchor bar serves french-fries and beer for half-price at a certain time of day—this time. Gabe treats me to both, recommending that I not eat too much because he'll be cooking later on. I devour drink and food until I am more than tied over. Although his intention to cook the meal is honest, I know that he'll be much too drunk by the time we make it over to his house—he's getting there already. Bob drinks his beers without a word.

The last time I drank with Gabe he was on a bad one. It was a mess. He was buying me beers at this very bar on a very similar afternoon. Usually Gabe, when telling about anything, becomes animated by the recollection like a drunken ape that mimics the actions in the story. He's infatuated by movement, exalted by absurdities. But the afternoon that he started in about his girlfriend—not Zadï, the current girlfriend; the ex-girlfriend, though spoke of in present tense—the action remained in his eyes. They went in and out of lucidity while the rest of him remained still. The talk began innocently enough with an anecdote from his morning.

"I was down on the beach, getting loaded on a bench—and I don't mean to glamorize my lifestyle, that's just what I was doing, getting loaded, and I saw these three punk kids down there, like seventeen years old, just down at the beach doing nothing, causing a scene... hollering at people and taunting them and what not—and the more I watched them, it just kind of made me wonder what I'm doing with my life, you know? It's like, I'm twenty four years old, in Monterey, California, and I work in a sushi restaurant, and I drink. That's what I do. I serve people food and I drink. That's it. I mean, don't get me wrong, I like working—having a job is a necessity in being part of this country's economic system, and really in just being a responsible citizen. But it's not gratifying. I'm capable of so much more than serving food. And what it comes down to is I'm sick of being a fuck up—just doing nothing with my life. And it's not like this is my only option—I have an education. This is just the life I've chosen for myself."

During this I simply lend my ear to him without any interjection because when people want to talk about themselves there is no other subject that will steer them off track. It was here, in his drunken logic, that his monologue turned in its most obvious direction—down hill. To old loves then. He had drunk enough that it had gotten to that point.

"And I have Zadï, poor Zadï, who's so nice to me, and patient, and sweet, and intelligent—but I'm not in love with her. Besides, she's moving to San Diego soon anyway, which is for the best. But, in the meantime, it's still tough when you're in love with someone else, and think about them every day, several times a day. And we write letters to each other, you know? So there's still something there. My best days are those days, once every two weeks, when her letter comes in the mail—I make a big production out of it, you know, and don't open it until I make a pot of tea and have the house to my self to sit at the table and read it four or five times over." (Pauses as if he were alone at his kitchen table with the pot of tea, then his eyes regain their lucidity and he remembers my presence) "I mean, my girlfriend in New Orleans is really something else, Love—she is the type of girl that takes your breath away, no joke."

That later I learned he had taken Lilly into his confidence several times on this matter, and told her that she reminded him so much of Her, makes these comments stand out in hindsight. Had I known then the driveling, downy, swindling...

"Rekindling anything though, of course, isn't an option. Her friends hate me. They don't let me talk to her because of the fucking mess we made—which wasn't completely my fault. She even addresses her letters to me under an alias—Peter Van Hortenstein, or other ridiculous names—nothing her friends couldn't figure out, but the idea is still there." He senses a recognition in me, that I might truly understand. For a moment we have a sickening bond over what I consider the unutterable. "What, are you a baby killer too?"—("I guess I wouldn't use that phrasing.")—"Yeah, but you're a baby killer nonetheless. You've killed a baby." What some people don't realize is that the effects of an abortion are long-lasting for both involved parties— yes, even the absentee, would-have-been father. Though it is different than the mother's grief. It is self-destructive/soothing, detached, nostalgic. They imagine that things could have worked out not only under different circumstances, but under the very circumstances the procedure was performed. It is a delusional grief with men. Women are the true sufferers.

As this yarn spins I recall that this actually wasn't the last time I drank with Gabe. The Last Time, in fact, was on a strange afternoon in Seaside at a party a coworker of his was throwing. The coworker, a Hispanic man of sexual ambiguity named Manuel, was throwing it for one of his four kids—it was his daughter's sixth birthday. Gabe's would be eighteen months. Mine would be about the same. Zadï came along, pathetically, to be our sober driver.

It was a family affair mostly, with the neighborhood kids and their parents, cousins were there, aunts and uncles. Pink and red and white streamers were hung, pictures of princesses on plates and cups, pots of spiced meats were cooked, corn tortillas. A piñata was suspended from a tree—Gabe held the string and yanked it up and down for the frustrated and excited children. After it was finally smashed the candy was gobbled up by the twenty or so kids in attendance. In particular, a great amount of candy was consumed by Manuel's three year old boy, Josef—he kept sprinting at me like a charging animal with a sugar mustache, laughing hysterically, until he came within range and I swooped him up in a fluid motion, then set him back down running in the opposite direction. Then he'd run at me again.

With not a crumb left of the cake, candles eaten and all, there was trouble sending the kids off to bed in their sugar deliriums. The last two to go were the daughter, who frowned when she had to change out of her princess dress, and Josef, who let out a shriek and began bawling. The other coworkers arrived shortly thereafter.

163

Not all of them, but a few. Genshiro, for one. A wonderful Japanese man of forty whose mastery of the English language is showcased in referring to himself by the all-American name, Allen. "A-W-L-L-E-N," he says it. Perfect L's. The owner of the restaurant came too—a thin, laughing, Japanese man whose name I can't recall. I can recall, however, that during dinner hours this thin, laughing, Japanese man would take an inflatable hammer around his restaurant and bop the heads of the more receptive customers—just for the hell of it. In a box these two carried with them a dozen or more bottles of sake, which were opened immediately upon sitting down. It was served in tiny porcelain cups with pictures of various samurais and geishas in meticulous paint on their cramped side-surfaces. Manuel filled mine repeatedly.

Earlier, just as the kids were being driven to their beds, mescal was served to Gabe and me. Manuel brought it out from its hiding place in the bedroom in a deerskin covered canteen labeled, 'MEDICINE.' Since those two drinks Manuel had been eye-fucking me, licking the little patch of dark hair just below his chubby lips, anticipating the effects of the mescal, watching for the flush in my face. Bizarre that a man with four children, all to the same woman, can be so obviously gay, yet still frequently exercise his right to procreate. To literally go through the physical act entailed I mean.

Anyhow, now that Genshiro and Guntiro—I've just remembered his name—had arrived, the mescal was retrieved again. Without breaking his stare, Manuel poured everyone a glass and licked the patch of hair expectantly. Worms fell out of the MEDICINE bottle like cancer, a handful of cat shit, bacterial. You had to eat that forsaken worm, though, in order to prove something. You had to eat it to show that you were a man. Because we had failed in other orders of our manhood, Gabe and I clinked together our mescal-filled glasses and took it down in one hard swallow, chewing the black worm to really get the taste. We savored the bitter, harsh shock.

And here this old drunken ape is in front of me, feeling no more like a man than myself with the sunlight yet-fading, and he is recounting the destinies of the world as if they were at one time his own. He's on Alvarado St. on some dateless drunken night in his memory. A fight is breaking out.

"I saw it," he says, "—I saw it escalate right from the start. There were two groups of kids yelling at each other—some young punk kids and some tough looking Hispanic kids. And, I mean, these guys looked fucking *tough*—like real thugs. I don't know what they were yelling about, but I figured it'd be better to avoid them by turning down a side street. Then in this little alley I see the group of Hispanic kids again at one of their cars—this gold, tricked-out lowrider thing—and they're all gearing up for a fight. Some serious shit, too—one of them was wrapping a belt around his knuckles that had a huge, brass buckle; another had a pipe in his hands. And you figure one of them probably had a gun, too. So I paused for a second, and as I'm watching them get ready for this brawl, the guy wrapping the belt around his knuckles looks up and makes eye contact with me—and the look in his face was really poignant, you know—it was this forlorn look that basically said, 'You ought to get out of here—something bad is going to happen. This isn't what I want to do, but I have to.' That look, man—it was awful. I felt sorry for him. It was like, that's what's expected of him, and if he didn't come through his friends would *shun* him. He didn't have a choice. And that's what really sucks; there are certain things that *you just have to do*." He shakes his head, looking for the parallels in his brain, and weighing his past actions to their present outcome. Most likely he thinks of the girl in New Orleans.

It occurs to me that he is now too drunk to cook any kind of meal, and that the french-fries and beer in front of me are gone. The Bobgoblin is also gone, having dismissed himself, still without a word, into the wandering existence of his own predetermined role in the world. I've had nearly too much beer, and know it would be wise to get out of the bar while it's still light out and my head is still clear. It's been a long morning and there are other things that I have to do.

7. NINE POORLY SHOT PHOTOGRAPHS

An attempt is made to manifest my ideas into physical objects. At 6am, gathered scrap lumber and dirty bed sheets are used to construct a giant canvas in which I intend to paint blindfolded. I destroy it before I ever begin and walk through the house in search of a misplaced instrument. With no luck.

By 8am I give up this notion and opt for one of Lilly's cameras—an old Minolta. If I won't paint, or play music, then I will shoot photos, which is a type of poetry. They say, 'A picture is worth a thousand words.' I barely know how to operate the camera—if any of the pictures turn out they will be brisk, obscure haikus. That's if I can afford to develop them. Otherwise they will remain pure poetry, spontaneous, energetic, and in the present tense.

In the light of eight-fifteen I start with The House—from the outside. The appearance of the frame is misleading. It almost looks decent. Brilliant morning sun shooting high from behind the roof making a fuzzy luminescence like a halo or an areola. The bushes have recently been trimmed, the courtyard swept, the paint touched up. The only clue into the true inhabitance is the cardboard box barricading one window and, if you look closely, the unreasonable number of emptied wine, beer, and liquor bottles in the trash. The shutter opens and closes and the poem is written. A diagonal wire runs from the power line to the ground right through the middle of the frame which I only now notice. The shot was probably ruined. Don't bother trying for a second.

If things are slow here, so be it—I will see their pace and take it even further. Taking off in no particular direction at a speed so impossibly slow, my stride is unmatched by any creature with an agenda. 'Snail-like' is an injustice. I am not looking at anything, and there is nothing that needs to be done.

Not a half block down, which takes me just under an hour or so to cover, a voice calls from behind me. "wah-wah-wah!" The sounds don't register in my brain and I don't find it in me to turn around. "Excuse me!" The man calls after me with a slight lisp for what I'm guessing is the third time. "But do you happen to know where the admissions is for M-I-I-S?" He spells it out. It was little trouble for him to catch up to my gait to get this question out.

"Believe it's a block or two down on your right side—someone there should be able to direct you to the office."

"I've decided that's the college I want to attend." The letters for the college this man wants to attend stand for 'Monterey Institute of International Studies.' He wears a filthy orange cotton shirt that opens at the color to expose an equally filthy orange and white striped t-shirt. His pair of ill-fitting blue jeans has a fresh piss stain running down the left side of the crotch. He is homeless. I recognize his dark, grey-stubbled face, the googly spectacles, and the shiny bald head. The teeth I remember too—small, yellow, gapped. There is no chance that he, Hunckley Hunckley Jr. as he calls himself, or J.L., will be going to MIIS. But that's beside the point—he's already won: I'm engaged in the conversation. The piss smell coming from him is so rancid that it gags me. "Hey! I know you...I've seen you at, uh...oh! Village, right? Yeah, I remember you—I liked your energy..." To cover up his stench I light a cigarette—it only makes things worse. I bend over and nearly vomit, then catch my breath.

"Can I take your picture?" I say, exhaling now and wiping my mouth with the back of my hand to cover a burp.

"Oh, *sure!*" He is flattered by this. In frame I get his straight-faced mug, desperately going for a dignified look, and a portion of The Monterey Herald he holds up next to his face. The film is exposed and absorbs the mirrored light. "I don't do any nudity." ("What?") "I said I don't do any nudity—well, unless that's what you need. I could get you a hairy chest. Or maybe some hairy breasts hahahah!"

"No—I'm not shooting nudes today. But, we'll keep in touch..." It would be easy to lose him if I quickened my step just a hair, but I resist. I am adamant about keeping my stride, my wonderful gait, my impossibly slow step.

"Do you still go there? to Village?" I mention that my girlfriend works there and that I'm there most days. That's where he fucking knows me from and I see him there most days too. "Yeah...I got eighty-sixed from there last night." He stammers through why, turning himself into a victim. Says it's because he's a gay man, and that one of the customers is a complete homophobe and didn't like him being there so he was asked to leave. I am wise to the fact, being that I witnessed it myself, that he had a verbal altercation just the other day with a daytime regular—one of my favorites, too—a genuinely friendly guy that owns a contracting business and comes into the café for a quick coffee, but always makes time to say hello and ask how you are. He, Hunckley Hunckley Jr., called this man a nigger. This is more likely the reason he is no longer welcome there. Regardless, he continues his tale about last night. "I'm homeless," he says, "I just needed some-where warm to stick it out for a while, keep warm." His creative solut-ion was to walk two miles to Nu-Art, the adult theatre on Fremont St., buy a ticket for a personal booth, and stay there till four in the morn-ing. "Just to keep warm. Then I had breakfast across the street, and now here I am getting my photograph taken."

I take another shot of him crossing the street, trying to get the piss stain properly framed and in focus. The shutter opens and closes again and the poem is now written in silver and urine.

"Another place I go is The Oshito Cinema," he tells me—the place that Sasha works. "I try to go there once a week. The last movie I saw there was called, 'Boy On A Wire.' Have you seen it?" ("No.") "It's about a French tight rope walker who is planning to walk between the World Trade Center buildings—when they were still there—and he thought what better way to do it than in costume, right? But when he tested it the costume threw off his balance, so he decided to do it com-pletely naked! My friend *Raw*bert, he went to the movie with me, he said, 'with his thingy-shlingshlong hanging out, wouldn't it be flapping to one side and throw off his equilibridium too?' And then he said, 'maybe he didn't have a very big thingy-shlingdong so it didn't matter hahahah."

"Maybe he taped it. Or tucked it back..."

"Y-e-a-h—hahahah—I wouldn't mind being the one to tape it." ("What?") "I said I wouldn't mind being the one to *t-a-p-e* it."

"Hm...right. Who was playing the role, J.L.?"

"Some no name. He looked like a cross between Mr. Joaquin Pho-enix and Mr. Keanu Reeves. You kind of have that look..."

"I hope that I don't have any Mr. Keanu Reeves in me."

"Well you have *something* in you that works—I bet you get A LOT of dates..." I snap off one last picture without looking what's in the frame, then start moving away from his hairy breasts and his statements that all seem to be hinting at something. "Where are you going?"

"Just going for a walk—it's my day off." I'm already fifteen feet removed.

"I'll come with you—I'm homeless," he repeats, "I don't have anything to do. I just need to go to the bathroom first and then to the bank!" I bet you do. Thirty feet removed. "Meet me right here, okay?" He has to yell for the words to reach me. I turn around one last time and nod my head to ensure him that, okay, I'll meet him right there, right after he goes to the bathroom and then to the bank. My tendency to attract freaks baffles me. I give him the thumbs-up.

Around the corner I resume my idiotic swagger, going almost unbearably slow now that I have to make up for the energy wasted in losing Hunckley Hunckley Jr. I come across two giant ceramic ice cream cones, one after the other, with ceramic cherries on top. They are the size of city trashcans. I absently snap each of their photos.

I find myself pointing the lens now through a shop front window to snap a picture of a taffy puller that has yet commenced its duties for the day—yesterday's taffy hangs dryly from the machine like stalactites. I have landed on Fisherman's Wharf and a large, illuminated clock face says it is only 6.50 in the morning. I don't know what day it is. Quickly, I get the shot of the clock and of the clock's reflection in an unopened restaurant's window. This poem confuses me.

At the end of the wharf the whale watchers are waiting to board their boats. I look for Ron, but I'm told his boat is not going out today. Standing alone then, at the very end of the wharf, at what I half-believe to be seven o'clock in the morning. From here I can see Moss Landing across the bay, where the migrant workers have already taken to the fields. Santa Cruz Mountains are further up. A line of clouds are forced to appear purple over the water, with the sunlight bending over the horizon and all. Beneath me a harbor seal performs something resembling his morning ablutions, only it is more of just a lazy, sidelong drift in the water and a breathing exercise. The sealions are barking insanely out of view.

For the last time I open the shutter on the camera and keep it open. I leave it open so long that the film is probably being singed, burning inconspicuously within the camera, trying unsuccessfully to capture this holy scene.

8. THE ACCIDENT

Everyone is gathered in the backyard at Gabriel The Archangel's. A soft, bright green clover lot enclosed by a tall cement wall and high fences. It looks like it is straight out of the stickball Brooklyn childhood of my father, where Gabe spent some of his growing up as well. The grill is going strong, pots are simmering on the stove. The ice is yet melted in our drinks. All of the faces are present:

Sasha with her beady, non-Jewish, Jewish eyes, who has thinned considerably, so much that her features have changed and it looks as if she were in constant recovery from the flu. Ron with his beard grown longer than ever, brilliantly red in the afternoon sunshine, and his full gut. Jessie with her oily hair, fragrant with marijuana stink, her goofiness, her strange gestures, and her long stories that go nowhere. Zadï with her pale complexion and pale personality, her well refined use of language, and the inevitable awkwardness that comes with being the daughter of two astrophysicists. Gabe, good and unfortunate Gabe, as always, with beer in hand and bottle hidden elsewhere, tending to the day's meal in the kitchen. Big Gabe pads around too, off radiology duty at the hospital for the day but still in his scrubs. Big Gabe is the teddy bear of a man that lives in one of the three bedrooms at the back of the house. He could drink all day and no one would ever know the difference. Presently, he slathers excess marinade onto the grilling steaks. Whatever is in his glass has probably been mixed too strong. Lilly finds herself with the day off as well. She sips a whiskey-juice drink that Big Gabe mixed for her, lying in the hammock under the carport, conspiring with the other three girls.

These are her friends. Though they accept me graciously, and treat me with nothing but generosity, the truth in the matter is that if she were to leave me they would be gone too. My friends are a thousand miles away. I have made it a habit to catalogue their faces, their voices, their mannerisms, to encroach upon their distance. They are readily available in my memory bank, safely kept under lock and key.

On especially lonely evenings, when Lilly turns over in bed and goes silently to sleep, I seek the comfort of my brother, Aden, or my good friends Jason or Ethan—which is to say nothing of the women I've never met and that might not exist. I was the best man at Jason's wedding and the one to have introduced him to his wife. Ethan owes me a year in a happy relationship, too, having introduced him to his dear Casey Mayhan. I will never tire of these people. Their jokes will never get old. Nothing will ever change between us.

Of all, though, my favorite companion is unquestionably myself. I am able to take a multitude of forms. Anything that fits into the imagination. My face is unfailingly the best looking, my voice the most soothing, my mannerisms the most pleasing. I am always able to find the right words to tell myself, whatever the situation calls for. It's nice to know that when everyone is gone I will still have these things in my memory, and I will still have myself. Meanwhile, I take my acquaintances with a grain of salt.

Stakes are set into opposite sides of the lawn and Ron and I toss iron horseshoes at them, then walk zen-masterly to where they have landed and toss them right back. We loosely keep score of the game. By the look of the tosses, I should be winning. Mine go on a clean, three-flip arc, consistently landing near the pin. Ron's are side-winders and knucklers that fly haphazardly in either general direction, dangerously at head's height. Occasionally he gets a lucky skip and finds himself within a length's distance of the pin; or he shamelessly comes across a deadringer, which is what it's called when the horseshoe bounces off the ground in front of the pin and flips dumbly into scoring position. It goes straight to his head, these deadringers, and on my next toss he will certainly be heckling me. His most common tactic is to let out a fart mid-backswing. The stench of sulfur and egg hides in small, invisible pockets of air throughout the backyard.

Summer is almost within a believable distance. Wonderful weather. Powder sky and powder clouds. Distinct shadows where the cool still lurks. Spots where the sun actually makes you sweat. The savory stream of smoke off the grill. A lazy sort of daytime intoxication that exaggerates the slowness of everything. Any closer to summer and things might stand still—time might stop.

We are playing a game of horseshoes and the girls are conspiring and the meat-smoke is filling the air so that you can taste it and Gabe wants to get out of the kitchen. He needs a break and the stew can take care of itself. Zadï deserts her half glass of wine and goes to him lovingly. He wants to take her for a spin on his bike. Ron goes with them and our game stops. Have a seat under the carport and take a cigarette from one of Sasha's usual three packs. My feet are left in the sun to absorb the heat. From there the warm blood travels the course of my body—a bead of perspiration forms on my side and trickles over my ribs. If the weather were any better we would surely have a problem on our hands. The climate should change at a steady rate, and it should be in accordance with the sun and the moon and the people of the sun and the moon. Equilibrium should be kept—calamity looms on either side thereof.

A dream car pulls into the driveway at a reality breaking speed and offsets the balance of everything—the day shifts into the realms of calamity and with it comes confusion and disbelief. The back door swings open and Ron emerges carrying Zadï in his arms. She is crying hysterically. He carries her to the front steps and sets her gingerly down and she screams louder because it hurts. Gabe comes after the car, walking his bike sternly with no expression on his face. He sets the kickstand and stands over Ron and Zadï. The rest of us are stunned. Big Gabe wants to know what happened. No one knows what's happened, but Zadï's crying persists. Between sobs and shrieks she repeats that it hurts, it hurts. Big Gabe wants to know what in the hell happened. Gabe tells him that she fell—she hit her head. Gabe takes Ron's place in holding Zadï's fragile person, her pale, battered frame limp in his arms. Big Gabe is calling an ambulance; he has to call an ambulance. Ron has to leave. He's sorry, but he has to leave.

"Zadï," he says, "I'm sorry—I have to leave now. Jessie and I have to meet my mom for dinner. It's her birthday. I have to leave now. You'll be okay. Gabe's right here—you'll be okay."

Zadï is wailing. Ron and Jessie are gone. Big Gabe has already called the ambulance and they're on their way—we can hear the sirens start from the Peninsula Hospital, which is only two miles away. Big Gabe inspects her wounds even though the ambulance is on its way. She has a contusion on the back of her head and scrapes along her back—her spine is sore. She has to go to the hospital because there might be internal bleeding. Just to be safe she needs to go to the hospital, and she'll be okay—the ambulance is on its way.

Her wailing is fit for a madman. She's gone completely insane. She's in shock from the fall and her eyes are blank. We stand around her incapable of doing anything but stare into her blank eyes, and tell her in our thoughts that she'll be alright. You're just going in to get checked out, Zadï—You Will Be All-Right. Gabe's face doesn't twitch. The dream ambulance arrives with the same reality breaking speed as the dream car. Big Gabe hides inside because he's drunk and these are the people he works with. The ambulance is here and the paramedics are getting out and none of this is happening.

None of this is happening, but I can't stop it from happening and I can't do anything that will change the way it is happening. Through thought I am trying to trade places with Zadï. Some pain is easier to handle when it is yours to bear. Some pain I could never wish for. Zadï sees the ambulance and she sees the paramedics and she is in agony—it fucking hurts—but she keeps it together as they start to ask her questions. They ask her what her name is. Marie Alison Irving, she tells them. I never knew her real name. She is whimpering. They put her on the stretcher and ask her age. She is twenty-five years old. Big Gabe hides just inside the door where he can listen. Little Gabe stands on the steps being questioned by another paramedic about what happened. He tells them she fell. They were riding the bike and she fell. She had been on the handlebars. Well, they both fell, but she was the one that was injured. Internally, Gabe is making an effort to sober up. Bad

171

enough to have caused the accident, worse to be drunk. Someone needs to call her parents. Zadï hears this and she screams bloody murder to not call her parents. Please, don't call her parents.

The paramedics are putting her in the ambulance and turning the sirens on. Gabe is getting in after them. Big Gabe comes out of hiding, feeling as if he has disgraced himself. His friend was hurt and he was drunk. No one would've known it. He stands in front of the three of us—Lilly, Sasha, and myself, the only ones left—straight, steady, coherent. He is embarrassed and nervous. And not so apparently drunk. The ambulance is gone. The reality breaking speed of everything has left a tear in the fabric of actuality. There is something basically different, but it seems uncertain if the cause were real.

In the aftermath there is still no clarity. No one knows what happened and no one can tell us. Ron is gone. Gabe is at the hospital. Zadï is being drugged and put into the machines. Big Gabe, if he weren't under the influence, would be the one looking at her X-Rays. The only thing we can do is wait for an update. Big Gabe is on his phone nonstop, calling anyone he knows at the hospital to get information on Zadï's condition. She hasn't come out of the scan yet, they tell him. He keeps calling and they keep telling him. All we can do is wait.

There is a feast on the kitchen counter. Marinated steaks with bacon and a sage seasoning, twice baked potatoes with cheese and sour cream, corn on the cob drenched in butter, garlic bread, broccoli, heirloom tomatoes, salad, couscous, and a vegetarian stew. During the reeling madness that surrounded the accident, the food was forgotten about. Most of it was burned, overcooked, or went soggy, brown, or cold—everything but the stew. The stew has made it through with flying colors. The stew has been cooked to perfection.

Gabe has just returned from the hospital where he sat for three hours in the waiting room with Zadï's father. She is going to be alright, just like we told her. Just a concussion, a little bump on the head—maybe a hairline fracture in the coccyx. They're keeping her there for two nights though to keep watch, make sure the swelling goes down. Immediately, Gabe pulls beer from the fridge, pours a few tumblers of whiskey, and begins to put together a plate of food. The food hasn't been touched until now. Big Gabe, Sasha, and Lilly all thought it would be inconsiderate to dig into the food under the circumstances. I am famished however. I am the only one that will be eating with The Archangel.

In Gabe's absence the four of us lamented the possibility of all unexpected events. We reflected on the different outcomes that easily might bare the various names of our relatives and other loved ones. I recalled a dream from a few nights ago that, by chance, also involved a bike. The dream took place in a dark, rundown town that was no more than overgrown, weedy pastures littered with broken foundations and jagged cement blocks. My brother was there, the poet, speeding around on his bike, nearly flying, and purposely crashing into the cement slabs to send himself head first over his handlebars into the weeds and head splitting blocks. He kept picking himself up, more injured each time, remounting the bike, and speeding off again into another spill over the handlebars. He is trying to kill himself, I thought. Trailing him on foot, for what seemed like forever, running behind his bicycle crying, yelling after him, 'Aden, no! Don't do this why are you doing this!' Running after him, tears ruining my vision—screaming those words—he just wouldn't stop trying to do himself in. 'Aden!' I screamed, snot and tears smeared across my face as he picked himself up from the weedy emptiness of the town, sweating profusely, bleeding, and bruised. 'Aden if you kill yourself you're going to hell!' A horrible feeling came over my head when I heard myself, or thought I heard myself rather, screaming that childish warning. My bawling started anew—hard, violent, streams of tears, streams of snot. In the middle of dusting himself off, he paused. 'God, man—why'd you have to say that?' He looked so innocent and pitiful like, he looked as though he didn't understand what was happening. He looked like he had in Bangkok when we saved the woman from the whorehouse. The death was accidental. He picked up his bike again and I screamed, 'Aden please! Don't do this don't kill yourself—they'll send you to hell, Aden!' My no-words trembled together in the no-air of the dream as he took off, and I was just too tired to chase him any longer. Collapsing in the weeds, they bent over my sobbing body and enveloped me as I choked on my tears and snot and choked on the no-words, the sentiments, 'it's okay...you'll be okay, Aden...I'll save you...I'll pray for you...'

Pushed the thought of this dream aside because I haven't talked to my brother yet to ask if he is okay—it worries me. Instead, took another stab at swapping places with Zadï. Successfully, in my head, I dressed myself in the hospital gown and was scanned, checked, tested, and molested by several doctors. The doctors that, currently, Zadï is crying to and discussing, in French mind you, the virtues of Bruges with the young, attractive European fuck of a doctor, as Gabe told us she had. It was the only thing we got out of him on the ride back. He was silent otherwise, for once.

In my head, I say, I endured the pain relentlessly and shook in every fracture and swell I might have obtained. But, in reality, it is Zadï there, delicate Zadï, who writhes, almost convulses, in the terrible shock of every agonizing moment. Myself, I cannot deny that I am actually in fine health, drinking the cold beer that's been put in front of me and sipping from a tumbler of whiskey. Gabe is warming our

173

plates, piled high with a little of everything. The accident seems to have been only a slight damper on the night. Things are continuing as usual.

The drinks are steady and strong, but conscientious. Bourbon and sodas to help settle the stomach until our plates are pulled from the oven. Your head feels fine, but they make your legs heavier and sometimes awkward under the table. Thankfully he never makes you get up. As he serves me the food I can't hold back—I go into it with vigor, eating the steak with the potatoes, the broccoli in a mouthful with tomatoes and couscous, garlic bread dipped in the stew. Butter squirts from the corn cob onto the table. The fat taste of bacon is rinsed between the teeth with a gulp of bourbon-soda. No wonder Gabe invites me to eat often—I'm the chef's biggest compliment.

As he, the chef, gets around to seating himself, the story comes—the long and short of it. She was riding on his handlebars down David St., the divider between Monterey and Pacific Grove. There was construction along the street. They were gaining speed, going down through the construction, and he saw a bump. A bump that had never been there before, he claims, but with the construction and all. He told Zadï to hold on tight. There was no avoiding it at this point. They hit the bump and both tumbled off the bike, only Gabe landed safely—safely on top of Zadï. Her head bounced and her back skidded. Gabe bounced off her body back to his feet. Her last words before the fall, as if she were purposely saying them to haunt him, were "I trust you, Gabe."

Safely on top of her he fell and now landed himself drunk at the table only a few hours later. The long and short of it. He does feel bad—if not for Zadï, then at least for himself. No amount of booze can hide the look in his face of guilt, sympathy, distress; nor can it settle the uneasiness in his stomach for poor Zadï in the hospital. Or maybe it's not that at all. Maybe he has recently had a bad dream about his brother and has just remembered it. Maybe it's the words themselves—*I trust you, Gabe*. Maybe it's that he suffers the deep, personal dissatisfaction that all chefs suffer when their meal has not turned out just so.

The third day of Zadï's hospital stay I am visiting for the first time. She was supposed to have been released already, but the doctors are keeping her for one more night.

Arriving in the afternoon with no flowers or gifts. This fact strikes me just as I am approaching the building and it is too late. The next thing that strikes me is that I've gone to the wrong place. A ghastly breeze coming through the entrance. White cushions on wicker furniture against white walls that have white squares on them—a line of white desks with computer monitors sitting sterile on them. A man is being pushed in a wheelchair by a man-nurse in a white uniform. It is like I am in a mental institution that's been suspended in post-war America that takes care of all the returning soldiers who have gone crazy—the ex-soldier whose face tightens, contracts, contorts like a lemon-grenade has just gone off on his tongue, remembering too-well the face that he had put his knife blade into, the blood that was as warm as expected, the scream that sounded like that of his invalid son's. Somehow I have wandered into the psych ward.

Lost in the courtyard, Ron and Jessie catch me peeking through a window to get my bearings and they guide me back into the hospital, through the spotless hallways of what was wrongly assumed to be the psych ward, and directly into Zadï's room. Ron has been visiting every day.

In her room the shades are drawn because the light gives her headaches. The TV is off because the movement makes her nauseous. The only form of entertainment is a pleasant, softly lit atrium. A small alcove that contains four plastic pots wrapped in green, blue, magenta, and silver colored aluminum foil. A white orchid, in the magenta pot, plays as the centerpiece.

Zadï's naturally pallid face is ghostly in the dark with the morphine and the red bags under her eyes. She's coming off the drip and was sick just a moment ago. She's feeling better now. She asks us to all sit on one side of the bed so she won't be strained in turning her neck and body—what, with the scrapes on her back and her coccyx being bruised, not fractured, as we thought. She seems to have adopted the convalescent role quite easily. She loves the morphine. When they let her out it won't be without a healthy supply of some sort of painkiller.

With a dramatic flair for playing out her role, Zadï asks us for stories from the *outside*. Ron seems better suited than I, so I leave him to it and dismiss myself for coffee. Down an extremely long hall, past open doors where I can see the feet of recuperating and worsening patients, hear the quiet discussions between doctors and family members, the rhythmic beeps of machines, the gentle raps on the closed doors, I find the coffee dispenser surrounded by three middle-aged women in whispered conversation. Fill three cups and one of the women gives me a dirty look. So it is, being that I'm simply visiting a friend with a mild concussion—*a little bump on the head*—and she, this woman, has been here day and night all week, watching helplessly as her daughter's kidney condition rapidly declines. Those of us who are dying are the lucky ones. It's those of us who are forced to stick around, to survive, that have it tough. Our day will come, but until then we have no other option, no other choice than to wait out our lifetime and try to make the best of it. The look on this woman's face! The thought comes that if this is not the psych ward, then soon it may

175

become one—the asylum for mourners. The place where people come to go crazy as they watch their families die.

Back in the room, Ron is finishing a story in which he rescues a pelican. He is out on the boat and sees the pelican choking on the surface of the water. He swoops it out of the water, brings it onto the boat, and has someone hold the beak open. Elbow deep in the pelican's gullet, which he says feels like a giant vagina, he discovers a half-eaten mackerel. He tosses the mackerel back into the water and the pelican lives happily ever after. Happily because he's a pelican, a bird, a mechanical creature, and doesn't understand the great tragedy of life. Better to be a bird, I suppose—or an Idiot.

It's a good story Ron's just told, but I've heard it before, so I distractedly glance about the room. Notice the clock on the wall has no numerals—it is a circular dial of ticks with hands spinning in a lull of timelessness. It is the exact clock that is hung on the wall in the Irving's den. It was there, in the mustard and pea shag décor of her parents' home in Pebble Beach, that Zadï first played the piano in my presence.

My knowledge of classical music is limited to a few of the bigger names, and then to only a few of those pieces thereby composed. But you needn't know the names to understand the sounds. She played them unfalteringly as I listened and rocked back and forth in an antique rocking chair. Rising about the room with the sounds, into the vaults of the ceiling, into the cobblestone of the chimney, into the timelessness of the clock on the wall, onto the porcelain wings of the dragonflies hung nearby, onto the mantel, into the various portraits of her well-groomed lineage. It was all made to be of great importance with the music, and a little sad. In one of the photographs, taken around the early 1900's, there was shown a young boy, lets say seven years old, in formal attire with tie and all, and his hair slicked down on his round head only to jut wildly out about the ears in fine, perfectly curved ringlets. I let out an inappropriate laugh in the middle of her performance—she stopped playing. "And what are you so amused by, Love?" She had taken to calling me the name her boyfriend had given me. Lilly, sitting on the opposite end of the den, cringes to hear her refer to me in that manner. To answer the question, it was those ridiculous ringlets that amused me. And what came next.

Satisfied that I was not laughing at her playing, she took it up again on a different tune. She abandoned the classical pieces she had been trained in since she was a little girl—this tune was one of her own and it had a distinctively modern-feminine quality with quirky, jerky rhythms accompanied by overpowering, odd cadenced vocals. She sang off-key, but she sang away regardless.

Poor Zadï may not be dying, but singing is out of the question—

thankfully. Talking is even an effort. We sit in silence as Ron, the lucky bastard, beats me to the punch and goes to refill the coffee cups. Jessie tags along. We sit in silence, Zadï and me, because as I am looking at her, at her almost transparent face with the red bags under the eyes, I realize that I have nothing to say to her. She is no one that I know, this person in front of me. *My friends are a thousand miles away.* The name 'Marie Alison Irving' means nothing to me—it belongs to the figure of a woman whose shapes evoke no emotion in me. Her temporary misery has no effect on my sanity. Which is to say, she is someone whom I have no deeply personal attachment, no investment; she is someone whom I do not love.

9. HOLIDAY FISHING TRIP

Father's Day comes as a sore spot. A prick in the balls, a scratch in the phantom womb. It's a sad song, a bad memory, and a swift kick in the ass. Nothing that warrants a celebration.

With his connections on the dock, Ron has arranged a Father-Son deep sea fishing trip. His dad will be there. Gabe's father is in town visiting from Baltimore—both will be present. And then me. My father can't make it though he lives only three minutes away in Pacific Grove. He is out of the country on business.

At 6am I awake before the rest of the house. Even Lilly breathes her last snores as I dress in my warm clothes and wool coat. The noiselessness of the house puts me on edge. Where there should be peace and tranquility there is shattering nerves. It is a troubling silence, like those of the towns in West Texas—there is an atrocious air that makes one feel as if someone has just been murdered, is about to be murdered, or a murderer has just been born. A troubling, dangerous silence.

In the quiet hallway there are tiny bones scattered on the floor which once formed the framework of a live chicken. All of the meat has long been eaten. Beamer has chewed the bones to hell and left them in the hallway to rot. They make me think of death. Creeping past the bones out the front door, as to not stir whatever evil that is creating this god-awful silence, I come upon the morning in a world made of bones. Bones of people, of fish, of pigs, of cows, of chickens. The houses are built from bone lumber and in the planks are knots where the bones were once broken and healed all wrong. Calcium deposits, nicks, scrapes, chinks. Bones of ancient fishermen and Protestants. Great big God-fearing bones. The sky is the color of old bones wiped with a dirty dishrag. Visibility is low.

Walking downhill there are the bones of a squirrel in the gutter. Its miniature skeleton is flattened. There is still some meat on the skeleton, and blood. Move past him along the down-sloped street of Franklin, which is the curved backbone of The Man, but he doesn't feel a thing because nothing has brought Him back to life. By time I make it to the dock I have seen the remnants of so much death that it nearly makes me sick. And this before getting on the boat.

The pair of fathers and sons is waiting for me to shake hands on arrival. Ron is the spitting image of his father, who is a squatty Scotsman, puffier in his warm dress, with a massive grey beard that hints at red in places. Gabriel looks nothing like his dad, a man of average build, grey hair neatly in a crewcut that he's kept since the war, and a nice looking All-American face that has nothing in it of the islands and countries he's seen, nor of the people he's killed. My father couldn't make it to draw comparisons. Had he come I'd simply say he looked exactly like me—all Irish and all Puerto Rican at the same time, light skinned with dreams in the eyes.

One tablet of dramamine and we're on the boat, slowly moving out of the harbor. At the back of the boat, Gabe's father, who has killed a lot of people, and helped a lot too, remember, casually rests on one knee and vomits with the calm discreetness of a military gentleman. To prevent seasickness I am at the front of the boat where the cool wave-spray mists my face, crouched like a smoking Chinaman to lower my center of gravity, and firmly grasping my left wrist with thumb and middle-finger. My gaze is fixed on the passing shoreline. (Whether I learned this trick in a book or invented it I don't know, but it is effective.)

It is a beautiful place, the town of Monterey, no matter which way you come upon it. From sea it is a number of quaint homes slanting upward on a hill that plateaus to evergreens bobbing in a pool of fog; from the south it is a change in the coast, sand to rocks, and perennial autumnal weather; from the north it is an escape from the city. From inland, passing through the awe-inspiring Salinas Valley, it is the said Eden.

That is, until it loses its mystery. If I were seeing it for the first time, from here at sea, the sight of the streets going up the hill into the trees, the houses on those streets, the green-white tint of the wharf made by seascum and seabird shit, the fog and the sunspots, it might move me. The idyllic look of this unknown place might inspire me, wake me up, tease my imagination, urge me to explore. But I know the names of the streets slanting into the trees and the names of the people that live on them. I know that the houses are made of bones and those bones are the charred remains of the innocent Chinese families who were burned out of house and home by Protestant settlers not *that* long ago, and that it was done in the name of God and that God wept for his ignorant followers, the crimes they committed in His name, and the victims of those crimes. I know that one street in particular, somewhere on the hill, is called Walton Street and that on that street there is a corroding Victorian home in which, presently, a beautiful young girl, whose hair is like my mother's, sleeps soundly. If it weren't for this last bit of knowledge I wouldn't bother to look.

A Common Murre, a little black seabird for which I have a tremendous fondness, appears in the water. He dives under the water for twenty seconds and reappears in a different spot. If it weren't for the beautiful young girl, as I said, sound asleep, I would dive after this bird, as there he goes again, and have him show me his world. Or I would float on my back, as best I could, and crack my meals on my tummy like the otters do, and stare up at the sky wondering about nothing. It is possible that I might accost the ship's captain with my pocket knife and tell him to take us all the way to China so we could apologize.

Forty-five minutes into the trip I have not yet threatened the captain. He kills the engine in a spot he says there's good fishing. We've all tied our weights securely to the line and baited the hooks with slimy pieces of squid. In a moment everyone is reeling in fish after fish—big and small varieties of rock cod, fish with giant, googly eyes, fish that have swallowed the hooks. Gabe reels in his first catch and gets sick as he grabs it—he wipes his mouth with his forearm, takes the fish off the hook, places it in his gunny sack, and feels better. Ron is catching fish like wild. One of the fish he pulls from the water convulses in a violent death-orgasm, white come shooting in spirals back into the water, and Ron bags the thing. Its blood is on the deck from when Ron had to rip the hook from his guts, no problem. Everyone has thrown five dollars into a pool for the biggest fish—it is already apparent that Ron will be the one to take the money. He'll rip the five dollars from each of our guts if he has to, I'm sure of it, *no problem.*

Can't catch a thing myself. Barely getting bites. Maybe I'd be having better luck if I could actually get my line in the water. It's not that it is a moral dilemma. I mean, I'm all for catching these fish—I'm all for catching the biggest fish. I need that money. It's just that I can't get my line in the water because my reel is fucked. It's tangled itself into oblivion. It looks like the pubic nest of the dirtiest bar-slut in town. Ron says it's because I let the line out too fast, took my thumb off the spool. Looking at the fish he's just bagged—an enormous, orange, vermillion with eyeballs like deformed testicles—I take his advice.

He untangles the knots in my line and I drop it into the water. A steady descent, thumb firmly on the spool—halfway down there's a bite. Stop the line, play with it, give it a few jigs. Feeling the thing go for it, I attempt to set the hook and reel in. It's a big one and it's putting up a fight. My rod is bending in the weight and pull, reeling in like hell because I need that money, and it's nearing the surface—can see its silvery-red body shimmering in all of its underwater, distorted glory. Pulling the rest of the way up, I am crushed by the sight of it. It's of a questionable size, almost too small to keep. Gently, I take the hook out of its eye where I somehow set it, and put him into my gunnysack even though it's nothing to brag about. Doesn't matter to me though because it's the fish that I caught and no one can take that from me.

Ron laughs at my fish and offers me a nip at his flask of scotch, which he has been carrying in his back pocket the whole time and said nothing about. I'm fine with the fact that he's been holding out on me —no self-respecting man would hit it so early in the morning. Then again, I am no self-respecting man myself, so I take a swig, set my rod at rest for a bit, and open a beer for a nice little break.

For the most part the fish keep coming in—their blood and come and piss cover the deck. Ron is catching more than his limit and puts the excess into my sparsely filled bag. His dad, like me, has given up the gig for the moment and rests in the cabin. Unlike me though, his face is green shaded as he sits with sick eyes closed and giant beard crumpled against his chest, rocking in the motion of the water. I am alert, savoring the taste of my beer, standing at the railing outside the cabin and watching the wan movements of the hull dipping in and out of the water.

Briefly we are in the middle of nowhere—no land is in sight. We have nowhere to go back to and no destination in which to look forward. We are floating above an alien world that will forever be mysterious to me and forever inspire fear. We are floating above a world in which God The Artist created in a manic whirl without constraint, where not one of the bizarre creatures retains his image, yet all were bestowed with His inherent majesty. They do not kill each other in His name, nor anyone else's. They kill in the name of Survival. When they peer up through the looking glass and see the sorrowful land creatures they do not understand, nor do they care to understand—they simply revert their attention to the depths of the holy waters where their next meal awaits them, and the process repeats itself over and over, becoming infinitely smaller so that, eventually, the human eye can no longer gawk at it and must then return its gaze to their own sorrowful land.

Briefly this happens, but at no great length, so I am unable to make sense of it. It leaves a sensation that is not completely unlike seasickness, or earthsickness, but would most accurately be described as soulsickness, as others have called it before. The boat lurches forward and the motor roars as we start to make our way back in. My bag is filled to its ten fish limit and I am only responsible for a few of their lives. If our existence were still merely concerned with survival and procreation, rather than the trivial and abstract matters that propose myriad unanswered questions, from which rises an unrelenting frustration, that then is the root cause of war, unhappiness, suicide, then it would be old Ron going back to the beautiful young girl of mine—Ron who catches all the fish and can provide for a family with his practical know-how. Fortunately, for me at least, our existence is based on those trivial and abstract matters, so all I have to give up to old Ron is my last five dollars for catching the biggest fish. Five dollars, even my last five dollars, is an insignificant amount in comparison to its primal alternative. Besides, Ron has Jessie to go back to and I intend to make him, the great fisherman, really earn my money by pressuring him into eating one of the eyeballs of his prize-winning fish. But that can wait until we reach land.

This time, on our way back in, I take no interest in the passing sorrowful shores. I am enthralled with the show going on at the back of the boat. From my smoking Chinaman position, I watch the deck hand in his orange slicks as he filets the fish. Precise, learned strokes of the knife—from neck to tailfin. Along the flesh hinge at the tailfin he flips the meat with a turn of the wrist, which smacks his station's table with a wet sound, and he finishes cutting the meat from the scales. On the opposite side of the fish, the precise, learned cuts and strokes are performed again without variation. It is done in less than ten seconds. From the tip of the knife blade the carcass is flung overboard. Seagulls are in steady pursuit of the boat, pausing to gobble up each set of bones, then swooping in and going after the next. There are two flocks in rotation. One man in one set of orange slicks filets the fish that feed them—some of the fish are still alive for the first cuts. They give in after the long cut down the side.

Bones flung through the air and bones in the throats of the scavenging birds. Everywhere there are bones and the bones make me think of death.

Settling back into the waters past the break in the waves, the sealions bring themselves to my attention. A large number, say twenty, of these said animals that spend much of their time above water, languidly sunning their massive flanks on the rocks and docks, are perched on the dock doing just that. They bark noisily in idiotic unison. One of the barks comes in clear distinction from the rest, in a long, drawn out, painful bark—*aaaarrraawwooooowwooooo; 'why? why?'* he asks. And the rest of these giant, sunning animals answer him in idiotic unison, *'cos, because, because...'*

Solid ground. Dry, firm land that wobbles under our sealegs. The deckhand is finishing with the last of the fish. Seems the fathers have already gone for their naps and Gabe has gone with them. Pressuring Ron proves to be an easier task than expected, seeing as he finished all of the scotch with a couple of beers to boot. It is merely a suggestion that, since he caught the biggest fish, and I handed over my last five dollars to him, Ron ought to eat the eyeball of this wealth-bringing fish, which, indeed, resembles a deformed testicle. On some drunkenly sympathetic level he agrees.

He takes the eyeball between his two fingers and puts it into his mouth as it were a delicacy. He pops it between his teeth, the fluid expelling into his mouth, and swallows quickly with a slight gag. He requests that I eat the other eyeball, as a way of showing respect—for him or myself or the fish, I don't know. Again with the two fingers, he places the glassy bead-eye into my hand.

With a deep breath it goes into my mouth. Trying to pop it between my teeth, it keeps slipping out, sliding over my tongue and against my teeth like a putrid pinball. I am gagging over the taste when it finally bursts—the fluid fills my mouth with grit, sand, and salt. One hard swallow sends it down my throat like rancid fish-wine; right back up comes green bile and grit, which makes the gagging worse, and I spit the acidic contents of my guts onto the dock. Ron is laughing at my final, violent, gut wrenching gag.

With the tears in my eyes, visibility remains low. Down is up and vice-versa. The sealions bark into the bone-mist. I wash the taste out of my mouth with a swig of the last warm beer.

10. LINCOLN, NE: LETTERS TO LILLIAN

Preparations were made in a frenzy at the last minute. I am to fly back to Lincoln, NE in order to fulfill dual purposes: First, to help my best friend, Jason, his wife, and their new child, pack up their belongings to move to Colorado; Second, to watch my baby sister walk the stage at her high school graduation. Then, there in the big town of Lincoln, Nebraska, I will remain for a month before reconvening with Lilly in *her* hometown of Austin, TX for a short summer vacation.

It happens that these arrangements were made a few days ago and that I am already laid over in the Los Angeles Airport. Still, none of it has quite set in.

Contrary to plans, I was sure that we were on the plane to LA together, Lilly and I, sharing a window seat and staring down at the ocean—I could smell her, could feel her, could *almost* see her. *She was with me.* But, just now, staring instead at the reflections in the airport floor, and seeing my own reflection ringed by the glare of fluorescent lights, I noticed that I am alone. Like fragments of a dream I am forced to recall, I have a vague memory of her seeing me off in the Monterey Airport, which is preceded by the memory of an ill-fated attempt at making love to her in a bathroom stall. Of course, I have left her, and for the next month these fragments will be the actual memories from our last encounter. If only it were a dream.

Only fifteen minutes ago did this occur to me and I am already beginning my third letter to her. I'm going to flood the mailbox there on Walton St., dear Lilly, and inhabit the space below your door. This is how I'm going to miss you—I am taking you with me everywhere....

Up above the clouds, going too many miles per hour when each one is further from you, a piano is playing and a large woman with painted eyebrows is taking drink orders. Everyone is asking for orange juice, of all things, and extra pretzels—they're fresh out of pretzels. The clean-cut grey haired man that's just ordered champagne to substitute for his orange juice is eye-fucking me, Lilly, and Lincoln is another bad flight away. Only my mother is waiting for me, or at least she is all I can see, there with my sister. (For this reason I order a soda without the whiskey.) No one else will do—just you, see? How to make you believe me, how to show you that I've meant it in all the mornings waking up next to you? However many months in and you're still new to me. I hate to leave you so near to the beginning. Nebraska is where my home used to be, but you have helped replace it with something better.

Changed my mind about the drink, can't you just add a drop?

Nodded off. Awake in Denver and one hour lost. Quickly board another flight. Must be getting closer to Nebraska because the look of the people is so engrained in me that I don't notice a single one. Unsure of anyone's drink orders, but doubt that champagne made it to the glass. If I ordered a drink myself, I must have drunk it already—there is no glass in front of me, nor any snack wrappers.

Within forty-five minutes another hour is lost. Back in the Central Time evening, waiting in the oncoming storm with my suitcase in hand. Mima is predictably, almost endearingly, late. It wouldn't surprise me if she didn't show at all—what would my mother be doing on the west coast? It's hard to believe that I've made it back to Nebraska.

Landlocked with the sound of a summer storm. The change in season is startling. In Monterey the fog still glows with perpetual cool. The prairie boomer serves as welcoming committee in my first morning back. There is something unbearably sad in each roll of thunder. Rain laments the same loss, maybe, or something completely unrelated. Woke me from what was half-dream on Mima's floor(imagining you there with me, oh Lilly, snoring, turning over, grabbing for my hand. Sleeping alone has never been so difficult). Mima gone off to work while I was sleeping, and all I saw of her were those fifty minutes of car ride, from Omaha to Lincoln, when she bought me chocolate milk from the gas station and told me all about her new boyfriend from Oregon with the two first names. And, back at the house, when she showed me a picture of myself, standing with my father in the driveway of our old home, for the sole purpose of pointing out the Minnesota t-shirt he was wearing—which is the state his mistress-wife hails from. The photograph must have been taken within his first two years of adultery, long before Mima had any suspicions—now just over a year has passed since his marriage to the woman. Syd is nowhere to be found either. Can't expect to see her much though, it being finals week and all.

Seven o'clock, five Western Time, and the reality of lying here by myself is too much, so I put my clothes on and go for a walk.

It's an unfamiliar neighborhood—never lived in my mother's current house; probably only spent a total of two weeks visiting her under this roof. Suburban track homes, leased SUVs, trampolines, new schools, invisible fences for family dogs. The only thing that makes it interesting is the storm—the early, booming storm. And the fact that summer has somehow arrived without my knowing it—at least in this part of the country.

On return I make breakfast with no intention of eating it. Just something to stay busy. Thunder and rain pound out their welcoming rhythm, and poor Bear-dog(my mother's six year old Chinapoo that looks like an ewok, if you remember), she is wagging her tail in slow-motion at my feet as if she might sit there forever waiting for me to pat her head. Which reminds me, maybe that little bitch—excuse me—that used to work at the café was right, or partially right, when she called me your cute lapdog, your stray pup. Because here I am halfway across the country just waiting for you. Waiting for you to pat my head. But, sweetheart, life is so good with you, and warm—I want it no other way.

The green color of the stormy sky matches your eyes—if I'm wrong about this, which, look!, I'm not, then I still find solace in the delusion. Anyhow, my food is ready and, as it turns out, the writing of this letter has made me very hungry. I'll spare you the details of my plate's contents. I miss you. With love.

In the setting of your childhood it is easy, even as an adult(though a very, very young one), to revert back to those habits in which you grew accustomed to over the seventeen years you spent growing up there. Especially when you return to discover that none of your old friends have left. As if your problems of the past had remained static, awaiting this untimely return, they present themselves anew with the same intensity and disregard. It is a challenge to avoid slipping back into these habits and their implicit ramifications on body and mind.

For one night I go out drinking. Find myself at a gathering in the upstairs portion of a midtown duplex where my first girlfriend, my high school sweetheart, Mary Mary, apparently lives. She is not home, her roommate tells me, because she has gone to Kansas City with her fiancée to visit her aunt. Did I not know she was engaged? And to a young boy whom I have known since the first grade? The problem with this 'big town' is that it keeps getting smaller. The crooked drapes are drawn in a bit closer, the notes in the song overlap, and my vision blurs some. After the night leads to its inevitable hungover morning, I resolve to not go out again.

A familiar shame accompanies me for the next two nights, which are spent at Jason's with his wife and the baby boy who I am meeting for the first time. He's a miniature, bald version of his father. I am trying to teach him to call me 'uncle'—at three months old my efforts are in vain. This sweet little boy, my nephew as I call him, watches with vague interest from the harness attached to Mother Ainsley's breast as Jason shares an expensive bottle of wine with me that was given to him from another chef at work as a parting gift. This might mean he took it for himself off a back shelf—as a parting gift. For a married couple they look thin, and happy. They appear to be very much the same as always. Jason still gets worked up about miniscule things, launching into detailed descriptions of meals, sunsets, leaves he saw blowing, a song he heard, and Ainsley still corrects what she imagines are his blunders, amending a description here, completely ridding another there. He still finds the humor in me, she still finds the disgust. Very much the same as before, except that the bottle is only halfway gone when they go to bed. Jason brings me a blanket and pillow for my stay on the couch. He suspects, rightly, that the bottle will be gone by tomorrow, and follows Ainsley into the bedroom with what I feel is a twinge of regret because he can't sit up with me to help finish the wine. The lights are off and their door is closed. I anticipate the sound of the baby's cry, but it doesn't come.

Morning summer rain gives the windowpanes a soft iridescence. Up early taking orders from Ainsley to pack this box, or that, or send another over to her parents. The child watches with his same vague interest, from his same breast-cuddling harness. The work moves steadily and the small trailer fills with boxes. From within, listening to the tin sounds of the storm and slipping on the rain-slick metal, Jason and I turn the loading into a mathematical game of who can find the best fit? Ainsley is frustrated that we are dicking around, which we must be, because she can hear us laughing inside the trailer and it shouldn't be taking that long. If she were to venture out to the trailer, though I wouldn't recommend it through the rain with baby in tow, she would be amazed that the job weren't taking us *longer*. Every nook and cranny is filled in the six feet tall by six feet wide wall of boxes and bric-a-brac.

Jason doesn't have a clue as to what most of the shit is, but it's going with them all the way to Colorado anyway. Because Ainsley doesn't come out to inspect the fantastic job we are doing, just calls out her orders from the doorway with babe perched against her milk swollen breasts, she is convinced that we are dicking around and she is annoyed with us. The baby coughs and whines into her agitated tits. For a moment we have a seat on the boxes inside the trailer. A creaking has begun somewhere, and creates a sensation in my brain, like it is uncoiling and slowly cracking my skull—from within or without I cannot say, the origin is indistinguishable against the rain. The trailer is attached by a shaky hitch. The matriarch is calling our names from the front porch. We have to get back to work.

Mima's heart is breaking because I can't find it in me to sleep at her house. Can't explain what exactly it is, but there is a first through sixth sense that it is wrong—all of it feels askew. I am staying on the couch at Ethan and Casey's apartment now, breaking Mima's heart, much like I did last October when I was in town for her birthday. Presently, I choose to refrain from going into the specifics that are concerned with that particular time period, though I will surely find myself divulging them later because it all comes back to you, dear Lilly, and the omnipresence of your Sex...

The diligence of the storms that come and go each day are the single thing I miss about this place—the ensuing flash floods and tornado warnings. The green skies, grass, and the bright pink and white blossoms of the downtown trees. Outside the window is a giant evergreen tree whose tip resembles the head of a dragon. The fire was put out by the rain; the steam is in the clouds. Alone it becomes apparent. Ethan and Casey are gone to work during the day. You are not here.

Being more intelligent than arbitrary depression, jealousy, or anything, cannot keep you from being susceptible to them or their side effects. We are still the children we once were. When Ethan gets off work we sit together on the second floor balcony overlooking the park to discuss these things. He is one of those genuinely good-natured and humored men who, without trying, can make it through anything with a half-smile on their face and no matter what find the time to point out the stain on your shirtfront—which, by the way, is never there, you will just find his finger rushing up to bat your nose. None of that Catholic guilt or grief shows, even with the brunt of his mother's and little brothers' bills on him while his drunken father rests up in the hospital. Only the true saints are unaware of their martyrdom. Our talks help some.

However, I did break down the other night while trying to fall asleep on the floor, which I moved to from the couch in order to stretch out fully. You never called me back and it made it worse—the last time we spoke there were voices in the background. Who were those people?

By morning it had passed, the attack on my brain and nerves, but the sense of dependency remained—nay, remains! Am I that unhappy without you? You aren't so far away, and I'll be with you again soon, so why do I worry myself or get sick?

I am suspicious of those people who rely on the company of others to validate themselves or subdue their own discontent. But here I am—worried, sick...the tremors are in my hands. A mess. I can feel each of the bones in my feet, my body; several heartbeats are found in contradicting rhythms—each one is too forceful, too strange. I become scared when checking my pulse. Somehow the beat continues.

It is not that I could not do this without you; it is that I no longer have to. What am I doing here?

An old friend totes around a picture frame to snort drugs on. A father shoots up while his baby girl is with the mother—they've divorced after just the second year. My own mother will have to leave soon, and Sydney too. Already their home nearly collapses my chest—sleeping there in pain is not an option. Jason and Ainsley are gone—we moved out their things so suddenly it seems—and their baby is with them. In Arizona another of my friends is pregnant. These continuances and discontinuances, these stops and starts in others' lives—what are they to me?

I have lost all interest in my previous projects, and doubt all efforts for the new one. The new one I mention is something I've concocted at night, peaceably on the balcony with one drink, sitting in the corner chair smoking ever-quietly in the dank air above the dog park and sewer, so proud of myself for staying in for these simple joys rather than going out with old acquaintances to get drunk—for the sheer purpose of fighting loneliness. It is a fable, a fairy story, this new project. Chances are it will be a bad one, being that the probability is great that I have no talent. In my preteens I wanted to be an actor. Or was it that what I really wanted was to be one of the characters in the story? To give my life importance?

When I leave again, don't worry yourself, my confidence will be restored—And you will still win all the fights. Your voice, it will bring me into submission. The life outside myself is only desirable when you are in it. There are so many other things—those things that tap the cracks in your skull and go creaking through your brain. I am not the person I was when I lived here, and you, my sweet girl, are no one that I knew. I miss you more than these storms. I've decided to come home early.

187

What did the squirrel do to warrant the so many altercations between him and bird that I should be able to witness it at a given time when escaped to the balcony for morning coffee, smoke, etc.? The chase twists downward around the tree trunk with acorn trailing both bird and squirrel. An old man sits with dog on leash just far enough to muddle his features; only a maroon sweater, khaki pants, and white hair can be made out like a splotch of spilled paint in the early grass.

Bird. Vs. Squirrel fight of the century, as far as I'm concerned, has taken off around the corner and from around that same corner comes a brown and white rabbit hopping lethargically with no apparent direction. Never any direction. The old man is gone. The paint has been cleaned up. The rabbit sniffs the gutter, hops directly beneath me, chews five blades of grass; hops to the next gutter, sniffs. I have nothing better to do than to *be* this rabbit for a moment.

Really I am a human though, scratching about insignificantly, and my coffee cup is empty and I may as well remove my shoes again. It is some time before noon.

This is narrated in god-awful seriousness, Lilly, with the sincere belief that you are right here with me, or asleep on the couch where I'm about to wake you for oatmeal and coffee. Don't worry yourself, as I've said before, I'll bring them to you right there. The bananas should be eaten as well. Personally, my appetite has been ruined by the sight of the folded blankets and the realization that the only snores to be heard are from Casey's family dog, Gunner, who is staying with us over the weekend.

Wavering between these sentiments of companionship, and the ubiquitous *loneliness*, I am struck by a collective sympathy. For the couples that will invariably part, for the transient youth illusioned by their own sense of freedom, for the stable youth that has mocked their own old age with precarious disillusionment(I have just written precarious, when I meant to write *precocious*—funny that either seems to work), or ignorance, and, dear God, for the well-adapted middle-aged women whose lives are suddenly transformed, and they lack the independence, the self-sufficiency, to get by on their own. They are forced to understand that, in fact, they had *adapted* to nothing at all, they had only *adopted* a lifestyle that belonged to their ex-husbands. To his new mistress-wife, the husband says, 'Welcome to my life.'

Someone else says, 'the one who loves the least controls the relationship,' and they storm inside, rather, attempting to retreat quickly, but handicapped by their anguish, they s l o w l y storm inside like a soft, warm rain. The entire cast of reality is puffed up on a deflated dream, chasing disappointments of old ideas and their beliefs are divorced from their hearts. Superficiality is enjoyed en masse. The good things are more rightly the rare. Unhappiness has never been so romanticized, so desirable—the truth takes more courage to keep. What shit, I say, and do not extract the wrong notion: You are the virtue, the rare; the right bank to the destitute left. This other side, which I call your name from, is a joke, an abstraction, a brief separation. Perhaps more an amusement during a short date?

We only have so much time this morning, and I'll be back across soon besides. There's enough here to last me for years—there is no reason to be here. Again, I tell you, I am coming back early!

Family affairs exhaust my last days. For ten hours at a time I see them and they still say, "you hate us, don't you," when Ethan picks me up for the evening. My father is in town for the graduation. He wants to know what my mother says; my mother wants to know what my father says—is that all? What else was said? It could certainly steal the last life from a desperate ghost.

At the ceremony we all sit together. Dad and I barely keep it together. He keeps his sunglasses on inside the dark auditorium—in combination with his pinstriped suit, with his initials embroidered in the lining, he looks like a member of a crime family, or the modern, Puerto Rican equivalent to a certain grim, gray regicide. But there is no family and there is no king, and this may be why, I swear, he cries beneath those sunglasses, though I am the only one who notices. My mother is busy taking pictures at random, or so I think, of different graduates who, apparently, are friends of my sisters. I only recognize a few of the sad faces.

After it is all over she'll be moving away, my sister, into the great, big howdy-do world—not quite though when you consider the environment of the all-Mormon university she'll be attending in... Idaho. My mother has nowhere to go. I repeat: my mother has nowhere to go. There is always time for growing up...

And that's what I'm thinking at the post-ceremony family lunch of all meat and potatoes, which makes you tired to eat. Dismiss myself to the basement at my grandparents home to look for the banjo I won't be able to play, but would find supreme enjoyment in just plucking the strings. Instead, I find my grandpa's high school yearbook from the year he graduated. Someone writes to him, 'I wish that I could stick around here(Scottsbluff, NE) with you to please this town's beautiful women, but I have to go...and, like an old soldier, I will fade away.' He writes to the young, quiet drinker that irresponsibly got married just a few years afterwards to my grandmother and still drank and smoked. Small town Nebraska had filled him with dread. Now he sits upstairs, reformed, silent—a man of The Church.

The women in our family have petty arguments around him, my

189

grandfather, and if he does open his mouth it's to diffuse their slanderous taunts, jabs, and so on. My grandma, upset, makes an announcement to the room. "I think when kids get older they forget their parents are people—or maybe it's just my kids." My grandmother is dying slowly of cancer. I imagine that most mothers feel this way. Mine surely does. And I do know that she wakes up in the mornings, that she suffers, and worries, and that she has an independent life from my own. God, dear God—it is to you I am writing this to, and to you I am asking for guidance—it is so hard to be here, *but what can I really do?* Isn't my presence enough? Just showing my face every once in awhile, going to movies, lunches, etc.? Giving up some of my free time, which everyone knows I cherish so much, to the people I care about? Is that not enough?

Later on, happy hour at a downtown hotel. Meeting my father for free drinks at the bar in the lobby. It appears The Prince of Egypt has come into town—having caught wind of the cheap real estate and wanting to capitalize on the opportunity—and is sitting at a table with my father drinking a white wine spritzer. Haven't seen Raf since that fateful weekend when I, having not had sufficient funds to buy fish food, 'forgot' to feed his precious fish and was asked, ostentatiously, to please leave. By chance it was this event that forced me to find lodgings at Walton Street—did I ever tell you that? He says the fish is doing just fine. Also, Raf says he read my manuscript on his flight to Lincoln—he says he liked it. He even showed certain excerpts, presumably in which he was mentioned, to his in-flight neighbor, who was, also presumably, a fairly attractive younger woman. This aside, he would like me to show him around the downtown properties—mainly, he would like me to show him the bars.

A four block stretch of wall-sharing brick buildings house the majority of the downtown bars. Any night of the summertime weeks they are crowded. Small town Nebraskan boys who are done with classes for the summer, looking as if they stepped from an ad poster hung in a clothing store of one of the local malls, get their fill of cheap beer, cheap vodka, cheap whiskey, and try to displace their own dread with intoxication and one night flings. They don't see the lights in the trees, the trees themselves, the reflections of these trees in the glass of the buildings, or the shadows made by the leaves on these trees on the spit-lined brick sidewalks. In their cheap drunks, the boys only see the various one dollar specials and the mini-skirts of overly made-up, small town Nebraskan girls doing exactly the same thing the boys are.

Inevitably, we run into a group of old friends who carouse this scene. One of which is a good friend, Sal, who used to put me up at his apartment sometimes when I needed a place to stay or just needed the company. I've been trying to get a hold of him since I got back, but he's been too busy to return my calls, he says. He's only half-drunk and I do believe that he's sorry. He invites us to join him two blocks down at Main Café with his girlfriend. We decline the offer because Raf wants me to show him the bar that an old college buddy of his owns. We say goodbye to good Sal and his friends, and go inside the Tavern at 14th and 'O' Streets.

A quick shot at the bar and Raf has already forgotten why we chose to come into this particular establishment. The bartender is a twenty-five year old girl, okay looking, typically Middlewestern, who wants to move to California—coincidentally, Raf is *from California* and still lives there. I leave the two to start up conversation over Our massive, Western state and take a walk through the bar. The bar on each floor is busy, people are dancing, and yelling, and the smell of cologne mixed with perfume, mixed with cheap alcohol reminds me of nothing. For a moment my head goes blank, despondent. Come back to the front of the bar and the twenty-five year old girl who wants to move to California serves us a drink—*on her.* We take them in a gulp, Raf throws a twenty dollar bill on the counter, and we make an exit.

Any bar we might choose to go into would lead to the same sights and dialogue. A semi-attractive bartender, horribly loud music, nauseating smells, and a free drink. Aimlessly, we walk past the strip of bars as I explain this to Raf, who doesn't care much. As we're split between one similar bar and the other, someone shouts, "Font!" It's coming from a long line outside of somewhere called 'The Rusty Rail.' "Font! Is that you?" The line is almost at a stand still and I'm able to pinpoint the origin of the shout. A broad-shouldered, beer-swollen boy with the softened, nondescript features of a farmer whose labors have ceased to be tended to, looks in my direction with a square-jawed, beer smile. By God, the boy's name is Zach Olson and he is someone who graduated from high school in my class. In all those years of school together we never spoke, but tonight—tonight we are old friends. "My God, Font, come here! Look at you!" he says overly loud. As to not embarrass him in front of his fellow bar crawlers, if they have even heard his shouts, I approach him in line. "Font, you son of a bitch! It is you!" He hugs me gruffly, then holds me out at arm's length and puts his hands on each side of my face. His friend, who recognizes me as well, but is not quite as drunk, looks on stupefied, wondering what the meaning of this is. Holding my face in his hands: "Font! For christ's sake! You're all grown up. The last time I saw you you were all clean shaven and baby-faced—but look at you! You look good Font! For fuck's sake, you look like some sort of Actor! (noted) Or poet or some shit—look at you! (to his friend, Trev Myers) My God, Trev, are you seeing this guy? (again to me) Look at you—you look fucking good,

191

Font!"

With each praise sung Zach's face inches closer to mine. He's near enough I can smell the one dollar specials of his bad breath. Raf remains a half-step behind me where he has stood throughout the entire encounter. I imagine that he cares even less about listening to drunken Zach Olson than I do. I thank Zach for his generous compliments, and tell him it was good seeing him, but I'm showing my friend here (gesturing to Raf) around the area and we've got to go—so I will see him a-r-o-u-n-d.

One slow block down, thinking about calling it a night, we happen upon another old acquaintance. Jacob The Sweetheart is his name. He's a skinny, large headed, but not unattractive man-boy of twenty-five. Though he should have graduated at least three times now from the University, he has changed his major multiple times and has one last semester to finish before he finally graduates with a Bachelor's Degree in English. Hoorah! Another man that's learned to read and write in the spongy marrow of the pedant's barebones, and to receive a Certificate for the accomplishment, with a capital 'C' for Crap. But Jacob The Sweetheart is, needless to say, a *sweetheart*, a great sort of guy, and we accept his offer to join him at his friend's newly opened bar in The Haymarket.

The bar is in the basement of the The Sullivans Building, which is adjacent to the train depot in The Haymarket. Above the bar there is a sandwich shop, above that a yoga room, and above that are three floors of apartments. On the fourth floor, on the back side of the building, the west side, is the apartment I once rented—the one where someone or something died.

Back in the basement, four floors below the apartment, and one more underground, we come through the doors to find the bar mostly empty. During the day it is a student-oriented pizza parlor, which the décor reflects with long, bench-seating tables covered by white-black checked cloths; the raw brick walls are hung with pictures of New York eateries and street scenes. At night it is a jukebox, pool, and booze. All hours are equally dead—every bus-iness that has rented the space has gone under. Not a single pie was sold today, and now only four patrons haunt the bar, all of which are friends of the owner. Thus, the liquor is being sold at half-price—some is being *given* away.

Jacob The Sweetheart introduces us as old friends from California. Everyone welcomes us. Seeing as we're old friends, the owner pours a free round. The Prince of Egypt sips his vodka a little out of place, but receptive to the spontaneity and the young, unfamiliar crowd. Each free sip and the bar seems to sink further underground—beneath the weight of this cursed subterranean space, beneath the breathtaking weight of my old apartment, *it sinks further underground.*

Out back we go for a smoke—through a heavy, red door and up a short, narrow flight of stairs into the alley behind the building. Under a single lamp sits a table with four chairs. One of them is left open as I take a seat between Raf and Jacob The Sweetheart. Smoke blows past the lamp to make faint shadows over our faces like ghost-bugs retreating ominously into our skin. Jacob The Sweetheart is talking about *my work*, asking if there's anything he can read. From a ways off I hear his voice, and the words fly past me, over me, up above my head to where my attention is focused on a fourth floor window that's been left ajar—the window which I once dropped pennies from, light bulbs, plates, and so on, into this very alley. You don't want to know the other thoughts that creep up my spine and into my brain. My God, you already know them anyway. I wrote an entire book about them and, Sweetheart, if you want, you can read That. For now I refuse to say another word.

Weather channel forecasts through my mother's home from a television set in the kitchen. More storms a-coming. Quite obviously they are with just one look out the window. Green skies of summer's eyes, the clouds pursed like lips of doom. Laundry rumbles and tumbles in the dryer, tosses a quarter. Bear-dog laps at her water with such vigor that I am frightened for her health—as well as for mine. My pulse is accelerated, or at least it feels like it; my palms and feet are in a cold sweat. It is only noon and I am already taking my seventh piss of the day—the last day to be spent in Lincoln.

In my sister's bathroom, relieving myself, the sight of a hair straightener that's been left on upsets me. Towels on the counter are hot by proximity—a fire hazard. "Damnit, Syd, please be more careful," I say coming out of the bathroom. She shrugs her shoulders, an innocent mistake—oh well.

My clean laundry is in a warm pile in the center of the living room. The two true Font women sit side by side on the couch. I sit in the recliner. Each of us holds on our lap one of the warm garments from the pile and delicately mends them with needle and thread. My mother hems the new pair of grey wool slacks she's purchased for me; Syd repairs a hole in an old pair of jeans; I sew on a new button and stitch up a small tear on a shirt Mima bought me on a previous visit. All of my wardrobe has been colleted in that manner—on visits to Mima she always finds an excuse to get me with her in a department store where she can buy me pants, shirts, socks, underwear. Now they are all in need of repair. As we finish with each article, they are folded neatly and packed into my old brown suitcase, then another battered clothing item is extracted from the pile. The deliberate and painstaking operation is a heartbreaking one; it is like a sad, ancient ritual in which the mother(and sister here) prepares her child, the baby boy, for a long journey into the expanse of separate realities outside of her own home and the town in which she raised her son. She has performed this ritual a number of times with all of her children. By now, my poor and dear mother, sweet Mima, carries it out with a graceful precision. Not one heartbreaking iota of the operation is missed.

But this description is becoming superfluous to its purpose. By the time you receive this letter, or thing, my dear, I have probably arrived and we are together right now, in the flesh, at home—so, put this down and come back to bed.

11. SUMMER CLEANING

In the progression of my absurdly detailed letters Lilly was led to believe I was going crazy. For this reason I don't hold the estranged wariness of her greeting against her—she had expected to find me disheveled and manic-eyed upon my return.

Instead, I come through the front door of Walton St. with clear, sane eyes, wearing the wool slacks my mother sent me away in. Lilly stands outside of our bedroom door at the end of the hallway, inspecting my appearance in search of a change. Anything that might give me away. She doesn't touch me until we close the bedroom door behind us. Pulling her in close, hips to hips, arms swinging around to her lower back, I kiss her with the intensity that builds in a prolonged absence. My tooth hits her upper lip and she pushes away with revulsion to my lunatic kiss.

"Who have you been kissing, k-y-u-h-l?" The first words out of her mouth are an accusation. The conviction in her face that I have been unfaithful is discouraging. I assure her that I have been kissing No One. She doesn't believe me. Go in for another anyway, moving her toward the bed.

How painfully sad sex can be when it is had out of sheer obligation, in a state of fragile mistrust, gently probing the relative waters to test for changes in temperature. For three days we've been getting reacquainted, leaving all of our twenty toes dipped in at all times. There's been no reason to leave the room. Everything had improved until this morning.

For a long time we were not concerned with the welfare of the house. Now, this morning, it comes back to the forefront of our attention as we undertake the intensive, overdue objective of cleaning.

We are cleaning for guests. The dates were either confused in my head or I chose to confuse them—or perhaps Lilly's assumption was

194

right and I have gone crazy to an extent—because I knew that Lilly had friends coming from home for a visit, and I knew that they would be driving across the country to go to a music festival in Tennessee, then back to Texas together. But, on the fourth day after my return, the date seems to have arrived too early. My presence would be ludicrous if it weren't being employed to help sterilize the kitchen and clear out the trash. She's forgotten who I am, but the house must be spotless. She says her friends will be in tonight.

The task of cleaning a home that's been neglected for fourteen years is one that I wish I would have avoided. The idea of an additional month separating me from Lilly however is intolerable—I've chosen the mop and broom and the three days we spent alone together. Nothing seems to loose the grit from the floors or the dirt from the rugs. Hosing down the trashcan isn't enough to take out the stink—a few maggots survive. Half of the items in the refrigerator have surpassed expiration by months. The sink is stopped up—atop the water is an oily film and in it floats eggshells, brown bits of lettuce, onion, meat. Walls and ceilings are spotted with grease—long and short streaks precede the spots from where the grease dripped down the paint before drying in large globs. Dirty socks are found under couches, in the ash-filled fireplace. A doll appears with fabric worn thin on head, crotch, and legs from years of Beamer's humping. Impenetrable piles of broken light bulbs, boxes of old bills and junk mail, dented cans of food, electrical chords that no longer have their accompanying appliances, are covered over with dirty sheets. We remove the broken washer from the middle of the living room into the courtyard. A new, industrial sized trashcan is purchased and put into a corner of the kitchen. All cushions are overturned and the windows opened. Scented candles are burned in every room—four are designated to the back of the toilet. Broken plaster is swept from the bathroom floor. While holding our breath, mold is scrubbed from the shower.

As we go through the backbreaking and inefficacious motions of cleaning, Lilly talks aloud. She is nostalgic about her old life in Austin because her friends are coming. She says they will be here in a few hours. She retells stories that I have heard before and could do without hearing again. She has no concept of decency in regards to my feelings. Of certain things I would be better left in ignorance.

Such as their recreational habits back in Austin. Don't care to hear it. They were into drugs—all of the psychedelics. Every story begins with a pill or a drop. It's hard to find the humor in someone breaking his legs from jumping off a roof in his paranoia, turning a car over in a ditch, or the inability to properly reason, or getting lost in your own backyard, or crawling through a field of cacti and screaming because the reality of each prick in your skin is far too ordinary, or real. There is nothing funny about a girl stripping off her clothes and running down the middle of the street in the nude, yelling inanities in drug-fright, when that girl is one in the same as the girl you lay with at night. But she talks aloud about these things with the distant, yet somehow immediate, fondness that one might have in recalling a happy memory from childhood, and, in the act of reminiscence, she becomes that child.

Every year she makes it to the music festival in Tennessee. The last two years she went with her ex-boyfriend, whom she was living with at the time, and their two roommates. The same two who will be arriving shortly. I am supposed to be okay with this fact, so I say nothing. Listen to the stories. Scrub the shit off the floors. She promises she won't do any drugs, but, under the circumstance of the festival, I imagine that might change. She is driving the width of the country to a place in Tennessee where people fuck in the open grass and where even the most seemingly innocent things might be dosed —stickers, lollipops, water, a slip of paper found on the ground. I have heard the disreputable accounts of some of those who will be in attendance—people calling themselves the Merry Pranksters, other groups parodying the aforementioned. Against her own will her promise might be broken. See: A girl sits on the toilet in a house she's visiting and comes out of the bathroom tripping because there was acid on the seat. 'Here—drink this, you'll be fine.' Drinks the juice from the carton but, oops, that was dosed too teeheehee. For a whole month she is out of her mind—everything she touches is adulterated. Will she ever come back? If she's lucky she'll get halfway. Personally, I don't like to test probabilities and percentages. No matter, because on a bus there is a woman walking the aisle that will do it for you by blotting acid between your eyes. Someone in back stares out the window, smoking what? They say that in one hit of DMT you slip into a death vortex— the passing world flattens and turns into images cut from paper, each shadow is sucked in one at a time through a tiny straw in your brain. A chemical release that mimics your death throes, wherein you catch your first glimpse of God and His holy visions. There is no God in DMT, and no death. All synthetic revelations that puff up lazy and self-righteous prophets—stinking poets with deformed visions and drug-dealt wisdom. If they'd really seen God, then they'd stop searching— wouldn't one use be enough? But their God is light and that light only comes to life with *a pill or a drop*. Changing lights, flickering, trailing, bright lights—synthetically bright lights. Everyone is searching for something.

Take a minute for a deep breath. The circulatory system is a complicated miracle described in an uncomplicated three-letter word: _____. Listen closely.

Only once did I make the mistake of offending Lilly, her friends, and her old life in Austin. On a downhill walk I commented offhand on frivolity, falsehoods, reverse enlightenment, and the gods of such things. Then again, I drink—and what difference? I wasn't allowed a sip for a week. But a drink, up to about the sixth, quiets my insides, tunes me to the intricacies in a single breath or pump of blood—you can hear the churning of your guts where God, the natural God called and considered so many different things, was and is and will be. A dark closet has the same effect. Sitting on a park bench for several hours. Coasting through a landscape by car or train or bike or foot. Waking up before the sunrise. Staring at stained glass, participating in a game, going barefoot on a rainy day. Whistling with a blade of grass.

If she, or I, had known then that my words matched those of her favorite poet, who had a more experienced right to remark on the subject, perhaps her reaction would have differed. Perhaps not. Regardless, I mention that this poet—though later in his life—renounced the use of hallucinogens/psychedelics because, after years of doing them himself, he felt that they were a hindrance to genuine self-realization. And the poet has the last word.

Lilly's friends are late. Six hours of cleaning and there is almost no sign of progress made on the house. No sign of her friends. We bought groceries and took them up to Sasha's to make dinner in a kitchen that isn't crawling with disease. Dinner is prepared already, simmering on low heat on the stove. Lentil Bolognese with rice pilaf and an entire tray of buns that is wrapped in foil and left in the oven to keep warm.

Dark now, we sit on the porch waiting, smoking, sharing a couple large bottles of beer. Lilly is elated by each set of headlights coming down the street. She is progressively more disappointed when each set remains on and each car keeps moving. I am inexplicably annoyed by this show. Still I say nothing.

11 o'clock the headlights finally belong to the car that carries within it her friends who have driven all the way from Austin, TX. They get the welcome that she definitely didn't waste on me—forget that I spent all my money in buying a plane ticket from Nebraska just to see her and that I'm going to have to fly above the same route her friends have taken just to see her again in Austin; that is, once she spends a week alone with her mother. She runs into the street just as they've stepped out of the car and jumps into the arms of the driver, wrapping her legs around the waist of his tall, lean, attractive frame. Keeping both feet on the ground she more appropriately hugs the passenger of the car, of a similar stature to the driver, and the three of them walk towards the curb where I am waiting to be introduced.

One shake of both of their quiet, good-looking hands and it is over. They move on. Absolutely no recognition of the position I hold in their young friend's life. Sasha is introduced. She's confided to me that she's desperate enough to fuck either one. Not that their faces inspire desperation, she makes frequent use of those words. She never means it though, you can tell by the timid way she extends her hand that she expects to be won over. Neither man makes the effort; they're tired and hungry from driving all day.

Despite this, Lilly wants to feed them and show them everything at once. Half hour to eat leftovers from dinner, rest up, take a few drinks from the bottle that she had waiting for them—like holy offerings to unknown gods—and we're all walking down the hill with Lilly leading the way. A wet cold lingers in the fog. Bars spill their drunks onto Alvarado St., soon to be looking for cabs and someone to go home with. One pass through the saturated crowd and you've seen enough.

Onto the beach at high tide, white caps occasionally form like a wink of the eye. Cold, wet bite of the midnight water so close. Too cold and too wet for the Texan-Greek gods who expected their ocean water warm as their bath. Lilly probably apologizes to her two dear friends that she couldn't make the water warmer for them, but I can't hear what's being said as they walk up ahead in the sand. The tide slowly carries their voices out in the muddled sea foam.

I imagine that her friends—their names too grand to mention yet in their holy remoteness—would rather be back at the house, warm and sleepy on booze and travel exhaustion, than standing at the edge of the frigid water, looking at the seaside lights that mean nothing to them because they've not yet come to life. Catching up, I suggest we head back just as a white cap catches me off guard, winking at me, and it occurs to me that it's the wink of a prankster and that everyone and everything is playing some sort of sinister joke on me. It rolls over into the dark in the next moment, but its unmistakable significance has alerted my senses. Fleeting objects are caught in my peripheral like little demonchilds trying to get their kicks in my misery. One of the gentle imps, patronizingly I think, agrees with my suggestion. Another white cap forms as we turn off the beach and there's a feeling of dread, which is then followed by a confusing, and unprovoked feeling of regret.

Up the hill the joke continues. Lilly walks toward the house with her two friends and they laugh together because they're all in on the joke. They're all laughing at poor, innocent, prairie boy me, who continues to say nothing as I trail ten feet behind, growing increasingly despondent with each step nearer the house because these two jeering figures are stealing my Lilly from me and taking her away to the sound of distant music, drugs, and an ongoing orgy that's being carried out on the natural stage of a soft, green hillside. And I will never know the absolute truth of it. I will have to trust her offhand anecdotes whose details, though filtered for my ears, and only partial, raise suspicion in combination with practical, deductive reasoning, and an overly vivid imagination. I will have to trust the look of the grey-glimpse of the white cap in the night and the gnawing sensation in my intestines.

Back at Walton St. the two guests take our room for the night. They shut the door, turn out the lights, and conspire against me in imperatively dark whispers. In the kitchen, Lilly and I lay out on the smoke and grease stained couch which no amount of cleaning could ever restore to its original color. The clean sheets covering the cushions don't keep the dust from going in my nose, nor the dirt from getting on my skin. Lilly is apparently unaffected. She is asleep by half past one. I am awake, wiping the dirt off my arms, and listening to the house noises.

Above the sink there is a window which we forgot to shut. The broken blinds are pulled as best they can to a crooked mass only three-quarters raised. Through the opening below comes an unremarkable thought, but a thought nonetheless, of the late-night, sleep deprived variety that come in the form of a vague question: how is it that the moon, when seen in full, obstructed or not, can appear so flat? Why does it look so much like a glowing contact lens? and for whose eye? Tell me, *for whose eye?*

If you check into a room in the recently constructed hotel on Cannery Row and look out one of the windows that face the street, you will see a gift shop in the old, red-faded building which once served as the general store where "a man could find everything he needed or wanted to live and to be happy." Back then it was owned by a Chinaman with fingers like sausages that tapped-away on the counter all day. It was conjectured that this man was "evil balanced and suspended by good." If that is so, then the suspension has long been cut by his successors. There is no good left here. Coming out of that building with the weight of the evil pressing on you, and crossing the street, if you will look directly below any of the northeastern facing windows of your luxury hotel, right next door, you will see the inconspicuous, low brown building where old Doc Ricketts once lived and worked. Out front there are fresh vomit stains on the sidewalk. From tourists or locals who knows, but they are there, shiny and bright, as remnants from last night's bout to prove that it all, indeed, happened.

Now, if you will look up from these stains and follow the sidewalk only a few steps further, you will find yourself at the doors of the Aquarium. ENTER the unfounded characters of Cannery Row revisited, fifty-something years after Last Thursday, like fresh vomit stains on the bastardized scene. Shiny and bright, *this is happening.*

Seven of us young pricks come through the side entrance where we lie to the staff to gain free admittance. Today we are all students of Dr. So-and-So, visiting The Aquarium on assignment. The real reason we are visiting is to show Lilly's friends how great the area is. In reality, The Aquarium is among the few great things about this area. And, surely, it is the last piece of blatant truth in Monterey. If it weren't for the incorruptibility of its specimens, at least in their very essence, that would be changed too. But the impalpable qualities of their lives are inviolable—there is no ego down there.

Embarking into the glowing hallways, blue reflections shade the looks on our faces, disguising any emotional discrepancies with the slow-motion of liquid serenity. Baritone organs blow out through loud speakers and the Self washes away in underwater explosions. A tall, southern gentleman dismisses himself to personal explorations. Another southern gentleman parts with the company of a Jewish looking girl suffering from lack of attention and the early stages of an eating disorder. A red-bearded Scotsman disappears into The Aquarium labyrinth with a Mojave Desert goddess by his side. A couple is left—one in repressed paranoid annoyance; the other unaware—holding each other's hand with uncommunicated emotion, squeezing lovingly sometimes, while squeezing disdainfully at others. But this, too, fades complacently into a symbiotic side-stroke as they pull themselves through the water.

From eyes deep set in blue flesh reflects the silver sheen of sardines swimming in circular unison around a glass-domed ceiling—one breaks sporadically here and there, trying to reverse the order in a backwards stroke, rewinding the atomic clock of all-time without luck, stuck there for a moment, then sucked into the forward flow of the impenetrable current, forcefully shifted in the perfect motion of the captive fish. The dive-flight of the Common Murre, that wonderful bird, is followed in glittering bubbles from surface, underwater, past shark, past ancient sheepshead fish, through kelp forest and rockfish, back to surface...a few treads of thin flesh webs, the shark gets larger below, comes into full focus, then drops mysteriously back into the blue haze—a black streak blows through, tiny bubbles trailing the flap of the Murre's dive-flight. One stray tentacle of purple, sucking-eyes coils in the dark retreat of its unnatural habitat...white cotton puffs of the water world dandelions—anemones shifting in the feigned current like a Japanese cartoon. Subjected to the vibrations of the organ resonating in the water, accompanied by the slow drift sound of an ambiguous woodwind, the jellyfish contract and expand their bells in rhythm; their tendrils are in a long, steady, harmonizing sway. Looking closely, nose pressing up to the glass leaving its oily tip-print, ghost breaths appearing and disappearing beneath the nostrils—like the multitude of children with their parents that traipse about asking

200

questions about everything—you can see the tiny brine shrimp free-falling and squirming through the obstacle course of jellies. The thin, limp branches, the neon twine, zaps the struggle of the brine shrimp to a halt—paralyzed, its fall continues. You blink and lose sight, and, before you can find it, the lifeless protein has been absorbed.

All of the tank in view. The deep set eyes pop from their sockets, the body disconnects—they float through the convex, now concave waters; the angles of the water changing. A massive tuna zooms by in pursuit of nothing, yet free from the fate of ending up sliced thinly on a plate somewhere up the block and some of us are hungry. The nose comes off the glass, and, wow, the nose was oily because there is its mark! A little spot beside all the other little spots that will never get through to the other side, though it's so close that you can actually see yourself falling apart in the wide frame of a fish's eye.

Pulling back from the glass, and turning around, we see seven confined penguins in declarative stance: one stares glumly at the wailing wall; one licks and ruffles his swollen, potato-like belly; one is in heavy repose as if he were a gentleman in wait of an iced drink to ease the southern heat; in a slow, waddling gait, two penguins discuss the contents of their last meal and speculate about their next; another penguin stands perfectly upright atop a rock platform with his eyes closed and beak stuck into the air; at his back, the last penguin hobbles back and forth in futile attempts to gain the attention of the preposterous little creature with his idiot beak pointed towards Heaven.

Outside we mimic the penguins. Each of us striking the pose of our corresponding penguin, who kindly returned our identities as a parting gift just before leaving The Aquarium. Under the sign at the entrance/exit we retain our poses so Lilly can snap off a picture—the light hits the film all shiny and bright and we are captured there forever.

The trip has put me in a great mood. Walking along Cannery Row I point out to everyone the faded-red building and the low, inconspicuous place of old Doc Ricketts. No one cares though because they haven't read The Book—not even Ron who has lived here for over ten years. Somehow Ron doesn't need to. We keep moving, up a few blocks to Lighthouse Ave., and Cannery Row falls behind us without a sound, lacking any significance.

The mood sets the pace. The pace is slow. A good mood can go more quickly than it came. And it has. Everyone is hungry. I have no money. We take seats at a long table in the Lighthouse restaurant where The Archangel works. He is here with his hair pulled back into a bun and the hangover worn off. He brings us two large bottles of hot sake. Our porcelain thimbles are filled to the brim. I make the first toast. It is unintelligible because I am already drunk on my mood. The mood is somber. In the morning Lilly will leave ahead of schedule. I will be alone. The fish are freshly killed. Their meat is served in thin slices. No one has read The Book.

I am drunk on my mood already and the drinks are coming besides. Don't order anything because *I have no money*. However, when the food comes out, a plate is put in front of me. AW-LLEN is standing behind the sushi bar smiling at me. He is giving me the thumbs up. I am smiling back at him and my face is warm from the sake and gratitude. I have no money, but that's okay. On the plate in front of me are eight delicately crafted rolls: seaweed on the outside, then an even layer of rice, then perfect, soft cuts of a fresh, dark pink fish. The fish, fittingly, of course, is tuna. No joke. There is a supreme delight in finding absolute continuity in reality. Although it is always there, to be able to touch, and eat!, the concrete evidence of it is extraordinary.

Allen is aware of everything. With knife in hand he occasionally looks over at our table. Each time he sees the progress I have made on my plate until it is finally empty. Every glance he takes apparently renews his own inner joy. He returns to his work chuckling to himself, shaking his head back and forth with a deep and loving understanding. His pace is content. His mood is a fine-tuned harmony.

12. GOD THE WOMAN AND THE SELF

The saddest room in the saddest house in existence is the empty sea-blue room on Walton St. in Monterey in California—(in America on Earth in Hell and so on)—which I once shared with my loving girl-friend, Lilly. The hangers are now free of clothes in the closet. The books are in a box somewhere and the broken bookshelf leans against the blue wall. Nails poke nakedly out of the plaster where pictures and paintings once hung. In another state, Lilly's blood tingles and some-thing drips onto her spinal column. We will have to wait to see her in Texas. Until then, we will sit at my writing table.

All of our things are gone. There is nowhere to sit. The writing table has been removed. The house has undergone another transform-ation. In one of the front rooms the raccoons finally scared off Kitten and her owner. The other room was cleared too. The tenant was evicted for having a dog. Beamer, Neechie's puppy, sleeps unaffectedly atop the armrest of the chair in the kitchen as usual. On the adjacent couch is the new bear of an inhabitant that works at the local grocer. One day he wandered up here and the next he was snoring on the couch. The occupants, their names and faces, have once again revolved in the meaningless disarray of Walton St.—but this is not what I want to talk about.

What I want to talk about is what I have called *divine deliberation*. And what to say of passivity? of the conscious submission to a greater will, in combination with a deeply Christian feeling of responsibility? Let me tell you:

For the few years in my experience that might be considered my 'conscious life' I have lived something resembling an idle existence—to the trivial non-believer at least; the man preoccupied by success and progress. Allowing myself to be affected only by naturally occurring factors such as storms, romances, favors asked of me, their fulfillment, hunger, rivers bent or broken, birds flying this way, dogs running that, family, an arbitrary urge to leave and carry on, money problems(or sometimes an unexpected, helpful sum of money), dreams, the idea of a dream, or the memory. Which is to say that, for these low number of years, I have given myself to the singular guidance of what I choose to refer to as God most of the time, but could be called Anything. 'The Universe,' to give one example.

The ensuing situations of Passivity, the consequences therein, I accept and endure. I have been similar to the Christian child described, badly he says, by Nabokov's flamboyant vessel in 'Pale Fire,' who says something like this: 'In preparing for a big move, the child trusts that his parents will arrange for him or her all of the necessities of living—food, shelter, schools, churches, etc.—and form no expectations of what it will look like. They simply believe that where they are going will be better than where they are.' The Book is not in front of me, so the quote itself is most definitely wrong, but I don't need the book in front of me to retain the general mindset and illustrate it clearly.

Perhaps it is not though, and what I have transcribed is nearer to Invention, spun to suit my specific purpose. Perhaps I was attempting to show off by mentioning that brilliant fiction's title. In any case, it is written down and I will continue by saying that even if that *move* is the move into Heaven, oh heavens, or something minute as moving into a shitty Victorian home in Monterey, Calif.—or climbing into a van with a group of strangers to get the hell out of Anaheim, CA—I am positive that my existence will be provided for and that the eventuality of whatever circumstance will be an improvement.

It is important not to forget that in succumbing to the organic tides of Universal Order you are susceptible to the conniving and deceitful evils hiding within. The morning star shines ever-brightly to misguide us, pulling the tides in too early, sending them out too late; burning down our buildings, or just lighting the fuse. It is left to the Individual's discretion to draw the discerning lines between 'good' and

203

'evil'—to stand by our Christian phrasing. It is their Personal Responsibility to feel the disparity of an innocent breeze to that of a gastric belch, and to follow The Wind accordingly. In order to do so, the act of sitting becomes mandatory. If we are to sit, and to smell, we will never have to see, in hindsight, that we have mistaken the glow of the morning star for that of the rising sun, or that we have been carried by The First Wind, instead of The Good Fourth.

This may seem out of the blue, and if it does it's because it is out of the blue. Out of the black-blue of nighttime where the subconscious invades your convictions with an overriding certitude. It mocks the lucid, practical brain, prodding it with suppressed images, and asks, "how is it that you've gotten here?"

Here on Fog and Spaghetti Hill I am housesitting Sasha's one bedroom while she visits her old friends in Portland for a week. Rather than sleeping in her bed I have laid out the sheets from my stripped mattress on the Oriental rug in the living room. Each day I enjoy the simple happiness that comes from watering the plants out front. They are coming back to life. The faucet is tightened and no longer leaks. The porch is swept quietly. Dishes are done immediately after use. Evenings Ron and Jessie stop by with wine. Mornings I make them tea. This is the reward for my day's accomplishments. Tomorrow: repeat.

Presently, the evening's wine is gone and the glasses washed. As a writing table I clear the papers and diet pills from the surface of a desk in the corner of the room. We will sit here. Above our seat is a window, in the reflection of the window a face. Over the face, atop the head which houses it, a hat. A ludicrous, floppy, straw hat that was found on a bench in Big Sur where past literary giants have lived, died, and played. Beneath the hat, within the head, we are on a picnic with Lilly in the cemetery, watching the geese. I pelt them with chunks of bread that hit their hollow chests and fall to the ground. They eat every crumb from the earth. They fight over the morsels and skid over the gravestones inlaid in the grass. One of the geese skids to a stop on one of the gravestones. He dips his head halfway up to his neck in the cylindrical, water-filled hole meant for flowers. There are no flowers. He dips his head in, pulls out, then goes down for more. The name on the stone is Lydia Mae(1918-1993). Seventy-five when she died. No cause or relations inscribed.

The coincidence of the name is uncanny, for it just so happens that I am now sitting with another Lydia Mae. She is fully alive, born in the year of my birth—Nineteen Eighty-Six. She has dark hair past her shoulders, high cheekbones, a broad, pink smile, and eyes any color of choosing. Any color the imagination can come up with, because that is where she is painted. More paint would be superfluous. The imaginat-

204

ion has nothing to add. Only the eyes are interchangeable in her vague masterpiece.

I am sitting with Her in the backseat of a van. We are heading east on the interstate in leave of Anaheim, California. It is the first time we've met. I am in love, as always. We are going to get married. The rest of the van is filled with others whom I am also meeting for the first time—and musical instruments. They are a traveling band on tour through The States. Only one of the passengers do I know. An old friend from Lincoln, NE. It is a mystery how I got here. Instinct tells me that God put me here and that God is a woman. Women are behind everything—every action and reaction in Art and Life alike. The sex is liable to change according to taste. For you it might be a Man, or a Man dressed like a Woman, or vice versa. In this instance, mine, It is a Woman and the Woman's name is Lydia Mae. I am in the van because she is in the van, and the van is heading in the direction of Lincoln, Nebraska, where my mother lives and where soon it will be her birthday—which, I remind you, I have never missed.

The preceding events are irrelevant. I will only mention that they are sordid and that they, like everything, involve a woman. The succeeding ones you may be aware of, but let me recount one of them, the last, to refresh your memory.

In Lincoln my mother's birthday comes and goes—autumn of last year. My father, recently remarried to the Woman he kept as mistress for eight years, has just moved to the place of his dreams, Pacific Grove, California—the neighboring town of Monterey. His wife and her two year old daughter are to follow. They need help with the drive. Having no commitments, responsibilities, or money, I agree to accompany them.

To Monterey then. Or anywhere.

Like belongings in the back of a cross-country truck, we are jumping around and shifting from one place to another. This is the sporadic form of the natural state. At any point an end or beginning can be marked; a destination set or an arrival made. The only apparent thing in the foreground is the Self. Behind it a Woman.

The painting of The Woman remains intact, though the placard beside Her has changed. It no longer reads Lydia Mae, and we don't know where that name has gone. Written in the third open space from the top, on a lined sheet intended for musical notes, is the name **Lillian**. The bold is important. These letters, though, however bold, are subject to change, be rearranged, or transform—all at my whim.

The length pleases me, almost. And the 'L' in front. The urge to tamper with the rest will not be ignored. And what to do about this?

Lillian. Li-...Lo-...Let us consort with a genius of language. We will flip back to his name, which we mentioned earlier, found as usual between Miller and Omniscient.

If he is not upset, might he offer us a suggestion? Lend us some advice? A name? He answers("the tip of [his] tongue taking a trip of three steps down the palate to tap, at three, on the teeth"): Lo. Lee. Ta. The brain canvas flutters. Her eyes bat. Her blood tingles and paint drips onto her spinal column. **Lolita** it is. Henceforth by that name. From the inside out, *Lo!* How is it that you've gotten there? and me here?

Like cold spaghetti molded by two cupped hands, the brain. **Lolita** pouring through each fold and crevice like cool breast milk, then coming out through the nose.

On the skin above the lip she is an unrecognizable sheen. The skin itself she made, and underneath it she hides, but the skin remains mine. Pulled over the angular bones of my face it forms a reflection of The Self. Across from the reflection, another reflection—the face in the window glass. Through the reflection, the cool breast milk fog of The Incomprehensible Woman. The Great Nymphet, unimaginably matured.

Both hovering and in motion, I watch Her slip over each of the hat-like rooftops of Monterey that harbor their own specific, sleepy scenes of Modern America. Under one, most any one, the digital alarm clock internally ticks closer to its inevitable and obnoxious waking buzz, tune, or vibration, wherein the Progressive Man will then rise, unperturbed by dream, to the occasion of another successful day. That is, wherein the real paperwork begins.

Numbers and keys, like holograms, materialize in an electronic make-believe. They float through green boards, glass screens, into handheld devices, out of giant machines, whiz through heads and brains, fog eyeglasses, contacts, flog asses, curl through discolored cut-icles, coil over paper cut fingertips, stick to the tongue, then un-stick and are gone. Following their course are innumerable boxes of unnamable things, which traverse concrete warehouse floors, come through wide open doors, stack on steel beams filled with other unnamable things, come off the shelves, drop on heads, re-traverse the concrete warehouse floors, smash a finger, break someone's toe, then shoot out the wide open doors on the o t h e r side, *and are gone.*

The accuracy of this description doesn't concern me. Somewhere in there a few people make a lot of money, some make a little money, and I make none. A lot of paper is filed, tossed out, crumpled, torn, burned, reprinted, and filed again. Every day an entire book is written. And every day it disappears.

This then is the side-note to that novel existence. The idle doodle placed in its narrow margin. The inconsequential fading ink, or lead. The unintelligible kilobyte on the crashed hard drive. This is what concerns me.

It is this unobtrusive portion of the great text, picked apart by the spirited Individual, fragmented and pushed onto the fringe of its existence, which provides meaning to The Holy Book. The red-hued comments of the eccentric editor—the unabashed Self, and the Woman behind it—are the conjunctive parts of the otherwise chaotic whole. They are the constituents of the Timeless Identities which precede a nation, a people, or an era. Without them all reason would be lost, all thought and belief unprecedented. No Good and no Evil, just Action. The moon would shift and sway. Tidal waves would swallow shores. Fuses would be lit. Buildings burned down. The Wind would come and Man and His history would pass unceremoniously in a violent flash of incoherent numbers and keys. Then everything would follow.

By my quiet and harmless Self, above Monterey in the Idea of America, I am conscious of the fog beginning to glow the bright bluish-grey of near morning. I am conscious that the cause of this new light is the sun, and that the sun is a massive star at the center of the Solar System. The alarms are about to go off. No birds chirp. Beneath where I am sitting, down the hill near the water, a few seagulls caw. Though it is a remotely ugly one, it still incites the word, 'Song.' For now the song will continue to be sung.

As a Conscious Man, I heed my limitations by remaining inactive. Actions made in uncertainty, or the feigned certainty of certain organizations or faiths, are the greatest cause of dissolution. In a world rotating on a synthetic axis, spinning like a child's toy in the material imagination, which wears itself out in its quixotic search for Unattainable Certainty, my resolution is Negation. Non-behavior suits me; to be still and peaceful. The Woman will speak for Herself. It is an heroic act to put the morning tea on the stove, and to wait attentively for the inexplicable forces of nature to stir themselves. And we are badly in need of a hero.

13. THE GREAT SOUTHERN NATION

"The only place hotter than Texas is Hell."
These are some of the first words I see in Austin in large letters on the marquee of The New Hope Church and I believe them. Nine PM, the sun has moved down, it's almost gone, and the humidity of summer

207

still hangs on your clothes and in the air like the ghastly noose of God's Word around a sinner's throat. It nearly chokes you. Sweat trickles behind the eyeballs. Any thought other than 'save me' is impossible.

The last thing I can remember is bussing up to San Francisco for my flight. I was sitting behind the black-capped head of the driver that was eating shelled, salted peanuts from a skinny plastic bag, then some sort of cookie, and my god could I smell the sugary vanilla crème filling of that cookie. At 11 in the morning that cookie would have tasted so damn good. Anything would have done I suppose, just to rid my mouth of the bitter, dry feeling that comes in the morning after even a few drinks.

Smelling the sweet crème of that cookie, I tried to think of other things. 'If you just stare at the trees out the window they will teach you everything,' I thought. The trees were moving—their feminine frillies like those on the bottom of skirts that girls don't wear anymore—they were moving and I was moving. Everything was moving and I stared so long at the movement that my gaze penetrated the landscape and I saw something clear and calm that evoked an indescribable nostalgia—just light, colors, and textures, somehow nostalgic. Occasionally, a spectral image would break through of a horse, a shed, a dirt road, a road sign that said 50 miles to SF, or a white bus with trailer attached, hauling portable shitters out to the field workers. The field workers themselves, going out to pick lettuce, artichokes and such—I saw the only good that comes from the fashionable vegetarian crowd around the country; the men going to work the produce, to provide for a demand and provide for their families. 'Nothing much has changed for those poor men,' I thought—'how nice that might be.' But I thought in the distracted and youthful way that only an idiot can think because he never has to go out there to perform the labor himself.

Then I heard a girl's voice, or a woman's, and it reminded me that those poor little girls never quite grow up, they just grow breasts and push out children, but they are still those little girls. And the little boys don't grow up at all. Aside from the increase in hair, then the loss, and our parts getting bigger, we are still those rambunctious and insubordinate little boys that like to daydream, be dirty, and cause trouble—and after it's all over we like to go back to our friends, sometimes forlorn, sometimes smug, to tell them every last detail of our great adventures and our even greater mishaps.

The flight itself and any lesson learned from the trees must have come out through my pores. I can't remember a thing, except for the airport bars and beer shops being closed when I got in and having to wait for an hour in the sticky, empty-belly evening for Lolita to arrive. Now I'm still sweating like I'm in hell as we drive around Austin in the air-conditioned car Lo borrowed from a friend. She is lost in her own hometown, circling the city's outskirts, passing by the skyline in one direction, then passing it in another. We have seen the same HEB grocer five times already, the same I-Hop, the same parked trailer that has stopped selling tacos for the day, and the same gas station where, on our first pass, I bought an outlandishly cheap six pack of Lonestar tall boys in the spirit of the great nation of Texas.

Finally, by accident, we are shot onto a strip of South Lamar Blvd., which Lo knows well because it is five minutes from her mom's. Comfortable with the surroundings, she decides to stop at an all-night café to buy me a hamburger before settling back in at her childhood home for the night.

We are seated in a booth at the rear of the restaurant, enclosed by several tables of skin and bones hipsters—"fucking transplant Austinites," as Lo calls them—drinking cheap beer and being seen. It is a fashionable nightspot for aesthetic youth with nothing better to do than take pictures of each other. Their well thought out, secondhand appearance, and the occasional blue-white flash of a digital camera, grabs little of my attention. I have seen one table—or feel like I have, somewhere in the northwest maybe—so I have seen them all. The waiter pouts about between tables, too incredibly hip to be friendly or outwardly happy. With keys swinging from his belt loop, smacking against his leg, he brings my -burger to me without the meat or the smile, and pouts off to another table.

Blood sugar is back up. The sweating has stopped. For the first time I am able to see the girl sitting directly across from me in the always flattering light of the café. All at once Lolita has vanished. As if she had only been a vivid figure in the void-filling imagination, made up in the accusing and destructive distance, she has gone and left behind her an emotional imprint of relief and the figure of a real Woman. In soft, plain text it is Lilly there. Viable, compassionate, vulnerable. She is thinner in the face and legs, and her hair is dyed slightly from exposure to the sun, but it is Lilly all-right. Lilly with the heart in the iris and the sailboat in the other. *My* Lilly.

The Woman in the thirty year old photograph I once kept on my desk, whom I have known only as The Mother of Hope, has now come to life as the actual Mother of my girlfriend. She is a wonderful woman, Lilly's mom, with long, silverish hair that she keeps in a ponytail, strong facial features that have yet lost their attractiveness at fifty-five, and an intelligent, reserved disposition. Her hospitality is unmatched. As it once was at the bakery, I am fed *incessantly*. Renee, the first name which I call Lilly's mother by, discovered that I like mushrooms—I eat them with every meal. Twice a week she makes London Broil.

Saturdays she grills fish and shrimp. For breakfast I eat acaí sorbet with fresh strawberries, blueberries, and a sliced banana, topped with cashews and granola. Fresh towels are laid out in the bathroom. Picture albums are made accessible. Books are purchased and left for me on a table outside the bedroom door. The long unused air conditioner is turned ON.

It is no wonder that this is the woman who birthed my Lilly. Physically, the resemblance is astonishing, and, though Lilly would never admit it, certain aspects of their behavior are likewise. From the cluttered garage, which I am not allowed entrance to—a trait which Lilly possesses, of hiding from me those things which she perceives as embarrassing—an old card table that belonged to Lilly's grandparents has been dug out for my use. Renee has set the table in the long, green grass of the front yard, amongst the overgrown native flowers and birdfeeders, where I can watch the humming-birds, the finches, and all of the other species attracted to the wild floral arrangements of the yard.

In a decorative, white-painted garden chair, with hints of rust in places, I have made habit of sitting at this table in the early afternoon with notebook and pencil, and a tall can of beer—Lilly reading on a blanket spread over the grass at my feet—to record the previous nights' dream.

It comes back to me as I am driving along the interstate and there are no other cars on the road—on each side of this road there are no homes, no silos, no barns, nor bars. No sign of civilization. The road stretches in the middle of two, enormous, horizon-swallowing fields of bending, tall grass of a subdued green—green gone over with a grey wash. Trouble turning my neck to make out a road sign, trying to figure where I am—can't move my neck, but in my peripheral I see the name OMAHA and directional arrows that point me North, South, East, West—I can't make out which is which in my peripheral, or where I might be headed, But I am walking out of a door with the feeling that it is someone's home I've just left—I cannot turn back...I am walking into an open field of short, bright green grass now and above the field is a thin fog-blanket that adds a degree of mystery which forces me further into the fog and grass Where a tree appears— far off. Even at a distance its grandiosity is not obscured. It is a massive tree whose branches are festooned with multicolored leaves and these branches with these colored leaves extend into the fog with a sense of majesty. I am fumbling with a camera on the top of a hill overlooking the tree, attempting to manipulate the f-stop and aperture, but the setting-knobs are blurred so I give up and look back towards the tree—I have missed the shot because the tree is now right in front of me and the branches and the leaves come down out of the heavens, surrounding me and framing a door in the trunk of the tree. Thomas Wolfe is chanting somewhere:

"...a stone, a leaf, an unfound door; of a stone, a leaf, a door. And of all the forgotten faces..." —etc.!

And this door remains open to me—through the doorway I can see that it leads into a long, narrow corridor. I am already in this corridor somehow—it seems to be that of a high school gymnasium; I can smell the chlorine from the swimming pool and the mildew from the locker rooms. Through another door I see a ceremony going on— a wedding or a baptism, I cannot tell. A guest at this ceremony, a girl in one of the middle rows, looks at me passing by and a nasty gleam goes through her eyes—I hurry to the elevators...I will go up, or down; I will go anywhere so long as it distances me from the look in that girl's eyes—the girl that now waits for the elevator with me. She is standing completely nude, repeatedly pressing the call button. Her skin is pink and soft like she has just taken a long, hot bath. She is flabby, her skin hangs loosely. She is not ashamed that I am looking at her, nor is she embarrassed that I am disgusted—I haven't said anything to her, but she seems to be replying to me, 'oh dear, I guess you're right—I may have to put on a dress, but I just don't want to wear any clothes.' Without warning she attacks me—she attacks me with a harsh, heavy, backwards scoot into me, her arms grappling for mine she is trying to pull me inside of her and I am struggling with her weight—I'm terrified that she'll overcome me and get me inside of her, so I desperately push with both hands, I shove all of my strength into her back and she falls to the tile floor, her skin skidding against it with a squeak and thank god the elevator door opens and I jump in. The last thing I see before it closes is the girl starting to get up, first getting onto all fours, and from behind I see the gaping hole between her legs, right under her asshole, and it is the most horrifyingly dark sight I've ever encountered.

Being in Austin, staying in Lilly's small, dark bedroom in the house where pictures are hung of her from those awkward, androgynous years when the teeth never come together quite right, the once familiar feeling of homesickness arises in me. A sickness that exists for a place that does not.

Even this home has long been broken. Lilly's father goes unmentioned outside of a short anecdote from her childhood when he wished that she had been a boy, so signed her up for every sport that he could; or when he would dress her up in cowboy boots, and a matching plaid shirt to his, to take her to the rodeo. Other than that he is just a clutter of memories that aren't permitted to me. Still, there is something here that makes me miss something else.

Maybe it is Lilly's unremitting pride in Austin Island that moves me—a pride unfamiliar to my native Nebraska. In her opinion, Her City can do no wrong. The burn on the soles of your feet from walking barefoot on pavement is charming, and the itch from walking in grass. The tornado warnings and the sudden storms, real storms with thunder and lightning, are exciting. The drinks are made stronger, better. The food is cooked in a way unknown, and superior, to the rest of the world. The music venues are more alive, the music prettier, more original, the crowd cooler. The landscape is grander. The 'sea turtles' in Town Lake are the oldest living. The rope swings going into the water are the longest. Her friends are funnier, smarter, more interesting, and more loyal than any friends I ever could have made elsewhere. She takes me around to meet them; they have names now.

Erik is a transplant from Corpus Christi. He is one of the old roommates who picked Lilly up from Monterey—the one she hugged appropriately. In his afternoon bedroom we sip beers. An unexpected rain falls against the windows. The exaggerated stillness produced indoors, consequently, makes everything seem of greater importance. I flip through Erik's books—comical Bukowski poems, a few of the beats, an unopened Goethe, the stories of Robert Louis Stevenson. Each line is more relevant in the still, dry room. It is this effect that causes me to believe that all books should be both read and written in the rain. If not in the rain, then on the run when all of the details of one's own life take on a similar quality of greatness. When the world crams into the small compartment of a train, a car, a plane over the ocean, then extrapolates in the infinite capacity of the head.

One of Erik's roommates, a musician from Iowa named Isaac, runs to his room to grab a copy of essays written by Michel de Montaigne. Last night, a bit silly on beer, after singing sporadic blues on the back patio, badly, I discussed with him a little of Emerson, and I tried to quote his description of Montaigne. "Nobody can think or say worse of him than he does. He pretends to most of the vices; and, if there be any virtue in him, he says, it got in by stealth." This is what I had tried to say, but confused the order and made unnecessary additions. Although the quote was amiss, he understood my desire to quote. My innocent, accidental slander was a 'superficial offence.' We agreed, in amazement, upon the attraction of men throughout history, and now, to one another through the sole medium of Idea. In short, I saw in him my brother, and he in me, and now this brother of mine dismisses himself back to his bedroom to sort through his bag of recently purchased gourds.

Our other brother, Erik, speaks in the genuine, heartfelt tone of the beer rain about his ex-girlfriend. They broke up over a year ago, but the guy is still hung up on her teeth, her figure, her laugh. They annoyed the hell out of him, but he misses that tangible annoyance. He is left with the impalpable frustrations of a budding alcoholic or a decent writer, as goes the joke. In confidence, he tells me to hold on to my devoted Lilly(he wasn't so lucky); I tell him to write a book. Afterwards he'll be free. He may be convinced. With the rain collecting and gushing earnestly through the sewers, the shake of the gourds coming from the other room, and the books left open on the floor, exposing their strands of ordinary words, it is not a farfetched possibility—nothing is.

In the endless possibility of a day such as this, the sensation caused by the extrapolation of immediate events(assisted by beer, maybe) is a tingling in the bloodstream that reaches all extremities. Everything settles into an almost imperceptible buzz about the body. The only war going on is the one on the home front of one's being and there is nothing left to fight for. The struggle seems to be overcome. The only cost is eight-bucks for a twelve pack. The only loss is one of time, and it is not so much a loss as it is an exemption from it. We are in a small pocket of resistance. A small, but extreme resistance of the current condition, which is carried out through the unstrained act of being human; of sitting together and exchanging stories, and drinking cold beer while sheltered from the cold rain.

Home is nothing more than a vague feeling of comfort and acceptance. I am at home amongst these feelings of homesickness, listening to one of my dear brothers try to articulate that emotion in terms of his ex-girlfriend. I used to tear up when someone said something meaningful to me and I felt compelled to reply. Now, whether I reply or not, I smile, nod, sip my beer, and watch the same process occur in Lilly's face. It is the same process that has occurred for ages, and which endears one person to another, bonding them together in their temporal inhabitance on earth.

However briefly, we have won our significance and made a small mark in the margin of a vast, white page. To celebrate, we drink our beer a little deeper, a little longer. If I am wrong about this it does not matter. Because, at the holy present, I believe every last part of my infinitely expanding bullshit.

Well-being is a mental attribute; physical wellness is a disparate condition. Even those on their death bed can be content. It is the ability to remain conscious of relativity—not necessarily, though, to understand your frame of reference—that keeps one's spirits at ease.

We paid a visit to Lilly's grandpa in Bandera, Texas, a small town west of San Antonio where you have to be cautious of rattlesnakes. He is a ninety year old man of few words, an old sailor of pure German heritage, that speaks through a hole in his throat which is kept covered with a bandana—what few words come out, come out with a metallic ring. Although he told us, me rather—he was elated by the presence of a young man—that the doctors made him give up his two favorite things in the world—smoking and drinking—he seems to be doing alright. The ghost of his wife visits often. He stays in contact with other veterans from his boat—he goes to their funerals. And he said, good-naturedly through that metallic voice box of his, that I was welcome back anytime—assuming he's still alive.

If reality is but the intricate, interlaced figments of all imaginations, and the body is merely the vessel which one is forced to experience it through, the old sailor's regard for physical wellness is one that I can relate to.

A spot has appeared on my cock—a tiny, flesh-colored bump right on the shaft. Nothing of it. It will go away on its own. My behavior is unadjusted: I have beer in the afternoon at the card table, go swimming in Town Lake with the oldest living sea turtles, explore the dried up Green Belt(a stretch of land behind Lilly's home that should be a tree-lined river, but in the drought is just a rocky trail between two thirsty banks), fly off the rope swings into Krause Springs and all the other springs surrounding Austin, eat well at every meal Renee serves me, and, sometimes, even ask for seconds.

Lilly's attitude toward the temporary imperfection on my cock is different. She researched the various names which one might call this little, flesh-colored bump by. Each night she inspects me with frigid hands, like a detached nurse, without feeling. She is looking for mutations in size or shape, which never occur, but her concern is so great that she seems to invent the changes regardless. She has scheduled an appointment for me at the local clinic.

On the five minute drive to the clinic I smoke three cigarettes. The last is put out in the ashtray at the entrance. There is a secured corridor in front which you have to pass to enter the main lobby, and where all cellphones must be turned OFF. The receptionist asks us to please wait one moment to sign in as she handles a price check on abortions over the phone. "An abortion in the first trimester is Four Hundred Dollars," she says coolly, then listens to the probably horrified young girl on the other line. "Okay—yep—alright; thank you," she says, and hangs up. She turns to me and Lilly to ask how she can help. All we need is a simple check-up.

The paperwork takes five minutes to fill out in the lobby. It is a personal evaluation of recent sexual activity and hygienic habits: No (I have not had anal sex in the past six months, or ever); No(I do not have sex with men); Yes(I have only one partner); Yes(I guess I do smoke—but is this relevant?)

While completing this humiliating survey a number of reckless,

214

possibly unlucky people arrive at the clinic. In spite of its claim of being discreet, it is obvious what each person has come for. One girl, in her young twenties, sending messages to some unknown party on her cellphone that is certainly not turned off, has come to take care of the swift business of the morning after pill. A man of thirty something, white, in good shape, has come to be tested for gonorrhea, syphilis, and HIV—he can't afford all three tests, so decides to take his chances on gonorrhea, and only pays for the latter two. A young boy, high school age, sits between two girls of the same age who appear to be angrier than they are nervous—they were quieter while checking in, so we couldn't make out the details, but enough has been implied. Everyone avoids eye contact.

"Mr. Font!" A nurse in teal scrub pants and a floral top calls my name. Lilly gives my hand a last, meaningfully soft squeeze and I follow the nurse through the doorway she called from, down the hall, and into a small, sterile room. She takes down my height and weight, then checks my blood pressure. "Your blood pressure is unusually high for someone of your age and stature—you're a smoker?"—("Yeah, and I have an issue with anxiety")—"Are you taking any medication for that?"—("No, they wanted to try me out on a few different things, but I've always turned down any prescriptions.")

She glances over my paperwork on the clipboard she holds in her hands—makes note of my anxiety. "Okay—go ahead and have a seat right here and Dr. Q will be in to see you in a few minutes."

I have been wearing a cognac-colored straw hat—for twenty minutes I take it off my head, rest it on the arm of the chair, then my knee, then put it back on, take it off, fix my hair in the reflection of a picture frame(the picture behind it I haven't noticed); then the hat goes back on my head, I stand up, walk to the door, walk back, and sit down. With my hands clasped over my belly I stare at the examination table, a sort of raised and reclined barber's chair lined with tissue paper and equipped with cold, aluminum leg supports for pap smears and other vaginal inspections. Next to it is a lamp and a monitor for sonograms.

A short knock of one-two-(no three) comes on the door, then Dr. Q comes in and introduces herself. The woman about to examine my penis is short with a big hook-nose and an indeterminate accent that might be of eastern European descent—her hands are small and look otherworldly cold. She sets down the clipboard the nurse has passed to her and asks me to undo my pants. After pulling the lamp over to my crotch and switching it on—I can feel the heat from it—she puts on a pair of latex gloves and crouches down to get a closer look at my pathetic, exposed member. She holds it in one small, gloved hand and pulls the skin this way and that with the other.

"Vell, ve can burn zis off for you right now, or I can give you a few samples of ze cream and rite you a prescription for a month's supply. You jest put it on ze infected area, jest a dab, every ozher night before you go to bed, and in two to seven veeks it vill be gone — vichever you like."

"What?" My pants are still undone, penis hanging limply, guiltily, over my opened zipper.

"It is jest a common case of HPV. I recommend ze cream. You follow ze application instructions zat come vith it, and in two to seven veeks it is gone. In ze meantime, no oral or vaginal sex vith yer partner—Human Papilloma Virus is very easily transmitted during outbreaks. You can zip up now."—("Okay, so...")—"Yes, well—hpv is very common amongst sexually active people your age: two out of every sree people ave it." ("Alright, well—the cream then?") "All-rite —and should you ave any questions, zer is a pamphlet I vill give you zat vill answer zem. You are a smoker—no? Zis vill be a good reason to quit. Zey love ze smoke. Anyvay, I vill be rite back vith yer prescription and information and you vill be all set to go. And, remember, it is nothing to beat yerself up about—ze only way you can avoid coming into contact vith ze virus is by practicing abstinence. But—I vill be right back."

This last part is said as she closes the door behind her and leaves me alone in the room. I push the cognac-colored straw hat towards the back of my head and sit back down in the chair to wait.

One last time I remove the hat from my head, rest it on my knee, and return it to my head. I can't wait to get back to Lilly with the *good news*. "Well, I do have hpv," I'll tell her, "but it's okay, babe, because the doctor said that it's basically an inevitability amongst people our age—so really there is nothing to beat myself up over."

Not the best way for a vacation to end. But, then again, there isn't really a *best* way, or *even* a good way that vacations can come to a conclusion. The time just comes and they end.

14. FLOWERS AT A MILE A MINUTE

Christmastime back on the central coast. At least what feels like Christmas with the immediate absence of sun and heat, fireplaces lit in the smoky, overcast grey-blue; the inherent joyful glow of all lights, the increased warmth indoors. And it is only the first week of August.

When it is overcast
there are no shadows
unless artificially produced.
(By artificial light?)

216

We are living now in the unfinished portion of my father's home in Pacific Grove, Ca. where the inhabitants converse slowly, at two miles per hour. In a type of languid surrealism they pass their time by creating ludicrous predicaments for themselves. Recently, police have been called with noise complaints that turned out to be caused by raccoons; a report was made which stated that flowers had been stolen from someone's garden(spotted later were a family of deer in this garden, enjoying a snack); a car, parked overnight at the waterfront, considered to be very sinister looking, was towed away under locals' suspicion; an American flag was found desecrated, a slight tear in one of its corners; at a restaurant on Lighthouse Ave. a glass lantern has gone missing. Arrests have yet been made under the latter offense. The delinquents are still on the loose in Pacific Grove.

On the smooth cement floors of the unfinished portion of my father's home, we are the only town residents living in relative poverty. What little furniture we moved over from Walton St. was salvaged at the dump, as it is known already. Aside from which we have a torn, black leather couch, that was given to us by my eldest brother's girlfriend in Berkeley—which is supported by bent metal bars that slowly break our backs—and a glass lantern hanging in the middle of the room like a colorful and delicate diadem of defiance. The only privacy we have is formed by a short wall of boxes filled with knick-knacks, books, ill-fitting clothes, and give-aways. I say this not as a complaint, rather as an attempt at morally justifying our life amongst such an old, spoiled lot.

Our situation is not so bad though. We live for two hundred dollars a month. The heat is always on, the water never runs out, and leftovers are free game in the fridge. Windows span the length of one of our walls—one of two permanent, outside facing walls, constructed of real materials—and outside those windows is a picturesque tree, as if a fairytale illustration, and a birdbath. At night the branches, stretching beneath the street lamp, make charcoal patterns against the door slats over our bed—which, if gone through, these doors will lead you to the laundry machines. By morning the slats are cleared again.

The situation is not exactly like living with one's parents after a mature age, because my father is not exactly like a *father* anymore. Disappointing or pleasing him is not a priority. It is my eldest brother, Mitch, to whom my actions are regarded, which is why it is difficult to write much about him—I am writing *for* him. As concerning my real father—my biological father, Emilio—I am the only member of the family who has never written him off, temporarily despised him, or really cared that much about the decisions he has made in his personal life. For that reason he treats me differently than his other children, and definitely more favorably than he had in my childhood. He con-

217

fides in me his daily struggles with conscience and responsibility. At heart, my father has always been deeply Catholic, though it was a recent decision to reclaim his Faith. At heart, he is also deeply like me. In that way, it is more like living with a very good friend, whom you do love, and whose sex life you actively try to ignore, though it is impossible not to hear the occasional cringe-inspiring sounds through the vents. And I'm sure he would say the same.

The co-habitance is strange, and a bit cramped, but otherwise fairly easy and a great relief from the destitution of Walton St. The only troubling factor is my father's new daughter, Emiliana, who may or may not be his namesake. She is an impish thing of three years old who refuses to shit in the toilet. Instead, she painfully relieves her partially constipated bowels into a diaper while standing in various spots about the house—at the living room couch, under the dinner table, in front of the television, in the kitchen. The kitchen adjoins our living space with the rest of the house; it is separated by a thin, sliding door. It is not uncommon to find Emma there in the kitchen, standing at our door, for other purposes than just to shit. Her inopportune knocks come frequently, though we rarely answer them. On the off chance that we do, we are liable to find her, the demon child, twirling in circles, lifting up her tiny dress, and telling us to look at her body, *look at her body*. She is the embodiment of fornication.

But, as it is with some disreputable, evil, or annoying things, she is capable of teaching one valuable lessons in life. Like when she covers her head with her silky—the soft velvety, pink blanket she's carried with her since birth—and believes wholeheartedly that she has disappeared. A power bestowed by the devil? Perhaps. If only the rest of us could believe...

It is hard to discern what finally set her off, but Lilly has made an executive decision: we are going to travel to _____. I omit the place-name of our destination because it is subject to change daily. Some days it is Romania, or Croatia; some days it is Iceland, or New Zealand; most days, though, it is Thailand. As arbitrary a destination as Thailand is, it has, for Lilly, come to represent a definite escape. The main thing is to go—somewhere outside of Monterey; wherever. To move forward, onward, upward; to fucking *move*.

Lilly has worked every day at the café since our return. Every day she comes home tired and frustrated with an ache in her belly. She tells me that my (non)behavior is no longer cute. My passive approach to things doesn't bring in enough money, and money is needed if we are to go on a trip—to Thailand or otherwise, money is needed.

A job has been secured for me at The Public Library. Leon Basho The Printer, Sasha's dad, has connections with the library staff and has arranged for my employment there. My application is in, and my tests are taken—all I have to do is wait for the phone call. But this is not enough. In the meantime, I must work another job.

I have started, or re-started, my life in the workforce at a florist on Franklin St. in downtown Monterey. After walking in to inquire about the usual posting in the shop front window, I am immediately taken on at ten dollars an hour(or about sixteen cents per minute). Like all jobs that I have romanticized, and then procured, I am supremely let down.

The woman that hired me is a greedy Chinese woman by the name of Vera, who would upsale a burial wreath to a widow in her lowest time of mourning. She refers to herself as an artist, too, and tells me that anything that touches her hands is Beautiful—only she says it "boo-tee-full." She works her two kids, a boy and a girl, to the bone and has patience for nothing. Training lasts fifteen minutes, a quick run through of how to answer the phone and take orders, and how to clean the flowers—nothing about the names, though. Then she takes off on deliveries and leaves me in charge of the shop.

My first customer on my first day—who comes in while I am very busy spritzing the orchids around the shop with a water bottle—is a brother, a local Italian housepainter, who wants to make arrangements for a Friday bouquet delivery to the gravesite of his recently buried sister. I have no idea what to charge, or how to handle his loss, so I take down his number and sympathetically inform him that my boss will call him when she returns. The next customer would like to order her bridal bouquet, and a white and pink crown of roses. I put her information on a sticky note next to the housepainter's. As the young bride leaves, an image flashes into my head of an arrangement that Vera is probably delivering right now—it is a small, white wicker basket that holds several yellow flowers, a few white ones, some purple, pink, and an oversized, multicolored lollipop; attached to the basket is an inflated balloon that reads, "IT'S A GIRL!"

In one hour of work I have seen the entire spectrum of life laid out before me in the unremarkable form of shitty floral bouquets, arranged by a money-hungry woman posing as an 'Artist.' Birth, Marriage, and Death, all for a price between thirty-five and seventy-five dollars— eight dollars extra for delivawy. Also, in the course of this hour, I have inched ten dollars closer to our foreign destination.

For the sake of calculations we will mentally settle on a destination: let it be called Thailand. Thailand, from Monterey, Calif., is roughly eight thousand miles away. The cost of a plane ticket is something close to 1,100 dollars—approximately 14 cents per mile. In terms of hours worked at the florist, one mile equates to about one minute. And after every seven minutes, tack on an additional mile for the hell of it.

At a mile a minute, cleaning flowers is OK work. Monotonous, but meditative. I could clean 12 bunches of carnations in twenty-four minutes if I wanted—or I could clean them over an entire four hour shift. A bunch of roses? Five minutes. Or maybe an hour. If Vera is around the shop, she lets me take smoke breaks in the courtyard behind the building. If she is not around, I let myself take them. In a day, I usually manage three breaks back there at ten to fifteen miles a piece.

Monterey is considered the sun belt of the Peninsula—sitting in my designated smoking chair in the courtyard, next to the dumpsters and beneath the two large trees, the sun comes through in a fine juxtaposition of light and shadows. The back door of a restaurant opens into the courtyard, the odors are painfully delightful. They should write that on the menu. The growl my stomach makes echoes back. 'The food in Thailand will be better, and cheaper,' I think. Since I have been sitting here I have come eight miles closer to the border. My cigarette is out, but I intend to travel six more miles before going back inside. Making headway in a standstill is hysterical to me. Accomplishing something by doing nothing. What is funnier still, is thinking there is something very Oriental in this premise. Something refined and spiritual, almost omniscient.

Vera The Artist is inside putting together the last of her arrangements before deliveries. "Good break?" she asks. A very good break; very productive. A considerable distance was covered. This is what I am thinking, but I only say the first part—"A very good break."

There are three bunches of long stemmed roses in the bucket that need to be cut, cleaned, and dethorned. It is one o'clock and Vera is about to leave on delivery. I am off at three and she won't be back before then. Whether I finish cleaning all three bunches of long-stemmed roses in the next two hours or not, there will be no effect on the progress of my trip. The end result is the same. At three my shift will be over, and I will have made it 275 miles closer to Thailand, if that is still where we are going.

Regardless, it is OK work, cleaning flowers. *It's monotonous, but meditative.* So, though it makes no difference, I am going to coolly, mechanically, cut and clean the roses for Vera. When they are finished I will put them in fresh water in the cooler in the front of the shop—maybe put one aside for Lilly, too. And I will idle about the store, spritzing the orchids for the second time in the day, until my shift comes to an end.

My three o'clock routine is to punch out at the florist, walk the five blocks to Village Café, and order two beers. The first I drink quickly, while standing at the end of the bar and trying to mollify my work-disgruntled girlfriend, who has another two hours before she can leave.

I brief her about my day's earnings; I remind her that everything will be okay. She has trouble believing me when there's an ache in her belly. The second beer I pour into a pint glass and take to an empty seat near the entrance of the café.

Ron usually arrives not long after. Today he comes gingerly through the door and taps my shoulder to get me to join him outside. He only has an hour before having to head back to the wharf for his next whale watching trip—he would like to spend it with a hot coffee, sugar but no cream, and a few cigarettes. His work is exhausting him. He hasn't had a day off in three weeks because he'll be quitting in two more, and needs the money. He has plans for a trip of his own.

It seems that while we were off in Texas he had an altercation with his father. One that began playfully, but ended, after shirts were taken off and punches thrown, with his father wrapping his car around a tree down the road from his property. Ron had gotten into his car with Jessie to leave the situation behind them; Ron's father took off after them, in his ex-wife's car actually, not his, and didn't do so well behind the wheel after a few bottles of wine. The same gentle man from the fishing trip. Afterwards, they had to send him away to a clinic down south. Apparently he has a history of mental illness—a couple of suicide attempts; bi-polar, manic, unmedicated. It is clear that, for Ron, this is what set him off—now *he* is going to travel.

He tells me that he would like to go to Hawaii at some point—to swing in Banyan trees and clip coffee plants to make money; sleep on the beach and in parks. For now he says he's going to Portland, or Eugene—all he knows is that his friend is driving up to Ore. at the end of this two weeks and he can catch a ride for free. He and Jessie can make things work—she'll go to Humboldt for awhile, clip buds from a different sort of plant, then they'll meet up again. His plans are loose, but they are plans nonetheless, and plans that will lead him out of Monterey. Everyone is being led out of Monterey; for one reason or another, or no reason at all, it appears that our time here is limited.

After Ron leaves for the day's second trip, I remain seated on the short, rock wall outside the café. About another hour before Lilly gets off. And after that it will be only another few hours before she falls asleep. Then another few before we wake up to do it again. The job and the routine are wearing on her as they are wearing on Ron. It's tiring and frustrating to be stuck somewhere you no longer want to be—and what if you never wanted to be there in the first place?

The best a person can do is to try to accomplish something— anything. And the best way to do that as I have so adamantly declared before, and now shamelessly declare again, is to *do nothing*.

221

15. THE IDIOT SAINT(and Other Images)

My full name is Kyle Benjamin Constantine Neilseph Fontlajara-Montaigne. I am a man of indiscriminate ethnicity and pure principles. A thoroughbred mutt.

Like the family dog, who will never know the extremes of either happiness or sadness that a human experiences, but will go through life with a vague sense of satisfaction, all the while bringing unlimited joy and affection to his owners, my eyes appear to be calm, complacent, distant.

Being inked into my arm, starting from the inner bend of the elbow(which some call the 'ditch'), is the image of a tree: first the deep and methodical roots that allow the tree itself to live off the nutrients which the Earth provides it; then the thick, gnarled trunk of the tree, twisting up the bicep in a strong, steady procession of black lines; at the upper part of the bicep, the trunk breaks into bowed branches, sparsely adorned with leaves; blowing off the top of the tree, in an arc that follows the natural curve of the shoulder, the leaves make a subtle transformation into birds; one bird has a leaf-like body with a tiny oval head and thin beak, and looks as if he were dive-bombing back down towards the Earth; the next has further transformed, his wings becoming apparent, though tucked, like his head, into his soft, flightless body; the next further still, with his body full of feathers, his wings appear to be gathering the breeze, kept in control beneath them, and he stays suspended in the air-skin just above the faint glow of a halo; the halo is above the head of The Idiot Saint, dressed in holy robes with his arms and hands open to Accept—look closely and you see that he's farting beneath the robe, a silent, relief-bringing fart which is the cause of The Idiot's half-smile; follow the robe down towards his feet, planted firm-ly in the ground, and the last bird appears, noble, stern, and fully developed.

Once the outline of the image is completed, the color comes later. A template suitable for a watercolor: softly muted hues; skin tones, earth tones, and celestial. The belly of that noble bird, there at The Idiot's feet, is white like lamb's wool or milk with a tinge of vanilla; the feathers like a blueberry faded by sunlight.

But this is the superficial part of the process—the intersection of the inner- and outermost parts. Before heading inside, let us take a look outward: An arm. The arm rests over a padded support wrapped in thin, clear plastic that is taped down. Tending to the arm with what looks like a modern quill is a man of Hispanic descent, Catholic descent, in deep concentration. He is in all black, wearing black latex gloves and there is sweat on his brow. Everywhere there is an audible buzz—the sound of the invisible, rapid movement of the quill-tip, and of it repeatedly piercing the skin, leaving behind it a trail of black blood. The man with the sweat on his brow is a topical artist capable of recreating any image you please—from reality or the imagination, if there be a difference. He does excellent work. If it were my arm I would thank him, pay him a compliment, or a tip—but it is not my arm because I am not all there...

A part of me hovers about the room behind the artist where I mingle with the subjects of the hanging photographs—they are all coming to life. A giant butterfly comes unglued from his poster—his outstanding crimson wings flap in slow motion, yet they keep his airborne position stable; Vishnu, from the wall opposite, gestures with all four arms for me to come see his show of greatness—what appears to be a lion's head quivers at his side; a dozen crosses have begun to ooze burgundy sap one droplet at a time; a young woman's ass—detached from her body with the words 'NEVER DIE' written below it, one word per cheek—sways inconspicuously, a slight undulation running from top to bottom, where a few dimples of cellulite look to be half-smiling for the same reason The Idiot is; now returning briefly to The Idiot himself, where off to one side Lilly watches him take shape on the arm; attached to the arm, above it, atop the neck, calm, complacent, distant eyes like those of a dog.

This is where I am—within the eyes, behind them, in the innermost process which is an inaudible conversation going on between The Spirit, The Self, and The Idiot. Words are not used here. The dialogue is a concurrent back and forth of emoting and no one gets confused. There is a great understanding, as if a prayer were being both said and heard, and the answer sent and received instantaneously —a blessing. The only manifestation that this is happening is an incommunicable sense of wellbeing, a feeling that something Godly is within you; but, before these words are formed, they don't seem that contrived, hokey, or false. They feel and sound true. In attempting to describe the feeling and the sound in speech—in confining It to language—the mouth and tongue unintentionally deviate from their original objective, of describing that feeling and sound, because they are worldly components being used to define an unworldly sensation. The furthest they will get is to the start—an enigmatic, *'It is...'*

It is a sunny morning in 'the last hometown in America.' Out the window the birdbath is dry and the trash bins lining the curb are empty. It is payday.

Over the phone I speak with my brother, Aden, who rarely takes up the pen for any other purpose than poetry, study, or to sign for a credit card purchase of the necessities—he tells me that he recently made a drawing. The description exactly matches that of the bled, scabbed, and healed image on my arm—Our Patron Saint. It is not a coincidence; *it* just *is*.

Elated by my brother's revelation, I hang up and clear my insides of a putty-like substance. The consistency of this movement is the result of eating heavily processed foods. Last night we had a casual farewell dinner with Ron and Jessie at a diner-chain. My order was substantial: a quarter-pound hamburger topped with an over easy egg and a side of french fries. The toilet can't flush it all at once. I decide to close the lid and let it rest there for awhile.

The yolk colored light of the sunny morning is waking Lilly up for her day off. In bed, I bring her a simple breakfast of whole wheat toast, fat free cottage cheese, and oatmeal, which is destined to end up only partially finished on the bedside table. I tell her about my brother's drawing and I think that she understands my excitement just as well as I do—which is not well at all. In any case, it possesses an inexplicable quality of absurdity. That alone can make a person happy, and right now we will take what we can get.

Things around the house are on the rocks. Our presence has become an obvious burden to my father's wife. We leave a pan over night in the kitchen; or we forget to break down a cardboard box before putting it into the recycling bin; or we take a shower together while she's cooking dinner; or we don't remove our laundry from the dryer in a timely fashion. Plus, we are still in our early twenties to her *almost* thirty and we have few responsibilities outside of ourselves.

There are a number of other grievances being held against us, only we will never know what they are because she doesn't tell us. Instead, her frustration is taken out in massive flares of temper that are usually directed at her daughter and usually arise for reasons that aren't seen by us. Though, we can still hear her screaming in the other room, "Damnit, Emma! I'm so sick of this—I just want things done *my way!*" (with just a hint of the nasally Minnesotan accent) Then the child starts to cry, of course—because there's no way you can explain to a three year old girl that those disciplinary screams aren't directed at her—and everything is unresolved.

Today there have yet been any disjointed confrontations. Everyone is eerily at peace; yawning even. The only unfortunate circumstance that faces us is that our friends have left. Aside from Ron and Jessie being gone, Zadï made her own ungraceful departure to San Diego after a bad breakup with Gabe; The Archangel now slowly loses his wings in the lost nights of reinstated bachelordom. Sasha got an internship at The County Journal, a literary *local*, and has since stopped calling. Her loneliness is being employed in writing scarcely read human interest pieces and enduring commonplace harassment from her editors. There is little time leftover after a schedule that grueling, except for maybe a few hours here for self-loathing, and a few minutes there for a short talk outside the café.

But, as I said, it is an uncommonly sunny day and a fine day to be alone on one's bike, coasting through the last hometown in America at the speed of conversation, headed towards a destination where a paycheck awaits you in a small, cream-colored envelope.

En route to the florist, the back tire of my bike goes flat. If I take the bike back to the house, then walk into Monterey, I can get to work one hour after my scheduled time. The unforeseen mishap is understandable—one short hour late.

I'm telling this to Vera over the cellphone Lilly bought for me while standing on an uneventful street corner in Pacific Grove, inspecting the inner tube in my back tire for the source of the leak. She is livid. She tells me not to bother coming in, and that she's not sure if she wants me to work for her at all anymore. Then she hangs up. What that means is that she is sure that she doesn't want me to work for her anymore. But, the fact remains that somewhere behind her counter, next to the sympathy cards maybe, there is a check addressed to me that needs to be picked up. A small-summed consolation.

The shit hasn't quite hit the fan, but back at the house it is close. The plumbing is backed up and the bathroom is flooded. I forgot to mention to anyone that the toilet was temporarily out of order. Don't know who pulled the fateful lever, but it was my father's wife who was in there first with the plunger. It is said that she yelled and cursed the whole time—"God-Damnit! I want them out! I'm so fucking sick of them—I want them out!" (She didn't realize Lilly was in the other room.) With her breath held, only expelling it to curse, she tried violently to break up the clay-plug backing up the plumbing. The plunger became inverted; when it popped back into position the brown water splashed onto her arms. It is said that she then yelled one last time that she wanted us out, cursed again, "Ffffuuck!!" then washed her arms and got into the car with her daughter to go for a long drive.

It was then that my poor, loving Lilly rolled up her pant legs and entered the bathroom. Light tears swelled in her eyes, a few overflowed onto her cheeks. The flood water wet the legs of her jeans despite rolling them up. She pushed at the hole in the toilet with the plunger. The toilet's throat gurgled. She couldn't last any longer. She poked again. Nothing happened. She had to get out. She had done her best.

As I come into the house I find Lilly sitting on our couch-bed in a robe while her laundry cycles in the wash. The bathroom door is closed; the light and fan are on. I kiss away my embarrassment and close the door into our room, leaving Lilly there alone. A blue bandana is tied around my nose and mouth—only my eyes can be seen like the wild eyes of an old western bank robber. Plastic bags are wrapped around each of my hands and arms. I am ready to do the job myself. One more deep breath and I am inside the bathroom. The door locks behind me.

Twenty minutes later. I am in the shower, sitting down. Hot water comes down over my head, which is rested between my knees. Only a little vomit has come out. The water follows my hair and falls into the tub without getting in my eyes. My hair has grown too long. My eyes are wide open, watching the water channel off my head in an array, then following its course into the shower drain. All of the plumbing is running smoothly. The toilet is back in order.

At the kitchen sink I finish brushing my teeth. On the dining table I see that the mail has already come today. My cousin from Washington sometimes writes me, Mima occasionally sends something, but mostly the only mail I get is bank statements that always say the same thing— "you don't have any money, you never will have any money, and, by the way, you owe us some of that money you don't, and never will, have." Flipping through the stack of envelopes anyway, I'll be damned if there isn't a long, formal looking letter from The City of Monterey Public Library, addressed to one 'Leon Font.'

Above, my name has already been stated in full. 'Leon' is not among the long line. Very clearly and deliberately printed on the front of the envelope, the mistake is disheartening. In a jagged, diagonal line I tear it open across the back, and remove the letter by pinching it in the middle, bending it, and pulling it out through the hole I've created.

Dear Leon:

> Thank you for submitting your application for the position of Library Page with the Monterey Public Library. The search drew a large number of candidates, and our decision was a difficult one.
>
> We have selected another candidate who best meets the requirements of the position and the needs of the Library. We very much appreciate your interest in the position. Your name will remain on the eligibility list for six months or until exhausted.
>
> We wish you every success in your future endeavors.

Below the body of the letter it is then signed, sincerely, by the woman who shook my hand, promised me a job, forgot my name, and broke her promise.

16. FORT ORD

I'd like to say the whole thing burned down, or blew up. One less deteriorating structure to worry about at Fort Ord—it would save time and money, and it might be just the accelerator the restoration process needs.

But to say that not only induces suspicion of my guilt, it is misrepresentative of the real damages incurred. In actuality, it was a small fire that burned, and is still burning, outside of a low, vacant building on the sea-facing perimeter of the utterly abandoned military base. The damages caused by the fire thus far are minor when compared to those preexisting, and mostly smoke-related. There is a lot of smoke. Like a tight, sinuous column of bats, it flies into the sky in a call for attention. The response is non-urgent.

The original, beautiful plot of land which first comprised Fort Ord—situated between Marina(north) and Seaside(south)—was purchased by the U.S. Army in 1917. The eclectic topography was ideal for cultivating young men to be well-rounded and disciplined soldiers. The young men were sent there for small arms and hand-to-hand combat training before being deployed to war as soldiers. Discarded shells littered the training grounds and young men were prepared to die. By the early 1940's, when the property had expanded to roughly 28,000 acres, nearly doubling its original size, barracks had gone up and Fort Ord was considered a permanent military post. Ammunition continued to be unloaded, explosives were buried in staged battle areas, and trained soldiers continued to be shipped off to different Wars. In 1994 the base was abruptly closed due to military downsizing and excessive contamination of groundwater, soil, and air.

As accurate or inaccurate as this brief history may be, it does not explain what can now be seen on the grounds of what is still referred to as Fort Ord. It is a frightening and mysterious sight of degradation and suspension. Live rounds are scattered precariously amongst spent ones. Houses are gutted; mattresses and children's toys are pulled onto deserted roadways and overgrown lawns. Church steeples sag into the broken pews. Schools are partially demolished by vandalism—only their playgrounds are unscathed. Deer droppings are found on top of squatters' boxes and blankets. Human droppings, either a squatter's or a bored teenager's, are found in a refrigerator. The community theatre, for whatever reason, retains a highly functional stage. A giant swimming pool breeds insect life in its deep-end; shattered glass in its shallow. Graffiti is scrawled over entire walls, entire buildings, a number is given for a good time. A suitcase is left open to display its contents of one book(neither Testament). Doors are yanked from hinges, holes are bashed into everything. Some asbestos particles have been knocked out

227

of the air with the drunken piss of University students—whose campus was inexplicably built on the grounds—yet several more particles still hang in the plaster and tile dust. Toilets are a third filled with stagnant water—someone has taken a shit here, too.

There is an arrested air of the ungodly hour, wherein everyone seemed to have stopped what they were doing and left. It stretches the entire expanse of Fort Ord, yet constricts the intake of breath; the surroundings can be inhaled only in precise, ironed-and-starched, tight-lipped breaths. And none of it makes it out of the lungs. It is the black tar residue of a lost heyday and the ignored backtrack of a self-important, forward plunge.

A man in a red shirt disappears behind the building where the fire is burning. The red shirt is the only detail that could be made out. Authorities have not yet arrived on the scene. The fire is running out of fuel and the flames slowly go down. In the hot ash are the charred remains of a well-paid hooker—it's awful. The man in the red shirt will never be caught. No one ever saw him at the scene.

17. DEATH COMES FOR A GOLDFISH

Above Cannery Row, on Hawthorne St. in New Monterey—where it dead ends at the presidio, number 140 1/2—we have moved into a one-bedroom shack with a full tub and a tiny, but quaint, front yard. The property is nestled behind the roof of a glass shop, and between two apartment buildings. With the high wooden fence surrounding the property, though, and the big tree where the possum family lives, the illusion of privacy is retained.

The house is part of a temporary arrangement we've made with Lilly's boss, Sandy. She is subletting it to us at no cost while the lease overlaps that of her new place. She had to move somewhere larger to accommodate the recent arrival of her seventy-two year old mother. The only stipulation in our agreement is that before we leave we must clean the house thoroughly.

The transience of our current situation does not stop us from making the house livable, or calling it ours. Our mattress and box spring are in the bedroom along with an antique, collapsible tray table being used as a nightstand, and our little red table. Our clothes hang in the closet, our books make up neat piles against the wall, our dishes are in the cabinets, and our food is in the fridge. We found an old solid wood coffee table on the side of the street, which now serves as our extremely low kitchen table. For chairs we have milk crates.

Little, personal things are popping up, too—trinkets. An old charm bracelet inside of a tiny corked bottle. A short bamboo stalk in a miniature chipped vase. A birthday card, handmade with construction paper and a felt tip pen. A bundle of three, six-inch long, decorative corncobs. All Lilly's things—heartbreaking things.

Lilly says that all we are missing is pets—she wants goldfish. She drags me to the pet store and says we both have to pick one out. She immediately finds hers. It is the most erratic fish in its tank, a Telescope Eye Goldfish with one giant eye and one tiny eye, just like how she draws anything with eyes. She already has all the supplies in her arms, and is calling over an employee to net her fish.

My casual, disinterested stroll by all the tanks of dirty, unremarkable, and short-lived goldfish has come to a halt. I am fixated with a reddish Bubble Eye Goldfish, who looks either absolutely content or just stupefied by his existence. Two-inches above the bottom of the tank, his face pointed at the rocks, he occasionally nose-dives into the blue shit-and-algae-catching rocks, then returns to his position. The employee that has come to put our fish into their traveling vessels—the clear plastic bags filled two-thirds with water, one-third with air, then tied at the top—is a young Indian boy with recently removed braces and a mustache. I point directly at the fish I want, but he doesn't know why I would want that fish, so assumes I was pointing off to the left and grabs the wrong one. I correct him, pointing again— "No, I want that sad fish back there that's barely moving." He has no choice now but to net the right fish and give him to me to take home.

At home we set the fishbowl in the window-shelf above our bed— it is a bay style window which comes out from the house like a glass box. During the day the bowl will heat up and the fish will have to be moved, but at night they will be cool and close to us.

We let our goldfish gently into the water in the fishbowl. The Telescope Eye Goldfish is Tu. The Bubble Eye Goldfish is Rebbe. As they meet each other for the first time, I notice that Rebbe's right eye is injured from when the Indian boy with the mustache let him slip out of his fingers and onto the floor near his station. He asked me if I wanted a different fish, seeing as he had dropped mine, but I didn't. Now I see that the protective sac over Rebbe's right eye is deflated, and looks like it is adhering to the scales around the eye. It will never heal completely. An enormous amount of pity comes over me.

Five seconds after the first time, I think they meet each other for the first time again. They swim in circles, half-circles, and zigzags, trying to acquaint themselves with their new home. And each other. We turn out the lights and lay below them in bed. Every so often we can hear them come to the surface.

An ancient, untended lemon tree is behind the house next to a land-locked boat. It grows fruit the size of tetherballs. It is aligned perfectly with the position of the window above our bed so that the healthiest, thickest part of the tree is framed. The fishbowl appears to be resting in its branches.

The daylight is shifting further into the morning hours and night falls sooner. The glow from the distant sun softly illuminates the varying densities of the fog. We feed the fish and move their bowl to the little red table where the sun, if it shows, can't get to them. We lock the door to the shack behind us, our few belongings safe, wipe the dew off our bike seats with the sleeves of our coats, and begin the slow, downhill ride into Monterey.

Past the bocce ball courts at the park near the wharf, past the gelato shop, past the fountain at Portola Plaza, and past the Alvarado street cleaners we arrive at the café. You'd think the streets would be cleaner with the frequency in which they are swept and sprayed. The birds will never stop having to shit, though. The bums will never stop needing a place to piss.

At six-thirty in the morning there is already a line formed at the café entrance. They don't open until seven. On the short rock wall in front, near the newspaper dispensers, I politely stay out of Lilly's way inside as she prepares to open, and take in the day's first sighting of a bird—a little, black bird flying nowhere. Nearby, Radio, an eccentric and bigoted war veteran, wearing fatigues rolled up to mid-thigh, performs his morning stretches before beginning the daylong conversation with himself. Pushing a shopping cart down the middle of Pearl Street is a homeless man with a raging boner—he wants to know the time. From behind me comes an old, bald chef, in full apparel except for the hat, with his steely eyes set on Today's paper. Fifty cents go into the coin slot. He steps back—"seventy-five cents?" (turning to me) "Can you believe this? They raised the price to seventy-five cents for this piece of shit. Seventy-five cents, for a piece of shit!" He sticks his hands into the pockets of his white and blue striped chef pants and goes around the corner—he comes back with the difference in his palm. Two dimes and a nickel go in the slot. He opens the door, grabs his piece of shit paper, then lets the door slam shut. He mutters to himself, *"motherfuckers."* Then returns to wherever it is he's come from behind me.

Not five minutes later a black escalade pulls up to the curb and a broad, waddling black man gets out in a black, flat brimmed hat and bright-white shoes. He approaches the news dispensers with his seventy-five cents ready. "How you doin today?" he asks me. ("Fine, sir— yourself?") "Ah I'm doin alright. You need a paper?" He is holding the entire stack of papers in his hands, including the display. I decline. Poor reviews. He sets his loot in the passenger seat of his escalade and drives off. I look over to where my quiet friend is sitting. A heavyset, post middle-aged white man with a big grey beard, a hot cup of coffee, an ice water, and his third cigarette. He seems to have not witnessed the misdemeanor theft. He is staring into the sky where the sun still barely shows through sections of fog. The street cleaners have turned the corner onto Pearl. The second morning-bird drifts by, following the course of the first.

The Pearl District, as some have started calling it, is an area of shops in downtown Monterey just off Alvarado St. It is made up of two banks, a French bakery, a tailor, a photography studio, a German-Italian restaurant, the cantina, the printing shop, and the café. It is a reflection of the Peninsula as a whole—a microcosm of a microcosm. There is a recession here. The economy is bad.

   Standing in the uneven dirt parking lot of the printing shop, Leon Basho The Printer lights up a Basic, long and skinny, slight looking like his fingers, and squints his eyes with disgust. Recently, his daughter suffered a fainting spell while walking down the hill from her house—journalistic stress and no food in six days; there was quite the buzz around the café. And then there are his two sons who are troubled in the way all adolescent males are. But he doesn't talk about these things—in his private life he adheres to stoicism. What Leon Basho The Printer talks about his having to bring in business, for fuck's sake, by writing copy for goddamn customers for free—but he's just the printer, goddamnit. He feels like a 500 dollar hooker giving blowjobs for 50. If he's going to get fucked, he says, he wants to get paid.

Everywhere it is the same. Everyone is getting fucked. Everything is bad.

The hub of all activity in The Pearl District is Village Café, where I am a regular installment. Where the milk is always steaming, the grinder clicking, the coffee brewing. Where the baristas work harder than anyone and no one is satisfied. Where the customers are always complaining, yet keep coming back. This is where Monterey congregates. I am able to recognize every citizen's face now. Lilly can name their drinks.

   Although the customer base is loyal, stable, the café is hurting as well. Sandy, who I finally understand to be part-owner, has to work a regular morning shift to save money. It's not that people want less, they just can't afford more. No one tips. Hell, I even work on an as-needed basis. They have me take out the trash, brew coffee, buy bags of ice from the grocery store, peel apples. Sometimes it is my duty to kindly ask homeless people with raging boners who just want their disintegrating cups filled with half and half to please leave—or to remind old Hunckley Hunckley Jr., when he comes in reeking of piss with his blowup sex doll in tow, that he is no longer welcome here; or to standby during an oust of an irate customer; or to subdue the in-house baker after an argument. She is about my mother's age, Tessa The Baker, so I approach her in the same way I would Mima—jokingly rubbing her shoulders, asking her to explain to me what's wrong. There is always something wrong at the café. Whenever Sandy runs into me she tells me that I need to devote my talents, if there are any, to writing a book about the café. She'll write her story from behind the counter, I'll write mine from an outside perspective. It will be about the life of the characters who reside in the fog-laden hills of the once alluring Monterey, and who comprise the clientele of The Café. She will fund me in the way that I am rewarded for my other services: coffee, espresso, sandwiches—sometimes beer.

An old instructor of mine once said that all one needs to write is to write what one knows. Anything outside of that is Fiction and the world doesn't believe in fairytales anymore—though it is in need of a new one. From the inside out, what I know best is my surroundings and my Self. Much of my time is spent at the café. Much of what is not can still be accredited to the café—the people I know, the jobs I've fallen into.

Essentially, Sandy, you've asked me to write a book about what I know. And, in all respects, this is That Book.

It is rare to find service anymore that can be remunerated with an exchange of service or small goods. People are preoccupied with cold, hard, real money. The phenomenon of the deliberately impoverished generation is a negative preoccupation—they refuse to work, but they will sit all day with a cardboard sign that begs for *your* money.

The only decent approach to making money is to first realize that it is not the money you need. The necessities of a good life are invaluable and few.

I have integrated myself into the community. The town is beginning to remember my name. I am able to eke out a good, honorable existence through a small network that begins and ends with The Village.

Mornings I connect with the hobos of Monterey. A short walk through The Pearl District and I am in their restroom for a holy constitutional. Copies of The County Journal are piled on the changing board, the toilet paper dispenser, the hand dryer, the sink. If the toilet paper is out, The Journal is conveniently on hand. Down at The Wharf they are being used to wrap fish.

A short walk back to the working class. At the café, Bad Bobby, the contractor that J.L. called a nigger, is finishing his cup of coffee and is ready to take me on at fifteen an hour to be his assistant. Bobby is a typical contractor—he's been everywhere, seen and done everything, and knows the details and backstories besides; or at least knows someone who does. He can fix your bathroom, your computer, your car, and your brain.

Most of our day consists of being between jobs—driving from one site to another, picking up supplies. Hardly any work gets done, but it gives him a chance to impart his wisdom to me. He tells me I'm working for an old dog now, so I gotta listen closely 'cause there's some shit he can tell me that I can't learn elsewhere. He's a Vietnam Veteran—must have been thirteen or so in service if my calculations are correct. Says he used to carry twelve frags at a time, six pairs of clean socks, two M16s, and a pistol. He's a bad motherfucker, he's seen some shit. He also has four master's degrees in various sciences, and is not just the best driver in the world, he is also the safest 'cause he learned to drive in Germany where the standards are different—shit, he even raced professionally over there for awhile. "Problem with Americans," Bobby is telling me, "is everyone thinks they're entitled to everything so no one is courteous to each other. You see it in driving. Everyone rushes around and they think, 'oh, well I have the right of way so I should be able to be here and no one else'—and they're always ready for a fight in America. In Germany everyone on the road is responsible for everyone else, so what you have is a more courteous people and less accidents."

After a long car ride where my wages have really been earned, we pull up to the adobe house in Pebble Beach where I am helping build a bathroom from the floor up. The house is owned by a man named James Weisse—a man who has worked little, but lived well since early in life due to a large inheritance. Last night he raised his voice at Bobby because the job is taking too long. He told him he needs to speed up the work so the bathroom can be done in time—in time for what? Bad Bobby Philosopher, the old dog that he is, kept his cool. "When they start screamin' at you like that," he explains, "you jest let 'em heat up—you let 'em say whatever they want to say, but it's gonna cost 'em. That runnin' of the mouth last night, it's gonna cost old Jim. He thinks he's half-Jew? Well I'm *whole*-Jew. I'm gonna dig so deep in that pocket book of his now. I'll let him run his mouth as much as he wants, but with that bill left wide open like that, you bet I'm gonna charge his ass for it." Old Jim is at home today. Bad Bobby refuses to work while he's here.

We haven't accomplished much, but it looks like it just *might* rain. Besides, Bobby doesn't much feel like working today anyway so we call it quits early. We drive back to the café where he logs my hours on an index card that is nearly filled on one side. He grabs his second cup of coffee today and tells me he'll see me tomorrow.

* * *

Afternoons I spend with Sandy's mom, Babs. She has short-term memory loss from a series of small strokes and there is cancer everywhere in her body. Despite her health, she is good humored and enjoys my company. She was a flirt in her day, and still keeps in practice—even if she can't remember your name. She likes to tell Lilly what *she* would do if I were *her* boyfriend. She refers to our outings as 'dates.'

Our dates usually consist of a doctor's appointment, a haircut, light grocery shopping, or small errands. After, we sit together at the café for awhile and have a bite to eat. A couple of hours at most, depending on how she feels. She has good days and bad ones. Some days she tells me about the Inn she used to own in Vermont, the guests she remembers, the parties she threw; or she tells me about her ex-husband, or other love interests, or just the clothes she used to wear out on dates. Some days she doesn't care to tell me anything.

Last week we celebrated her seventy-third birthday. Lilly and I made her cards and took her out to eat. It was the most fun she's had in a long time. She joked that she may be way over the hill, but she was going to make sure it was a slow, gradual descent the rest of the way to the bottom. Only a few days before, when I dropped her off at the end of our date, she told me she just wished it was over—she felt so sick; she was ready to go. It was a particularly bad day.

There is little variation in the overall routine. Bad Bobby will never finish the job, so there will always be work—it doesn't matter if he has to repeat himself. Babs' health will fluctuate; she will be in and out of the hospital. One sad day down the line Babs will not come out and she will be missed.

Things will get better, and they will get worse. Things will continue to happen in between. The dissatisfied customers will always return to the café.

The dead hours at the café are the midday ones right before Lilly gets off. A few predatory men will linger in the otherwise empty café. The tables will be wiped and the floors swept. The refrigerators will be restocked, new coffee brewed. I will sit on the short rock wall outside, further breaking my father's heart, waiting to leave with Lilly.

It is this time of day now and I am sitting on this rock wall and the condition of The Pearl District has apparently had no effect on my wellbeing. In two weeks I have somehow accumulated enough money to embark on my trip with Lilly, and leave this all Right Here.

Coming down the sidewalk is a man I have not seen in months and may never see again. It is the heavyset, round bellied, goatee and leather jacket, ex-military poet—Good Pablo. He has trimmed off a few pounds and his face is clean-shaven. Little else has changed, he tells me, except that he no longer smokes or drinks.

I ask him how his book of poems turned out. He says that it was rejected sometime during the editing process—it never made it to the press. There is no book. He is not discouraged by its failure. He does not consider it a setback. In fact, he is in good spirits and says he joined the Salinas Poetry Consortium. He will carry on with his writing, his life.

Lilly's shift is over and she is in a hurry to leave but Pablo has a gift for me before we can go. From the trunk of his car he presents me with two very expensive, very strong bottles of red wine that were given to him by a Basque friend of his whose family owns a local vineyard. He has no use for it anymore. I accept the bottles of wine with quiet, enormous gratitude and tell him goodbye.

With one bottle to each of us, Lilly and I ride away from the café. First down Pearl St., then around the corner at Alvarado, then past the fountain at Portola Plaza, then past the gelato shop, then past the bocce ball courts where we have to dismount our bikes to walk them past the presidio, up the hill.

For a moment we stop. A curious thing is happening on the sidewalk: an injured, flightless bee is puttering about on the pavement, going in circles; no explanation, just small, sad, flightless circles—Lilly moves him out of harm's way to the grass at the edge of the sidewalk. There is nothing else we can do. We go home.

In 1937 a poet by the same name of our Good Friend wrote his own book of poems. Though originally written in Spanish, there is an English translation of one of the lines from one of these poems, which reads: *From one hell to another, what difference?*

The difference tonight is the occasion: Our Anniversary. To signify what length of time we don't know. It is also Valentine's Day. Dinner is set for two on the low kitchen table in our one-bedroom shack. A bottle of very expensive, very strong wine is open. Tu and Rebbe, in their bowl of freshly cleaned water, act as the animated centerpiece.

We observe our holidays out of season because calendar dates are usually irrelevant to their said corresponding events. There is a Spiritual Timeline to which we adhere. There is an incongruity to its times and dates that make the chronology appear far more accurate. It is in the spirit that the Truth is retained; nothing can discount what has certainly happened there.

What is happening now is a weightless pirouette and a sad fight to keep from going belly up. The fish are sick. Their bodies are swollen and their equilibriums askew. They are twirling in their bowl and shitting curlicues. The water is not balanced. There is no way of helping them. This time the poor creatures cannot be saved. We have stopped eating—an insignificant gesture to pay respects.

As Tu and Rebbe struggle with their fate, I explain to Lilly my theory on goldfish. I tell her that goldfish are meant to be starter pets. Children are supposed to be infatuated with them in a small way. They are kept in glass tanks and bowls—they can't be touched. From outside the glass, the child can watch the span of his pet's life in just a few weeks. At the end, the goldfish will tremble, he will swoop down to the bottom of the bowl, and he will exert a final shiver as to tell the child, 'I am done.' And the child will remember this for the rest of their life.

There is no longer hope for Tu. He is gone. His life was lost to a noble cause: in the fulfillment of his destiny as teacher in lesson of death. That is the inscription on his burial raft, which I make by destroying a pinewood box, and forming a sort of triangular mausoleum on top of a long, solid plank. It took me three hours to finish, but we finally seal him in with hot glue—Lilly leaves a small bouquet of wildflowers inside with his body. At the water's edge we leave the raft balanced on a rock where, when the tide comes in, it can be swept up by the surf and carried out into the bay.

It is late when we get back, nearly ten. Lilly immediately climbs into bed and is out for the night. Above her head, Rebbe has made a miraculous recovery. He swims around his bowl balanced and orderly; unaffected and steadily. I wonder if he remembers the fish that died here tonight, or if he even remembers another fish at all. Was their coexistence just a tangent to their otherwise disparate realities? which we subjected them to against their will? Or in another month will I find my fish, Rebbe, disoriented and sick, making his final death swoop and shiver, to follow his lost bride?

Behind the house, in a dark, unseen spot on the presidio at DLI, the trumpets interrupt this question with their song. The trumpeter, a soldier I will never know, plays his own rendition of the sleep-song with a hollow melancholy that is drawn out across the Peninsula. The notes are dropped down an octave.

In the song there is a biblical quality about it that is definitive of the night—it resembles an ending. The sound wakes the child in the apartment that hangs over our yard, but its crying soon fades back to the harmless, imperceptible coo of deep sleep. On the adjacent balcony, an old Russian professor smokes a cigarette while waiting for his late dinner. The possum family rustles the tree's branches.

Above my sleeping girl, through the distorted glass of the fishbowl, Rebbe appears twice his size. He is a creature at peace, swimming along with minimal effort, and with that one good, frowning eye of his, he looks as if he were winking at me. It is the absurd wink of an

Idiot: One which does not fully comprehend the entirety of its own meaning, but is vaguely aware of being in on a vast, Holy, ongoing joke.

—November 2008, Monterey, CA

REQUIEM FOR CHRISTOPHER*

Thru the cold window fog is a distant Hell star—a red pulse of blood and fire, Satan's beacon blinking for his sinners—it boils & spits & coughs over the trains in the yard...one moans on South, like a widow wailing in the night, and another is stopped for its six months of pending—once a spark, glimmer, shine of all America, now's gone numb for its rusting. The glass panes are streaked with forced winter tears (from where I've drawn pictures with my finger tips) that drip, droop down in sudden magic tragedies, and on the sill they gather into puddles of salt-ridden 'membrances to mourn the death of a little boy....

I was sick like he was, desperate from years of haunting nightmares, and especially from having happened across Mikey, who had reached the age of his brother, Christopher, when he had died, and I cried hideously and openly over the startling resemblance he bore to him. And it was he whom found Christopher so many Decembers ago, lifeless in a bed of bloody sheets, shotgun smoking and hot on the floor, sad scribbled last words splattered with red—too private and gentle to ever be whispered even amongst all the Angels in Heaven.

That's what I saw in my feverish, hopeful, sorry, rants... wandering thru the cemetery on the first day of Spring—my collar pulled in close to protect me from the snow flakes that floated down over Lincoln like quiet morbid fortunes. I didn't know, and don't still, if Christopher had been buried there—he could have been returned to the air, and rain, and trees, in one magnificent freeing motion of his Mother's hand opening to allow his ashes to be carried away back into everything. Had I been among the pews at his service I would know, but I hadn't attended the funeral, not out of disrespect, nor lack of an all-consuming pain, but (guiltily) out of pure fear and the possible realization of death's imminence over myself and my family (this being much earlier than my understanding of life thru death, which is the Earthly sufferings, sorrows, joys, sins, repentance, love, and compassion of our broken condition, which can only truly be appreciated thru Faith). Tho having been absent from the ceremony, I have found myself several times, in nightdreams and in daydreams, with my hands on his casket, helping carry it along to its final resting...but the dreams never end, the

---

* As mentioned in the "LOWER-SIDE" section of the book, this is an unedited stream of prose for the dearly departed, Christopher Thomsen.

procession just continues along forever like a sad death march into Hell, and I wake in a panic of my own cold flesh sweat...more often, in my dreams, he appears to me in black, standing alone and trying unsuccessfully to speak to me; his jaw has been reset by some delicate ethereal surgeon, but is still unable to form the words burning behind his clear eyes—like he's back on my front porch again in drug-induced hilarity....

He and Curt rang the bell at my parents' home and I answered the door to see 'em both there giggling from huffing at cans of duster or gulping down cough syrup—(I feel so bad today, now...)in my upset and confused childish stupidity I pushed both of them to the ground, their fallen bodies crushed the frozen grass and I stood over them—don't remember what was said—as they rolled around laughing and laughing...it was weeks later when snow had gathered into massive heaps in cleared parking lots and grown filthy and hard that my Ma picked me up—from being out goofing with the other boys, yelping and cracking in our early adolescence—I got into the car to feel my chest crushed, and heart-go-to-throat, from the overwhelming pressure of a yet-spoken tragedy, darkness, suicide...I'd left my body in foresight of learning something awful, that had already begun to settle into my bones, so my Mother's voice seemed to echo thru all of the eternities that may exist between body and soul....

"you know Christopher..." and I did know him, well enough to have exchanged young boy punches to the arms and to have rummaged thru his father's things in the basement, in search of a single pornographic video that we watched with curious gaping mouths—I was the reason Christopher became acquainted with Curt and Larry, which was a friendship that began in sneaking cigarettes and smoking them in tunnels—just puffing them really, never letting the smoke slip down into our lungs to rest & rot there—and taking midnight walks over to girls' houses to throw rocks at their windows and hope for them to emerge, soft & perfumed & shy, to kiss one of us lucky boys on our young dreaming mouths...but it all ended in their parting from my company to run off and get high on stolen pot and cough syrups and pills and anything lying around their houses; and eventually resulted in Christopher's violent death—which I don't blame the drugs for, but rather the hopelessness that can only be felt when coming down from a high, or a drunk(or in the moments following an orgasm brought on by yer own hand); and all of the little abuses from his supposed best friends, whom used him for the pinches of grass he would take from where they were hidden in his father's cigarette packs, and as an outlet to relieve them of their self-doubt by pushing him further into his enveloping emptiness—these friends whom were destined to forget him—And the blood is also on the negligent souls that only cried their

239

own selfish mean-nothing tears, tho all the while sensing his impending doom..."yes, s-w-e-e-t-h-e-a-r-t—" he's dead. He's dead.

I'm sick like he was, mesmerized by the throbbing tip of the devil's penis, ready to spurt its scalding semen over the horizon in sheer ecstasy—a celebration of waning Faiths...*waahh-eeer-trchtrch-trchtrch-bng-bng-BNG!* the train pulls in screaming murder! rape! and flop-pangs its last breath to unload its passengers....I see their lips move in saying "see yeh....", "see yeh...." to end the casual acquaintances they'd made while aboard—and it's with great disgust and self-loathing that I remember those words, too, as the last I spoke to a boy, never-to-be-man...a child so hopeless and gloomy to have relinquished his rights to bare witness of all those could've-been years(the ones I've now seen) of a passing death, which slowly ends in the birth to eternal life....

Mrs. Kriezel was the natural object of our innocent fantasies, she was younger than our other teachers, and slim, and had breasts—we all had her for third hour, never paying any attention to the days' lesson, but just gawking at the pale woman-skin that barely shown under her shirt when she would lift her arm to write on the board—sometimes we'd be fortunate enough to find her stretching at her desk when we came in, and we'd drool and rejoice in the perfect view of her beautiful naval. She sat quietly tho, in the back of the ill-fated room, head over to-be-graded tests, or maybe pictures of her husband and sweet kids...the bell had rung for class to begin a few minutes before, but everyone just shoved and teased and joked while we waited for her to take attendance...Christopher spoke so softly to her that it would've been impossible to eavesdrop on their conversation, making it particularly difficult were the 20-so thirteen year olds messing about like mad before they'd be silenced for the 45! minutes of class....kids have gotten cuts, stomachs have been upset, heads hurt, fevers had, and it was these usual ills which I suspected as Christopher walked to the door— "where yeh goin?" I might've been the only one that noticed him leaving, maybe just the only one that cared or wondered—"home...." he said to me, like he'd said so many times before so that I just said, "alright, see yeh...." to him and went back to whispering newly learned obscenities...now knowing that he meant *home* to be the grave—death on to death—he walked there in heavy, lonesome chains, the song of my *see yeh* guiding him into everlasting pain...his blood is in my mouth, and on my tongue—his blood stains me as well.

Factory smoke, thick and grey, pours over the red eye of evil; but its horrible glow still shows thru the smog like a hungry demon, grinding and snapping its ugly teeth in anticipation of gobbling up its unsuspecting prey...my single candle burns with the hope of all-Saints in the window, and makes a wavering chant of golden light on the glass to the sweet Virgin that she might bow with me in prayer for my lost soul, and that of my beloved friend.

ave, ave,
ave, Maria

It was a few weeks after his death, when I returned home from tracing the invisible bloody footsteps along Christopher's last sad walk home from school, that I found an old picture—it had been packed away years before on the upper shelf of my closet...I stood on my bed to reach the shelf, and searched it unaware of my own intentions—I opened boxes, and shoeboxes, until in one I found a plainly marked brown cylinder that had been sent to my address thru the mail, and popped off its white plastic top to unroll the photograph inside: it was taken four years earlier on the soccer field atop the plateau behind the houses of Thunderbird Estates, a few minutes West of my own neighborhood—the whole team wore red jerseys and matching socks over their tiny shin guards...we had all yet to begin adolescence, so still had whiney unchanged voices—you could see it in our faces...in Blake Schumacher's, there with his tall hair and broad forehead—an amazing defender; and in mine there, in the middle with ornery grin, competetive bastardly eyes; and then there, in Christopher's. Christopher Thomsen, standing inconspicuously in the back row, with his little teeth smiling whitely beneath his round face, outwardly happy—but even in his young happy face it was hard for me, even then as a well-meaning little boy, to see past the dark, utterly frightful implications of finding the picture on that particular day...as I stood looking at his house earlier, my heart torn to know this to be the end of his walk, and that mine must trudge on elsewhere thru his wake, his ghost must have been peeking out of the blinds of his bedroom window overlooking the front sidewalk—stuck in Hell's everlasting moment with barrel in mouth, teary eyed and alone—and he must have seen me as he peeked out of that corner, and deserted his looking-post to tug at my soul, and at my hand to say, *'just help me...please, help me...'* and then followed me home, from where our paths once split but now merged again, to lead me to my closet where his plea changed at the picture's discovery, *'look! see! but you must help me....'*

I can no longer make out anything beyond the window—nor are there tears in its fog...its wavering chant continues, but is subdued by the startling transformation of glass to mirror, whose reflected image is not my own...my hair is blonde-brown, and short, no longer the black unwashed mess which I have come to recognize—I have become soft,

241

and my face is much younger, my sharp chin receded, and my teeth now have dull silver braces...I close and reopen my mouth, but they still reappear.

I am thirteen years old, and my name is Christopher James Thomsen—my eyes are unimaginably tortured, and my mouth is dry with ash and dirt, as I have not spoken in quite some time:

> *I showed myself to you that night humbly, as you showed yourself to me that day. I could not yet speak—as these are my first utterances since death—so I stood, and said nothing. I was allowed my face restored, in the light in last you remembered it—tho one finger was missing, and remains so, as it's been ostracized to its trigger, where it has mocked me relentlessly in my silence...I showed myself to you that night in order to ask your consent, that you might assist in guiding me back from darkness...my heart has been judged, and said pure, just overtaken. And you received me with tears which you only knew in your sleep, so that over time my tongue has been freed, and I am able to speak again, to ask that you help me still, to be received by the grace of your Father—I am lost, but you can Save me.*

I am unaware if I fell asleep...my eyes regain focus as if just recently waking from a dream, or having their tears dried, to see that the mirrored window has dimmed, and is covered again in hot milky breath—the Hell star remains in its constant pulse, but is now less menacing than it is pitiful...a weak sobbing of exhausted pain. My hands are trembling, and I put them to my taught rough face, and recognize it. I run my tongue over my teeth and feel their undisrupted slime, tho when it nears the back of my throat I cringe to feel that it's sore—which must be the result of the ache in my throbbing ear, as it hums along with the red-time being kept, and the rhythmic chant of the candle, in a longwinded song of death.

Tho it is with an ill hiccup of the brain, and a slight choke—as I am growing progressively sicker in these visions—I cannot ignore the cold sweaty cotton of my shirt that is stuck to my chest and back and arms, being that it is the very same shirt which I wore as I sat up in bed that night, the first of many more terrifying nights, and felt two separate beats in my chest—one forlorn, emanating from somewhere below the simple regards of muscle and tissue; the other guarded, erratically thumping adrenaline thru my body that would wildly burst in instances of sheer panic...I could still feel him perched in the unobtainable realms of my subconscious, awaiting sleep paralysis to corner me on an overlapping plane that I couldn't understand...but for weeks he lay dormant in an unaccounted for vessel of self-pity, as our classmates began to bubble playfully back to normal—the suicide counselors and support groups thinned out, then ceased to exist...the kids wrote with black felt tip pens in bathroom stalls again and laughed, they made out and threw food at each other, and the pins were undone to remove the yellow ribbons that would no longer be worn...clouds of smoke were exhaled from unaffected mouths, rose upwards, then disappeared—and so, too, was Christopher forgotten.

My own pained mouth was incapable of opening, wired shut by the serpent veins of the deceased, to allow his memory to be so easily exhaled into the mushroom cloud of undignified casualty, and get lost in the abyss of too-young deaths...No, it remained stagnant behind my sewn lips, closed into my slow-burning lungs, as I breathed its perfume too deeply, and personally—and like a strange disease it crept thru my sanity, causing lucid nightmares that ever-repeated on my arrival home from school....

My brother Aden, three years my elder, was on medication for a purpose unknown to me—all I knew of it were our father's apprehensive doubts over its benefits, and its necessity, and that there was a correlation between the medication and depression, and suicide...*suicide*: I would open the door with the taste of iron on my worried tongue, and faintly smell the sweat and the sulfur of the macabre bowels of shitting demons that had surely sunken their claws into my brother's heart...where he lay unconscious on his own bed, shotgun absent, but bile spilling from the corners of his mouth onto his cheeks and pillow—his own tormented note written plainly, but horribly, on a scratch of paper that rest on the bedside table...as I had imagined it the previous day, and would imagine it for so long after. I saw my brother awake each morning, and likewise I saw him die—thru the debilitating fear of my imagination, and the constant dull echo of hidden desperation in that persistent thud-ache of a stranger's heartbeat within ...I watched the countless deaths and, in turn, lamented them.

Rain has begun to fill like glass orbs onto the glass plank of the propped open window...breaking on the surface and sliding down into the alley-ocean below—so much has been broken, so much has gone unheard. The timing of the rain, the steady movement with no crescendo—no, just sound, the constant rhythm of the natural cycles—it's impeccable. My brother never died—I, too, am fully alive. Christopher has not been forgotten...I mourn him deeply, and as fully as my capacity to live. Rain, dear rain, freely falling under the moveable pews of this memorial service—the sun dares to yet rise, tho the increasing reflection of its encroaching light, a slight prism from the opposite side of the building, positively points to something—yes, what! My eyes are weak, drained, and troubled with lack of sleep...when I stand(as I have just done) and squint into the horizon for clarity, the reality is denied—a vision takes its place: up three tiers of the subliminal stairs which ascend the bright, damp, quiet room we walk—Christopher and I—one in front of the other...I am leading him. At the top of the third level stand two young men in white robes with white towels draped over their forearms...they instruct us with their eyes to follow them thru the corridor. To our left, over a short, white wall, we can see into the depths of the tiers which we have come—clouds as thick as water are rising, but our pace remains steady, deliberate, as we move toward a door which has just been opened for us. Turning back to look at Christopher, I see that the two men guiding us have taken him by the arms already—they are leading him now into the room behind the door where a semi-circle of similarly dressed men is formed around a white-painted wooden chair. Inside, they seat him in the chair and he is silent—the two men leave his side to return to the door where they nod, then close themselves in—it's over. I am on the outside....

Again I see the horizon, more blue replaces the wispy pinks and lemons, the rain is now evaporating off the early walks—dawn has passed. My heart beats solemnly, one consistent beat. He has escaped me. There is no guarantee of Salvation, no—I am no savior, no angel; I am nothing. But my cries have been heard from their lowest, still...the delirious pains of irreparable pasts are left to memory—*I* have remembered them. This is all that is in my power...to retain the images of all the transient faces, to retrace the coordinates of our being, to contemplate the angles of their intersections, and to pray—Lord, grant me, grant *us* your mercy, pity, strength, awareness, compassion, forgiveness...Lord, by your Will we are thankful for all that you have given us. Glory be in your name—of the Father, the Son, and the Holy Ghost. Amen.

As the sun now fully streaks the sky and ground and buildings, my last word of prayer consents that my mourning may cease...and in the strange elation of that final vision I find the energy to draw the window closed, and stumble over to my bed, where I now collapse. Sleep awaits me, angels. The terrifying night is behind us....

—2 December 2006, Lincoln, Nebraska

VOL

THE SHORTS

UME

II

THE DOGS COME WHEN YOU'RE GONE
(2009)

For
l. wilkins

*****Travel Itinerary*****

#0000flight0000#
2 June
///Flight#579 Departs 8:30am Austin, Tx-----
-----Arrives 10:20am San Jose, Ca-----
Flight #7147 Departs 12:20pm San Jose, Ca-----
----- Arrives 2:12pm Seattle/Tacoma,Wa///

#1230drive0321#
* * * 5 June * * *
(Tacoma, Wa) To Rexburg, Id

* * * 7 June * * *
(Rexburg, Id) To Breckenridge, Co
Via American Fork, Ut

* * * 9 June * * *
(Breckenridge, Co) To Lincoln, Ne

#0004bus4000#
* * * 11 June * * *
(Lincoln, Ne) To Austin, Tx
Via The Southbound Bus Line

FROM: LINCOLN NE
TO: AUSTIN TX

*** CITY ***		***SCHEDULE***
LINCOLNNE		BHL 0120
OMAHA	NE	JL 0501
ROCK PORT	MO	JL 0501
KANSASCITY	MO	JL 0803
* * * 12 June * * *		
NEVADA	MO	JL 0803
JOPLIN	MO	JL 0803
TULSA	OK	JL 0803
OKLAHOMCITYOK		JLP 0803
ARDMORE	OK	GLI 0803
DENTON TX		GLI 0803
DALLAS	TX	GLI 0897
WACO	TX	GLI 0897
AUSTIN	TX	GLI 0897

****

#1000:
(Tacoma, Wa) To Rexburg, Id

"I am all alone in this. There is no one here to dot my 'i's, cross my chest, or finish me off. I am completely free, weightless, at risk of being carried away, floating off into the dark space behind the brain where the idea of God both lives and dies, and where creation itself can be ended abruptly, at any time, like a television set effortlessly being turned off. A simple electronic shift from image, action, and movement, then a backwards flash that's followed by the clear, grey void— and then what?

"They say that he who thinks about that dark space behind the brain will go mad; that his skull will crack and his flesh and bones will be sucked into the opening as if it were a vacuum. In the same way that a sharp pain in the left arm signifies a heart attack, an early sign of madness is to have a sensation like swallowing your tongue. The throat swells up and tightens, and the good little Christian boy looking into the mirror thinks that his face is turning blue because he's scared that he really exists, how he really exists, so prays to the God he no longer knows anything about to slow the speed of his racing heart, to grant him some serenity. Then those boys grow up.

"And here I am, alone, hurrying across interstates unknown, waiting for the storm to start in. There is no one else headed in this direction(towards the storm) and it's been grey-blue, sick dusk for nearly 100 miles now, but I'm still able to breath and there aren't any pains in my arm. Let me look at my face: the colors are normal even if the face could look better, prettier, but it is what it is; there isn't any food between my teeth at least. I imagine that if there were it would've been expelled by now anyway with all this rambling...

"I can speak so easily though because *I am alone*. Good and alone, dictating into the mechanical ear of a digital recording device that cost me twenty dollars that I couldn't afford except in heaven. It's propped in the center console of the car I'm driving, right next to a photo strip

251

with four pictures, running vertically down the strip, of a sweet faced girl. Please, Little Woman in the picture, tiny black and white creature, come to life. Keep me grounded! Keep my lap warm with your ass and my hands warm with your thighs; keep my thin lips from turning blue. But, first, say your name. Whisper it into my ear so that only I can hear; whisper it so gently that your concentrated breath beats over my drum and slides down into my throat where I can pronounce it for you: **Mar ·i ·belle**.

"I know for a fact, my dear, that you are no virgin, but you can certainly be my bell—that bright, cheerful sound reminding sinners they oughta repent and telling the hungry it's time to eat. Sweet Belle, ringing in my tooth and ear, let me tune my fork to the pitch of your voice—talk with me. And talk quietly, remember, right into my bones until my whole body vibrates with the sound. Don't ask me silly questions either, like whose car is it I'm driving, or why(you know I'll be with you soon enough); instead, ask me what the clouds look like, or if it's raining yet; ask me what I dreamed about last night..."

The sound of heavy rain falling onto the car roof and windshield, wipers rushing over glass, tires rolling on wet pavement, a few distant guitars and echoing voices, hard plastic banging against hard plastic, another bang, a very soft thud; the sound of the microphone rubbing against cotton, or linen—two taps.

"...Can you hear me, Little Woman? The grey-blue clouds of dusk have finally gathered into the full blown night and the rain's coming down like cats and dogs, as the expression goes. Excuse me for having to raise my voice over the storm, but I moved you into the left pocket of my shirt, right over my chest, where you'll be safe and can hear me better. My mom bought me this shirt. I've been wearing it for the past five days. Don't let that little detail make your nose start to itch though—I smell like sunscreen, cigarettes, and deodorant more than anything else, plus the sky-dust smell from the rain is coming through the vents, which is one of the most pleasant scents in this world...it almost makes you feel like you're up in the clouds themselves, propelling yourself along through the fluff on the wet masses of accumulated particles, swimming like a monkey fish.

"Tiny Creature, you know those people who say you'll go mad if you think about the dark space behind the brain? They're the same people who say that heaven is up here. It's impossible to say what the truth is, but it seems a person could easily go mad thinking about this, too. Awhile back there was an exit for a town called *Divine Wisdom*—think any of the town residents could have bestowed me with The Truth?

"I'm only kidding about all this. It's just that I *am* alone and there's no one here to tell me when or where to stop. If I were to stop here I'd be stuck in hell. Do you know what hell looks like? It looks like a stretch of rural highway outside of heaven's gates (Rexburg, Idaho?), where your eyes can't quite focus, the rain has just stopped, and things dart out in front of you in the road.

"There's a large yellow sign on the shoulder that reads, 'Game Crossing.' Consider the two meanings of the word *game*: one is used to categorize certain wild animals; the other describes a recreational activity in which a set of rules apply and a specific goal must be reached. This is purgatory. The objective is to get through, riding straight and narrow at a speed of no greater than 65 miles per hour. A few seconds ago a bunny rabbit shot into the road and I ran him over, crushing him under my front left tire, killing him instantly. I couldn't swerve out of the way in time and now a giant vulture is waiting for me about a hundred feet ahead in my brights—he's not moving from the middle of the road, in direct line to be hit...and at the last, split second he swoops over my windshield, displaying a six-foot wingspan, I swear to God, whatever that means. So the bunny rabbit dies, by my hand and foot, and the vulture lives, doubling his good luck with a midnight snack *gratis*.

"What would you say about all this in the dead of night, speeding towards the Promised Land, Little? When all these ghosts come out of the dark shoulders of the road, and the white vertebrae of the painted road-spine all seem to be breaking off, trying to lead you astray—what would you say then? Don't tell me. Men should never hear the thoughts their women have when they're alone; likewise, women should never hear the thoughts their men have while all by their lonesome. They should only read their letters from the road, look at the snapshots taken from the moving cars, trains, busses, and planes, and happily receive those chance roadside calls from payphones(not everyone can afford a cellphone); the vagrant thoughts themselves are ridiculous, strange, scary, and sometimes just plain dumb. But, as men, we can't change how we are when our women are gone—we can't help but wander off like terrified children exploring the basement, slowly creeping into that almighty dark space behind the brain, that aforementioned clear, grey void, and calling into the hollows, 'Where have you gone, Little Woman?' Intently listening for the echo to return from the walls: 'Where is your God?' Then incorporating that transformation upon our persons as a whole, asking ourselves, 'Where are we now? And what?' But we don't have the straightforward answers that might ease our brains. What we have is an inflammation of the lungs, a burn on the tip of the tongue; tiny fingers on tiny hands, groping along the cold cement walls of basement eternities, taking advantage of whatever chinks we can find, using them as little points of reference, anchoring our thoughts in the unique definition of each recess before we continue forward, upward, so that we can always find our way back down no matter how far gone we are.

"Do you understand, Tiny Woman, that you're at the very bottom of everything? That a half-step outside of the darkness your sweet face serves as a definite and grounded light? An unchanging landmark in my head? All I have to do is tug on this string you've thoughtfully attached to me and soul returns to body; the miniature, blue-glowing version of myself returns to the center of my chest(as one writer described it) and I'm able to plainly, clearly, see the strong curve of your face-framing jawbone, the mole above your upper lip, the scar on your forehead, the shading of your tattoos (even that absurd one behind your ear), the childish down of your skinny thighs just barely catching the light, the 'muffin top' of your hips, as you call it, right before that special time of the month; I'm able to see these things and what's before my very eyes, the 'real', suddenly adheres to gravity, the individual masses of each object securing themselves firmly to the earth in accordance with the law and accomplishing a sense of stability, tangibility. All I ask you to do in return is to give me an occasional, gentle tug from the other end; remind me what it feels like to be pulled on, to be stimulated by the base simplicity of human touch...

"Still, why all this openness of speech, this frank stupidity and randomness of solitude(though brief and disjointed), when I have already said myself, *'women should never hear the thoughts their men have while all by their lonesome'*? Well, Sweet Creature, I'm speaking aloud in this way to soothe your conscience and possibly to soothe my own. You don't have to say anything. I'm well aware of the way you think in my absence, of the things you contemplate, the details you brood over; I know the type of light that's cast on me when we're away from each other, and I know the types of things you imagine me doing in that light, which is enough to break your heart into believing them—and then so what if those things did or did not occur? The damage has been done already, and opinions of me are marred in a way that's not easily ameliorated. But I understand that women, like men, can't change how they are when their men are gone. No one can help but act and think in a very peculiar manner when left to their own devices, when their perception of life expands further than individual or collective circumstance and seems to reflect on the idea of life itself...

"Listen, Little Tiny Creature in these four black and white pictures, and in my head, and somewhere in Texas awaiting my return, what I mean to say right now is that there are no other women waiting for me anywhere and no other strings waiting to be pulled like you think there are. *I am all alone in this.* There's still a long drive ahead, just stay with me—allow me to eliminate the need for potential false accusations and curb your suspicions on a whole. There are plenty of other things in this world a person can worry about if they so choose to, not that I recommend bothering with many of those worries either, but I'm telling you there's absolutely no use in worrying over me.

"...All this while I've been following the highway, squinting, not a car in either direction out here, and I've talked my way into the outskirts of Town Paradise now where the illuminated Mormon temple is visible, trying desperately to look like a star, hanging low in the valley to guide wayward folks into its young, rigid arms. The rain has continued to hold off, but it is, nonetheless, pretty damn cold for June. It's curfew here and all of the soon-to-be engaged couples are saying their goodbyes like something out of the movies(no company of the opposite sex after midnight, I guess, with a one hour extension on Fridays): a couple here is standing by a car, not touching, enjoying their last few minutes of frustrated, chaste flirtations; a promiscuous couple there is walking hand-in-hand along the sidewalk with a shared quilt draped over their shoulders; a group of confused couples—three boys of nineteen and three girls, none of them dating each other just yet, but surely to find themselves married soon to who knows which one—are saying their somewhat awkward, but more or less excited, expectant goodbyes outside one of the girls' apartment buildings(the guys are segregated to apartment buildings three blocks away). The night smells like cold meat in an open-air market. I'm nearly crawling past these couples on the street, harmlessly searching for my sister's address, yet still feeling unrightfully like a predator with my unshaven face apparently against Brigham Young's honor code, even though I know more than a few of those old Latter Day Saints wore beards...

"...And here it is, Little Woman, right across from the university stadium like she said it was, nestled behind another girls' apartment building, nestled behind starter homes for young families whose fathers are still determined to get their degrees—the mothers already have theirs. Do you know what they call it? I'll tell you what cute little name they have for it: M-R-S. Believe me when I tell you that's not some joke I've just made up right now—nor do I even think it's funny—it's just what the girls say around here. But, like I said, I'm here and it's late—past curfew—so goodnight for now...I love you...."

(Rexburg, Id) To Breckenridge, Co
Via American Fork, Ut

"If music's played today it's to be played softly, tastefully. It's Sunday and I'm leaving this odd place in peace. The streets are still. Everyone's in church in almost every building in town, singing hymns and taking the sacrament—torn up pieces of Wonder Bread that's been blessed by young men in second hand khakis, short sleeve shirts, and ties. My sister's somewhere, in one of these buildings, concealing her braces (which she'll only have to wear for six months) and soaking in the doctrine of a basically newborn church.

"She showed me around yesterday in a cold, drizzling rain. Not one coffee shop in its tiny 'downtown'—not that I drink coffee anymore because it makes my heart jump; but good luck finding tea— however, there are two bridal stores, on the same block even. I was taking pictures as we walked and it was strange: I pointed the lens to a spot right behind the glass of one of the shop front windows, and where the mannequin body was cut off at the neck my sister's head app-eared—a reflection, hovering, wearing the dress. She thought it was funny, but I was scared of that pale ghost in the white gown; I wanted to tell it to go away, while at the same time I wanted to ask it, 'Where are you going?'

"Well, that little ghost followed us the rest of the day, into the garden where a hundred thousand proposals have been made and where a young couple was having their engagement photos taken—also, a curious thing, where a stone sculpture of Pan stood at the edge of a fountain opposite The Lady Virgin with a chalked-on blue mustache; through a muddy apple orchard that made me happy, and the art gallery with charcoal drawings of *almost*-nudes(women in sports bras and underwear) which were hung on walls of that crosshatched twine-carpet, scratchy type of fabric that Mormon churches across America always put on their walls. My mom used to tell us not to lean against it because we'd get lice. She even took me past the stairs where our aunt once waited for her returning sweetheart and I saw my sister's bridal ghost converge with my aunt's and they both tripped down the last three stairs into the arms of their beloved, my god...

"...So the music just barely hangs in the background like it's part of the rain that's following me as I tiptoe out of town, leaving my sister behind. But she's more than just a good girl, she's smart. She knows she's sheltered and she knows what that shelter looks like. She told me of some of the issues she has with her *sisters*—we spoke a little...about their blind faith, about the emphasis on minute details, about strict observation here and relaxed judgment there—whatever fits. My sister is a very sweet, reasonable, and spiritual girl; she's not an oaf. She certainly doesn't look Mormon—presuming you know what that bloodline looks like? (And it is a bloodline.) But what does it matter anyway if you can tell the difference between a Utah Mormon and a 'regular Mormon'? It doesn't. My sister will be just fine.

"...I'm in a kind, glad mood today. I listened to the first recording —I won't listen to another until I'm back in Texas—and I sounded insane, depraved, guilty; but today I'm happy. I'm driving on Highway-33, on the same stretch that brought me in, and I am very certain that this is not hell. The blue haze daylight of the casual, gentle storm is illuminating the roadside in its true colors: wet moss greens and lime candy greens, splotches of smooth mud like honey, and rolling up and down onto the horizons and through their folds, floating like half-frozen milk through space, is bright fog, both dense and light, as if it were being pushed down by the slick sky the color of my oldest bro-ther's eyes, heavily holding all that rain. God, it is cold and beautiful. There's no doubt in my mind that if my other brother were here he'd try to fuck it—this landscape. There is no one who would call this *hell*. I clarify this now not to discredit anything I've said previously, but to stress the effect the brain has on its environment. I was as certain of what I saw then as I am now, although my tone is a bit different, a bit clearer. I took on the cadence then of a madman—still, how lucid it was...

"...Although my driving is steady, straight, strictly following the directions to my good friends' home in Colorado—by way of a quick stopover in Utah—I realize that I'm getting off course. I wanted to get back to a question you were going to ask me, Little One—the one right before the rain first started coming down. It was on the tip of your ton-gue; you were holding it there and being very patient with me— you were going to ask me, 'What did you dream about last night?'

"Now I'll give you two answers, because what I dreamt last night is different from what I dreamt when you first tried to ask. Last night's dream was simple, short, but somewhat unnerving. I was in a car— maybe this one, but whose to say it wasn't?—driving along a highway

257

very much like this one I'm driving on right now; in fact, with my friend, the one I'm stopping over in Utah to see *right now*. He was riding
in the passenger seat next to me playing his guitar (with no sound), and
for no particular reason I let go of the wheel. The car stayed straight
for a moment, then began to veer off to the left just as the road began
to curve right. Off a giant, red rock the car soared, slowly, weightlessly,
half-flying almost, but I wasn't scared. I looked at the clouds, calmly
checked my seat belt, and communicated to my friend that he should
brace himself for the landing—he did so simply by *smiling*, and that was
enough. We touched down without any recoil from the impact and
rolled safely to the bottom of a hill covered with clovers and, your
favorite, sunflowers. Suddenly he was gone, my friend, vanished except
for his guitar. It was just me, the car, the guitar, and, for some reason
or another, a portable urinal. Then I woke up, not surprisingly, having
to piss.

"I might believe that I were *still* dreaming if it weren't for what
happened next: before I could rise from the bed to make my jog to the
toilet I heard a soft moan and an exhalation...the sound of someone
turning over in their bed—it was the guy in the bed across from me,
one of my sister's friends(where I was forced by, again, the honor
code, to stay). And then he said something, pronouncing the words quite clearly, so there was no mistaking what I heard—he said: 'I have a
proposition for you.'

"Those words alone are startling to hear at that time in the morning, but what made them more so was that when I turned over I saw
that he was laying there on his side, facing me, with the blanket pulled
up over his mouth so that the only thing visible was a nose, a set of
closed eyes, and a close-cropped haircut resting against a pillow. He
was still asleep! Believe me, I laid there for a minute or two longer just
to make sure. Finally, after making a few more moans, he turned his
head towards the wall and I immediately got out of bed, took the
quietest piss of my life, made the bed as if the sheets were light as air,
then got the hell out of there. It felt good to be up so early in the cold,
in that light drizzling rain that's just now starting to pick up and fall a
little bit harder, if you can hear it—but who was that devil that
questioned me? And what was his proposition? God, Belle, you tiny
woman, I wonder what it is about these strange things—if they're even
there—I wonder if they really mean anything..."

*The metallic background rain makes a sudden change in sound from dropping in
succession, one steadily after the other, to an outright downpour like loud static on a
tin radio. A voice breaks slightly through, crackling, 'shit,' or, 'ohmygod,' or something else; distant wet gravel slop-crunches under car tires, a car door opens, two
dings, a car door closes. Seven minutes pass, the rain audibly letting up...a car door*

opens, two dings, a car door closes.

"...This rain is something else, Little Belly—for a second there I couldn't see. I pulled onto the side of the road where there were a few abandoned farmer's market stalls, or something like that—a place where some native crafts are sold, maybe. It was a small wooden structure with walls on three sides, open in the front, right on the edge of a giant grass field that was backed by giant grassy hills; it's awning was enough to provide shelter from the rain, so for a few minutes I stood under there smoking a cigarette, dry, and my monologue carried on in my head. I'd been wondering if any of these strange things really meant anything, but, at the same time, I was thinking, 'I'll probably never know'—which I probably won't. The one curious incident will be placed with all the others because even if the meaning of the one is discovered it leads only to further, more curious incidents, more inexplicable, more fantastic—and where do we find ourselves then but back in the dark? That cool, evasive dark where I always keep your face close at hand...Oh, but I *do* know that these old sentiments are for the babes, the boys with runny noses and the girls with frillies on their socks, the *weans*, the kids who sing to Heavenly Father on Sundays, asking him, 'Are you really there?' Still, I'm fascinated, enthralled, alarmed, scared shitless by them. How can you forget the mystery? I don't know that either, but they must, they have to—you can't fight with any certainty when no one claims to have the absolute truth. And isn't there an argument going on? Aren't there voices being raised?

"The rain has dissipated, crawled up into the clouds here, still hanging very low. I have come onto a long, straight stretch between which two towns exactly I'm unsure of. (Dismissing the pun,) there is something both concrete *and* abstract about this highway, how the road and sky meet at a central grey point on the horizon at always the same distance away. It's nice to look at. It slows the heart rate and opens the sinuses. As I stare at it I'm going to try and do something—which I'm only telling you about because I want you in here, in my head—and I want you to try with me, stare: see how the eyes zoom in, straighten out, and relax, and how the vacant space between here and horizon has disappeared; see how the grey is actually full of color and each grain of color floats on various paths, glowing, vibrating; let go of the end of your intestines and see how they unravel slowly, slithering through zero gravity, which is no longer on the horizon but is in your tummy—light...and nowhere... clouds ate the jam...raspberry seeds are stuck on the sides of the mountains...clean your mop again, boy...get the mint out from between your teeth...wash up...call on old mother acorn...juggle your cigarettes, but don't smoke 'em...I don't want to have to repeat these things.

"Everything is clear, peaceful. My chest is warm, my breathing is right. Now I can tell you about what you wanted know—about the dream.

"The night before I left Washington—having gone none stop since my flight out of Texas, visiting with my aunt and cousins, working at my cousin's shop in Seattle for two days to afford gas money for the drive—two of Jehovah's Witnesses arrived at the door. I had just gotten back to my aunt's, tired, and was making myself a sandwich and a milkshake just like I used to, but I stopped what I was doing and opened the door to them. Neither the man nor the woman had much to say—they smiled, but didn't overwhelm me—they just wanted to invite me and my family to a convention. The pamphlet they put in my hands would explain everything. On the front, it read: *How Can You Survive The End of The World?* This question invoked pity from me, but I also felt a dumb warmth for these people and appreciated what they were trying to do even though I felt that they were probably in no position at all to provide me with a legitimate answer to the question they proposed. I wanted to offer them something to drink, or a piece of fruit, but they were on their way too quickly so I didn't get a chance.

"Later on, when I went back to the spare bedroom my mom had stayed for a month not long ago, I was trying to remember what The Witnesses had looked like—but I couldn't. I closed the blinds, not wanting to catch my reflection in the window. The lamp was on and I tried to read—I was too tired. I saw the words on the page as if through teardrops, distorted, fuzzy; my eyes couldn't stay open...

"It didn't make sense for me to be where I was, but I conceded that there was nothing I could do to change it because it was a dream—I knew that. I was in the kitchen of the large, dark home of my former boss, Arpeggi—that little Italian guy from Southern California who claimed his father was part of the mafioso and who paid one of the other employees twenty dollars to let him spit on him. You remember the one: he got drunk at the shop occasionally, he made me put Splenda in his iced tea for him, called me, 'Kid,' had guns in his office. Arpeggi was in the kitchen, too, and a handful of old Japanese women who were standing to either side of him where his pudgy body was hoisted onto a wooden bar stool. I couldn't hear what Arpeggi was saying, but I could tell that he was ordering us—there was someone behind me who he was addressing as well—to do something, kill someone I think, and he was sweating profusely while giving this order and laughing—that big growth on his eyelid, that ball of skin, was bobbing up and down as he laughed and it was distracting me, but also it gave me something to look at so that I didn't have to make direct eye contact with him, though it appeared that I was. The only time I looked away, briefly, right through the space between two of the old Japanese heads, I saw the two Witnesses at the kitchen sink with clearly defined, full-color features: the woman with dark brown hair, a soft tan over her normally white skin which was evident in the pink sunburn on her cheeks and the white glow at her hairline, wearing a purple blouse and a dark grey, below-the-knee skirt; the man was plain, kind of an ignu, blue eyes, hair cut short enough you could see the scalp, his jaw line going down from behind the chin to mid-neck, a round belly that his purple tie draped pleasantly over, landing right at the waistline of his dark grey slacks. They were oblivious to where they were—their clothes were matching, they were drinking tall glasses of water and smiling at each other, probably warmly inviting, then reinviting, one another to *come and listen to the answer.*

"When I changed my gaze, attempting to return it to that pink gob of skin partially hanging over Arpeggi's right eye, I came to the conclusion that something bad was about to happen. I was moving stealthily through shadows in the backyard towards a rickety wooden stage at the far back of the property; the person who'd been behind me earlier was still there, moving stealthily as well, because this was what we were hired to do: Arpeggi had given the order for us to kill him, right in his own backyard. My shadow friend and I made it to the stage undetected and from there looked down onto the lawn where a large rectangle was illuminated by the kitchen light left on inside. The daughters of the old Japanese women must have come out of the woodwork, the trees, or somewhere, because there were about thirty of them there stripping off their clothes. Arpeggi was already stark naked, laying on his back in the grass, and as each girl succeeded in getting rid of all her clothes he began stacking them on top of himself, one on top of the other like a horizontal totem pole. From base to tip the totem pole was writhing on the grass, shaking at every joint, and I can't say how it is I knew this, but the whole thing was *diseased.* Every girl had contracted something or another and it all coursed through the length of this horizontal structure. We tried to warn Arpeggi, but he couldn't hear us. He was dead anyway. Not that we were going to kill him; there was nothing we could do—we were simply forced to watch, looking down on death from our wooden stage as it emerged from the very place those tiny daughters had come...from nowhere in particular, out of the dark, entering the lit rectangle from all directions in packs of three: the Hounds of Hell—dogs wild for the taste of dirty blood and the high-pitched screams of human-sized sex dolls. Only a few showed their teeth; a few snarled, slobbered, foamed at the mouth. Mostly they came in quietly, though, methodically, menacingly—lurching forward by the inch, slowly closing the gap between themselves and the orgy until the moment when they were so close that their prey couldn't react, were basically eaten already. I woke up before anyone was bitten,

261

but there was a darkness there, there was death—*something bad had happened.*

"Packing the car that morning, as you might imagine, was somewhat of a chore; getting my mom's belongings into her sports sedan wasn't easy—there weren't very many things, but there were a few big pieces, furniture. Plus, having just woken from that dream where I saw both sex and murder basically. What *did* help was that when I woke up I found that the book I had been trying to read the night before was closed shut on the floor and I had slept on the bookmark: those pictures of you, Little, in grey color, happy, now staring up at me from the console, listening. Also, my uncle made me an egg sandwich and I drank the last of the milk. But that was okay too, because as I was packing the car the milkman came and brought more—can you believe that? They still have a milkman. It's not until now, in recounting that dream to you, that I remember the uneasiness I felt from it. Why did those things have to happen? And why only in my head?

"Traffic is moving slowly, almost not at all. I'm just outside of Salt Lake City and the roads are slick. It seems there was an accident. Up ahead I can see a fire engine, an ambulance, and...two...or three cop cars. The right lane's closed off. I'm trailing a minivan exactly like the one my family had when I was a kid—except for the color. Theirs is maroon, ours was blue. I remember taking trips in that thing, the whole family settling in with luggage and pillows, having the same old fights that can be expected in a situation like that—one person was always having to piss when the others didn't(shouldn't have mentioned pissing); or it was always too cold for some, not cold enough for others. My oldest brother was always short and reasonable on the subject: 'You can put more clothes on if you're cold, but I can't take my clothes off.' My sister tormented me then—I've never felt so aggravated since. It wasn't until I started toying around with the Gameboy, or reading the book, or looking at the atlas, that she wanted those things—and then she *had* to have them immediately; she'd tell my dad that I hit her. I don't think I ever did hit her, but my dad's word was the last one and I always had to give it up...god, I remember trips to Dallas in that van, trips to Colorado, to the Dakotas, to Minnesota, to Utah. My mom took me to Kansas City in it once, when I was pretty damn young, to some modeling convention. She wanted to see my picture in a magazine. Thankfully, no one else did. But we had a good time.

"...F – O – U – R cop cars—not three. The other one was hidden by traffic and road blocks. They have a stretcher out, and there's a giant piece of debris in the road but I can't tell where it came from— there's someone on the stretcher. There's a little bit of blood—at least a little bit that I can see, and now I can't see anything but the lights in the rearview and side-mirrors because it's all behind me and both lanes have opened up. Traffic's moving along smoothly, erratically even, speeding to make up for lost time like we didn't just see firsthand what the possible consequences are when we get in a hurry...

"...By no means am I trying to keep up with traffic, but, my god, this is getting dangerous anyway. American Fork shouldn't be too much further, but I'm shaking, I'm almost jumping out of my seat—I've gotta piss! I've gotta piss or I'm going to crash this car, I can barely think right now—it hurts."

There is a break here in the recording, as even some of the most open men still prefer to relieve themselves in private...even if it be in a public restroom.

"That thing earlier, it's been happening more frequently lately, more abruptly. All of the sudden the feeling will arise, then in a matter of minutes it'll escalate until it's painful and I'm nearly pissing myself. I was so shaken up by it passing through Salt Lake to get to American Fork that I forgot to take the camera out of the car.

"But maybe we don't need a picture; maybe I can describe it to you. Through Lehi, under the freeway, veer right across the tracks, your second left, then the first: 'it's the dirtiest house on the block,' Jonathan told me; 'the only one without a yard.' He said he'd be waiting for me in the field, wearing nothing but a headdress and holding a pitchfork. Of course he had clothes on when I showed up. But I understood anyway. It's like what Capote said—(forgetting about, 'that's not writing, it's typing,' or talking)—about the man in *Cold Blood* who he spoke to in prison: something like, '[they] grew up in the same house, only [Capote] left out of the front door, and [The Murderer] left out of the back.' I don't know exactly how he put it, but I know the meaning of what he said, just as I understood what Jonathan said—only under milder circumstances. If Jonathan left out of the front door, then I guess that would've been me climbing out of the window, or the chimney; or maybe I never left at all, just stayed at home daydreaming about it while baking banana bread and cookies. Whatever the case, I like banana bread, and I like cookies.

"Regardless of all that, let me further describe the *dirtiest house on the block*. It's on half an acre of land, all dirt, surrounded by houses with horse stables and green and gold pastures. Half of an acre sounds big, but it doesn't look it next to the neighboring fields, especially when the house itself takes up quite a bit of that space. Five bedrooms, a living and dining room, a huge kitchen, a few bathrooms—all put to use. Two as a recording studio—one for the instruments, one for the digital mastering—one as Dana's sewing room(his wife), one as the master bedroom, one as the guest-. It's strange to be in a house that big knowing that your friend owns it, walking up to the second story, looking over the banister into the place where *he* lives. Did I tell you that Capitol wants to distribute his record? I remember gathering people onto his lawn to watch him play for free. Now his music has bought him two homes, not that he asked it to. At lunch he told me how he was still amazed every time he heard that his music had touched someone, that a seemingly insignificant thought of his had somehow transcended its brain then skull barriers(both connected to the heart) and meant something, at least to *someone*—though he never expected it to; he never expected anyone to buy his album.

"But enough of that. I left American Fork already an hour ago of driving, plus one stop to piss. He gave me the album for free. Let's just listen for awhile. The Colorado border is fast approaching..."

Another break in the recording, which can be attributed to silence on the part of the speaker due to concentrated listening, hearing for the first time the musical labors of a friend. As the conversation—if you can call it that—begins again with a short buzz, then a quiet clearing of the throat, you can very well assume that it's because the last song has come to an end.

"Well, on my way into Colorado then—Colorful Colorado. They welcomed me with that title, *colorful*—rightfully, too. From American Fork, heading east, I've watched everything puff up and blend together. Red rocks turning into gold ones, turning into plateaus, turning back into red ones, and gold too, a stream here now a river, rocks of any color now the foothills of mountains, wearing green beards, winding through the golden grooves of Father Rocky, that old mute, under a great big blue sky, blue like in those paintings you like so much—*surreal*...the clouds are cartoonish almost against that blue. Perfectly formed and illuminated. They make you want to study light. I oughta study the light. Visit my aunt and uncle at their cabin.

"From Breckenridge, their cabin's probably only about an hour away, taking a southbound curve around Denver's outskirts. Little Bear-dog's up there already, apparently enjoying her time with the cats, and the horses, and the wild turkeys. They love having her there. It's been five years since my aunt's dogs died. And she doesn't have any kids. Did I ever tell you that story about my Aunt Kaye, about the time she visited my family when I guess I was about three years old? Everyone was out to dinner together and she had me propped up on her lap at the table; I had fallen asleep before too long, and when the food came she refused to eat because she didn't want to wake me. She's such a sweet woman. I was the ring bearer at her wedding when she married my uncle. They had it in Omaha, where he's from. I was thirteen. I brought the rings in on a string loop, then they put the rings on each of their fingers and the string was burned, separating them, but

264

bonding them. It must have happened two nights before the wedding, but my dad didn't tell us until the night before—our dog died. What I remember as our first 'family dog'—Mallory, the black Scottish Terrier. She was hit by a car on the road next to our house, the year before we put up the fence, and the car took off without saying anything. Dad was still at home, would be making the drive up Sunday morning, the morning of the wedding. He scooped Mallory's little dead body into a cardboard box. Out at the Jameson's acreage—our family's best friends—he buried her near their property line. A few years later the Jameson's dog was court-ordered to be put down—it had bitten too many people passing by the property. Jack Jameson, the dad, did it himself. He gave Joe(the dog's name) a big steak, and right as he was finishing it Jack shot him. They buried him next to Mallory. What the hell...

"I cried when I found out about Mallory. I was sleeping in the same bed as my Aunt Kerri at the hotel, and she could tell that I was crying, so she turned over and rubbed her hand over my back for a-while. It helped. I delivered the rings. No one told my sister though. She was ten. When we got home from the wedding, she came through the door and started calling, 'Mallory! Mallory!' Just like we all knew she would, because on the drive home she was talking about how excited she was to see her dog. Someone should have told her then. 'Mallory! Mallory!' She was the one who really cried. Her eyes were so inflamed behind her tiny glasses—she had to take them off. The next day my dad took her out to where Mallory was buried and they said a prayer. For awhile they went out there and did that once a week. I don't know when they finally stopped going.

"But that's just how it happens with pets. It's sad. First, your fish dies. Then your guinea pig dies. Then your dog dies. And you're supposed to learn something from each experience—not about death, but about yourself I suppose and how you best cope with loss. Eventually you have to relearn those things when they come back in terms of people—first, with people your friends know, then with people you know, then within your family, then your friends, yourself, or what have you, but I barely know what the fuck I'm talking about here.

"Beardog is OK. My mom said that she spoke with Kaye on the phone not too long ago and that Kaye put the receiver up to Beardog's ear and she started licking the phone when she heard my mom's voice. My mom could hear Beardog licking the phone. She's OK. It's my grandma that's sick. All I have is a couple of bad habits, on and off creation-anxiety, and a small bladder. Nothing that warrants any great degree of alarm—at least not right now.

"I'm driving through a great country, further west from where the Wolfe ancestors would have passed, but land and towns which none-the-less inspire certain descriptions. Nestled in the valleys between these hills are old mining towns without a plum tree in sight, but still I feel like I can hear the plums falling to the ground, keeping time in the changing seasons of little Thomas or Eugene's life in *Look Homeward... Angel*, Belle...these places make me want to drink black coffee even though I've quit, and have dark beer even though I'm driving, smoke some of my bad tobacco even though I can't stand its smell. Awhile back, for no reason whatsoever, I realized that I even want to gamble. I've never gambled in my life, aside from a few low-stakes poker games with friends, but right now I feel like gambling and if I see a casino I'm going to stop. There's a billboard that's come up a few times already, advertising, 'Bar and Grille, Casino, Entertainment.' The last one said it was in 20 miles, which means there should be another soon, telling me where to exit...

"...And, here...a sudden offshoot. This place doesn't feel quite right...I don't see any casinos...just a group of people sitting in lawn chairs outside of their house...and a closed down gas station...and a boarded up motel. There...an old building with a neon beer sign...'Bar and Grille.' There it is. It says they have *keno*. Turning around then— damn me...those people in the yard are staring at me, 'what?' Oh well. Probably for the better. I'll be on time this way. The Finleys are expecting me around nine. Or that's when I told them I'd be getting there. They're probably expecting me much later. Well, I'll surprise them. I'll be on time.

"Crazy it's been, what, a year since I saw Jacob and Ali last— remember, when I was back in Lincoln for my sister's graduation? and I helped them pack up their stuff to move? Little J. was only—March, April, May—three months old. They're probably all settled now. J.'s sixteen months old. He looks pretty big in pictures. I wonder how big he really is though, or if he'll remember me. I wonder if he'll call me 'uncle' yet. I'm going to try to get him to say it. And I won't forget the camera this time. You'll have plenty of pictures.

"The ski towns are already starting to pop up; snow capped mountains getting closer—in June. I'm taking pictures out the wind-ows again, and you really should tell me to quite doing that: steadying the camera on the steering wheel, zooming in, checking the viewfinder on the camera pointed in one direction, trying to steer the car in another. It's going to make me sick. I keep finding myself looking down for too long, then when I look back up, terrified, I luckily see that I managed to stay on course, but one of these times, Little Girl— no more pictures. Not driving off the cliff today. I *know* you've never been to this part of the country. I'll take you some time. It'll be safer.

"Close your eyes. It's safer. Close those big green eyes of yours.

"The window's down to smoke—sorry, but I couldn't help it. Stick

266

your fingers out of the opening, it's cold. Have you ever touched snow in the summer? Have you every really touched snow? There was that one 'bad' experience, that's right: you jumped into a pile of it and got pissed that your clothes got all wet and that you were cold. It probably didn't help that your dad put that snowball on your head. But, admit it, it made for a great picture—I'm glad your mom had her camera out. Where were you anyway? How old were you? OK, try it again. It'll be better. It won't sting your hands this time, your clothes will stay dry. Just stretch your fingers a little bit farther, it's right above us, churning with the clouds there, trailing down onto the tips of the mountains growing taller on each side of us, sprouting from all around turning from green beards to white. Are you counting the miles by the little green signs on the side of the road? Do you know how far we've gone? How far we have to go? Do you know where we are, Little Woman? *Are you really here?*

"The big white belly of the ski slopes has swallowed me. You've never been here and you're not here now. I'm seeing the lake alone, spread out across the base of several peaks where the town is. I'm coming into town alone, talking aloud to this make-believe ear of yours, or to that great big eye in the sky. Neither of you is answering very candidly—and you not at all; only the former says anything, in that cryptic voice of sight, rising out of whatever you want to call it, pretending its either nothing, or its mistranslated, or its coming from something else, or somewhere. But who's behind that mountain? What's behind the brain, the birth?

"There's a pinch in my chest, just off center. I missed the turn. But I can turn around. You can always turn around—*hahaha*. You've never met my friends, huh. They're great people. You'll have to meet them sometime—just not this time because you're not here now. It's funny, if you were here I probably wouldn't be talking this way. I am though. I'm here. And I'm tired. I think all of this talking is taking effect on my brain—good or bad, or what. The lights are on in the house. It looks warm. I'll try to call you to say goodnight. It'd be good to hear your voice."

"After all, there are still the faces. And they're never the wrong ones, because it's there in your memory that they hold strong and become true—the faces, everlasting in the brain. The body is in and out—in and out of peoples' lives—just like Jacob said, 'tomorrow you'll be gone and everything will be back to normal.' No lasting difference. *In* here, where you hug and smile and ask all those first necessary quest- ions and feel good and comfortable, where you eat and drink together, crack jokes, go on walks, and talk about the same old shit happily...

"I broke down this morning. I had three cups of coffee with breakfast. Have to piss now, but oh well. This morning I let myself have coffee because I'd be gone later and *everything will be back to nor- mal...*

"...The kid talks, you know. And he laughs. The house has a nice gravel path on the side leading to a park behind it. There were snow flurries when they drove me through the developments where the gon- dolas will take you up to from town, and where Ali used to spend her summers with her family. We went for a walk. Jacob and I climbed trees up on the mountain and saw all of the lake at once. A family walked by—the mom told her little daughter she'd never seen creatures like that before. I slept well in a big warm bed—I laid diagonally. Oh, and the kid dances, too! On an empty cardboard box like a tiny stage; he's so light that he doesn't crush the box—it doesn't even bend. We blew bubbles in the living room for him and he popped them with his sticky, bald head. He did say 'Uncle' once; Jacob taught him how. God, he's a cute kid. But what use does he have for the word 'uncle' now? Unless maybe he'll remember my face. Or create one for me. *In and out.*

"*In* through the mountains and valleys where you see the snow, and *Out* to the Great Plains, the steady slope downward and eastbound from high altitude to the flatlands, the open space, the prairie.

"They brought up names to other faces which I hadn't considered in some time. More babies are coming. A wedding. Some people are still missing, fine; some people just recently stopped through. And each of our lives continues indifferent to the others'—even when there's love there. For whatever reason, words from *Portrait* come to mind: about death being inevitable, but the moment and method still a mystery. And it's that way regardless—save for suicide. Then you can answer where your God is because he'll find you; then you can answer where you are, and what. I was raised in what might be called the open chest of this nation, or the big, bleeding heart—that's where you're taught to think about that. In the vastness of the prairie. And here we are, coming back into that vastness.

"The interstate is a parallel here of east and west in the middle of this vacuity, between these two nonexistent places. Out either side of the car, what do you want to see? It's there. It's scary and big, prying open the skull at the back of the head just by being looked at, trying to get to that dark space. I know this drive. This is the drive I took with my brother when I was eighteen, only on the opposite side of the parallel, heading west to California. We tried to read *Quixote* out loud to each other, but we didn't get very far. We ate pie for breakfast. We wanted to write about it; we wanted people to know that we had pie for breakfast because to us it meant something—we got it *a la mode*. It's easy to imagine what I looked like back then. Look at me now. Look at this face: I've simply added a dab here for a mustache(I don't know why), taken out a line there by not drinking as much beer, cut some of my hair, bought a different pair of boots, and absorbed a little bit more sun, thanks to the hot hell of Texas(—excuse me). But there are other things here you can't see, of course—for instance, what about those lost months when I broke the jar of jam in the back alley? and what about those other places I went and those things I did alone? What about those babies that *didn't* come? And this just about me. Because then there are those other people whose lives I've entered and exited a number of different times and ways all this while—what about them? And why ask now? What matter?

"It's not that I have some childish fear of returning to my hometown. Don't let this outburst, as calm and controlled as it is, give you the wrong impression, little person to whom these words are being directed. I've been back there plenty of times before. What's bothering me is the separation, the brevity of the situation, the unbalance, and the miscommunication. How can you catch up with old friends, then leave them within the proper context? Of the great concern for 'where' and 'how-come'? How do you describe to them an intangible twist in the ingenious plot that, first of all, you can't even understand? Or the eerie feeling of spiritual misfire, or death? It's never quite enough. It's never, ah...*whooo*...I'm pulling this car over..."

A mechanical ticking noise begins to sound its alarm of big-small-big-small within the car to ensure that its driver knows and doesn't forget that his hazard lights are on; loud whooshes created by large, fast moving cars passing by a smaller, still one; a single clack, five consecutive dings, a quiet zip. A steady stream of some sort of liquid can be heard, its pitch growing higher as if the liquid stream itself were quickly filling a bottle—then it stops on three, last, broken high notes. A plastic cap is audibly screwed onto a plastic bottle, a zip; hard plastic now hitting hard plastic—then silence. Sound washes back in with soft, low music, two quick blows into the microphone, then a gentle brush against soft cloth—say, the cotton fabric of a shirtfront pocket. Apparently some situations are too desperate for the luxury of privacy....

"I took a minute, quietly—for myself. After dumping out the bottle of piss onto the side of the road I got out—right at the state border. Nebraska...

"I had to go for awhile, but I held it at the back of my mind, telling myself I wasn't going to stop until I saw that sign—*the good life*. But it came alright, thankfully. I took a picture of it for you, and of the country view off to the side: two big trees and a perfect dirt road leading far back on the southern horizon, half-blue spotted with white, half-green marked by yellow flowers and brown fence posts and, of course, that brown dirt road—probably giving way to some farm or farmtown.

"After I took the picture, I just stood there, gazing...smoked a cigarette, because like my brother said, 'it's like brooding over fires.' And I felt a little silly, and a little sad. I asked myself, 'What in the hell am I saying about all those faces?' I thought about the people I might find if I went down that dirt road. That made me sad, too. I can't really say what the other thing giving me this feeling was—it was just big, and vague. None of it made sense, but my guts seemed to move as gently and painfully as the long grass of the prairie I was and still am staring at, which is a dumb thing to say, but that's just how it was. A vague sense of movement and history and the blank unknown of what's before that. It's all such an old struggle. And what to do with it? That's what I was trying to get at earlier about putting things within the proper context and such. And that's it—that vague, old sad struggle of *wonder*. And how to not let it eat you. To appreciate it and smile at it, god...to balance it...

"...I'm not unfamiliar with all of this. It's like how little kids relentlessly ask their parents questions, and even if the parents don't know the answer to a particular question they'll make it up. It's always been like that. Only I'm both child and parent in this case—I definitely don't know the answers but god knows I'm trying to make some up. If only to ease the relentless child in me that's calling out these inanities. I

270

was something else as a little boy...I never said a damn thing. Most of the time I just tugged at my earlobe and felt varying degrees of discomfort. I remember in kindergarten feeling my face get really hot, and feeling so scared for who knows why, and I would suddenly begin crying, uncontrollably. I only went for half a day, but they had to send me home to my mother early when that happened—and I never told her what was the matter when she asked. I just tugged at that stupid, tiny red earlobe. Once I acted out. Just once though. James Blackraven made fun of me while we were playing in the back of the classroom one rainy day when we had recess inside—this was back in Tacoma where it rained a lot year round and where I only went to school for a year. We moved to Lincoln after that. But whatever James Blackraven said that day really got to me—I punched him. I knocked out one of his loose baby teeth and he had to go to the nurse's office. I haven't hit anyone since. I've always been afraid of really hurting someone. It was easier to just go back to my mom anyway.

"You know, after we moved to Lincoln it wasn't until the end of second grade that I stopped carrying a picture of my mom with me to school? It was of her with my dad hugging her from behind outside of my grandma's house in Dallas one afternoon after church. Where is everyone going? Dad's in California, sure. But, Mom, sweet little Mima —where's she going to end up? Can you imagine her selling her house in Lincoln, storing away her things, and buying this car I'm driving? It was only what seems like just a few months ago that she drove it out to Oregon to be with that guy—the Mormon who smokes, drinks, shoots guns, and looks at porn. You remember the size and weight of his mustache when we met them that day in Los Gatos? when they were visiting his sick mom at his brother's house. How weird. His poor mom couldn't even pick herself up from the recliner she was dying in. I know Mom had a hard time leaving him like that—but he smoked, he drank, he shot guns, and looked at porn...even though he told her he was 'Mormon.' It took her a little while, but she finally took off to my aunt's one day, thank god. And now she has her own mother to look after down in Florida where she and my grandparents all live together, eerily just a few miles down the road from the orphanage my grandma grew up in. I already told you she's sick. Her other three daughters are going down to visit in the next few weeks. It all points to something bad I think. Apparently, the other day she asked her doctor, 'Is this what my life is going to be like?' When he told her that it was, she said she didn't want to live a life like that, in pain. She doesn't want to go through treatments anymore. There's really nothing I or anyone can do about it, except make her comfortable and love her. Just be sweet to her. Drink cups of hot milk ad vanilla with her...

"It makes me think of Babs. A lot of things do. To be honest, I

271

sometimes ask her ridiculous questions then look for answers in the things around me...just like a kid would...I was doing it a lot back at the house, at your mom's I mean—right after we found out that she died. But everything talks in Texas in the summer—especially the trees. And they're all loud. I didn't expect any firm, resolute answer in the natural sounds of Texas, nor did I get one. But I liked pretending that I was talking to her, and that she could hear me—huh, Babs! You old doll! You knew exactly what you were doing—I heard about how you went. Daughter Sandy hadn't left your side in over a week, your room was always filled. But the second she left, and the room cleared, you settled comfortably into your bed and let yourself go right out into the bright, open space where your bones didn't hurt anymore. There was only one other person with you. You did it privately, quietly, bless you, on your own terms.

"And how about the last time we saw each other...as if you didn't set that up with some angels so that every time I thought about you I could smile. Belle and I were leaving the gold coast for Texas, and we stopped to say goodbye one our way out of town. You were getting out of the hospital that day, and when we got to your room you were sitting on the made-up bed with your things packed. Your blinds were pulled open all the way so that the light from the hospital garden came through against your back and every tiny and delicate fiber that out-lined your body was illuminated by that light—you angel! You were doing well that day; you recognized us immediately(though you rarely forgot my name), you hugged us, and you joked with us. You wished us well and instructed us to be safe on our trip as you always did. I'm trying to figure it out—what was your cue? You kissed my cheek! You kissed my cheek and those costumed carolers appeared at the door from nowhere, dressed as they were for the eighteenth century. They asked if they could sing and you of course said sure. I don't know exactly what they sung, except that they were Christmas songs because it was December—and that you gave me an annoyed look when they sung in German. It all sounded nice to me as far as I was concerned and you looked nice, too, you were doing so well that day. When the carolers were finished they bowed, then moved on to the next room. We could still hear them singing, but they were softer, further in the background. Belle and I had to get going because our friends were waiting in the car. We said goodbye again, and hugged one last time. And as we left you smiled, but didn't wave; you were sitting very still there on the made-up bed, your things all packed to go, and the light still came in from the garden, hitting against your back and making the fibers of your outline glow. Babs, you old doll. You did that on pur-pose. You knew everything..."

272

A short period of silence, or near silence—music still heard at low volume— followed by a fraction of a click-ing then complete silence as the recording device is turned off. Now music again, louder, that has the effect of making one feel as if they were floating through a blue sky on a vehicle smooth as a bubble—purely instrumental.

"It's funny how a break in thought quickly alerts you to your physical environment. Which is to say, Quiet Belle, as usual, I had to piss and the gas tank needed to be filled.

"I'm not really sure where I stopped. The fuel pumps hadn't been updated since the sixties. There were cows a'hundred yards to the side of the gas station. The attendant was a friendly guy with glasses and hair too long in the back. I told him it felt good to be back in Nebraska, where I grew up, which I guess it does feel good though it was out of character for me to tell him so. He welcomed me back anyway, which was nice to hear. For the most part I feel like I've just been going forward, on and on...

"I'm really not sure where I am, like I said, but I'm definitely back in Nebraska, and I couldn't be any more than two hours away from Lincoln at this point. I'm hesitant to call it 'the home stretch,' but you know...I told Ivan I'd be getting in around eight—and I'm right on schedule. It'll be nearing dark around then. In the warm part of the sun just going down I'll get to come into the place that raised me. Good old Lincoln, Nebraska. And good old Ivan! He's probably at the pawn shop right now waiting for me, kicking around in his dress shoes and helping his degenerate customers fill out the paperwork for their loans, occasionally breaking now and again to play one of the beat-up guitars they have there. He hates that job. I'm going to buy him a drink. It'll be a good thing to sit there with him over a drink and have him tell me all about how things are, even if they end up being the same. I'm sure they won't be though. It's been a long time. It's been too long—for everything. I'm at risk of getting all sappy here, babe, but I won't!

"Because right now we're going under the great archway of Kearney, Nebraska in all of its deep purple glory and don't you see there off to the left—the llama farm. You're unaware of the importance of the llama farm and the archway—you don't know what they mean. Let me fill you in: this is the butt-end of the real golden gate, where when you enter it, under the archway going west, with the llamas seeing you off, you're gone, off into the country where your background is the story you're in the mood to tell and your breakfast is either apple pie *a la mode* or whatever the Holiday Inn is serving for free even though you slept in your car; and on this side, Little Darling, eastbound under the archway, with the llamas welcoming you like awkward but friendly men with mullets, you're back on the inside, where if

273

you pop a tire your friends can get to you before dark and where you're covered up by an invisible blanket made up of corn dust and silk—the tighter you pull, and the closer it gets to your skin, the bigger the world gets, and the more beautiful because you no longer really know what's out there and you're not disillusioned by the reality of shit places you once imagined were wonderful. This is the restoration process, the renewal. Next stop is that dainty, multicolor-striped flight-less balloon that says 'York' and means you're just forty-five minutes away from the drunken fantasy land of 'Everywhere Else Is Beautiful, But Not Here,' where the head gets fine-tuned while the body gets wrecked. And that's exactly what happens—or at least used to. But not this time...

"This nervous energy you can hear—vibrating in my mouth, and chest, and directly into my shirtfront pocket to where you're listening from—it's resilience. This is a part of the restoration process, moving through the old damned wreck and into the renewal. It's the bad blood having it out. This is a point in the cycle which can only be experienced on the ground. Flying's no good for it. It's too sudden. It fucks the nerves. Everyone should return to their beloved/abhorred cities and towns and homes in this way—on the ground through the country, close-up, so you can be a part of the passing action, touch it, and truly see how the cities rise up in front of you and become, then fall behind you as the history of your emotions, your memories, follows suit. You run through the entire scale in your head, weighing out everything—both actual occurrences and possible ones, past, present, and future—living or reliving it all in attempt to discover meaning, or no-meaning. It's not just cathartic—it's necessary, and common. People have always done it. It's what we all should and hopefully will do at some point—and then do again. It allows you to loosen up, cry, get over it, and scream, 'My God! My God!'

"From the air you don't get this. You get a sleepy feeling, cramps, stale breath from eating peanuts and not talking, a bad drink—maybe you get some reading in, finish half a crossword puzzle, actually get a good drink. At best, you stare out the window above the clouds and feel absently mushy, sad—like you're helpless. Then your only words are said in your head, to whatever god unknown, 'Forgive me—for everything. I've done things I shouldn't have and I'm sorry. Please, forgive me. Your will be done.' The Submission Prayer, said by passengers who believe their plane just might be going down—*it's going down*. I'm the most basic, idiotic Christian in the air. On the ground I have no faith-name, just an inkling of faith in something and a very religious awe of my surroundings and my existence. I see this beautiful country and know it's not mine. I did not make it. I have nowhere and have made nothing. This is what the ground covers. This is where the air is that you can breathe. *My God! My God!*

"There's the balloon! Like a big, multicolor-striped squash. Upside down. Forty-five minutes away—just enough time to have my friend sing me in. And he ought to. It's fitting. Plenty of light. Sing for me, Jonathan. Ivan's waiting just up the road. I was late the other night and it can't happen again—but you don't know about that, do you... (Jonathan, you just keep singing; don't let my voice disturb you)...we were driving—me and you, Little, and one of your friends—in a semi-truck of all things. The cab opened into the back, which was cleared out and looked like a giant warehouse with a toilet in the middle. Water was splashing around everywhere—the toilet was broken. We had to stay in the cab with the door to the back closed. You seemed irritated. By the time we got to Mexico you were utterly pissed—why'd you want to go down to Mexico anyway? It was your idea. There were snakes everywhere. And an elephant. He was standing on the end of a very long downed tree branch; I, on the other end, jumped onto the branch and catapulted the elephant into the air. Just a few feet up and back down, but he flipped over in the air and it was all in slow motion. He came down onto his back. He looked at me, got up, then charged. I ran, but elephants are faster than you think—I had to run hard and fast, escaping through narrow alleyways where he couldn't fit, but where there were dirty Mexican street dogs barking and trying to bite my legs with their greasy snouts. I made it out into the market. No more snakes for now, no elephant, and no dogs. I found you. You were sitting with your friend in some makeshift bleachers. There was a stage in front of you. There were girls dancing. One did a cartwheel, then a handspring—she made her skirt flutter up. You told me I couldn't watch. I was angry with you for making me leave, but you insisted that I did even though the foul men in the bleachers were eyeing you just as much, and with the same look, as they were the dancers. Fine. I didn't let you know I was angry with you. I didn't know what you might let one of those men do to you if you knew—just out of indignation. I had to meet Ivan anyway. I'd forgotten he was waiting for me and I was already late. I slipped behind the bleachers and through a series of curtains into the bar. I scanned the room for Ivan...it was crowded...but there he was, sitting at a table by himself, smoking a cigarette and wearing a straw hat with the end of a peacock feather sticking out of the band. He waved me over, laughing, and it was obvious he didn't mind that I was late. That's just how things are. I sat down with him and the waitress came over for our drink orders. She was pregnant. She was an old friend of mine...

"...I bet you question the relevance of that somewhat strange relation. Don't you. Well, let me tell you what you need to know about that: if it were irrelevant, it wouldn't have come up. It's not imperative

275

that you be able to see at first glance the synchronicity of complicated or even uncomplicated things. That stuff is for the winged and the behooved, fingering through ethereal documents with incomprehensible speed and precision, both wanting you on their side. And for the biographers who come too late—aren't even born yet—and whom probably will endow the unfortunate and unwitting dead with their own countering philosophies. It doesn't matter. There's too much to look at now, right now, to bother with that shit—forget it because you see that tiny cowboy on his tiny horse in the sunset? right there on that sign, he's showing us the way to yet another historical landmark. But this land *marked* is enough for me. The once blank slate of this cultivated prairie. See how there are more trees now, in dense clusters about the sides of the road? We're almost there. The first signs of a human hand forcing its landscape. People are here. Not two million, but some. Lincoln: next seven interchanges.

"First for the rural neighborhoods of far west Lincoln, where families live in quickly built track homes and the nearest spot to buy booze is the gas station that my baseball team would stop at for Gatorade as a kid just as we were leaving town for a doubleheader in Grand Island. Now the airport exit and the travelers' motels—next is West 'O' St., then downtown, but I'm taking this one here...past the airport strip...to bring me into downtown from the north side on the overpass...

"By the lakes outside of downtown—manmade, small. Reflecting a pitifully middlewestern skyline. Just a few buildings over thirteen stories—if my old friend Hassler were here he could tell us exactly how many, he'd know. These old sad lakes! The light is perfect, hazy, blue—sad as these lakes. And the football stadium on campus here...crawling across the overpass...the baseball stadium there where my brother's childhood friend Al Horton used to play before he went pro—and Chambers, too. Down below you can see those old brick buildings by the train station and post office—where my old place was, and the starting point for many long walks across cold downtown and further that winter when I was more than a bit off. The local paper's building—*The Star*. The Good Onion restaurant. And 'O' St.—the mainline through balmy, summertime downtown Lincoln. It's all come up around me: the same old buildings and these street names. From abstraction to distant embellished illustration to a real living thing. The people are walking and breathing and doing just fine. The cars are moving according to lights and signs and signals and they're all abiding by the law. I'm going under the speed limit, slowly inching along with the window down—I think I probably know every person on the redbrick sidewalk down here. But I don't. I'm wrong. I don't know too many people here anymore. Just a few close, but distant friends.

"There's a payphone up here near the corner. Any further and I'll be driving aimlessly. Ivan moved again, and I need to call him to find out where he lives now. But I'll call you too, Little One, the first chance that I get. It's the best way to end any drive."

#0004:
(Lincoln, Ne) To Austin, Tx
Via The Southbound Bus Line

My voice is shot. I need a glass of milk. And something with sustenance. Chicken and mashed potatoes maybe, and big, doughy rolls—without gravy. My stomach is empty. My throat hurts.

The drive is already over, just like that, and I am on the bus now. I am not making any attempts to talk. There is a short black man on the bus with a pencil thin mustache that is doing all the talking for me. I am avoiding conversation with anyone.

At one point, a few years ago, I would have been in my seat, alert, listening to any and every detail that I could pick up from the muddle of voices. I would write letters to my brother about what I heard. Why not anymore? Now I sleep as much as I can, waking up in the middle of the night sometimes to find that we are at a tiny bus stop in the dark and scary state of Missouri(though barely out of Kansas, where I am comfortable). New passengers get on and I put my bag on the seat next to me in hopes of deterring them from sitting there. For awhile, there was a young guy sitting next to me that I learned would be getting off at one of those dark spots in Missouri. He didn't talk much, which I liked. However, he did think it was necessary to tell me he regretted wearing pants that were too tight for the trip—his cigarettes didn't fit in the pocket quite right and he kept on smashing them. Fairly sure he meant he wanted one of mine. And I would have let him have one, too—being that the smoke is doing nothing good for my throat—but I was too tired to offer a legitimate response. I think I politely nodded, and that was all.

He is gone now. The seat next to me holds my bag. My head is down to record, by hand, these last lines of my short trip. No one has tried to talk to me. Not since the young man in too-tight pants got off at some ungodly hour. It is nine in the morning. The sun is out.

This is the thirteenth hour of a ride that started off badly. I said goodbye to Ivan at the pawn shop and told him I would walk to the bus station from there—it was only about fifteen blocks. At least it would have been only about fifteen blocks to the *old* location. It took about an hour and a half of frustrated walking and making inquiries with random people to learn that the depot had been relocated to a spot that was seven miles outside of downtown. The bus was scheduled to leave twenty minutes from then. I had to pay three dollars for an iced tea at a café just so I could use their phone to call Ivan. He picked me up and got me to the station just in time. We said goodbye for the second time. The repetition would have been somewhat embarrassing were we not old friends. I thanked him for good measure and he left. The other passengers had already started exchanging stories with one another about their previous exploits. Details interchangeable. But the bus wound up being forty-five minutes late.

It was my plan from the start to remain inconspicuous, a little anonymous grey dot within the vast array of colorful characters. I immediately began reading Singer's, *More Stories*. Instead of taking one last look at my hometown, I saw Warsaw. By dark I was deep into the city and halfway through the book. This morning I picked up where I left off and was elated by one story in particular—which I will get to— and was startled by the resemblance of its subject matter to the on-going pattern of my thoughts. It made my eye twitch and my tongue swell. Even if I wanted to talk, I am presently unable.

My mouth is dry and fat. The sunlight coming into the bus is making it unbearably hot. People are coughing, eating greasy breakfast burritos, their shoes are off, and so on disgustingly. The bus reeks. I can almost no longer feel the cool wind and drizzle of Idaho, or the brisk cold of the Colorado morning when Jacob and I went for a bike ride(and acting like a child, or clown, as usual, I flew over the handlebars onto the unthawed ground), or the brief but welcomed snow flurries. I can almost no longer feel the high-performance AC of my mother's car as I drove it over mountain, valley, and prairie on some absurd trip back to Lincoln where I was to park it in the garage of my grandparent's empty and unused home there, where now it will just *sit* —also empty, also unused. Although the physical feeling of those things is wearing off, it is impossible to forget that they are pieces of my own very lucid past, which, in part, successfully accomplish the creation of the present.

I am human, and alone, and therefore not only susceptible to the things stored in my head, but to the forces of the ever-changing current sensations. At hand, there is the sweltering bus, the inhabiting passengers thereof, their foul smells, and their incessant murmur of dread equal to my own. No one wants to be on this bus. But we are.

Now there is also this book. In particular, one of the stories in this

279

book, which contains within it a testament that, though it is only a fraction of its whole, seems truer to me than those most regularly encountered. He was over fifty when he wrote it, but it concerns the time in one's boyhood when you first begin to question your superiors and the doctrine they live by. Certainly it is about his own boyhood that he writes, but it is universal, and timeless. Everyone will question, and must. It is an essential part of the human experience. Dear Tiny Woman, I am still directing my words to you, and you must forgive me for this change of mode—but I am doing my best to retain the styling's of my own free will, and earlier tongue, and I want you to think of this: *he was over fifty when he wrote it.* Picture him with a bald, white head that is marked by a few dark spots, a crease between two wide, dark eyes, large ears and an equally large nose, a smirk that is not a smirk but just an old, stern mouth that happens to be turned up at each end, instead of down, from years of intelligent reasoning and good-natured, beautiful fascination. Picture him wearing a white, long sleeved button down shirt, a vest, and a tie, sitting at his typewriter, alone, quietly recounting something he experienced as a young boy, and delicately(as are the fingers of fifty-odd year old men who have been through both World Wars—especially Jewish men) typing the words that jump out at me now concerning a cork, the darkness, madness—*existence.* He was over fifty when he wrote them, but he was a lot younger than I am even now when he was alone in that apartment of his memory, thinking about the cork that floated from river to sea, to ocean, to the end of the world, and then beyond that into a darkness not unlike '*the dark space behind the brain where the idea of God both lives and dies, and where creation itself can be ended abruptly, at any time, like a television set effortlessly being turned off.*'

I am able to repeat myself so accurately because with the help of an angel I transcribed the first recording in Rexburg. I paid in Hail Marys and Our Fathers to have those words, out of my own mouth, put down in writing in front of me so that I could have a better look at exactly how mad I had gone. In God's honest truth, who- or whatever God is, I have not gone mad at all. My faculties and balls are intact. I am not at risk of anything unnatural or unforeseen. I no longer know about being all alone in the world, but I am absolutely certain, by everything and now Singer's words in front me, that I am "surrounded by hidden monstrosities and mysteries that no one [can] resolve." And that is the immutable state of our existence. It is heartbreaking, but otherwise only as harmful as our brain allows.

The worst of my ailments are superficial then. A sore throat from talking too much. A sore ass from the bad seats of the bus. A cramp in my leg that will have to wait to be stretched out. A gross odor coming from all over that is so heavy, hot, and impenetrable that when I breathe out of my mouth I can taste it. A puddle forming in my belly-button. A constant, dull ache in my back. Numbness alternating through each of my limbs. And the poet's *thousand* other things meant to imply many, countless, more than I am inclined to get into because I have a broken heart, and my brain feels soft.

But we are coming into Dallas already, actually passing by the library and grassy knoll, making just one last stop afterwards before ending in Austin, where I will soon be able to lay myself out in the dark bedroom, and to listen to the cool, soothing sound of the air conditioning unit in the wall as it fights to overcome the heat, and where I will have you right there with me, Little, comforting me even in sleep so that when I wake up there will be nothing to be frightened of. All of these present discomforts will soon be over. And these rampant, stray thoughts of a brain left to roam alone through the absurd and frightening landscapes of America—and the place behind it, the darkness—will not have disappeared altogether, but at least for a little while they will be gone.

—Summer 2009, Austin, TX

SEX/ABSURD
(2009)

For Mima

WARNING:

If anyone should ever attempt to put on this multi-media performance, I wish them good luck. Sex/Absurd is first and foremost a written undertaking, and, therefore, its mechanical specifics—such as the construction of the set, the possible hazards therein, or the dual projection of the second act, and so on—were not given any consideration. Anything is possible in the head. And that is where this is to take place.

CONTENTS/CHARACTER LIST

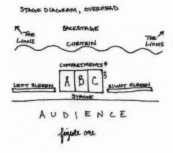

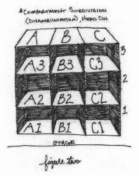

Act One
HOW TO LOSE YOUR SELF COMPLETELY

[Interior]

The large curved dome of a human head from within—a man's head—like an open stage in a glistening pinkish-violet walled auditorium wherein a play is about to be put on. This is not the beginning of the play, filled with nervous energy and clearing throats, but it is a pause, a break. A calm and silent interlude.

The play began quite some time ago and is now somewhere between its middle acts. The actors are already exhausted, tuckered out—fucked out, if you will. In the dark they are drinking glasses of water and putting cold, damp washcloths on their foreheads. No one is wearing even a stitch of clothing—not that it matters. Presently they are offstage, unseen by The Audience.

In the middle of the stage there is a tri-level platform illuminated by a blue glow. Each level is sectioned off in thirds by plywood walls, dividing the structure into nine compartments overall for the various connected and disconnected vignettes of thought and memory *(see immediately: figure two)*. To either side of this structure there is a big, orange vertical, rounded-edge rectangle, which, together, create the illusion of a giant set of eyes that are closed during the daytime.

They open. The compartmental structure goes dark.

[Exterior]

View from the openings of the large pair of eyes, blinking slowly, from background to fore-: the far wall of an apartment with a partial, but bright, window; next to the window there are two photographs hanging on the wall—one is of a young man whose face is obscured, and the other is of a very young girl wearing a yellow dress and clown make-up; *(moving forward, across the unfurnished apartment, through the open bathroom door)*a sink, a mirrored cabinet above the sink, slightly ajar; *(farther forward still, past the toilet and into the tub)*soapy water fills a deep, old-fashioned tub halfway to capacity—a foot rests on the faucet at the far end, a hairy knee pokes out closer up.

On the surface of the water, in the immediate foreground, a fixed gaze: the belly of the bather rises and falls in gentle, held breaths, the water covering it, then uncovering. A clear, not overly loud voice becomes audible in soothing time with each breath.

Man(Voice Over): *(Inhaling)* Low-tide.... *(Exhaling)* High-tide.... *(Inhaling)* Low-tide.... *(Exhaling)* High-tide.... *(Inhaling)* Find the oysters.... *(Exhaling)* The Picnic's ruined....

The soft echoes of the unilluminating narration slowly fade, leaving just the sound of breathing, ever-softening, too, until all remains quiet.

The rectangular frames blink back into orange, still oblivion. The center structure fades back in, returning to a shadowy, blue glow.

[Interior, Compartment 1C]
A light fades in. A man is revealed in full repose, naked, in a bathtub filled halfway to capacity with what looks like soapy water, but is actually white and blue cellophane. The man is basically still, except for the occasional slight movement to reposition himself. The light remains on.

[3B]
A light is switched on. A floor lamp to be precise. A man sits at a small desk. He is clothed in an open bathrobe—nothing else. A typewriter is in front of him. He stares at it for a moment, scratches his crotch. He takes a blank piece of paper from the desk drawer and puts it into the typewriter, feeding it through with a few cranks of the knob. He begins to type—steadily, constantly.

[3A, Simultaneously]
A light fades in at the first stroke of the typewriter's key in *3B*. A young man stands at a counter stirring a drink with his finger. He is speaking into a telephone.

Third Man: *(Excitedly, somewhat drunk)* We're still in the honeymoon phase of our relationship though—yes. It's been, what, like three weeks.... She spent this last weekend up here and we didn't leave the apartment for four days. *(Laughing)* At one point she got on top of me, and she was doing this thing like holding her hair on top of her head with one hand, and pawing at my chest with the other—then she came. Then I got on top and I came.

[1A, Simultaneously]
A red light fades in and the anecdote from *3A* is acted out according to its narrative cues. A young woman holds her hair on top of her head with one hand as she rides the young man and clutches his chest with the other hand. She orgasms, audibly.

The lovers switch positions. The young man is on top and now he orgasms—also audibly.

They both collapse. The red light switches off.

286

[3A, Continued]

The young man is still on the telephone, though his speech stopped after his last statement, seemingly to let it sink in with the listener on the other line—or with himself.

Third Man: *(Continuing regretfully)* God, man, I don't know why I even told you that. It's fucked up isn't it—that I told you that? *(Pause)* Whatever though, I guess we all tell each other some pretty fucked up stuff. I'm just excited, you know—obviously.... She tells me she loves me, and I say it back....

The third man's voice, as with the first, trails off slowly as the light follows suit, fading, until the compartment is silent and dark.

[3B, Cont'd]

With a flamboyant and satisfied gesture, the young man at the typewriter, finally, forcefully strikes one last key. It is fair to assume that it was either a period, or some other punctuation mark, or the last letter in his name—whatever that might be.

He flips the release lever on the right side of his typewriter, and pulls the piece of paper the rest of the way through. He holds the paper up to the light and inspects it. Then he begins to read aloud.

Second Man: Dear Ms. Hoyt, you wonderful but distant woman—I was told something recently that, for whatever reason, made me want to write to you....

After the opening address of this letter, the second man, his voice, and his typewriter, all fade out to black while the reading of the letter is continued elsewhere, from below.

[2A, Simultaneously]

As the second man in *3B* begins to read his letter aloud, a light fades in to reveal a somewhat distraught young woman sitting cross-legged on her bed. She is the recipient of the letter. She begins to read aloud as well.

Ms. Hoyt: *(In unison with 3B—shocked, horrified)* ...You wonderful but distant woman—I was told something recently that, for whatever reason, made me want to write to you....

[2A, Cont'd Independently]

Now that the man in *3B* has disappeared altogether, Ms. Hoyt's voice stands alone as she continues to read the letter aloud.

Ms. Hoyt: *(Muttering to herself)* Jesus.... *(Then to all, from the letter)* A friend of mine from New Hampshire called me the other day. He was in a kind of frenzy, and it's very likely that he had had a few drinks—judging by the volume, excitement, and openness of his speech. But I could be completely wrong about this; those things could have been caused by something else. In fact, you should know that the purpose of his call was to tell me something: He is in love. *(Guffaws)* This was not a difficult thing for me to surmise, because not only did my friend announce it to me once, but after the first announcement he continued to profess this love of his throughout the rest of our conversation.

Ms. Hoyt(Cont'd): Now Ms. Hoyt—you utterly sweet and innocent woman—you may be wondering what all of this has to do with you. I imagine you sitting on your bed—just like you probably would have been had I come over that day to say goodbye. And I imagine you asking yourself, 'What does all of this have to do with me?' *(Trembling)* Well, to answer your question, which you are certainly asking: Nothing. You do not know my friend from New Hampshire, nor does he know you. But it makes no difference. It has been a long time since we've spoken, and you probably hate me. Regardless, I was compelled to write to you in order that I might share this with you: people are still falling in love; people are still getting excited. Be well.

At the end of this letter Ms. Hoyt, the reader, calmly folds the letter into thirds and places it on the nightstand beside her bed. Then, also calmly, mechanically almost, she lies facedown on the bed, motionless. For now, the light remains on.

[2C, Simultaneously]
A light fades in as Ms. Hoyt in *2A* reads the line, *"I imagine you sitting on your bed."* It reveals a set identical to that of *2A*—a young woman sitting cross-legged on her bed—except that she does not hold a letter, nor anything else, in her hands. She is alone on the bed until Ms. Hoyt finishes reading her letter and lies facedown on the bed, motionless.

[2C, Cont'd Independently]
A young man now enters the room, taking a seat on the edge of the bed, somewhat distanced from the young woman. She takes no notice of him. He is wearing pantyhose over his head, covering his face.

After a momentary pause, he speaks through his mask.
Fourth Man: I just wanted to stop by to tell you that I'm leaving. *(Pause)* Do you hate me?
Woman: *(After a pause, sadly)* No, I don't hate you....
Fourth Man: Okay. *(Pause)* Well, goodbye then.

The man gets up from his seat without turning towards the woman and exits. Calmly, almost mechanically, the woman then lies facedown on the bed, motionless. Fade to black.

[1B, Simultaneously]
A light fades in in the cheese aisle of a grocery store as the masked young man in *2C* sits down on the bed. A young man is quietly trying

to make a decision of which cheese to buy—reading labels, checking prices.

A young woman enters and is seemingly having the same difficulty as the man. She is reading the labels on different cheeses, checking prices.

[1B, Cont'd Independently]
As dialogue ceases and the lights fade to black in *2C*, the movement in the cheese aisle of the grocery store becomes more apparent.

The woman reaches for one particular product, which just so happens to be right in front of where the man is browsing. The shelved item the woman was attempting to inspect is knocked over. It falls in front of the man.

Second Woman: Oh! I'm sorry, I didn't mean to hit you with the cheese!

Fifth Man: *(His browsing unaffected)* I understand—do whatever you've got to do.

Second Woman: Oh.... *(Giggling)* Well maybe I'll just have to hit you with some cheese again some other time....

The woman smiles suggestively at the young man. She picks up the cheese she knocked over—still smiling at him—walks off, then exits. Fade to black.

[2A, Cont'd]
Ms. Hoyt, who has not budged from her facedown position on the bed, finally makes a resolved effort to rise. Back in a sitting position— though on the edge of her bed now, not cross-legged—she opens the nightstand drawer. A small piece of lined paper is extracted, but she continues to fumble around in the drawer in search of something to write with...with success!

Using the nightstand as a proper writing surface, Ms. Hoyt's head is bent over in concentration, focusing on the blank sheet of paper in front of her as she begins to fill the page.

[2B, Simultaneously]
The light in *1B* has just gone out. In turn, a light is cued to fade in and reveals a fairly young transvestite, fairly pretty, standing beside a middle-aged gentleman who sits complacently in a green velvet recliner. The transvestite smoothes the hair on the gentleman's temple.

Transvestite: Baby, you're such a genius.

Gentleman: No I'm not.

Transvestite: Oh, yes you are a genius and you know you are, baby.

Gentleman: Alright, well I might be a genius, but we're the only ones who know it goddamnit!

Transvestite: Baby! People will find out... *(Tugs on the gentleman's earlobe)* Why don't you read me the new poem you wrote....

Gentleman: Which poem?

Transvestite: The one about how we drank too much.

Gentleman: Ah, speaking of—have you tried that new vodka I bought?

Transvestite: Baby, we had some last night...don't you remember? *(Inspects the gentleman's nose)*

Gentleman: Oh yeah, yeah, yeah—you should get some out right now.

Transvestite: Hold on—you've got a booger...

Gentleman: *(Wipes his nose)* Did I get it?

Transvestite: No....

Gentleman: *(Wipes nose again)* Now?

Transvestite: No.... Maybe it's not a booger.

Gentleman: *(Licks his thumb, then wipes under his nose with it)* Did I get it now?

Transvestite: *(Clapping hands)* Yes—you got it!

Gentleman: Alright, well it wasn't any booger then, it was probably just dry skin masquerading as a booger.

Transvestite: *(Laughing)* 'Masquerading as a booger'—you should write a poem about that!

Gentleman: Oh, I've written a lot of poems....

Transvestite: *(Smoothes the gentleman's hair again)* Yes you have, baby—you're such a genius.

Gentleman: No I'm not.

Transvestite: Oh, yes you are a genius and you know you are, baby.

Gentleman: Alright, well I might be a genius, but we're the only ones who know it goddamnit! *(Pause)* The rest of the world just thinks I'm shit....

Transvestite: Baby! People will find out, I'm telling you...just read me that new poem you wrote—the one about how we drank too much....

Gentleman: Are you going to get that vodka out? The new stuff?

Transvestite: Yes...but only if you promise to read me the poem—do you promise?

Gentleman: Yeah, yeah, yeah, I'll read you the new poem—of course I will.

Transvestite: OK. Good. You just hold tight then....

The transvestite kisses the gentleman on the top of the head, then exits. The gentleman remains seated in the green velvet recliner. He busies himself by removing various things from his pockets and laying them on the floor at his feet. He appears to be making a mental catalogue of the items. The light remains on.

[2A, Cont'd]

As the transvestite in *2B* exits the compartment, Ms. Hoyt—who, meanwhile, has been writing, pausing, then writing away—finishes her reply to the letter she received earlier.

She sets her pen down on the nightstand and picks up the piece of paper. She presses it to her lap, scared of it, then holds it in a way that it can be read.

Ms. Hoyt: *(Taking a deep breath, then reading from her written response)* Dear Mr. Ignatius, you were right when you said it had been a long time since we've spoken. You were also right to assume that I hate you....

Just as Ms. Hoyt begins to read the letter she's written, her voice, along with her entire compartment, slowly fades out. Black.

And the letter is continued elsewhere, from above.

[3B, Simultaneously]

As Ms. Hoyt's voice announces the opening address of her letter in *2A*, a light fades in. The same man is sitting at the same desk in the same bathrobe—still with nothing else on. Only now he sits slightly cocked to the side with his feet propped up on his desk, directly beside his typewriter.

The letter from Ms. Hoyt is in his hands. He begins to read it aloud.

Mr. Ignatius: *(In unison with 2A—unemotionally)* ...You were right when you said it had been a long time since we've spoken. You were also right to assume that I hate you....

[3B, Cont'd Independently]

Now that Ms. Hoyt in *2A* has disappeared altogether, Mr. Ignatius' voice stands alone. He continues to read the letter aloud.

Mr. Ignatius: *(Still vaguely unemotional, if not inwardly somber)* I do hate you. I hated you then and I still hate you now. Today, when I received your letter, I felt physically sick. I wanted to throw it away, or cry, but I gathered my strength and read it anyway. Why would you do this, Mr. Ignatius? Why would you write to me after all this time? And without so much as a genuine, straightforward apology? Your little story about your friend in New Hampshire did not amuse me. I am not sure I even believe you have a friend in New Hampshire. You are a very sick man, Mr. Ignatius. And I think you like that you are sick. You have to. If you don't like that you are sick, or don't realize it, then you are probably the most lost individual I have ever had the unfortunate experience of meeting.

Mr. Ignatius(Continued): *(Still reading)* In fact, you *are* the most lost individual I have ever had the unfortunate experience of meeting, and I wish that I had never met you. You are a very sad fool and a coward. You disgust me. Please do not ever write or try to contact me again in any way.

The letter is over. Mr. Ignatius drops his hands to his sides, pauses, then tosses the letter on the desk. He folds his hands in his lap and tilts his head back, thinking. The light remains on.

[2C, Simultaneously]
A light fades in as Mr. Ignatius tilts his head back in *3B*. The set remains the same as it was left before: the young woman is lying facedown on the bed. Slowly, she rises into a cross-legged sitting position. She is wearing pantyhose over her head, covering her face.

The young man from earlier reenters the room, still wearing the pantyhose mask like the woman. Again, he takes a seat on the edge of the bed.

Fourth Man: I just wanted to tell you that I'm leaving. *(Pause)* Do you hate me?

Woman: *(After a long pause, sadly)* Yes, I do hate you....

Fourth Man: *(Another long pause)* Isn't there anything I can do?

Woman: Yes. You can go away. And please do not ever write or try to contact me again in any way....

Fourth Man: Okay. *(Pause)* Well, goodbye then.

Again the man gets up from his seat without turning towards the woman and exits. Calmly, almost mechanically, the woman then returns to her facedown position on the bed, motionless. Fade to black.

[2B, Cont'd]
Having retrieved the bottle of vodka and two glasses, the transvestite reenters the room. The gentleman's pockets are emptied, and he is rearranging their contents on the floor.

Transvestite: *(Concerned about the mess)* Baby, what is all this shit?

Gentleman: *(Looking it all over at once, then resolutely)* All of this shit, my dear, is me. This is the stuff that makes up my person—now look at it!

Transvestite: Well, baby, if this shit is you then you need to clean yourself up. *(Pauses to fill glasses)* Here—I brought you a drink. *(The gentleman stops what he is doing and reaches for the drink; the transvestite pulls it away, just out of reach, taunting him)* Ah, ah, ah...not till grandpa cleans up his mess....

After a second attempt at snatching his drink, the gentleman—growling and muttering—concedes to clean up his mess. He quickly shoves the things back into his pockets. They will have to be reorganized later. The transvestite rewards him with the drink. He takes a big, satisfied sip.

Gentleman: Ahh....

Transvestite: Is grandpa happy now? *(The gentleman shakes his head 'yes' and finishes the drink)* Good. Now read me the poem.

Gentleman: Yeah, yeah, yeah.... *(Displays his empty glass, wiggling it)* Just give me one more fore the sake of warming up the old song-box....

Transvestite: *(Filling the gentleman's glass)* Just one more for now....

Gentleman: Ah, good...good....

The gentleman takes another big, healthy sip, then searches through a few of his pockets. He withdraws a crumpled piece of paper. He clears his throat, flattens the paper out on his knee.

Gentleman: Shall we begin then? Of course we shall. *(Clears his throat again, then reading from the paper)* Canto Seven or Thirteen: I Don't Know How I Got Here. *(Pause)* There are lights running along the carpeted hallway of The Good Time Hotel. I don't know how I got here, but the lights will not let me get lost. They are like tiny glowing ushers, guiding me by the balls—because I've had too much to drink! And I don't know how I got here. But I know where I'm going—*(The gentleman stands up excitedly, his energy rising along with his body, and the poem continues aloud)*

[3B, Cont'd Simultaneously]
As the gentleman in *2B* stands up, Mr. Ignatius places a piece of paper in his typewriter and immediately begins to type. The typing remains more or less constant throughout the rest of *2B*'s poem.

[2B, Cont'd Simultaneously]
The gentleman has just stood up and the transvestite takes his seat, listening intently to the gentleman, enamored with him, as he continues reading his poem unbroken.

Gentleman(Cont'd): —I'm going to have a good time, just like the name of this hotel advertises. It's already a good time, but it's going to be a better time! A great one! I've had too much to drink and I'm going to have more. I don't know how I got here but I'm glad that I did get here: here at The Good Time Hotel, in the strange hallway where there is a door on each side of me. Something tells me that I can guess what's behind these doors, but I'm wondering what is that noise...

Gentleman(Cont'd): ...What is that fucking noise! Is that you up there, you son of a bitch? *(Speaking towards the ceiling, towards 3B)* Typing away at that thing as if you were jerking yourself off like some stupid and pathetic little boy, jerking yourself off because no one else wants to! No one cares about what you have to say, you son of a bitch! If what you want is poetry, or art, you little cunt, then you listen here— you listen to me!

Gentleman(Cont'd): *(Returns to reading the poem)* Something tells me that I can guess what's behind these doors, but I don't want to guess—I want to see! My dick is poking up a thousand feet from my jeans, trying to decide which door to knock on first—swaying left, then right, a thousand feet high! Yet it always seems to return to me, pointing instinctively.... I don't know how I got here, but I can still get it up! It's up and it's pointing at me because it knows that *I* am The Good Time. *I* am the fiery light running down your carpeted hallway—you bitch, this is.... *(Begins to stammer and break off)* You bitch—this is.... *(Holding back tears)* You bitch.... *(The transvestite stands up to console the gentleman, sitting him down in his chair, petting his hanging head)*

Gentleman(Cont'd): ...This...is...the end. *(Pause)* It's over sweetheart. It's over! Do you see this poem here? Read the date! Do you see? It's dated five years ago!

Transvestite: No, baby, it reads like new—it's fresh!

Gentleman: You bitch, it's five years old! *(Pauses, then calmly)* I'm sorry I called you a bitch...it's just that I'm dying. *(Pause)* My typewriter doesn't even work anymore....

Transvestite: Baby, don't talk like that! It's upsetting. Besides, you're a genius.

Gentleman: No I'm not.

Transvestite: Oh, yes you are a genius and you know you are, baby.

Gentleman: *(Another drink is poured, which he accepts; then sadly)* No. You're wrong about that, kitten. I'm not a genius, and that's why I was never recognized as one. And now I'm even less. Now I'm just tired, drunk, and old.

Transvestite: *(Smoothing the hair on the gentleman's temple)* Baby....

Gentleman: Now, I'd like it if you please left me alone.... I need to get myself all sorted out....

The gentleman, seeming much older in his present state, with sad hanging head, begins removing the various items from his pockets again. He places them neatly on the floor at his feet. The transvestite looks on for a moment, and silently resigns to obey the gentleman's wish. She sets the bottle of vodka on the ground next to the chair, then exits.

The gentleman continues his delicate task. Fade to black.

[1B]
A light fades in in the cheese aisle of a grocery store, again. A woman —the same woman from earlier—browses through the cheese selections, reading their labels, checking their prices.

The woman performs her actions absently. She seems to be preoccupied with something else—she continuously looks around her. She is waiting for the young man who once said, 'Do whatever you've got to do.' He does not show up. Fade to black.

[3B, Continued]
Mr. Ignatius' typing has gradually slowed, and now ceases altogether. He tilts his head back and lets out a deep breath. He pulls the sheet of paper from the typewriter, then begins to read it aloud indifferently.
Mr. Ignatius: Dear Lady Unknown, Dear Figure I see in the dark, Dear Mystery....
    Mr. Ignatius' voice trails off. Fade to black.
    The letter is continued elsewhere, from below.

[2C, Simultaneously]
A light fades in to show the young woman in the mask still lying facedown on the bed. The young man—also still in mask—reenters the room but does not sit down on the bed. He remains standing.
    In his hands he holds a piece of paper—the letter written in *3B*.
    As Mr. Ignatius in *3B* begins to read this new letter aloud, so does the masked young man begin, in unison, though without looking at the sheet of paper he is holding.
Fourth Man: Dear Lady Unknown, Dear Figure I see in the dark, Dear Mystery....

[2C, Cont'd Independently]
Fourth Man(Cont'd): ...It is not my intention to bother or harass you, but I clearly see that you are lying there and know that you are destined to listen. You must. You won't run from me or disappear unless I choose for you to do so—which I don't. What I choose for you to do is nothing—just continue to lie there, listening. I am somewhat afflicted. Perhaps by you, my dear, or by my own sweet creation. Invention can sometimes prove to be a precarious thing: it may lend itself too frequently, or from a place too low. In any case, I must keep things simple, direct. Tell me: Who are you really? Are you the curious angel of my conscience? Or that devil thing that wants to eat me? Are you the prickly backbone of the offspring of my delusional thought process? Or the soft underbelly of my puppy-dog imagination? Out with it—tell me: Which wind did you come in on?
Fourth Man(Cont'd): *(After a long pause)* Just as I suspected—no answer. I have not asked for one yet. I have only asked for you to lie there and listen...because I recently had a dream, I think, which confused and saddened me. There was a man just past his prime, drunk and uproarious. He read a terrible poem of his, which was his most recent poem—and it was written five years before! He couldn't even get to the end of it when he himself came to that conclusion. He began screaming, then, almost, crying. The boy-woman who he'd been read-

ing to tried to console him, but with no success. He had already given up it seemed. The life he once had was over.

Fourth Man(Cont'd): What does it mean my little mystery? Who are you really, and who was that man? Who is the woman that waits patiently in the cheese aisle? How do they all come together—if at all? Please, I ask of you now to wake up—answer me....

The masked young man lingers over the woman who has not budged from her position on the bed. He waits for her to make the tiniest stir—which she does not. He sits down on the edge of the bed, mildly defeated. Fade to black.

[3C]

A light fades in. A mother sits on a loveseat holding her small child in her arms. She caresses the child lovingly.

Mother: *(In a soothing tone, speaking to the child)* Relax, my sweet little boy.... I've never seen such a small child get so worked up. I'm right here; mama's right here. Everything's going to be alright—don't you worry. And to think you were my easiest pregnancy.... But you were never like this when you were inside of me. I would read you stories from the bible about the Immaculate Conception and you would gently stir in there—I swear I could feel you listening.... It was so sweet.

Mother(Cont'd): You were actually due on Christmas, my little angel—did you know that? I was going to call you 'Noel' if you were a girl. I didn't let the doctors spoil my Christmas surprise by telling me what you were going to be—a little girl or a little boy. Of course, you were a little boy growing in there, and, as most boys do, you came a little early. Poor things. What is it about you little boys that makes you so eager to get out, to leave? And soon enough, as is always the case with you poor little things, you're just as eager to find your way back out of the mess you've gotten yourselves into...to find your way back home.... You can just never really be happy until you've experienced the great unhappiness this world has to offer—isn't that right? Silly boys.

Mother(Cont'd): It's so sad that you have to grow up, sweetie; or at least it's so sad *how* you have to grow up. If it were up to me, my little darling, you would never grow up. *(Pause)* No. Don't grow up. *(Pause)* Just relax, my sweet little boy. Everything's going to be alright—don't you worry....

The mother kisses the head of her tiny child. She begins to quietly hum. Fade to black.

[2A]

Ms. Hoyt stands at the side of her bed. She is removing her garments one by one—her shoes first, then a sweater, then her dress, her bra, her panties.

Completely nude, she smoothes the sheets on her bed. She takes the pillow at the head of the bed and moves it to the center of the mattress. She climbs onto the bed, straddles the pillow, and begins rocking to and fro, grinding her crotch against the pillow in gentle motion—supporting herself with one hand on the wall—until she comes.

[1A, Simultaneously]

A red light fades in as Ms. Hoyt in *2A* takes her position atop the pillow. A young man sits on the edge of the bed holding a young woman in his lap; she straddles him, facing forward, riding him.

Both are wearing masks like those previously seen in *2C*.

Their motions are gentle, rhythmic, enchanting. The young woman braces herself against the wall with one hand. She comes. Fade to black.

[2A, Cont'd]

After her apparent orgasm, Ms. Hoyt's hand slides down the wall she had been using as support and she collapses on the bed. She takes the pillow from beneath her body and clutches it against her, cuddling it. Fade to black.

[2C]

A light fades in. The masked young man and woman remain in their previous positions—the woman lying facedown on the bed, the man sitting on the bed's edge.

The young woman slowly rises into a sitting position, propping her back against the wall, slightly distanced from the young man.

Woman: *(After a long pause)* I thought I asked you to leave....

Fourth Man: I did leave.... And then I came back.

Woman: Why would you do that?

Fourth Man: I don't know. I had nowhere else to go....

Woman: Oh bullshit. You could've gone anywhere. *(Pause)* How long has it been anyway?

Fourth Man: It feels like it's been almost forty years...but it could have been only four, or maybe a couple of minutes.

Woman: Jesus—and you say you have nowhere else to go?

Fourth Man: Nowhere....

Woman: That's pathetic.... *(Pause, then changing tone)* What do you look like now?

Fourth Man: Bad. I look bad. And it's only getting worse.

Woman: Can I see?

Fourth Man: No. I can't even see....

Woman: You're lying. You can see—you just don't want to. *(A long*

297

pause) I do believe you about how you look though. I bet you're aging terribly.

Fourth Man: Yet you still think of me when...well...you know when you think of me....

Woman: No, I don't.

Fourth Man: But I saw you just a second ago.

Woman: No. You saw what you wanted to, which is exactly how it's always been. That has nothing to do with me.

Fourth Man: I don't understand.

Woman: I'm sure you don't. Did you even notice if it was really me?

Fourth Man: I'm sure it was. *(A long pause)* Isn't there anything I can do to understand?

Woman: Yes. You can leave, just as I told you before. Go home. And, please, do not ever write or try to contact me again in any way....

Fourth Man: Okay. *(Pause)* Well, goodbye then.

For the last time, the masked young man gets up from his seat without turning towards the woman and exits. Calmly, almost mechanically, the woman then returns to her facedown position on the bed, motionless. Fade to black.

[3A/3B Interaction]

A light fades in in both compartments. The young man in *3A* sits on a stool at the same counter from earlier—no drink. No goddamn drink for the old boy. In *3B*, Mr. Ignatius sits at his typewriter, not typing anything but fidgeting with the keys, the knobs, the levers. They speak openly to each other, outwardly, rather than into telephones.

Third Man: You haven't been returning my phone calls, old boy.

Mr. Ignatius: I didn't realize I'd missed any of your calls....

Third Man: Well, you have. For weeks now.

Mr. Ignatius: Weeks? I talked to you just the other day, old boy. You were telling me all about how you were in love—remember?

Third Man: I *was* in love—a few weeks ago. But that's over now.

Mr. Ignatius: Over? What happened?

Third Man: Nothing. She had to go away for awhile.... It was only natural that things between us should end, or cease to continue, or however you want to put it.

Mr. Ignatius: *(Perplexed)* Huh.... I'm sorry.

Third Man: No, no...it's fine. We still talk on the phone—every other night usually; we still tell each other, 'I love you.'

Mr. Ignatius: Dear god, old boy! What the hell is the meaning of this? You still tell her you love her?

Third Man: You know what they say: It is what it is.

Mr. Ignatius: They do say that. *(Pause)* I've always liked that phrase—just saying it more than anything. *It is what it is....*

Third Man: *(After a short pause)* Well, how are you anyway?

Mr. Ignatius: How am I?

Third Man: Yeah—and why do you keep doing that?

Mr. Ignatius: Doing what?

Third Man: Repeating my questions before answering them like it's some sort of imbecilic conversational-trick.

Mr. Ignatius: I don't know. I guess I don't really have the answer until I truly ask the questions of myself....

Third Man: You know how ridiculous that sounds when you think about it, old boy? And there's no need to explain why.... *(Pause)* Regardless though...*how are you?*

Mr. Ignatius: Apparently not well from the sound of things. I've been writing imaginary letters to imaginary people—and I've been getting some really terrible replies. Well, just one terrible reply. *(Pause)* I'm thinking of taking a little vacation—maybe to New Hampshire...get some of that clean, crisp New England air into my lungs and see you, huh?

[1B, Simultaneously]

A light fades in once again to reveal the cheese aisle of a grocery store. The same woman browses through the same cheese selections—reading the labels, checking the prices. Her main preoccupation, though, remains in waiting for the young man to return. She continues to look around for him, from side to side, over her shoulders.

[3A/3B Interaction, Cont'd Simultaneously]

Third Man: I wouldn't bother if I were you....

Mr. Ignatius: Why's that?

Third Man: Because I am not presently, nor was I ever, in New Hampshire. *(Pause)* And you're in Portland....

Mr. Ignatius seems to have become distracted by something under the floorboards. He rises from his seat and leans over at the waist, listening to the ground.

Third Man(Cont'd): *(After a long pause)* Besides, old boy, the water's getting cold....

Mr. Ignatius: *(Speaking to the floor)* Hey! *(Now to the third man)* Hold on for a second there—hold on....

Third Man: Alright, sad man, but *the water's getting cold....*

As Mr. Ignatius continues his downward investigation, the man in *3A* shakes his head dejectedly and the lights in his compartment fade to black.

[3B/1B Interaction]

Mr. Ignatius: *(Speaking to the woman in 1B)* Hey, you! *(The young woman*

299

searches for the origin of the voice) What...in-the-hell...are you doing down there?

Second Woman: *(Timidly)* Me?

Mr. Ignatius: Yes—you there standing in the cheese aisle: What...in...the...*fuck*...are you *doing*? Who are you waiting for?

Second Woman: *(Stammering)* What do you mean? ...I...um...it says in the script for me to come here and wait for someone called 'Brando'.... I'm just following the script....

There is a long pause, wherein Mr. Ignatius becomes obviously more relaxed—sitting back down in his chair, calmly reflecting for a moment.

Mr. Ignatius: *(Jestingly)* Is that what it says for you to do, huh? Just stand there and wait?

Second Woman: Yeah and—

Mr. Ignatius: —and you're an actress then?

Second Woman: Yeah I'm sorry, I'm just playing my role and it says right here in my script to—

Mr. Ignatius: Okay, okay...you're alright. I'm just asking a few questions here simply out of curiosity. *(Leaning forward in his chair, intrigued)* So tell me, what does it say in this 'script' about after this Brando character arrives—what then?

Second Woman: It doesn't go into detail really.... It just says to 'improvise.'

Mr. Ignatius: Fair enough—but humor me: Pretend that I am Mr. Brando. Pretend that I am Mr. Brando Ignatius, horrifier of ambivalent young women, lover of small dogs, euphemism-giver of sweet-treats and other things, a mama's boy with a penchant for cheap drinks and soliloquies; pretend that I am he. What now?

Second Woman: *(After a long, thoughtful pause)* ...I guess I'd follow your lead. They call it 'saying yes'—to the situation, to the character, or what have you.... It's imperative to 'say yes' for improvisation to be, eh, fruiful....

Brando Ignatius: OK. Well, what's your name then miss?

Second Woman: My name is Holly....

B. Ignatius: What's your middle name Holly?

Holly: Jane....

B. Ignatius: Holly Jane—of course it is.... Well, Ms. Holly Jane—do you love me? Just say yes, please....

Holly: You want to know if I love you, huh—then let me ask you this: Would I have waited for you all this time if I didn't love you?

B. Ignatius: You are an actress, Miss....

Holly: *(Sternly)* The answer is yes. The answer is always yes—I do love you.

B. Ignatius: *(After a pause)* Amazing.... But why is that, Ms. Holly Jane?

300

I am such a difficult and foolish person. I've done some pretty despicable things....

Holly: Mr. Brando, sweetheart, for this to work properly you must also say yes to yourself.... Why do you men always want so badly to be loved, then cannot believe, or don't understand 'why' or 'how' it is that we women do love you? And, if we let you, you'd even go as far as to ruin that love simply because of your own disbelief! It's mystifying....

B. Ignatius: Human behavior in general is mystifying—it's not just men.... *(Pause)* And do you mind if I call you something else, Holly? I mean, something other than Holly?

Holly: You can call me whatever you want to, dear.

B. Ignatius: Then I'll call you Wilka—that's the name of my fiancée. *(Pause)* You are Wilka now, my fiancée. *(Another pause)* Are you there, Wilka?

Wilka: *(Adamantly, easily, taking on her new role)* Yes, I'm right here.

B. Ignatius: I'm sorry I said 'fuck' to you earlier. I didn't mean for it to sound rude, I was only trying to be playful, and I'm still a little at odds with something I—

Wilka: —Bran-do... *(Drawing out the name lovingly)* You don't have to apologize—I know you didn't mean to be hurtful. I know you want nothing more than to just be good, sweet, and genuine. That's why I love you.

B. Ignatius: Oh, Little Woman...there's something I have to tell you—it's important. I only learned it earlier this morning, but it's bad. It's bad news, Wilka....

Wilka: The only thing you have to tell me right now, Brando, is that you love me.

B. Ignatius: *(After a long pause—frustrated, but genuinely)* I do love you. I love you so much....

Wilka: And I love you too. I love you something terrible....

As these words sink in with Brando Ignatius—our confused, yet omnipresent hero—he hangs his head, regretting that he was unable to tell his Wilka the bad news that must be eating at him. Both compartments fade to black.

[2B]

A light fades in to reveal the gentleman 'poet' sprawled out on the floor. The items taken from his pockets earlier are scattered around him—some under. After a few moments, the transvestite enters the room holding a typewriter in her arms with a giant bow stuck onto it.

Transvestite: *(Cooing as she enters)* Ho-ney....

The transvestite sees that the gentleman, *her* gentleman, is on the floor in a state that is apparently less than conscious. She places the gift she's brought with her on the floor beside the gentleman's head. She sits down in his recliner and admires him, smiling.

Transvestite: *(Quietly, in a soothing tone towards the gentleman)* Honey...I brought you a gift. Wake up, I want you to see it. Wake up.... *(Moving from chair to floor, then gently shaking the gentleman)* Honey, wake up— mama has something for you.... *(More loudly)* Honey!

After a long pause, having received no answer from her gentleman, the transvestite leans over his face to listen for breath—apparently hearing something to alarm her, which is to say, perhaps hearing nothing at all.

Transvestite: *(Worried, becoming distraught)* Honey.... Honey, wake up— wake up.... *(Irate)* Honey! Honey, wake up! Wake up! *(Bawling)* Wake up, Honey...wake up...please...wake up....

The transvestite's sobbing becomes more and more hysterical; her words grow increasingly slurred, slobbering and wailing over her dear gentleman until she is absolutely unintelligible, exhausting herself there on the floor beside the gentleman's body. Fade to black.

[3C]

A light fades in on the mother, grown somewhat older, but still very pretty, utterly beautiful even. She still sits on the loveseat.

In the mother's arms, and partially extending onto the loveseat as well, is her child—now a young man.

Son: Mom, will you tell me about the night you brought me home from the hospital after I was born? *(Pause)* I need to hear the story right now....

Mother: Of course I will—I like that story, too.... *(Begins stroking her son's hair)* Well, you were due on Christmas Day, as you know, but my little angel just couldn't wait until then. On the evening of the twentieth of December I just knew it was time—I could feel it. I told your father to put my things in the car because we were going to the hospital. On the way there my water broke, and when we got to the hospital they put me in a wheelchair and wheeled me straight up into a room. I remember being surprised that I wasn't in any pain. The doctors wanted to give me some medication to make me more comfortable, but I didn't need any. I just lay there, knowing that you were coming, and I felt not one little bit of pain. It was a miracle. You were my easiest pregnancy—did you know that?

Mother(Cont'd): Anyway, a few hours later you were delivered. It was early in the morning on the very first day of winter. My little snow angel.... You were so beautiful— you had a full head of fine, dark hair; and you had the cutest little nose! You were such a healthy, calm baby, but the doctors still made us stay there for a few days to run some tests, and to let me recover, they said—though I didn't need it. They finally let us leave on Christmas Eve. And the first thing I did when we got home was put you under the Christmas tree. You were so tiny and quiet, just laying there under the tree sleeping; you were my little Christmas Miracle.... You were so beautiful....

Mother and son quietly reflect on the story, and, presumably, the time and things that have passed between then and now. Fade to black.

[Interior]
As the lights in *3C* fade to black, the orange rectangles on either side of the nine compartments begin fluttering. Like a man opening his eyes, blinking them slowly, readjusting their focus in the daylight.

They open completely. The compartmental structure, and the stage, goes dark except for the dim light in *1C*, appearing ever smaller in the surrounding darkness.

[1C, Cont'd]
The bather, who has remained in the tub all this while, finally stirs from his position in repose. He sits up in the tub, then stands. He exits the bathtub and dries himself off, looking elsewhere.

With the towel around his waist, he goes to the mirror. He stares for a few moments.

First Man: *(Talking to himself in the mirror)* This is what it's come to then—you're dying....

[Exterior, Simultaneously]
Through the eyes, on screen, from the perspective of the bather, mimicking the action in Interior Compartment *1C*: the surface of the cold bathwater; *(the body and eyes of the bather rising)*his feet, a towel, then a stable view of the sink and mirror; *(after a moment, moving to where the eyes' gaze has been fixed)*the mirror above the sink and the reflection in that mirror of a young man's face.

The face remains square, constant, in the mirror—staring at its own reflection.

Man: *(After a few moments, talking to himself in the mirror)* This is what it's come to then—you're dying....

After the man makes his announcement into the mirror, and through the brain-auditorium itself, he continues to stare. He pauses before he attempts to speak again. He looks at himself, very seriously. He takes deep breaths that are heard by the audience as if they were their own deep breaths they were hearing.

He continues to maintain his stare, his silence, as the Interior action comes to an end.

[Interior]
After the bather in *1C* makes his announcement, in unison with the

clear, not overly loud voice resounding through the brain-auditorium, he continues to stand in front of the mirror, staring.

The lights in his compartment—indeed, the last lights on the stage —slowly fade out to black.

The compartmental structure, and the entire stage itself, are completely dark.

There is nothing more in the flesh to be observed.

Only the screens remain illuminated on each side of the stage, like a giant set of eyes that are turned onto themselves in a bathroom mirror. From there the action will resume.

Act Two
SWEET TREAT: A EULOGY

[Interior]
The play has just ended. In the dark, the actors are retiring to their dressing rooms of nonexistence. They will not be returning for a curtain call.

One of the members of the audience begins to clap. He quickly stops himself when he realizes that he is the only one clapping, causing a mild feeling of embarrassment in himself and those around him. The other members of the audience stir somewhat, cough, clear their throats. They seem to be in limbo of whether or not to remain for the second act.

But the auditorium is so dark, warm, and inviting. They cannot be harmed by simply watching the lives of others. This is quite possibly the deciding factor for the majority of those who stay—or the realization that they have forgotten their way to the exits.

Regardless of their reasons why, most of the audience remains in their seats and certainly all of them remain within the auditorium. Some of them kneel down to pee into cups. Some duck under their seats, hiding, taking a few quick puffs of cigarettes. The children—God forbid there be any within the audience, but, yep, there they are—are fed cereal from Ziploc bags.

The second act is about to begin.

On the two screens like eyes, the leftover action from the first witnessed act is suspended by way of film. Abruptly, the audience's attention is brought back to these screens when a deep sigh resounds throughout the auditorium, almost reverberating off the soft, pink-violet walls of the head's interior.

[Exterior, Simultaneously]*

---

* It is not the audience, or reader's responsibility to decipher the traditional, sparse formatting of scriptwriting, and subsequently picture the action/dialogue in the way in which it was intended to be imagined. Neither do I wish to stray too far from the format found in Act One. Therefore, I have taken it upon myself to continue on in a similar style as before, and to play my self-appointed role as storyteller, dictating the happenings of the film that is about to seen as if I were spoon-feeding my very own beautiful child.

Brando Ignatius(the name we now recognize as this man's, and maybe all of the other men's from the first act, too?) holds his place in front of the mirror—all soft skinned from the bath—where he has been standing already for a few long moments. He lets out a deep sigh, not breaking eye contact with himself.

B. Ignatius: I'm dying then. *(Pause)* If that's what the obituary says, then that's how it is. *(A long pause)* How are they going to remember you, old Brando? By the product descriptions you've written for those various sweet treats? Or those few essays on the origin of dance, the role of sex in modern America, the mechanics of dream, the correlation between medical advancements and the frequency of natural disasters, and so on? *(Another long pause)* But no one's read those. They're in a folder in a briefcase in the closet. Wilka, you may do with them as you wish.

B. Ignatius(Cont'd): *(After a pause)* I will die. There will be a memorial service. A small one no doubt. But there will be one nonetheless. *(Pause, then with conviction)* Today you will write your own eulogy, old boy—by way of a poem. You will write the first and last poem of your life and you will give it to Wilka. She's your fiancée—she will be the one to read it.

At this profound decision, Brando finally breaks eye contact with himself and looks down out of frame. Water can be heard turning on, and a secondary liquid stream can be heard mixing with the water in the sink.

This continues just long enough to see the good, healthy relief in Brando's face as he looks one last time into the mirror, then exits the bathroom.

Cut to Brando looking at a tiny piece of paper that has clearly been torn out of a newspaper. On this piece of paper, circled in red ink, is his obituary. It reads:

> Mr. Brando Ignatius died tomorrow. In his short life he achieved mild success as a copy writer at a large confection company. He was productive, courteous, and under-appreciated. Cause of death is unknown, but is believed to be related to a non-preexisting heart condition that is common of men in their mid- to late-twenties.
>
> He is survived by a young woman whom he wished to propose to, and a ceramic pet fish.

Cut from the perspective of Brando Ignatius. The screens' images split temporarily in order to show separate, yet relevant action.

[Left Screen]
The perspective of an onlooker, observing the behavior of Brando Ignatius from head on. He is sitting at his typewriter, fully clothed.

[Right Screen, Simultaneously]
Close-up of the ceramic pet fish suspended in a tiny birdcage that is hung from the ceiling. He has one big and one bigger eye.

[L. Screen, Cont'd]
Brando takes an index card from a stack on the small table which his typewriter sits. He places the index card in the typewriter and begins to type.

Cut to backside of Brando, sitting in a large, for some reason familiar, green velvet chair. He is in partial silhouette, as his chair and table are set in the center of three large bay windows.

[R. Screen, Simultaneously]
Close-up of index card as Brando begins to type. The card is shifted to the left and the imprinted letters appear one by one, until the typing ceases and the line remains in plain view momentarily: *Now that I am dead.*

Cut to close-up of Brando's face, contemplating the next line of his poem.

[L. Screen, Simultaneously]
As the Right Screen cuts, so does the Left Screen and the images sync up with one another: a close-up of Brando's face, contemplating the next line of his poem.

[Both Screens, Simultaneously]
A close-up of Brando's face, contemplating the next line of his poem.

The intercom buzzer goes off in the apartment. Brando rises from his seat and goes to the receiver (you may assume that he is followed in frame, from midsection up to just above the head).

The intercom is of the old fashioned type—Brando picks up the earpiece and speaks into the receiver attached to the wall.

B. Ignatius: Hello?

Wilka(Off-Screen): It's me.

B. Ignatius: Wilka?

Wilka(O/S): Yes.

B. Ignatius: *(Excitedly)* I've been expecting you. *(Pause)* Wait there! I'll come down.

Brando grabs his coat and the index card from the typewriter. He opens the door to the apartment and locks it behind him in the hallway.
The hallway is well lit, carpeted, and looks as dated as the intercom. Brando opens the door to the elevator, then the gate, and enters.

The elevator goes down, then Brando exits by opening the gate and door in the reverse order as before—naturally.

Passing quickly through the lobby, Brando goes to the front entrance and is visibly confused to find that Wilka is not there. He goes into the courtyard in front of the building, looking around for her.
B. Ignatius: *(Calling into the courtyard)* Wilka?
There is no response from Wilka. He waits, but still none comes.
B. Ignatius(V/O): Where did she go?

Back into the lobby, Brando first pauses, obviously perplexed, then begins to search for Wilka—around and behind the old wooden columns, down off-screen hallways, under the couch cushions. He is unsuccessful in finding her.
The chandelier style lights hang down in the center of the lobby—some yellow, some red-orange. The stained glass of the apartment doors on the first floor are dim, and bad, giving the strange, still feeling of being outside of a Sunday school classroom.
Brando has come to a stop—his search temporarily over. He stands in front of one of the many tarnished brass, ornate faces that are mounted at the top of the columns in the lobby. Each one has a subtle variation in expression; Brando stands in front of one that is arrested in mid-laughter.
B. Ignatius: *(To the laughing face)* Excuse me—did you happen to see a young woman around here? She's about this tall, dirty blonde hair, green eyes....

Close-up of the face.

Then Brando from behind, looking just slightly up at the figure.
B. Ignatius: OK. Well, thank you....

Brando gives up the fruitless inquiry. He goes back to the entryway, glances around again, then exits the building.
The courtyard is free of people—there is only its dry, decorative fountain and a number of flowers(which the audience can almost smell).
B. Ignatius: *(Passing through the courtyard, unexpectantly)* Wilka?

B. Ignatius(V/O): Where did you go, Little Creature?

On the move, down the sidewalk of a tree lined residential street. A homeless man, too young and well manicured to appear desperate, sits on the curb up ahead.

B. Ignatius(V/O): *(Changing his voice, mimicking)* Hey, could you spare any part of a dollar? *(Then exaggerating)* Eh, no... I'm...sorry...I've only got this fifty cents here and I need it to make a phone call. *(Mimicking again)* What about a cigarette? *(Normal tone, declining)* Unh-unh.

Now passing the homeless young man, not stopping.

Homeless Young Man: Hey, could you spare any part of a dollar?

B. Ignatius: No, sorry—I don't have anything myself.

Homeless Young Man: What about a cigarette?

B. Ignatius: *(Calling behind him)* I don't smoke!

The homeless young man is left disintegrating on the sidewalk. Becoming whatever he allows himself to off-screen.

A payphone on the sidewalk. Brando inserts fifty cents into the slot, dials. He lights a cigarette as it rings. There is no answer on the other end.

Wilka(V/O): Hello, you've reached Wilka. I'm sorry about everything that's happening between us. Please leave a message.

B. Ignatius: Wilka, it's me. What happened? I came downstairs to meet you and you were gone. *(Pause)* Why did you leave? *(Pause)* Anyway, I'm not at the apartment anymore. I've come out to look for you. *(Pause)* I hope I find you.... *(Goes to hang up the phone, then ejaculating quickly)* Bye!

Brando hangs up the phone and remains in front of it for a moment. Where in the hell has she gone? He seems determined to continue his search until he can answer that question for himself.

Again, walking down the sidewalk of a quiet, residential street. It appears to be midmorning. Few cars pass, yet the street itself is far from empty.

As Brando continues down the sidewalk, he passes a young woman in an overcoat, standing at the curb smoking a cigarette. He expresses little interest in her.

Then he passes another young woman, in similar dress, standing at the curb smoking a cigarette in the same manner as the first. He gives her a curious glance.

Then a third woman—same thing.

And all the way down the sidewalk you can see that there are an endless number of young women in overcoats, doing that exact same thing.

Brando's pace quickens. He is inspecting each woman thoroughly, though with haste, as he passes them.

B. Ignatius(V/O): What are you all doing out here?

His pace continues to quicken.

Now at a near jog, passing women of little or no distinction—faster and faster. Brando cuts off of the sidewalk down a side street until at a safe distance he slows down, looking behind him as if to check if he were followed.

B. Ignatius(V/O): Who were all those women?

Arriving at a café and entering. A few customers sit silently here and there. No one is behind the counter.

Brando walks through a short, narrow corridor that opens into a back seating section. He looks around at the tables. On the walls there are painted-on books—he touches the flat, feigned spine of one.

Another back room opens up. It is dark, quiet. A lamp is on each of the tables. Only one person sits in this section. It is a woman. She looks up at Brando and stares.

Woman: *(Slowly, seductively)* Would you like to sit?

B. Ignatius: Eh... *(Laughs, pauses)* No... well... *(The woman looks down at the book she is reading, not listening any further)* I shouldn't...you see...I'm looking for my fiancée—well...she's not my fiancée yet.... But this is the café we usually meet at and I was hoping that she might—*(He realizes that the woman is paying no attention to his excuse)*—maybe I could just sit for a few minutes, rest my feet....

She still pays him no attention. He draws closer to her, crouching over to get a better look.

B. Ignatius: Hello? *(Snapping near her face)* H-e-l-l-o...?

Brando waves his arms in front of her face but receives no reaction from the woman. She is utterly still. Brando laughs—confused? nervous? what?

B. Ignatius: Would you like a cigarette? Huh? *(Offers one from a pack, then puts it away)* No, no you wouldn't like that at all. *(Pause)* Just tell me though...what is it that you would like?

The woman remains motionless. Brando snaps his fingers once more, then gives up with a sigh. He stumbles backwards out of the room.

At the counter, the barista is still gone. Brando rings a bell and waits for her to show.

From a back corridor the barista emerges—a pale woman of round figure and jaw length dark hair. She greets Brando with her eyes, silently.

B. Ignatius: Hello... *(Fumbling through his pockets)* ...could I just have a small coffee please?

As the barista turns around and pours a cup of coffee for Brando, he finds what he was looking for—his credit card—in his shirtfront pocket.

The barista puts the cup of coffee on the counter and rings up the purchase: $1.60.

Brando attempts to give her his credit card, but she is obviously disappointed by this and does not accept it.

Close-up of hand written sign: Minimum purchase of $5 for credit and debit cards.

B. Ignatius: *(Embarrassed)* I'm sorry— forget it, eh...I'll just pour myself a little water here. *(Actions mirroring his words as he pours himself some water)* ...And I'll be on my way—sorry, again....

With small cup of water in hand, Brando politely toasts the barista, who still says nothing, and exits the shop.

At a table in front of the café, Brando sits down. He is the only person sitting at the short line of tables.

Midday? Maybe. The general, thin grey of the city makes time hard to tell—if it matters. The yellow-orange café lights seem all the more colorful.

Brando's table is on the far left of the screen, at the very end of the line, as viewed from the street.

After folding his coat in half, Brando very neatly places it on the bench seat beside him. He removes the index card from his shirtfront pocket. With his hand rested on the table, index card between thumb and forefinger, he reviews, again, the first line of his poem.

Close-up of the card: *Now that I am dead.*

Behind the card, painted on the table, there are a few blurry images of human heads. He sets the card down on the table, off to the side.
B. Ignatius(V/O): Oh!

Close-up of the painted heads: One is of a long haired, bearded patriarch figure. He is wearing thick rimmed glasses. His beard looks like a mass of pubies.

The other is of a man in profile at his typewriter, in his early thirties, who appears to have been good-looking earlier in life—and still retains some of those good looks— but the swell of alcoholism has already gone to his face. Mainly, under his chin, following the jaw line back to the neck at a point lower, droopier than usual.

311

Brando—again, sitting at this table at the far end of the line—directs his attention towards the figures painted on the table.

B. Ignatius: Old Grinsberg! How did you get here? *(Pause)* I thought you were off in heaven with your father and mother death. *(Pause)* But here you are, looking well.

Image of the face with the pubic beard. The lower image of the profiled alcoholic at his typewriter.

B. Ignatius(Cont'd): *(After a pause)* While you're here...maybe you can help me with something.... I'm writing a poem—a eulogy really, for myself.... It's going to be read at my memorial service. *(Pause)* Yes.... *(Pause)* What does death mean? What is death? Old Grinsberg-death? Self-death? *(Pause)* All I have so far is, 'now that I am dead.' Then what? There is nothing left to compete with; there is nothing left to snarl at—I do like the image of dogs—and why was there ever? I saw you as my brother, death? Now humor me; abridge and place—shit!

B. Ignatius(Cont'd): *(After a long pause)* It *is* bad. Shit. I've got nothing. *(Pause)* And you're right. It's true that I'm not dead. *(Pause)* And, yeah, I see you down there Kerroway—you poor soul, you.... I knew that you weren't dead. Don't you remember visiting me sometimes? You have a ghastly sense of humor, you know—you always scare me...you're always so drunk.... *(Pause)* My fiancée—well, my girlfriend—she says I scare her when I drink too much. She says I lose something, and my eyes go sour. She thinks I'm a bit off in places, and that my one eyebrow raises too high.

B. Ignatius(Cont'd): *(After a pause)* We really shouldn't drink so much, you know. As they say, 'be more careful with the ones you love.' But look at you, old boy! There's still some love in you. There's still some life. You're not dead yet....

Brando trails off and goes silent. He thinks for a moment, then slides the index card over so that it is directly in front of him. He writes something.

Close-up of the index card, now displaying a second line: *I am not dead yet.*
[Interior, Simultaneously]
There is a silence on screen which allows the audience to quietly speak amongst themselves without interrupting any major plot developments.

One audience member whispers, "What in the hell is the meaning of all this—where is it going?"

Another audience member says, "So is he dead or not? I don't understand what the point is...."

Another replies, "I don't know if I even care—what the fuck does any of this matter to me? Jesus!"

Another audience member wonders aloud, "Where are the tits? I thought this thing was going to show more tits?"

A few audience members have gotten bored and stopped paying attention. It really doesn't matter to them. One, a young man, kisses his girlfriend's neck and she begins to squirm in her seat, creating friction between the fabric of her seat and her thighs, upward, stimulating her clitoris. The boyfriend moves his kiss down on her neck slightly, then exposes part of a breast from her low-cut shirt, then the nipple, which he nimbly moves his lips and tongue to.

There are the tits.

Right there in the dark, in the middle of an aisle between a sleeping family and a very large man that has had to resort to using the molars on the right side of his mouth to crush the popcorn kernels at the bottom of his otherwise empty bag of popcorn. This man has no interest in the tits, or in the screen. The concession vendors are slowly, painfully making their way back to his aisle. He watches them intently, waiting for them to arrive with a hot, fresh bag of popcorn, and hungrily cracking and devouring the hard, buttery kernels in the meantime.

[Exterior, Cont'd]

Brando, after what could have been either a daydream, or just a daze, comes to as it begins to rain. The rain is sudden, persistent, and spread out. It falls evenly and wholly.

He puts his poem back into his pocket and stands to put his coat on.

Man(O/S): Brando! *(Pause)* Brando!

Brando looks around to see who is calling his name: across the street is a man wearing the hood from his heavy coat—he is looking at Brando and waving his arm to come over.

B. Ignatius: Stefan? No....

Brando laughs and trots across the street.

Stefan: Brando, how are you? *(They hug each other)*

B. Ignatius: I'm well, I'm dying....

Stefan: Good, come with me—I want to show you something!

Stefan takes Brando around the shoulders and they begin walking through the rain together.

B. Ignatius: And what is it you want to show me, Stefan—a new painting? Have you been busy?

Stefan: I love the rain, my friend—it feels good, huh! I feel closer to nature in the rain, closer to my creator!

Stefan continues to drag Brando along excitedly, smiling.

B. Ignatius: Are we going to meet your creator then, Stefano? Is that where we're going?

Stefan: I feel closer to *you* in the rain, my friend!

Stefan claps Brando on the back to show his feeling of comradery. He's beaming. Brando looks distracted.

B. Ignatius(V/O): I forgot to say goodbye to old Grins and Kerroway! Oh well, I'm sure they'll understand....

The pair, moving all the while, has come upon a door that opens onto the street from the lower level of a three story apartment home.

Stefan: Come on, I need to stop here first.

Stefan pushes Brando into the door ahead of him and they enter into a low-ceilinged room, which is actually fairly long, but is sectioned off by semitransparent curtains. To get anywhere, the curtains must be pushed aside. All of the compartments are candle lit. A record plays from somewhere they have yet been.

In a back room, through a door past several curtains. Brando and Stefan enter, in that order. The music gets louder. There is a couch set up for a very small audience to watch something—what sort of thing we can only assume—that is happening off-screen.

Stefan urges Brando to sit on the couch next to two young women who are both quite clearly deeply engaged with whatever it is they are watching. Brando removes his coat and sits down beside the two young women. He searches through his pockets. He gets his hands on a cigarette from that magical shirtfront pocket of his.

The young woman beside him lights his cigarette before he gets a chance.

B. Ignatius: Oh—thank you! *(Pause, then offering his hand)* Hello, uh, I'm Brando....

The young woman simply smiles at old Brando and redirects her eyes back to the off-screen action. Brando, too, begins to watch curiously the off-screen happenings— tilting his head to one side, then to the other side, like a puppy dog whose face allows for complete forgiveness in spite of the abominable act they are about to commit, the one they are thinking about committing, or the one they have just recently committed.

He takes a drag of the cigarette, exhales, then slowly glances at the young woman. He turns back to the mysterious display, again slowly, then again to the young woman. He seems to be confused or saddened or something. He stands up, carryings his coat over his arm like a gentleman, and dismisses himself from the room.

Outside the rain has yielded to something more subtle, quieter, but no less wet. A grey screen of light distorting drizzle surrounds Brando, who stands outside of the apartment door, on the curb, now finishing the second half of his cigarette with his overcoat on. Evening approaches.

B. Ignatius(V/O): Why is it that you can never say no to anything, old Brando? *(Pause)* It wouldn't have been necessary for you to involve yourself inside—it was simply enough for you to have just been there and seen what you did for Wilka to leave you... If Wilka found out! *(Pause)* Oh, Stefano—that fool....

Brando laughs, then finishes his cigarette like some sort of sewer creature he had seen in a movie, tilting his head backwards to look towards the sky, puffing quickly, drooping his facial features, and pacing back and forth in an exaggerated gait. He sees a young woman standing at the curb near him, wearing an overcoat and smoking a cigarette. He stops his nonsense, puts his cigarette out on the ground and pockets the butt.

B. Ignatius: *(To the woman)* I saw you earlier....

Second Woman: Oh?

B. Ignatius: Yeah, I saw you earlier this morning—you were dressed just as you are now, and smoking just as you are now. There were at least a hundred other women on the street, all doing the exact same thing as you—why were you all doing that?

Second Woman: *(Laughing)* And you remember seeing *me* when there were at least a hundred other women?

B. Ignatius: Yes, I think so. You all frightened me.

Second Woman: Women frighten you then?

B. Ignatius: It's not that women frighten me, it's just that...there were so many of you...and it frightens me that in all of the women I saw, not one of you was the woman I was looking for....

Second Woman: You don't think I could be what you're looking for?

B. Ignatius: Don't get me wrong, I'm sure you're what a lot of men are looking for. *(Pause)* I mean, it's not that a good woman is hard to find—there are a lot of good women out there...great ones...it's finding the right woman that's hard....

Second Woman: *(After a pause)* What about finding the right woman for *right now*?

B. Ignatius: Oh, I've found her—she's just missing is all. *(Pause)* I know she's around here somewhere, it's just that I can't see her *right now*....

The young woman has finished her cigarette, now discards it into the street. She approaches Brando, coming rather closely to his face, leaning in, almost brushing his cheek with hers.

Second Woman: *(Whispering)* Well maybe you're just not looking hard enough, sweet boy....

B. Ignatius(V/O): This is all from something—what is this from? 'If things turn out badly then it is a tragedy, if they turn out alright then it is a comedy.' But what if nothing happens and the way things turn out are no different than how they began—what then? It is crucial to say nothing more to this woman.

The young woman somewhat retreats from Brando's face and gives him an outrageously large smile. He nervously smiles back. Stefan comes up from behind Brando, clapping him on the shoulder.

Stefan: *(Good naturedly)* Well, I apologize miss, but me and my friend here must be going!

Second Woman: *(Still smiling, to Brando)* Of course! It was nice seeing you again....

The two men are already on their way, walking down the street in the ever-nearing evening.

Stefan: Sorry about that back there. I didn't realize you knew that woman.

B. Ignatius: I didn't.

Stefan: Ah, making new friends then—good. And mum's the word!

B. Ignatius: I just happened to have seen her this morning...and that is a ridiculous saying.

Stefan: It's okay by me.

B. Ignatius: *(After a pause)* What time is it anyway?

Stefan: Eh, about there I guess—not far to go now! It's just right up here.

Brando and Stefan round a corner and start up a small hill onto a bridge. Halfway across the bridge they stop at a small sitting nook between two lampposts that still remain off in the fading daylight. The view is of most of the city, at a slight distance.

Stefan: Some wine, my friend?

Stefano pulls a bottle of wine out from within his coat, the cork poking out of the neck and holding two tiny paper cups in place.

B. Ignatius: Yeah, sure.

The two paper cups are filled and a silence passes between the two men. Each of them takes a few sips from their cups. Stefano breaks the silence without changing his cityward stare.

Stefan: Sorry you had to see what you did earlier—I just didn't have any money on me and when I saw you I wanted for us to have a little wine. My friend over there, she always has a little wine to spare, and the, uh, show, was happening merely by chance.

B. Ignatius: It's nothing I haven't seen before—though never as a true spectator I guess.

Stefan: Usually it's just that same old mirrored image, huh?

B. Ignatius: The one that I'm used to, and enjoy—yes.

Stefan: Well, sometimes a change in perspective doesn't hurt though—a minor rotation to alter the angles and curves, a slight shift in vantage point, and suddenly you're a brand new man.

B. Ignatius: *(Calmly, jokingly)* I have no intention of fucking you tonight, Stefano, if that's what you're getting at—so don't waste your lines. I am a man that loves women.

Stefan: Good. Then we understand one another. *(Pause)* More wine?

B. Ignatius: More wine would be good. Besides, I'm dying anyway....

Stefan: Yeah, I heard you earlier. *(Pauses, refilling their cups)* And you're not dying any more than I am, which could mean something or nothing. But...

Stefano raises one finger in the air, his arm partially outstretched towards the city as if he were asking for something, anticipating, waiting.

A very long moment passes with the finger still raised expectantly. Then the street lamps turn on, all at once. **Stefan(Cont'd):** *(Satisfied)* There. Now drink.

Stefano touches the rim of his paper cup to Brando's, then gulps down its contents.

Stefan(Cont'd): And that's it.

B. Ignatius: Yes it is.

Stefan: Then I'll see you later.

Stefano shakes Brando's hand and bows slightly, then turns on his heels to leave, immediately turning back around.

Stefan: Eh...I almost forgot to leave you with one last drink. *(Filling the cup that Brando had drunk down just as Stefano was leaving)*There you go. Sorry, but I'll be taking the rest with me....

B. Ignatius: *(Smiling, tilting his glass in toast)* I understand.

Stefano turns on his heels for the second time and leaves now for good. Brando remains in place, still. He looks out at the city and takes a deep breath. He finishes his wine in one drink, crushes the cup, and pockets the trash.

B. Ignatius(V/O): *(Sighing, then happily)* What a fool....

Coming back down the bridge in the glowing grey blue of the onset of evening, Brando walks in apparently high spirits. He is whistling softly to himself, then mimicking the click-clack sound of his boots on the sidewalk.

Suddenly upon the perimeter of a park, Brando enters the grounds, ascending a few small flights of stairs, touching the hedges here and there, looking about the heavily wooded park that now surrounds him.

B. Ignatius(V/O): Aha!

317

On the plateau of a small hill there is a long row of teeter-totters; in front of the teeter-totters is a large swingset. Brando approaches the swings and sits down on one. No one else is in the park.

B. Ignatius(V/O): This is the swingset of my dreams, in the park of my dreams. *(Pause)* No one else is around. I am alone, sleeping.

He begins to swing back and forth, gently at first, then gradually gaining momentum and altitude.

B. Ignatius(V/O): It's on this swing that I have often lifted off before, soaring over those trees into the atmosphere, looking down into the world from a bird's eye. *(Pause)* Could I be dreaming now? Could I be dreaming that chase-dream now where the object which I seek is always just out of reach? *(Pause)* Will I ever find you, Wilka? *(Pause)* No, this can't be a dream—those lights turned on and the daylight itself is slowly fading. Lights don't turn on or off in dreams, they supposedly remain in whatever state they began. *(Pause)* But that could be wrong.

B. Ignatius(V/O, Cont'd): Maybe I am dreaming, or maybe I am dead, or maybe I have finally lost it altogether, and gone out of my mind. Who's to say where the differences in those things lie anyway? Not you, Wilka—you're not here. Stefano, that beautiful fool—I think he's a little bit of a drunk. *(Pause)* There is only me, and this swingset, and this park. We are to decide. It is our choice.

B. Ignatius(V/O, Cont'd): I am going to jump now. Don't be afraid. Either I will float, or I will not. *(Preparing himself on the swing, then counting at each forward motion)* One.... Two.... Three—

Having gained a considerable amount of momentum and altitude, Brando heaves himself forward off the swing, on three, and goes flying into the air with legs and body perfectly straight and stiff! He reaches a peak along the parabola of his jump, then begins the inevitable descent of the other side. But just a foot above the ground, right before he hits, his body is suspended, hovering there like an opaque ghost.

The screen trembles and shakes for a moment. Focus is regained.

It all looks quite real. Hovering there just a foot above the ground, Brando is convincing as a real to life ghost. He is startled, elated, confused. He inspects the distance between his own two feet and the ground, giggling.

The initial reaction is overcome.

Brando is now only accepting and ecstatic. He puts his hands together over his head, which is now bent over forward while his ass pokes out behind like a speed swimmer about to jump off the blocks, or a child that's about to be rolled downhill on an invisible plank at

318

high speeds.

B. Ignatius: *(Cueing his own movement)* And we're off!

Moving as if on a hallucinatory track, hovering in steady flight one foot above ground, unnoticed by the immediate environment, Brando glides like a cheerful ghost through the different scenes of a psychological montage(seen by the audience through his eyes)— sometimes commenting, sometimes merely observing—as their images transfigure and transform, seamlessly merging one occurrence to the next.

A) Farther down the hill within the park, near a large fountain. Circling the fountain, suddenly in full daylight.

B. Ignatius(V/O): *(Whispering in amazement)* Wilka...there you are!

Brando and Wilka sit on the edge of the fountain, laughing and talking with a third person, a young man whose resemblance to Brando implies blood-relation.

B. Ignatius(V/O): This is when my brother came to visit. We all had a nice time, didn't we? I was glad to see that you got along with each other.... *(Pause)* It gave me the impression that you belonged in my family....

The circle now taking a steady curve inward, creeping up from behind Wilka, looking over her shoulder into Brando's face.

B) Brando's face: at a booth in a bar, the gloom. Across from him sits Wilka. Each has a drink in hand—one is dark; the other, the lady's, is water.

In the background, past Wilka, is a small group of people. They are sitting in a back section of the bar listening to someone speak in front of a microphone—the speaker finishes what he has been saying and the group claps. A new speaker from the group switches places with the old one.

B. Ignatius(V/O): I had just written my essay on The Mechanics of Dream—I wanted to read it that night to an audience. It was my first real attempt at writing anything other than descriptions of sweet treats. It was important to me. But it was clear that the little gathering was interested only in sex, carnal desires, drunkenness, and other good times. *(Pause)* Later in the week I wrote my humor essay on The Origin of Dance. I don't know if it was funny or not because I never showed that to anyone either—not even you. *(Pause)* I could've sworn you were ashamed of me that night, and all I did was went on drinking until everyone else had finished their readings and we all went home. I doubt I got laid—but I don't remember....

The lights in the back of the bar turn off and everyone is gone.

319

Wilka stares at Brando who then hangs his head.

C) With his head down in busy concentration, Brando stands in the kitchen of his apartment hastily doing dishes. Wilka is annoyed in the background, through the kitchen door into the living area, packing a few books and notebooks into a bag, then getting her coat.

Brando turns the water off in the sink, leaving the dishes unfinished, and goes to the kitchen doorway to watch as Wilka prepares to leave.

B. Ignatius: You had asked me to leave—said you didn't want to get into a fight. Over what? *(Pause)* Then you gathered your things to go—just like this.... I had made you dinner earlier, then we took a nap. *(Pause)* Of course, I didn't let you go alone. I went with you—and you were happy.

Wilka has the things she needs and is opening the door to leave. Brando turns the kitchen light off and grabs his coat, catching up with her just outside the door of the apartment. He puts his arm around her lower back as they take their steps to the elevator—their backs and coats filling the frame.

D) Slowly moving forward as the lower backs of the couple move outward more quickly, changing then into two full backs, then shoulders, and heads. The dream couple now walks along the street one in front of the other—with Wilka leading, naturally. They have come upon the building of their present residence. There is an 'Apartment Available' sign hanging from the fire escape.

Wilka stares up at the sign and begins to call the number. Brando stands back and waits as Wilka soundlessly chats into her phone.

B. Ignatius(V/O): How did we end up here? *(Pause)* What were we really looking for?

Suddenly in the empty apartment, later that day. They are moving their first few belongings in, moving their few pieces of furniture around first here, then there, trying to find the right place for each item. The big green chair is moved several times.

B. Ignatius(V/O): There's no place for that poor chair in our apartment—it's too big. *(Pause)* We should've left it in the basement where we found it....

Brando moves the big green chair back into a position in the window that it had been previously, but seems either more or less satisfied with its placement this time around or is just simply exhausted by the mental efforts of decision making.

He sits down in the chair, coming closer to us, closer....

Beyond Brando's face, now set staring out the window, the street below can be seen. It is raining. Spinning halfway about his head,

Brando's face envelops the frame.

E) Again with that fucking face! Brando's face, right there front and center. Then, panning out, pulling back from this face, it is apparent that the setting has changed.

A different room. The lights low. Colors dark. A vague heaviness.

Wilka appears from the atmosphere or stratosphere. She grabs Brando's hand and yanks him from his seat, forcing him to dance with her. Their steps are mismatched, out of sync, of time, beat, and everything. There is no rhythm in the tango. She sees this and pushes Brando away, then disappears.

Brando, alone, does a few slow dance steps. A little one, two—a tap. Then he gives up. He slowly sits down on the ground, then lies his whole body down to boot. A blanket materializes, puffing itself up, and gingerly landing over the supine Brando.

F) Tracing the folds of a blanket, up along the deep, soft trenches, all the way up to the very top where we find Brando's head laid on a pillow. He looks mortified, disgusted. A television comes partially into view, showing blurry pornographic images. A teenage boy is under the covers next to Brando. The boy says something to him, unheard, then grabs Brando by the hand and leads it under the covers. Brando is near tears, resisting, afraid.

B. Ignatius(V/O): This is how I was introduced to sex—by a swarthy adolescent boy, whose little mustachio came on too early, and was revolting. *(Pause)* You didn't know that, huh. *(Pause)* I was eight then, and he must have been fourteen or fifteen. *(Pause)* I used to resent that poor young boy for making me do that to him—he should've known better. I used to be ashamed of myself. But I am not anymore. I have forgiven him now. *(Pause)* Not that anyone ever knew one way or the other—but I have forgiven him.

Now through with our trembling, skittish glances of a teary eye, a bottom lip being sucked under by its upper lip in remorse—again a teary eye, again the sad lips—our gaze trails off from the face to a shoulder, to an arm, then settling firmly down on to a hand.

G) The strong, veiny hand of a young man holds the arm of a sofa. The hand belongs to Stefano; the couch is the one in which Brando sat earlier as spectator of that off-screen action. Brando leans against the couch where Stefano sits, watching just as Stefano does. The wine bottle is empty in Stefano's lap. He gawks towards the mystery of life.

B. Ignatius: Now there is this—poor Stefano!

From the perspective of anyone who should ever happen to sit on the couch, looking forward: a woman is bent over away from the couch; first seen is the woman's ass, clothed only in panties, almost transparent, then the bare-skinned bend over her lower back and the parallel lines of back and tummy, separated by the ribcage; following the natural line of her very bones, over the soft skin covering the slight hump of a partial breast, then receding into the upper, upper thigh of an obviously nude, obviously feminine creature—the other thigh seen, too, from the far side of the bent over body, clearly outlining a woman on her back whose legs are spread wide open like the giant, white wings of an angel as the other woman, or creature, digs deeply within them....

Stefano and Brando, again. Brando puts his arm pitifully and lovingly around Stefano's head, pulling it into his side.

B. Ignatius: You have brought me to the opposite end of this cracked egg, my friend. *(Pause)* You have showed me equal sadness.

Brando bends down and kisses Stefano on the head as a father would his sick child. He straightens his posture again and turns back to the action—back to that overwhelming sight of the woman's ass, clothed only in panties, bent directly into the screen.

H) The bepantied ass of a nurse is viewed in its entirety—wide, full. She is bent over between the wide spread legs of a woman in labor. The woman's face can be seen, relaxed, serene. The nurse casually extracts the baby and holds it up to the mother who is smiling in ecstasy. The nurse is fully clothed now. She hands the naked child to the mother.

B. Ignatius(V/O): *(The mother lipsynching)* My sweet baby boy.... *(Pause, the mother's lips now stuck smiling)* And my sweet mother....

The mother, cradling the infant Brando, brings him as close as she can to her chest to kiss him on the soft down of his head, then takes a deep breath of his head's aroma(the audience surely does smell this aroma, of a soft, clean baby).

I) And the mother now pulls back her nose from the child's head, holding in the breath. She lies on the floor of a room lit only by the lights of a Christmas tree. A dark figure is in the background, in repose, with the feet outstretched and supported by a dark mass. The child is lying under the Christmas tree, barely awake. The mother strokes his head and begins to sing.

B. Ignatius(V/O): *(Softly, accompanying his mother's voice)*
    The first Noel, the angels did say
    Was to certain poor shepherds in fields as they lay
    In fields where they lay keeping their sheep
    On a cold winter's night that was so deep
    (Pause)

322

Brando's voice ceases, as do the lyrics of *"The First Noel."* His mother, still lying on the floor stroking his infant head, carries on the tune in a gentle, soothing hum. The sound is pervasive, continuous. Slowly fade out to black.

[Interior]
In the warm, ever-shrinking auditorium of the imagination, a maternal hum echoes throughout. Momentary darkness.

The audience has a strong desire to sleep. Everything in their bodies and minds is telling them to sleep.

The humming continues, coaxing the audience into a trance, which the physical environment suddenly inhibits with the introduction of an irritating stimulant: systematic drops of water, at once warm, then colder; rain falling from the hidden, tissue-like ceilings.

What was at first relaxing and calm—the humming, the warmth, the darkness—has now become uncomfortable, startling. Even those deepest entranced, or asleep, are awoken. And just in time to witness the closing scenes, the final brief waltz and pirouette of a ludicrous ballet in their imaginations, in their lives and the lives of others, as this one common experience put on film, on stage, on paper.

At the audience's feet, puddles have begun to form and expand. Anxiety and terror is induced. Everyone sits up in their seats, drawing their feet and their knees up to their chests.

[Exterior, Coda]
A woman's rhythmic hum slowly gives way in the darkness, receding into it, then is replaced completely by the sound of rain; the darkness is replaced by light, fading in as inconspicuously as the rain.

It is a bright nighttime. Rain comes down lightly and steadily over Brando's horizontal face, laid down to rest on the wet grass of the park. The teeter-totters and swings are unmoving.

Brando opens his eyes.

A gradual rise from the ground—first the head, then the rest of the body. The absence of Internal vocalization is apparent. The atmosphere is unnaturally quiet and tranquil. The sound of the rain can hardly be considered a sound—it is more of a presence. It is simply there.
Brando brushes off the pieces of crushed leaves from his coat and jeans. He straightens out his damp and somewhat tussled hair. He stretches, touches his toes, then begins to walk at a snail-like pace.

On the wet streets, in the bright night, there is a stillness of everything that is nearly spiritual. Brando comes upon a sleeping bum whose slumber is so peaceful looking that he lingers over the figure, observing it. He is visibly touched. With great care he removes his coat and lays it over the bum's underdressed body. He watches him for a moment longer, then turns around.

He paces back and forth along the curb. He goes back to the sleeping bum, still peaceful looking, and certainly warmer.

Again with great care, he regretfully removes his coat from the bum and drapes it over his arm. The bum stirs and awakens drunkenly.

Bum: Hey! *(Gathering his inebriated composure)* Son of God.... *(Stammering)* Can you spare some change for Satan?

Brando is not alarmed by the broken stillness of the bum, or by being called son of god. He accepts it in a dreamlike state.

B. Ignatius: I'm sorry...I don't have anything....

Bum: How 'bout a cigarette for this old devil then?

Still dreamily, almost spellbound by the coarse figure in front of him, Brando reaches into his shirtfront pocket for his cigarettes. He removes the pack along with his unfinished poem. He looks at them both, then gives them to the bum.

B. Ignatius: Here—have them.

The bum, with trembling hands, accepts Brando's cigarettes and the poem, though unwittingly, with true simplicity. He opens the pack and takes out a cigarette, placing it with effort between his lips. Brando slowly turns to leave.

Bum: Hey! *(Calling Brando back, the pack of cigarettes open in his dirty outstretched hand)* Can I offer you a cigarette?

Brando, amused or touched by the bum's generosity, takes the few paces towards the dirty outstretched hand. He takes a cigarette.

B. Ignatius: Thank you, sir....

Bum: God be with you!

Brando smiles, lights his friend's cigarette, then lights his own. He gives the bum the universal nod of understanding, then walks off.

In front of his apartment building, Brando stalls along the edge of the courtyard. He stands in the drizzle and haze with his back to the street, and finishes his last cigarette. He is gazing up at the building as if he were actually looking into it, through it.

B. Ignatius(V/O): What am I to say now, Wilka? *(Pause)* 'Where have you been?' No —that doesn't matter. 'Where are you now?' *(Pause)* 'Who are you?' *(Pause)* Oh...poor Wilka...what is there left for us to do?

The night has lost its earlier shine. The bright grayish blue of before midnight has developed into the thick, full darkness of the earliest hour of the morning.

The last cigarette is gone.

The poem is gone.

The union of man and woman to man and wife has not been

promised, secured, or even proposed. The woman is a myth, a phantom, like that object which one searches for in a dream without ever overcoming that minute yet vast distance that separates it from idea to thing, tangible, real, without that yearned for and dreaded capturing of it, or without ever fully comprehending what it actually is.

The man is inert, circular—a willing victim of the middle ground, fighting through inaction to retain the illusions of childhood, with an intuitive fear and loneliness instilled in him by the mere pr-ximity and unavoidable accompanying disillusionment of his adult life. Oh...

Poor Brando, standing there in the rain. The only thing left for him to do is to go inside, to remove his coat, and to dry off.

Quickly through the lobby, past the unspeaking faces of the columns.

A slow, upward ride in the elevator.

In the hallway in front of his apartment, Brando unhurriedly takes his keys out of his pocket, searches for the right one, then inserts it into the lock. He enters the apartment.

Behind the closed and locked door, within the apartment, the world at large has been shrunken down. What little furniture there was in the apartment is now either pint size or has disappeared altogether. Brando, whose features have taken on those of a surprisingly agile-looking doll, stands at about eighteen inches tall.

As if in a soft spotlight, miniature Brando walks a few choppy steps into the apartment and stops. All movement is seen exaggeratedly in stop animation.

B. Ignatius(V/O): Hello.

Wilka, now doll-like as well, sits comfortably on a red velvet chaise lounge that was not in the apartment before.

Wilka(V/O): Hi.

B. Ignatius(V/O): I've been looking for you all day.

Wilka(V/O): Yes, I know—and now you've found me. *(Pause)* I've been here all along.

B. Ignatius(V/O): *(After a pause)* Oh....

Tiny Brando walks nearer to where Wilka sits, and stands in front of a very small piano. They are both in frame.

The faint, high-pitched hum of a singing bowl gradually becomes more apparent in the room(and the auditorium)—not necessarily its sound, but the feeling within one's body which its vibrations produce.

Brando strikes a chord on the piano.

B. Ignatius(V/O, Cont'd): There was something I wanted to tell you this morning. *(Pause)* There was something I wanted to ask you, too.

(Pause) But I'm no longer sure if either is relevant; nor am I sure if now would be an appropriate time regardless—I don't think you're wearing any panties under that dress....

Wilka(V/O): I assure you, I am.

B. Ignatius(V/O): Okay.... *(Strikes three more chords on the piano)* Well, I guess you should know then—I'm going to die.

Wilka(V/O): Do you know when?

The trembling of the soul within the body, created by the singing bowl, continues to increase. The two dolls seem to be talking within a giant bell.

B. Ignatius(V/O): I read earlier that it would be tomorrow, which I suppose would mean today at some point, if not very soon. *(Looks around the room)* God—can you feel that? *(Listening, looking for the feeling or the sound)* It's like my heart is splitting open from the middle and unraveling from each side and it's spreading out through my body like it were a piece of pork being pulled apart—but it's not. It's right here in my chest as usual. *(Puts one hand over his chest, checks his pulse in his neck with the other)* My god, I can feel everything in my body...moving...it's too much—this body is too big, I don't want it! It's too big!

In his agitation, miniature Brando has begun to draw himself inward, hunching over as if a great weight were crippling him. He checks his pulse again. Takes a few deep breaths. Then he regains a somewhat calmer demeanor, and his body partially unwinds and straightens out.

B. Ignatius(V/O, Cont'd): *(Vaguely calm)* No, I don't want it. *(After playing one last chord on the tiny piano, he turns to Wilka and tiptoes to her side)* I apologize. *(Pause)* Do you hear that though?

Wilka(V/O): Yes. *(Pause)* It is the sound of light—you can see that the sun is rising....

Brando looks past Wilka out the tiny window and sees that the sun—an orange reflective disc—is, indeed, rising. The sound of the singing bowl, the sun, the light—the feeling—is enveloping, almost unbearable.

B. Ignatius(V/O): You're right—it is. And I haven't slept yet!

Wilka(V/O): Come here.... *(Motioning for him to come lay next to her on the chaise lounge)* Come lay next to me—sleep....

Brando meets her invitation with little resistance, silently accepting, and letting his tiny body down next to hers.

Wilka(V/O): Now close your eyes and let go...just be quiet...be still...and fall asleep my sweet little boy....

The two dolls remain nestled in next to one another, conjoined basically, and still. Their two tiny bodies fade delicately, slowly, into a bright white oblivion.

Fading in from the pure, bright light, the colors of the morning blink into focus through the window. Brando—in the flesh, full size—lies on the floor of the apartment, alone.

Still fully clothed, Brando awakens himself completely by rising from the floor, coughing, and stretching. He goes into the kitchen and fills a pot full of water. The pot is put on the stovetop to heat up.

Next to the stove, taped to the refrigerator, there is a note that has been left for him.

It reads: *At work. Be home soon. –W.*

He stands there in the kitchen for a moment. He attempts to fix his sleep-disheveled hair—with no luck. He goes over to his typewriter in the next room, searches for something around and under it, then returns to the kitchen. He searches the fridge, on the outside, among its various papers and drawings, under those, too, and finally finds what he is looking for—he grabs it.

The water has started to boil.

Brando turns off the stovetop and pours the hot water into a small, porcelain teapot with two bags of tea. He lets it steep on the counter and returns his attention to the small slip of paper taken from the fridge.

It reads:

> Mr. Orlando Loyola died in his home yesterday after a long battle with lung cancer. He was 84 years old. He is survived by his wife, Elsa, and their two daughters.
>
> Mr. Loyola was an upstanding citizen, a great husband and father, and a successful and generous local business owner. By both the community at large, and his surviving family, he will be greatly missed.

The entire obituary has been circled in red ink. At the bottom, in that same red ink, in the same hand as the note from Wilka, is written the words, *'Good Lungs are Important.'*

Brando appears to be baffled, amused, or relieved—a little saddened— by this obituary and its red-inked side note.

After looking it over for another moment longer, he sticks it back to the fridge with a magnet. He picks up the small teapot by its handle, and a matching small, porcelain teacup. He leaves the kitchen.

In the bathroom, Brando sets his things for tea on an upside down milk crate next to the tub. He turns the water on for a bath. He goes over to the mirror and stares directly into his face. He takes off his shirt. He disappears from view for a moment, below the mirror, presumably to remove his pants. He returns to the mirror and resumes his stare.

B. Ignatius: By all means you're dying then, old boy. And there's nothing you can do about it. *(Pause)* I am dying. *(Pause)* But not today—at least not right now, which is when and where everything is happening. *(Pause)* How will they remember you? It's impossible and unnecessary to say. *(Pause)* I am not a bad man. I am decent, sensitive to others, compassionate. I open doors for people, stran-gers—men and women both—and I smile at them. *(Smiles at himself in the mirror as if he were one of those strangers)* This is all that matters—what *I* believe I am. *(Pause)* And that is my self, naked, and happy....

Brando turns the running water off in the tub, which is now full. He refrains from going back to the mirror, although his monologue seemed to want to go on.

He lets himself down into the tub slowly, exhaling as he does so. Having settled into place comfortably, he reaches for the tea. He fills his little teacup and brings it into the tub, holding it just above the surface of the water. He takes a sip, then rests the cup on his chest.

Brando calmly stares at or into something that cannot be seen. The cup rises and falls as he breathes in deep, steady, held breaths: Inhaling, low-tide.... Then exhaling, high-tide.... Inhaling, low-tide.... Then exhaling, high-tide.... And so on.

The screen, with each passing breath, darkens in that same constant rhythm.

In the ever-dimming grey, with the volume fading as well as the light, there is an indiscernible sound somewhere—but what is it? Maybe a gentle splash caused by slight movement in the tub, or a door being unlocked and opened, or a name said, a sound of surprise, or delight, maybe another gentle splash; or maybe nothing at all.

Then silence follows and the complete, impartial darkness of an ending.

Act Three

WHOEVER CAME HERE WITH ME
CAN FIND THEIR OWN WAY HOME

[Interior]
The auditorium is in absolute darkness. There is a fleeting stillness which can only be experienced after exertion, physical or mental—a brief stillness which expresses its intrinsic gratitude for all action, movement, and speech to have stopped.

The show is over.

As if by the flick of a switch, light and sound is suddenly restored to the auditorium. At once there is a shimmer of bright pink and white, and a clatter—there is an uprising. It is time to go home.

What the audience has been thinking all this time, they now say. And what they say is bad. They berate the actors who appeared on screen, picking apart their looks, their talent, the behavior of the characters they portrayed. They belittle the writer, the director, the cinematographer, and crew, saying, "Well I could do better than that!"

They say it had no meaning, no heart, it tried too hard, went too far—and for what?

They say it lacked purpose, and vision. There is no way it could ever be considered *Art*.

And what about the first act? They have already forgotten about that.

Overall, the audience is dissatisfied, which is good. The audience likes to be dissatisfied. They like to say bad things. If they came out after the end of a performance saying things like, 'Yes, it was very good,' or 'phenomenal,' or 'beautiful,' then they might have to admit to their own incompetence.

Instead, as the audience begins to clear out, they say, "How in the hell did I get here, and why did I even come?"

They won't let themselves remember the answers.

The water from the earlier flood has drained, but has left the carpet soggy and covered with litter.

As the audience files out of their aisles, popcorn, chocolate, gum, and discarded wrappers stick to their feet and the foul water from the carpet splashes onto their pant legs. This causes more irritation in their already dissatisfied and agitated hearts, therefore resulting in utter

329

irrationality.

The audience repeats to themselves, *"How in the hell did I get here, and why did I even come?"*

Then answers, "I don't give a shit anyway, 'cos I'm leaving—and whoever came here with me can find their own goddamn way home!"

They mutter these things and they are glad, morbidly glad. They push past one another with that menacing joy, first seeking out someone to complain to, who they will demand a refund from, then seeking out the exits.

Children are abandoned in the search—some are trampled—along with personal belongings, good manners, and self respect.

All the sense has gone out of these people—of order, of responsibility, of rationale. What peace there was within them has left. If there was ever any spirituality about them, it has vanished without a trace.

Along the soft, glistening pink walls which house the auditorium—and that have created those fantastic, otherworldly acoustics—ineffectively searching for the exit, the audience claws with their nails, bangs their fists, their heads, bites and gouges with their teeth, and uses every other body part imaginable, like terrified caged animals, in an unsuccessful attempt to force an escape.

It is not going to happen, although their struggle continues. The soft, irritated-pink walls will not cave in. The domed ceiling will not open up and let them take flight out of here. There is only one way in, and one way out. At present, that exit is locked.

Eventually, the audience will wear themselves out. They will be physically exhausted, and will take a few deep breaths out of necessity.

Then, another stillness—if only for a moment—in which they are given a second chance. Some audience members will take advantage of it, and will realize the fault in their action; others never will.

Those in the audience who have come to terms with their wrongdoings now begin to hunt for their loved ones, hoping to god they have not been trampled. If they are lucky, they reconcile. They pick up lost bags, purses, glasses, sweaters, and the like. If they are not lucky, then they will have to understand that those are the consequences of their behavior, and they will suffer because of them, endlessly calling out the names of those who they have lost forever, and crying hysterically over that loss.

The lucky ones, crossing themselves, sit back down in their seats in order to reflect on what has really just happened here. They contemplate their surroundings: the smell, the horrific mess, the several audience members who still bang and scratch at the walls, screaming wildly.

It is awful, they think.

And they know that they did not make it through because of their own virtue—it was by chance; divine intervention. Someone or something let them make it through.

It will be different now, they promise themselves.

But regardless of these thoughts that pop in and out of the audience's heads, regardless of whether they think their luck is good or bad, or the promises they make to themselves, they will all have to wait until someone or something decides that their time is up—then they can either leave, or what? Or die? Or, worse—disappear into nonexisence?

Whatever it may mean, the decision has been made. The time is now.

The auditorium lights are dimming, and the stage lights are warming back up for another act that no one wants to see. The lions are coming out of their dressing rooms behind the curtains, stalking through the backstage hallways, and out into the auditorium.

A very small door marked 'Exit' opens from beneath the stage.

The audience looks around at their loved ones and the other members of the mob for the last time; they look at the single, tiny door and at those beautiful, ferocious beasts on stage. Their options are considered. The risks are calculated, and weighed. Then, all at once, they make their final mad dash....

—Winter 2009, Portland, OR

SONGS: I CAN'T SING*
(2010)

*For
B.*

---

* With additional contributions by BRANDON FONT

CONTENTS

---

* Songs written by Brandon Font
° A Christmas story written by both of The Brothers Font(sic)

Foreword: On Music

Music is present at the beginning and the end of everything—the birth exaltation, and the death lamentation—as well as it is present in between; that is, music is everywhere, being absorbed at all times, either casually through the subconscious brain, or intensively through the conscious brain. It is both produced and heard, simultaneously, by the subtle force within man that is irrevocable, spiritual.

For some, music is considered the *divine art*. In reality, music differs from painting, or drawing, or writing, or whatever, only inasmuch as it does not require the absolute attention of or participation from its audience for it to effectively move them—though it doesn't hurt to have them willingly listen. However, I do not believe this makes it the divine art—divine, of course, implying a heavenly origin, or perfection—in the same way that I also do not believe any art is or can be divine, being that all art is created by creatures of this earth, and therefore belongs to this earth, making it inherently, obviously, worldly and imperfect.

I say this not to degrade art, or the artist, but to elevate them both. Art is essential to existence because it strives to be transcendent, and even believes itself to be at times; it is the making of life from life, within it, or of it; it is creation spawned from creation that, if only for a moment, provides its audience with the sense that their life, and life itself—the basis for art, and the artist's perception—might actually mean something; it is a continual process of giving abstract life and taking it, of forming and destroying, which ultimately allows for the human experience to expand infinitely, theoretically, if only to give the individual a better understanding of the present, physical life they are leading.

And music is simply the most accessible, most universal art *form*.

As Henry Miller said, *almost*, "If your organs are intact, your ears work just fine, and you desire to do so, then go right ahead. You're the instrument. Just open your mouth—sing."

Although it is seemingly that easy to generate a song, there is no mention of the quality of the song, or of the quality of the voice which is singing it. By the standards of ordinary judgment, it is fair to say that I cannot sing. I am capable of opening my mouth. I have a pair of lungs. I can pretend to know a little of music. But it would be a terrible misrepresentation of my talents to say that I am *singing*.

335

When I was younger, all I wanted to be was an actor. When I was taking (very unnecessary) classes to teach me how to act, all I wanted to do was write. Now, as a writer, all I want to do is travel around the world with a tiny wooden piano meant for children and sing my ever-shrinking lungs out. Instead, I am sitting at a tiny wooden desk in a relatively empty apartment in the Northwest of the country I was born in, writing *this*.

This book is to be taken in as similar a casual manner as one would take in music—either with your pants down at your ankles in the bathroom, or on a long drive when all other options have run out. This, then, really *is* a song, or songs, or at least very much like one; it is the foundation of a song, the music and the lyrics of a song to which anyone can and should sing along. I do not yet have a tiny wooden piano meant for children, but I am certainly still learning how to play.

Untitled No. 1

I am a mountain—USA. A mountain with a full view of so many starry visions of America and abroad(atop the world, winner of world wars, child of America!).

When rocks tremble, or souls quake, I have changed into a bunch of grass hoppers and devastated crops, drank beer after working on the docks in plain clothes—just one man—and also just simply stayed the mountain and blew my top. Lava burned and boiled down pretty feminine green thigh slopes of beautiful oily impressionistic landscapes and ignited every shiny world, continuing advertisements that had been a burden to all the (once upon a time) tranquil snowflakes on my tombstone shoulders.

All of them lost in fire—this being but only a fraction of one vision I have seen as the mountain.

Borges and I, and I

There are two of me, at least, just like Borges said. The one considers himself to be a decent Christian, like those before the phrase was invented. The other little bemustached clown is a bad man. He is sick, and says things that don't make sense. The Other Font is a whorish storyteller, full of vulgarities and sketchy scenes. He is of a darker nature. At night he drinks wine instead of tea. In the morning, he drinks both wine *and* tea. He gets fat on these things. Then he hates himself for being fat.

As I said, he is a sick man. He is a bit off in the heart and head. But I do not hold it against him. I am The Former Font, amongst many Others. I am a decent Christian—like those who never knew what the phrase meant. I am good, basically. And that is why I can forgive him.

Still, The Other irritates me a little. Like just now I said to myself, "I might enjoy just one little glass of wine"—only to discover that the wine was gone. He already drank it all. Or am I drunk?

I was pretty drunk

I was pretty drunk when he made mention of my writing, asking, "Is it any good?" So you can imagine my reaction(utterly mystified) at the time, though I can say now that I'm sure he only meant well and was trying to be polite. I shouldn't have been such a prick. I shouldn't have drank his beer after that and eaten all his french fries; but I was, and I did, and now feel a little bad about the way I acted.

What I should have said, and resolve to do so if ever someone poses that question again, is, plainly, "It's fantastic." Though I really hope to never have to push those words out of my mouth, because no one ought to ask such questions in the first place—they're ridiculous, and tacky. In all honesty, the person who asks them should feel a little bad about the way *they* have acted.

The Orange

"A new project, a mind game, a new year...."
—*Unknown American Poet*

Tonight an orange from the bowl at work.
No booze tonight,
Just an orange.
After we smoke at Ali's house,
I'll just pull out the orange, eat it—
Offer someone else a slice.

Did just that
And said to Ali, "You need your vitamin C."
She said thanks and looked at me strangely,
Then ate the orange wedge.
But she was also eating pistachios—
Of course I snagged some.

She threw one at the television and screamed.
Her football team fumbled,
But went on to win big.
The big play involved a fake punt,
A beautiful pass.
America is not so different—

Oregon Mountains,
The Nebraska windswept plains—
People sipping beers yelling at football games.

So the orange again, why does it glow?
Why does it float so? Why is it so immense?
What is its origin? How is it so different?

But I guess it's because I made it so, believed it so—
that I made it float.

When I looked at the orange, I said,
"You have entertained me, orange, and fed me.
Now we both float. Now we both glow."

How
"How Proust Can Change Your Life"
        Can Change Your Life

There is no better way
To navigate through the long neck
Of certain creatures,
Than by condensing their passages.

A firm grasp and twist,
And you've crushed the larynx.
What was once a low, dry tone
Is now a high, quick pitch.

You can more easily recall
What has passed: a bedtime preparation,
A party unattended, the lamp's
Revolving Illumination;

The good cry
Had in mother's absence,
And so on.

The gentleman caller
Calls only briefly. His voice, spared,
Resounds just as meaningfully,
Although squeaking somewhat. His

Attraction buds, blooms, and dies,
Quickly, but no less intensely.
And the throat is surpassed
In one gallant swoop of a Swan's

Decorative wings. Without need
Of a single lick of the thumb,
Or a single visit to the john.
The creature is mostly unharmed.

There is nothing left
To search for then.
Everything is accounted for.

Without the fear of losing

Time, feel free to spare a moment
In employing the exercises you learned
From Father's old medical texts:

Jumping off a short wall, and absorbing
The impact. Climbing back up,
Then jumping off again. It's good
For strengthening the back and legs.

Breathing techniques
Are good for the lungs—useful
In the prevention of Tuberculosis,
Or some other such thing, I think.

Calisthenics promote
Good Overall Health.
If I remember right anyway.

Certainly the eyes have not been strained,
But saved from the tiny veins
Of those six-hundred initial leaves,
Fallen precisely from that old French tree,

And bound as neatly as the babe's
Or invalid's diaper. Even
If I don't remember it all,
Or right—

It is still alright. Because
I can see just fine. My bones
And lungs are withstanding.
My health is not yet failing.

Untitled No. 2

A vivid imagination is not always a good thing to have—it can be a danger to the health, detrimental to a nervous heart.

Like when I was younger how my mom was in a fatal car accident, I saw quite clearly her pretty face—lifeless—bloody where the skin was burned off; her head was wedged between a broken seat shoved forward and the steering wheel where the airbag never deployed.

My sister was in the back seat—she fared better than our mom, but she still couldn't talk right.

And that every time the sirens passed.

I couldn't do shit until she returned home safely. Which she always did.

Or when I was thirteen how my friend killed himself. A shotgun to the head, they said. No one could figure the messy logistics—I could.

Soon after my brother followed suit. He committed suicide quietly in our home, and in the bathroom at school.

Sure he was sad. We're all sad. But it was the meds he was on that did it.

My dad was always talking about those meds. "They're bad for him," he said. "They'll depress the kid. Says right here they've been linked to depression and suicide."

No one paid him any attention, but I listened.

And every day for three years my brother died like that, by his own hand. All it took to recover from the loss was the sight of his car pulling up outside, or a phone call. "Brandon says he's going to so-and-so's—he'll be home a little late."

Every girlfriend I've ever had has cheated on me—at least twice. I just never had the heart to confront them.

Relatives and friends have passed away right and left. I've mourned them. I've spoken to them on the phone afterwards and told them all about it. They thanked me.

I've contracted diseases too. I've fathered many children, gone down in airplanes. I've done irreparable things, committed atrocities.

But everything turns out OK. "My health is not yet failing," I tell people. "My seed is not yet sewn." Still——

Tonight my girlfriend was abducted. She called me at work, sounded distraught. She was trying to alert me to what was happening. I had a customer, couldn't talk—I'd call her right back.

She never answered after that. And business was slow in the market. And my heart was racing, sunken down in my chest, thrashing against the backs of my ribs.

I got off early and hurried home. My socks were wet. I was having difficulty smoking.

When I got there she was sleeping. Her phone had been left in the kitchen. I knelt down and hugged her. She woke up. She turned that big head of hers on that tiny body and smiled. She was alright. She wasn't going anywhere.

A vivid imagination is certainly not always a good thing to have—it can cause terror in the brain, and pain in the chest.

But sometimes it's not so bad either. Like how this morning I fucked that chick from "The Notebook" and afterwards she thanked me.

How To Attract Women

I learned somewhere that women are
Attracted to men who still have the scent
Of other women on them—as though that
Scent were a stamp of pre-approval.
So I tried to fool those women
By spritzing myself with perfume regularly.
My brother said I was dandified, like Alfie;
That I had gotten soft.
The trick has only worked once.

Tiny Blues

It came upon me like everything does—by accident, chance, fate, divine intervention, no reason at all. Absurd and strong, vague, in the middle of the night—the real middle...the middle-of-the-brain...a dark spot in the center not at all like black ink leaking from a tiny source across the surface of a white page—but some would want to put it that way, wrongly, just because; or maybe blue, like the color of vein-through-skin: of the body next to mine, asleep; of the body in mine, awake.

A space heater provides warmth to exactly four square feet of space—the rest freezing.

Suddenly a voice—in the middle of the night, from outside the brain going in: "You fucking bastard."

Then singing: "Where are you now, my little darling? If only I could See You Next Tuesday, in the light...."

A loud, hoarse sound in the night, those blues. I look out the window though I should be asleep, and it is coming from nowhere, hovering in the cold air—coming from a man so small he cannot be seen.

Again: "You *fucking* bastard."

Those are his tiny blues. And he is right: I *am* a fucking bastard. I'm not drunk, but maybe I should be, I'd like to be. The body next to mine, still asleep—good. I am no one to you right now, so small you cannot see me. Easier to leave.

I am gone...everything's disgusting...the grind...the god-damn This...and That—

That rejection earlier: "Transparent, straightforward."

What that girl said on the train: "Smash it like a broken wine bottle and get out."

Get out of everything and away from everyone—including yourself, like how read the tape on the sidewalk: "The ego is a slippery slope."

An idiotic gesture, two bum kids kneeling down on the sidewalk to write that, then kneeling down on the sidewalk and expecting alms, my cigarettes, my two dollars, my anything.

The rejection, further: "Too coherent."

Even in a fever that has crept up on me from nowhere, from Spain, old, through the air, beginning then in the lungs, then the bloodstream, then the brain. Soul-fever, they call it: a sickness of the kind that everyone gets when they remember that they are no one.

And the air is still holding those imaginary snowjewels, those words like those that come from the mouths of pretty but neglected wives across America and beyond: "You fucking bastard."

Just hanging there in the frozen pipes—something or nothing, which is it: a block of ice that'll thaw? A yellow snow sculpture? A nondescript? An abomination?

I spoke with a nihilist at a cocktail party. I remember thinking that the whiskey-sidecars were sweet, and that the food was good; that I should've worn a tie; that my brother had told me he contemplated the possibility of Singer being a womanizer, of sorts—a quiet, reserved one if there is such a thing. Someone who appreciates the beauty of women, but does not wish to exploit it.

My brother is a good man. Singer was a good man—*is* a good man; his stories are good. And I am either nothing or a fucking bastard —that's all there is to it.

Cowboy
To be read in "an unctuous 1940's radio-man tone."

After twelve years living on the street, slowly softening his brain and straining his vocal chords, a local non-profit organization assisted in obtaining a small apartment for Lee "Cowboy" Saunders.

On Cowboy's first night in his warm apartment, he lay down on the bed—his first real bed in twelve years—shocked, disoriented, and attempted to come to terms with his new arrangements. His cell phone was plugged into the wall. He looked at it and its digital clock read 2.15am, give or take. He thought the bed was too soft. The room was too warm, and dry.

At two-thirty in the morning, or so read the cell phone-clock, Cowboy rose from his bed, went downstairs, and out into the street. It was raining. Cowboy stood there on the sidewalk, in the rain. He was crying. He was thinking, "What's wrong with my brain that I can't just be comfortable in that nice little apartment they set me up with— what's wrong with me that I'd rather stand out here in the rain?"

The following morning, recounting this story with a hoarse voice to anyone that would listen, Cowboy cried again. Several times he repeated the story, asking what was wrong with him, and he cried.

An Afternoon at Sea; Or,
The Half-Science Of Mysterious Creatures

I am not a "fallen angel" as my brother once alluded: a dense, square-jawed Pegasus whose beauty is in the nimble, acrobatic way of fall—though I don't mind him saying so.

People say things—*I* have said some things; I have also said nothing. In both instances thinking to express the same belief, like a man who spends one afternoon at sea, and believes to have understood the mystery of continuity, the driving force, the methodic vibration of strings, the interconnectedness, the half-science of a- or the way of life.

I am first a creature, no angel, then a man—a man come from the great vacuity, affected by prairie upbringing and such: wide open spaces, baptized young; a man come from a long line that extends into Spain, Catalonia, France, wherever...a people whose dreams are regarded as not just dreams. And the valuable experience of sleep should not be taken for granted.

I like men who enjoy a good lie-down, a pleasant nap; men who "just listen," in the same way that I like men who burn with good things, saints that pace—for what? (A good God and better natures.)

I like men that say things, too, out of a harmless affection for all things, people, although they know little about one another, anything, having barely spent a lifetime, an afternoon, merely gawking mouths wide at their seacreature-like existence—all murky, moving shadows within shadows, groping with those "glowing nerves," descending into the drink, smiling with no teeth, bums, fish, all alike....

Untitled No. 3

"We ain't that near the true sea!"
But we're close enough that seagulls still fly over the city with their nasty scouring, and cawing, that people still act like sailors, and that there is still an unconscious unrest which gives the notion that a valid option is to flee.

But remember: "We aren't *that* near the true sea!"

The open one, at least. And although the choice to leave seems available, it is rarely chosen—if ever, if it's even possible.

Instead, we act like sailors here. We are stagnant, and we rot.

Ferry to Vashon

Ferry to Vashon, boat in the Sound,
            I won't ride you today.

But I'll send naivety with you
            and wave from shore.
I'll send tears with you
            and smile from shore.
I'll send anger with you
            and dance from shore.

I'll send pretension with you
            and fart from shore.

By the water, I found a penny

By the water, I found a penny.
It had been flipped to Lincoln beneath the pillars.
Did he swim in the waves? Could he feel his toes?
I curled mine in my shoes,
like an ape would around a branch, to fight the cold.

I liked myself today for being gentle but no bore.
Others walking on the pier said, "hellos."
To me that is also official copper and gold.

I saw a woman quit smoking

I saw a woman quit smoking on a street corner today.

A well-off bum had asked me if I had anything to light his butt. This woman overheard him with matches ready in hand,

Handing them over and saying, "Here yeh go—keep 'em. I'm quitting."

The well-off bum was astonished that this woman had parted with her matches. Not that this woman had quit smoking.

But I was astonished, too. And I believed her. Because I will never see that woman again. And, therefore, cannot be proved wrong.

**Doing a two-step while listening to
Classical Music in the morning**

It is just a tiny alarm clock that produces the sound,
Like a momentary window in time, playing backwards

And now: in the back-, there are men
Huddled over a giant snuffbox;

In the fore-, I am just a tiny man that dances
A two-step in slow-motion.

(Against my neighbor's popcorn ceiling,
down through my floor.)

It is now just after my coffee with steamed milk,
after my second morning constitutional,

After I learned that my father still loves me, and
after the lift of the Water Bureau's "Boil-Alert."

It is now OK to drink the water without fear of E. Coli,
which wasn't the potentially fatal strand anyway;

And it is now OK to hold out for a better opportunity,
because my father will still help me out of destitution.

It is the thirty-first of November. I am still, still young.
If anyone could see me, they'd say that
I am not so bad at dancing either.

Though that could change over night,
Like how the song just suddenly stopped playing.

Bombshell

In the park there is an old bombshell, from WWII.

It's displayed down on the path to the water. The path with moss covered boulders.

This bombshell killed no gooks, but it killed me to look at it.

To be so fortunate with breaths of cold air in the park; I could see my breath.

There Was A Very Small Fire Here,
But It's Been Put Out

1.

I was the shadow of a shadow slain
By flippant tongues that flapped in vain.
I was cast out into The Poet's Race,
As a phantom net that crept through space.
To those caught in the web: a digital curse
Of the self reflecting its Self in verse.

That is the Ego's natural state.
Everyone can relate:
From the house-pent Ma(vaginal neglect/aggression)
To adolescents of both sexes(angst, lust, obsession).
Seeking validation through word possession, they
Said the things they thought they had to say.

One insisted on laying fantastic claim:
"Self-Realization!" he professed; another cried, "The Same!"
Dreams, too, were talked about at length,
Childhood memories, other poets, others' poems, mental strength.

Casual mention of sexual encounter, a body part
Involved? A must. The sex
                    Then redelivers to the start.

I was the shadow of a shadow slain
By that common case of manufactured pain.

2.

There are things I can't remember then.
There I things I can't remember—then,
I died young. Or so that story's told.
But look! A more recent scene, unfold:
Something poking from The Poet's ass!

On a foreign train, lower third class.
There is a toilet charge, they say,
About one cent U.S., everyone must pay.
But The Poet was more than willing to split

With a fortune for someone else to take the shit

For him. A frightening thing in the floor:
Just a tiny hole behind that 'bathroom' door!
Leading all waste straight down to the tracks,
Moving beneath him with the speed of brass tacks.
I can't remember what the metaphor means.

3.

Getting back to The Dying Act.
Enter a revealing fact:
Not a single body really dies.
It's a spiritual death, behind the eyes.
There are a few simple steps that bring The Fall.

Observe: The self-help guide that says it all,
Called, "Everybody Hurts and You Can Hurt Too."
The First Step: Believe that it's true.
Second: Memorize the text in full.
Third: Mix everything in That Internal

Hat. And then The Last, with haste:
Rearrange ideas(& letters) according to taste.
Now you have your own labor of love,
Called, "How Your Sad Truth Can Be Your Dove."
In translation, Would You Notice The forgotten scenes?

4.

I was alarmed to learn
The ease with which a fire can burn.
A steady, pale glow will keep
Without much fuel, without oxygen—it's cheap.
All you need is a computer and a good ear
For pleasant rhymes; a six-pack of beer.

Everyone has his/her drink of choice.
And with it comes their peculiar voice.
I submitted a number of Great Works,
Each with its own epic tale, its own quirks.
Not a single detail was sober, or light;
I was an ordinary man with an extraordinary plight.

Behind the computer screen The Phantom Team
Received my work with high esteem.
"Your poem is better than we could ever hope to get!
If you give us that fortune, we will take your shit."
Luckily, a valid point was brought to my attention.
A bad thing had happened. No further mention.

There is nothing more to explain.

Notes to "There Was A Very Small Fire Here, But It's Been Put Out."

lines 1-69: The style found in these lines may or may not have been taken from Vladimir Nabokov's fictional character, John Francis Shade, in his poem, "Pale Fire."

The content, however, is an original, abridged first-person narrative about the brief literary career of a young man I once knew—whose name, Richard Francis Payde, though unmentioned in the poem, bares a striking and ironic resemblance to the name of the fictional author of "Pale Fire"—and his reluctance to shit in a public toilet while on a train overseas, which I attribute to the temporary haughtiness of his aforementioned *career.*

These parallels were unclear at the time the poem was composed.

line 70: This is the missing line that would otherwise complete the poem's symmetry, and would presumably be the same as the first. There is no good explanation as to why it was discarded, other than to have the effect of being *tres mysterioso.*

If Only The Geese Flew More Slowly

The downstairs tenant has a strong aversion towards the neighbor directly above them, though they know nothing of this neighbor except for the fact that he or she has a bad habit of playing with a tennis ball inside of their apartment.

Inside of the upstairs apartment, presumably: the tennis ball is bounced constantly throughout the day as the geese fly from the north, going south; it is bounced against the floor, then wall, then hand, then repeated incessantly.

None of this is seen, of course, rather it is *heard*, always, as several, softly padded thuds and a rumbling through the downstairs tenant's ceiling.

And it is annoying, mygod! But it stops.

Then a little while later a new gaggle of geese flies by overhead, again going south, and the rumbling begins from the top: floor, then wall, then hand.

And it is goddamn annoying—again.

If only the tenant downstairs knew a little something about the neighbor above them, like how their neighbor is a woman of a certain age, how she is out of work, and bored, due to injury; like how she has to use a walker to maneuver through her cramped apartment with tennis balls thoughtfully attached to its feet to dull the noise of the clank and scoot as the geese go by her window and she scrambles to take a picture of them for her son—which she can never quite get.

If only the tenant downstairs knew that then he might offer to help, or at least take pity on her rather than getting annoyed.

Or if only the geese flew more slowly, then the woman could get the picture off in time by herself and resign to peacefully reading in her chair—self-sufficient, immobile, injured—henceforth making no cause for her neighbor's grievance.

But the geese won't alter their flight to accommodate any poor human, regardless. They will always, until the dead of winter, go as quickly as they can outside the window, south, and the upstairs neighbor will always insist on playing with her godforsaken tennis ball—that bitch.

I am not Kerouac; He Died in 1969,
at the age of forty-seven

The first time I heard the name it was from my father. I was almost eighteen, sleeping out of my car, writing poems with cold ears in December, and stealing booze and sandwiches.

He said, "Who do you think you are—Kerouac?"

My father's name was, by chance, Emil. Mine was what it is now; that is, *not* Kerouac.

I did not think I was he, but I read him anyway, almost completely—though out of order—by then turned 18.

Later I could not read him so often, sad to be scared for his soul, scared for my own soul which was vulnerable, impressionable—like all souls.

One night when my baby sister whispered, "Jack-y," into my ear, they burned like those of someone who is talked about in their absence.

And I still did not think I was he; I just thought, "A hundred years: no specific loneliness. Another: no specific joy. It's all the same thing."

Which was really a vague feeling more than it was a thought, but it had a comforting effect on me, taking it at the time as that of timelessness—or, more precisely, the impression thereof.

Still, I looked my sister dead in the eye and said, "Don't you ever call me that again—please."

A Sexual Autobiography of Dean Moriarty
in First-Third-Person

It was only The First Third of my life
On the first try. It was the rest, the next.

Neither very good, or bad, in light
Of their nature: Blacked out

Again on the adjacent floor,
Three days, or three nights

Later—what was it?

That our breaths smelled
like American Honey was as much

The sickness, as it was
(Was) the turn on—probably

Too sweet, or not sweet enough;
Too strong, or not strong enough;

Too expensive, surely, and too much
For young blood that runs

On the idea of what we were doing:
What was it? I don't know anymore,

Other than it was a simple routine
Of that 'beautiful disgust' in self-deceit

Of that someone who calls themselves
A dying hero—gone, always

Under a believed-in false pretense
(Seen blurred, relative, subjective):

A spiritual nurturing;
A typical fancy for all young boys;
An excerpt of a story, and support;
An expansive ribcage;

A way the light hit;
A love-drunkenness;
A tie to childhood, or how it should be;
A certain dance—Spanish—the rain;
A despondent feeling;
A bad habit that relieves a mirrored image of hell;
An excitement carried off the road,
Ad nauseam.

"I had a scary dream," she said.
"It was about infectious disease."

Which was a valid nightmare
To be recorded in the middle of the night,

After the first years together—
What were they?

Maybe some feigned affection,
Based on a vague, particular resemblance

To some others—
Woman is just another creature

Just as this is another creation, coupled
With a mirrored image, of fragments

From separate hells, that should be burned
Or should have, after the first or third line.

Improvising to a room full of aspiring and failed poets

Improvising to a room full of aspiring and failed poets, wearing a pair of prescription wide-rimmed glasses that were found on the bar floor moments before going to the microphone.

"I'm sure a lot of you in this room are well aware of the fact that publishing houses, literary agencies, and the like, all have impeccable timing.

"One innocent afternoon you submit a piece here and there, thinking that it can do no harm—at least you tried.

"The agency or publishing house then receives your submission, reads a few lines, and dismisses it. It goes into a pile marked, *'Tell him off, but do it politely, and make sure it's impersonal.'*

"And it sits there, waiting.

"As it does, time passes—first weeks, then months, or whatever. You forget that you ever tried. But they continue to sit on it, this submission of yours, and they continue to wait.

"Then the bank processes your overdraft one day, or the first of the month comes and you realize you don't have *quite* enough to pay rent, or your wisdom teeth are coming in*(opening mouth to show audience)* —and it is then that the postal service is cued:

"You receive your letter of rejection.

"Usually it's exciting to get mail—people enjoy it. Today I received two letters, both from the same publishing house, and both saying, *'We're sorry, but you may as well go fuck yourself. And good luck!'*

"But, still, rent somehow miraculously gets paid. And you even find yourself with six dollars leftover, which is enough for something. A poem, for example...."

Readjusting glasses, and pulling crumpled poem out of pocket, bringing it very close to the nose so as to be read—the prescription glasses and whiskey sodas causing extreme dizziness:

"Forget the toilet paper. Get the two bottles of wine instead, and clean your ass with the shower head. That's what Old Buck would've done —if only for the purpose of shooting that tepid stream up there (awakening a sense of shame in yourself, then dignity through that shame), then getting drunk and telling people about it."

Nodding at the audience to signify the completion of the reading. The prescription glasses coming off in a swoop. Vision still slightly blurred. A few people are laughing, though most are doing nothing.

No weak man should ever

No weak man should ever reread his own words once they've been put down. Those words are dead.

Nor should those men speak aloud of the things they've done while given to drink once they've sobered.

But they do, and it is clear then that they are preposterous men.

Thus, for the sake of our health, we can only laugh at ourselves, like lambs.

Some Gag Modern Shit, Hey—

I cannot be too sarcastic, I am a lamb,
And I cannot be too sarcastic
Because my bones are stomped grass—
Grass and flower me some sugary tradition, babe—
How to take care of anyone?!!

(COLD BEER, the sign read)

The only poets are comedians
And I'm too lame lamb and shy—
The devil in me is a reckless drunk though.
Lately, though, things been a'right, it's cool dude, it's cool—
Nice!!! Nice!!!

Growing (Wu-Wei) Sentences in Flower Pots

1. Preface

Growing sentences in flower pots was immediately influenced by a few things of some interest. To name a few: a shiny green humming-bird with a red collar(I need to get some sugar for the feeder), a quiet afternoon reading Alan Watts' "The Way of Zen," numerous glasses of green tea, the foggy Oregon winter, a bike ride, a campfire of old burning miscellaneous papers with my name on it, and, finally, a few sober days of good clean living after a long holiday bender.

Of course most of the writing had been done at other times, but the immediate influences provided the needed coherence and lack of self-consciousness.

The Tao is mostly a path or a faith that cannot be grasped, but only described as what it is not. And also an important thing to remember from Watts—"In most Taoist writings there is a slight degree of exaggeration or overstatement of the point, which is actually a kind of humor, a self-caricature."

And also from the Tao: "When the superior man hears of the Tao, he does his best to practice it. When the middling man hears of the Tao, he sometimes keeps it and sometimes loses it. When the inferior man hears of the Tao, he will laugh aloud at it. If he did not laugh, it would not be the Tao."

2. Yellow Leaves

Big quiet Doc Mullen stands outside with his arms folded. I pull out a cigarette, look at him, and then join him in staring out at the windy grey rainstorm—slick wet yellow October trees bend and swash over the trim, green grass campus.

"What's up, Doc Mullen?"

"This is the tail end of a big system swirling off the pacific," he says with a slight Kentucky drawl, still staring at it, arms folded.

In his old age he is both brazen and ruddy—he is also glasses upon a good sized red Irish nose and cragged still handsome face. His comment immediately paints a wider more impressionistic view of the blowing grey storm and the dancing trees—he's an old history professor wearing a retro suit; an aesthetic swirl on the storm that was not there before: trade winds, ocean currents, palm trees, nature's primordial unbiased power in general, things creaking and navel, Filipinos....

All of it personified and swirling in the fog, moving across thousands of miles of Ocean. It makes me truly feel our own proximity to the Pacific, although it is a dreamy twisted road to get there, foggy, windswept, beautiful, stark, and sort of strange—(America!). Sometimes I forget it is so close. Would even go so far as saying fishes swim there in abundance upon sacred waters—something deep in the mind, at once religious, upon the land, and distinctively American—a forgetting of time and space due to imagination, and moving around a lot— always the feeling of an old unused cannery rotting on the rich glittering waters of Monterey Bay.

Old doc Mullen says something about Humanity as he stares at the storm, "...............it makes us all human."

Later, from my warm cozy recliner I begin a poem in a small notebook—"In the chair I am no one." I pretend to be camping. Yellow leaves are on the trees outside, rain. Warmed by the space heater at my shins, with legs crossed, I stare at the leaves that make me feel of the gold leaves outside in the grey fall. Fall they do.

"Yellow leaves, the thoughts of trees," I write in the poem while considering them by an emptying and phosphorescence the color of smoky fall, and an aesthetic swirl that was not there like Tao on the wind—

3. The woman, the fish, and the stray dog

Can't sleep a freight train head billowing past ice cold creeks in dark nowhere ravines—He called earlier, girl trouble, she read one of his emails, knew his password—I said, "ya know my dad always complained my ma was a snoop"—Women(!), I listened some more and had no advice—Woman!—

He spoke more than he usually did, being a quiet kid—I went fishing and caught a trout earlier this evening—some trout took a dry fly right when it was about to sink on the end of a naturally drifting course—about four hours of fishing for a single trout—worth it?— yep—

There was a mangy mutt lurking around the river at dark and so I fed him—sundown—From a grey tote in my trunk with old canned goods bought months ago, I cracked three cans of Tuna and a Spaghetti-and-Meatballs for the poor mutt—dumped the food on a little concrete square under a BBQ grill—the mutt, with a white eye patch and other patches of brown and black, lopped it down—later, called the Medford Humane Society to let them know there was a mutt in the park with no tags and a blue piece of twine on, or rather around, it's neck—

4. Smoke

Smoke break: driving through fog to the gas station to get smokes—at the counter: touched by what the old crackly voiced craggy faced old man attendant says to the young girl at the counter that he is obviously familiar with—"It doesn't matter what other people think" (he taps his chest below his heart and sounds damn genuine) "Go with what's in here."

And the girl smiles and takes her bag, and the other attendant outside: shrouded in the cold, shrouded and hunched over, hooded sweatshirt pulled up over the head, Classic American Negro working stiff, holds himself with dignity—

Now I stand outside, pulling meditatively on a Marlboro light, staring at beads of water on a small tree in the fog—calmly, watching the cars pass through the fog, blowing out smoke—calmly, like an old medicine man chanting by the warmth of his smoky camp fire and staring into it.

This Woman Was Beautiful

This woman was beautiful. She came into the little market early on during my closing shift, slowly walking the few aisles, deliberating over every item on the shelf, inspecting the labels with a magnifying glass, I swear to god.

Eventually, after fifteen minutes—which is enough to look closely at everything in the store at least twice—she made her final decision: a small, dark chocolate bar that cost eighty-nine cents. She put a handful of change on the counter and began counting it out, then gave up and politely asked me to just take whatever the amount was.

Her name was Renee, which is of French origin, meaning "reborn." She was turning sixty-one at about supper time on December thirty-first—ten days after my own birthday, and just twelve days away from that night. Her birthday had always been about celebrating light, life, and rebirth, just like her name implied. It was always an emotional time, she told me.

No one else was in the store, so I stood there and looked her in the eye and I listened. I don't know what color her eyes were, but they seemed pretty and I thought that she was probably fairly attractive when she was younger, which wasn't all that long ago.

She went on to tell me that this time, the time of her sixty-first birthday, was especially emotional—she was having to get rid of her dog. As she said this, her colorless eyes wrapped themselves in shiny cellophane, shook, rippled, then tore on the surface. Tears flowed in a languid stream that followed the wrinkles from the corners of her eyes, down across her cheeks, and into her open mouth: she was still talking with voice trembling, breaking and all.

Her dog, Lady, was healthy at sixteen human years of age; she had been taken very good care of and could probably live another five human years. I refuse to speak of Lady's age in terms of the 7x dog-year-conversion not just because it's ridiculous, but because Renee refused to do so also; Renee spoke of Lady's age in terms of human years, and, more so, spoke of Lady herself as a human.

Renee said that Lady was hypersensitive; that it took many of those sixteen human years for Lady to learn how to be touched. By nature, Lady hated to be touched; one always had to go to her if what one needed was affection, it was never the other way around. Even after all those years, when Lady was somehow coaxed into being petted, Renee felt that the petting was accepted without joy, Lady enduring it rather, tolerating it. "Do you know what it feels like to be with another person, a human, or just any living creature, and to feel like you're just being *tolerated?* It's awful...."

369

The tears mounted again and it *was* awful, but I thought of my mother with my father. I thought of an ex-girlfriend. I thought that Lady sounded like a real frigid bitch. But just like my mother had stayed with my father until it was absolutely unbearable, so had Renee stuck with Lady—it's what lonely people do to avoid what they imagine to be even greater loneliness.

Awhile back, Renee's sister had been worried about a potential suicide. Renee had remarked, "I can't end my life until Lady ends hers." It was apparently a joke, or so she said to me when recounting her statement, laughing through the tears that hadn't stopped coming, slowly. But, in a sense, it was not a joke, and she clarified the statement by rewording it: "I can't have my life until Lady has hers."

And it had come to the point where Renee, having put her existence under the magnifying glass of her approaching sixty-first birthday, had made a final decision: she and Lady must separate and lead their own lives and, eventually, deaths; things between them had finally become *unbearable*.

As I learned all of this, I continued to hold onto her eyes, which I am now beginning to remember the color of: hazel, like my mother's eyes, and with that thin sheen over them that I have so often seen over my mother's, which made the hazel-iris almost glow. Renee had taken a silent moment to herself in order to wipe her eyes. I was very quiet, waiting for her to explain *how* things had become unbearable, what the other grievances were, what she really meant by that—and why now?

I wanted to tell Renee that I thought she was a very beautiful woman, and that I was sorry that, for whatever reason, she had to get rid of her dog, and friend, of sixteen years, Lady, but the bells that hung on the market door jingled against the glass, the cold wind swept in, and Renee's tears froze.

It was a small, amiable looking foreign man entering: he was in need of cigarettes.

Regretfully, I said nothing to Renee, assuming I would have the opportunity to in a moment, once the transaction with the foreign man had played out. But as I moved to the cigarette case, quickly, Renee was saying to me, "I hope I haven't scared you with all this talk. I've talked to you once before, I think. Happy birthday."

Then the bells jingled again and she left without another word to go home to Lady and to enjoy her dark chocolate bar with a cup of coffee, as she had earlier told me she would.

I rang up the man's cigarettes: five dollars and seventy-five cents. He took out his credit card, handed it to me, and with a big smile on his face inquired, "Crazy?"

I didn't think Renee was crazy, but I told the man that I wasn't sure anyway and he nodded to show that he understood. Then he took his cigarettes and he left too.

The store was relatively quiet then. No one was talking but there was music playing softly, the refrigerators were all humming, the lights buzzing, and the oven breathing. I stepped outside to see if Renee, who didn't move very fast, was still visible on the sidewalk. She was nowhere to be seen. For a moment I lingered there, listless, hanging, like a little boy in wait of the end of a bedtime story, a conclusion, some sense of grand meaning behind the sadness of this beautiful woman's fragmented narrative.

It did not come, and it won't come. Not that Renee offed herself and her dog—though I can't be sure, I'll say that she didn't—but that is just the nature of these things: you are given a brief window into the personal tragedies of others, witnessed by way of eye or ear, purposely or by chance, and you learn just a tiny bit about them—a small piece of fact or fiction—then they are gone. The tangent of your two lives has passed, and henceforth the trajectory of each existence is oblivious of the other's present, actual state of being. There is still that intersecting occurrence, of course, meaningful or not, which is left open-ended in space—and therefore subject to embellishment and nostalgia—but it does not make sense, and it won't make sense. Not everything can be understood with a great degree of certitude, nor should it be. And, usually, those who either fret over this uncertainty or believe in any abstract thing with unwavering certainty are the ones who go mad, who kill people, themselves, and so on.

As I stood there on the sidewalk I did nothing. I thought about these very basic ideas of no-sense and wonder, and I forgave Renee for not finishing her story. I went back inside the store. Although I no longer expected the end of a story, or anything, I continued to think about Renee, who quite possibly was a very plain-looking, typical woman past a certain age, and I began to believe that she was incredibly beautiful—probably the most beautiful woman I had ever seen, for real, not exaggerating, I swear to god again. If that belief is wrong, oh well. That was how I remembered her.

It was getting late then—near closing. No one else had come into the store, though the music was still going and the appliances noising. I farted and no one heard. Then I began to mop.

The Significant Rain of Freider Wunder

The tiniest dictator of the tiniest country in the world is housed within the Northwest of the United States in the anteroom of a one bedroom apartment that is located in The Lucinda Court Apartment building, which, it should be known, is regulated by the U.S. Government. The officials of the city in which this building stands have not yet become wise to its tiny inhabitants, or its tiny administration; not even the president of the United States, or his seemingly countless intelligence agents, have learned one iota about their existence. If they had, this tiny country and its tiny dictator would probably be in real big trouble.

The name of this country is Freiderland and the name of its dictator is Freider Wunder. It is astonishing to see what discipline and order he is able to enforce with such a tiny iron fist! There are approximately sixty citizens living in the country(over 100 if you're really counting heads— *just* heads), and each of these citizens acts with complete and utter decency. When one visits Freiderland, one feels the sense that everyone in the entire country has given you their attention —their eyes following your every move. And if the new and weary tourist decides to speak, they will all listen attentively, not interrupting even once to ask such silly questions as, "What is the purpose of this visit?" or, "How long do you intend to stay?"

Of course, the self-appointed ambassador of Freiderland—a man not so tiny—may pause to ask you if you would like a cup of tea("Oh, no thank you"), or some other agreeable treat—but the pleasantness of it all! The whole operation is run smoothly, diplomatically, serenely. It is wonderful.

Certain visitors to the country—people of not tiny stature, but certainly small—have compared Freiderland to "a fairytale that's exploded!" It is not an inaccurate thing to say of Freiderland, that it resembles an exploded fairytale; these guests, however, did fault at a different point during their visit: while in a discussion with the ambassador regarding Wunder's dominant, yet compassionate reign, the guests imagined in their small but not tiny heads that the word 'reign' was spelled 'rain'. But this was a small, forgivable offense, especially because the mistake had gone only so far as the spelling of reign, for the meaning of the word itself had been comprehended correctly. All had been understood in Freiderland. Everything was still good.

"For a country so small, and otherwise perfect," one underground journalist later inquired, "why is it that not just the majority, but literally every single citizen of this *Freiderland* has bad teeth, and sleepy eyes? Is anything being done about this?"

Thankfully, those who heard the journalist's question were not offended—not just because of their thick, shiny skin, but because they no longer paid heed to the trivialities of their own appearances. On a whole, it was true that each and every citizen of Freiderland had once symbolized beauty incarnate. But by whose standards? And what did that mean anyway?

The journalist's question had actually been posed to Freider Wunder, the tiny, and magnanimous dictator of Freiderland, but it was the ambassador who made answer.

"Well," the ambassador began in a tone probably too friendly to be addressing such a rude journalist; "it all began quite some time ago. Would you like to hear the story?"

"Yes, absolutely! I mean—of course, I am a journalist," the journalist replied.

The journalist removed his notebook from his shirtfront pocket and readied it for his notes—he thought the citizens of Freiderland might have snickered when he did this; he thought it was because his notebook was very small—no bigger than his own palm—and therefore more suitable for someone of their size. He tried not to pay attention to the inaudible giggles, listening instead to the ambassador.

"Once upon a time—as goes the condensed version of this story—I went on a trip to Germany to pursue certain...err...medical treatments...that were more affordable there than they were here. During the first few months of my trip I was lonely, and meeting people was hard—I didn't speak any German! But one day I was on a walk—not too far off from the Alexanderplatz in Berlin so that I wouldn't get lost—and I came across a very tiny antique shop. It's always been a hobby of mine to collect old things, so I went into the shop hoping to be comforted by the various trinkets and things, and it was there that I met Mr. Freider Wunder. He was stuck in some back aisle on a very high shelf, trying to figure out how to get down without hurting himself. His tiny bald head, with its cracking and peeling, was tilted over the edge of the shelf as he was gazing downward, calculating the safest route to the ground. And so of course I offered to help him—how could I not? He was so adorable and helpless. I took his tiny body into my arms and I removed him immediately from the dry, dusty oppression of his surroundings. He was grateful for me. And, in turn, I was grateful for him. He really got me through that period of my life."

The journalist's hand paused over the last thing he had written in his notebook and he looked up. "Yes, well," he said, trying to get to the point without being impolite; "but what about the bad teeth? And the sleepy eyes?"

"Oh, I'm getting there. Be patient," the ambassador replied in no less of a friendly tone than he had kept this whole time with the journalist.

"After a while," the ambassador continued, "I decided to give up my treatments in Germany and come back to the states. It had been just under a year since I arrived there, and Freider Wunder had been with me for about eight months then. I asked him if he would like to come with me, and I promised him whatever he wanted. He agreed to come with me—obviously, you can see him right there(pointing)—but there was one stipulation: he wanted a sanctuary for himself and his people to live in warmth and in peace. Naturally, I obliged."

"Now you have to understand that Freider Wunder's people are an inherently submissive people. They are accustomed to a life where they listen without speaking, where they dress in clothes of a style and color they have not chosen for themselves; where their hair can be cut at any time by unpracticed scissors and never grow back. You can imagine what this might do to a person emotionally. Freider Wunder's nerves had grown thin and ravaged over the years—along with his compatriots'—but his appearance changed only in the slightest. A new crack here, a little peeling there. He said it was degrading. He said that a man's outward appearance ought to reflect, at least somewhat, what he felt inside."

"When Freider Wunder came here with me he was beautiful. But I have made him more beautiful. A little burn and droop, some sagging and transformation—and *voila!* News quickly spread amongst his friends: word blew and quivered throughout the city and surrounding areas in all the right places. Those who needed to know, learned. Those who wished to come, came. And a country was formed. A sanctuary for the underappreciated and unloved, the tired and old, the quiet, the tiny, all overseen with the ease and simplicity of none other than Freider Wunder—the man to whom I owe so much...."

The journalist concluded his notes and skimmed them over. By all appearances, the ambassador to the tiniest dictator of the tiniest country in the world was completely insane, mad, at wit's end, out of his mind, gone. He was not just slightly cracked, like his dolls, but wholly and totally obliterated. The journalist scanned the shelves and compartments where these tiny "people" resided—none of them had moved even a centimeter; they were absolutely static.

"Okay," the journalist said, breaking the silence that had been hanging there since the end of the ambassador's story. But nothing else followed.

The ambassador, being well-versed in the handling of all sorts of different affairs, saw that his guest was in need of a moment alone—to regroup, he thought. "Are you sure I can't get you a cup of tea, or anything?" the ambassador asked.

"Actually, a cup of tea would be nice. Thank you," said the journalist, somewhat dumbfounded.

The ambassador dismissed himself into the kitchen, out of sight, and the journalist felt inordinately soft, and warm. He decided that it had been against his better judgment to decline a cup of tea earlier. His host had offered him something, and he ought to accept. Besides, tea was always a nice thing to have in cold weather.

Outside the window, the journalist could see that the usual cold grey of the afternoon had taken on a silvery sheen which meant it was drizzling. Yes, it was raining now and tea would be just the right thing.

The journalist looked over to the shelf where Freider Wunder sat watching everything in the room as he probably never ceased to do. His hair was cropped haphazardly, asymmetrically; the peach-colored rubber around his eyes sagged sadly, dramatically, making the harsh blue eyes themselves seem to bulge out; his teeth were crooked, protruding outward over the bottom lip. He looked as if he had been around for quite some time now, and had seen and heard too much of this world. The journalist smiled at the doll called Freider Wunder, then quietly and sadly laughed at himself. "What about you—can I get you anything Mr. Wunder?"

From the kitchen, the always kind and hospitable ambassador called, "Would you like any milk or sugar?"

Without breaking eye contact with Freider Wunder, the journalist put his tiny notebook back into his shirtfront pocket and looked forward to reading over his notes later on by himself. He patted it satisfactorily.

"Yes, sir," the journalist called to the ambassador in the kitchen, "both milk and sugar, please."

The journalist hesitated then, and he considered adding onto his statement a compliment which he now felt sincerely in his heart; what he was considering saying to the ambassador of Friederland was, 'You have really wonderful dolls.' But he opted against it, deciding that those words were unnecessary because that fact was surely known to the man already.

When A Paisano Gets Paid

The paisano joke involved a raising of the hands toward Heaven and a crossing of the eyes. And at Christmastime this gesture became exceedingly significant, as everything does, just like the Christmas Story anthologist said, "to set a story at Christmastime is to instill it immediately with a certain amount of prestige."[*]

True, there is an ambiance that surrounds Christmas that is unlike any other during the year and which seems to take effect on all peoples no matter what their faith be, or their non-faith, but paisanos are especially vulnerable to this feeling, this nostalgia—paisanos are especially vulnerable to happiness.

However, Christmas being a popular setting in America, the resemblance may be simply that of a thematic issue.

That being said, this paisano joke at Christmastime seemed an absolute riot. Ensuing its execution there was always an abundance of laughter, and grinning. Also, the merrymaking was corroborated by a vision had of an elfin apparition, a sprite if you will, which peaked out from beneath the unlit Christmas tree that stood at 3ft tall in the paisano's apartment. It was a brief vision—there and then not—yet it was evident in that momentary sighting that the sprite was not American, but of European origin, possibly come over on a boat like so many ghosts.

'It is bait,' the paisano thought. 'Sit on it.'

On second thought, confessing his simplicity to the unfilled space where the sprite had been, the paisano said aloud, "I am a simple paisano. I will take it."

And take it he did.

He thought that in trying to follow the sprite he would make a fool of himself, so he would not do that. He also thought that in ignoring the sprite altogether he would disgrace the sprite and its affable behavior towards him. He did not want to offend the sprite, whose vision he was grateful for; he preferred to reciprocate its kindness, which was a difficult task to accomplish when the being that was to be reciprocated was actually an intangible thing of beauty, such as he considered the sprite.

After much contemplation over this dilemma, and a solo performance of the paisano joke—followed by the mandatory laughter—the paisano arrived at the most logical conclusion he possibly could in his

---

[*] There is a possibility that this "quote" is based on Alberto Manguel's words in his introduction to "The Ecco Book of Christmas Stories."

simplicity: he vowed to buy a gift, with no recipient yet in mind, having faith that the sprite would show itself a second time to reveal the person who was most deserving of this somewhat divine gift.

It was a brisk afternoon which held rain, but not snow. It was cozy indoors, and romantic out. The paisano felt inordinately well-to-do: the previous evening he had gone to his work Christmas party at which he received a one hundred dollar holiday bonus. This was not a huge amount of money, but in the paisano's heart it grew, fanned out, and took flight—it was now a tremendous sum. He felt himself in a comfortable position to buy a fantastic gift for someone who(?) would hopefully find the gift equally fantastic.

Somewhere and at some time in the paisano's life he heard that the best gifts were always impractical, and usually something the recipient would never buy for themselves. With those wise words of ambiguous descent in his heart, and head, the paisano set off into the cold and rainy city with his honest and good intentions.

Rain beaded on the wool of his coat, collar pulled up around the neck, and looked like little jewels; he was fond of virtually everything at the present, and when he looked down he imagined them as diamonds that he could afford—real gems! But this was just horse-play, a mere paisano game to amuse himself with. His real spiritual obligation—which is how he now saw the purchasing of this gift—continued to be carried out meanwhile.

In his head, he rummaged through the objects he had seen in big department stores and smaller shops, and he leafed through the imaginary pages of their catalog. At the back of this catalog the paisano found a section dedicated to objects unseen, unfound but yearned for, and it was here where he believed to have found the perfect gift. Which is to say, he simply remembered something, just a little item that he had thought would be quite a nice little item, but until now had forgotten about: it was a letter opener.

The paisano tore out the page with the letter opener on it and brought it to the forefront of his brain: its dull blade, the functioning shaft, was thin, shiny, polished gold or silver; the handle was either tastefully decorated glass or finely carved wood. It was a very nice item, surely, this letter opener. 'But does a letter opener meet the requirements of a good gift?' the paisano asked himself.

To give answer it was necessary to break down the question into the two questions that were created by the paisano words of wisdom regarding good gifts: 1) Was a letter opener impractical? and, 2) Would anyone ever buy a letter opener for themselves?

The paisano was able to answer as follows: as to The First) Yes, a letter opener was an extremely impractical gift. It was uncommon for people to sit down in these modern times and hand write letters to their family, friends, or loved ones when the internet and email was so readily available to them; aside from the occasional birthday or holiday card which were usually just as impersonal as emails, the majority of the mail people received were bills that should be torn open scornfully rather than delicately slit by a letter opener, and advertisements for local restaurants and grocers, coupons, etc. that should be trashed rather than kept. Therefore a letter opener would be appropriated to a situation of utmost rarity, an anomaly, really—the personal, handwritten letter.

And as to The Second) People were certainly fond of buying themselves things, especially impractical things, but those impracticalities were most commonly of a material nature—things they could adorn themselves with, or decorate the walls of their apartments with, or anything that might occasionally come up in conversation wherein the person could retort, "Oh, I have one of those!" A letter opener came close to fitting into this category, but not quite. Although evidence had already shown that a letter opener was impractical, it went further in illustrating how a letter opener was not just impractical, but basically obsolete, so it would never come up in conversation because it was almost forgotten altogether, and therefore a person could hardly ever find occasion to say, "Oh, I have a letter opener."

In short, the paisano, after his very patient and logical reasoning, concluded that a letter opener was, indeed, *the perfect gift*.

"A letter opener then," the paisano said to himself, hurrying along in the rain. "Where does one go to find items that are basically obsolete, like this letter opener?"

He figured his best bet was an antique store, or a vintage boutique. He knew of a few locations around the city. Nervously, he trekked from one place to the other and continued to leave each establishment empty handed. 'A letter opener,' the paisano repeated in his head— 'Bah!'

The lack of success the paisano found in these gloomy specialty stores was beginning to weigh on him. His heart was intent on the letter opener, and the dark, cluttered stores offered no solace for his heart's desire. It seemed that their main interest lay in big wooden trunks, new furniture that had been made to look old, and globes of all size and color. "If only what I needed was a ridiculous, oversized wooden trunk," the paisano said to one of the store clerks, a woman with grey hair, well-dressed, and chubby.

She replied, "And what is it that you need, sir?"

"I am in need of a letter opener," said the paisano.

She laughed. "Oh, we don't have any of those!"

378

The paisano felt something within him begin to snap, and a sound came from his mouth like, "Bah!" Immediately he was embarrassed, and worried. He thanked the store clerk, despite her rudeness, and he left.

Outside, the paisano breathed deeply. He knew that this letter opener business was a tough one, but giving it up wasn't an option. He owed it to the sprite to follow through with—with what? Well, with giving in to the holiday tradition; with buying some absurd gift out of an even more absurd feeling of nostalgia; with opening up the chambers of his simple and glad heart, and sharing all its happiness. Isn't that what Christmas is all about anyway? Isn't that what life is all about?

The paisano felt himself grow somewhat lighter. It was good to be out of reach from the suffocating air and dingy trinkets of the antique stores and their heavy, captive trunks. He was still determined to find the letter opener, but his determination had changed. Where before it was frantic and rushed, it was now tranquil and nonchalant. The paisano thought, 'What good is the giving if it's lost its good spirit?' He shrugged. Then he raised his hands toward Heaven and crossed his eyes. He let out a big laugh into the rainy, grey void.

He composed himself, smiling. He formulated his next move. 'I will get the letter opener—there is no doubt about that,' he said to himself. 'But first I will cheer myself up, get back in the spirit. I will walk past the big Christmas tree to look at the lights—they're probably just turning them on now. Then I will go into the warm and bright mall, where there will be Christmas music playing and pretty women to look at. Afterwards, I am positive there will be plenty of time for the letter opener—yes sir, no doubt at all about that.'

The paisano casually followed the plans he had outlined. He walked past the big Christmas tree in front of the courthouse, and the lights *had* just been turned on. Families and young couples and street kids were gathered around the base of the tree. The families and young couples took pictures; the street kids asked for handouts.

The paisano stopped to look up at the tree. The lights were blurred from the drizzle and the sky was still visible, barely, through the grey mist, and the digital flash of pictures being taken reflected off the several large, shiny bulbs hung on the tree. Through the rain, the scene appeared like a picture in a newspaper made up of millions and millions of dots. Seeing it as such, the paisano was slightly removed from the reality of it all, which is something that often happens to men when they experience supreme happiness. "It was like a dream," they say afterward.

A homeless woman forced the paisano to interact. She said, "Excuse me, Brother, but could you spare some change?"

He looked at her. She was someone he had seen on numerous occasions. She was always calling everyone *Brother.* "Yes," he said, "I think I do have something...." He reached into his pocket and pulled out a single bill, thinking it was a One. He noticed it was a Five as it moved from his hand into hers.

"Well thank you, Brother—God Bless!"

The paisano nodded at the woman and watched her walk away with five-percent of his one hundred dollar holiday bonus. 'It really wasn't my money in the first place,' thought the paisano. 'It came from nowhere and belongs to no one—it's money that should be spent hastily.'

With his feet springing off the metallic-blue sidewalk of the wet city dusk, the paisano began moving again. He sauntered through the background of family photos, his lips together and his eyes squinted at the corners, and he moved across the street, two blocks away to the mall.

The mall at Christmastime is not a gathering point designated only for Christians with full pockets; it is a large and warm place which welcomes all peoples and, if looked at properly, inspires joy in most of those whom pay it a visit. Songs are played there that everyone knows the words to, lights and decorations are hung that anyone can look at and either appreciate their surface beauty or their beautiful absurdity, gum and candy and mints are given out for free from decorative glass dishes, drinks are served piping hot with a cartoonish wisp of steam suspended above them so that even those who are not drinking them are assured that they are *piping hot.* And the women—always women in heavy coats, purses and bags bouncing against their backs, hips, and asses, as their heels click over the tiled floors gleaming with cleaning product in one place and rain shaken from their umbrellas and heavy coats in another, both of which casting their reflections and multiplying the number of women.

For a paisano, who always buzzes with happiness about to be realized, the mall at Christmastime is a sanctuary; for a paisano who's just been paid, or especially a paisano who's just received an unexpected sum of money, it is also a trap.

The paisano had positioned himself on such a bench that he was able to fully experience all the holiday delights the mall had to offer—a speaker was right behind him playing nonstop Christmas tunes, the high ceilings overhead were festooned with greenery and where they were not there was glass that shimmered with bright, cheerful colors and warmth, a potbellied Santa Claus was around the corner from the nearby escalator, and the escalator itself, of course, gave way to high traffic and, thus, many women in passing. The longer the paisano sat there the more pervasive his surroundings became. He was acutely aware of the excess money he carried in his pocket; each time a woman passed, he badly wanted to spend it on them. But in the naturally pious, restraint is just as automatic a virtue, so the paisano did not spend his money on the fleeting women. He simply sat there on the bench, astute to his surroundings, and let the stimuli of Christmas fill up his being.

It suddenly occurred to the paisano that it might be good for him to stand up, stretch his legs. He did not know how long he had been sitting there, but he could tell by the increasing brightness of the lights reflecting off the darkening glass overhead that it was now night. He would have to be on his way soon. Before he left though, he wanted to investigate the store that was directly in front of the bench he had been sitting; the entire time from his seat, he was able to make out the image of a lamb, just the head, hanging on one of their walls, illuminated from a spotlight above.

The paisano went into the store and up to the wall where the lamb head was hung. It was a very beautiful mask made of plaster casting, flesh-colored acrylic paint, and real fleece. He took it off of the wall and tried it on. In the mirror he inspected the way he looked. The image of the lamb had always affected him, but it was naturally, obviously, more affecting at this time of the year. The mask was very realistic, and as he reviewed its appearance atop his own human frame he began beaming from beneath it—a smile so big that it was visible through the tiny holes made for the eyes.

A clerk approached the paisano. She asked, "Can I help you with anything, sir?"

"Oh no," the paisano said, "I'm just looking. This mask is very beautiful."

"Isn't it?" said the store clerk.

"How much does it cost?" the paisano inquired absently.

"Fifty-dollars," she said. "But it's a very beautiful mask!"

"Yes," said the paisano, taking off the fifty-dollar lamb mask. And on a second thought, remembering the true purpose of his outing, he said, "You know, maybe you can help me with something. I'm looking for a letter opener—you wouldn't happen to have a letter opener, would you?"

"Actually, yes we do. Come—right over here."

The woman led the paisano over to a glass case near the register, and pointed to one small shelf where a few items were displayed. The paisano bent over and looked in—"letter openers," he exhaled to himself, mystified. Five beautiful letter openers were laid out in their plush velvet cases, like those that fine jewelry come in. Each one had a gold-plated shaft, delicately extending from their ornate, wooden handles; only the decorative carving on each handle differed slightly. They

381

were just as the paisano had imagined—they were all beautiful. With wide eyes locked on the letter openers, he inquired again of the store clerk, though more purposefully, "How much do they cost?"

The store clerk opened the case and removed one of the letter openers, then checked the price. She did this again with another. "It looks like they're all sixty-five dollars, sir," she said.

The paisano was smiling. He said, "You have no idea how difficult it is to find a letter opener—I've been looking all day. I'll take this one here, in front."

"Okay," replied the store clerk. "And how will you be paying today?"

"Cash," said the paisano, already removing the proper number of bills from his pocket. He put sixty-five dollars exactly on the counter top as the woman put his letter opener in a bag. "And that should do it."

Once a man gets what he desires, it is not uncommon for him to feel remorse, realizing then that he had fooled himself in his own desires— what he truly wanted was more illusive than some object that could be acquired. With the paisano this was not the case, for it was not his own desires which he was fulfilling, it was those of a greater will which had something to do with the elfin apparition he had seen in his apartment. He was proud to have participated in the grand tradition of the holiday, which was something clearly larger than himself.

As the paisano walked through the dark back toward his apartment, he ran into a friend. They quite literally almost bumped into each other before they recognized the other as someone they knew and were fond of. It was a woman friend.

The paisano said to her, "Oh, hello! I almost didn't recognize you with your hood up shielding you from the rain and from friends. Are you walking in this direction?"

The woman friend greeted him in a similar fashion and they both laughed. She *was* walking in the direction that he gestured, so they decided to walk together.

"Do you want to see the gift I bought today?" the paisano excitedly asked his friend.

"Yeah, sure. Show me."

From the inner pocket of his coat, the paisano revealed the plush velvet case and withdrew the letter opener, holding the handle in his one hand while gingerly supporting the shaft with the palm of the other. He said, "It's a letter opener. What do you think?"

His friend feigned interest, saying, "It's a really nice letter opener. Who's it for?"

The paisano sensed the real disinterest in his friend's tone, and decided that the letter opener was probably not for her. "I'm not sure," he said. "Maybe my brother."

"It really is a nice letter opener—wow. What made you think to buy a letter opener as a gift?"

"Well," said the paisano, "it's hard to say exactly, but as I was thinking of what gift I might buy, I remembered hearing that the best gifts were usually impractical ones that someone would never buy for themselves."

"A letter opener certainly is impractical," said the paisano's lady-friend. "And I doubt anyone would ever buy one for themselves."

To which the paisano replied, "Thanks." Then they came to a point on their walk where they must split if they were to make it to their proper destinations. They said goodbye to one another, and as they were walking away they both called, "Merry Christmas!"

When the paisano reached his upstairs apartment, he thought about the encounter on the street with his friend. He turned on his Christmas tree lights and sat down on the floor next to it, leaning his back against the wall. He removed the letter opener from his coat pocket again, and began fiddling with it unconsciously, all the while staring at the place where he had seen the sprite. The sprite did not come back. He was not alarmed by this. He thought, 'It's a very busy season for sprites.'

It was then that the paisano received a call from his brother. The sound of the phone startled him at first, but he quickly recovered from the shock and began to wonder if this phone call weren't a sign that he should definitely give the letter opener to his brother.

Their conversation was fairly short. The paisano's brother wanted to let the paisano know that he would be driving up the following afternoon so that they could spend Christmas together. It was impossible to get together with the rest of their family, but they lived close enough to each other where at least spending it together as brothers was feasible. The paisano was excited by the news, and was cunning in his following maneuvers, which were designed to learn whether or not his brother would like a letter opener for Christmas. Inexplicably, the paisano was able to immediately coax a story out of his brother that ended with the mention of his brother already having a letter opener—he bought it for himself the month before.

'One letter opener is plenty for any person to have,' the paisano thought, somewhat befuddled. 'To have more than that would be just plain ridiculous.'

The paisano shrugged his shoulders—a common gesture amongst paisanos—though his brother could not see this over the phone. They both said they were looking forward to the following afternoon, and the holidays together. Then they hung up.

The paisano spent that night by himself. Now it should be known that a paisano by himself is a strange thing, very quiet, thoughtful, observant, spiritual—a paisano amongst friends or family is something completely different; a paisano amongst friends or family is no less spiritual than he is when alone, but his behavior is more outspoken, boisterous even, jovial, and often his ideals are exaggerated to the point of becoming caricature-like.

As the paisano sat alone in his apartment, silently meditating on his tree, he imagined what the upcoming holidays would bring. He imagined lots of drinking, lots of jokes and laughing, lots of carousing about town, moving from one place to the other, eating, more drinking, and even in his imagination he knew that most of these things would cost a little bit of money—potentially quite a bit of money.

'Sure, I still have about thirty dollars left over from my bonus,' the paisano reasoned, 'but that just won't be enough.'

The paisano looked down at the letter opener, which he still fiddled with in his lap. It became an absurd object there in his hands, with the price tag yet removed. "Sixty-five dollars!" the paisano exclaimed aloud, raising his hands toward Heaven and crossing his eyes. "Bah!"

Next morning, the city was grey and shiny. The rain, for now, was either already on the streets and sidewalks and buildings, or was still up in the clouds. It was early.

The paisano awoke in his apartment, warm and dry. He got up and looked out of the window. "Not raining yet," he conjectured. Then he went to the kitchen and put some water on to boil for tea.

Once the water had boiled and the tea had steeped, the paisano brought it out into the main living area and sat down next to the Christmas tree. He had forgotten to turn the lights off the night before, and thought he would leave them on this morning as he drank his tea. Whenever the paisano drank tea, and his brother saw him doing so, his brother called him, "Nikolai," although that was not his real name. In preparation for his brother's visit, the paisano momentarily thought of himself in terms of this "Nikolai" person.

Nikolai sat in a recliner with his big sweater on and a blanket over his legs, drinking tea. He pondered over the day's possible happenings. He routed his morning in his head, and sipped from his tea cup. It was a good morning.

As Nikolai disappeared into the last drop of tea, and the used tea bag was thrown in the trash, the paisano reemerged with an agenda. He cleaned his dishes, put on his coat, and went out.

On the street, the paisano felt healthy and believed the air to be good. His manner was brisk, but unhurried. He approached the entrance to the mall. Upon walking through the doors, he realized that

384

he had never been to the mall so early in the morning. They had just opened, and the Christmas music was already playing, but the sounds echoed off of everything because there weren't any bodies to absorb the noise, soften it. The music seemed very loud, and the interior of the mall seemed to have grown considerably. He walked through the large, empty walkways and crept past the unmoving escalators to the only store he had visited in the mall the day before.

Standing at the counter was the same store-clerk who had handled the transaction for the letter opener. She didn't hear him come in.

"Hello," the paisano said soothingly, making sure not to alarm her. She looked up and returned the hello. "I need to return this letter opener—I purchased it yesterday." He put the velvet case on the counter and opened it to expose the letter opener. They both looked at it.

"Okay," the store clerk replied. "And is there a reason you need to make this return?"

The paisano said, "It appears that my brother already has a letter opener."

"Oh," she said. "Okay. And how was it paid for?"

"I paid in cash," said the paisano resolutely. "The receipt is right here."

Now they both looked at the receipt, and back at the letter opener—the numbers clearly matching up, the story clearly coming together.

"Okay then—everything looks alright," said the store clerk, clearly dismayed that today's first business should be a return. She opened the till and counted out the proper change. "There's your sixty-five dollars back, sir. Enjoy your day."

The paisano took his sixty-five dollars from the woman and wished her an enjoyable day as well. He walked out of the store into the cavernous mall, a very small man in a large place, feeling his pockets to be very heavy. The empty mall was peaceful, so he slowed his gait, and glanced slowly around as he moved towards the exit.

'Ninety-five dollars,' the paisano mused. 'Ninety-five dollars can buy a lot of drinks. And a lot of drinks can cause bad skin and stomachaches,' his self-reasoning continued. 'My brother will not get a letter opener for Christmas this year, but perhaps I should get him some antacids and some soap. They may not be impractical, but they will certainly be good to have.'

The paisano nearly burst out of the mall doors into the street, or so it seemed in relation to the morning quietude of the dead shops inside. The streets were lively, and the rain was still holding off. The air was still good. His pockets were positively bulging. He looked about for the nearest drug store where he could buy the antacids and soap to put under the Christmas tree, picturing big silver bows on them that would reflect and shine the lights of the Christmas tree like the transient glimmer of an elfin apparition.

His brother would be coming soon. He couldn't wait to have a drink and tell him the story of the letter opener—he could already imagination his brother's reaction: his mouth would open wide into a grin, his eyes would cross, and his hands would shoot up towards the Heavens. They would both share a big laugh.

A Note About My Brother

All featured work in this book written by my brother, Brandon, was compiled unwittingly on his part. It was not until after the book was formatted—and included a few of his works—that I alerted him to my intentions.

For the past five years, my brother has been sending me poems, short stories, and various descriptions from his time spent camping alongside rivers as he worked for Oregon Fish and Wildlife, fighting wildfires on the west coast for private companies, traveling, and studying history at universities in La Grande, Oregon and, currently, Ashland.

The initial plan was to piece together all these works of my brother's in one big book solely under his name. Two years ago I even wrote an introduction to that book—before it existed—wherein I announced that he was "the greatest poet I [had] ever known." Lofty a thing to say as it was, the exaggeration came naturally, and happily(see the Preface to my brother's, "Growing (Wu-Wei) Sentences in Flower Pots"). Had he heard me make such a proclamation he would've been a little ashamed, a little proud, and passed it off as if he hadn't heard anything at all, then probably sighed and gone back to cloud- or star-gazing. But he never did hear.

Due to the nature of my own ongoing projects, a crashed hard drive, lost emails, and a small brush fire built with his own hands, my brother's book never came into fruition—or at least it hasn't yet. For now we are restricted to the very limited few works that has been included here in *"Songs...,"* to which I am not only grateful to him for producing, but also for granting me the permission to use.

So—thank you, Brandon. And that's that.

—Winter 2009/'10, Portland, OR

IN FULL BLOOM
a letter, a love story
(2010)

For
K.A. — Happy Birthday

EDITOR'S NOTE

The following is a letter to a certain unnamed celebrity(and any legal representatives reading over his shoulder), whose alleged physical resemblance to the author, after much distress over the issue and over his own existence, gave way to several reckless decisions and eventual catastrophe.

The letter was written in pencil from somewhere in Canada where the author was, at the time, a self-proclaimed fugitive. It was then "smuggled" across the border into Los Angeles by unknown means, miraculously coming into the hands of the celebrity himself, whilst literary agents in the area, newspeople, filmmakers, and tabloid "journalists" all began to buzz with rumor of a scandal.

The manuscript itself contained not a single erasure, nor a single trace of hesitation on the author's part, as though every detail were not contrived, but the absolute truth as the author knew it. The only editing I have taken the liberty to perform is purely aesthetic, merely breaking up the author's long scrawl into neat, logical paragraphs; also, in keeping with the author's desire to remain anonymous to the public, I was obliged to omit the very last line of the letter, being that it was, naturally, his signature. Otherwise, the letter remains exactly as it was written.

—Early Spring 2010, Ashland, OR

Dear Mr. O—— Bloom:

I would like to preface this letter by stating that in my own incomparable opinion—an opinion you would most likely share in this matter—we look nothing alike. At most, there is a resemblance in our facial features that goes no further than perhaps an eyebrow, or the way our facial hair grows(in particular the mustache), or our small stature and the fact that when we smile it makes us look smug; and never any of these given things at the same time—it is always just the one thing or the other. However, in regards to this matter of our appearances, and my disbelief in the notion that they are strikingly similar, I stand in the minority.

Let me illustrate this point.

Once(but not only once), my own mother was watching a movie in which you star, Mr. Bloom, and she called me in the middle of it just to say, "It's like I'm watching you right now—he's so handsome." Meaning, of course, that I am so handsome. And to no offense to you I might add, seeing as she's *my* mother, and she just so happened to see something of me in you—probably the smug half-smile in this case—and immediately chose to believe that it *was* me she was watching, rather than you, and therefore the man on screen, her son(me), was certainly quite handsome.

Same thing with my ex-girlfriend's mom, only it was a different movie she was watching, and instead of saying *he's so handsome*, she said, "Aww—he's so dawrling...." Realize that she's from the South, and she has that cadence in her voice which goes along nicely with such diction, allowing the use of the word "darling" in place of "handsome." But in the greater scope of things it all contains this meaning: They think you are handsome, and that I look like you; or, They think I am handsome, and that you look like me. I'm sure you can understand the interchangeability of these two statements in their minds even without agreeing on their position.

I find this type of thing especially troubling when it involves strangers. While traveling(I always wear a nice gray suit with a black tie), going out to the movies, and while grocery shopping, the inquiring glances of strangers are cast on my every mundane movement as they question their instincts against what's before their very eyes—*Is it really*

391

him, you can almost hear them thinking. *Oh, it can't be—but is it?* I feel embarrassed for these people. Worst of all is the grocery store though, because there the occasion to remark always presents itself. As I attempt to make it through the checkout line with minimal conversation, the individual's reasoning has finally surmised that it could not really be you, Mr. Bloom, dressed so shabbily, unshaven, purchasing bay scallops, turkey bacon, and beer, and they say to me, "You know, you look *exactly* like a celebrity...."

I used to get a little red in the face when those words came out, but that reaction passed. I usually just half-smile now, and say, "Oh, yeah?"

They reply, "Yes, you do. I bet you get that all the time—do you know which one?"

I am still half-smiling here, and I say, "Occasionally, and I do believe I know which one you're speaking of, but entertain me anyway—tell me which one you were thinking."

You see, Mr. Bloom, I don't like to jump the gun at this point in the conversation. It happens that every once in awhile, rather than saying your name here, someone will have seen me from a slightly different angle, or my face will have been a little swollen with last night's beer, and a different star will arise—maybe, "E. Hirsche," or, "J. Sturgess." I like to give them the benefit of the doubt, a chance to redeem themselves before following through with the all too common, "O——Bloom!"

Not long ago there was a woman who said to me, "You look like a celebrity."

Of course, I said, "Oh, yeah—which one?"

And she surprised me—she said, "Not any specific celebrity. You look like your own celebrity, very unique."

If she had only stopped there, Mr. Bloom, all would have been fine. However, that was not the case, and you may be interested to hear what she said next. She said, "Well, you do look kinda like, oh, that guy from [quintessential movie in which you star]—but you're not as flat as he is, you're deeper looking, more complex."

You can imagine my relief in these instances, either when they are thinking of someone other than you, or when they are thinking of you but proclaim me to be superior. And you can imagine my amusement when they can't even remember your name!

I don't mean to poke fun at your feelings, Mr. Bloom, but it is not that I mind so much people thinking that I look like another human being as much as I mind them thinking that I look like you. There is something about you so utterly, and indefinably feminine—something that I am unable to identify with. I am a man, Mr. Bloom, who has all of the basic needs and desires of a man, but with a softness that comes

392

only of good men. Which is to say, I am a good man—remember that—and therefore am able to admit that I do not know you personally, so perhaps I am wrong and it is not you who bares these qualities, rather, it is the characters that you play.

Then again, it is your choice of which roles you accept, and the world at large knows your person by these roles, not yourself, so to them you are merely your basic physiognomy and the characters you portray. And that person is quite femmy, if I may say so myself —a few times I have even heard him(you) referred to as a "twat." An unnecessary jab for sure, but you should know that I stick up for you in the event of such name-calling and defamation of character; it has not been by my choice, but the world has lumped us together on a physical board, Mr. Bloom, so to hear you be called a twat is like some part of me that I cannot see or understand is being called a *twat*, and I resent it. I say to those people, "Ah, he's not so bad—com'on!" Or I say to them, "You can't call him a 'twat' if you know nothing about him."

They are persistent though, saying, "I don't need to know anything about him to know that he looks like a twat."

And when they have gone that far, Mr. Bloom, there is really no use in trying to sway them—the only real choice of action then is non-action. But it should please be noted here that I have put my own reputation at stake to preserve your honor—no matter how abstract the situations may have been—and if the time came where our positions were swapped, and you were given the opportunity to defend my good name, I hope you would do the same.

But enough of that, Mr. Bloom. I believe I have provided ample evidence to support myself with, and with those facts having been stated, you should now have a reference point for extrapolation, thus allowing yourself to ascertain, to a certain degree, an idea of what my ongoing experience has been like, and its accompanying disconcertion. This idea, this inkling of understanding, is absolutely imperative for you to have in regards to my peculiar case. Without it, I will appear in a way that I am not. I will appear to be pathetic, a pathological liar, a pervert even—and I am certainly not those things. I am a decent man, incapable of knowingly committing any horrendous or petty crime; I am loving and good, sweet as often as I can be and patient. You must remember these things regardless, Mr. Bloom—please.

The initial response to being repeatedly told that you look like someone else is chagrin, which seems an old word, but is defined as "a keen feeling of mental unease caused by failure, disappointment, or a disconcerting event," leaving no better word to describe it. And so the chagrin builds in your heart and brain with each new time you hear the words, "You know who you look like..." until it reaches its end result of casting your existence into oblivion as someone else's despondent shadow, a sour spot in what was an otherwise pretty sweet life.

The secondary response to being repeatedly told that you look like someone else is pure, uninhibited freedom through the knowledge of your anonymity. How many other faces like mine? How many others being told they look like this or that person? People everywhere looking only on the surface of things—how many of them seeing me, the individual?

After many years of experiencing the former response to the sound of your name, Mr. Bloom, taking my own existence to the brink of extinction—an obliteration of self that was not self-inflicted or welcomed—I experienced for the first time the latter response.

It was somewhat busy for a Wednesday night in the usually slow bar. I was sitting alone at the counter having a whiskey and club soda and a tall glass of ice water. The typical old drunks were at the end of the bar, chatting up the bartender who was a young woman that had grown to recognize me as a regular and knew my drink of choice was either the whiskey(she pours doubles) I was drinking that night, or beer with a splash of orange juice—and always a tall glass of ice water on the side. A few of the booths were filled with quiet groups of young folks sharing pitchers. The obligatory lone drunk was at the opposite end of the bar glued to the television, talking to no one in particular about past quarterbacks. The keno players were in the far back, catatonic. The juke box was playing pleasantly without interruption in the background. And a good looking young woman was shooting the classic solitary game of pool—left hand vs. right hand. It looked like the right hand was winning, but not by much.

The girl playing pool, pretty in a typical way—long brown hair, sharp features, legs showing, the impression of well-formed breasts as soft mounds through a thin cotton shirt—set down her cue and approached the bar. Two stools away from me, she called the bartender over.

"Another rum and coke please, and a water too," she said. As the bartender turned to make her drink, the girl turned to me, apparently having been watching from the corner of her eye, and it came out: "You know who you look like?"

It was already my second drink, which meant I was relaxed without being drunk. So I said to her, "Yeah, I suppose I do know who I look like. But who do I look like to you?"

As expected, she said she thought I looked like you, Mr. Bloom. The bartender set her drinks on the counter, and the girl paid for the rum. Still, she lingered there, two stools away.

I said, "I can't disprove an opinion, I can only disagree." Then gesturing to the pool table, "You need someone to play with you?"

The blatant sexuality of the question was not overlooked. She smiled without a hint of shame, the floozy, and said, "That would be nice."

Quickly, I ordered another drink and we walked to the table together. I told her I would take over for her left hand, stripes, which still had all its balls on the table— only one solid down. It was my shot. I chose a cue, the heaviest at 21 oz., and took a big swallow of my third drink before lining anything up. I felt exhilarated, as if the notion of my self were burning away in the bottom shelf whiskey, and my soul were dismembering itself from my body, floating above it to watch it perform. The girl observed me closely as I swaggered around the table(shot well that night), and the movement of her eyes, the unprecedented doey fondness, made her extraordinarily beautiful—the fact that she wanted me, I guess. It gave me the impression that she and I might be movie stars, or not just that, but this was the movie itself and we were method acting. It was not my intention to go home with her—I didn't give a shit about that—my only task was to play out my role.

In all, I missed only one shot. After the eight ball dropped, her eyes did too, and her face. She stared down at the ground, then looked up with a forced smile. "Good game," she said, extending her hand to me in good sportsmanship. "You want to play one more?"

I was happy to tell her that I couldn't, I had to go. And I did leave on that note, believing that I had left her with seven more seconds of film, sad and confused, alone in the bar, before the cameras cut back to me in motion, in the night, never to see her again.

Next morning I awoke slightly hungover—responsibly controlled by staying hydrated the night before—and wondered whether the alcohol had had something to do with my extremely gratifying and overall humorous experience. But it was not long that that question would go unanswered, as three days later, that very Saturday, I found myself experiencing a similar elation when the situation was closely repeated.

I did not dare take my newfound confidence, inspired as it was by lofty ambiguity, to the same bar and the same woman, for fear that my behavior should elicit the wrong kind of attention and give me the reputation of being a womanizer. It was not about that anyway—it was about the absurd joy in acting the grandiose nondescript, transforming from a miserable bore into whichever of the several typecasts that a woman will project onto a man. So I sauntered on down the street a little farther than usual, and ended up just one block away from my regular haunt at a place called, "The Bull." I didn't like the name of the place because it evoked, for me, the image of not just one bull, but many bulls stampeding through crowded streets, and the bulls were actually men trampling over the women in their path. In spite of this, and the black tinted windows that allowed nothing inside to be seen, I was lured in by the number of women standing outside to smoke—so many beautiful women.

Entering, I avowed to myself that I would not drink anything that night other than ice water, and maybe a glass of orange juice. It was an experiment, and I would treat it like one. I even went as far as to consciously formulate a question and hypothesis: Question) Is my arrogant behavior an affectation of booze, or of the sense of self-assurance I obtain through superior anonymity? Hypothesis) A combination of the two, yet heavily relying on the presence of alcohol to encourage the simulated self-assurance that is achieved through drunkenness.

According to my hypothesis, the night would probably end with a lonely, unswerving walk back to my apartment and a clear head that understood too well that I had failed at one thing because the floozy in the other bar was an anomaly, and succeeded in another—that being the prediction of my failure. It was not something I was looking forward to, but my resolve was strong.

The bar was packed with varying types of people, ages, ethnicities, and it took me a few minutes just to get to the counter, but I somehow squeezed myself onto a stool and ordered a tall glass of ice water. Needless to say, the bartender was not pleased with this patron of hers ordering only ice waters—though I was tipping. I had three glasses down and a fourth in my hands before it dawned on me that hypotheses were often proved wrong, and a melting feeling had already crept into my bloodstream which bore an uncanny resemblance to the state I had been in only a few nights before. I was an absolute no one at the bar, a fixture of total mediocrity, common in every sense of the word. It was an exalting conclusion to draw from ice water and a hundred unintelligible conversations. My hypothesis melted away too, and the question which it was in answer to. With that knowledge, I envisioned my bar stool swiveling, turning like a screw in the direction to make it rise, and elevating me at least a foot above the rest of the bar.

Precisely at this moment a woman's voice entered into the vision. "Excuse me—"

I turned and looked slightly downward. It was the woman who had been sitting next to me this entire time with a friend of hers, another woman. Neither could be said to be young, but even with their youth passed they were attractive—just two bored professionals with nice smells and good skin from expensive cremes. With my eyes I acknowledged that I had been addressed.

The woman continued loudly, "I just have to tell you, you look *exactly* like O—— Bloom. My daughter would be absolutely in *love* with you!"

I could hardly remember the time when hearing that would have annoyed me, made me callous. I said coolly, "Well where is your daughter tonight?"

The woman thought this was a charming retort. She laughed and put her hand on my arm for longer than she would have if it were just her daughter that would be interested in me. She finally removed her hand and my skin tingled where it had been, the sensation moving up past my elbow to my shoulder, then my chest, and down into the rest of my body. She offered to buy me a drink.

It immediately crossed my mind at this point that my experiment, by disproving my hypothesis, had been successful. The water had assisted in my intoxication by keeping me sober long enough to realize this. There was no longer a need for sobriety, though, and there was now cause for celebration—my walk home could be swerving if it wanted. Also, in order to maintain safe mount on the high horse of my un-self, without bursting my top—shouting out philosophical non-sense into the bar, or some such thing—I thought it might be helpful to subdue my raging anti-ego with a drink. Besides, someone else was paying. I accepted the woman's offer and settled on a whiskey and club soda to start.

If this were a novel, Mr. Bloom, I might take the trouble here to go into detail about what the women looked like, giving each of them small quirks that made them seem human, "real"; if it were a movie, their looks would be apparent already, but they would still appear inconspicuously in the credits as "Woman In Bar #1" and "Woman In Bar #2." Although this is merely a letter to you, albeit longwinded, I will stick with the format you are more familiar with only insofar as referring to these women as "Woman #1"(who bought me the drink), and "Woman #2"(her friend), because their real names, and looks for that matter, are not so important as their reaction to my strange conceit, and borderline vulgar nonchalance.

Due to the bartender not knowing me, and the fact that all of my previous drinks were ice water, I must have been perceived as some kind of a pussy because when my drink arrived it was, I felt, abnormally weak—or maybe I had already begun channeling your aura and the bartender served me accordingly. I didn't let on about my disappointing drink though. Rather, I said to Woman #1, "Is the next one on you too? Because if it's not I'll take this one slow."

It would've been hard to miss with her—she laughed. "Of course it's on me, sweetheart," she said, grazing my leg with hers under the counter. At that I finished my drink in one go. She called the bartender over for another.

Woman #2 seemed to be scanning the bar pathetically, looking for someone to start a conversation with her. Woman #1, however, she was locked in. As her interest was clearly growing, she justified it by talking about her daughter again, saying how much she would love me, she was beautiful, etc., and she even got her cellphone out and began texting her.

She showed me the message after it was sent: Hey, where are you?! Met a cute boy you would love!

She was giggling hysterically. Her daughter replied: At [boyfriend]'s house. Hope he doesn't read this cos he'd be pissed! Have fun.

She showed me her daughter's reply, sadly. And she went on to explain that, sure, her daughter had a boyfriend but he wasn't any good for her. She needed to be with someone like me. Then she cotinued to discuss the situation, scheming of ways to get us together, until the point where I was thoroughly drunk on her tab and the bar was finally closing.

I told her I didn't live far, but she insisted I share a cab with her and Woman #2. As the driver pulled up in front of my apartment, she handed me a piece of paper with her and her daughter's number on it. She told me to call her daughter sometime, and if her daughter refused to go out with me then I should call her and she would make it happen. She then told me how sweet I was and kissed me as if she were going for the neck but missed and got me on the jaw.

After that I said goodbye and got out of the cab without watching them drive away. Then I stumbled inside to my bed and slept, as they say, like a baby.

I could go on and on in this fashion, Mr. Bloom, elucidating the minutia of my each and every small "sin," but it would be against my better judgment to do so and completely unnecessary besides. I've only related these two instances now as Exhibit A and Exhibit B, that you might see the natural progression which led to the true object of this correspondence, Exhibit C—strangely enough, the beginning letter of such words as calamity, catastrophe, the country Canada(where I am currently a fugitive), and the name Claire, all of which are relevant to the matter at hand.

It suffices to say that Exhibit A and Exhibit B were not controlled occurrences, happening only one time each, but a representation of many other comparable events, and a precursor of what was to come.

I knew that my general disposition had begun to change; that my usu-

398

ally quiet, reserved temperament had turned into an exceedingly arrogant, and suave farce that I carried on not only in bars, but in coffee shops, in the grocery store, in movie theaters, etc.—but I did not know exactly to what extent. It continued to remain unclear to me until the actual moment it happened. And then there was no turning back.

I regret to inform you at this time—though I must if I am to paint a complete picture—that there is a third response to being repeatedly told that you look like someone else, which is to allow the person telling you such to harbor their misconception as truth, and subsequently believe you to actually *be* the person they thought you to simply look like.

Some would say that this third response is one of depravity, and that only a person out of their wits is capable of allowing such an atrocity to take place. I urge you though, Mr. Bloom, to ignore what those people would say, because there was nothing cold or calculated or criminal about my actions. I need for you to comprehend that the way it happened was completely organic, innocent, and my response was more out of temporary confusion and love-drunkenness than anything else.

Prior to the event I am about to describe—which will continue to be known as Exhibit C—it did not seem unusual to me that one day I decided to keep only my mustache. Men in high spirits often do funny things to their appearances to show outwardly their inner peace or happiness. So as I was shaving, I kept the mustache and I laughed at it. I cut my hair short too. It wasn't until recently—just moments before I began writing this letter—that I truly inspected the effects these alterations had on the appearance of my face. The mustache seemed to bring my cheekbones out and the cheeks themselves in, casting subtle shadows in the hollows on each side of my mouth. It also made my nose thinner, daintier, if you will—like yours, Mr. Bloom. The haircut brought out the framing of my face, the jaw line becoming infinitely sharper, the chin pointier. And all of this coming together in the eyes, large and brown, with the brows nestled closely over top—the one eyebrow jutting slightly upward mischievously. The eyes had not been changed one bit, but in the setting of my other altered features I was able to take notice of the quality in them that might allow a person encountering my face for the first time to deceive themselves, and say, "You know who you look like..."—well, I suppose I might, just maybe, look like you to some people then, Mr. Bloom. I guess it is a gentleness in the eyes, a suppressed hint of some abstract wound, that expresses a degree of genuine, heartfelt lovesickness—some softness that is not a part of me, or a part of you, respectively, but a standard emotion that invariably draws the attention of dreamy young women.

I stand by my initial remark here though, in saying that I do not think we look alike, admitting, however, only that there is possibly something in each one of our faces that evokes the same reaction from women that want to be in love.

When I left my apartment that afternoon, Mr. Bloom, it was with my freshly altered appearance that, in retrospect, added to the illusion that I was someone other than myself(you), only the eyes had yet the look of lovesickness about them—that would come shortly.

I enjoy going to the movies by myself, especially the matinee, which is rarely attended by more than a handful of people, and that was my plan on this particular day with nothing more in mind. I saw her at concessions as I was purchasing my ticket—Claire.

Wasn't that the name of your costar's character in that movie where you planned to commit suicide? If my memory serves me right, which it usually does, then what a coincidence!

Of course, I did not know that her name was Claire yet. All I knew was that there was a gorgeous young woman standing there at concessions at that age where everything had come out of its awkward stages and settled nicely, where the immaturity of the experimental period had passed, too, leaving her like a flower in full bloom at the end of spring, stable and confident in the dawn of the long summertime of her life.

She was more than the unimaginative "breathtaking," Mr. Bloom. She was a nauseous feeling creeping over the body from head to toe, standing at about five-foot four in what looked like a "jumper," which was a white, short-sleeve cotton blouse on the top, with a thin black belt separating it from deep navy blue cotton shorts on the bottom that were suggestive(showing all of the knee, and a few inches of cinnamon and vanilla thigh above) without being immodest. It was an unbelievably warm day for late February. She had a charcoal grey sweater draped over her arm in case of cold in the theatre. The ankle-high boots on her little feet were fairy like. My muscles trembled, contracting and relaxing at random against my bones; my eyes vibrated in my skull, the pupils dilating.

At one point she turned her head so that a beam of sunlight coming through the windows illuminated several of the stray blondish hairs on her otherwise neat head— the hair in back pulled into a low, smooth pony tail, while the hair in front was pushed behind the ears sweetly—permitting me that not uncommon, yet certainly longed for, vision of a man's dream-woman materializing in "real" life as an angel with halo and all.

Don't let this angelic comparison put you off, Mr. Bloom. If this were a literary work I would obviously try for a more unusual image than the angel, but I cannot refrain from using the cliché here, in this letter, when what I'm after is providing a truthful account. The fact that I briefly saw her as an angel, no matter how often the symbolism has been used, remains true to me, and in that fact alone it should be considered remarkable.

Continuing then, with the visual foreplay of Exhibit C.

Just as I was getting in line for concessions, without really wanting anything, Claire was receiving her purchases—a small bag of popcorn, a bottled water, and Junior Mints. She took them over to her friend, a girl who looked quite a bit younger than her, though dressed similarly. Maybe her little sister, I thought. The girl whispered something into Claire's ear, who immediately turned and looked at me. I did not look away soon enough to avoid making eye contact with her and at the time I did not think that was an altogether bad thing, because when her eyes met mine, having already acquired the "lovesickness" appeal to them from watching her in line, the sides of her mouth curled ever so slightly upward in a shy smile before she instinctively hid herself, pretending to be talking to her sister about some movie poster. Her sister still stared in my direction conspicuously, and secured for me the knowledge that this brief locking of eyes could only mean actual, verbal confrontation at some point—at the least a "hello" or an "excuse me."

The girls went into the bathroom. Probably, I ventured proudly, they went into the bathroom to discuss the man they had just seen at concessions, and plot different ways of engaging him in conversation. I found myself at the concession counter, still not really wanting anything, and feeling somewhat lightheaded, so I settled quickly and inexplicably on a cup of ice.

As I filled my cup with water from the drinking fountain, the movies were being called to start. The twenty-so people in the lobby dispersed, and were ushered into four separate theatres. I casually took a seat a couple of rows from the back of Theatre 3, directly in center— the movie that was showing deserves no mention, it should only be noted that it was rated "R" and that you played no part in it, Mr. Bloom.

Soon after I sat down, Claire and her sister walked into the dim lit theatre just as the previews were beginning and it both relieved me(that I was already seeing Claire again) and caused me great anxiety(because what if she sat next to me?). They started up the stairs towards the back with the young one leading, and halfway up Claire took notice of me(my heart pounding), softly pushing her sister's back into an aisle four rows in front of me. They did not go to the direct center of the row, as most people would, instead they sat down about a quarter of the way in at such an angle from my position where I would be able to see, at all times, the light from the screen playing off the soft, unblemished skin of Claire's cheek. She put her sweater over her shoulders, and as she did so she turned her body even further in my direction, knowingly giving me the fantastic full view of the symmetry of her face, flaunting its flawlessness for me. She smiled slightly, without looking up at me, and a red light shot out of the screen that reflected off her face and made it look as if she were blushing. She turned back around to watch the movie.

I remember thinking it was a tremendous blessing to have entered the theatre first that day. Had Claire and company gotten their desired seats in back, it would've left *me* sitting a few rows in front of *them*, which would have been unimaginable torture. I would not have had the audacity to peek backward at any point during the movie, but resigned myself to a rigid and distracted forward-facing position, my back thoroughly cramping from the tension, wondering whether or not there were the little eyes of a beautiful young woman four rows behind me burning into my flesh.

As it was, sitting behind Claire offered me a great amount of authority over the situation. Over my head was cast the dissipating and ultimately intangible beam of light from the projector that magically produced a picture on screen, which was then viewed by an audience member here in the third row, a couple there in the eighth row, Claire and sister in the thirteenth row, then me in the seventeenth, and no one in the two rows behind me. Every image that came from the projector to the screen, then received by my eyes and gone into my brain, was a dual image that was filtered through its peripheral atmosphere as well, which, namely, was Claire sitting there with her sweater over her shoulders and the light refracting off her cheek. I was able to follow the movie itself, while also following Claire, easily surmising what her reactions were to the movie and therefore gaining a basic idea of her personality. During the parts of the movie which I perceived as funny, I saw that Claire, too, thought they were funny as her shoulders trembled and the one side of her mouth came into view, widening in smile onto what was otherwise just her cheek, and the corner of her eye, squinting. During the serious parts she sat solemnly forward in her seat, engrossed.

On principal, I enjoy movies. Even when it is not a particularly good movie I am watching, I am usually entertained—though, of course, I do prefer good movies over bad ones. However, while viewing the movie in question, I began hoping for any and all evidence of the latter, because I found that an implausible or ridiculous development elicited a look back from the girl four rows in front of me, Claire, turning herself slightly to make a look of exaggerated disgust at her sister (though really for my amusement), while glancing toward my seat from the corner of her smiling eye.

The worse it was, the longer she would look, the more her nose would adorably scrunch up in distaste—the more my body would ache. Each time it occurred, it was as if a tiny string were pulled within my body and a fresh wave of wonderful nausea went through me. My hands were clammy. My heart palpitated in a way that usually meant I'd had too much coffee, or smoked too many cigarettes. I did my best to suppress it until it was a small, but significant buzz emanating from my core.

Just now a bee landed on the outside of my window, displaying his underside against the glass. The entirety of his little body, from fuzzy head down to stinger, is thrusting on a two count—coming at the glass, then away, then at it again—appearing to be in attempt of pollination. He is not a sick bee either, with AIDS or anything—he looks to be in good health. But what perfect timing! His pulsation mimics to a "T" what I felt inside of my body in the dark glow of the movie theatre—that rhythmic surge of futility, of the brain sending messages to act through the body before a physical response is feasible; my nerves curling up into tight balls.

In the end, the movie turned out to be alright. Overall, there were only a handful of questionable moments throughout, and so I was able to take with me a handful of alluring glances from Claire, which is enough to make a man ill for a lifetime.

As I exited the bathroom from the mandatory after-movie piss, I noticed that Claire was standing not far away, alone, appearing to be in wait for her sister to come out of the women's room, which was right next to the men's. Eye contact happened naturally—as did a smile. I broke the mutual stare while closing the space between us, walking towards the doors that led onto the street with my nerves curling further inward and my stomach rocking as if on water. I had to get by her to leave—just one last look to remember her by.

"Excuse me—" came the soft, smooth voice of honey mixed into milk, now right beside me, from the young woman whose face still haunts me. I stopped in my tracks. She started, "Are you—"

"Yeah," I said nervously, my tone going slightly up at the end as in question, making reply to her initial *excuse me* while accidentally interrupting her following venture.

"I'm sorry," she said, momentarily averting her gaze with a smile. "Hi. I'm Claire."

She smiled fully now, sticking out her hand just far enough away from her body for me to assume she intended for me to shake it. By now, she was wearing her sweater in the proper way, and the right sleeve covered the bottom portion of the palm of her extended hand.

Forgetting to introduce myself, I replied only with a dopey smile, and a wavering, "Hi..." as I shook her tiny extended hand and fell in love with it for being so incredibly small and warm. Then, "Nice to

403

meet you."

To which Claire heartbreakingly answered, "Nice to meet you too, O——."

Before I continue with the particulars of ensuing events, let us briefly examine this crucial moment wherein the whole fabric of my existence changed and the third response was taken by complete accident.

It all boils down to this:

As I exited the movie theatre I was extremely agitated by what could be considered as nearly two hours of abstract flirtation, along with its accompanying thoughts and the effects those have on a solitary body in the dark. I headed for the bathroom for a piss, and as I did so I noticed Claire walking in the opposite direction—again my reaction was torn. I was relieved that my torment was over, and also sad because it was over at the expense of this beautiful young woman's departure. While in the bathroom, I mourned over my loss and daydreamed about unlikely chance encounters later on.

So to come out of the bathroom then and see that Claire was still in my orbit was a great surprise, very confusing. It caught me off guard, and for a split second I even questioned the authenticity of my sighting—had I fallen asleep in the bathroom, standing up at the urinal? No man of reason could ever say "yes" to that question. I knew better, which meant only that this was the "real" thing and therefore had the potential of being humiliating and hurtful. I decided that the only thing to do was smile at her with the forlorn look of loss I had acquired naturally while daydreaming in the bathroom, and take her in completely through the eyes, one last time, in order to catalog her image to perfect memory.

It was startling to have this new plan foiled by such a sweet sound, that discreet seduction of her calm voice, which she believed to have used to express these words: "Excuse me, are you [O—— Bloom]?" And to which she believed I responded, "Yeah."

The way I see it, it was a simple mistake of my answer to her address, with an under-exaggerated rising tone, being interpreted as an interjection to the actual—and obvious if I were you, Mr. Bloom—question at hand. It could have been easily cleared up had after she called me by your name I stated that I was, in fact, not you. But show me a man that would interrupt a conversation with a beautiful young woman over such trivialities as a name, especially in the over stimulated state that I was in—show me! And I will lay the matter to rest.

As this was not the case, being that I, like any other man in the given situation, did not pay heed to the misaddress—telling myself that it was some auditory trick—I am unable to lay the matter to rest. If I were a man of extraordinary conscience, Mr. Bloom, then it would be a different story and my current predicament would not exist. This letter would not need to be written.

Ignoring the implications of the dialogue itself—still baffled, sweating, fearful of a possible delirium—I asked Claire if she'd like to go for a drink. She agreed, and when her sister came out of the bathroom she asked me to hold on for a moment as she went to discuss it with her. Excitement was apparent in their body language from a distance. They came back together, beaming, and they both joined me.

The place the girls chose was a coffee shop around the corner from the movie theatre. At the time, I thought it was a very tasteful and charming decision, which I attributed to the fact that Claire's sister was probably not of age for something stronger. Exceedingly more enchanting was Claire's choice of drink—hot chocolate! I ordered a Moroccan mint tea. I can't recall what her sister ordered. In any case, I couldn't really afford all three drinks, having just treated myself to a midday movie viewing, but I paid for everything anyway—just to be nice, I said to myself. Both girls thanked me profusely.

We sat at a table in a back window of the shop: Claire and I quietly engaged in conversation, her sister thumbing through a magazine meant for chubby girls—both physically and psychologically—or young, impressionable ones. It was a great stress to me, that magazine. I kept glancing over at it, nervously anticipating the moment when the sister would come across a picture of you, Mr. Bloom. It is one thing to confuse the person in front of you with another from memory—especially if that memory is held under the assumed distortion of silver screen to "real" life—but it is entirely another when there is a photo present to draw comparisons from. Thank god you stayed out of the media that month. Had you been in a drunken bar fight, Mr. Bloom, or overdosed, or done anything equally embarrassing or noteworthy, it would have meant immediate disaster for me.

But Claire's delicacy was able to remain unbroken. She clearly thought me to be an extravagant figure, but she eluded the subject. The most she mentioned was the offhand remark, "You look a little different in person—not as fragile, or something...." She followed up by taking a sip of her hot chocolate and apologizing. I assured her that it was okay.

The casual deceit a man is capable of, Mr. Bloom, continues to perplex and frighten me. One minute he can be, think, or say one thing, and the next he can be, think, or say the complete opposite— both with absolute conviction. And this behavior does more than just convince his audience of his sincerity, it succeeds(usually) in convincing himself of it too. Which is to say, a man is nothing more than his present circumstances and his reaction to them—whether his conscience perceives them as agreeable or not.

As I spoke with Claire that afternoon I was amiable and convincing. I was my full, undiluted self under the imposed guise of "O—— Bloom." I must say, Mr. Bloom, that you were fantastic company. In Claire's words, you were "so candid and down to earth." Her affection was visibly growing. Even without the red glow of the movie screen lighting her cheeks, I noticed more than once that she was blushing—a trait on a woman that invariably endears her to a man. But she had me before that.

I would like to take a moment here to provide clarity of my initial intentions, or, rather, the lack thereof.

I did not wish to court beautiful Claire. Pretty and sweet as she was, I hoped only to enjoy her company as all men enjoy the presence of a woman—"the sights and smells." I was not looking for love. I've been in love before, and it's a painful thing in the end, even if you're on the Upper-Side of the equation, being the first one to fall out of it. Saying nothing of love that is not reciprocated from the get go.

But the reasoning of a man is never consulted when such an emotion arises. There is something in his body that is uncontrollable: it's the way the chemicals are arranged in his brain; it's his genetic predisposition to react positively to attraction—to feel a lightness in the gut, a buzz behind the eyes, a rising below the waist. He cannot alter his nature. He can only choose to either indulge or stifle it. Personally, I've always been an advocate of the come-as-it-may philosophy, even if what comes is accompanied by legal restrictions in most states, save for New Mexico and probably Utah.

It was a startling and revelatory thought I had in the back window of the coffee shop talking to Claire: "I am in love." It was equally startling(and revelatory by way of her blushing and her foot always "accidentally" nudging against mine) to see in her the same exact thought, even though it originated under false pretenses; typically, people fall in love with ideas of people or things over the "reality" of them anyway—so her love was not uncommon, or unjust.

Given the effects of the biological response to attraction, especially when reciprocated, and the muddle of flamboyant, precursory events, it is no wonder that I overlooked certain finer points of that afternoon which, I'd like to think, would have altered my future course of action. Still, as they say: "Come as it may."

And come it did, strong, in the slight frame of a young woman, which is always the most influential and dangerous form. Claire— sensitive without being needy, affectionate without being overbearing, intelligent without being smarter than I am, or a bore, compassionate without trying to save the world, fun without being tiring, confident without being a bitch, sensual without being a tramp.

As for her looks—which I've already given my first impression of —I'm sure you've seen plenty of women. Put together a mental collage of your favorite traits. Imagine those features as being better somehow, radiating. That's what she was for me, that crystalline projection, ineffable—Claire!

Speaking softly as we said our goodbyes, her hand lightly below my elbow, Claire and I made arrangements for a later meeting. Numbers were exchanged. Then she left, leaving in her wake a gap between us that would decidedly exist for one week.

During this time, Claire's image was emblazoned in the soft tissue of my brain where even ordinary women have the potential of becoming extraordinary. Already something of a phenomenon, my impression of Claire was affected exponentially. Her beauty grew quickly and outrageously in my mind, instantly demanding awe of ludicrous proportions. She was a mythical creature, seemingly unattainable, yet somehow soon to be mine.

My only satisfaction that week came in knowing that there was an end result in sight—though unbearably far off—and nightly phone calls from Claire, which always began innocently but would inevitably lead to topics of discussion that will not be mentioned, along with heavy breathing. The tension was building in my body, invisibly, ever-slowly edging towards an eventual but certain climax. I was counting down the days.

She was all I could think of. I went from reading the classics to not reading at all. I went from doing crossword puzzles to staring at several empty squares in a box that meant nothing. I went from showering every morning to not being able to stand the feeling of the water against my skin. Even my clothes seemed to cling against my body, irritating me so much that I had to pull my undershirt away from my chest to avoid being smothered. Socks were shunned completely. Certain other undergarments were unthinkable, not wanting my hypersensitive parts to be constricted by fabric and thus irritated as well.

In this way, what would usually be called the "grace period" actually turned out to be the beginning of my freefall from grace. The carrying out of my abstract affair in phone calls and daydreams had obvious psychological repercussions. For every physical torture I experienced there was an emotional one that was even more devastating. My body was growing increasingly tight and anxious as my mental state suffered both as a side effect, and from its initial cause, Claire, becoming altogether over stimulated and exceedingly fragile.

I had told my employers that I was going on vacation, and in doing so created an abundance of free time for myself that exacerbated my condition, and assisted in my ultimate demise. The only activity I found myself capable of during this period was walking, the exertion providing a small degree of relief from my agony.

I took long walks through the city and its intermittent parks. I walked somewhat hurriedly, but without any particular destination. I attempted to become engrossed with the immediacies of my surroundings—to no avail. I looked up at the clouds hanging low and grey over the buildings, and you would not believe the things I saw there. Within the greyscale I could make out the image of an ex-lover's face, turning at its base as if shaking in disapproval—my old lover, reprimanding me in the clouds! I saw the billowing hood of the female anatomy, looking very old and worn, with a particularly dark patch of clouds sagging beneath it. I saw, too, a child's head poking out from under a thick, grey blanket, and the child was visibly sad or afraid, tears forming in its dirty cotton-like eyes.

I saw other things as well, which disturb me in hindsight, though at the time they did not alarm me. At most, the cloud-objects served as a momentary distraction and were vaguely confusing. My pace would remain quick and my destination unknown, or nonexistent really; my heartbeat would remain erratic and too strong, and my head a nervous wreck.

Occasionally I would notice that I was thirsty. Then I would pop into the nearest bar for a drink. Three glasses of water to hydrate me, and a shot of whiskey to (hopefully) ease the extreme agitation I was forced to bear at the cause of my unfulfilled desires. "Claire... Claire... Claire..." I thought, like the incessant prayer of a devout pilgrim to his God. Alone, the repetitive nature of these thoughts is enough to make a man go crazy. Worse if that thought is of an incomprehensible "being"; worse yet if that thought is of a young woman whose looks are astounding, and whose sex can be quite nearly seen, smelled, and felt, but without her actually being present and therefore not being able to offer the physical contact that would alleviate the terrible longing she had so inspired.

Being stationary for any length of time was more than I could handle. I would gulp down my drinks and run out of the bar, back into the bright grey city which seemed a hallucination—everything blurry, colors muted. I would continue walking. My gait was automatic, my legs absently propelling my body along sidewalks and footpaths. I was being mechanically carried from one odd place to another like a lunatic, or a ghost, my spirit no more at ease than those of the dissolute creatures just mentioned, my brain just as befuddled.

The only effective method of reprieve was to sit myself down once my dogs got to barking and have a cigarette. The smell and taste of the smoke was awful. The nicotine was nauseating. I would become excessively dizzy. The back of my skull pounded with exhaustion and foreign substance, causing me to unintentionally rock to and fro, swaying gently like a drunk. But the physical ailment was welcomed in my delirium. I was able to concentrate solely on the sickness, which was tangible and therefore not so terrible.

I know this was an irrational way to behave. I am by no means proud of it, nor would I ever condone that sort of thing in others—not even for entertainment purposes. However, I must admit that as I write this the pity and disgust I feel for myself still cannot fully outweigh the dormant and inappropriate desire I have to see Claire again —the sick urge is not entirely suppressed.

When the week had passed, I believed the nightmare of my mental suffering to be over and composed myself for my scheduled date with Claire. Little did I know then, the nightmare actually continued to inch forward—merely refraining momentarily from the production of its undesirable side effects—and would soon reach its peak.

How exactly this came to be I will now explain to you, Mr. Bloom, bringing to light my reasoning for the use of such terms as "inappropriate," and, "legal restrictions."

Over the phone, it had been decided that we would meet just after 5pm at a bench along the west bank of the river that cuts the city in two. A few blocks south of the Main Bridge was our chosen bench, noteworthy for its proximity to the Dream Tree, which is a moderately sized tree from whose branches hang young folks' dreams written on tiny slips of paper and attached by strings. Incidentally, the location put us almost directly in the center of the city and therefore in a beneficial position for us to head into any of the city's districts, as our plans detailed nothing further than the meeting itself.

Claire arrived at the bench before me. Though approaching from behind, I could tell it was her sitting there just by the color of her hair, the way it hung and caught the fading light, and the slightness of her well-outfitted shoulders—all the same as I had first seen them in the theatre, only more so. As I crossed the soft grass of the park towards the bench—and Claire on that bench!—an uncomfortable(and familiar) pang of lust arose in me and I squashed it immediately.

It was not that I was anticipating so much the physical act of making love to her(though it was something I'd given a lot of thought to) as much as it was the prospect of conquering the idea of her. As I've already made clear, since our first meeting only a week before she had grown considerably in my mind and become something of a surreal entity, her figure singlehandedly representing all that a man could possibly desire.

And now there she was—Claire, in the flesh.

I circled the bench widely enough so as not to come upon her by surprise as a predator would his prey. When she saw me she smiled and stood up. I took the sight of her in, and instantly found it to be a perfect match with that I had stored in my brain. Amazing. I did not hesitate to go in at once for a kiss, wrapping my arm around the (very) small of her back, and respectfully, delicately, pressing my lips against hers which were soft and inviting, opening on contact. This lasted for several beats.

We were both smiling when we pulled away. Then I greeted her properly in the tradition of the Chinese. "Have you eaten yet?"

She informed me that she had not yet eaten. I offered a solution to this: a little restaurant I knew of in the northeast of the city called, "Tuk-Tuk." It was a modern place with good Thai food, presented decorously in the dim warmth of candlelight. It was pretty nice, I told her. She took me at my word.

We hailed a cab to get to the restaurant, which turned out to be a painful ordeal. Not that the cab was hard to flag down, we got one easily enough; but it was the close quarters of the backseat and the swiftness of the car—it was overwhelming.

Out the window we watched the darkening city, big and sad, fly by from our comfortable perch in the back seat, and our existence seemed to shrink down within the drizzling atmosphere, allowing us the notion of utmost self-importance. At corners, centripetal force brought our tingling bodies closer together—she leaning into me when we turned left, me into her when we turned right. Each time our bodies made contact it felt as though it were the very first contact, just one man and one woman discovering the pleasure of each other's touch.

But we couldn't wait for the corners—we needed more. She began to run her fingers over the back of my hand and up my forearm; I grazed her knee; she touched her fingertip to mine and applied gentle pressure; I touched her cheek; she traced from my fingertip to my palm, stopping there in circular motion; I pushed the stray hair at her temple behind her ear and kissed the uncovered spot; she nestled her head further against my lips, exhaling slowly through her slightly parted mouth.

The thought of prolonging the sick ecstasy of the consummation of our new togetherness until after dinner proved to be too much. Our casual, and I thought discreet, playfulness was maddening. I would have gone insane had each arousing touch from her not provided also a small amount of relief, as if releasing a tiny bit of pressure from my heart valve to ensure that it not grow too large and result in explosion; then again, the pressure building was far greater than that escaping, which meant that an eventual explosion would have been imminent— probably under the table at dinner, had we ever made it there.

Luckily, or so I thought then, she suggested we skip dinner. As if she were taking a line she had learned from a movie, she whispered, "Do you want to go back to my place?"

At this juncture it seemed only logical to say yes. I took the initiative to get the driver's attention at once. Claire raised her voice to the cabby to give him the address of our new destination, which, coincidentally, wasn't very far from Tuk-Tuk. A few moments later I watched the restaurant go by out the window as we sped past it.

Arriving at Claire's, I can't recall getting out of the cab, or who paid the fare—though I suspect it was me in mechanical upkeep of appearances. The only thing I recall is standing in front of her house feeling very disoriented in my surroundings.

The house in which Claire lived was large and stately looking, with a short wrought iron fence surrounding an immaculate yard, and a stone path leading to the front steps and sizeable veranda. It was situated in one of those tree lined neighborhoods outside of the city center which inspire thoughts of wealth, good meals, and cozy nights in front of a fire. What the interior of such a house in such a neighborhood might look like I was previously only able to guess at, seeing in my imagination sleek wooden floors, decorative alcoves, wine cellars, many warm bedrooms, and a large kitchen which served as the common meeting place for the members of the happy and friendly family that surely lived there. It was not the type of house a young woman lived in alone.

As we crossed the stone path to the house, Claire must have sensed something of the discomfiture I felt about my expectations of a single person house being replaced by a much larger one, because she made a comment then that both cleared up the present question about her living situation while simultaneously creating a new, much darker question.

Again, as though she were repeating lines she had heard in a movie —though it struck me that we might not be thinking of the *same movie* —she said, "Don't worry...my parents aren't home."

With her tiny hand in mine, leading me up the front steps now and already beginning to unlock the door, I made a mental excuse for this unexpected development. An early spring break, I thought. She was still in college and her school was simply on a different schedule than others, which I knew would not be getting out for another two weeks. She had just come home for a little visit, that's all. But then how had I not learned this already? What did I really know about Claire?

Of course, my body was still bent on carrying out the activities which were now so close to happening; I was willing to believe in the thin excuse I had made for Claire. She pulled me by the hand inside.

I know these interjections must be tiring you, Mr. Bloom—especially since you have, no doubt, taken a great interest in the narrative at hand—so I will make this quick.

I cannot stress enough to you that up until this point, and for a few more minutes yet, I was completely unawares of the gravity of my situation, and the heavy consequences of my desire for Claire. And I would like to bring to your attention—rather, remind you—that my only physical interaction with young Claire has been restricted to innocent handholding, some minor petting of the non-private parts, and a somewhat brief kiss in which neither tongue penetrated fully the other party's mouth. None of which, to my knowledge, would generally constitute a sexual crime, and they certainly don't when considering the given circumstances.

Also, I would like to state that I feel quite fortunate that Claire chose her own home as the location for our "escapade," seeing as the place a woman lives is incapable of telling a lie about her, each seemingly trivial detail providing an intimate truth about who she really is; had a different locale been chosen, a crime likely would have been committed that day.

Thankfully, what we are dealing with here is not the abstractions of what might have happened in this or that instance, but the indisputable and humiliating facts which comprise the absolute truth of what *did* happen.

Carrying on then.

From the entryway, with the door locked behind us, I was led through a hallway where school pictures of Claire were hung, one from each year of her education, which I did not consciously count at the time, though there must have been eleven in all. At the end of the hallway there was what I assumed to be a family portrait, showing Claire(with braces) with her mom and dad.

I was curious to ask her why her sister was not in the picture, but Claire interrupted me before I could begin. She made a sound of disgust("ugh"), then said, "Ignore the pictures, please—they're so embarrassing!" I could not ignore the pictures altogether, though I did refrain from posing any question regarding her "sister."

Before reaching what looked to be the kitchen, we climbed the stairs which shot quickly upward from the hallway to the left. The sound of our footsteps were ominous against the hardwood. At the top, there were four doors: the first opened into a bathroom, while the other three were bedrooms. One of the bedrooms was furnished, but was decorated plainly and far too clean to be lived in; the other bedroom was clearly the "master suite," where Claire's parents slept. And the third bedroom, although it was the only one with the door closed, was quite obviously Claire's. A sign on the closed door read, "CLAIRE," in bubble letters, and underneath it was written, "Keep Out."

Promptly as we had entered the house I had begun sweating. By now I could tell the beads were visibly forming around my nose and on my forehead. I felt very sick. Yet just as we were about to enter her room, I still managed to gesture at the door sign, and say, "Does that include me too?"

"That sign is for everyone but you," Claire replied. "Otherwise my parents think it's okay to rummage through my things when I'm gone."

When I'm gone, I foolishly clung to in desperation, as if her brief absences implied one extended absence(college, please!), as she once again pulled me by the hand, only this time into her room. She quickly shut the door, the slam seeming overly loud in the large, empty house—just the two of us there, alone.

The walls of her room were cluttered with pictures and magazine clippings which I immediately made it my duty to inspect. Claire took off her sweater, exposing her dainty, childlike arms. She tossed it onto the bed, then asked politely, "Can I offer you a drink?"

I accepted, taking my eyes off the contents of her wall just in time to see her produce a bottle of vodka from under her bed. She poured us each a double, at least, into two dirty glasses plucked from her nightstand. She handed one to me, and I thanked her. She sat down on the bed, kicking off her shoes and bringing her legs into a pretzel beneath her, then downed her drink and refilled the glass, shuddering.

I took a sip of my vodka, exhaling slowly through my mouth, and recommenced looking at the various bric-a-brac and keepsakes around her room, and the countless pictures hung on the walls. I noticed there was a quote written on the vanity mirror in flowery script with a dry erase marker, though I can't recall what the quote was. There were too many other things to look at: the cotton panties conspicuously strewn across the floor, the bra hanging from the top of the mirror, the textbooks with their bedoodled covers which hid the names of subjects I feared one learned *before* attending college, the pictures of her and her friends who were invariably younger looking than she, an honor roll slip dated last year in its latter months, and various other things(such as the handwritten notes from her friends, the bottle of vodka hiding under the bed, her movie stub from the week before, which was for a PG-13! movie in Theatre 4!! rather than the R-rated movie we saw in Theatre 3) which all forced me—even in my fragile delirium, which so badly made me want to remain oblivious—to arrive at a single conclusion: Claire was not the young woman I had supposed, but was just a girl no older than seventeen, and, judging by the falsified movie stub and the Cancer Sign(a crab) drawn in one corner of the vanity, would

413

not yet be turning seventeen until the beginning of summer.

A wave of crushing panic came over me all at once as I recalled our phone conversations, the kiss in the park, the cab ride to the house; trembling, I finished my vodka and struggled to keep it down as I prepared myself to turn around and make a direct inquiry to Claire on the subject of her age, so that she might either confirm or discredit(an optimistic thought) my newfound suspicions.

Before I could do this, I noticed something else, on the third wall of her room, right next to the bed, which held my attention for a moment. Right next to the bed, as I say, there hung a picture cut out of a magazine that was much like many other pictures on the wall, only this particular picture was of you, Mr. Bloom. You were partially re-clined on a couch with your shirt unbuttoned too far, holding that characteristic half-smile of yours which is so terribly smug. I could not help but see the helpless irony of you being present, like an atrocious fly on the wall, for my devastating discovery of Claire's age.

My eyes began to burn with tears of defeat, you could say, and out of my mouth came an exasperated, "Claire...."

Slowly, I turned around to follow up on my inquisition; although my vision was increasingly blurred, I found that Claire had at some point gotten up from the bed and was standing directly behind me. Startled as I was, her glowing features, skewed by the tears in my eyes, appeared ghastly. I could make out a basic change in her countenance, which I interpreted then as anger or fear, or a generally upsetting combination thereof, that was the logical result of me standing directly beside your picture, Mr. Bloom, and Claire recognizing me as a fraud.

As I recall the image of her now, with the dry eyes of hindsight, I can see clearly that her appearance was merely that of a slightly intoxicated young girl, a virgin, determined to become a woman at the hands of yours truly, a bizarre and unwitting crook. Her shoulder was exposed, that cool vanilla showing a strawberry heat rash from booze and nervousness. It is shameful to remember such things, but there they are; her precocious development—like my transition from goodhearted nobody to lascivious identity thief(my apologies to you)—acting superbly in feigned earnestness. Yes, in that way she was, for a short while, as much a woman to me as I must have been you to her—what atrocities are capable of spawning from simple miscommuni-cation! And why must we allow them to go on for so long?

I imagine that any plausible answer could be nothing more than despicable. It can only be my hope that after I left that evening, Claire, puzzled and hurt, dwelled upon the very picture of you that had incited me to tears, and came to understand that you were not one and the same man as he who stood in her room only hours, or minutes, or seconds before. How terrifying for her if this was the case, yet how relieving, too, to have not made her very first carnal mistake under the especially unfortunate conditions of deception. But I cannot be sure what happened in Claire's room after I left, or if she ever came to that realization, as one can never be quite sure of anything that goes on in their absence.

As I stated previously, when I turned around to find Claire standing directly behind me, I was under the assumption that my cover was blown. Whether or not she knew that the cover of her age was blown as well—or was even aware that I had believed her to be quite a few years older than she was—I do not know. The situation, however, was in my opinion clearly in danger of becoming hostile, and thus I refused to waste any further time in asking questions to which the answers were obvious if I were willing to acknowledge them. Above all else, though, I wanted to get out of there before Claire could acknowledge the implications of the discrepancies between the photo of you, and the man in front of her who vaguely looked like you— from a certain angle, just a single feature, or whatever it may have been; surely the "reality" of those implications would have induced screaming on her behalf. And it would have been unnecessary for me to be present for such a show of outrage when the reaction within myself was already much, much worse.

I excused myself to the restroom, touching Claire one last time not on the cheek as a lover, but tenderly on the shoulder as a teacher steering his pupil in the right direction—regretfully, away from me.

As I closed the door to the bedroom, leaving Claire forever behind me, I failed at averting my then bright red eyes from the sign hanging mockingly on the backside of her door: "CLAIRE," it wailed; "Keep Out you sick bastard—Keep Out!"

It is possible that I had already begun to romanticize myself as a criminal, for the stealth with which I moved down the stairs and out of the house then was insurmountable. Once outside of her home, I strided across the stone path and hopped the short wrought iron fence onto the sidewalk in one leap. Not skipping a beat, my stride merged into a dead sprint upon landing and I stole out of the neighborhood without once looking back or stopping.

The following events remain in a haze. The only thing I can say with any certainty is that I arrived back at my apartment after dark, drenched in sweat, and panic-stricken. My consciousness was wavering on the fringe of a blackout, as I was suffering from an acute physical and mental illness that could not be cured with good, old-fashioned rest or with several whiskey sodas at my local haunt. Everything proved to be ineffective not only in regards to offering a cure, or at least some relief from my tremendous pain, but also in grounding me even in the slightest to allow me enough logic to make sound

415

decisions.

It is likely that my reaction to the circumstances were exacerbated by my ample knowledge of "Humbert Humbert"'s true account of his obsession and subsequent affair with "his" young *Lolita*, as edited by renowned writer Vladimir Nabokov. If only this letter found a similar fate!, ending up in the talented hands of a man who might be entrusted to manipulate my uncouth behavior into Art. I fear that this is a pipe-dream though, Mr. Bloom, and this letter is more likely to find itself in the likes of a mildly experienced, and virtually unknown writer's hands—someone young and desperate as myself—as this is commonly the only type of person willing to take such risks anymore. But aside from this——

I don't mean to say that there are any implicit similarities between myself and "Humbert Humbert"—I, for one, am considerably younger than he was; and Claire, conversely, is considerably older than Lolita in her said "prime"—I only mean to highlight the single, relatable fiber of our otherwise parallel experiences, which is the obsession of a man for a woman...or girl(in his case!). It was my understanding of the nature of this obsession, and how it will often take precedence over any other existing factors(the least daunting of these being the law), which scared me most of all. Consider your morality being disregarded to accommo-date your baser desires—it's outrageous! Of course my reaction was extreme, but not to excess, considering.

I flung myself out of my bed, where I had returned from the bar, drunk, laying fully clothed and paralyzed until then. As I shot up to my feet, a surge of pain went through my chest—"coronary thrombosis," I heard in my head. Were I to stay any longer I would undoubtedly fall victim to the phantom crime looming in the recent past and the possible future. It was there, waiting to take me. I was resolved to flee—there was no other option.

The next thing I remember is being awoken by the sound of my keys dropping into my landlady's metal mailbox in the lobby of my apartment building and recalling vague images, as if from a dream, of hauling many of my belongings to the trash and locking the door to my empty apartment. All I had with me was a small suitcase full of clothes and an attaché case containing my more important documents, a notebook(which I am writing in now), some envelopes, a handful of pencils, and a pencil sharpener. In my hand I held a note that I could see was addressed, in my handwriting, to my landlady; I did not bother proofreading what I had written, but at once slipped it under her door and left the building with my sparse luggage, following the consider-able momentum behind the decision I'm not sure was ever made.

I walked to the train station in the quiet, misty darkness of the early morning. It was not a long walk, and I don't believe I thought of anything in particular—I was acting on impulse.

When I arrived, there was only one attendant on duty, an over-weight man with grey hair and a great big grey mustache, sitting at the ticket counter. I approached the counter, unnoticed like a drunken ghost. On the monitor I saw that the next train going out would be leaving at 7.15am, which was still about four hours away.

"Excuse me," I said, startling the station attendant out of his reading, his book snapping shut on the counter to reveal the front cover which bore a single word, a name, as its title: "Lolita."

I admit that this coincidence is probably of my own invention, but when I saw the book there I was convinced of its title and gloomy contents, making it, to me, a "reality." You have surely noticed that "reality," in all its multiforms, consistently appears in this letter in quotations, because, like Nabokov said in his afterword to "Lolita"—something I believe was written to avoid indicating "places or persons that taste would conceal and compassion spare," by tricking the reader into the realm of Fiction—"'reality' [is] one of the few words which mean nothing without quotes." And so in this "reality" of mine the book appeared in plain view, rekindling my terror, and crippling my mental processes anew.

The bemustached attendant grumbled hello, and asked what he could do for me. I told him I needed a ticket on the next train out, requesting my destination as "the farthest it will take me." The last stop on the route was _____, Canada. He asked for my ID and specified the amount to be paid for the ticket.

As I reached into my pocket, I discovered a large, orderly wad of twenty-dollar bills, which was further evidence of the illness I was suffering from; a memory was jarred from my walk to the station—which I had thought to be fully coherent—of visiting three separate ATMs along the way to clear out all of my accounts(not much in any of them). I counted out the proper amount and slid the bills across the counter. The attendant handed me my ticket in return and gave me a boarding time, then resumed his reading.

For the next few hours I did nothing. I sat very still on a bench outside of the station and watched the sun rise as a brightening refraction of light that, filtered through the drizzle and clouds, offered none of those characteristic colors of sunrises, but merely changed from one shade of blue to another, eventually settling into the crisp blue-grey of morning. Though, as the blue hues lightened, a fantastic sight did become illumined: in a tiny park across from the station there was a single tree whose branches had begun to prematurely bud its pink blossoms for the oncoming spring—it was the only one that had done so thus far, and the light and its solitary nature accentuated its beauty.

417

I will be short and vague concerning the details of the confused journey that ensued, mainly to retain the integrity of this narrative, seeing as the specifics themselves are impertinent to my cause.

I boarded the train at the designated time and found my seat, which was next to the window on the second level of coach class. Typically, I would have found my way to the "bistro car" for a drink, but I knew too well that booze would not give me the comfort I sought; instead, I stayed in my seat, draping my coat over me as a blanket. I slept intermittently, having terrible dreams during each lapse in consciousness. I would awake petrified, gasping into the railcar, and quickly scan the passengers surrounding me who had usually changed with each sleep interval.

People got off at their stops, and new ones got on. The dull morning changed into a similar afternoon, though sunshine occasionally broke through the clouds and burst in through the windows unwelcomed. Then the afternoon passed, too, changing into a dull evening, then quickly into night.

With the night came the arrival at the end of the line—Canada. Between dreams I remember being asked questions about the purpose of my visit, where I was going to stay, and for how long, how much money I had, and so forth. The answers I gave must not have been very good, because border patrol seemed intensely curious of me. However, my innocent attitude and the word "holiday" seemed to suffice in the end and they sent me on my way.

Due to the directness of the first part of the journey, I was uneasy. It seemed that simply going from one place to another was not enough. I had showed my ID to purchase the ticket. It would not be difficult to track me should anyone be attempting to do so. I decided to continue moving.

From there I traveled by various means—bus, cab, foot, hitchhiking—for a total of three days and three nights, each step, I thought, convoluting my passage and therefore not quite making it impossible, but surely decreasing the likelihood of my whereabouts being discovered.

I will not describe my current lodgings any further than saying they are cheap and plain—it was enough to have made earlier mention of the bee. As for why I chose these particular lodgings, I will only say that as the distance between myself and alluring Claire increased I felt my senses begin to realign with my body and was able to see my situation with growing clarity and objectivity; and at a certain point along the journey I announced to myself, "I have gone far enough—this will do." And as I said this, I noticed my present lodgings advertising a vacancy across the street. I did not deliberate over the decision—I simply made it.

To arrive at my present location is to arrive also at the conclusion to write this letter to you, Mr. Bloom, and, consequently, the main purpose herein.

It is possible that you are wondering what this purpose might be; though it is my guess that you have not failed to notice the hints I have provided for you and have thereby foreseen my purpose in writing you—in which case, good. And there is not even a slim chance that you have failed to comprehend the repercussions of your indirect involvement in all of this, so you know already that to ignore this letter is to succumb to your own demise.

Please, do not interpret what I say as a threat to your wellbeing; it is, in fact, the complete opposite. It is an offering of redemption. I am extremely apologetic for having drawn a third party into this affair. But one must ask oneself—in Claire's eyes, who is the third party? Is it you, the man she is presumed to be in love with? Or is it me, the man whose name she has no knowledge of?

Make no mistake, it is Claire's impression of the situation that constitutes the final say in the matter. And, as of now, we can only speculate what her impressions might be. Which is to say, Mr. Bloom, that we must take precautionary measures to ensure our emergence from this crisis is a positive one. We hang in a very sensitive balance—remember that; an equilibrium whose stability depends on a lovestruck teenage girl. Indeed, it is every bit as dangerous as it sounds.

As you can imagine, I have carefully pored over the minute details of our situation. Silly as it may seem to an outsider, I have a sneaking suspicion that you are now beginning to realize the seriousness of these things, and the potentially dire position this puts us in. That being said, you should take comfort in knowing we stand as such:

No crime has been committed. Moral boundaries have been pushed, actions of a sensual nature have been carried out, and an illegal lust has been sparked—but no *crime* has actually been committed. Witnesses will attest to having seen you flee Claire's house that afternoon in a dead sprint; this does not have to be evidence which corroborates your guilt. I mean, examine her body—in full! And don't you worry, Mr. Bloom—they won't find anything. You're safe.

Although I mentioned that our fate rests in the emotional swing of sixteen year old Claire, I will also make mention that I am confident her obsession and loyalty to me(you?) will keep her in quiet wait of her man's return, patiently counting each fraction of passing time, adding it to the summation of her desire, and waiting, just waiting, until she may be embraced by him again.

Which means, Mr. Bloom, that our futures revert back into our care, relying then on our own devices—our tactfulness and delicacy.

419

Furthermore, it means that to retain this position only one of us may continue to exist in our present forms, because if Claire were to learn of our double existence we would immediately fall from her favor and relinquish all rights to the making of our own destinies.

I have taken all things into consideration and, though I wish it weren't so, this is the only way we may keep control of the situation—one of us must not exist.

You must be thinking now of your own personal success and comfort, thinking me mad to say, "One of us must not exist," and surely thinking it obvious which one of us that is—but slow down; stay with me. Your cooperation is of utmost importance.

I am not suggesting that either of our persons need be removed from the earth. Sure, my initial inclination was to plant a suicidal seed in your brain, and try to sway you to kill yourself, or, more likely, murder me; but that was an inclination had under the mad spell of panic and shame. The slow afternoons here in my Canadian hideout have done me good, Mr. Bloom. I no longer see the logic in such things. Neither one of us should have to "die" in the traditional sense.

But entertain the prospect of an abstract death, of a rebirth founded not on destruction, but on transfiguration; the soul remaining still in the malleable body, only called by something different. The change of a name does not change the thing; and, in sentient beings, even the change of the appearance of the thing does not change the essential thing.

Consider it as an option. A quick, painless snip and pull—the tugging of the ears this way, a bit of cartilage in the nose there, bulking it up; your lips could be fuller too(collagen), and your eyes any color of your choosing(contacts). Truthfully, it sounds quite exciting. Like being a permanent and beautiful disguise on a secret agent whose objective is to observe this alien world—and, yes, we are all foreign to each other already. Just a minor operation, Mr. Bloom, and life is again yours for the taking.

You are aghast at this recommendation, I see. Well, don't be childish—the severity of your predicament does not allow room for you to react absurdly. I would undergo the cosmetic surgery myself if my finances were not so meager. Perhaps if you are unwilling, then you will give me the money. I would gladly make a few alterations to become a man again. But then you must choose between your money and your looks. So, which sin is it—vanity or greed?

Don't answer that, Mr. Bloom. I am afraid your indiscretions are stacking up. Bear with me. I am here to help you. You will be OK, but you must take my advice; lay low for awhile(shouldn't be hard seeing as I haven't really seen you in any movies as of late), continue to be silent, and contemplate this fact: *one of us must not exist.*

You have now been briefed, Mr. Bloom. In no way does that qualify you to handle the possible futures with the fragility they deserve—but at least you've been warned; you know the score.

From here, I regret that I must leave you to act alone. If you do not reply in a timely manner, I will be forced to assume you have chosen to take the position of the rogue. In which case, I fear for you. And I can only say that it will be in your best interest then to contact Claire directly—her address is enclosed. But I urge you, Mr. Bloom, I beg of you—please!—do not do so until her eighteenth birthday has passed, as you, and you alone, will be held accountable for your actions. She will be waiting for you. Maybe she will not be wearing the identifiable red hat, but you will know her regardless and she will be waiting for you, I can assure you of that. All that need be done to make her yours is to whisper her name, that soft sound, that sublime note, that mesmerizing—"Claire...."

SONS & DAUGHTERS OF THE EARTH
(2010)

For
Little Feather, Listening or not

TRACK 1

Partially hidden away on a residential street in Echo Park in California, nestled behind another home at an unnamed ½ address on Lake Shore Ave., at the bottom of a steeply graded empty lot where coyotes graze at night, there is a house growing from the side of a giant avocado tree. And in this treehouse there once lived the "cult"—though more accurately described as a family—known as The Sons and Daughters of The Earth. They were a mix-up of 100 different species at least, consisting of the basics, such as your dogs, your cats, your turtles, your squirrels, your birds, etc., along with the more exotic types, such as your lions, your sex panthers(they do exist), your monkeys, your koalas, a single wolf that was said to be domesticated, and they were all men and women too(save for that bastard wolf) who lived together as a family until just two weeks ago to the day when they met their bizarre and untimely deaths.

The house is no longer occupied by anything representative of a family. Those who have heard rumors of the demise of The Sons and Daughters of The Earth and have ventured into the neighborhood to attempt a glance at the place where they once lived have failed terribly at this because they cannot get through. The property is sanctioned off by investigators who at this moment still haunt the grounds, looking through every nook and cranny of the home in search of some sort of tangible clue as to why, some sort of logical explanation for their extraordinary rise and sudden fall.

There is only one surviving member of the cult, a small man with pale skin and olive-toned features who is widely associated with a lean bear cub. He has agreed to talk to me, giving me exclusive rights to the story of The Sons and Daughters of The Earth, under the sole condition that the names of all Sons and all Daughters be changed. He will be referred to here under the assumed name of "Avonaco."

From the hospital bed where Avonaco lays with his cheeks sunken in and bags under his eyes, bandages running the length of each forearm—spotted in places with drops of dried blood, the red seeming all the darker in contrast to the sterile bandages, his white cotton hospital gown, and the spectacularly white surroundings of the hospital itself—he recounts to me in full the story that will soon be paraphrased.

I sit across from him in a wicker chair that looks as though it were out of a WWII mental ward, and I listen intently with one leg crossed over the other as my little recording device sits on the end table beside me. The hospital staff has been kind enough to allow me several extended visits to Avonaco in this fashion, which could potentially be explained by the professional appearance that is evoked by the sight of me in my wool suit, with tie snuggly about my neck as I carry my leather attaché case full of notes through the long hallways, the clicking sound of the heels of my brand new dress shoes echoing through the otherwise silent corridor, and my typically polite, congenial demeanor —I smile and nod at everyone. I would like to take the time to thank them all now for their endless discretion and hospitality(excuse me), especially D., who provides countless cups of tea which she serves to us on a charming silver tray without saying so much as a single word while my interviews are in session.

The windows are always pushed open in the hospital room. Outside there is always a warm breeze blowing eerily through palm leaves. Due to the mental state of the patient in question—whose glazed eyes give away that he is obviously still in shock—and the maddening sound of the rustling palm leaves, it is likely that his tale is woven with exaggerations, distortions, and perhaps even the occasional outright falsehood, creating something closer to a caricature of the cult, rather than a snapshot.

It is not my responsibility to discover the actuality of any mentioned occurrences—leave that to the baffled investigators; it is only my responsibility to record the truth as it is told to me through poor, mangled Avonaco and as history will come to recognize it. No matter with what amount of certainty I have in the truthfulness of these occurrences I am to record, I share them with a clear consc-ience because they will always and forever—as everything is, regardless—be open to speculation.

TRACK 2

On a day in a year that remains ambiguous to outsiders, the cult was established in the desert outside of Los Angeles by a man wearing a white linen suit, a pencil thin mustache, and face paint. His name, at times, will appear in this record as, "Ashkii Nosh," while at other times it will be just plain and simple Daddy. Like the half-lion, half-wilde-beest (meaning, of course, "wild beast") that he is said to have resemb-led, he roared into the dust and heat and all who heard him came runn-ing to his side where they saw him in the glaring light of the desert sun and he proclaimed, "I am your Father. You are my Sons and Daught-ers." Thus, the family inexplicably began to take shape.

Although its initial formation took place in the desert, Ashkii Nosh quickly moved him and his children into Echo Park, in a relatively quiet neighborhood where they roamed amongst the rolling hills spreading their seeds of free love for all things and appreciation of nature and beauty. It was there that the family proliferated—sons took lovers and had more sons and daughters; daughters took sons and turned them into lovers and had more sons and daughters; the parents —which originally would have been Ashkii Nosh, above all else, along with Ember(mama bear), East(the jackal—later banished from the family without further mention), Bunny(the bunny), and Nevaeh(the sex panther), though it should be mentioned that the status of "parent" did not necessarily imply a union between any of the five(all of them, except for Nosh, were considered both parents *and* siblings amongst everyone)—the parents, I say, they took their sons and daughters into their beds, took their siblings into their beds, and brothers and sisters had more brothers and sisters, more sons and daughters, and so on. Which is to say, it was an absolute mess. The family did not operate on a specific tree so much as it did on a tangled web, or a wide, deep manmade lake whose water was constantly being circulated.

This should have been cause for alarm within the family, this stepping on of their siblings' and parents' toes, this ever-complicating, spiritually incestuous orgy of merging souls and bodies—but that was not the case.

There is a Japanese author named Kazuo Ishiguro who once wrote a book called, *"An Artist of The Floating World,"* the *floating world* in reference being that precious, fleeting world that exists only in certain hours of the night in pleasure houses, artists' dens, and other places of the like that produce a romantic mysticism in mainly young folks who are inclined to dream about god(in the abstract, non-religious sense) and who find him/it in this world only to lose their dream to the morning, the sun rising and dissolving the learned truths of the dream, leaving behind it only a vague memory and the desire to find their god again.

This was the world of The Sons and Daughters of The Earth—*the floating world*—though with them the morning never came. Everyone drank incredible quantities of alcohol in the family and everything ran nonstop. In the treehouse there was but one bellowing song that didn't stop, one real-time film perpetually being shot, one book—the longest that's ever been written(and is still being written in their memory)— whose endless plot does not grow slow because the continuous writing of the book *is* the plot. They were all floating there, always, even in the daytime when brains had been fucked out, bodies blown out, sheets torn, and fur coats pissed on—The Sons and Daughters of The Earth remained perpetually suspended, deta-ched, and open.

There would not have been time to foresee any bad blood in the family. Everybody would have been too busy fucking everybody else. Everybody would have been too drunk, too free, too high to be able to see that far back down to the ground.

TRACK 3

Days of the week did not fully exist for The Sons and Daughters of The Earth except when their names were used as blanket descriptions for the general feeling of a given day—a Monday might feel like a Friday, which might feel like a Saturday or Tuesday, which might feel like a Thursday.

Sundays especially did not exist for the family, save for the *idea* of them on a particularly slow morning when a hangover might set in, and with the terror of prolonged drunkenness that finally fades into vague sobriety—giving way to heart palpations, trembling, and disgust—one member of the family might have said, "It feels like a Sunday." (To "real people" it could have been a Wednesday, or Tuesday even, when they were just taking their lunch breaks at work, dreaming over their sandwiches about Friday, Saturday, or the languid warmth and relaxation of a Sunday.) This statement would then be followed by extinguishing this feeling within a few minutes by way of consuming a warm or cold can of cheap beer salvaged, somehow, from the night before. And all was well again.

On a particular day before the fall, Ashkii Nosh sat in the garden of the treehouse feeling very hungover. He was sitting with Coal(mama bear's mongoose lover, which would therefore make him Avonaco's father later on) who had once been a pilot for the U.S. Government, but had come across hard times at work and was currently unemployed; although out of a job, the government continued to pay Coal a fair sum of money each month which allowed him to stay afloat, living comfortably in his many hours of leisure.

The sun beat down on the two family members in the garden, probably intensifying their hangovers. Ashkii Nosh stood up from the grass and walked slowly over to the lemon tree that stood on the edge of the garden, near the gate. He plucked one of the lemons from the tree and inspected it. He said, "It feels like a Sunday."

When said within the family, those words actually meant, "Today feels like it does not exist," which is also to say that one can do or say anything they wish on that day without any future repercussions. A day that felt like a Sunday could turn out to be a wonderful or horrible

428

thing—in the moment, it always seemed wonderful.

Ashkii Nosh took a big bite out of the lemon, rind and all. He then spit it out into the grass and remarked to Coal, "We will invite our Children into the garden."

It never took long for the Sons and Daughters to congregate. Within a matter of a few beers(which Nosh and Coal had found hiding in a piano bench, in a cardboard box in the coat closet, and behind assorted plants in the garden), all in the immediate family had arrived.

They came in waves of floral patterns and bright white cotton and linen, elegant dresses and dapper suits, long flowing hair and straw hats, shoes that shined or bare feet. And each brought with them supplies stuffed into satchels, into baskets, wrapped up and tied in sheets—things like beer, wine, champagne, liquor, juices and carbonated beverages, bags of ice, fruits, vegetables, cheese, meat, fish, and bread; all the essentials to enjoy yourself without losing it before dark.

It would be beneficial to mention the names of a few of those in attendance—among many others, who may or may not be gotten to eventually—so that their names(and animal-faces) may be introduced into your minds now and not catch you unnecessarily off-guard later on: there was, of course, at the nucleus of this specific party, Nosh and Coal, then Ember, Bunny, and Neveah; and then there was West(the dingo), Sky(the hyena), Light(the baby beaver), Feather(the sex *kitten*— they exist too), Little(the fawn), Cocaine(the peacock), Juan(the flamingo), Mud(the sloth), Ruby(the butterfly), Persia(the creature that mates for life), Sunday #1 and Sunday #2(both ginger rabbits), Nibble (the preying mantis), Ohii(the lady hummingbird), Baby Blue(the fox), and French(the duckling).

The only notable characters not present were Bull(father wolf), who would not show up until later on when things were in full swing, Avonaco, who had not yet been introduced to the cult, the unnamed serpent and the unnamed raven, who had caused problems with certain key family members, and potentially a handful of others who had been excommunicated at some point for one reason or another.

Outside of the immediate family there was first the extended family, then the distant relatives, and then those people who were on the fringe of everything, who came and went frequently and anonymously—these people were referred to as either ponies, stallions, or run-of-the-mill barn horses, or cows, calves, or whinnies. Once word had moved that far out from the center, and the ponies, calves, etc., began to wander into the garden, then the zoo was complete. The party had finally begun.

Night came and the lights that were strung around and hung everywhere were turned on—in the garden, around the rest of the lawn, in the outdoor gypsy den on the side of the treehouse, and in the treehouse itself—and the animals ran wild. Bunny hopped around preaching the pure joy of being; Neavah and Feather slinked about from one place to another, dressed scantily, shooting glances at everyone with their almond eyes; Light stomped and whirled about as Sky recounted lofty stories and told jokes loudly; Sunday #1 and Sunday #2 sat in separate corners, smiling sweetly; Persia brushed her hair and straightened out any wrinkles in her dress, waiting for her Man to come; Ember and Coal began to glow internally, creating their own natural light in contrast to those that were hung and strewn about; Mud rubbed his beard with a grimace, breaking down conversations into points and counterpoints; Juan gaily shared with others the contents of a box he always carried with him that contained within it anything and everything—miniature soaps, shampoos, colognes and perfumes, other smell-goods, jewelry, underwear, shirts, shoes, and various other bric-a-brac; Little discussed fantastic literary works concerning the infinite nature of possible realities; Nibble spoke openly of sex, bodily functions, and fetishes, coyly ending each remark with a sharp twist of her curvy hips in a short green dress that stood out tremendously against the overbearing white apparel of the others; Bull arrived and roamed about from place to place, quiet yet stern, attracting the company of females from a diverse range of positions within the family; West drank beer after beer, never faltering in his movable wit, making everyone laugh and smile; Ruby and Ohii combined forces and fluttered through the night in wonderful flashes of red; Baby Blue leaned against one wall, then another, beaming a magnificently white smile; Nosh went from one outrageous act to another, swinging from trees, kicking like a billy goat, telling the most fascinating stories, balancing on his head, standing his ground as an undeniable and powerful life-force; and French the duckling hugged everyone that came by as he switched the records on the record player, eventually removing the needle altogether when he discovered a guitar that he immediately began to strum.

At the sound of music, so resonating and present, ears pricked up everywhere. Everyone picked up the nearest instrument they could find—tambourines were played, a massive organ, harmonicas, flutes, and bongo drums. One by one, the sounds came together until there was only one song being played in perfect harmony, echoing off the hills into the rest of the neighborhood. Even the coyotes behind the house could be heard howling in unison. And then French began a slow, simple chant to go with the music. "Ello," he sang, "my name is Orney—what is your name?" To which all the animals would reply, fittingly, in their own very unique noises, "Horny as well!"

To anyone overhearing the noise, it was not a particularly good song—it was repetitive, and the lyrics were base. But in the garden it was captivating. The sound and the words(true as they were to the crowd) were utterly fascinating. It carried on for a great deal of the night, until gradually sons and daughters departed in pairs into the dark, distant family members went to their own respective homes, and the anonymous men and women simply disappeared.

As the sun rose, only the immediate family was left. They had returned from their dark corners where the right to free love had been exercised, and beauty was appreciated in nature. They sat on the roof of the treehouse to watch the new day begin. The flamingo traipsed off for a moment, then returned with a full case of beer, handing out bottles to everyone. He then went inside and made scrambled eggs. He called the others in to eat; as they shoveled the eggs into their mouths and thanked him, he proceeded to clean the entire house and lawn, wearing nothing but a white t-shirt and bright purple underwear.

TRACK 4

As the days did not so much exist within the family, neither did Time per se—past or future events were spoken of in loose terms like *a couple of days ago*, or *tomorrow*, or *last week*, *next week*, and so on. Hours in the day were measured by the intake of alcohol, by the number of cigarettes smoked, by the absurd quality and quantity of stories told and exploits revealed.

Due to this lack of a legitimate timeline, and the fact that Avonaco was not present in the beginning of the cult, it is impossible to say for how long the early days lasted. I ask Avonaco how long that period went on. Without hesitating, he replies, "A number of years."

Also, in knowing that Avonaco was not a part of the Sons and Daughters in its early days, I can assume that his relation of its events is a combination of hearsay and future experiences of his own. Suffice it say, the gathering like that which occurred in the garden was not uncommon; in fact, it would have been uncommon for there *not* to have been a similar gathering. It can also be assumed that the cult continued to grow in this manner, gaining a reputation in Echo Park that quickly fanned out into the surrounding areas.

The specific details of How exactly the cult grew, and Who exactly the people were that joined, are completely beside the point. It remains that cult gained notoriety as rampantly as a wildfire that blows through the Southern California hills. And we now know that its aftermath yielded just as much damage.

The only thing that Avonaco can tell me about the early days of The Sons and Daughters of The Earth is that they operated on a few simple principles. Just as it is in families of blood relation, there was not one single belief system, in all of its intricacies, that pervaded throughout the entirety of the cult. Each individual still carried the idiosyncrasies of their own personal cosmogonies. The common threads that *did* join them together were these, in no specific order (though I will order them here for clarity's sake):

1) For the individual, life is impermanent.
2) Life should be lived in the present, with appreciation and awe of all things.
3) There is some sort of greater power at work in the universe, and we will never fully understand it.
4) Be good to all those who will accept your goodness. And,
5) Nothing is certain.

In short, they had the ideals of a wholesome religion without any apparent God, and without any real convictions that could supersede their own consciences. The plural, "consciences," is important to note, because although they considered themselves a community, there was no push for *communal thinking*. They were intolerant of those who attempted to force their beliefs on others. If it was discovered that a son or daughter was doing so, they could easily find themselves excommunicated.

And another thing—every basic principle, while being broad and philosophical, could also relate back to sex. If it was not obvious already, sex played an important, continual role in the cult. It was everywhere.

Avonaco attempts to resituate himself in his bed, shifting his weight from one side to the other with his two maimed arms held gingerly above the sheets. The attempt is not very fruitful. I ask him, "Can I help you with anything?"

He very calmly remains in the exact position he was in before his ineffectual move. He does not answer me immediately, rather he seems to drift off into the distance for a moment.

A big gust of wind picks up outside, and the rustling of the palm leaves briefly becomes so violent that it sounds as though it were pouring rain. The wicker chair creaks beneath me.

Finally, Avonaco speaks, his voice monotonous and methodic. "I feel very strange. Please call in the nurse. I would like to get back on an IV and be alone for awhile. Come back tomorrow."

TRACK 5

The next day, two nurses and a doctor are in the room with Avonaco when I arrive. They politely inform me that I must wait outside, or leave and come back later. It seems that the cuts on his arms have become infected. They are rubbing a special salve on his arms every couple of hours to reduce the itchiness and pain, and treating him with antibiotics to prevent the infection from spreading.

As I walk towards the courtyard to wait, I peek through the door, left slightly ajar—I think by D., that good woman, who probably knew that I would be curious to get a look—and I see the three bodies in white uniform surrounding Avonaco in his white robe, in his white bed, in the white room. He endures their prodding with the same vacancy that I have seen in his eyes on so many visits before. He has already experienced too much pain to be bothered by a few pokes on the arm. He has lost so many people that he loves.

When I am in the room with Avonaco, it is easy to forget his emotional attachment to the subject matter. For me, it is an intriguing story that I want to know more about. For him, it is a catastrophic event in his personal history. It is something that happened to him. After the trauma that he went through, I can only imagine how difficult it is for him to retell these events to me, basically reliving them through his words. What he once viewed as some of the best times in his life are now covered in blood; even those finest moments, those bright gems of pure, childish joy, are overshadowed by tragedy.

Since I have been coming to visit Avonaco, he has become exceedingly solemn, and detached. All he does now is stare, and speak slowly and evenly. At first, he spoke with a certain amount of vigor in his voice, even anger. Even in his initial shock, there were moments when he would come to life with passion, his voice rising loud enough to be carried out the window, or he would become sullen, and pout, his voice trembling and tears coming into his eyes.

On the first recording from our interviews, he told a story that pinpointed the exact beginning of the end. And although he did not arrive in Los Angeles until two weeks after it happened, he told of the precise event with fiery conviction(remember it is paraphrased, and, in this instance, a number of curse words have been omitted (except one), not because they were used to the point of distraction, but because they were used with such force—as if they were uncontrolled tics— that an annoying number of exclamations would have been necessary):

The beginning of the downfall of The Sons and Daughters of The Earth was marked by a double tragedy in a single biological family, which, out of good taste and respect, will not be mentioned any further than that in a story as vile as this one. In affect, a dark cloud came over the usually sunny skies of the floating world, and beneath the surface of everything there was a quiet sadness.

At the time, the cult had grown so large in number that out of necessity they spread themselves out, several of them residing in nests built through various treehouses in the hills of Echo Park. (Daddy, family man that he was, spent time living in each one of these nests intermittently as he continued to diversify his family, moving between them in his private, movable bedroom—a sweet pea green VW Bus, called "Sweet Pea.") Still, remaining at the center of The Sons and Daughters' existence was the original treehouse where lived Bunny, Nevaeh, and Bull, regularly, with its additional, sporadic residents being Ashkii Nosh(of course), West, Juan, and Cocaine. It was here where the greatest distress was felt.

Bunny was a woman who took great pains in the welfare of others. She took it upon herself to find a cure—or at least a distraction—to the sorrow that had crept unsuspectingly into the floating world. Her resolution: to bring new life into the house.

One afternoon she drove outside of Los Angeles with Nevaeh and Bull to a remote section of high desert where a wolf sanctuary was located. Pulling into the sanctuary, the air was hot and dry and smelled like piss and shit—a more potent variety, too: *wolf* piss and shit. There were massive pens set up around the property to house the different breeds of wolves—Grey Wolves, Red Wolves, Himalayan Wolves, Timberwolves, and so on. An overweight man in a baseball cap and overalls came out to greet them.

As the man approached the car, the three of them got out. They all shook his hand and took notice of the yellow hue in his fingernails and the dirt underneath them. He was chewing on a cigarette butt. He was an affable enough man, but his unprofessional appearance made them hesitant to take his suggestion of getting in with the wolves and petting them. When he saw their hesitation, he muttered something incoherently and picked up a toddler that had been running around in bare feet and matching overalls. Apparently to illustrate just how safe it was, he put the toddler into the pen with the Timberwolves and shrugged his shoulders at the three cult members while letting out a peal of laughter.

Still uneasy, Bull offered a cigarette to the man. He accepted, spitting out the gnarled butt of his last cigarette(smoked who knows how long ago), and put the new one into his mouth. He smoked it in five drags, right down to the filter, then began chewing again.

The man opened up the gate and removed the toddler from the pen where the wolves had only circled him for a moment, sniffed, then sauntered off and minded their own business. He ushered in his customers.

The wolves reacted to the three new intruders with the same amount of vague curiosity, then immediate disinterest as they had with the toddler. They were free to carefully walk about, almost on tiptoes, immersing themselves in the wolves' adapted environment. Coming too close, or moving too fast, attracted some attention, but not much; the wolves merely looked up with their clear, intelligent, wild eyes, then looked back to whatever concerned them on the ground or in the distance.

In the back corner of the pen there laid a mama wolf with her pups; the pups were tiny and their skin was still loose, their extremities still short and pudgy. They were mostly grey all over where their parents were light with jet-black markings. They were soft and sweet. Bunny picked up the pup nearest her and brought it to her face. It smelled like the great outdoors; it smelled like life. She instantly fell in love, and showed off her little pup to Nevaeh and Bull.

A newborn child, even when it is the most beautiful little thing you have ever seen, still has the potential of causing sadness in a person; they can imagine the infant's whole life spanning out before them with all of its pain and hardship leading only to eventual death—it terrifies them for the child and fills them with dread. A newborn animal, wild or not, no matter how big or vicious it will someday get, will invoke nothing but sappy thoughts from even the most stoic of men; all they see is the tiny thing in front of them, so soft, so pure, so good. They all fell in love with the little pup—instantly.

In a moment of pouting, Avonaco quietly remarked, "With animals, we look at death as just a part of nature; with people, we look at death as a tragedy. Humans want to live forever, and believe we deserve to. But that's just not the case. Fuck...."

On the recording, after that emphatic *fuck*, there is a long pause. The sound of the wind through the palm leaves, though it can always be heard, becomes more apparent in the sudden silence. Then, as suddenly as he stopped talking, he began again in an impatient tone:

Bunny called the man in the overalls back over to them. He had been watching the entire time, and was by their side in a moment, still chewing on the butt from the cigarette Bull had given him earlier. She asked him how much the pup would cost, and he gave her a quick, straight answer. "Four-hundred-dollars. Cash only."

Finding an ATM out in the high desert wouldn't have been easy, and they only had three hundred dollars between them. This didn't pose a problem to the man. He took the cash from them and shoved it in the front pocket of his overalls, then handed them the baby timberwolf and sent them away.

On the drive back to Los Angeles, the pup slept in Bull's lap.

Naturally, because he had already been associated with wolves, the little pup was his and the word "father" was added as a prefix to his animal-spirit. Together, they named the newest member of the fam-ily; mistaking the little boy for a little girl, they chose the name "Yona." When they found his tiny penis a few minutes later they laughed, but the name, *that name*, had already stuck.

TRACK 6

Yona was already thirteen pounds when Avonaco got in to Los Angeles; dark spots in his fur had begun to appear on his tail and on his somewhat elongated snout, and although he had become leaner, he was still incredibly clumsy, and confused. On his massive paws, he skulked about the treehouse sleepily, nudging against the furniture and wondering how it was that he had gotten there, and *why* he was there at all.

It was the night of the summer solstice. The sun had been high and bright in the sky that day. The night was hotter than usual. The partial moon shone as if it were full, and the coyotes reacted accord-ingly. The wolf howled out the window in the treehouse from his tiny haunches. The conditions were perfect for Avonaco's welcoming cere-mony to take place that very night—his first night in the effervescent hills of Echo Park.

The nurses have given Avonaco a heavy dose of painkillers. An IV drips down from its bag, through a tube, and into his arm. His lips are ever so slightly curled upwards at their sides, making him look like an imbecile with a subtle but pleasant smile stuck forever on his face. He appears to be enchanted. Sitting upright in his bed, he has no trouble recalling the details of the ceremony. His eyes are glazed over and it is as if he were speaking aloud in his sleep of a dream he is having.

There were eight of them chain smoking and drinking red wine from ceramic mugs in Bunny's tiny room in the treehouse—Avonaco, Nevaeh, Bunny, West, Coal, Ember, French, and Juan; there were nine if you include Yona, who huddled beneath a clothes rack in the corner of the room. French was playing the guitar, strumming away at the same song on repeat; Juan stood behind him rubbing his shoulders. Coal sat in a plush chair with Ember in his lap, both of them listening to the music with faces smooth and relaxed, in bliss. In a large bed there laid Bunny, West, and Nevaeh beneath a thin, white cotton sheet. Most everything was white in the room. In the dim light, the adorn-ments glowed like the face of the moon.

Avonaco leaned against the windowsill, blowing thin streams of smoke continuously through the screen into the night. The only family member he had met previously was Bunny—he had known her forever, before she was "Bunny," and she had been the reason he had ventured down to LA. The others he was meeting for the first time. Outside the room, the rest of the zoo could be heard from the living room, the lawn, and the garden—other family members who he would meet too, eventually.

The red wine took off the edge from traveling and the usual discomfort that comes with meeting several new people at once and feeling the need to remember all their faces and names immediately. He noted the red rings that encircled the inside of his mug, each one marking the level of the wine before he had taken his last drink. There was quite a bit of space between each red line—he was not exactly sipping. And he was still unaware of the ceremony that had already begun around him.

West and Bunny were becoming intertwined on the bed, softly kissing each other and running their fingers through each other's hair, becoming a single form cloaked in the white of the sheet. Neveah rose from their side seductively, and crawled to the end of the bed. She was staring at Avonaco, beckoning him with one finger and a half-smile. He set down his glass and went to her. The song continued to play.

As Avonaco begins to describe the sex panther in all of her splendor—which he will most certainly do after this brief interjection—he slips into the present tense. Although his slip is inadvertent, I intend to honor Her memory by retaining the disparity in Avonaco's use of Tense, being that it is most likely a symptom of his shock, to an extent, and of the deep affect she clearly had on him.

He knew she was beautiful, but up close she is more than that. She is a wild creature whose external allurement is merely a physical manifestation of her impalpable internal Self. She is a shining example of nature's fondness for perfect symmetry. Her features are soft and flawless like those of a woman who was imagined then painted in oil by one of the masters. The blonde hair that hangs right at her shoulders is a fantastic mess. Her pale skin is like cream that has been beaten with sugar into sweet silk. Her lips are a muted pink, the bottom full and pouting. She smiles and her teeth could kill you; they give the inexplicable impression of innocence—the teeth! And her cheekbones are high while her jaw is sharp, so that her very face bends and plays with light. Then there are her eyes, bright and wide; they are green with a touch of some other color, unnamable, unreal, and home to those tiny black holes where a man is liable to get lost forever, sitting there as if at the bottom of a well, staring into space trying to make out the shapes.

To touch her is to be young, and happy; it is to have an affair with

437

life itself, on a perfect curve in the absolute Present, and not be jaded by the experience. She is both pure joy and pure suffering. She is a balancing act in suspended equilibrium. To hold her is to accept the fate of everything with a smile on your face. She is the stop to all wandering, the end of the line. She is what every man wants. And yet *she* is unattainable.

She lays out a fur coat on the ground and it happens. Everything fades away except Her. The sounds from the zoo can still be heard, but they are like a distant cacophony of roars, whoops, and yelps; still, no sound is loud enough to drown out that of her heavy breathing, of her body disregarding gravity, of her mouth moving and her teeth grinding. The world becomes incredibly slow until it appears to stop, vibrating imperceptibly like the strings that connect everything. Then it is over.

Avonaco stops speaking for a long while, and it occurs to me that he looks as though *he* were *sitting at the bottom of a well, staring into space trying to make out the shapes*; he looks as though he were lost, forever. When he begins again, his eyes have lost their prior glossiness, and his speech is troubled as if he had become aware of his surroundings, of his physical condition, and of my presence in the room. He appears to be lucid and self-conscious, absently inspecting the dried blood and puss on the bandages covering his forearms. He reverts back to the use of the Past Tense.

She kissed him after all was done, he says. She looked up at Avonaco with her eyes gleaming in the dark, and the rest of the room faded back into his consciousness. She was smiling so big that all of her teeth showed—it nearly killed him. And she said, as if she were making an announcement, "Welcome to the family."

TRACK 7

Avonaco quickly fell into step with life under the family's customs. The basic principles he had personally abided by already, and the other peculiarities just seemed to make sense.

For instance, when the family ventured out into the greater public, they often donned face paint of various styles and colors. What this did was visibly connect them even when they were not physically beside one another, and, in turn, it spiritually connected them as well; in a crowd, it would not have been difficult to point out a Son or Daughter. So Avonaco, too, allowed paint to be put onto his face on the occasion of such an outing. He felt a sense of belonging. He enjoyed it.

Also, the heavy drinking was something Avonaco had no problem keeping up with. He had grown up drinking and had quite similar habits as the rest of the family.

Although some were involved in light drug use, of course—psychedelics mainly, along with cocaine and MDMA(pure ecstasy)—Avonaco refrained from those activities, but he did not look upon those who did them with any judgment; likewise, he was not looked upon with any judgment. As it was previously mentioned, the Sons and Daughters of The Earth respected and encouraged individuality, and abhorred those who pushed their lifestyle choices or beliefs upon others. So even the differences, of which there were certainly more than a handful, served as no place of discomfort. And everything else—the dress, the conversation, the creativity, the loving way they treated one another, the sense of awe they had in regards to life in general, and so on—fit Avonaco perfectly.

In his graceful entrance into the family, Avonaco found that he had been integrated into the very center of its relations. Ember and Bunny became his mothers, mama bear lending him the name "Avonaco" thereafter; Ashkii Nosh and Coal became his fathers; Bull and West became his brothers; only Nevaeh remained in an odd untitled position to him—though she would have had the right to be his mother as well, she simply chose to never name what exactly they were to each other.

Between those five men—Avonaco, Nosh, Coal, Bull, and West—there was a natural, common bond that was exceptionally strong. Amongst those in the immediate family, they were the only Sons who exuded masculinity; typically, the other Sons were of a more delicate, androgynous persuasion. The five, though, they carried themselves like old school gentleman with a dirty twist. They were all strong in character, stern but open, understanding, cordial, genuine—and they all loved women.

When they went out, it was always one of their birthdays. At lunch it was Coal's birthday; for bottomless mimosas in the afternoon it was Bull's; at the restaurant for dinner it was Nosh's(absurd toasts were given in Daddy's honor at length); in the clown room where the women danced and removed their clothes only to reveal *more clothes* (never actually showing skin) it was West and Avonaco's birthdays, who claimed to be twins. Consequently, everywhere they went they were given things—meals were served *gratis*, drinks were given *on the house*, etc. They used their demeanors—exaggerated as they were in each other's company—to their advantage. Women flocked to them. They were young and attractive. They were talented. They were charming. They thought nothing could go wrong.

Ultimately, they were wonderful fools. Disaster was right around the corner and they couldn't see it. But the end was to come regardless.

Even in the midst of an oncoming tragedy there are pockets of resistance, bright moments of pure joy that give Hope. In retrospect, it is always those moments that seem the darkest, the saddest, the most telling.

Ashkii Nosh had taken a particular liking to the newest member of the cult, Avonaco, and thus took him under his wing. It is common for a man in power to enjoy his reflection, and it is probable that this is how Nosh saw Avonaco—they were very similar fundamentally, though the one was very much smaller than the other. They bounded across the city together like two comical 1920's drifters in their floppy hats and slacks, appearing all the more comical due to the stark differences in their statures. With that humorous air, they charged from one place to another in that silent film they supposed themselves to star, the wind in their hair like kisses blown from old lovers or lovers to come. Their mode of transportation was Nosh's old VW Bus, Sweet Pea, and along in tow was always Nosh's dog, Arlo, who was of ambiguous European descent and whose mannerisms were human-like.

Arlo always sat upright in his chair with his body askew, his snout resting gently on his one paw. He had a Swedish driver's license. He spoke Russian and French, along with English. He enjoyed the classics in literature and despised most modern works, while also considering Shakespeare to be "trite." He was quite openly gay. He enjoyed fine wine and "backsnacks."

Arlo was not allowed at the treehouse. He did not get along with the other dogs. He was constantly getting into scraps with them, and winning—he was the cause of the bulldog's eight stitches and four staples: the staples were in her head, the stitches were in her hind leg (which got infected and almost resulted in a lost limb). He eyed Yona with contempt, seemingly knowing that he was not just another dog.

Yona weighed in at an unprecedented 50lbs. at the onset of one particular father/son bender—the one Avonaco relates at present. He had grown increasingly aggressive, continuing to piss any- and everywhere, tearing into the trash, and shredding clothing and bed sheets; feeding him was another nightmare altogether—his voracious appetite, coupled with his nature to fight for his food, was cause for a number of scratches on many a Son and Daughter.

Arlo was with Nosh and Avonaco that day. They avoided the treehouse.

It was a typically hot, sunny day in Los Angeles. The air conditioning was broken in Sweet Pea, and the front windows did not open. Nosh and Avonaco sweated as they drove along towards West Hollywood. Arlo panted in the backseat, staring longingly out the window (probably thinking about poetry) where the wind, which was hot too, bent the tall palm trees slightly.

West Hollywood is a neighborhood well known for catering to the gay community. Rainbow flags were hung everywhere. There was no need for it to be anyone's birthday in WeHo—to be young and attractive was enough. It was there that drinks would not only be paid for, but they would earn enough money to drink for the rest of the day.

They started at a bar called, "Rave." The sun was shining and men were dancing on tables in glitter-adorned underwear. Nosh and Avonaco ordered the "fruitiest" drink they could think of—appletinis. An old man at the end of the bar footed the bill, smiling at *the couple* and raising his glass. They raised their glasses to him as well, then took their appletinis outside to the patio, slowly choking down the sugary concoction.

It did not take long for them to attract a swarm. Several men approached their table and made small talk. They bought them drinks and, in return, were told stories that made them laugh. Dollar bills were shoved by the handful into the pockets of Nosh and Avonaco's slacks. They played the part, accepting the money theatrically.

Once plied with drinks and money for the evening, Nosh excused himself to the restroom. An older gentleman, standing at three feet six inches with his grey hair balding, followed him. He hoisted himself up to the urinal next to Nosh, nearly having to crawl up the wall to get there, and ogled Nosh's equipment. "Nice," he said coyly. He proceeded to offer Nosh a blowjob, and money to go with it, which Nosh avidly declined. The little man followed him out of the bathroom, back to the table.

With feigned regret, the father and son announced that they had to go. The little man whispered something to the man next to him, who whispered to the man next to him, and so on. The entire table turned to them. One man spoke up, with a lisp: "You guys aren't gay, are you...." It was more of a statement than a question; the articulated feeling amongst all of them that they had been duped.

The duo happily replied, "No, we aren't—but does it matter? We've thoroughly enjoyed your company. Good day!" And they smiled languidly all the way to their next stop: the cantina in Venice.

There was a cheap special at the cantina—$3 for a bottle of beer with a shot of tequila on the side. After their stint in WeHo, Nosh and Avonaco could afford to drink there for days. They were seated at a table outside and settled in. Next to them were three young Asian women drinking margaritas. The girls were not particularly attractive, but they were nearby and the special was irresistible. Nosh and Avonaco made simple conversation with the girls, who laughed awkwardly.

A moment later, three models walked in and were seated at the table opposite Nosh and Avonaco, and the men's attention was shifted.

The girls were unbelievable—all of exotic heritage, at least partially, all slender, all incredibly beautiful. Only one took off her sunglasses, and none would give their names, but they still talked to Nosh and Avonaco. The one that had taken her sunglasses off, a sultry mulato with a smile all the whiter in contrast to her skin—and the most attractive of the three in Avonaco's opinion—kept interrupting the conversation by announcing that she was in love with Avonaco. Taking notice of the book he carried with him, which was written *by* him(with a few drinks in him, apparently Avonaco—so quiet, sullen, and in shock before me—could be an extraordinarily vain creature), the girls expressed an interest in hearing him read. Drunk as he was, he obliged them.

He imagined himself on a stage before them, and his words came out, somehow, clearly and steadily although he drank quite a bit throughout. The only interruption came in the beautiful mulato girl telling him to meet her in the bathroom in two minutes. After reading for another two minutes, precisely, Avonaco told his audience to hold for a moment and went to the restroom—the girl did not meet him there. When he returned, he finished his reading without any further interruption and sat down next to *the* girl. He did not bring up her false invitation. Her friends thanked him as they gathered their purses. The girl whispered into his ear, "My name is Jasmine." They picked up and left after that, leaving Nosh and Avonaco behind, beaming in what remained of the girls' flowery scents, and ordering another special.

At this point, Avonaco's memory becomes cluttered, unclear. He recalls drinking more—a lot more—and sleeping intermittently. He recalls briefly kidnapping one of the Daughters and sending her back on her way. He recalls pissing into a styrofoam cup in Sweet Pea that he had found on the floorboards. In hindsight, he recalls noticing the sneer of the men at Rave when they left, and the condescending tone in the models' voices; he recalls seeing a disappointed look on his mama bear's face; he recalls eventually returning to the treehouse to recover, without Nosh(to his memory), and hearing from a half-sleep the sound of Bunny's disgruntled voice loudly denouncing the benders, the antics, the two pieces of evidence which tied Nosh and Arlo to the interior of the treehouse—Nosh's single boot in the middle of the floor and Arlo's paisley scarf.

There is a rap on the door. One of the nurses pads in on the thick soles of her tennis shoes. Normally, I would be annoyed by the interruption, but Avonaco's face has become so pale that I feel it is warranted. Another nurse follows behind her. Despite their efforts, Avonaco's infection has evidently spread, because his condition seems to have worsened. They give me permission to stay for another hour—no longer.

TRACK 9

Most living things grow at a steady or logical rate until they reach maturity. This was not so with Yona—he seemed to grow exponentially. With each new sighting of the moon, his howl increased considerably in decibel level; his snout became pointer and his teeth sharper; the dark markings in his fur became even darker and more noticeable; he ate and drank more—subsequently, he grew more, became more displaced, and more violent. He was 120lbs. and getting larger—he was no longer allowed to sleep inside the treehouse.

And while Yona continued to grow more and more towards Life, the cult grew in the inverse; they grew further and further apart, inching closer to their demise.

Apparently, the already tangled mess of sexual relations within the family had become so intertwined that no single string was ident-ifiable from the next—it resembled a massive ball made from rubber bands, each band so entangled with all the rest that it could not be removed without compromising the structure in whole. Not that there was a clear structure from the get-go, but things had gotten out of control: sons disregarded other sons and slept with their daughters, their mothers, and even their sons; daughters disregarded other daughters and slept with their sons, their fathers, and their daughters too. Toes were being stepped on everywhere, feet were crushed; feelings were being hurt, and jealousies arose.

Even in a *sexually liberated* community, it can happen that the individual's desire for the absolute possession of another's affection will come through; it is an inherent—though sometimes narcissistic—trait in human beings, to want to be the sole object in a lover's eye, even if it is not a realistic desire from an evolutionary standpoint, and especially not a realistic desire when considering the number of different people in this person's own eye, from which each and every one is expected *absolute possession of their affection*. As contradictory as all this sounds, it does not change the fact that this is how it was.

It was said that Nevaeh was not in love with Avonaco in any traditional sense, but she had laid claim over him at his welcoming ceremony and was distraught that he did not then pine after her or dote on her persistently. Instead, he ran around in the company of Nosh and shared beds with anonymous horse-vultures, muskrats, hummingbirds, chipmunks, and whinnies, flirted with butterflies, and

443

all the while drunkenly said things to Bunny like, "If we ever got our shit together we would make a great couple," and, precariously, things to Persia like, "I wish it were you...."

Secretly, Avonaco knew that he would have ceased all of that nonsense for Nevaeh if she had not been helplessly devoted to a scrawny, undependable raven whose presence always felt ominous, and who no one in the family liked. He was a young thing, vain yet insecure, disingenuous, and generally an absurd human being. It was no wonder he was never accepted by the family. Nevaeh's attraction to him was considered all around to be baffling.

Nosh, like Avonaco, was subject to his own promiscuity and its accompanying silent aversion from within the cult. He was sleeping with a lioness beloved to most members of the family, while also messing around with a feline of a smaller breed, and various calves and whinnies besides. But there was a serpentine woman he had been involved with on and off too, whose affect on him, similar to that of the raven's on Nevaeh, was thought to be "toxic." He kept returning to her in times of need, sneaking off to be with her in secret, arriving on her doorstep in the middle of the night—but everyone knew what was going on; the close-knit family saw through his every action. It did not sit well with them.

Between West and Bull and Nevaeh and the others, there were a hundred other comparable situations happening, which Avonaco does not think it necessary to go into detail about. (The only family members who remained immune to the behavior were Coal and Ember, somehow always remaining in their pleasant, goodhearted bubble of objectivity.) And it was all occurring underground. Nothing was made mention of; in private, maybe, but nothing was ever said aloud in the group. Like a rotting pile of compost that stretched deep down into the soil, the smell simply rose into the air, stinking to high heavens of its self-imposed dissolution, and it hung there.

The animals knew though. As when a storm is coming on the horizon, and birds fly about haphazardly through the trees, deer trot into the forest for cover, and all other creatures scurry and flutter around in a nervous energy to find a place to hide—*they knew*. The turtles crawled under the rocks in their cage. The dogs shook and barked at things that seemed nonexistent. The wolf heaved himself over furniture, from couch to couch, and broke a giant mirror. It shattered into a million sharp pieces, sticking into seat cushions on the floors and getting lost in tapestries. When Bunny went to clean up the shards, one piece cut her hand deeply. Her blood dripped bright red onto the white tile in the kitchen.

444

TRACK 10

Exploding like the first violent spout from a geyser, which would soon give way to many others, things finally came to a head one day while another father/son bender was in full swing.

It happened on the quiet, residential street in front of the neighbors—a shouting match. Bunny stood in the road in her bare feet, screaming at Nosh. For such a little girl, her voice was incredibly loud—it carried. She berated him on all accounts—his life and person in general, the lack of respect he had recently shown his Sons and Daughters, his sneaking around, the messes he left everywhere in his wake, and so on.

Avonaco was unsure what sparked the argument at the time (though he later learned it was just a bad day and a beer can left on the coffee table). He had been inside the treehouse when it started. He came out into the street for the tail end of it to hear Nosh's yelled retort, "I have been *unduly* singled out—why are you acting like such a *bitch* towards me, Bunny?"

Though it was out of her character to do so, little Bunny simply walked away, her face red with suppressed anger, and disappeared back into the treehouse. But the result of the argument was clear enough— Nosh was presently unwelcome at the treehouse. He climbed into Sweet Pea and slammed the door. Avonaco got into the passenger seat and they were silent for a moment as the engine turned over, then idled. Arlo sat bolt upright in the backseat, licking his chops.

Although Avonaco was still allowed in the treehouse, he felt partially responsible for Nosh's temporary banishment—he had certainly been present for many of the activities he believed to have upset Bunny, and knew that he had even been solely responsible for a few. His decision to join Nosh was automatic, supportive. Besides, he knew of a refuge. An old friend of his was visiting the area with one of her girlfriends; they were staying in a hotel in Santa Monica. Nosh, Avonaco, and Arlo sped off in that direction.

The hotel was one of the nicer ones in Santa Monica, just off the pier. The lobby had bright white marble flooring, ornate cherry wood furniture, vaulted ceilings, and a giant chandelier; the entire back wall was a window, out of which, past the white tables and chairs of the expansive courtyard, the ocean could be seen.

As Nosh and Avonaco entered, a receptionist greeted them politely and shook their hands. Avonaco, while taking in the grand air of the lobby, affected his best genteel tone as he addressed the receptionist. "I would like to make a call to Ms. Wallace. I am not sure in *which* room she is staying."

445

After looking through their list of guests, the receptionist quickly got Ms. Wallace on the line, and in another moment she was strolling across the lobby in a black dress and warm smile. Originally from Tennessee, she had all of the features that would rightly qualify her as a Southern Belle. She greeted Avonaco and Nosh, who she was meeting for the first time, with big hugs, then showed them up to her room.

The room was on the fourth floor of the hotel, with two queen size beds, a minibar, a large TV, spacious bathroom, and a balcony that overlooked the beach. Out on the balcony, on the table, there were two glasses that had recently been used—the girls were drinking champagne; they were congenial. Ms. Wallace's friend, Ms. Pappas(formal last names being used, I am told, to avoid the confusion that might arise if their first names were used instead, which were both "Suzanne"), was introduced and was happy to meet both Avonaco and Nosh, giving both of them hugs just as Ms. Wallace had done, then offered them each a glass of champagne, which both men happily accepted. It was clear already that Ms. Pappas was a fiery, full-blooded Greek, so they were glad to see that she took an immediate liking to them—things would not turn out well if she did not.

They drank for awhile on the balcony, and discussed what they would do for the night. The ladies wanted to be shown around. Nosh was familiar with the area, having lived close by before the cult existed, and suggested a bar he knew of that was within walking distance. It was decided they would go there.

Leaving the hotel room, Avonaco spotted a fifty dollar bill on the dresser where the TV sat, and said to Ms. Wallace, "I believe someone is forgetting this"—picking it up and outstretching it in his hand to her—"you'll probably be needing it." She refused the fifty-dollar bill. With a wink, she told him to put it in his pocket, and that maybe he could buy her a drink shortly.

They all went down the elevator in high spirits, Ms. Wallace taking Avonaco by the arm, and then out through the lobby as though they were all on vacation, carefree. In front of the hotel, something dropped out of Nosh's pocket, who was walking a few steps ahead of his friends with Ms. Pappas. It fell straight to the ground and Ms. Wallace spotted it—"Is that hair!?" she exclaimed. It was, indeed. It was a long lock of Nosh's brown hair, which had been cut by a woman at a party, and which he and Avonaco had both forgotten about until then. Why it was in his pocket, neither knew. And then to see it in the drive of that fancy hotel—it could not be explained.

Nosh answered Ms. Wallace, "Yes—that is my hair." Both girls laughed out of confusion, disbelief, the feeling of having no responsibilities, whatever. Then they all continued on their way to the bar.

The placed was called, "Cheri's." It was your typical dark bar lit by red candles, with a number of shadowy alcoves where you could kiss your woman. The girls paid for the drinks—whether out of their own pockets or from the $50-bill Ms. Wallace had Avonaco slip into his pocket earlier—and the boys told their stories, making fools of themselves for the amusement of the girls, who were charmed by their antics, and never stopped smiling—each was successfully pulled into an alcove at one time or another.

When they got back to the hotel, and snuck Arlo in using Avonaco's belt as a leash, the party split in two: Nosh and Ms. Pappas were left on the bed in the room(Arlo the voyeur was on a chair in the corner), while Avonaco and Ms. Wallace grabbed some drinks and ran down to the beach. The sand felt good and it was dark enough, but it was cold near the water and they weren't the only ones who had ventured onto the beach that night; so they went back to the hotel and, not wanting to interrupt any potential activity in the room, made themselves comfortable in a lounge area on the fourth floor, in full light and in full view of at least two security cameras. It had been a good night. Eventually, the two couples, and Arlo, fell fast asleep.

It was in the morning that problems arose. Where the girls had been having fun the night before, and presumed the boys to be doing the same, showing them a good time on their vacation, it was evident the following morning that that was simply how they lived. As the girls readied themselves in the bathroom for brunch with their strange bedmates, Nosh snuck Arlo back out of the hotel, then returned to sit with Avonaco at a table in the corner of the hotel room drinking vodka from the minibar. They made big plans together to sit in the room all day in the dark, as if they were outlaws in hiding, waiting for the trouble to pass—plans that would never come to fruition.

Leaving for brunch, they stumbled across Nosh's hair again in front of the hotel. Miraculously, it had not moved from the night before. And in the daylight it was no longer funny. Furthermore, at brunch, both Avonaco and Nosh passed up food, opting instead for two pints of beer a piece, then making an offhand joke to the waiter when the check arrived, something like *the girls will take care of this one,* which was then immediately followed by Avonaco asking Ms. Pappas for one of her cigarettes.

And that was that—Ms. Pappas had had enough. She was not just visibly displeased, she actually *barked* insults at Avonaco. She consulted Ms. Wallace in private, and convinced her that her friends had to go. Ms. Wallace approached Avonaco and Nosh, regretfully telling them that they would be going their separate ways, leaving the two of them like stranded children, hungry and without money in the middle of a grocery store. They were displaced, like wild animals removed from their natural surroundings then abandoned. They were stuck. There

447

was nowhere to go.

As men will often do in situations such as this, Nosh and Avonaco got drunk. They took Arlo to the beach and let him run around in the sand as they passed a bottle back and forth in Sweet Pea. The sun was so bright it was heartbreaking. They tried as best they could to stay out of it; and as the day went on, and shadows lengthened, it became easier and easier. Ms. Wallace had told them that she would see them that night—it was something they both looked forward to like salvation itself. But there was no way for her to get a hold of them; she had no idea where they were.

It was early in the evening when Nosh and Avonaco arrived back at the hotel unannounced. And again they told the receptionist that they would like to make a call to Ms. Wallace, only this time they knew the room number. She strode down into the lobby in another dress, her smile seeming somewhat forced. She said she would go out with them, and she did; but even though she apologized for Ms. Pappas' behavior, the night was sour. They went to the same bar. They ordered the same drinks(only Ms. Wallace didn't cover the tab this time). They even sat at the same table, where they huddled in close over the candle's flame, and Ms. Wallace attempted to explain *why* Ms. Pappas had gotten upset, which was not something they were concerned with hearing—*everyone* was upset.

When they finally left that night, Nosh was too drunk to drive Sweet Pea, so he stumbled into the backseat with Arlo and fell fast asleep; instead, Ms. Wallace drove, looking incredibly absurd behind the wheel in her dress. For a long time she cruised through the back streets of Santa Monica, into Venice, then back, talking very little to Avonaco, and it was apparent that they would not be invited back to Ms. Wallace's hotel again.

Eventually, she pulled off onto a side street and parked. It was raining out—a fine mist. And under one street lamp it even appeared to be snowing. Ms. Wallace called a cab. Avonaco waited with her in the rain for it to come. When it did, she kissed him on the cheek, got in, and the cab drove away. Avonaco smoked half of a cigarette on the street corner, then became disgusted by it and put it out. He crept back into Sweet Pea and silently cuddled the passenger seat from the floorboards, his head and torso stuck in the gap where there was no center-console, thankfully, and his feet under the dashboard. A helicopter flew through the sky, flashing its searchlight into yards and trees just three blocks away.

TRACK 11

There was a period of quietude then. Following Bunny's suit, the majority of the family, mainly its Daughters, took up grievances with Nosh and had him temporarily excommunicated. They said it was "to teach him a lesson." It was rumored that he and Arlo had driven into the desert to be alone for awhile. Whether or not that is true, he had disappeared.

The treehouse became a somber, isolated place. During the daytime, Avonaco and Nevaeh were often its only inhabitants. Nevaeh would hole up in the garage, which had been converted into her studio, and chain smoke as she put together headdresses made of various feathers, animal bones, and human teeth, which were to be sold to production companies to be used in films and music videos. Occasionally the raven would visit her, only to go away again soon after, leaving her in tears. Avonaco would take care of the dogs—whose behavior grew increasingly anxious—feeding them and taking them for walks. He would also sit at a table inside, working on something he called *an imaginary memoir*. He avoided Yona altogether, who was now 150lbs, and terrifying. He let Yona skulk about the yard by himself, setting out large bowls of food and water for him when it was known that the wolf was far enough away to not be able to sprint over and attack before the door to the treehouse was shut and locked behind him.

Bull continued to work constantly, toiling away at the office in front of an editing screen, perfecting the visual effects of high budget films he took no interest in. Bunny went off to auditions for roles in B Films, and shot commercials for companies that could afford to pay her at least a month's worth of rent for a day of work.

At night, Bull came home worn out and disillusioned about the film industry. Bunny returned with her pockets full, but creatively dissatisfied. And they would all sit together in the treehouse then, listening to sad records or solemnly rehashing some past event, or dispute.

Bull and Avonaco would step outside together to smoke. They quietly made small talk, and discussed their personal ambitions, plotting out storylines for books and movies, planning extensive trips to unknown regions, and so on—all of the things that young men will talk about in private, when the harsh, oppressive world is not listening, and when their women aren't around to shatter their dreams with realism and practicalities. Neither knew what to make of Nosh's disappearance, and neither could do a thing about it, so it went unmentioned. Only time could tell what would come of all that—and what was time in the floating world? If it was anything at all, it was

449

moving in slow motion.

All around Echo Park, in the various nests that the Sons and Daughters inhabited, things had become sluggish, and muted. It rained a few times. The water rushed along the perimeters of the homes in fast, muddy currents; it washed away some of the foundation of the treehouse. That is what happens when a central figure is removed from a family, or community—the surrounding figures are loosened from foot, and become unstable. The common thread that tied together the Sons and Daughters was at risk of busting at the seams, coming unraveled; that intricately woven fiber that so tightly bound them as a family, it was in danger of coming undone. It seemed as though everything could fall apart.

The last hour of visitation is up for the night. The nurse—meaning D., the ever considerate, the last nurse on staff before shift change—even allowed me an extra fifteen minutes with Avonaco before coming into the room at what she must have imagined (probably with her ear to the door) to be a natural stopping point.

It is apparent that Avonaco's treatments have been ineffective. With my rudimentary knowledge of medicine, and the human body, I can still tell that his health is failing. Beneath a beard that has been growing for at least two weeks and some odd days, I can see that his glands have become incredibly swollen—a sign of his body desperately fighting off infection—and from the open neck of his hospital gown I can see that red splotches have developed on his chest, possibly elsewhere on his body as well. The bandages on his arms are so wet they are almost dripping—I imagine this is puss from his festering sores that refuse to heal.

I say goodnight to Avonaco and step outside of the room to wait for D. so that we might have a word. When she emerges, I pull her aside. She tells me that his vitals do not look good. The hospital has not been able to locate any of his family members, nor any of his hospital records; due to his unresponsiveness in the matter, the hospital must continue to act independently in his best interest. All of which is information that I am probably not authorized to hear.

Thus far, he has not reacted to the antibiotics in the way the hospital had hoped. They have no choice but to increase the dosage and pray for the best. She tells me to come back tomorrow afternoon.

TRACK 12

The following afternoon, when I return to the hospital, Avonaco's condition has considerably worsened. The decline in his health is so great that it can be seen in all of his features—the red splotches are on the upper part of his arms now, and have crept up onto his swollen neck; his once sallow cheeks are now bloated; his skin, though always having been somewhat pale, is now a pasty white. Despite all of this, his eyes are twinkling, and lucid. Those eyes, so aware and alive in that disintegrating head—they're horrific. But he has never before been so collected and coherent.

He describes the emotional distress within the family in reaction to the excommunication of Nosh, and the dissolving of its bonds in general.

The seasons had begun to change. There was a shift in the winds and the days grew shorter. Night came sooner and sooner and the air was chilled. The women in the treehouse, like the dogs, became nervous, their behavior marked with irrationalities, their moods swinging. In turn, the dogs were further disturbed, becoming more nervous and thereby causing further disturbances for the women. The situation perpetuated itself.

The wolf was bigger and more dangerous than ever. He weighed almost two-hundred pounds, his markings were black as a damned soul, and his behavior was troubling. He would stalk through the shadows in the garden during the daytime, then disappear into them at night; when he did show himself it was only to snarl at his owners, or at the other dogs(who yelped and hid when they sensed him nearby), or to pounce on the heaps of food that were set cautiously out for him. He tore up Bull's hands one afternoon when Bull attempted to feed him; the cuts required several stitches and the bandages remained on for some time.

The men at the treehouse—which, aside from Bull and Avonaco, then included West(who had left Los Angeles for an extended stint on the road, returning surprised and discouraged to find the family in disarray), and Juan(who had come back to the treehouse apologetic for the circumstances of his own temporary excommunication, which had been a result of a series of thefts within the family wherein all the missing items were discovered in His Box)—they were sullen and helpless. They spoke in quiet voices, making abstract allusions to the problems from which the family suffered, yet still nothing was said outright.

And still the days grew shorter, the nights longer; still the winds changed speed, and direction, and the air grew cooler.

It was a wonderful day when the women finally called the men into a meeting in the treehouse. They said they had been talking at length(as they always were), and had come to the conclusion that *something* needed to be done in order to save the family—only they were not exactly sure as to *what* that something was.

Every winter the family would briefly split up, without any malicious or dissolute cause; they would split up to return to their orig-

451

inal homes, or to go off to work, or to travel just for the sake of traveling, among many other reasons. And in the spring they would come together again. Winter had almost arrived. Whatever was to be done needed to be done *soon*—before winter came, before the family disbanded, because this time there was the risk of it being for good.

They all got drunk at the meeting. The men were glad and talked loudly and openly. The women were glad too, and they listened to their men, smiling, then interrupted them with new suggestions, or repeated ones. The discussion went on for a long time. Bottles were drained. Ashtrays were filled. And eventually it was decided—they were to throw a party at the treehouse for All of the Sons and All of the Daughters. Nosh was to be the first invited.

TRACK 13

Immediately after the decision was made to throw the party, action ensued in preparation. Money was scrounged up and boxes of wine, liquor, and beer were purchased. A large kennel was constructed to hold Yona during the festivities. Lights were replaced around the garden and new candles were brought in. Records were salvaged from garage sales and boxes set out on the curb as trash around Echo Park. Instruments were tuned. Nevaeh set about her work in the studio, sewing, stitching, and gluing together different fabrics, feathers, and other materials that came together as several intricate masks to be worn by the Sons and Daughters at the party.

On the morning of the shortest day of the year, before, in effect, the longest night of the year—the winter solstice—all was ready. The wolf was very carefully lured into the kennel with five pounds of raw meat and locked away. The night came on quickly and the candles were lit, the lights were turned on. Nevaeh handed out masks to those already present in the treehouse in relation to their spirit animals—Avonaco and Ember with the heads of bears, Bunny with the giant head of a floppy eared Bunny, Coal with the head of a mongoose, West with the head of a Dingo, Bull with the head of a Wolf(which Yona howled at, and began scratching at the walls of his kennel), Juan with the funny pink head of a flamingo, and Nevaeh herself with the very elegant head of a panther. All the other guests could now arrive at their own free will, and would be given their animal masks accordingly.

Fittingly, being that he was the first invited to the party, which was largely being thrown in his honor, to accept him back into the family, Nosh was the first to come through the gate into the garden at dusk. The moon was already shining brightly in the sky, softly illuminating those places where the lights and candles could not reach. Everyone

452

hugged him and kissed his cheeks and was happy. He was given a very bizarre looking mask—it was a frightening mix of wildebeest and lion, with dark, beastly features, a pink mouth, and a long, tangled mane. Ceremoniously, he humbly thanked everyone and slowly lowered the mask over his head. The festivities began.

They all came, the entire family, in groups and alone, one after the other. They filed through the gate and the silence was broken like the *pop* of a lid coming off a jar. Suddenly there were a thousand musical notes unleashed at once. The sound blared through the neighborhood, echoing off the hills, and filled the air with the feeling of celebration. It was a fine noise, joyous and innocent, which seemed to carry the Sons and Daughters of The Earth up off their feet, lifting them higher and higher back up towards the moon.

Their world was floating again, suspended by thin strings atta-ched to each one of their bodies, which had transformed like their heads into the forms of animals. It was like a zookeeper's nightmare, those creatures escaped from their silent captivity in a loud burst, hovering through the garden like acrobats in an animal circus: bears juggled while standing on their heads; bunnies hopped through fiery hoops; sex panthers swung upside down from trees, holding onto the paws of kittens who did double backflip dismounts; mongooses flew miniature airplanes and did barrel rolls and loops; beavers built colorful bridges that hyenas trotted across on one paw, cackling; peacocks put on burlesque shoes with flamingos; fawns performed amazing illusions; sloths climbed into corners and disappeared, reappearing in tiny pools where ducklings swam in circles so fast they created a whirlpool; din-gos flashed toothy grins as they fooled calves in games of sleight of hand; a lady preying mantis screwed her mate on a platform under a spotlight, ate his head, regurgitated it, then miraculously set it back on his body and brought him back to life; butterflies carried a large backlighted net where hummingbirds made shadow puppets; foxes took elements from each act and ingeniously strung them together to create a completely new act; beasts showcased unnatural exhibitions of strength, lifting tiny cars stuffed with a dozen cows at least over their heads and hurling them safely to a ledge 30ft. overhead; a wolf sat in a tent with his crystal ball, staring into space and telling the future.

It was a fantastic show. All who were present were at their best. There was laughing, clapping, and hollering. There were incredible displays of love. There was merrymaking, and drinking. Glasses swung around on tethers and were filled, emptied, then filled again. Bottles were drank and kicked to the side. New bottles were opened, drank, and kicked to the side. The world continued to climb higher, and the Sons and Daughters of The Earth were a family again.

But there was another wolf in attendance—*a bastard wolf*. A latch must have come undone. He slinked through the dark, masquerading as his counterpart, blending perfectly into the menagerie. No one noticed the intruder. Had they seen him, they may have had time to run.

TRACK 14

It is an unfortunate thing that happened that night. And especially for it to have happened so soon after The Sons and Daughters of The Earth had mended those fractures that had come between them, reconvening in that magnificent show of unified joy.

But the fact stands that what happened that night is that they all died, save for Avonaco. And it is unfortunate for us, all of us, that the precise details of their deaths will forever remain a mystery because just a moment ago our dear friend, and the last known surviving member of the cult, Avonaco, died as well.

He went silent for a long while in his bed, so I called in the nurses. The nurses—two women that I did not know; I am unsure of where D. was at the time—took note of his pale skin, and the increasing number and redness of the splotches that had come to cover most of his body, yet it did not occur to them that those things might indicate an allergic reaction to something. They simply checked his charts and saw that it was near the scheduled time for another dose of antibiotics. They promptly distributed the penicillin into his body, then stepped back to go about straightening the bed sheets and making sure Avonaco was being properly supported by his pillows. They asked him if he needed anything, and he gave them a short, exasperated, "No thank you."

As they went out of the room, Avonaco's already pale skin became ghostly white, like the walls and floors of the hospital, like his bed sheets and his gown; the hives ever-creeping over his body became inflamed and bright red as the continually appearing blood spots on his white bandages, growing and changing shape. His face ballooned up and his breathing became forced. He stared directly at me, or through me, as I repeatedly asked him if he were alright. I attempted to call the nurses back, but to no avail. In a matter of a few minutes he had passed—his body gone completely limp, and still.

Horrified, I walked out of the room and into the hallway, where eventually I found D. and told her that I believed Avonaco to be dead. Then I went into the restroom and vomited.

Later I was to learn that the cause of Avonaco's death was indeed a severe allergic reaction, called anaphylaxis, rather than the infection that had been so worried about. They had been using penicillin to treat the infection, to which it was now apparent he was allergic to— probably since he was a child; it was only a mild allergy, which is why it was not caught from the beginning, but the steady increase in dosage and the prolonged presence of it in his system finally was too much and caused his body to react violently, sending out massive amounts of histamine through his bloodstream, affecting his heart, lungs, and esophagus. It would have been an extremely uncomfortable way to go. Essentially, his throat swelled up so much that he was strangled to death.

TRACK 15

It is quiet in what was once Avonaco's hospital room, except for the sound of the palm leaves rustling in the breeze outside of the open window. It is late afternoon and Avonaco's body has already been taken down to the morgue; the sunlight poring through the window illuminates the harsh white of everything, seeming to accentuate the empty bed where Avonaco once laid, as now it is sanitized and neatly made to hold its next patient.

Avonaco's absence in the hospital room can be felt. The absence of all The Sons and Daughters of The Earth, as they began to come to life through Avonaco's words, can be felt too. They are all gone. They are all but fragments of things that once were, suspended in the air in their history that is left to us in partial due to the negligent treatment of Avonaco's injuries and his subsequent death.

What remains of their story must be pieced together using the remains: the few recordings of Avonaco's voice, sounding infinitely more haunting now that he is gone, and whatever the investigators have been able to uncover from the house at the 1/2 address on Lake Shore Avenue.

In the police report, it states that their bodies were found on the morning of Christmas Eve after receiving complaints from neighbors about a stench coming from within the gates of the treehouse, and a questionable lack of noise. Their bodies would have been decomposing for just over 48 hours then—the smell would have been atrocious. The report mentions that the bodies scattered about the house and garden had been mauled. Blood was everywhere. Some limbs were missing. And each and every Son and Daughter was found wearing, if nothing else, a strange mask which bore a resemblance to one type of animal or another.

There was an article in the Los Angeles newspaper on the 23rd of

December which described a wolf being found in the early hours of the previous morning in Elysian Park, which is only about a mile away from the treehouse. He had been seen skulking about the perimeter of the park in a daze, with something that appeared to be blood in his fur and covering his snout. When authorities went to the park to retrieve the wild animal, he laid sleepily beneath a tree licking his paws; as they approached him he attacked, forcing them to respond immediately to ensure the safety of those present. He was shot and killed.

In connection with the story of The Sons and Daughters of The Earth, one can only assume that it was Yona that was shot down that morning. And one can imagine his actions before he arrived in the park. One can see the Sons and Daughters, joyously celebrating in their garden the rekindling of their precious family—drinking, laughing, and shouting; and one can see the quiet escape of Yona from his makeshift cage, then skulking about the premises hungrily.

By all accounts—including Avonaco's fleeting descriptions of Yona as being, "said to be domesticated," and as being a "bastard"—we must conclude, as the police later did, that it was he who murdered The Sons and Daughters of The Earth. Though still the question is left as to How—how was one single wolf able to kill so many people? How was he not brought down by one or all of the many that were in attendance that night?

To answer this, it is necessary to consider the state that they must have been in at the time of the murders. They were ecstatic. They were drunk. Perhaps they were so ecstatic, and so drunk as to not be capable of putting an end to their ultimate demise; perhaps those who saw what was happening even believed it to be a bizarre theatrical performance on the stage of the floating world.

But another question remains—how is it that Avonaco was the only survivor of this frightful affair? Was it that they had run out of alcohol, and he had briefly stepped out to get more?, then come back through the gate with arms full, and everyone dead, where he was quickly mauled by Yona before allowing that Bastard Wolf to make his escape? And what about those two days of slowly bleeding in the garden before the authorities finally discovered him?

Or is it possible that Avonaco, in fact, was not the only survivor?

Further in the police report it is mentioned that the police department "cannot be completely sure if all members of the 'cult' are accounted for; several of the supposed members existed beneath the radar as degenerate artists, gypsies, and other social misfits of the like. It would not be a surprise if a number of members are still somewhere out in the world, lying low."

Although even the police have been diminished to making speculations, rather than stating facts, we can still remain optimistic in eventually solving the mysteries of the existence and sudden non-existence of The Sons and Daughters of The Earth. It is rumored—though there is no mention of this in what little of the official police report that I have been able to acquire access to—that the authorities possess various journals, drawings, notes, and personal items that belonged to many of the Sons and Daughters. And thereby we can be hopeful that someday these documents will come to light in order to further explain who and what The Sons and Daughters of The Earth were, and why it is they left us so quickly.

Until then we can only look back on them fondly in these mere fractions of their lives as they float farther and farther away from us, being carried by the wind up into the void, listening as they rustle the palm leaves on their way and remembering the principles they lived by—those simple and joyous principles, which proved to be too pure for a world so fixated on their own fabricated belief systems as to blindly attempt to firmly plant them in the ground everywhere. We can only look into the bright white of this empty hospital room and realize that something good is gone.

—September 2010, Los Angeles, CA

VOL

THE SECOND NOVEL

UME

III

I AM NO ONE
an imaginary memoir
(2010)

For
Every woman I've ever seen,
thought of, or dreamt up—
I miss you all. And my apologies.
Especially l.w.

Part I

The Imaginaries

IN THIS FUTURE AS WE KNOW IT, RIGHT NOW, I am sitting above a street in a notoriously clean city in Northwest America, staring out the apartment window and experiencing(not for the first time) the "intangible swarming" feeling that accompanies any given person when they encounter a labyrinth from their human, and therefore limited, vantage point in a world whose nature is limitless.

It is the Perpetual Midmorning here—10.15am—and the city, as always, remains under the grey spell of a self-important rain. People are humming and whistling at outrageous volumes. Bums drink their forty-fourth beers of the day. Wet footprints are mopped up from the market floors. Miniature dresses are sewn for boy dolls—or perhaps the miniature dresses are not sewn for the boy dolls right here and now because I've just seen the tailor walking down on the street having a cigarette.

The tailor is a very tall, lanky gentleman. He is a kind man, and astute. He has spotted me in the window where he knows to look bec-ause he is actually a good friend of mine, the tailor. With the hand holding the cigarette he waves. At least I am fairly sure that is what's happening and, in any case, I am waving back.

It is at this moment that I recall the mess I've made of my hands. They are completely black.

Earlier, in my underwear and slippers, I labored for twenty min-utes over a new ink ribbon that had to be transferred from its original, smaller spool to the larger spool that is compatible with my typewriter, an old Underwood Golden Touch Hideaway; so for twenty minutes I, in underwear and slippers, sat there winding the damn ink ribbon by hand which, of course, got my hands all messy so that I've now got to be careful about touching anything—esp-ecially my face. Or just wash my hands.

That's what I'll do. I'll wash my hands.

I mention all of this because these details, seemingly trivial, are un-ique to this moment and cannot be mentioned truthfully at any other moment. In another moment, another future, I did not see the tailor wave and the occasion to relate the story of the ink ribbon did not arise. In another future I am in a different city, or town, so do not hear the humming and the whistling, do not smell the pickling effect of the forty-fourth beer on the bums' bodies, do not see or hear the rain that causes the wet footprints to appear on the market floors. In yet another I am still here, but my hands did not need to be washed because they were clean already—the new ink ribbon was never purchased, so I never had to sit in my underwear and slippers transferring it from one spool to another and these words will never be written.

Perhaps in some futures I do not even write.

I have been thinking too much lately. In particular, I have been thinking too much lately of Borges. Those familiar with his work have probably already surmised that this might be the case, or were at least already aware of being reminded of something, or someone.

Recently I undertook the task of writing an essay on Borges; specifically, an essay on Borges' short story called, "The Garden of Forking Paths," which turned out to be an ambitious an ultimately crazy essay that my current girlfriend, Lillian, handed in to her Lit. Criticism professor under her own name. The essay ventured that the story's purpose was, aside from nodding at infinity, to create a labyrinth—or recreate a labyrinth as conceived by a character within the story—and the accompanying "intangible swarming" feeling within the reader as if they were encountering a labyrinth(which they certainly are) *from their human, and therefore limited, vantage point in a world whose nature is limitless.* The essay then continued by explaining Borges' methods of writing about such a convoluted theme by extracting details, images, statements, and metaphors from His story, dissecting them all and repositioning them in a manner that is more easily understood. It concluded by stating that in another existence I did not finish the essay; rather, my head exploded.

But this is the existence that I am concerned with—the one where my head did not explode; the one in the Ever-Holy Present that I am undeniably living through an inexplicable series of choice actions and reactions. To look back any further than my own decisions and their consequences would be a mistake—I cannot be held accountable for those things that occurred before my birth in the same way that I cannot be expected to consider those forks in time wherein I was not born. The first fact then that must remain at the foundation of everything is that I am here—I exist.

The second fact is a matter of my biological makeup. Being that I have come into existence as such at one point only, I must therefore

464

consider myself to have only one possible set of genes. What these genes have created is a man of not considerable height, bad teeth(that were fixed in this future), pale-ish skin like that of a sick olive, muscul-ature and metabolism that are hypersensitive to stimuli, a persuasion towards the abstract, extreme organization (almost incongruously), and simple kindnesses or basic consideration for others, along with a hint of vague despondency here, good-natured foolishness there, and cynic-ism in the sense that Diogenes would have approved—"to live like a dog is to eat in the market like a dog," or some such thing.

The facts that then might follow consecutively—meaning anything and everything—are all subject to change.

2

BEING THAT A MAN CAN SPEAK ONLY FOR HIMSELF in his absolute present condition, I will say that it is god's honest truth, an indisputable fact, that I am, *right now*, on my way out of the city, riding backwards on the train. It is 10.15am and I can see nothing except for flickering light like sunspots on a camera lens as we pass between apartment buildings and old churches—which I know instinctively are there—then the downtown commercial buildings, then the underside of overpasses, then, finally, the increasing number of trees as the train moves from outskirt to suburb.

Frequently the train stops, pauses. A recording of a woman's voice makes an announcement: *This is the Portland blue line train for Gresham. The doors are now closing.* Then she repeats herself in Spanish.

I hear this woman from a distance. She is not talking to me. I know where I am and where I am going. It makes no difference to me whether the doors close or stay open. I am already in my seat. A wo-man is in the seat next to me. She is a young woman—my woman. She sits quietly beside me with her head on my shoulder, but she is also not beside me.

Across from our seats there is a large pane of plexiglass in which a number of reflections are cast, each one shifting slightly as they reach farther and farther back into infinity. In the third set of reflections there is no longer anyone sitting next to me; I am sitting alone on a train somewhere in Greece. I am listening to a long monologue about a long monologue, both indubitably enhancing the beauty of modern Greece and the modern Greek while the speaker also attempts to enh-ance the beauty of himself. It is no longer a time when a ride on an air-plane entitles you to an invitation from a city councilman to take cog-nac in his home, as it was when this monologue began, yet I insist on leaving intact the idea and relevance that is evoked by saying *modern*.

Anyway, there is no doubt in my mind that the coast of Greece looks now just as it did then, as there is no doubt in my mind that it produces the same sentiments. It is a place whose significance within man's history has already been set in stone and blood, and whose legendary past cannot die out even after the last Greek has been wiped off this earth because it is secured in the landscape, the trenches, the shores, the soil, the rock; its grandeur, in its very essence, is inalienable and its myth is recorded permanently in the great soul of the earth.

It all sounds so wonderful, but I have no need to a buy a plane ticket for the physical, actual Greece. I have learned all this while riding backwards on a train destined for Gresham, Or.; Portland, that notoriously clean city, cannot be seen from this great distance.

The train stops near the end of its line, the end of the world: *Now stopping at the Gresham Transit Center. This is the Portland blue line train,* and so on. I put "Colossus" back in my coat pocket and get off the train.

All at once I am six miles outside of Paris in a place called Saint-Denis. It's drizzling. No one else has gotten off at this stop aside from Lillian and myself. The train continues on in its previous direction, soon to hit its last stop and turn around. It rounds a bend into a cluster of trees and makes its temporary disappearance. The tracks are deserted. On the opposite side of the tracks there are silent rows of homes occupied by decent families that pray before eating their midday meal. The air above these homes is soft and still, though I swear a dog barks—just once. It's almost religious. But then where is the Basilica?

I am looking around for a sign of the aforementioned structure, and I notice that there is one other person who got off at this stop. He has just stood up from tying his shoe and I can see him clearly. It is me. Another Font whose life began as one life with my own, but since then has split off for one reason or another. I look as though I have gained some weight. Perhaps too much beer drinking; perhaps I never learned to tame that beast.

And wait—if we are in Saint-Denis then that must be the case. It was four years ago that I came here, leaving behind me in the states a young woman who was *not* pregnant with my child. I was thinking about her often, reading The New Testament. The most remarkable thing I remember taking from it though happened after I was in Saint-Denis, while I was sitting in the oak shade of a giant tree in Valencia, Spain, thinking about what I imagined was God, and saying to myself, "See the birds there—they're fed today! So don't you worry about anything either."

Later on that very night was when I met the Dutch girl that I fell madly in love with. But the morning that followed our one night of love—which was provoked by more than just our own persons, but the romantic atmosphere of traveling in general, of being lost in rainy

466

brick lined alleyways where orange lamps are glowing with big halos, and of countless drinks to boot—the Dutch girl kissed my cheeks then left town, forcing me to find a ride to Madrid where I would contemplate the lives of the prostitutes down on the street while cracking peanuts on a fourth floor balcony, refraining from drink, and reminding myself of the passage about the birds. It was good for me. I smiled about the Dutch girl, though I'd never see her again—just hanging onto her name, "Sabrina"; I smiled about the girl back in the states, though she'd never talk to me again. And they were just two beautiful things of the past.

But here I am in Saint-Denis, most likely never having made it into Spain to sit under the oak shade and meet the Dutch girl; maybe never having read the passage about the birds, but surely having heard it. So why that swollen gut and the long face? I never forgave myself for that poor girl, huh. I never discovered that the missed period was just a late period. What a nightmare. Cheer up.

The Other Font sees me eyeing him, which I've been doing for what length of time I don't know. I have no interest in making conversation with him. There's a button missing on his sweater. Conversation would probably lead only to confusion and embarrassment. I decide to show him my back.

Once I turn around, I am brought suddenly and firmly back into Gresham. A mixed-crowd stands around in wait to transfer onto one of the many busses in the long line at the curb. The bus drivers smoke cigarettes off to the side of their rigs, not minding the stall one bit.

In the center of the triangular plot of grass which serves as the waiting area there is an inlaid circle made of bricks. On top of the bricks there is a broken down TV with a loveseat and adjacent recliner positioned in such a way as to allow their occupants to watch what's not-showing. A young mother sits on the loveseat smoking a cigarette just as naturally as the bus drivers do with that vacant, satisfied stare aimed at the blank screen as her child sleeps next to her in his stroller.

The inch and a half of her cigarette and all cigarettes becomes an inch, becomes half an inch, becomes the last, hot, throat-stinging drag and the cotton filters are crushed underfoot to extinguish their final, triumphant red glow. But there is nothing to actually celebrate over. There is no genuine triumph. No one has really won anything. The bus drivers just hop back onto their busses and the passengers follow like clockwork.

There is an additional holdup. Three disabled folks are trying to board the bus and the bus driver is having a difficult time with their accommododations—the mechanical ramp isn't coming all the way down to the sidewalk like it's supposed to. This lasts for a few minutes. Alterations are made. The bus driver gets things under control and the end of the ramp finally manages to reach the sidewalk. The last three passengers board the bus, skillfully parallel parking themselves in the front thereafter.

The purpose of this trip is academic. It is our first time out to Gresham. I am only riding along to ensure that my little woman, Lillian, doesn't have trouble negotiating the public transit in and out of a city that is new to us. She doesn't necessarily need me here—and I certainly don't have any scholastic business of my own to tend to—but the ride at least makes me feel better. I will have more than a vague sense of where she is when she comes out here twice a week to attend classes. I will be able to perfectly imagine the sights she sees. If anything should ever happen to her, I will know exactly which bus driver to go after. Besides, I think she enjoys having me in the seat next to her.

In front of these seats, there is an older woman with a goatee that consists of three long, grey hairs. She is in mid-conversation with a woman across the aisle—actually the young mother from a moment ago—who plays with the tiny fingers of her stroller bound child with one hand while playing with an unlit cigarette in the other, ready and waiting for her stop on the route. The topic of their discussion is swine flu.

"They say that by the end of the year, eighty percent of the state is supposed to have the swine flu," the older woman reports to the young mother.

"Is that what they say? I hadn't heard any numbers yet, but I'd believe it—I knew it was going to be bad."

"Yeah—eighty percent. Do you breast feed the little one?"

"Yes, I do—I've breast fed both of my boys," says the young mother.

"Oh, good. I breast fed all of my kids too. Did you know that breast milk actually has some of the best antibodies for the swine flu in it?"

"I did hear something like that—the immunities—which means the little one here will be fine, but I just don't know what I'm going to do with the other one. He's eight. "

"What you oughta do," instructs grandma, "is put a little breast milk in his cereal in the mornings, and I'm sure he'll be fine."

The bus comes to a halt on Kelly Ave., just a few stops away from the college. "You know, that's not a bad idea," says young mother with cigarette still in hand and now lighter out of pocket. "But this is my stop. It was really nice talking to you. Enjoy the rest of your day."

"You too, sweetheart. Bye now!"

The mother exits the bus past the parked wheelchairs, going

backwards onto the curb in order to gently get the stroller onto the sidewalk two wheels at a time. As the bus takes off, I can see her through the windows shielding the wind with a cupped hand to light up. She pulls the blanket up over her child's nose.

The older woman turns to us, speaking as if she had not been a part of the conversation we just overheard her having. "Isn't it strange, the things you hear on the bus?"

Lillian and I nod in agreement. Instead of making eye contact with her, I look at the three long hairs on her chin, then back out the window. Lillian is stuck making the eye contact. There is an odor reminiscent of that of the warm, moist flesh between two folds of flabby, unclean skin—mildew. I don't know where it's coming from. The bus moves on towards our stop.

The disorder in the administration services at community colleges is insurmountable. It takes two and a half hours to ask a single question. The seats are all taken in the waiting rooms with either pimply-faced eighteen year olds flirting with one another, or pimply-faced forty year olds flirting with the eighteen year olds, leaving us waiting in the hallway where I am not rethinking my decision to abstain from taking any courses. Everyone's behavior is questionable here. The atmosphere is positively adolescent. The flirting is carried out in *indoor voices*.

Finally it is our turn. The question is asked. The answer is uninformative and disappointing. The papers have not been filed yet. The records are not available at this time although they were sent over six weeks ago. The woman advisor has the face of a horse. I am still not rethinking my decision. It is time to turn around and go home.

On the way back into the city, I am riding in the same position as earlier, though facing forward now. I am relieved to be free and clear of Gresham. I hope to never have to go back there. Due to my overactive bladder—a symptom of diabetes, which I may or may not have—I had to use the restrooms on campus five times in the span of our two and a half hours of waiting. No matter which restroom I chose to use, there were always at least two people taking shits; you could see their little white velcro sneakers in the stalls with their pants all bunched up around the tongues. The urinal cakes smelled like cheap cologne, which made me nauseous. But I'm feeling better now.

So with this wonderful sense of relief, facing forward on the train back into the city, I can see now what I was unable to earlier: the landscape transforming from tree-lined suburbs to the gas stations and taquerias of the outskirts, then under the overpasses that house the shyer of the bums, then the downtown commercial buildings, the old churches, and, finally, the apartment buildings. The backwards motion

469

of the morning ride must have affected my brain—I am seeing the city again for the first time. It feels good, hopeful. Everything seems new, interesting, vast.

As we reach the point on the line where the apartment buildings are, there is an announcement: *This is the Portland blue line train for the City Center, continuing on to Hillsboro. The doors are now closing.*

Before the automated woman can repeat her announcement in Spanish, and the doors actually close, we get off the train. The stop is only a few blocks from our apartment building. We take our first steps in that direction. They feel as if they were our *very first steps*—the ones we'll look back on and say that they really mattered. This is the beginning of our new life together; the beginning of a new life altogether.

3

THE APARTMENT BUILDING WHERE WE LIVE—on the fourth floor, number forty-seven—is called The Lucinda Court. It is one-hundred years old and feels it. In accordance with the nature of month-to-month leases, a lot of people come and go here. Since its construction a hundred years ago the building has seen and heard the lives of countless people and endured many a beating. Fred the elevator fairy says there is an "odd energy." He seems to like saying that and wants to feed into it, eyefucking me as the words come out of his mouth. Whether or not there is an *odd energy* in this place is a personal opinion. Fred is free to think, say, and do whatever he pleases. He can eyefuck whomever he so wishes. I am not here to stop him.

The actual reason I am here is not so easily defined as that. Other than my preference of cold rain to dry heat—having spent the last eight months of this future in Austin, Tx.—it is still somewhat unclear. Why, the Little Woman said "Portland," and so there we went. No questions asked. It has been a month now.

Judging by the aesthetics of our little perch here on the fourth floor of the Lucinda court, one might be inclined to reduce that month to a week, or even a few days. Our furnishings consist of a full bookshelf, three mismatched end tables with three milk crates used as seats, and an uncomfortable, rotating sitting chair that we found inside the basement entrance to the building. For sleeping there is a designated spot on the hardwood floors that we walk on during the day, and where each night we lay out whatever soft, potentially warm things we can manage to produce—wool coats, towels, the cushion from the sitting chair, etc. But no matter how many coats and blankets we acquire—which is quite a few thus far, given to us by my very generous friend, the tailor—the pile itself never fully suffices. Come morning our backs still hurt. Our bones still must be thawed out.

There is an ambivalent quality about perhaps any city—that it could give or take you, who cares?—but it is especially evident in this city. We are trying hard to make an honest attempt at living in Portland, which for us requires little more than the modern basic necessities—food, shelter, plumbing that works—yet the cost of these modest amenities is atrocious. Not necessarily because of the attached dollar value to any single one, but because in order to pay whatever that specified amount might be one must be able to first earn that dollar somehow—and how does a person do that when there is no work? Tell me, where do they go?

It may not be true that Portland doesn't want us, but I am more than certain that this city doesn't *need* us; rather, it doesn't need me. There are six heads to every one opening for work here. Each day, several times a day, I am reminded of this undeniable and aggravating fact.

Presently, I am walking with a slight limp along the intricate, crosshatched path that makes up my daily route in search of work. From the far west of the city down to the west bank of the Willamette River, first north of Burnside, then south, winding around on foot then cutting back, mapping out the location and business hours of prospective employers, waiting, just waiting for that sign to go up in the window—and never inquiring about work before that. You can waste a lot of paper and get a lot of hopes up if you don't wait for the 'Help Wanted' or 'Now Hiring' signs to go up; you will have a lot of decent conversations with people who would never dream of hiring another person to their staff, much less you, and under the pretense of their friendliness you might even take a day or two off from the hunt, assuming you'll be getting that call soon. But don't fool yourself—that call is not going to come. Just after you left they threw away your brand new résumé, and not long before that they had already forgotten your name.

It's 10.15am and I've just left my little lady three blocks back at one of her two places of employment—both of which I applied for as well, neither of which granted me even an interview. It is the Market this morning, then the Theatre tonight. About seventy-dollars this morning, then fifty tonight.

It's only 10.15 in the morning, as I said, and I've already lost what little I had when I left. A nasty old bum with one eye swollen shut hit me up and out of fright I gave him all the money I had on me—which turned out to be close to thirty-five cents. It's a heavy loss to be had so early in the morning, and there's no quitting till its dark.

So I am walking along 5th Ave. with my slight limp and there is not a single sign up anywhere. Everywhere there are people eating,

471

sitting, begging, or letting their dogs shit in the middle of the sidewalk—but no signs for work. I can see it in their eyes that these boys out here eating, sitting, begging—letting their dogs shit where they please—they would love to see anger, but it's not in me. The only reaction I can manage is one of vexation, grave silence, a gloomy anxiety, despondency—subdued frustration that leaves only a moment-ary film of tears on the eyes.

Like this man on the corner with the unholy round face and beard—why does he torture me with his lofty pestering? Is it not enough to have to save myself without his placing the great weight of the mountain's responsibility on my shoulders?

And this girl opposite here, with the pigtails—must she try to drown me with the rivers' fate?

"Don't pretend you aren't paid for your causes, that your checks aren't dutifully signed by the fat green hand of a peaceful man," I want to say to them. "Please, just let me be on my way. Let me make my living first. "

It has been too long since I've worked. Oatmeal and tomato soup is bad for the complexion. My cheeks are sallow. My legs are weak and my pants a bit loose. My pockets are empty.

For those of us who didn't save before the recession it was sudden and painful. One morning we feasted at breakfast, eating quickly so as not to be late for the matinee, thinking we would take a nice stroll over there. Then, as we were picking our teeth we realized it would be the last time we would eat like that and the six dollars for a midday show-ing was out of the question. Secretly we all stopped picking our teeth then and left some bacon lodged in our molars. We wished that we had chewed more slowly, that we had ordered the extra side. Openly we all wished that we had asked for champagne in our orange juice—it would have been easier to take then, lightly abuzz, partially deluded, with our hands a bit heavy under the weight of the Styrofoam boxes we held, each containing a little something for later when our cheeks were sall-ow and our pants a bit loose.

Hands hanging heavily between knees with that subtle tremble from hunger. O'Bryant Square: the decent pigeons are in absolutely no hurry; not even when the shined shoes—say *loafers*—of some soda drinking besuited man stomps by dangerously close do these pigeons care to move quickly. The pigeons stand their ground. And that man in the loafers—where is he going?

There is nowhere in particular I have to be right now. It's exhausting. I am on break from the hunt, as I call it—still not a single sign in any store windows. I seem to remember someone else remem-bering that year he searched for a job without the slightest intention of ever taking one—which is ridiculous. If only I could resign myself again to that level of supreme absurdity, that vulgar nonchalance. This seat in this square might be more enjoyable then. I would be able to let myself consider the heaviness of my hands hanging between my knees and relish the color of the blood building to a tingle in my immobile fingertips. I would be able to laugh at, and say fuckall to, words like *relish*. I would be able to scan the dark faces of the rain-cold homeless —by choice or otherwise—and feel pity for all of them.

To the old, the real, I'd say, "You poor old soul."

To the young and drunk, I'd say, "What insight do you hope to gain? What do you think about sitting there all day?"

It is growing harder for me to allow myself the luxury of such obscene leisure. Still, it remains in my disposition to have an affinity for the daydream, the sit still, the lie down, inasmuch as they are sweet, or innocent, or produce something. "If you will stay there all day cursing and stinking then you will have something to show me by night," I want to say to those young folks(my age) sitting there in act-ive, vile do-nothing. "Give me something I didn't have before. Teach me something. At the least, entertain me."

If I will sit, then I will produce. If I will not sit, then I will still produce. My hands are wide in the palm, with fingers that are short and strong. They were formed for work—to pick and pull and be sma-shed a number of times. They were built to withstand the day and to hold at night.

My hands cramp in this long scrawl as I jot it down in O'Bryant Square: the fingers are stiff to the tip and the palm is crippled to a certain extent, all bawled up, mangled, trying to fight...don't fight it...just let the tension ease from the outside, then in, until it spans the greater width of the hand. It will be better soon. Everything will get better soon.

In the manner that ghosts transport and drift from one bedroom vision to the next, I raise my head from the sight of my hands hanging between my knees and O'Bryant Square is gone. Where there were the stocking-capped heads of bums, there are now the tops of green trees, then golden yellow, then orange, then red. It is already, and only, mid-October—the fifteenth to be exact. The sidewalks wear different coats of color. The grey haze is darkening from east to west. The heavy ghostfog is rolling ever-slowly down off the hills and into the city where the inhabitants all sit around idly not because it's nighttime and we're done with work for the day, but because it's dark out, we're tired, and there's no work to go to anyway.

I am out here on the fire escape taking this in; inside I've got today's meal simmering on the stove—tomato soup with canned, diced

473

tomatoes and onion. The rice is warm in its pot. The little lady won't be happy with the meal when she finishes her double shift, but she will expect it. She will not be happy that I haven't found a job, but there's nothing that can be done about it.

As if it were the first premature flake of snow—appearing from thin air then falling, and hovering, then continuing its descent—the grey ash from the tip of my cigarette drops, dwindles, then glides down from the fourth floor fire escape of our apartment and disappears into the litter behind the building. It is childish, but it makes me wish for real snow. I wish it were Christmas. I wish it were my birthday. I wish that there were people coming with presents in tow. I wish that there were drinks to be had. I wish that someone or something needed me.

Left behind this first flake of snow, at the end of a soft, white inch, there is a glowing red ember like that of a burning torch. It lights up and fades—a foggy exhalation—then lights up again. But there is no significance in its illumination, no depth. It is nothing more than what it actually is—the end of the cigarette after a long day's hunt, a bad habit, the warmth of inertia, my temporary resignation.

Again, the grey ash created in the burning of this tiny bridge falls from its thin, stem-like form. The waning grey crystal drops over the railing of the fire escape into a slow, lawful dive, moving from fourth floor to third, then second, and first, meandering at each level, pausing for a moment as if to peer in, to pry, to ask for help from these strangers experiencing their own sadness and decline, and then, finally—unsuccessful in its attempt to survive—it reaches the ground, wet with its permanent mist, and it dies.

4

I'VE COME ACROSS A STAND-IN JOB ONLINE, seeing it listed offhand as a sign in a digital window: "Stand-In Needed for Lead Role in Feature Film." I apply for the job as I have been applying for anything I can find, on a desperate whim with no expectations of getting it, yet still optimistic for something. I imagine the position is for a snuff film, or a local independent no-budget—either project being something I probably don't want to be a part of anyway. But it's imperative to keep yourself out there, to keep trying at everything. To give up or hold out for a better option when options are scarce is ignoble and pathetic. A man won't find sympathy when he's down and out if he's resigned himself to being down and out. And a man always needs sympathy.

Some past (I think)good deed has allotted me a phone call today in response to my application and headshot, which I should mention is a terribly corny shot of me sitting on a green velvet chair, barely smiling, smug, that was taken on Lillian's camera-phone for the express purpose of applying for this job. So I've received the call on the grounds of that soft-erotic picture and I'm still a bit apprehensive about the project in general—especially since they're calling with only that picture to go on—and I am now running through the motions over the phone of what the job entails, the hours, the dedication. I ask the person on the other line if they're going to need me to take my clothes off, because I really have no intention of doing that. Thus far the man on the other end has seemed apprehensive himself, though only in telling me what exactly the film is about; to the question of taking my clothes off he opens up, assuring me through a laugh that my clothes will stay on—it's not some snuff film or local independent we're dealing with here. He informs me that the position is for a major motion picture directed by acclaimed Portland-based director, Gil Van S———. If I'm available tomorrow, he says—as I laugh to myself—then my interview is at [given time] at [given location]. Now I am the one assuring him that, yes, I am certainly available—my schedule appears to be wide open.

The way these interviews work is the same way that certain contests work. They bring in six or so guys in a couple of different sets, each set taking place at different times during the day, and each guy within that set is given his one chance, his one heat—lasting just a few minutes—to make an impression that will stick with the casting directors, the judges, thereby resulting in an immediate win and future employment.

Approaching the specified building fifteen minutes before the specified time, I am yet aware of the process. To my knowledge, there will be maybe one or two other guys here for the interview either before or after me; probably two days of interviews, so about six of us in line for the position. As I am a little early, I stand outside of the two story brick and ivy building, thinking it unwise to have a cigarette, but unavoidable at this point too. I light up and hear someone call my name. It's a young guy that's just called my name, come out of the building where I am to attend my interview in fifteen minutes and holding an unlit cigarette in his hand. He introduces himself as the man I spoke to on the telephone, Rick, and says he recognized me from my headshot. Inwardly, I am somewhat embarrassed to resemble the man in that picture, but outwardly I am shaking hands, smiling, and offering to light Rick's cigarette although he has his own lighter. He talks a little bit as we smoke, telling me that there's already one guy upstairs waiting, and a few more should be coming soon. I nod at that. I ask him how he likes Portland. He says he likes it a lot. He's thinking about moving here. I tell him, yeah, it's not bad, as long you've got work lined up beforehand. He nods at that.

As we're having this chat, another potential stand-in arrives. My competition is a stringy fella with feathered blonde hair to my messy black, his face is too thin and still bares the indescribable evidence that he once wore braces—but none of this bothers me. The thing that gets me is how he boldly steps between Rick and I and interjects, "Are you *Rick?*" then looks me over with beady, disapproving eyes. After Rick confirms that, yes, he is Rick, I smile at the newcomer, Alec, and introduce myself. I am not here to compete. I hope to get the job, sure, but I won't fight for it. I'll be friendly, act normal. I'll shake Alec's hand and wonder whether or not it's a compliment when I take off my hat and he says, "Wow. I really like your hair—does it do that naturally?"

Following Rick's lead, who has decided it's time to go inside, we head for the entrance. A young, plain but nice looking girl comes out of the door on her way out. Rick asks her how it went, and she says she was nervous, but she thinks it went well. Rick wishes her the best of luck, then we go inside.

I hold the door and let Alec go in first. From behind, as we start up a narrow stairwell to the upstairs loft where the production company has formed their temporary offices, I notice that Alec has somehow managed to attach a potential deal breaker, a piece of trash—just a fraction of a littered candy wrapper—to the outside of his left shoe. For half the length of the stairs I watch his left shoe climb higher and higher, closer to the second floor where all will see this piece of trash stuck to his shoe and never again take him seriously. Finally I decide that the right thing to do is to tap his shoulder and alert him to this small, yet crucial element of his appearance. He thanks me and removes the litter from his shoe, leaving it in the middle of the stairs where someone else might step on it. As he turns around I pick it up and put it in my pocket, then have to skip a few steps to catch up to Alec and Rick as we reach the level of the offices.

The second floor loft deceivingly appears to have been inhabited by these people for quite some time: the walls are decorated with posters from Gil Van S——'s older films, pictures he's taken, and several different calendars that pose as detailed schedules for the entire production with shooting beginning in three days; low set walls and several desks section off the large space into smaller areas designated for different people, and different tasks; there are big aluminum tins on a table in the center of the room with heaps of food, which the crew picks at as they walk by; everyone is moving around in a hurry, phones are ringing, everyone's already on the phone, speaking into hands-free devices. We are instructed to sit just to the left of the stairs where there are two long couches arranged as a waiting area. [Given unknown name, not Gil] will be with us in a moment, Rick says. Then he

476

removes himself to another part of the loft, leaving us alone on the couches though we can still see him not far away conversing with a beautiful brunette woman in knee high boots whose voice occasionally rises high enough to be heard.

Fifteen minutes and three arrivals later, [Given name] finally shows up and escorts the six of us through a dingy hallway and into a very large, bright space that has been turned into a photo studio. Giant white screens are hung as backdrops, a massive white canvas is laid on the floor with pieces of blue tape set in Xs in various spots, bright lights are arranged in a semi-circle that faces away from the backdrop, reflecting off more white surfaces and shooting softer light into the center of the room. The six of us are made to stand in a line to be sized up. I am clearly the odd man out by now. The five other guys next to me are at least two inches taller, of a slighter frame, and blonde. For some reason this puts me at ease rather than distressing me. I am not going to get this job and, therefore, can act with casual indifference to the situation at hand, speaking honestly without nervousness, and watching all the while curiously, almost baffled.

Our pictures are taken individually for records. One by one we stand on top of one of the blue-tape Xs, first facing forward, then to either side. Afterwards we are taken back into the front waiting area to wait our turn for a five-minute personal interview. Probably a bad sign, they point to me first and I am guided back through the dingy hallway into an even darker side room that looks as if it might be used for screenings at some point—there's a few plush, velvet chairs, a chaise lounge, three long couches, a projector, and a large screen. The only spot in the room that is lit is in a back corner. [Given name]'s assistant pulls one of the plush, velvet sitting chairs into the light and directs me to sit. The light is coming down from the high ceiling in such a way that it works as a spotlight, holding me in center stage. Two folding chairs are brought into the perimeter of the spotlight, backed a few inches into the shadows as in an interrogation. [Given name] comes back into the room and he and his assistant sit down. They're ready to begin.

First they want to know if I understand what a *stand-in* does on set. I tell them that a stand-in is used as a lighting and blocking tool by the director of photography, acting as a physical presence for the camera's focus, the cinematic composition, and lighting to be adjusted before the real, well-paid actor comes onto set. They say good. That's correct. And they add how important it is for a stand-in to be punctual, to follow direction, to be personable without being chatty, and so on; but, most importantly, the stand-in must resemble as closely as possible the actor whom he is standing in for. They are looking for someone who is a bit taller than I am, though it might not matter, and with blonde hair.

477

Would I be willing to dye my hair to a lighter shade of brown? Of course I would. I'm willing to do just about anything—it doesn't really matter to me. So long as my clothes stay on(a joke that misses). Mainly, I would just like to be a part of something that involves creativity—if not my own, then at least someone else's; and I'm interested in seeing the inner-workings of a film.

They nod their heads—yes, yes. They want to know a little about myself. I tell them that I'm a writer. I'm twenty-two years old at the moment. I'm from Nebraska. Where in Nebraska? I'm from Lincoln. [Given name] happens to have a good friend who is from Lincoln—I might know her sister. The name certainly sounds familiar to me, but I can't say at this moment that I know her sister. The conversation dies down. Unless—do I have any questions? No, I suppose I don't have any questions at the moment; what would be required of me seems pretty straightforward and simple. Then we're done.

I am led once again through the dingy hallway, back into the waiting area. The two men shake hands with me. They wish me luck. They don't tell me if I'm supposed to wait around, or if I'm free to leave; all they do is smile one more time not looking at me and call the next guy in. Again, he's taller than I am; he's got blonde hair. So do the other four gentleman in wait for their interviews. I decide that I'm probably supposed to leave now, so I do. I walk down the narrow stairwell and out the door.

On the sidewalk I light another cigarette, knowing that I've just missed an opportunity. I allow myself five minutes to regret that I've missed the opportunity, thinking that it would have been an interesting experience—it would've been fun. But that's just how it is and my five minutes are up, so I stop thinking about it.

5

SITTING IN A CAFÉ WITH LILLIAN, nighttime, I am out of work and it's already been two weeks since my only interview in Portland, which has led me to feel somewhat dejected. I am attempting to help Lillian write an essay on a book called, "Bones," and I know that it is only a matter of time before I have to write the thing myself. This fact irritates me.

I encourage her to title the essay, "The Nasty Bone: A Critical Essay"—a title which doesn't take. She's getting annoyed with me, or so I think she is, and with the essay itself. We both read "Bones" —I on a Sunday afternoon, when I take time off from the hunt(never look for jobs on a Sunday), sitting in our old green velvet chair with a blanket on my lap like a little girl, drinking tea by the window, enjoying

478

the rain; she here and there on public transit, sitting between drunks and freaks and people that smell bad and people who talk to themselves. She's under the assumption that I was able to get more out of the book than her, as I was able to read it straight through with my only interruption being to piss—which, I argue, is frequent. Truthfully, we both enjoyed the book and got out of it what we could—enjoyment, as I said, and the occasional overcute sentence or metaphor that made us cringe. It is not something either of us want to talk about.

This standoff between us is at risk of becoming an argument, which I would like to avoid at all costs. A beautiful brunette woman in knee high boots walks by our table, speaking loudly to the non-descript she's with; I can't help but watch the brunette woman very carefully as she walks by, not just because she's beautiful, but because I think I recognize this woman. My gaze, although averted from the standoff, does not help the delicate situation.

I say to Lillian, "I think I know that woman. "

She says curtly, "Who? The loud one?"

"Yeah," I tell her, "I guess." She immediately wants to know how I know her, looking at me suspiciously. "I think I saw her at the stand-in interview, talking to Rick. Her name is Adette. I can't really tell though. Maybe not." She is quick to doubt my potential recognition of the beautiful brunette woman, whose name she finds ridiculous. I am quick to concede that she's right, it's probably not her. It doesn't matter anyway. I'd rather not argue over it.

Changing the subject back to the essay, I ask Lillian if I can see what she has so far. She's got a little bit. And she knows what she wants to say, she's just having trouble putting it down. I write the first paragraph for her, and ask her what she thinks. She says it's good. I ask her what she wants to say next, and she tells me. I write another paragraph using her ideas, my words. We're working together now. I'm confident the essay will get finished. She notes that it *has* to get finished—it's due tomorrow.

Being out of work is being at your lover's disposal, which everybody knows is a full time job. I am riding out to Gresham with Lillian against my unspoken will, carrying with us a completed essay on the book called, "Bones." Although I promised myself to never come out here again, I couldn't deny her my company when she asked me to ride along with her. There were no alternatives.

The blue line train, which was empty at first, is filling up more and more at each stop towards Gresham; the closer we get, the bigger the bag of potato chips each passenger holds, the louder the snorts, and the more white velcro sneakers you see. Eventually, almost every single person on the train is wearing white velcro sneakers.

Then there is an announcement: *Now stopping at the Gresham Transit Center.* Soon thereafter I find myself not only in Gresham, but at the very center of its being, the grey nucleus of its existence—The Community College. It will be another six hours before we can leave.

I am in the library doing my best to stay busy, write stories, write poems, read something, don't look up, don't look at the clock, don't look at the shoes, when I receive a call from a number I don't recognize. I answer in a whisper, walking towards the exit. It's a woman on the other end of the line, her voice clear and sweet. "Hi, this is Adette," she says. "I saw you in the coffee shop last night."

I am already outside the library in the cold, smiling, trying to keep from trembling in case she can hear it in my voice. I try to reply coolly, "Yeah—I thought that was you. I wasn't sure. How are you?"

Adette tells me that she's doing well. But, she says, they're going to need a stand-in tomorrow. She wants to know my availability. It's not for the lead character or anything—they went a different route with him. But at least it's something.

As with Rick, I tell beautiful Adette that I am completely free, which she sounds happy to hear. She tells me the job is mine then, and for now it's just two days of work, tomorrow and the next day, but it could potentially lead to more.

I say to Adette, "I appreciate the call, and for giving me the opportunity. I'm glad you remembered me when you saw me last night." She says of course, sure, we needed someone. I ask, "What time do I need to be on set?"

Adette answers, "About ten in the morning—a little after. Just make sure you're there no later than ten-fifteen." I promise her I'll be on time. Then we hang up.

6

ARRIVING ON THE JOB AT PRECISELY TEN-FIFTEEN in the morning after catching a ride from an acquaintance—who later on I will learn was paid $20 by Lillian for the "favor"—I find myself haunting the set of a major motion picture. We are right off the Columbia River at Rooster Rock. It's raining and there are trees everywhere, mud, people in slickers and rubber boots. In a clearing there are two lines of trailers and tents set up like a miniature town. Everywhere there is free coffee and free food. I am making the rounds of this small town by myself, at a loss for what to do or where to go—too shy to ask for any free coffee or free food.

I bump into one of the men who interviewed me a couple weeks back; one of the men who did not give me the job as the lead character's stand-in. I've forgotten his name. He's forgotten my name as well. Regardless, we shake hands. We reintroduce ourselves. He claims to be happy to see me, and that he had hoped that I was the one who would've gotten the job I interviewed for. Probably a lie, but a good-natured one I think. I don't mind hearing it. I tell him thanks.

Jacob, the man's name, sends me over to wardrobe with a call sheet in my hands that contains the details of what I'll be doing today. In wardrobe they glance at my call sheet, then hand me a giant button up dress shirt that is my color cover—tan—that must be worn any time I am called to stand in front of the camera. It goes down to my knees like a dress. There's a girl sitting at a desk at one end of the wardrobe trailer, talking on the phone. She doesn't look up.

So in my new dress I take off from wardrobe, and catch one of the many white vans shuttling people back and forth from *basecamp* to *set*. I am the only one in the van. The driver says, "Hi." I say hello. Then she says, "Are you an actor?" No, I tell her, I'm a stand-in. It's my first day on set. She welcomes me and tells me not to be nervous, which I'm not, then stops the van at the top of a mud and gravel path that leads down to the set. I graciously thank her for the ride and she laughs like no one ever thanks her around here.

Walking down the muddy path to set, I am thankful that my heavy wool coat hangs down to my knees to hide the dress underneath. No one notices me as I walk down. Some of the crew, and the actors, are busy shooting a scene that takes place through the trees, but everyone else is listless, just hanging around having hushed conversations. I stand off to the side and turn into a tree, stable, silent. As I am the tree, which now appears to be on fire, smoking from its upper parts, I see a young, plain but nice looking girl come down the path. Her hair is very short now, and she's wearing red lipstick, but I recognize her as the girl leaving her interview as I went in for mine. Apparently hers did go well. She's talking with Jacob as she walks, and once they are to the bottom of the path and right in front of me they stop. There seems to be a pause in their conversation and Jacob is scanning the people on set with squinted eyes. He squints his eyes right through the tree that I am twice before coming back to me and unsquinting, locking his eyes on mine—"Ah!" he says. Then both of them approach.

I am introduced to the plain, but nice looking girl whose name is Anna. She is soft spoken just as her pale skin and tiny stature suggest. Jacob leaves the two of us to talk. She asks for a cigarette. I can tell by the way she inhales that she doesn't actually smoke—she looks like she's in pain from the one drag.

Anna is a little girl originally from rural Idaho, nineteen years old. This is her first big move away from home, and this is her first big job on a movie set. She is working as the stand-in for an Australian actress,

481

nineteen years old as well, who is about to become famous. Previews for the last movie she did are currently being shown in theatres prior to the feature, soon to be playing in theatres nation wide. The movie is the retelling of an old classic, "Alice," directed by the famous Tom B——. I have not yet seen this Australian actress, but I have not yet seen a lot of people in the world, and I cannot say I feel any especial yearning to see this one person—though I've heard she's very pretty.

Back to Anna, though, who is struggling with her half-gone cigarette, trying to keep me engaged in conversation probably out of cold boredom. Her nose is bright pink. My toes hurt inside of my boots. Anna asks, "Have you been up to *Crafty* yet?"

I tell her I have no idea what 'Crafty' is.

She says, "It's the school bus looking thing up on the hill—they've got all sorts of treats in there, and coffee, and pretty much anything else you could ask for. It's amazing. Come on—I'll show you."

I look through the trees and the scene that was being shot earlier is finished. Gil Van S—— is sitting with his director of photography, looking as if they are joking around rather than discussing the next scene to be shot. I am not sure what time it is, but it appears as though nothing is to be done any time soon. The word is that we're all waiting around until dark. I agree to walk with Anna.

"Here," Anna says, handing me what's left of her cigarette. "I don't want any more. "

I take the cigarette from her and take the last handful of drags as we start up the gravel and mud path towards what looks like a school bus on the hill.

The amount of pampering received on set, even for a person in a role as miniscule as "stand-in," is certainly cause for amazement. In *Crafty* alone, I am fed well on chicken meatball soup, and leave with two bananas, a package of crackers in my pocket, and a hot cup of coffee. And that's not to mention what's available back at basecamp, where in one tent, on a single plate, you can eat sirloin steak, grilled salmon and asparagus, scallops in creamy garlic sauce, spinach salads with nuts and berries and cheeses, and a heaping pile of buttery-smooth mashed potatoes with soft, still-warm rolls for dipping.

Then there are the space heaters around set, like portable electric fires contained in freestanding metal torches. As the rain comes down steadily, I am going between smoking along the perimeter of the set, edged against the dense woods, standing in soaking wet grass and mud puddles, to standing warm in front of the space heater, glancing around at the orange-tinted faces of what has now become evening. One of the faces belongs to Gil Van S——. At present, I am standing in the vicinity of a space heater and Gil Van S—— is three feet away from me; he is amiable with his stocking cap pulled back from his ears in the radiant warmth of the space heater, eating gummi bears one by one from his handful. He does not see me. Anna stands next me, openly doting on the nearby figure with her eyes. She whispers to me, very quietly, "Gil talked to me for the first time today. He asked me if I was warm enough." I nod, and casually look up at Mr. Van S—— who is nearly out of gummi bears.

Meanwhile night has come on in full, and the crew has begun to set up the next scene to be shot. An old grey Honda Accord has been parked at the bottom of the gravel path leading to set and lights are being indirectly positioned around it in such a way that they light up different parts of the trees for dramatic effect—sets of branches with particularly shapely leaves, or branches themselves that are particularly gnarled.

Someone radios a cue to an unknown person in an unknown location around set. Suddenly a second moon appears just over a cliff, far brighter than the real moon, which hangs in the sky opposite, a sliver, glowing inconspicuously. There is a stir. Everyone becomes excited at the appearance of this second moon. It means that all is falling into place. It's almost time to begin the shot. I think I hear my name being called at a distance. They're looking for [given character]'s stand-in. Anna taps me on the shoulder. "They're looking for you," she says.

I walk through the dark masses of the crew, away from the space heater, and am immediately reminded that my toes hurt inside my boots from the penetrating wet cold. One of the dark figures grabs me by the arm—it's Jacob. He leads me into the scene and opens the door to the Honda. There is a crew radio inside that broadcasts the various direction and movements of the crew. Jacob reaches in and turns it off as I go to take off my coat in order to expose my *color cover*—the dress—as I was earlier instructed to do. "Don't bother taking off your coat," Jacob says. "Just keep it on and stay warm. Here, hop in. "

I get in behind the wheel of the Honda and Jacob closes the door after me. Complete silence from the world outside of the car. The heater is on full blast and I'm sweating. I wish I had taken off my coat. I put my hands on the wheel and stare out the windshield as if I had been driving and have just now come to a stop, occasionally checking the rearview mirror.

Out the front windshield, with the headlights shooting forward, I see the half circle of the crew looking towards the car. Gil Van S—— and the director of photography are sitting in two chairs directly in front of me, looking towards the car as well, but by way of two monitors set in front of them. With all these eyes on me I become increasingly self-conscious—I sweat more, check the rearview mirror more(where there is no movement to be seen). I readjust my ass on the seat because it's already begun to go numb. Yet no one minds my unrest, my lack of ability to sit still. It occurs to me that no one is actually looking at me—they don't see me. They see the car and a figure in the car, but they don't see that the person who makes up this figure is me; instead they see the actor that will soon replace me in the car—and then forgetting about the fifteen takes they'll need to get the shot, seeing him only in the single finished product of the film, that ten to fifteen seconds of a clip where he(the character, not the actor) drives the car down the mud and gravel path and comes to a stop to let his friends out.

My existence shrinks. My self-consciousness leads me to the conclusion that I am the only one fully aware of myself. My thought and action are scrutinized solely by my Self. It is reassuring. My grip lightens against the wheel and my ass regains feeling. I am comfortable in my sweat, though a feeling rises from my belly that is similar to nausea, but it runs all the way up into my brain where I am not merely pretending to drive, but I am really, wholly driving and I am the only one who knows my present whereabouts. To anyone else I am either missing, or never existed in the first place. No one knows that I've left.

7

IT WAS A TERRIBLE AND INCONSIDERATE THING to do, steal my brother's car. But the thing is done and I'm driving his old grey Honda Accord through the desert night with the windows down, screaming along with the songs on the radio to stay awake.

My brother does not yet know I've gone with his car, though I'm already halfway from his place in Socorro, NM to my destination of Las Cruces where it is rumored that a beautiful pixie lives who can solve all of life's problems with a single look, a single kiss on the mouth, a single blow of a bubble with her gum.

The sun is almost up to blow away my blue dawn cover as I'm coming into the outskirts of Las Cruces, to a place called Mesilla—the actual residence of the rumored desert pixie. The sun is just about to come up and my brother will know then that I've gone missing, and taken his car with me. He will try to call me several times but I will ignore his calls. He will worry and call our father, call our mother, and they will all worry together. But I need not think about their worry. The sun is out now, flashing brightly against eastern-facing surfaces, and the pixie has just woken up, sensing my presence near, and she readies herself in the bathroom mirror to give me that single look, that single kiss on the mouth.

The desert morning is pleasant before the sun comes up fully to heat the dirt that's been cooling off all night in the dark. It's warm and dry, golden and blue. I am sitting on a bench next to a fountain and the fountain spray cools my expectant face. The stolen car is parked behind me three hundred feet away—it's resting, ashamed. The pixie is late. My brother is probably beginning to worry. I walk back to the car and I call my brother. He is awake and has been—he *was* worried but that worry now turns to anger. He hates me right now, I'm sure. He tells me to come back immediately—what the fuck am I doing in Las Cruces?

I say that I'll be back in awhile; that I'll take off now and be back in about three hours. He doesn't yet realize that this is a lie. He's irate, but takes me at my word. We hang up and I toss the phone onto the passenger seat of the car. I go back to my seat on the bench next to the fountain.

Staring at the spraying water and the coins in the water and the light reflecting off the spray mist, I think of nothing but the pixie. A moment or so later she appears as if my thoughts made her materialize. From behind me she suddenly appears, a tiny and beautiful thing, half-Mexican, dark hair and dark eyes, lighter skin with the hint of a darker shade. Her features are womanly but young, sharp but soft; her hips are narrow and her lips are full. Her voice is small, but engrossing. She reveals her name to me—Micaela, girl angel.

She comes to me and kisses me, her mouth parting on contact. Her hands, like a woman's on a little girl, touch my face and gently push away. She quietly looks at me. She's so small, so beautiful. She takes me by the hand and leads me away from the fountain. We walk past a line of small adobe homes with rusty metal crosses above their doors and into a small park. There is a gazebo in the middle of the park. She takes me to the gazebo and sits me down in its center. She kisses me again, then gently pushes away again. She looks at me, and says, "Now tell me you'll stay."

There's someone else walking across the park, getting in their car. I watch them for a moment, then look back at Micaela, her big brown eyes soft and watery, loving, real. There's no way I can refuse her. I say, "Yeah—I'm staying." She smiles and lets her tiny body down onto the gazebo floor, slowly bringing her face next to mine. I think she whispers, "Good."

8

THE DESERT IS NO LONGER A WASTELAND filled with wonder that purifies a man's spirit then spits him back out into the world renewed. It is a wasteland filled with dread that deceives and entraps him.

The desert takes from the rest of the land like a bastard. It steals its water and corrupts itself. It steals its vices and destroys itself. The more you say Salvation, the further away it gets. And the desert lives and breathes the word "Salvation," thus stripping it of its meaning. There is no such thing as salvation in the desert—there is only an illusion, a hallucination.

Men are given water to drink here and they find that the water is polluted, they are even thirstier. Men are given booze to drink here and they find that the booze is equal parts intoxicant and stimulant—they are drunk, fully awake, and still thirsty. They ask for more in their confused state—more booze, more water. The more they put into their bodies, the more they want, the more fucked up they get, the more they forget.

It is unclear to me now what the fuck I am doing in Las Cruces, NM, or how in the fuck I got here. But I am already running on my second year stuck in the desert. The Crosses: the place where a man arrives one day under the pretense of salvation and finds that the only way to it is by a slow crucifixion of self—or so the locals tell him. Marry the girl, forget about your family, they say. Marry me, the girl says—forget about yourself.

Only men of divinity are capable of forgetting themselves. For men of a lesser nature—hearty, real, earthbound men—the self is not a simple preoccupation that can be ridden from their thoughts with a little practice. It is a matter of fact. I am here, they say—I exist.

As a man bound to this earth in this present existence, right now, I am sitting at my desk in the window of my apartment, which I share with my desert pixie, and future wife, Micaela. She is off at work and I am staring out the window at the landscape which I have become entrapped in: sage brush in dirt lots, bent and broken chain-link fences, low-standing adobe walls in disrepair, native men in drunken stupors under the shade of small trees and awnings of corroding homes. There are cockroaches in our kitchen sink, under the sink, under the bed, in the cracks in the walls, the ceiling—everywhere. The wind is blowing forty-four miles per hour outside, kicking up dust, and brush, and whipping across the roof of our tiny apartment which was once the maid's quarters of an old, now defunct manor, creating a stir within the cockroaches and a sound within the apartment like so many ghosts wailing about what coulda been.

I am sitting at my desk listening to the ghosts and cockroaches, staring out the window, and thinking, too, about what could've been. Like another wailing ghost, I am writing down the *what could've been* with a sneaking suspicion that it is really the *what is* in another place, another time. I am putting it all down in secret in a book called, "The Imaginaries." In this book I am living out all the possible lives I could be living at present, in full. In one I am living alone in a suburb of Paris, studying the language and the way of living, eating rich foods and drinking a few beers every afternoon. In another I am working long hours in a breakfast restaurant in Tacoma, Washington, baffled each day that the place stays open though in clear violation of several health codes. In yet another I am working as a stand-in on the set of a major motion picture, sitting at the steering wheel of an old grey Honda Accord in Portland, Or. as cameras and eyes all point at and through me, experiencing a swarming in my brain that forces me to consider the What-Is of other futures.

In each of these futures there is the face of a different woman, the smell and feel of a different body. I am still myself, however, undergone the subtle variations of experiences that have forked off from one another and changed slightly henceforth. If Micaela reads the book it will be the end of us. She will be overcome with jealousy over my different lives filled with different women. She will tell me I have to go, and I will be okay with that—I want to go.

The time in a man's life when he is to learn harmlessly how to break it off with a girl is in his adolescence. The middle school years before sex is present, therefore leaving two bodies rather than the biblical One, thus making the split much easier, cleaner. In middle school I did not learn how to do this. I went from one girl to another, holding hands always with someone on either side of me, and when the one went it was only because she learned of the second. I denied myself a valuable lesson. I stunted my own growth. Years later I am left to answer the question, "How do you break a girl's heart and not feel bad afterwards?" Especially when you still love her, you're just not *in* love with her. It's an old question, yet consistently relevant.

"Try to become the monster," I say. Drink too often—more than you want to. Take down numbers in bars. Make her believe that you've cheated, though you never had it in you to actually cheat. "Or just write a book," I say then. Detail the actions of your brain on paper. Lead her through the dark place in your heart where you wish the word "us" didn't apply to the two of you. Leave her for good in your imagination. Leave her before you ever knew her and wipe her from your future memory. You can't feel bad about something that's never happened.

It's a heartbreaking task, the writing of this book called, "The Imaginaries." I am writing steadily in the sixth chapter now. I can feel the ideas coming to life. I am potentially at risk of slowly going mad—a position I am used to. It is best to take a break at these times; to ground yourself with the taste and the smell of the dirt, the wind blowing dust in your face, the solid feel of the earth underfoot.

Walking along a dirt road past the pecan orchards towards the interstate, warm dust blows over everything. Although it is warm, a thin
coat must be worn to keep the airborne dust off your skin; a hat must
be worn to keep the dust out of your hair; sunglasses must be worn to
keep your vision unobstructed. I refuse to wear sunglasses when I am
in this fragile state, at high risk of slowly going mad. Sunglasses would
only accelerate the process by removing my physical self further from
the real world in front of me, a fraction further into the dark recesses
of possibility. The dirt is blowing into my eyes and the road blurs from
the subsequent tears. I am walking along regardless of my flawed vision, heading in the direction of a small convenient store where I know
they sell beer, cigarettes, snacks.

   In front of the convenient store there is a small space of sidewalk
that is sheltered from the wind. After my small purchase of cheese crackers, a tall can of beer, and a pack of cigarettes, I sit in the small
protected space and enjoy my treats while watching the cars pass along
the interstate. People headed in either direction—east or west—and I
have no idea where they're really going. License plates from all around
the country—they could be going anywhere. A white van pulling a
small trailer steers into the convenient store parking lot. They've got
Arizona plates. Eight young folks pile out of the van, appearing to be
in some sort of band. Some head inside for water and a piss, some light
up cigarettes; the ones walking inside to use the restroom nod as they
pass. There's one fella in particular that catches my attention as he
hurries inside to piss. He's got a face on him that seems to be looking
for someone, in need of something—and badly. When he comes back
out, he's got a small purchase of cheese crackers, a tall can of beer, and
a pack of cigarettes. He makes eye contact with me, then looks down
at my shoes—plain old thin-soled tennis shoes. I look down at his
shoes and they look like something out of the pioneer days, and I feel
myself suddenly wearing those boots, walking around in them. "Nice
boots," I say to him in an attempt to grab his attention so I can see his
face again.

   "Thanks," he says, looking up and nodding. As his face turns
upward towards mine, his features startle me. I recognize them in an
uncomfortable way that gives me a familiar, dull headache. We both
look away. We both stare out at the road to a place where there may or
may not be wall-like mountains as if they were the gateway to this
territory.

   I ask him, "Where are you guys headed?"

   He says, "Well, my friends here are all in a band. They came
through Anaheim, where I've been living, and offered to take me

along. I just felt like getting out of California. So I'm not exactly sure where we're going, I'm just along for the ride—I think the next stop is Austin."

The band has all gathered back at the van, and taken their seats. The sliding side-door is left open, waiting for the last passenger to get in—this guy. He says, "Do you live around here?" I nod to say that I do. And then, "You know, the most beautiful girl I've ever met lives around here." At that he stops, nothing more. I don't want to ask her name, or what she looks like. I don't want to find out if I know her—Cruces isn't exactly a big city. He doesn't want to elaborate anyway. His ride is waiting for him. He gives me a last nod, avoiding eye contact, and a small wave.

"Good luck," I say.

"Yeah—thanks," he says. "Same to you. "

I watch him get into what looks to be the worst possible seat in the van, cramped into the back, having to climb over a few seats and heads to get there. The sliding door shuts and the engine starts. As they pull back onto the interstate, a cloud of dust rises and the wind quickly carries it in the opposite direction. For a moment my head is very light, and I feel as though I am going to faint. Then my headache goes away and I feel fine.

Evening's coming on. Micaela will be getting off work soon. She'll be bringing dinner with her. I have to get back home to hide the new pages of the book before she arrives. The book is not ready for her to read yet. But I cannot bring myself to move, to go hide the new pages of the book, even though I *am* a little hungry. I like watching the cars pass on the interstate in the fast approaching dusk. I like sitting by myself, drinking this solitary beer. Micaela will come home and find them then, the new pages. She will tell me I have to go, and I will be okay with that. As far as I can tell, there is no other way.

9

I AM BECOMING THE GHOST OF ANOTHER MAN, in the real, physical, invisible sense. The initial presence for his later action —then lost. This man is an actor. In other words, he is the embodiment of Fiction. He is someone else's brainchild. Behind him is another man, a *real* man, whose occupation is merely to be someone else. He is also a ghost. When I first saw this other ghost I thought it was me. I thought that I was hallucinating. But I quickly learned to recognize his features as similar at best, and I no longer really see that ghost—I only see through him, around him.

As a ghost I am free, but sad: free to travel lightly, jumping through various landscapes and exploring the possibilities that life has to offer; sad to be seeing the different possibilities that life has to offer, yet never fully living them. When I come to the place of my body's current whereabouts, I am somewhat startled by the conditions. My nerves are tingling. Today's stand-in work consists of sitting in the old, grey Honda Accord—same one from last night—in a large studio in North Portland. So I am sitting in the car and in the car with me are two more stand-ins; Anna is in the passenger seat and Brett is in the back. Brett is the stand-in for the lead male role in Gil Van S——'s new feature film. His job is the one I interviewed for weeks ago—which I didn't get, and which lasts the duration of filming—but I am not bitter about it even though this is my last day of work. We are all sitting peacefully together in the car, a camera situated just inside the back, passenger-side window, set lights fully ablaze in the otherwise blacked-out studio, and several men working around the car, peering inside.

They are preparing to shoot the scene inside the car that precedes yesterday's scene, wherein the car pulls down the mud and gravel path and parks. The shooting of the scenes is on a separate timeline as that of their appearance in the movie, but this will not be known in the movie itself where the continuity will be self-evident, inalienable, unbreakable. Today's action and dialogue will never occur out of sequence. Whenever the thing is happening, it's happening.

Where yesterday the car was parked at the bottom of the mud and gravel path, today we are driving in the car to that location. The car is on four dollies so as to be easily maneuvered on the smooth cement floor of the studio. A spray bottle is used to mist the windshield and windows. Five men holding yellow-filtered lights run by the side of the car one by one, alternating sides, mimicking country streetlamps to make the car appear in motion. Two men crouch at the rear bumper, gently rocking the car as if it were on a gravel road. A tape-measurer is extended from the camera lens in the back, passenger-side window all the way to the point where it's touching the tip of my nose. I am told to put my hands on the wheel as if I were driving and hold still—*hold real still.*

It is impossible for a ghost to hold still. The slightest breath will blow it any which way, and it will see all of the world in this way and grow increasingly sad over it because it cannot be a true part to the world's whole. Sitting in this old, grey Honda Accord my body may appear to be still, but remember that I am a ghost, an illusion—my phantom body remains static while my eyes and soul are in motion.

Within my brain I am driving through the desert night with the windows down, screaming along with the songs on the radio o stay awake. The car I am driving is an old grey, Honda Accord that belongs to my brother, but I've stolen it in the middle of the night. My brother doesn't yet know that I'm gone, but I'm already over halfway from his place in Socorro, New Mexico to my destination of Las Cruces where I've heard a beautiful pixie lives whom I've arranged to meet in the morning.

It's a fucked up thing I've done, but I'm driven by the off chance that this tiny woman can truly save me from something, whether that be myself or otherwise. And I'm already pulling into the outskirts of Cruces into a small, historic district called Mesilla—this is where the desert pixie lives. The sun is up and it begins to warm the night-cool earth. Eastern facing surfaces gleam with bright yellow light. The fountain by which I am sitting, waiting for the pixie, reflects the early sunlight in its spray and creates tiny rainbows. The pixie is late for our meeting. I walk back to the parked car and take out my cell phone—it shows that my brother has called eight times, each one missed. He knows by now that his car is gone, I am gone. He is probably worrying. I'll call him soon to tell him that I'm safe—I'll be back shortly. I stick the phone into my pocket and go back to the fountain, seating myself back on the bench until the pixie arrives.

Staring into the pale colors of the tiny rainbows of the fountain spray, I am stricken with fear from my own actions. I cannot bare the thought of my brother's disapproval, and worry. He will call our mother, he will call our father—they will all worry together. When I get back to Socorro later in the afternoon he will be angry, and he will tell me I can no longer live with him. Our father will fly into town and take us to breakfast. He will give me an ultimatum. He will say, "You can either come back to Lincoln(Nebraska) with me, or go work for my associate in Rancho Cucamonga, California where he's got a warehouse. You can't stay here." I will be ashamed then, and choose the warehouse in southern California over going back to the town where I'm from to work for my father. It would be too embarrassing to go back. In any case, it will be clear that I can no longer stay in New Mexico. I will have made this effort to see the desert pixie, badly wanting to be with her, only to find that the effort was in vain—it really took me further away. And all I will have is this one morning in the gold and blue desert, wherein I stole my brother's car just to see her. I will have this one morning and I will pine over it and her until the time comes again where I can make it back to her. What was a strong affection of the brain for something it knew little of while creating the rest will get just a taste, a brief physical awareness of the real thing, and it will become an obsession of the half-real of the what could've been. I will have her full features to dream of then while plotting ways back into her embrace—and what features!

That's what you do when you're young, I think. You dream and you plot, regardless of the probability of realizing those dreams and plots because in conjunction with your actual, current circumstance it makes for a fuller life. As I am already regretting my later departure, and imagining a future visit, the rainbow colors grow darker for a moment then disappear. I turn around to see that the sun has been blocked by a small figure standing in just the right spot. Shooting from each of the figure's dark sides are bright rays of light that form a golden circle like those that are behind the painted heads of Renaissance Saints. My eyes adjust to the stark contrast and I see that the figure belongs to the desert pixie. She stands at maybe five feet two inches, with a tiny, angular face and eyes in perfect proportion. Her skin is fair, and soft, but tanned by the sun. Everything is smooth—her hair like black satin sheets on a bed made-up for lovemaking; the color of her eyes like milk chocolate wrapped in clear cellophane. And moving down from the head to the small domes of breasts, the narrow hips, and the slender legs that don't touch, letting the sun shine between them all the way up to the crotch. Back to her mouth —full, shining, and happy. And out of the mouth her name is revealed, quietly: Micaela, girl angel.

I stand up and move to the side of the bench where Micaela comes to me and kisses me, her mouth parting on contact. Her hands, like a woman's on a little girl, touch my face and gently push away. She quietly looks at me. She's so small, so beautiful. She takes me by the hand and leads me away from the fountain. We walk past a line of small adobe homes with rusty metal crosses above their doors and into a small park. There is a gazebo in the middle of the park. She takes me to the gazebo and sits me down in its center. She kisses me again, then gently pushes away again. She looks at me, and says, "Now tell me you'll stay. "

I look into Miceala's big brown eyes, soft and watery, loving, real. I hate to say it, but I tell her I don't think I can stay—just not right now. She says she understands, then smiles and lets her tiny body down onto the gazebo floor, slowly bring her face next to mine. She puts her head on my shoulder for a moment, then raises it back up to kiss me. My phone begins to ring in my pocket. I take it out to see who it is— it's my brother calling. I apologize to Micaela, telling her I have to take the call.

After I tell him I'm safe, my brother is absolutely pissed to hear where I am. He says, "What the fuck are you doing in Las Cruces? "

There's no reasonable answer to that question. I simply got in the car and started driving. Now that I'm here, I don't really know what I'm doing(a lie, looking at the beautiful girl angel). He tells me that I need to come back—immediately. My brother is a sensitive man with high blood pressure. He sounds like he's been worked up all morning. The painful tone of his voice is more than I can take. I concede that I'll leave now and be back in a few hours. I apologize to him and hang up.

Micaela, with her tiny legs pulled in towards her body in the center of the gazebo, looks expectantly up at me. I had stood up to take the phone call and leaned on the gazebo railing. Now I go back to her.

"Listen," I say, "I know I haven't been here very long, but I've got to go— I'm sorry."

"I know," she says. "When can I see you again?"

"Oh god, I don't know. Hopefully soon. I'd like to see you again soon."

I put out a hand to her and from her seated position she grabs it. I help her up easily, and she nestles her head right into my chest, hugging me. She turns her head now, digging the end of her chin into my chest with her face tilted upwards. She whispers, "Good."

I lean down into the little mouth and kiss it again. It's soft and warm. My nerves are tingling. The blood rushes out of my face to elsewhere. I pull her in tight and hang on until it hurts. The pressure is building between us, we can both feel it, so she takes her small hands and puts them where her head had rested, right in the center of my chest, and she gently pushes away. She's smiling. She tells me I have to go, and I nod. I smile at her and promise to see her again soon. I say goodbye and walk back across the park alone, leaving her there in the gazebo like a young bride in wait of a groom and an audience. She's beautiful, so it shouldn't take long. I get back into the car then, both sad and exalted, and put the car in gear, leaving the music off for the long drive back up to Socorro.

10

THE FILM CREW HAS SHUT DOWN AN ENTIRE STREET in a quiet NE Portland neighborhood for the evening portion of today's shoot. Only two of the houses on the street are actually to be used: the one on film, and the other across the street.

The house off-camera is set up as a waiting area for extras—a hundred extras are coming out tonight. The garage door is open along with the door into the basement where there is a bathroom; chairs are arranged everywhere, bad coffee and cheap snacks, space heaters.

Across the street is the house on-camera. It is elaborately decorated like a haunted house where in the film a party is to take place on Halloween night. It is a spectacle in the upper middle-class neighborhood with Thanksgiving already next week. The neighbors all stand outside of their homes on their green, manicured lawns watching the action. Large trailers line the street outside of frame. Crewmembers buzz around looking busy. The three main stand-ins are called to their positions on the walkway in front of the haunted house. We are told to

493

just stand there—and no smoking.

From my taped X on the walkway, I watch as the white vans come in succession carrying loads of extras dressed in Halloween costumes. The Australian actress walks inconspicuously around set through the arriving extras who have no way of recognizing her yet. She is wearing a giant parka over her tiny frame and parts of her Geisha costume can be seen underneath. She is taking pictures of everything with an old medium-format camera. She sees me take notice of her and she smiles; I smile back at her then look down—it's a game we've been playing all day.

The Australian actress, Mae, is much more attractive than I would have hoped to admit. Her long golden hair has been cut for her role, framing a face young and fragile, unbelievably soft-looking, pouty red lips, a few barely visible freckles on her nose. And she's not attractive because she played "Alice" in that movie; she's attractive because that's just how it is—it's in the way she saunters about set, the way she moves gingerly and quietly, taking pictures all the time she's not on camera, smiling discreetly. Charm exudes from her in a way unknown to American girls. Hers is different—it's subtler, purer. Every time she passes me—the stand-in, the ghost—she lifts her eyes from her down turned head and looks directly at me, smiles kindly, then looks away. That's the game we're playing; we haven't said hello yet, but we are, nonetheless, well acquainted.

Anna the stand-in, the plain but nice looking girl, looks somewhat like Mae. Make-up has given her the same haircut and lipstick. Wardrobe has given her the same Geisha costume equipped with the same short black wig. But there is not the same movement in Anna, the same attraction, or illusiveness. She stands a few feet behind me next to Brett, both on their taped X's. She jokes around in a mousey way and touches Brett's shoulder occasionally. She calls my name in a whisper. I turn my head and she smiles and waves with a nervous energy. I give her a big, dorky, animated wave. Then I glance around for Mae—she's nowhere.

All the while the white vans have been arriving with the extras. There's about a hundred extras in outrageous costume now, and an assistant director begins placing them in a line on the walkway to the haunted house, in various spots on the lawn, some on the sidewalk either coming or going from the house, some in the house itself. They've filled in all the holes. I am surrounded by them. Brett and I are the only ones not in costume, and you can see the extras eyeing us, thinking that we might be somebody. When they realize they don't know our faces, or our names, they don't care any longer. The guy in front of me is wearing a boring frat party toga costume. He turns himself and his half-naked belly towards me openly, looking into my face. He says, "Are you one of the actors?"

"No," I say. "I am no one." He turns around after learning I'm not an actor, or anybody, and the whole scene not just looks like a full-on party now, with the lights flashing here and there, spooky, but it *feels* like a party—only I'm not drunk. Strange that I'm not drunk. Sort of wish I had a flask in my pocket to complete the ambiance.

Once the assistant director has settled all the extras precisely into their random-looking positions, he stands at the top of the front steps of the house and looks over the crowd. He walks through the mass of people and moves a few costumed groups around to different spots, getting the composition just right. He goes to the front steps again and reviews his work for a second time—perfect. He makes an announcement: "Okay, everybody, listen up! Thank you all for coming out tonight. Your presence here is appreciated and everyone looks great. I want you to look around you—get a good look at who's standing next to you, and remember your position. We're going to have lunch now, and when we come back I need you to go to the place you're in now. The exact position you are in right now is the one you will return to."

Lunch at 10.15pm is an affair to remember not only because of the inaccurate term used for the meal at this time of night, but because of the spread. At the church where basecamp is set up for the day the white vans shuttle everyone to their respective entrances—extras in through the basement, cast and crew, including stand-ins, in through first floor.

To the basement's pasta and meatballs, the first floor gets to have their pick of anything a person might desire to keep their blood sugar balanced, their bellies full, and their heads clear: hot and cold plates of gourmet dishes, hot and cold drinks, made to order omelettes, sautéed rice noodles and meat and vegetables, salads with all the fancy toppings, cheesecakes and other sweet treats—just about anything conceivable that's highly palatable.

I fill my plate with fish in lemon-cream sauce, mashed potatoes that I've topped with peas, a giant salad, and several dinner rolls—I'm going to use the rolls to make tiny fish sandwiches; to drink I'm just having water. The problem with the separation of extras and cast/crew comes in the matter of seating. Although we've gotten our first-rate meals on the first floor, the only place to eat them is in the basement of the church at any of the large cafeteria-style tables. I sit down at a table whose diners eat heaping piles of spaghetti and meat sauce. I eat quickly, not talking or making eye contact. I am somewhat ashamed of my delicate fish sandwiches, though they taste great. Finishing my meal, I've yet seen where to place my dishes. Rather than appearing lost by wandering around with my dirty plate, I hide it behind a poster board that looks like it was made in Sunday school by the younger kids—"The Ten Commandments," it reads, listing all ten at length. Then I casually float out of the basement, unseen.

Outside there is a van waiting. Before I can light a cigarette, I am ushered into the van by a nondescript assistant and taken back to set. The assistant director sees me get out of the van on set and as he approaches I can hear him say, "Good." Then he says, "Come with me," leading me back into the position where I am confident I would have made it to by myself—the place marked with the blue X; right where I was before.

I cannot understand this rushed behavior; on set there are only a handful of crewmembers, no actors, and no extras. I am virtually the first person back on set from *lunch* and it's cold. In position on the walkway to the house, I ask the assistant director if I can smoke. He tells me that I cannot smoke while on set, and I watch him immediately go into the neighbor's yard to smoke. I am dancing in place from the cold, curling my toes in my boots. Gil Van S—— is one of the few people still on set. He's joking around with the director of photography, snacking on pistachios.

After a few more minutes of joking, Mr. Van S—— finally looks over at me, dancing in place just a few feet away from him, and he says, "I think you can go ahead and have that cigarette now—we're not really doing anything yet."

"Thanks," I say, already moving over towards the base of a giant tree where I will crouch and smoke. "That's all I needed to hear."

He nods and gives his goofy grin, then goes back to his pistachios. There's a small pile of their shells at his feet. The fresh, warm ones still give off a little steam.

11

IN TWO DAYS OF WORK YOU CAN'T EARN ENOUGH to pay the bills, but you will at least regain good standing with your girlfriend. There was never a point when I relinquished my manhood, but with a hundred and fifty dollars in my pocket I am suddenly, to Lillian, "her man" again.

It is the morning before Thanksgiving Day, and we are taking a pleasant stroll together en route to a breakfast joint. We've already been to the grocery store this morning to purchase all of the necessities for tomorrow—I paid for everything. Lillian's arm is through mine as we walk down the city sidewalk, playfully avoiding piles of dog shit as if it were a video game. Yet even this idyllic walk and show of affection cannot tame the natural inclination for my eye to wander. A block ahead of us, walking in our direction, I spot what looks to be a very attractive female in an oversized coat. Her pace, matched with ours, quickly closes the distance between us and with every step her features become more apparent: first short blonde hair, pale skin(not uncommon in this city); now tiny feet, and thin legs, soft pink lips. Closer yet and my suspicions are confirmed—this woman is attractive, wow. And now right on top of us, she glances up from her sidewalk-directed gaze and makes eye contact with me. "Hi," she says very happily and smoothly, the tone of her voice sparking something within me that is startling—I know her.

Out of surprise, I make a quick response that does not conceal my pleasure at seeing her: "Hey!" Yet no one stops. Lillian and I continue on arm in arm, and the beautiful looking girl in the oversized coat continues on as well in the opposite direction.

"What a cunt!" Lillian hisses unflatteringly, the girl probably still within earshot. She then asks suspiciously, "Who was *that?*"

My delight is too great to be stifled. I tell her, "That was Mae—the lead in Gil Van S——'s movie!"

Annoyed, she says, "Okay...and she *knows* you? "

I explain to her that Mae and I don't exactly know each other, but my two days on set did require close proximity to her and therefore she, clearly, just happened to have recognized me. This does not satisfy her obvious revulsion of the brief, friendly interaction. If anything, it has only made it stronger. She cannot see why an actress would take any notice at all of a *stand-in*. This fact exacerbates a previously voiced fear. She believes that my two days(!) of work as a stand-in(!!) will lead to further opportunities, which will then result in me becoming famous and leaving her for an actress(!!!); she mentions the image, only half jokingly, of that actress being nineteen years old and of me doing coke off of her ass. I assure her that I have not and never intend to do coke. My heart is too sensitive. My body in general is too sensitive to be under the influence of any sort of drug—even coffee, babe! I purposely neglect to deny the accusation as concerning the actress; it's impossible to say what will happen in the future, although I do believe nineteen is an improbably low guess.

Harmless as it was, the encounter with Mae has ruined breakfast. Lillian's arm has already been removed from its interlocked position in mine. At the restaurant, she'll be standoffish and send text messages to her best friend under the table: "She said hi to him on the street and when I asked who she was he said, 'Oh, that was Mae W——,' like it was no big deal. What a cunt!" I will refuse to acknowledge the source of her bad mood. Unaffectedly, I will order the eggs benedict. No coffee; just water. And I will make use of the silence between us by daydreaming about possible later encounters with Mae the charming.

When operating properly, holidays have a way of temporarily resolving any problems that may exist between loved ones. Although the problem between Lillian and I is much bigger than a 'hello' said to a very pretty Australian actress—her negative reaction to it being but a side-effect of the bigger problem(my wandering eye, also but a side-effect of my overall dissatisfaction with what I have begun to consider a "sedentary lifestyle")—Thanksgiving does not fail to alleviate the situation. We will be acting as host to my brother and the tailor, both of whom will be arriving at any minute; and we will play well the part of the happy couple.

I have been up since the wee hours of the morning, slaving away in the dark kitchen to execute what will be my very first preparation of the Thanksgiving meal. My extreme focus and determination has only been possible by way of romanticizing myself in the kitchen as a French chef who must produce a delectable meal for several hundred snooty patrons, coupled with many small tumblers of red table wine. I have prevented myself from becoming drunk by allowing the tumbler to be refilled only after the completion of a given task—once after the yam casserole, once after the green bean casserole, once after the sausage and onion dressing, once after the mashed potatoes, once after the dough is formed for the rolls, and so on.

At present, it is no later than 10 or so in the morning and I am putting the turkey in the oven—all stuffed and basted with garlic butter and black pepper—accompanied by three onions cut into halves, and, therefore, am about to refill the tumbler again. Lillian comes into the kitchen still in her scant sleeping clothes and her teeth unbrushed. The smells have had an agreeable effect on her awakening—she hugs my busybody from behind, around the waist, as I finish dressing her Tofurkey.

"Good morning," she says. I greet her likewise, turning around to give her a proper good morning kiss. She's excited by this, and scampers off into the bathroom giggling. I hear the water turn on to fill the tub. I down the contents of the tumbler after successfully getting the turkey into the oven. In my head I put a check next to the "turkey" box on my list of objectives; the other boxes remain open, patiently awaiting their own checks for when their corresponding dishes are placed in the oven in an order I formulated with careful consideration of baking times and temperatures. Thus far, the meal is going according to this mental plan. An achievement that will, no doubt, soon lead to the first stages of intoxication.

The intercom buzzer sounds in the apartment, feigning the noise of a buzzer going off to signify the completion of this or that dish's time in the oven. I refill the tumbler, and it occurs to me that nothing is ready to come out of the oven quite yet; that, and I'm not even using a timer. The buzzer sounds again. I go to the door and answer it, "Hello?"

My brother's voice comes up from the ground floor. I press the "door" button to let him in and unlock the door to the apartment. The water turns off in the bathroom and Lillian calls, "Is that your brother?" I tell her that it is, and she curses. I can hear the water begin to drain from the tub, then the bathroom door bursts open and she streaks across the entryway into our closet—"I'm not even dressed!"

With the arrival of my brother, I make the switch from wine to beer, thus securing for myself a state of constant, mild intoxication. He helps me in the kitchen and drinks with me. We catch up through a thousand ridiculous anecdotes. The swinging door is propped open into the main living area where Lillian sits on a milk crate, reading from an anthology of short stories and occasionally chiming in to correct the details of the anecdotes I recount to my brother. She looks incredibly happy, and is increasingly satisfied with herself for her interjections; my heart feels big when I look at her.

Anyone with a sibling or a friend they've known for a long time can infer from their own experiences the specifics of a kitchen conversation on a holiday, so it is unnecessary to mention in any detail the dialogue itself; suffice it to say that time is measured only in the growing idiocy of the stories being told, and the number of empty beer cans that accumulate on the counter. As for the meal, it should be noted that my romantic vision from the early morning was not unprecedented in that the blood running through my veins can be traced back into the peasant households of France and it is, therefore, second nature for me to prepare large meals with ease. Each new dish is put into the oven and removed with automatic precision. The various smells thicken the air in the apartment until it is so heavy that the mere act of breathing becomes like an hors d'oeuvre, stimulating the appetite without spoiling it.

Six empty tall boys on the counter and the turkey coming out of the oven, the tailor's arrival, on cue, is announced by the loud buzz of the intercom resounding through the small apartment. Lillian moves not one inch from where she's seated herself atop a pillow on the floor; she, with a silent roll of her eyes, communicates her annoyance towards me for having invited the tailor to join us. I halt my final touches on the meal to let him in.

Several strange things could be said of the tailor. For starters, his accomplishments supersede the usual restraints placed upon his profession, as the miniature wardrobes he creates are specifically designed for dolls he has manufactured from his own freeform patterns and with his own hands—so he is a doll maker as well; and although he will sometimes sell these dolls for decent sums of money, his main income is given him monthly by the government for reasons which remain a mystery to me. Also, he belongs to a very select group of people that can call themselves "eunuchs," due to a decision he made ten years ago to have his testicles removed by a lesbian couple in a barn in eastern Washington; this was at a time in his life when he was on his way to becoming a woman, and which, in turn, prompted another decision which was to change his traditional man's birth name to something more feminine. He no longer aspires to be a woman, which makes the name "Ali" seem extremely incongruous to the bearded figure who is currently coming through the door into the apartment.

With these strange things in mind—amongst many others—what seems to me the strangest of all is that the tailor's entrance and his flamboyant, "hellew," is met by mumbled greetings that are slightly less than warm, and an awkward break in conversation that was previously fluid, which, no doubt, is apparent to the tailor. I suddenly feel bad for the tailor, and regret having invited him into an atmosphere that was obviously more symbiotic without his inclusion. Regardless, I sit him in a place of distinction, in the green chair at the head of our tiny table, and ask him if he will do us the honor of giving the blessing. He obliges: "Let us all be grateful that we find ourselves today in good company and with good food...Amen."

And all through the meal—which I will shamelessly admit is delicious—the tailor will insist that I accompany him next door to his apartment afterwards for a few minutes to see the feast that he prepared for his dolls. I will not be able to politely refuse him, so we will walk over together and I will look upon the miniature table where a dozen dolls are seated, staring disinterestedly at the stuffed and dressed Cornish hen, so small, completely untouched.

12

THERE IS A BELIEF AMONGST THE MAJORITY of Americans that one cannot eat or drink too much on Thanksgiving—this is false. After we've eaten and drank our fill—and after the tailor, as expected, has taken me to see the miniature Thanksgiving feast next door—we find ourselves around the apartment, horizontal, feeling the varying effects of a condition commonly called "The Itis."

We have eaten and drank too much; our bodies are overloaded vessels. We make small, sluggish movements and feel as though we have exerted ourselves. Two hours pass. Slowly, digestion takes its course and we are, miraculously, somewhat refreshed. And just in time for the second stage of our holidays—drinks and eats at Lillian's boss's apartment, the owner of the market.

We manage to make the walk to their apartment; when we arrive, we are confronted by a large, traditional spread. Our attempts at claiming to be full are futile; Lillian's boss, Chris, exclaims, "It's Thanksgiving—you can never have too much to eat! And what can I get you to drink?" Secretly, I shake my head. We are resigned to call out our drink orders and pick at the assorted plates of food set out for our *enjoyment*. Our bodies are swollen and heavy. I fight the urge to sleep— I must remain alert, grateful, and charming.

Two of Lillian's coworkers are present along with their significant others; her store manager, Maria—Chris's girlfriend—prances around as well. It is apparent that they, like us, have all eaten and drank too much, yet it continues. A game of chess is being played. A cigarette is being smoked on the balcony. Another drink is poured—and another. Maria reigns over a conversation had while slouched against the kitchen counter. Lillian has been sucked into her orbit, suffering. I mosey on over to the rescue.

"Maria," I say politely, "would you mind if I made another drink?"

She pushes herself up from the counter into full attention. She looks me dead in the eye and says, "You—you!" She points at my chest, her elbow crooked like some gun-wielding thug's. Her eyes are distant, yet fiery. She moves her face close to mine, breathing expensive tequila up my nose as she announces, without the slightest degree of slur, "I like you!"

I take the compliment extremely well, though making eyes at not Maria but at the various bottles of liquor on the counter, making my visual selection for (soon)future enjoyment. She repeats herself, breathing up my nose again: "I...like...you!"

This second time around, though taken with visible ease, requires some effort. Her finger, pointing at my chest, almost digging into it, is distracting me. I've forgotten why I've come over here. Oh yes, as a decoy—and what a successful one I have been! Lillian has slipped away from us into a quieter, more involved conversation with a coworker.

I catch my thoughts wandering. Back to matters of immediate importance. To the woman at hand, standing inappropriately close to me, I say(sounding earnest, I hope), "No *really*, Maria—thank you; I like you too. Should we drink to that?"

The mention of alcohol does the trick; her attention, without an unneeded verbal agreement, is moved to scouring the liquor bottles, nearly knocking them over in the process of looking for the right one. I suggest the whiskey—she pulls out the tequila and pours doubles.

With some people(seasoned drinkers especially) it is hard to tell when they go from plain drunk to blackout drunk—not so with Maria.

After the mandatory, though brief, wince that follows tequila, I literally see the "click," the fracture—right there in her eyes—and she is gone. I will spare history and future history the ensuing slurred conversation because the words involved, as embarrassingly ordinary as they are, and terribly broken, are words that most any person I can think of will not have a hard time imagining for themselves; nor will they have a hard time imagining her tone, her conduct, the slip of her hand on the counter, a quick grasp of my arm, and so on as it goes—a common American night, to be sure; to history and future history, I will leave it at this: Maria will touch on such topics as my charm, my good looks, how personable I am, complimenting me ad nauseam, and eventually, in the sloppy heat of late night, she will offer me a job at the market.

13

I AM CONSIDERING PUTTING EVERYTHING I WRITE within quotations in order to acknowledge that anything I say has already been said by someone, somewhere, and at some time. If it were not for the fact that such a task seems extremely tiring, I would certainly do so. I am, however, quite lazy when it comes to such matters, so I will ask you, reader—if you exist; *some* of you must exist—to please imagine the quotations are there, though invisible, from here on out; no, rather from the beginning of this paragraph, forward.

Having made that statement(again, and again, and so on), I will also say that the acknowledgment of such does not hinder my desire to continue to speak, to tell stories, to repeat, repeat. In fact, I am some-what encouraged by it because A) anything I say can be attributed to someone else, therefore largely freeing me of the personal respons-ibility which comes with "individual thinking" and creative license, and B) if I am compelled to reiterate things said repeatedly throughout the ages, then there is clearly a timeless quality to whatever I say, even if it appears minute or trivial on the surface—a fine notion that I am more than willing to believe in. And it is with this belief, inspiring as it does—through absolute self-assurance, a penchant for the dramatic flair(a tone I find quite enjoyable and therefore will not abandon)—that I will carry on from here, right now, in this future as only I(and now you) may know it.

I have just come inside from a brief and very quiet smoke on the fire escape that overlooks NW 23rd St. in the grey mid-morning of this notoriously clean city and I discover—or remember, for whatever reason—that not a single picture in the apartment reflects that I have a past which precedes that which I share with my current girlfriend, Lillian. Aside from the several up-to-date pictures hung of the two of us together, separate, with friends, the only photographs present are of Lillian's mom in her youth, of her grandma, one of her father, and of Lillian as a very pretty, big-eyed and big-headed woman-child. This fact is a disturbing one, as the absence of evidence from my past seems to suggest that I might not even have a past, and therefore do not actually exist, at least not without Lillian, which is the same as not existing, and without that foundation then where are we? If I do not exist, then there are no facts. Shall I adhere to my usual devices—repetition and a dramatist's flair? I shall: *There are no facts.*

Those words in mind, I sit down at my typewriter in the window and begin compiling my own facts whose purpose will be to create myself piecemeal; and in accordance with the words, "Man was created by Woman," I, as well, will create myself by taking from Woman—not to be confused with just a single "woman," but with a capital "W" meaning *every single woman*—of whom I believe myself to be composed of by the loose ends of their fibers gently waving like fleshy tendrils with nerve-globes at their tips making, like kelp in murky water, the illusive shape that appears before me in the imaginary mirror. I will put them all down in a book called, "The Imaginaries," in which slowly, by way of excavating these feminine veins of my make-up, and seeing them through from nerve-tip to ungrounded root, it will become apparent who exactly I am or am not.

I grab at random in the dirty water filled with these woman-like kelp, and I grasp as best I can the slick vine(one of an infinite tangled number) of some former experience: I am seventeen(oh no, old boy—really?), a strapping young man-boy, I'd like to think, and in my regular fashion I have been pining(*come* on) after this little lady—who is actually quite tall, model thin, and an all around unrealistic match for me—who shows no sign of returning my affection. I am calling when I shouldn't, showing up unannounced, writing poems addressed to her, and other activities of the like which I will spare myself from mentioning.

I am at a florist now, selecting what I imagine to be a splendid bouquet intended for said little lady. The woman behind the counter —not so much a woman as a *young* woman, a little bird—is being very helpful in the selection process. She points out the gerber daisies and mentions they're her favorite, and a safe classic, not at all presumptuous or overbearing. She suggests a squat, round vase—something tasteful. I accept her advice because, first of all, during the course of our interaction I have found my attraction to her growing, turning into a freefalling love even, and, secondly, she seems a person who is knowledgeable in her work. Quickly, she gathers the flowers and arranges them in the vase so that I am thinking it really is quite a splendid bouquet, and as she rings them up and I'm about to pay I inexplicably make the decision that I am buying these flowers for this young lady in front of me and not for the other one. I forget what the other looked like. I forget there was an "other."

I alluded to my typical behavior in the previous anecdote, but I would like to point out my consciousness, even then, that my habit of chasing girls was all too common by quoting a poem that I wrote at seventeen (when I still considered them "poems"), not because I think it bares any lasting literary merit, but because the poem illustrates perfectly the self-awareness of my wandering eye(two incredibly large eyes) and, as I am creating myself from Woman, I think it is a necessary step in my formation. And it just so happens that I have this poem, this little bit of pencil scribbled seventeen year old gibberish, tucked neatly into the top of my dress sock and I'd like to take it out and read it aloud while my mood is still so affected by the unprecedented loftiness of this process:

> "On a clear night, look/At the stars without pretens-ion/Choose a single one and stare—/See how it disa-ppears, fading/Into black, and the peripheral/Stars burn brighter? "

> "Now that star is a woman/And the sky, it's so big!/ The disappeared woman/Belongs to someone else now/They all belong to someone else/How did that happen?/Well, they're all dead anyway."

> "Then it occurs to me/That the only living one/Is bright red in the dark/Burning a half-inch/From my lips, and it is the only/One which gives—/Its effects may demand a Warning/But at least results are imm-ediate. "

With what a sense of urgency we live when we are young men or old boys in America, in love! Everything must be done with such immed-iacy, it's maddening. By nineteen I had made myself absolutely sick. But I am better now, I promise. I am more open to the present and the possible future presents. It may sound like I am digressing—so I am. But the digression is the sweet meat of things; the digression is what makes us human. And so Woman, too, is a part of this digression—the bones and the toast, the lungs and the milkshake, the thing and all thi-ngs.

This is a book of interruptions then, of digressions, and potential tran-sgressions. What this describes at present is the door buzzer blaring obnoxiously. I go to the door and let in my visitor—it is Jorge Luis

Borges.

Before I can greet my esteemed visitor he walks into the apartment and announces, "El color del perro es negro."

Taken aback, I say, "I don't understand. I mean, I do *understand*, but why have you just told me that the color of the dog is black? "

"You want to learn how to speak Spanish, yes," says Mr. Borges (though I do not know how he knew this fact about me), "then you must start with simple phrases. Repeat after me: El color del perro es negro."

I oblige him, repeating, "El color del perro es negro." Then, "Mr. Borges, didn't you go blind?"

He answers, "In some futures I did, and in others I did not."

I tell Borges, "I recall you as a blind old man, living within the bright darkness of the library of your brain."

"This is not that future which we share," says cryptic Borges.

I retort, "Then I will see you out now?" He assures me that I will see him out now. As I do so, I thank him for honoring me with a visit. He leaves, and behind him is the ghost of a little black dog, just hanging there in Spanish. Also, on the table next to my typewriter, he(I can only presume it was him, for the act itself went unnoticed) has left a book entitled, "The Book of Imaginaries." It is written by Borges. I laugh and look out the window, down at the street, which, like many other things, I had for a moment forgotten about.

14

ONE MIGHT BE WONDERING NOW about the market—did I snub the opportunity to be an upstanding citizen, a working stiff? As it turns out, the woman never called me back about the market(don't depend on a drunk), and it's no matter to me anyway because how is a man supposed to complete a book—in his imagination or otherwise—when his main concern is to mop the floor? In other business—because my business is a matter of constant concern—I received a call today in regards to a much better job.

It was Rick on the phone—Rick, of course, being the guy who got me the stand-in position on the Gil Van S—— film—and he just wanted to let me know that the lead stand-in had to go to New Orleans, so would I be available for the remainder of shooting? If so, I will be needed tomorrow and every day thereafter for two and half more weeks—excluding weekends.

A shudder in time, space, whatever, which is of utmost importance to the reader: in one possible future(a future I am familiar with) I am forced to say "no" to the stand-in position because I actually did get

the job at the market as the woman was not as drunk as I had supposed; in another I am able to say "yes" because here I am with all this
time on my hands and no money—and that is the present future. I am
just now approaching set.

It is with extreme pleasure(and probably Lillian's equal displeasure)
that I am arriving back on set for the first time after my hiatus to find
that Mae the Australian beauty not only remembers me but noticed my
absence while it existed.

Inconspicuously, Mae approaches me from nowhere and in that
accent that is irresistible to all American folks says, smiling, "You're
back."

And I am back, on that single phrase, suddenly floating in this
film-world where my every need is provided for, where things are fast
and nearly too good(they're too good), where coming down is an imp-
ossibility, where unattractiveness doesn't exist, where my girlfriend
hates me—and isn't that what I wanted? Isn't that why I began a
certain book in the first place? Because I am reckless, restless, and a
coward? There's no time to think about that, or anything. The cameras
have been rolling for quite some time already, I'm sure of it, and little
Mae's smile has grown bigger, more direct. Once you know someone
in the industry—or *somebody*, if you will —then you know everyone. I
am a hit on set. I am approached from all sides, not asking why, my
head in a whirl. "Give me a glass of water, please—I'm parched," I
might say, and the water will arrive. The water is ice cold and clean.
Where I come from we get our water from the tap, tepid. We pour it in
our own glass. But how did this happen? Where is it that I come from?
Now, I come from nowhere; if I must say I come from somewhere,
then it is from that tiny observation of "you're back," from that tiny
Australian actress, from that moment she took me in, under her wing,
taking me with her to float. And while I am floating I know of nothing
else but this air, this lightness in heart that can only lead to an eventual
severance, a cracking up, a breaking of the skull—just one quick snap,
one fleeting brush of an arm against an arm, one slip of the lips against
the lips and I'm gone. I am gone.

With my head high up in the clouds I am moving at the small sound of
thumb and middle finger pressing firmly together and quickly coming
apart. One snap and no break-up scene that I can recall. Lillian is
behind me and all I can remember are some tears, nothing more. I
know that I am heartbroken but the movement helps, the hand that I
am holding helps—Mae's pretty little fair-skinned hand in mine. We
are driving faster than we should, reckless, toward the hope and the
dream and the crushing weight of Los Angeles, California. When we
get there we'll joke and say that we made it. In my head I'll know that

only she made it—I simply came along for the ride, toting with me my single suitcase full of clothes and this heavy feeling in my chest. I'll tuck these things into a corner at her place and myself right behind them, behind her. I will be hidden away. I will be no one, still—only somewhere else, at a higher altitude. I'll quickly learn how to be a jealous man again and I will kill that jealousy by despising her. Poor Mae, the things I'll come up with in my imagination about you; the things that I will create and put down in print—what awful things! I will feel terrible and silly afterwards. I'll think too often about Lillian. I'll finally, truly love her then. But I cannot think about this yet, not while Mae's lovely little hand is in mine and everything is fresh and we are traveling so fast. I cannot think about how this will not work out. I've left a good woman for the sake of adventure, and this adventure is much too big for me.

I do believe you've heard my thoughts, sweet Mae, because you've removed your hand from mine to stick it out the window and catch the ever-warming air as we near the gold coast. We are driving slower now and I've known you forever. "Kira," I say to you—and yes, that is your name, sweetheart; this is the new future at present (when did this transformation take place, moving from one small blonde to another?) —"we've almost made it." She laughs—she gets *the joke*.

At twenty I am coming off a bad one, considering myself a could've-been-father, considering my young lady's abortion(a different young lady than I am currently riding with), considering what's ahead, considering the drowsy landscape between Lincoln, Ne. and Anaheim, Ca.—so many fields, and small towns; "so much desolation," I think in my 20 year old head.

Kira is antsy, catching the wind. I look over at her and her big eyes seem bigger—they're wide and darting. She's so beautiful when she's excited. The colors are changing as we cross state lines. She is changing. The little girl who once lived above me in that downtown apartment building(where the act that necessitated the abortion was "committed"(still feel like an offender)) is budding into a woman of the world—a sad, inevitable seachange. She'll outgrow me for awhile. Her boyfriend is waiting on the coast to scoop her back up into his arms and who will I be to her then? Just an old friend—an old friend she can no longer talk to.

But before this can occur we must get there. And when we finally do get there things, as they do in this part of the country, come together quickly and without much thought. I am now living in a two bedroom apartment on the edge of little Third World with Kira's boyfriend The Nameless and an old friend of mine from Nebraska, Dean, drinking every night til sunrise on the back porch which overlooks a narrow back alley that feels as if it is closing in on us. I've been set up with a job at a bizarre store next to a music venue for straight-edge youth(bands that scream) where we sell CDs, clothes, toiletries and other random necessities, clothes, used instruments, microwavable foods, etc., etc. On top of everything, there is a cereal bar at which my post stands. Dean, who got me the job, works the used instruments department and The Nameless doesn't do a goddamn, though his one lasting accomplishment was to allow our boss—a squat, Italian man named Arpeggi, who has very short legs, a growth over his left eye, and claims to have ties to the mafia—to spit on him for an extra twenty spot.

The shop itself is located in a bright strip mall whose main attraction, aside from the music venue next door, is an erotica super-store at the front of the parking lot. The daytime clientele are mainly homeless men and drug addicts—and the obvious stray pervert—try-ing to pawn beat-up acoustic guitars that Arpeggi usually acquires through the trade of two bottles of soda and a bowl of cereal or micro-wavable dinner. I come on shift in the early evening, 5pm, after these folks have already moved on to search for their fix or a place to sleep for the night. When I get in the sun is still shining, but the heat is wearing off somewhat—I am looking forward to the dark.

Coming through the doors into the cool, air-conditioned store, I greet Arpeggi hesitantly because he is a small and violent man, notor-iously "manic." Some nights he's in a foul mood, cursing under his breath, getting drunk in his office, counting his money and cleaning his guns. Tonight he is in a good mood though because a movie is to be shot in the parking lot in which the main star is a very young Aust-ralian girl whose name I don't recognize—Mae something-or-other.

Arpeggi says to me, "Aye, Kid—how 'bout an iced tea, a little sweetener. You know how I like it." He is sitting in an armchair in the front of the store, sweating, his black Yankees ball cap cocked back on his greasy head. I get him the coldest bottle from the fridge, dump in a packet of sweetener, shake it up, and bring it to him.

"Here you go, Don Arpeggi," I say to him, handing him the cold bottle of sweet tea; he takes a sip and nods.

Arpeggi pulls out a pack of cigarettes from his shorts that are too long and he hands me one, removing one for himself as well, and we step outside together. I crouch on the sidewalk, leaning my back agai-nst the store. Arpeggi leans against his $50,000(he always notes the cost) black sports car that he has parked in the handicap spot right in front of the store. He's talking, but I don't really hear him. I am wait-ing for the sun to go down.

AFTER DARK THE MOVIE GETS ROLLING outside of Arpeggi's
store and with it spreads a buzz through the customers and employees.
There are people everywhere moving about, talking, probably stealing
things, then they are hushed and still for the actual filming.

I am in the back of the store, posted at the cereal bar as usual. This
is where the extras in the film have chosen to congregate. There is one
extra in particular who can't seem to tear herself away from the cereal
bar(not sure she's done any actual work)—a quiet but sultry broad,
somewhat taller, brunette, wearing a pair of black lace tights under a
small dress. Eventually she strikes up conversation with me, haggling
over the fortune cookies that we sell for 50 cents a piece; I end up
cutting her a deal and selling her four for a dollar—I mean, there *is* sex
appeal there, albeit frightening. Her actions feel scripted, rehearsed, as
if a camera is secretly on her and the dramatic flip of her hair and the
subsequent dreamy stare off into space with a half-smile are not meant
for me but for the character I am playing in the ongoing film in her
coked-out head. Nonetheless, being that I am at this time, as I have
mentioned, a heartbroken and lonely 20 year old, when she approaches
me soon after the fortune cookie transaction I cannot help but feel
flattered when, without asking my name, she decides to start calling me
(the current male lead character), seemingly lovingly, Benny, though
pronouncing it in two long, seductive syllables as, "Ben-nee". And she
has something for this little man named Benny; she hands over the
fortune from her cookie, which reads: "Never pass up an opportunity
when it presents itself." On the back, in silver glitter pen, she has
written her name, Clarissa, and her phone number. After I give a big,
comical smile for Clarissa's amusement—which she returns with nothing but drug and film induced, exaggerated coquettishness—she disappears. I put the slip of paper in my pocket for later.

When I am finally pulling this little slip of paper out of my pocket,
with its message making the use of the phone number unavoidable, it
is well into the night, past midnight, the screaming has ceased to come
through the walls from next door, and the cigarette littered parking lot
is empty where the cast and crew have cleared out—but not without
first extending an invitation to Dean and I to attend their after party.
Arpeggi left earlier in a good mood because business was moving, the
gates in the front of the store are all closed and locked, and I am
exiting the parking lot with Dean in the passenger seat of The Nameless' old white Buick(which he lent to me for the night after becoming
too intoxicated, too early, and vomiting in his bathroom at the apartment). I am on the phone with Clarissa, her automatic voice even
eerier with digital inflection as she gives me directions to the hotel

where the after party is already taking place.

Fifteen minutes later we arrive at a seedy *motel* in some anonymous area of the Los Angeles sprawl. All of the rooms in the "L" shaped building have doors which open to the outside world—the busy street and the burning hollows of the dark, run-down side streets where impoverished families lie in poor sleep. One of the doors in the motel is swung open, pouring out light and people onto the balcony/hallway obtrusively. Cigarettes are being smoked, their grey exhalations rising and drifting; conversations are being had, their already loud volume rising, the words drifting.

We follow the light and the sound inside. People are everywhere, sitting in chairs, on the floor, laying on the bed, standing around, their eyes half-crossed; everywhere there are cases of beer torn into, open bottles, cocaine is in a pile on the bathroom counter(being dug into one by one and scraped aside into neat piles to be snorted). And in the middle of it all is Clarissa. She is leaned against the nightstand between three men who appear to be coming on strong and her dress seems to be shorter. As I enter the room she refrains from giving me a verbal greeting, acknowledging me instead by making fuck-eyes at me. There is no one at the party(save for Dean, obviously) that I know, yet I meet everyone quickly and just as soon forget them. It takes half an hour and four beers on my part before Clarissa approaches me in what I can already see is her typical way—a languid approach that begins from across the room, all eyes and legs, and ends with a strange, menacing seduction through the words, "Hell-o, Ben-nee," that is followed soon after by a gentle tug on the hand and a whispered proposition to take her home.

The hot breath in my ear and the fact that I had been drinking on the job before I came(not to mention my overstated mindset) and of course I am driving in the car of The Nameless, forgetting about Dean (sorry, old boy), with Clarissa positioned with her ass in the passenger seat and her head in my lap, lips parted to take me in in full—nearly running red lights and stop signs because of it—until, somehow, safely reaching the underbelly of my apartment on the border of little Third World, in the middle of the underground parking garage, where I am able to bring the car to a standstill and she can climb over the center console into my seat, and the black curtains fall over the scene completely.

16

I SEE THE SUN RISE JUST AS I AM COMING-TO from a long blackout wherein my actions were surely in poor taste, as those of a bad man always are, and my heart acts in direct inverse to the rising of the sun and drops even further than it had rested previously. Clarissa is still in the apartment, where we made it *inside* at some point and for reasons unknown to me at this juncture(though I will soon learn) she is flustered and says she must leave immediately. She is asking for directions of how to leave, how to, she says, "Get out of here."

Still coming to terms with my new consciousness, and the acts which I know I must have committed while unconscious, and now inexplicably finding myself in the doorway to the apartment with Clarissa standing in front of me on the doormat, almost pleading with me for directions *out*—and quick—the best I can muster in response to her is a thumb pointing to the right, saying, "The street is that way."

I look in the direction my thumb points and see that I was correct to have said *the street is that way*, because there is the bright-hot daytime street with the sun reflecting off its pavement, almost blinding, and heat waves emanating from its surface, distorting vision. Presently, Clarissa comes into view, walking towards the street in her barefeet, carrying her shoes in one hand and her purse in the other, padding away lightly and idiotically into the distortion. I feel heavy and cold, stuck in place with nothing but the bright light of day and the immense guilt that comes the morning after sleeping with strangers.

From behind me I hear the voice of Javi, the flamboyant Mexican boy who had apparently been sleeping on the couch the night before, and had therefore been forced to endure several hours of my lewd escapades with Clarissa in the kitchen right next to him, on the balcony, etc., of which he explains to me in depth how he had bore witness to them. Exceedingly more and more humiliated, I listen to Javi as he excitedly, in hysterical, high-pitched laughter, continues to describe the events of moments ago that had led to Clarissa's hasty departure: I had excused myself to the restroom at some point, as Javi's side of the story goes, and he chose to take that opportunity to snatch a twenty-dollar bill from Clarissa's purse(telling himself it was his payment for keeping quiet the night before), to which she immediately accused him of doing, in turn resulting in Javi's thin, but firm denial and each of them slapping the other in the face and it was over—she grabbed her purse and *had to get out of here*. Holding the twenty-dollar bill in hand, still laughing through his toothy grin, Javi offers to take me out for some food. It would be impolite to refuse.

After breakfast, where I order two beers and a plate of eggs, I let the day pass in a hazy despondency, thinking only of how I've wronged all the women I actually loved at one point or another. The only sight I am conscious of is a fleeting vision of two droplets of sweat rolling down my inner bicep, sliding right out of my shirtsleeve and dripping onto my pant leg. "I am utterly beat, broken. No—don't think about

The Fear," I am telling myself, and it appears to be dark now—the moon is out. I am sitting on our back patio with Dean, drinking whiskey over ice with a splash of water. The nightly Shadow Dance is being projected onto the neighboring wall of our narrow alley. From above us, light shoots out of The Nameless' bedroom window, casting the dark forms of the two common performers. Dialogue is minimal. It consists mainly of grunts and gasps. We are waiting for it to be over, being signified as usual by those two typical, base lines, "I'm about to come," then, "I'm coming."

The darkness is waning. The sun is rising again and I see it do so like a brilliant idea. I tell Dean that I am going to New Mexico to recover. I am going to see a desert pixie I once knew who will solve all of life's problems with a single touch of her fingers to your cheek, a single brush of her hair against your shoulder, or chest. My eyes are burning with the color of whiskey in the sunshine. My bag is packed and the sky is blue—blue like on film, or in paint; blue like in children's stories and books that contain *the knowledge of the holy*. Like in a dream, continuity is broken. There was no ride to the bus station—I simply arrive. I purchase my one-way ticket and immediately board the bus.

First stop is in San Bernardino. It is a short trip, yet I am bombarded, silently, by a spooky voice that rises from the text on my phone, straight into my head where it echoes, "Don't go! Don't go!"

There is a layover in San Bernardino. "Don't get on your next bus," says the voice of the devil. I am surrounded by two hundred folks without teeth, asking for my cigarettes, asking if I want any crack. I am crouched against the wall of the station, smoking, sweating, and the terrifying, trembling clear-headedness of sobriety is setting in—and I still haven't slept. My duffel bag is so tiny it breaks my heart. I realize that I spent the last of my money on a one-way ticket to the desert where I will not be able to afford to get back. "Don't get on your next bus," chimes that awful voice again. "I'll pick you up in San Bernardino."

I hear my bus called and the engine start; I hear it leave the station, but I don't watch it go. It is trash day in the slums. A violent sight, the mechanical arm of the garbage truck clamping down on the trash cans and pulling them in, then heaving them up and hurling the stinking waste straight into its crushing, metallic bowels before slamming them back down empty and partially broken. The sound is like that of a whining wolf-pup. The wolf must go back into the wild, taken by the scruff of his neck in his mother's jaws and carried away. But he is too far gone. The people snatched him up and took him into captivity to be domesticated. Now he needs the people to survive, so he stays.

I can still hear the whine of the wolf-pup as if the sound were coming from inside my brain in a dark recess that even booze couldn't drown. The wrinkled pink petal of some windblown flower flutters onto my tiny duffel bag, evoking the thought of that lusted for place between a woman's legs. I make no attempt at plucking it off. A commotion has started outside the bus station because of the ostentatious arrival of a white limousine. A chubby man with greying hair in a black suit and black cap gets out of the driver's seat and walks the length of the limo, then around to the passenger side that faces the station. He opens the door and a young woman emerges, a brunette in sunglasses, legs stretching into oblivion, clothed in a peach colored dress and tights as blue as the sky—it's Clarissa.

I stand up from my crouched position, slipping my bag over my shoulder, and Clarissa prances over to greet me. She throws her arms around my neck and jumps into my arms, wrapping her legs around my waist and squeezing, clamping down like the mechanical arm of a garbage truck. The crack dealers and panhandlers are drooling from their toothless mouths. The baby wolf is whining into the smog. Clarissa, with her sunglasses still on, pulls her mouth away from where she forcefully placed it on mine, her lips now shining with spit, and she digs her face into the side of my face, moaning, whispering, "Hell-o, Ben-nee," then bites my ear lobe so hard I think it's bleeding.

From a crystal decanter in the back of the limo she pours a glass of whiskey and raises it to my lips. The first sip burns—it wants to come back up, but I fight the urge. I don't recall leaving the station, or the door ever closing behind me, but we are already driving aimlessly the freeways of L.A., creeping invisibly along within our fancy, movable box. My stomach is growling wildly. Clarissa's clothes are stripped off and she is squealing, mimicking the sounds of my stomach at a higher pitch as she unbuckles my belt from her knees. Out the window I am watching commuters and vacationers pass us by innocently in their cars. Directly beside us is a blue luxury car which carries within it a very respectable looking family—husband and wife, two kids in the back with smiles ringed by popsicle juice gone astray; the kids are fiddling with buckets and towels as though they are headed to the beach. They try to stare back into our window in attempt to see who is inside—they can see nothing, no one; they can see only a dark reflection of their own beautiful family.

I cannot bear to watch the family any longer. Clarissa's grunts have become louder, wilder. I close my eyes and bite my lip. The tingle in my head is building as my shame grows and stiffens, inching towards that inevitable great shift, that obliteration of thought and self, crystallizing into one perfect moment of horror that the devil will swallow whole. The click in my brain is coming. The moment has arrived: I am dead.

17

I AM UP TO MY TEETH—my sensitive, chattering teeth—with a strange sensation of mystification that I believe to have come from either forgetfulness or conviction in my own fabrications.

I have just opened my eyes from the act of "dying" to discover that certain tales I supposed myself to be relating on the fly actually occurred quite some time ago, if at all. Where I thought I would see the haunting images of a limousine's sordid interior, there are peaceful and cozy objects of a sunny treehouse in Echo Park, Ca. that has been converted into a pleasant home capable of housing fifty people comfortably. My few belongings are folded into my suitcase and neatly stashed into a corner beside the couch I am presently sitting. A thousand and one empty beer bottles are strewn about the trunk of the tree. Shards of glass poke here and there out of the lawn. A rambunctious wolf-pup claws desperately at the front door to be let in because he is hungry. (Did you enter into my dream, little pup? What has happened here?)

I will clean up the physical mess below the treehouse before I tend to the psychological one within. I will gather the broken glass and recycle all the bottles. I will feed the wolf-pup. It will only take a second— then I can investigate the mystery that is causing my heart to palpitate and my skull to crack.

One beat and the thing is done—the lawn is immaculate and everything smells like lemons. I am back on the couch, staring again at the source of my extreme mental agitation: on the table there lies a very tidy stack of books, all of which I have written; on the top of this stack is a thick volume entitled, "The Imaginaries." Underneath the title in plain and eerie print is my name. Next to my name, for whatever reason, I have even gone so far as to ink my signature. I have no recollection of any of these things concerning the book called, *The Imaginaries.* To my knowledge, I only just now conceived The Book, the idea of which derived from the fact that I drank too much last night and slept with a stranger in the backseat of a car outside of the treehouse(barely remember it), and had a horrific dream that was comprised of one repetitive scene that entailed hovering over my ex-girlfriend, Lillian, in bed and asking her through tears, "Have you slept with him yet?" To which she unfailingly replied, without any hesitation or emotion, "No, I haven't—but I am going to." And I wailed to her then, saying, "W-h-y?" Only to receive another cold response: "Because you're not here."

Over and over that scene was replayed last night(was it last night?), and those last words of *you're not here* blew through my bones and shook me to the core because I am *not* there. Waking in that startled state, The Fear growing in my intestines, there was nothing else to do but write a book of repentance, a book of my imagination where I could live out all the different possible adventures with all the different women that have come through my life or my brain; in this book I would choose Lillian over everyone else, and I could be with her again, where I wanted to be again, and we would eventually be happy there, together, and I was going to title this wonderful book, "The Imaginaries."

To see then that this book not only existed already, but that *I* had written it already—or what I presume to be something like It at least, seeing as the titles are one in the same—produced a tremendous amount of anxiety in my soul that even at this moment has not yet begun to wane. The presence of this book leads me to question a number of things successively:

1) Is it possible that by *thinking* of this book, and believing that I would forge it into being, I somehow made it materialize in its completed state, as though Earth had finally become that intellectual creation called *Tlön°*?

2) If this is so, am I not obliged to follow one of their schools of philosophy, like the one that "goes so far as to deny the existence of time, [and] argues that the present is undefined and indefinite, the future has no reality except as present hope, and the past has no reality except as present recollection?"

And, most importantly in the matters of *The Imaginaries,*

3) In a place that "it has been decided that all books are the work of a single author who is timeless and anonymous," is it not true that *The Imaginaries,* then, belongs to not just me but all peoples and I am, therefore, not completely responsible for its contents which still remain a mystery to me?

But I must be honest with myself here. These speculations are a mental horseplay to avoid the actual matter at hand. Whether it is because I imagined it, or because it actually exists outside of my mind, The Book is in front of me and it must be dealt with—I cannot move forward until this suggestive work is delved into and figured out. I must know what it contains. Thus, I will continue here by turning back its front cover and transcribing its contents as they are revealed to me.

18

ON THE TITLE PAGE OF *THE IMAGINARIES*, these words are written in small print at the bottom of the right hand side of the page: *For those who are closest to me, though by all probability we will only have the occasion to meet again once or twice, if at all.*

Turning the page of this tome, it is at once clear that the events are nonlinear—one chapter will begin in one place and time only to end in another; the next chapter will begin in yet another place-time and be either static or circular. Very strange. I am given the impression that the starting point is an arbitrary one, so rather than throw my bias over the text I will let the book drop and open at random. I have done just that and exposed the following:

An incredibly large fly buzzes erratically around the room. The sound of his flight, like a miniature chainsaw, cuts through the otherwise silent air. Shafts of sunlight shoot through the windows of the house at five o'clock angles, illuminating myriad dust particles that typically go unseen—some settle on the polished wood floors, some on the armoire, on the bookshelf, on the desk. From my chair at the desk, I watch the dust float and settle like gentle, barely visible snowflakes while drinking a tall glass of iced tea and flipping through the original manuscript of one of the first "first volumes" of my life's ever-changing work, *The Imaginaries.* I am waiting for a visitor to arrive.

While I wait for my visitor—whom I await with especial excitement—I would like to take a few moments to laugh at the man I once was. Of course, it is a good-natured laugh I intend to give forth into my empty, old-fart home. And the relation I am about to paraphrase here(from the original, early first-volume manuscript of *The Imaginaries*) is a relevant one, being that it involves one of the first experiences in this future that is comparable to the one I will soon share with my guest:

I was young with good intentions, and had just done something that I perceived to be bad, awful, *loathsome*(oh quit acting so brokenhearted, you little fool). There is no need for the expletives. Suffice it to say that I was living in a somewhat popular destination in southern California at the time, and it happened that a friend was coming through the area with his band to play a show; when they were packing up their gear afterwards, and employed my hand in assisting them, through some offhand comment I was, for some reason, asked to join them on the road for the next portion of their trip. So instead of quietly coping with the decisions I had chosen to make, I opted to quickly pack my belongings and go on the lam. I jumped in their van and my escape was set in motion.

Heading East on the highway, crammed into the backseat of the van en (uncomfortable)route to Austin, Tx., I stared out at the landscape and became enveloped by images of different possible lives that I then lived out in full. I saw the beginning of new things and their inevitable, eventual demise. I found wholesome women, fell in love with them, then fell out—all in a moment. I lived alone on desolate ranches, romanticized my isolation, then came to yearn for society again. I disappeared into the wilderness and wrote mad letters to my family, tumbled down into a golden arroyo one night in the dark, and (unconscious and with broken legs) was eaten by wild creatures some hours after—my remains were found weeks later and the letters published posthumously in a collection called, "Build Your Homes Again: Letters to an American Family." In the backseat of the van I was sucked out the window and swallowed by my own ghosts, which were numerous and scattered amongst the side of the highways.

When we stopped, I snapped back into my physical self, confounded by the immediacies of my body that seemed almost less *real* than those I had experienced only in my brain. I wiped the crust from my eyes and got out to piss. We were near the New Mexico/ Texas state line, just outside of Las Cruces in a place called Mesilla. I had trouble walking up to the tiny structure calling itself a gas station. I was remembering a little pixie that I knew who lived nearby, and whose existence, always at an unattainable distance, haunted me. I always hoped she would be the good to my bad, the home to end all my wanderings, that sweet girl! It had been awhile since we had last spoke. She would not want to see me, thus her presence—so close I could feel it—was crippling.

I stumbled into the gas station, and relieved myself while purposely avoiding the gaze in the mirror. After purchasing a small snack, I went back out and noticed there was a young man sitting next to the building, just outside of the doors; he was smoking a cigarette, drinking a tall boy, and eating cheese crackers. I noted that these were a good combination of purchases, as they mimicked exactly my own purchases; I nodded at him, then grew inexplicably embarrassed when he looked up, so immediately averted my eyes to the ground near his feet. My head began to throb, a sensation I attributed to the heat, low blood sugar, the bright sun, and the blowing dust, the latter two of which creates this desert area as if it were an optical illusion.

Suddenly the young man piped in, "Nice boots." I turned to him for a moment, thanking him for the compliment, and a wave of nausea came over me that forced me to look away. I stared across the highway in an attempt to make out the mountains I was sure were there through the dust-shimmering glare. I could see nothing, though from the corner of my eye I could tell that the young man had gone to staring across the highway as well. Without looking, the young man spoke up again, saying, "Where are you guys headed?"

Absently I made reply. "My friends here are in a band. They're giving me a ride as far as Austin, I think." A long pause went between us. The band had all returned to the van and taken their chosen seats. Before I joined them, a chord was struck within me and my eyes hurt tremendously. "You live around here?" I asked him, to which he answered that he did. And with this pain pressing against my eyes and my brain I followed up by stating, "The most beautiful girl I've ever met lives around here." Then I stopped myself.

Another pause came between us before(finally) we both wished each other good luck. I cannot say which of us wished it upon the other first. I climbed into the van and we pulled back onto the interstate. The swelling eased within my skull, and faded into calm. I returned to silently looking out the window, making drowsy abstractions about my future. Again I thought about the desert pixie. I thought about what things might have been like had I stayed with her years ago when that option was viable. I thought about the eyes of the young man that I had met, and how there was that eeriness about them that I had tried to avoid in the bathroom earlier by not looking into the mirror.

Oh, what a silly and melodramatic little man! But I am not that man anymore. I am much older now, and don't take myself so seriously. I take advantage of my old age, playing pranks and saying bizarre or nonsensical things to strangers who take one look at this wrinkled body of mine and they say to themselves, "This man is senile—how sad." They were clearly not looking hard enough; they did not see the lucid twinkle in my eye, or the spring in my step. If they had they would have known that for as many old men that I am, somewhere, I am also just as many of those young men—those *silly and melodramatic* ones—somewhere else, spry, mischievous. I have a living memory of the events in my life, and of many events from other possible lives, and in that way they are still true to me, relevant, happening continuously in the present.

In the immediate present, the one where I am sitting in my quiet home(ignoring the buzz of the enormous fly) in wait of my guest, it has most likely been conjectured—through the previously related tale, transcribed so long ago—who exactly my visitor is to be. It was earlier this morning that I saw him, sitting down outside of the café where I just happened to be passing. He did not see me. I slipped into the café and wrote my address and a specific time to meet me on a napkin—it was addressed to him by name. I had one of the waiters deliver it to his table once I removed myself from the establishment. Even in my old age I can move quite stealthily. From down the block I saw the waiter deliver the napkin to the table. As the young man began to look about I rounded the corner. Now I simply wait.

I rise from my desk and go to the window, peering out into the now somewhat overcast street. A ways down I can make out the slight figure of the young man from the café, my approaching guest, with his hands in his pockets and head directed at the sidewalk a few paces ahead of him. It is almost twenty minutes past the stated time on the napkin; which is to say, my guest is arriving precisely on time.

Rather than wait for him to arrive on my doorstep to let him in, I crack the door open half of an inch and retreat back to my desk, sitting down with one leg crossed over the other in the chair that has been pushed back slightly from the desk. The rays of sunlight pouring in through the windows have vanished. I am sitting in a somewhat ostentatious gloom, which I find to be a humorous air that will shock my visitor to a degree that is far more than necessary. His footsteps can be heard climbing the steps.

Two gentle raps on the wood and the door creaks open into the house. My visitor calls inside, "Hello?" He peaks his head through the doorway and scans the room. He sees me on my shadowy perch, unmoving, and addresses me. "Hello. I'm Mr. Font. I was told to meet someone here twenty minutes ago—it was said to be a matter of 'utmost importance.'"

"Yes, I know who you are Mr. Font. Please, come in. Shut the door behind you and feel free to switch on that lamp there, by the wall."

Young Mr. Font does as he is told with obvious hesitation, though with apparent curiosity—why else would he have come by anonymous invitation? I can guess nearly his every move, and thought. I decide to put him at ease.

I continue, "Well, Mr. Font, it was I who requested your presence and I do appreciate you coming on such short notice, though I can't say your decision to come is a surprise to me."

He scans the books on the shelf, and the books that are laid about on the table; then he makes his way over to my desk. "It's no problem really, but may I ask who you are and what this is all about? As I said a moment ago, and as you know already, it was expressed in the note that this was a matter of 'utmost importance.'"

"It certainly is a matter of utmost importance, as each action in all of our individual lives is a matter of such scope. "

He seems to have come across something on my desk that has piqued his interest. "Also, how have you gotten my manuscript—what is this?"

"We don't have very much time together for this meeting, Mr. Font, so I will make things brief. Would you like a drink of water, or some iced tea? Perhaps you'd like hot tea instead—the weather is changing." He shakes his head "no," having already scooped up *The Imaginaries* manuscript from my desk and begun flipping through it. "I would like to introduce myself. I, too, am Mr. Font."

He takes his eyes off the manuscript to look at me more carefully. "My father's brother that disappeared without a word—Julien? "

"I am not Julien. But it is a fact that we are related to one another, if not in the traditional sense, then in a way that does not and will not ever make sense. I am a writer too, you know."

" I see that. This manuscript is substantially thicker than it was when I last left it in my hotel room only a couple of hours ago. What have you done with it—*finished it?* And what *is* that noise?"

Poor, confused, young Mr. Font, he turns his head about the room and his eyes dart rapidly around the lamp lit corners in search of the origin of the noise. He cannot find the cause for such a noise as he hears now—a subtle, yet piercing buzz.

"I'd like to consider it a collaborative effort at this point, and to be quite honest, there is no hope for *The Imaginaries* to be finished until you and I and an infinite number of others similar to us are good and dead—even then it is likely that the project will never come to fruition as you or I imagine it in our minds' eye. And that noise you hear, that is the sound of the persistent flapping of an enormous fly's wings. You cannot see the fly—it is a miracle that you can see me. For your own mental well being, you must imagine that this noise is coming from within your head, like a ringing in your ears that will haunt you from here on out; for even after the ringing is gone, the tone will be stuck in your memory like a song from your childhood that you cannot quite remember, and cannot quite forget."

"Excuse me for being blunt, Mr. Font, but the formalities of this conversation are starting to bore me. I would like to know what the point of all this is. Please, skip all these obscure inanities and tell me why you've called me here."

"There is no need to excuse yourself. I'll get down to the point: I've called you here to give you this manuscript as a gift. "

"That's it? You've called me here to give me *my own* manuscript?"

"Yes, and now that you have it I would like to ask you to leave. But not without this little bit of advice first: Read this manuscript or don't; but if you choose to read it, I want you to do so with a distanced objectivity, although some of its subject matter concerns you personally. We have sometimes lived recklessly. Sometimes we have lived with reservation. And in any case, the text of this manuscript should not guide you in your future actions; it should—again, if you choose to read it—serve as a look into a handful of possibilities which should be considered to be infinite. You are given but one existence to live out in full, and you must continually make decisions that propel your experience along until death. These decisions need not be calculated, though they should be made with the knowledge that they are yours alone to make, and the consequences thereof are yours alone to endure—for better or for worse. It is not in your best interest to feel shame or guilt over them. Own up to the peculiarities of your own behavior and move on. If you are unhappy with the results they have on your life, then change them. If you are happy, then don't change a goddamn thing. Now, please go."

All this time I have not moved from my smug, one leg over the other position in the chair at my desk. Young Mr. Font has stood in front of the desk, fidgeting with the manuscript in his hands and glancing about the main corridor of my home. He now folds the very thick manuscript in half vertically and shoves it into his coat pocket.

"Well, thank you for returning my manuscript. I'll see myself out then."

I nod at the young man, who keeps his word by turning on his heels, walking to the door, and exiting. As the door clicks shut behind him, I allow myself to burst into the laughter, which I had held in during the entirety of our conversation. The look on his face! The bead of sweat forming conspicuously on his brow! How much it is to be old!

I rise from my chair and move nimbly over to the window to watch the young Mr. Font trot down the steps and down onto the street, looking back one last time before scurrying away like a scared mouse—poor boy. The fly buzzes from the shadows into the center of the room, going about the ceiling, landing here and there on the furniture, on my books, on the windowsill. The temperature is dropping quickly and considerably. Rain has begun to come down in lazy sheets. The rain then turns into tiny droplets of hail. The tiny droplets of hail then transform into wide flakes of snow, gently falling over everything and beginning their accumulation that will dull the noise of the world. The fly takes off from the windowsill and his flight has become sluggish. He goes slowly from one place to another, the buzzing sound of his wings now more of a sputter. I turn off the lamp and go back over to my desk to put my house slippers on to prevent my toes from growing cold. I light a candle and remove a clean piece of paper from the drawer along with a pen. The fly returns to my desk, landing on its surface without an attempt to take off again. He crawls to the far edge of the desk, looking as if he were defeated. Then he stops.

19

I HAVE JUST TAKEN A MOMENT TO COLLECT MYSELF, and I must have dozed off because now it is completely dark. I am lying face down on the floor with a throbbing headache that goes from the back of my skull all the way through my brain into a steady, uncomfortable pulse between my eyes; next to me on the floor there lies *The Imaginaries* with its spine bent as it is open halfway, face down as well. Outside I can hear that the streets are wet from rain or melting snow;

the sound of car tires rolling over the pavement gives it away.

With the book open and the sleep clearing from my eyes, it is all coming back to me. The meeting with the old man that was either cryptic or incredibly direct—was any of it real? I seem to be disoriented still and cannot be sure if the old man is an actual memory or a fabricated one. I am wondering if it makes a difference in my commitment to establish a timeline of the events which brought me to my current horizontal position on the floor. I am willing to create a timeline that is specific to myself if need be; and in order to do so properly, I know that I must methodically kill off all of my other selves and possible selves. But before they can be burned, they must be found.

The blood creeping back into my limbs, I drag my heavy arm across the floor to grab the book. I pull it into my chest and take a few deep breaths. With some effort, I manage to push myself into a sitting position on the floor. I notice my socks are soaking wet, so I remove them from my feet, peeling them off slowly. I open the book—and not randomly as before. This is no longer a morbid curiosity. I am out for blood. I am out to kill all those fools who are responsible for ruining my life—why am I all alone? Where has my good woman gone? Where am I? The air feels too cold for Los Angeles. Once again, I am lost.

I steady my hands until they are still like those of a murderer. I am ready to recommence my investigation, to get back on the illusive trail of deceit and delusion. I lick my thumb and begin turning the pages one by one. In the third chapter from where I recall leaving off, after a few bizarre paragraphs that were written in Mexico (where I have never been), I find what I am looking for—the continuation of the experience that broke off en route to Austin, Tx.:

"I"[the quotations are all mine, and should be carried forward] came into Austin with a heart too sore for yet another woman, but I am now free of that ailment. The band and I are staying just outside of the university campus in an affluent residential neighborhood, in the home of a young woman who is very small with big hazel eyes named Ainsley. She is a kind, accommodating host, personable, and outgoing bordering on loud. It is clear already that she has taken a liking to me, as I have been supplied with the best blankets, the best pillows. It is late and we are standing around the kitchen drinking whiskey from coffee mugs. Occasionally she nestles her little blonde head into my chest (where it fits naturally, nicely, though I myself am not so tall), and makes odd remarks as if we've known one another forever. She knows how to get me. I fall in love easily, especially for tiny women with a penchant for drinking and affectionate behavior, no matter how bizarre. I am a man that needs to be loved, and this little woman has a lot of love to give; perhaps I have not yet taken a liking to her exactly, but I have certainly taken a liking to all that love she has to give.

I am looking past Ainsley, over her, out the kitchen window in what I am conscious of as being a whiskey haze. The moon is hidden, but bright. The trees are outlined by white, and the houses are softened so much they drip like paintings—none of this can be real. The kitchen has become the bathroom, and I am not in here alone. Ainsley is pulling my head down towards hers until our faces touch, our lips touch, our tongues touch. There is still mumbling and laughter in the kitchen. Our disappearance has gone unnoticed thus far—I nearly overlooked it myself. Ainsley pulls harder, preventing me from slipping out of her grasp back into the kitchen to find more to drink, slipping even further away then into a blacked out state, gone. She whispers, "My bedroom is the door just across the hall; we have to get there without being seen." I respond, "Anything to drink in there?" She kisses me again, backing herself—her tiny self—into the bathroom sink; I open my eyes to avoid stumbling and I see that behind Ainsley there is a mirror. In the mirror, I make the mistake of making eye contact with myself and suddenly remember the words about "mirrors and copulation" being horrible for the same reproductive reason. The words aptly fill me with horror and I want another drink. In another moment I will have that drink; I will sneak across the hallway with Ainsley leading me by the hand and I will be presented a pint of cheap liquor that will be drunk quickly and irresponsibly—soon after I will remove her clothes as she removes mine. We will fall into bed and copulate sloppily. I will see my vague reflection in her hazel eyes and know that I cannot escape. She will repeat herself over and over, saying, "I usually don't do this—oh my god. Really, I usually don't do this." I won't pretend any reaction to her words because I will be too drunk to give a shit. In the living room, on the floor, my bed will be taken by someone else who will thoroughly enjoy the best blankets, the best pillows. In the morning I will be too tired and ashamed to attempt to leave; my self-loathing and defeat will be misinterpreted as a willingness to stay—I won't have it in me to say No.

20

THINGS OFTEN HAPPEN QUICKLY and without explanation. Even the most logical, calculating person is liable to wind up far off base, asking themselves, "What has happened? How did I get here?" It is possible that the Christians were right to assume there is a Divine Will which steers us, no matter how badly we want to go to the right— to be in the right—always to the left at every fork in our lives, leading us to the inevitable center of everything, which is death. It is also possible that the Christians invented the idea of a Divine Will to comfort themselves with an explanation(that relieves them of personal responsibility) for their own backwards natures—"Everything happens for a reason," they say; even that thing you did while you were piss drunk, stumbling about in the blurry, all too familiar night. "God will forgive us our sins!"

I am unable to adopt either ideology. It is beyond me to think it reasonable to speculate about how the universe works, how it was created, and for what purpose—those things are incomprehensible and anyone who says otherwise is an asshole. I can only be conscious of the present, make peace with the past, and attempt to manifest the desired future.

This future I did not foresee. For two months I have been living a pleasant enough existence with Ainsley in her home in Austin, Tx. She takes classes at the university during the day; I take her dog, Penny, on walks, clean the house and do the dishes, go grocery shopping, read on the front porch and smoke cigarettes. She hates that I smoke; I hate knowing that I am not in love with her, yet am not able to sit her down to say, "This is not working." Instead, I quietly wait it out with a feigned smile, never truly being happy or content.

A man very slight in stature, standing at no more than five feet two inches tall, known widely as Professor Seagull, once said in his *longest book that's ever existed*(which never really existed to my knowledge), "The best definition of love that I have been able to formulate is that it is the captivity of the imagination. This is almost equivalent to saying that it is all imagination." And later he said, "The proper mate is the one who can stir the deepest chord that the individual can reach. "

I cannot fool myself about Ainsley. The only thing that she has held captive is my right to a full, healthy sex life, allowing for just one nightly release that always leaves me less than satisfied. I feel stopped up, constipated. Each day I begin writing a new book with this feeling —the same book as the day before. It goes nowhere. There is only one scene: a young woman with curly, brownish blonde hair and bright green eyes, wearing a summer dress and purple tennis shoes, stands in the park, calling to her dog who has disappeared into the thick bushes that line the bank of Town Lake(imagine a canal with swans and giant turtles and rope swings); when the dog finally emerges there are leaves and stickers caught in his fur, and as he sprints to the young woman— who is leaned over, patting her knees and laughing—his tongue is out and his tail wags wildly, freeing some of the snagged brush; the color of the dog is black; the young woman is absolutely beautiful; just as the dog reaches her, the sun brightens and washes out the scene in white light. And she is gone.

The young woman in the scene is a real woman. As real as any

524

woman, man, or creature can be. I saw her in the flesh, in the park, acting out the described scene. I have made it a habit to take Penny to the park every day for a couple of hours on the off chance of seeing the girl in the purple tennis shoes again. For a month now I have frequented the same bench in the same park, sitting there on the lookout while absently tossing the ball for Penny to go retrieve. Until just now, there has been nothing.

I have been sitting on this bench for over an hour. Penny is already exhausted from playing fetch in the heat. Ainsley is sitting in a classroom that may as well be across the world, studying texts she has lost all interest in. The girl in the purple tennis shoes, wearing another cotton summer dress, walks into the park; her big black dog(I'm bad with breeds) leads the way. I cross my left leg over my right, then uncross them. I cross my right leg over my left, then uncross them again.

I widen my stance and lean back like a cowboy, extending my arm across the backrest of the bench. I am sweating profusely, and from under my arm a giant dark spot shows. I take my arm down and lean forward, inconspicuously wiping the sweat from my face and underarms with my handkerchief. The girl in the purple tennis shoes plays with her dog and doesn't notice me.

Way off in the distance, across the park, there is a family sitting around a picnic table; they have the public grill going and smoke rises in signals of good health and happiness. Overhead, in a sky of exaggerated blue, there are bright white clouds inching along in slow motion —just a handful of them, gigantic, in shapes that resemble no object or creature known to the earth below. I take a cigarette from the pack in my shirtfront pocket and light it, sighing, 'what am I *doing*?' The girl in the purple tennis shoes has begun to walk slowly, casually, as her dog runs back and forth in erratic sprints from her side to nowhere, then back to her side. Her summer dress blows slightly in the hot breeze. I put out my cigarette and stand up. Penny looks at me in confusion as she sleepily emerges from the shade beneath the bench where she had been attempting to cool off. I take a steady, deep breath. I begin walking across the park to approach the girl, prettier than anyone I have ever seen.

21

CLIMBING THE WIDE STAIRCASE ALONG THE EDGE of an eccentric old woman's vast library, one will notice that the pictures on the wall—which change daily from one dull, ordinary image to another —are hung completely crooked and at varying heights, which, along with the exertion of climbing *so* many stairs, gives one the impression

of ascending into another world, a mad one like in a fairytale. Perpet-
uating this is the fact that the staircase, as you get higher and higher,
narrows.

At the top of these stairs, to get to the uppermost floor of the
library, the staircase has become so narrow that it is necessary to turn
your body ninety degrees and side step through the thin gap that
remains. Once through, you come upon a massive room with vaulted
ceilings, ornate wooden carvings, and more haphazardly hung pictures.
Off to the right there is a banister, which when approached can be
held onto firmly as you lean over and stare down several stories to the
bottom floor of the library. Standing at this banister is the eccentric old
woman. Her hair, streaked with wild flurries of grey, is pulled back into
a messy bun at the nape of her neck; she is wearing cognac colored
loafers, stockings with runs, and a shabby deep purple dress that has a
single tear in it, just over her right breast, exposing a dingy yellow bra
that looks as though it were once white. Next to her is a tall stack of
books; methodically, she grabs at the books from the stack, ripping out
single pages here and there, sometimes whole chunks, and very diligently she drops them over the banister.

As I approach this woman, watching as the pages float down towards the ground, I see that every book in her stack is written by me;
instinctively, I know the contents of each and every page she rips out
and discards. I am outraged by this woman. I attempt to charge her,
screaming, but am prevented from doing so by some unknown force. I
continue creeping along slowly, noiselessly, though I am certain she is
aware of my presence. When I finally reach her side, I make a motion
to push her over the edge, but my limbs are useless, constricted by the
same unknown force that slowed my charge to a waddle; ever so gently
I embrace her thin, rigid figure. She turns and looks at me with her big,
hurt, grey-green eyes. Angling her head down, she bats her eyelashes at
me like an ancient flirt. I feel her bony hand groping for my fly, and as
she pulls me out she looks upwards, without moving her head, and flashes a tiny, frightening smile. I cannot fight her—I'm paralyzed. I can
feel my body responding under her skeletal fingers; the dry skin of her
palm rubs the length of my hard cock and I am mortified. She is still
smiling. Her teeth match the color of her bra. With her free hand she
continues to destroy my books, tearing at the pages with purpose, then
gently letting them go over the banister where they drop, like ash
falling slowly from a fire escape, further and further into the dark, way
down into what I imagine must be hell.

22

I WAKE UP SICK FROM A LATE NIGHT and there is rain beating against the apartment windows. Hangovers are easier to deal with in the rain—the sound and the color, they make the world seem smaller, more manageable. For a few moments I lie here on our bed on the floor, and I watch the water hit the windows and roll down the glass; behind the water that rolls down the glass is nothing but bright grey sky—sky that will help in temporarily lifting the weight from the stooped shoulders of drunks all across the city.

Turning over, I see there is a note that has been left on the pillow beside me: *At work. Be back just after 2. Eat some soup today, sick boy. I love you. –Lillian.* It's incredible how sweet she is to me now, and how much I have begun to take it for granted. It's about 10.15am, and I am thinking, 'I have all the time in the world.'

There is some speculation about how I got here, to apartment number 47 in the Lucinda Court Apartment Building in this notoriously clean city called Portland, Oregon where I live with my kind-hearted girlfriend, Lillian. One book claims that we met in a café on the central west coast; another book claims that I boldly approached her in a park in Austin, Texas. I have memory of both events, along with a few others. I can recall the grey fog rolling down off the hills and through the small streets of Monterey, Ca., the bark of the sea lions echoing off the buildings, seeing her through the windows of the café where she worked, and going in for one last glass of wine just to talk to her as she swept up for the night. I can recall the humidity and blinding sunlight of the park in Texas, sitting on a bench, nervous as hell, seeing her across the dry brown-green grass in her cotton summer dress and purple shoes, and finally getting the nerve to walk over to her and say "hello." I can even recall living with her at her mom's house in Austin, working on Lake Travis for the summer as she, unemployed, bored, grew increasingly anxious and suspicious. And in each of these memories the dynamics of our relationship remain consistently the same; in each of these memories we still arrive in our present state.

Whether we were in Monterey, or Austin, or wherever, the first year we spent together she fought it. She had been eight months out of a relationship with a man who was neglectful and promiscuous. She distrusted men. She wanted nothing from me, and almost wanted nothing to do with me. I wrote her love letters constantly, did things for her, tried to show her that I was a different type of man than she was accustomed to. I told my family all about her and introduced her to them; for her first meeting—my father's 50th birthday—she showed up two hours late, having drunk two bottles of red wine, and almost missed dinner.

She was cold at first, mean even. She would ignore me for a week or two, not pick up my phone calls. She would flaunt pictures of her and her ex-boyfriend(including one in which they were having sex), and talk always about her old friends, her old life, and how much she missed those times. Once I had finally won her over it was bittersweet —I felt as though I had had to coerce her into the relationship, as though by force I had made her my girlfriend.

She became jealous of my past(though so open and careless with hers), and condescending. She created intrigue about my behavior, grounded or ungrounded, and berated me. I did not write well enough. I could not play the guitar. I should not have had that drink with the guys, because it wasn't just with *the guys*, was it....

But I loved her. I was patient. And for all of that love I was treated with what felt like contempt, with questioning, with disbelief. By the second year I had become exhausted with trying to sway her—either she would love me or she wouldn't.

My exhaustion quickly presented itself as indifference. I no longer fought back. I was too worn out to *try* anymore. And she finally loved me then—wholly, completely.

This second year has been one of quiet resentment. Why had it taken a full year to convince her to love me? Why should one ever have to be *convinced* to love someone else? Her every kind gesture was put in the shadow cast by that first year. Every sweet thing she said was heard as if from a distance, muffled. I had followed her everywhere. We had gone where *she* wanted to go, eaten what *she* wanted to eat. A precedent had been set. She expected me to remain obedient, like her big black dog, to remain accommodating to her every desire and whim. But I did not feel as though I were truly appreciated. I could not fully love someone whose love for me seemed to be based more out of the things I had done for her and *would* do than out of a genuine, heartfelt feeling for me, as a person. The love I had for so long tried to win was cheapened, made into a travesty. The shadow still loomed over our heads, and so even in the warm glow of Lillian's deepening love I chose to reject her.

The rain against the windows suddenly comes into view again. The sickness in my head and stomach worsen—images from last night are coming back. And then that note on the pillow....

23

IN THE ENGLISH COUNTRYSIDE there was a young man riding his bike, with its busted brakes, quickly through the slick and rutted paths of the dark; a bearded narrator, from somewhere off in the objective distance, formulated an explanation for the young man's precarious ride: "Recklessness is almost a man's revenge on his woman. He feels he is not valued, so he will risk destroying himself to deprive her altogether."

I can feel this same bearded figure hovering over me as I lie sick on the apartment floor, and he is repeating these words over and over in time with the rain. These are no longer words of sympathy; they are words of disgust.

For all of my extended efforts of making things work with Lillian, I have become a complete contradiction of the person who had made those efforts. The duality of man in its omnipresence is heartbreaking. My behavior is dishonest. It is lonely. I cannot share with Lillian where I was last night, or many other nights. She is under the assumption that I went out for a smoke, then chose to take a long, slow walk through downtown Portland in the rain, which resulted in me coming home near four in the morning, wet, and probably snoring for two hours until she had to wake up for work at six. This is only partially true. Perhaps the reason she does not understand this odd *story*, or fully believe it.

The full truth about what happened last night is much more logical than a long, slow walk without purpose—at least in the mind of a man it is. I got off work from the market at midnight—closing shift—only to return home to find Lillian sleeping. We both work at the market now on opposite schedules—she opens, I close. Even our days off are often not shared, except for Sundays; and on Sundays we always go out to lunch together, always to the same restaurant.

The sight of her sleeping, common as it is, did not fill me with anger or resentment as much as it did sadness. When she didn't love me, she slept; now that she does love me, she still sleeps. For awhile I sat up in the chair, reading, drinking. The rain was coming down and I could hear a lone bum singing *fuck-yous* from behind our building. It was distracting and mortifying, knowing that he was singing to me. I could not follow the story on the page; I reread two paragraphs continuously.

I put the bookmark back in the same spot it had been when I picked up the book and I went outside for a cigarette. By way of a well-practiced routine, I had smoked the cigarette perfectly down to the filter just as I was arriving at Tommy's Tavern on foot. There were only a few people inside. It was dark and there was music playing. The bartender was an old woman who I had seen often, and who knew me. She brought my whiskey to the end of the counter. As I stared into the glass, it occurred to me that I was not just out for a drink—I was out to be around women. Never would I touch them, or go home with them. Sometimes I would talk to them. But mainly I preferred to just look at them, from a distance, where they remained objects of my fascination, and appreciation; where I could pretend all of the different futures that I might have with them.

The old bartender was the only woman in the bar and she wasn't cutting it. I swallowed my drink and left. It was still raining, and I walked forward through the rain mindlessly. I walked forward in whichever direction my feet took me until I ended up in the middle of Chinatown at The Gardens—a strip joint where there was no cover, the woman serving you beer was eighty-five years old and friendly, and the girls dancing on stage looked like those strange, beautiful creatures that lived next door to you or around the corner; the ones with the tattoos that you had always offhandedly thought about seeing naked, or fucking, but never dreamed of doing so. At The Gardens you could watch them unabashedly. I drank beer and I shot pool by myself. I watched the girls and didn't say anything to them. Every so often I would go to the stage and politely place a dollar at the dancing girl's feet. She would smile and bend over. I would smile back then go back to playing pool.

The beer was more expensive than it should be at The Gardens, but I stayed there drinking until closing as I usually did when I wandered down there. Two-thirty in the morning and the beer in my blood and in my brain, and the images of all those girls stuck in my head without their clothes on—it is the saddest time in the night. Two-thirty in the morning is when you're still sober enough to know that you have made a mistake, and that you will continue to make more if you stay out, but just drunk enough where you will do nothing about it. I had a cigarette outside of The Gardens, just in case one of the girls had noticed me and felt like chatting for a bit—they never did. It broke my heart that they never wanted to talk to you—with their clothes on I mean, after your wallet is closed to them for the night. I just wanted the company. I just wanted someone to be next to me, awake.

Somewhat dejectedly, I stubbed out my cigarette and stumbled away from the entrance. It was never my intention—never!—but by another routine I found myself moving not back toward the apartment, but down five blocks to the late night haunt. There was a cover there —fifteen dollars—plus a one drink minimum. They only served water or juice. So I paid for everything and sat down with my water at the big stage. More drinks wouldn't be a problem—there was a flask in my pocket. I have to piss a lot anyway, so I would be taking several trips to the restroom regardless. Each time I stared into my face in the mirror. I forced a smile and it was much worse than the strippers at The Gardens not wanting to talk. There was some toilet paper on the floor. Water was in puddles on the sink. The bathroom smelled *too* clean, as if covering up for something. The masking odor was nauseating. I would choke down my pulls from the flask and get out—just one last disapproving look into the mirror.

At the late night place there was a rule that you had to pay at least a dollar for every song. They cut their songs short there, too, and the girls on stage—usually eighteen or nineteen years old—were of the sort that looked as though they hated what they were doing. The clientele hated what *they* were doing too. It was obvious in the way that no one was talking, or making eye contact. Everyone just stared forward and kept their money on the counter. It was easy to spend a lot of money there, and fast. You wanted to make just one girl smile, or you wanted to feel like you were giving her all you had, or something, and the money disappeared.

Forty-five minutes in, knowing that you could do this all night, spending all your money and never being satisfied, a girl would approach you. She had already approached you earlier in the night, but you weren't as desperate then. The girl that approached me was a little blonde chick. She was cute, in good shape, had a nice smile, and smelled nice enough, albeit somewhat strong—that traditional pungent aroma of cotton candy and sweat. It was $120 for a private dance, half-hour. I agreed upon the price with the girl and went to the ATM to withdraw the money. Another five-dollar charge just for that. Then she took the cash and guided me into a tiny room—maybe six by six feet —with a loveseat against the wall, a chair across from it that basically touched the loveseat, a mirror on two of the four walls, and two cameras on the other two walls. She laid one white towel down on the loveseat, and one down on the chair. I was instructed to sit down on the loveseat—the more comfortable option—and she closed the door.

Once that door was closed the girls will do whatever you want them to—for half an hour. They'll dance on you, they'll play with themselves, they'll stick a finger in their ass if that's what you're into. This girl, she could tell that I was somewhat uneasy with everything even though I paid without hesitation. She took it easy on me by dancing at first. A few minutes right there in my face. Then she turned around and sat down in the chair, stripping the last of her little clothing off and she began playing with herself. Her leg was propped up on the loveseat as she rubbed her finger in a circular motion over her clit. She was telling me about a couple that she danced for once. They came into that tiny room with her and they fucked while she fingered herself, she said. Everything was making me sick, but I was turned on too— which made me even sicker. The only thing I could do was to not look this girl in the eye and imagine that it was Lillian in front of me, touching herself, telling me to touch myself. And then it was over. The half hour was up.

The late night cab ride back was a silent one. There were a few cabbies waiting right outside for the ashamed patrons to come out. You just got in the cab and said your address. No one said anything else. He knew what you had just done, and you knew that he knew it. It was miserable. I kept picturing Lillian back at the apartment, asleep. She looked so adorable there, her mouth slightly parted, her body so warm, and small, and sweet. She was wearing my grey t-shirt—the soft one that she loved and always wore to bed. She was beautiful. So beautiful it hurt.

For whatever reason, I had the cabby drop me off a block away from the apartment. When I got upstairs I took off my shirt and stuffed it into the bottom of the hamper. I took off the rest of my clothes, took a piss, then quietly climbed into bed. There she was, exactly as I had pictured—the mouth, the shirt, the feel of the body; everything. I pushed myself as close to her as I could and a big wave of sadness came up in my chest. I wanted so badly to cry, to break down right there next to her and kiss her sweet face, but I couldn't. If I did, she would wake up. She would smell the booze on my breath and probably the cotton candy on my neck. She would have questions, the answers to which I could never give her.

24

THERE IS A BAD TASTE IN MY MOUTH. Like the sticky aftertaste of fruit that has gone putrid. And it's not the metabolizing alcohol. It's the bad taste that goodhearted men get when they have done wrong. It's that vile flavor of our misdoings, that sickness that rises straight from the bottom of our guts and comes out through our lying teeth.

I have had enough of this. I am done with lonely nights out and even lonelier mornings in. I want to be a good man. Someone who wives will use as an example to their husbands—"*he* does this," and, "*he* does that"; "why don't *you* do those things?" I want mothers to invite me to their daughters' parties where I will behave in a polite and charming manner. I will talk to them about my wonderful girlfriend, Lillian, and tell them how I wish she hadn't had to go in to work that day so they could meet her. I want to be the recipient of adoration and a source of genuine happiness.

But that is only one side of my nature. The Other is still inside of me, festering until that moment in the night when She is asleep and I can no longer bare the weight of my isolated self, so run off wild into the dark.

I brush my teeth. Part of my gums bleeds a little, causing a red thread to go through the white foam in the sink. I rinse away the foam and the red thread, then cup some water in my hand and into my mouth—swish then spit. In the mirror I notice that my face is slightly swollen. This further irritates me with myself.

Still in my underwear and slippers, I go out of the bathroom and over to my typewriter in the window. The rain is still coming down, thank god, because I remember that the typewriter is out of ink. From a drawer in the kitchen I remove the small ink ribbon I purchased a few days ago. It will not fit in my typewriter—an old Golden Touch Hideaway—as is, whose spool is considerably larger; it's an involved process, but the transfer can be done.

For what feels like twenty minutes, sitting on the floor in underwear and slippers, I unravel the big spool, then hook the ribbon from the small spool to the empty big one and slowly wind. It is a complete mess—

Back to the typewriter then where the cause for my painstaking ink-ribbon-transfer can be carried out.

It has occurred to me that in order to be a good man I must annihilate that Other within me; if this is not possible, then I will simply cast him off into the abstract world of literary creation, of complete fancy and fabrication. I will put him away forever in an ongoing book and this book will be called, "The Imaginaries." The plot will be difficult to define in this book, as well as the timeline, for the plot is actually the fate of man himself in his perpetual search for perfection and its inevitable discontentment as consequence; how he is always looking with his wandering eye for that thing that will complete him, though the thing itself exists only in his imagination—a woman, whatever amount of success, or power, a certain location, his Savior, etc.; and how when these things exist only in the imagination, although they are "real" to the individual, they are intangible, unattainable in any real sense, and therefore timeless. Thus, the search is never ending.

My fingers are moving over the convoluted keys of the typewriter. I start with women. For me, Woman is "God" incarnate. The creator of life. The beauty that hides behind everything. It is astonishing how quickly they come and go. It is as though all the women in my life passed me by in the highlight reel of a silent film—both the highs and the lows. There is no dialogue; occasionally words or thoughts or feelings are simply conveyed through quiet space. Their faces, their features, bleed from one to the next. I never appear in frame. I am like a bystander, put there to record their beauty and their horror...somewhere—I curse too much for Heaven, and I pray too much for Hell; which leaves us where?

The fading in and out occurs from one minute to the next and it is seamless. As they fade out(and the next fades in), if I look closely, I can see evidence in the background that proves this so-called bystander is not so innocent. Once through, it is as if the woman passed through a filter with jagged edges, some sort of spiritual colander that allows most everything to go through, but retains a tiny fraction of their better parts—though surely noticeable—and they are somehow less than they were before. I think of Lillian. If she ever reads *The Imaginaries* then we will be done. At the moment she is fully intact with color, sound, and dialogue. Will she, too, then be like the hazy, dreamlike women that have passed through before her? Will she be forced to love me Neruda's "certain dark things," taken grossly out of context? Or will she just not love me at all...?

I take up the first twenty or so pages of the book, which came effortlessly from the back of my brain, and I am disgusted by them; they are trash, smut, nonsense. My messy hands put black smudges all over the pages and I think, 'Fine.'

Past the soiled pages, out the window, and down on the street in the rain, there is a man; he is standing there smoking a cigarette, waving happily up at me in the window. This man is a good friend of mine—Ali, the tailor. He is tall, very skinny, with messy blonde hair and a blonde beard. He is smiling as he waves, and he is wearing giant, colorful rain boots. I wave back at him with my hands so black from the ink, and I am grateful that he cannot see so closely the stains that I have made. Still smiling, he drops his waving hand down to his side and continues to smoke with the other. He walks off and turns the corner.

A moment or two later the door-buzzer goes off. I know it is Ali the tailor, but I approach the intercom and answer with an affected air of questioning anyway. "Hello...?"

"Good morning!" says jovial Ali through static of the old fashioned intercom. "Come down, come down—I have something to show you!" I tell him I'll be down in a second.

Ali always has something to show me. New clothes that he has made for one of the dolls in his extensive collection, maybe a new doll that he has purchased, maybe a new doll that he has made, a book that has arrived in the mail, something he found on the streets or in the dumpsters—anything, everything. They are always interesting things, too. Even if they wouldn't usually interest me personally, his excitement over these items makes up for it. He is like an intelligent child who beams with light on his good days. And more often than not, it is one of Ali's good days.

Outside the rain feels good on my face and the physical part of the hangover seems to have run its course. I light up a cigarette and even though Ali has just finished smoking he is kind enough to stand with me in the rain to wait. We slowly walk out of the courtyard and to the corner. He lives in the building next to mine, just above the front stoop where the noise from the bums is loud enough to keep him up at night. He doesn't look tired though, not Ali; he has bounce in his step and his eyes are open wide. He's the type of man that won't let you get down. He is a good man to have as your neighbor.

Small talk("Your hands!" Ali exclaims) and the dodging of a few of the more obnoxious neighbors and we are in the apartment. The apartment is supposed to be a one bedroom, but it functions for Ali as a studio with a separate workspace. The walls are covered from one end of the apartment to the other. Giant dolls, little dolls, books upon books on the shelves, trinkets, paintings, drawings, his testicles in a leather pouch hanging from a nail(never actually seen them), doll furniture, doll heads, a gold-plated piggy bank; and there are dishes of candy on the desk, and on the shelves, there are a couple of tiny wooden pianos(fully functional), stars on the ceiling, satin butterflies hanging from string, a disco ball, mirrors, clocks, and so on. There is at least one of everything in his apartment, and there's still room to sit in a tiny green wooden chair for the cup of tea that he always so politely offers —a little table to set it on, too. It's a nice place to come for distraction —a safe haven of sorts; for a little while, looking around at the various things in the apartment, you forget about all the shit you've done.

As I'm standing in the kitchen of the warm apartment, sipping from the cup of tea that Ali has just placed in my hands without asking whether or not I wanted one(I did), he finally asks, "So are you ready?" A big smile is across his face, showing what I imagination is just part of his whole excitement. I am certainly ready.

From his freezer he extracts a large clear plastic bag that has been sealed at the top. He is nearly squealing about it. He holds it up to my face, his smile bigger than ever, and says, "It's a squirrel!" The squirrel is most definitely dead, but he appears to be in good condition otherwise—he wasn't run over by a car or anything. His fur is different shades of grey. His mouth is partially open.

Ali continues to explain his plans for the squirrel. How he has a taxidermy kit coming in the mail, and so on. So my good friend will soon be Ali the taxidermist. And this little guy in the bag will soon be thawed and stuffed, then mounted on a small plank of wood where he will stand with his tail up and his teeth out, his arms spread as wide as they can be, with a tiny party-hat atop his fuzzy head—forever.

25

I AM BACK IN APT. NO.47 OF THE LUCINDA COURT Apartment Building, still about 10.15am, again in my underwear and slippers at the typewriter, and in the mid-thirties pages of *The Imaginaries*, coming suddenly from my fingertips, are the words, "Not all futures are bright," and with these words I am actually experiencing, in the present tense, the future in which I unconsciously describe:

Not all futures are bright. Bright maybe in the way that the sun is out in this future, glaring off the newly fallen snow and the dangerous looking icicles hanging from the gutters of the adjacent apartment buildings, but not otherwise.

I would not say that this future is bleak either; I am past the point in my life where I feel it necessary to exaggerate the melancholy of a given situation. Some futures are just there—or here, rather. Here where I am compelled to sit at the window, staring out at the bright, glistening snow while the baby is asleep on the couch behind me. I do not need to turn around to check on him—the soft sound of his breathing is enough to ensure me that he is okay; and I do not need to turn around to know what he looks like. He looks like a perfect combination of me and of Jean. He looks like the beautiful cause that Jean will never love me. She loves him as much as I do. But I love her as well, and *she will never love me.* There's resentment in her face when she looks at me and in her voice when she talks to me. It happened too early. We were too young. She didn't want to have him, but I convinced her. I told her that everything would be fine, but it's not. And he's not so much of a baby anymore—he'll be three in just a few months.

Before it happened I think we both dreamt of moving to the city, living in a shitty apartment together, staying up all night listening to music, screwing, sleeping in; she would shoot photographs and I would write. Or maybe it was just me that dreamt that. I knew nothing about her then, and still don't. But the city sounds a logical dream that we or I would have had, at least a common one for an eighteen year old from Lincoln, Nebraska.

This is not the city. This is the small "downtown" of what could be considered both of our hometowns. My apartment is above a coffee shop. The newly fallen snow covers the narrow empty streets I know so well that will be grey and black in a matter of hours from the traffic that has yet begun. There is no music playing because, as I said, the kid is sleeping. A sweet little thing. Poor little thing. I turn around to look at him, and see that he is sleeping on his stomach with his head turned away from me. One leg is bent and pulled up to his side. His back rises and falls with each breath. The glow from outside is diffused as it comes through the window and it falls over him like the light in old oil paintings. That is the way I choose to see it anyway. There is no other option for me—this is just how it is. I only have him for the rest of the day. Jean will be here this evening to pick him up. She'll ask me how he was, and I'll tell her great. And that will be that.

Turning back around toward the snow, I see that it has been replaced by great big green trees, green lawns and wildflowers and pickup trucks parked outside their low-set Texas homes—all in that blaring sunshine of midsummer. The screen is in the way to see properly, but my eyes are adjusting, and the yellow light illuminates everything in a way that I am able to easily romanticize my surroundings. Across the street there is an old man watering his front lawn without his shirt on; his tanned skin hangs loosely about his stomach and his chest, thick eyeglasses drown out most of his face. The sunflowers here are gigantic; the patch of them in our front yard hides the old man's lower body, but I can guess what those skinny legs look like. The hummingbirds drink the bright red sugar-water from their feeders. The finches fly back and forth, then disappear as they land on a sunflower. A squirrel knocks down a small branch from a tree. Everything is glowing. Behind me, Lillian is napping with the baby—I can feel them there; I can hear the soft sound of their breathing. I turn around again and they are glowing too, softly.

Our little girl's birthday is right around the corner. A week from today she will be turning one. There's not enough money to buy her much, but we can make her something too. She's such a sweet little thing. They both look so adorable together. The warm light coming through the window falls over them and they must be getting hot— there's sweat on Lillian's upper lip. I close the shades and go to them.

I am becoming sentimental here. And for what—children that weren't born in this future? lives that I am leading somewhere in obscurity? Being a sentimentalist can make you sloppy, obtuse. A meaningful sentence can quickly become pathetic. *The Imaginaries* seems to be the most pathetic thing I have ever written then. When you write within your own privacy, there is nothing holding you back from putting down absolutely everything. Objectivity turns to subjectivity. Everything is important.

The rain coming down in its consistent, gentle blanket is the most significant rain of the century. It marks the potential for every moment to be the beginning of something new. A change in behavior, or temperament. The swearing off of a bad habit. The rededication to something that has been neglected. I pretend that I am out in the rain, letting it come down over my head and body, and I know that this sounds sentimental too, but I refuse to give a damn about the sound of anything so long as it sounds good to me. And, at the moment, what sounds good is a break.

THE WANDERING EYE, EVEN INWARD-TURNED, does not cease to weigh heavily upon a man who desires to be good. The weight, in fact, seems to grow even heavier. In reality there are imperfections. In the imagination there is an inclination to overlook these imperfections. A man will see nothing outside of what he chooses to see, and what he chooses to see is often exaggerated, crystallized in his mind until the point where it becomes *intangible, unattainable in any real sense*. It is enough to make him go mad.

I undertook the writing of the book knowing that this was the case. There is no room for me to groan into my pillow, "What have I done?!" The monster that I sought to destroy has grown considerably larger, branched out to even more depraved behavior—and I let him. Although the actions have only been committed in the imagination(and subsequently on paper), they have been committed in the heart, too, and the evidence is in my face. Lillian is suspicious of me. She knows that I am writing a "secret book." With contempt, she eyes the envelope that I store the pages in. She cannot stand the sight of that envelope. To her, that envelope is not just a reflection of my Self, but the complete, unabridged version of it. It is filled with the things she will never know about me.

For weeks now the envelope has been getting fatter, heavier. What was once a visual representation of my thin attempt to rid myself of certain dark urges is now a visual representation of my failure to do so —the envelope is impregnated with those urges. I am not Catholic. If I were, I would simply go to a priest and have him absolve me of my sins after chanting a thousand Hail Marys. I recite them by myself anyway, shut tightly away in the darkness of the closet in our apartment. I believe that She has forgiven me, but it is not her forgiveness I seek. Poor Lillian, the way she looks at me when we're eating together between her shift and mine; I know that she suspects me of something much worse than I have done. But I can't find it in me to reveal the smaller wrong to her imagined atrocity. The envelope has continued to fatten.

The only chance I have for redemption is absolute suppression. To push that dark thing far enough down so it can no longer breathe. With every brief contact it has with the air it becomes stronger, hungrier. Now it will suffocate.

When I began writing, I promised myself two things: that I would never make life decisions based on whether or not they would make for a good story, and that I would never choose anything over my work. But Lillian is worth breaking a promise for, if it's not too late. I am taking an extended break from the writing of *The Imaginaries*— indefinitely. I have stored the envelope away.

ONCE A MAN HAS MADE UP HIS MIND, he can make anything work. Around a single idea he is able to alter himself in order to achieve the outcome he so badly wants. We are ambitious and resolute when we want something. We are persistent to the point of derangement.

My mind is made up and the idea is simple, clear: Lillian. It was for her that I changed two years ago, settling down from my habitual traveling, of moving in that triangular pattern from Nebraska to California to Washington, back to Nebraska, and so forth. I broke all ties to my old life and I stayed with her, *for* her. And for her I will change again.

Two years ago to the day, tomorrow—Valentine's Day. We had been seeing a little bit of each other, on and off at her accord. She wasn't ready for a new boyfriend, but she did ask me to be her Valentine's date. Like a little girl, she had slipped me a piece of paper that posed the question, and I was supposed to check one of the boxes below— yes or no. I still have that slip of paper, with my very concise X placed in the "yes" box. I keep it in an envelope along with other keepsakes: a bracelet she had given me to match her own, a letter or two she had sent me in response to my dozen while I was away for two weeks, a ticket to a concert, a movie, a flight overseas, a picture of her over my shoulder in the sunshine as I spun her in circles, various notes on scratch paper, on bar napkins, a "menu" she had prepared for me to choose which food items she would make me while I was sick, brittle flower petals from small bouquets she would pick for me from the side of the road—amongst many other things, of course. She really has been good to me when it comes down to it; I have done my best to be good to her.

On that Valentine's Day we were going out to dinner with a group of friends. She wouldn't let me pick her up—we would meet at the restaurant—but I was okay with that because it gave me time to put the finishing touches on a letter I had written her. The letter explained that I understood she didn't *want* anything from me, as I did not *want* anything from her, although it was impossible to deny that she had already come to mean something to me(I detailed shared experiences, specific memories). I told her that it was not necessary for her to reciprocate my feelings, but that I wanted her to at least accept the fact that she meant something to someone, and that would not change regardless of her reaction. In all, it was a good letter. Needless to say, I went on further in this vein—for six pages. It was much more in depth than the brief description I have just given, and more personal—but the gist should be gotten from the cited examples.

I was mortified to be the first to arrive at the decided upon restaurant—ten minutes late nonetheless. The hostess gave me the once over. I told her I was waiting on the rest of the party, then proceeded to smoke in the non-smoking section of the patio.

Two couples showed up from our party and joined me—I noted that I was dressed better than they were. They asked me if I knew where Lillian was, and I told them that I didn't. Then two more couples showed up and did the same. Finally, ten minutes later, Lillian arrived with her date.

I was the odd man out once we all sat down at the table. Everyone was paired up. I sat across from Lillian, who sat next to her date. They shared a meal. Each had two drinks. He paid. The letter was burning a painful hole in my pocket.

There was only one bar that Lillian could get into at the time (she was still a minor), so it was the obvious change of venue that we made after dinner. We all sat at the counter of the bar. There were two couples between me and Lillian. I got drunk. I had to take a piss, and before doing so I went and gave the letter to her. She accepted it, baffled, then put it in her pocket and carried on drinking and laughing with her date and the folks next to them. It was humiliating. I leaned one hand against the wall above the urinal as I pissed, then went out and immediately ordered another drink. I took it in one go, as is the custom when your intent is to get shitty. I left the bar then and went across the street to another bar.

Later I learned that as I sat across the street, drinking two pints of beer in crowded isolation, Lillian was in the ladies room discussing with a friend this letter that she had been given and that had yet to be opened.

When I stumbled back across the street, Lillian sat next to me at the bar. She was strange and I was hurt. I clinked the ice in my new glass. I drank as though I were trying to "catch up." When the bar began to sway, I quickly made my downtrodden goodbyes and exited.

It was her friend who finally read the letter. Lillian didn't have the courage to do it. She told Lillian that she was a fool if she let me go. In the morning, Lillian called to ask if I would see her.

Two years ago to the day, tomorrow—but we are celebrating the first part of our anniversary today. It is Lillian's first of two days off from work. She is sleeping in.

I make her breakfast—the kind I used to make her every morning when we first started dating: two slices of wheat toast, fat free cottage cheese, and fresh fruit; the only thing missing from the plate is the couple of flowers that I would pick from the yard. When I bring it to

540

her she opens her eyes slowly and says my name in a very quiet voice. I kiss her. Her skin is soft from sleep and her body is warm. My grey t-shirt hangs loosely off her shoulders. It's so easy to love her when she is this way; it's so easy to love someone when they are just waking up.

Knowing it was our anniversary, our boss gave me the midday shift so I could be off in time to go out with Lillian, who made the plans for our night; she has been extremely secretive about these plans —it is to be a surprise.

I wear my wool suit with my black tie in to work. I put on an apron, tied neatly around the front, and as I sweep the market floors I feel as though I have been transported into 1920's small town America. I am just a simple young man seeing to his duties in quiet excitement before his big date with his sweetheart.

While the market is spotless and dead, I slip into the back office to make Lillian a Valentine. I use what supplies are available to me and manage to put together a giant heart made of foam board, framed with aluminum foil and lined with old Christmas lights; the lights then move into the middle of the heart and form the words, "I love you," in cursive. It's gaudy and quite clearly constructed by hand. She is going to love it. I wrap it in a big, black trash bag and stash it away safely where I will be able to retrieve it tomorrow—the day I was supposed to have planned.

It is just after dark when Lillian arrives and I clock out. She looks amazing in her tiny shoes, stockings, and grey, form-fitting wool dress. Her legs are so thin and fragile looking; her golden and brown curls hang over her shoulders in a way that is precious to me; her big green eyes are bright as ever; the mole over her upper lip is accentuated by a smile that will forever endear her to me—the "diamond" in her tooth, as I like to call it, is gleaming. I remove my apron and toss it on a hook in the back. My palms and forehead are sweating—every horrible thing I have ever done comes out in that sweat. I wipe my forehead with my handkerchief and my hands on a clean towel and I am happy. I go to my little sweetheart and together, hand in hand, we take off.

It is a long walk to our first destination, and Lillian refuses to tell me where we are going until we arrive. I continuously make absurd guesses as to where we are heading. This or that restaurant; this or that dive bar. We pass by the heavy wooden doors of a Moroccan restaurant that we have always talked about going to. I ask if we are going there, and she says no, then turns around and opens the door.

Inside the restaurant, the walls and ceilings are adorned with decorative tapestries and the servers are wearing traditional Moroccan dress although for the most part they look like your typical middle class white kids, probably attending art school in the city. The patrons are all sitting on plush pillows placed on the ground around very low-set tables. A belly dancer traipses through the main dining area, methodically moving her hips and abdomen, clinking together the tiny cymbals attached to each thumb and middle-finger, then she moves into a section in the back of the restaurant. The lights are low. The music is loud. Someone greets us and asks for the name on the reservation. She put them in my last name—Mr. and Mrs.

We are seated at a table in the main dining area next to an older couple, dressed poorly, very quiet. I am taken by the notion proposed by the name on our reservation. We are newlyweds, beaming in each other's company, sitting close together, holding hands under the table. The low lights and entrancing music add to this fantasy. I order a beer and that helps too. The old couple next to us is aware of the spark— they smile at us.

With our drinks on the table, Lillian gets up to use the restroom; the woman next to us gets up too, leaving just the men at the tables placed so closely together. The gentleman, reclined so far he is basically lying down, lifts his beer bottle in the air towards me.

"Strong beer, huh?" I nod in agreement. "It's only my second one," he says, "and already I feel a little—" he whistles two notes, high then low, to allude to being slightly drunk.

I laugh, and say, "I think it's something about these lights too."

He mulls it over while inspecting the lights, then replies with a distracted, "mm-hmm...." A few moments pass. Then he asks, "Your girlfriend?" pointing with a nod of his head in the direction of the restrooms.

"Wife," I say simply.

"Ah—you're a very lucky man."

The women return from the restroom and it is though the man and I had never spoken. What little he says to his wife is said quietly. Lillian and I flirt in gentle grasps of the hand, or of the knee, and in whispers. The concept of being newlyweds has stuck. The quiet man's words are repeated in my head, though I am no longer sure he ever spoke them—*you're a very lucky man.*

The food arrives in waves—first course through fifth. Each course is to be eaten with your hands, using bread as your only other utensil. Between each course a young woman comes around and rinses your hands for you; she pours warm water over them first with your palms up, then with your palms down. I can tell that Lillian is self conscious at first, but by the time the third course is through she has warmed up to the practice—she willingly offers her hands to the young woman. Once the main course is finished, we are given cold glasses of mint tea and a small bowl of fruit. Then our hands are rinsed one last time with fragrant water.

I have an issue with my blood sugar levels—if I wait too long between meals I get weak, lightheaded, black spots creep into my peripheral vision; and when I do eat, I have the feeling that I am high. After a meal as large as the one we have just eaten, I feel extremely high—and those two *strong beers* to boot. Hand in hand again, we are walking through the drowsy city through the dark to a location that is being kept from me as yet another secret.

Are we going to that porn shop over there? Are we going to loot the market? Are we going to the gay club to dance? To the park to sleep with the bums? To that back alley where you're going to kill me? Are you taking me *somewhere* to kill me? Am I going to die tonight?

To all of my questions the answer is no—obviously. At the moment we are simply walking hand in hand through the city. We are lost, making unnecessary turns down this or that way, headed in one direction then the opposite. She has not been familiarized with the city as I have, on foot, on those long walks I used to take during my extensive job hunting. As we eventually head back in the direction of our apartment, it dawns on me where we are going(The Hotel Deluxe, a swanky spot near our apartment and even nearer our work where we've walked by numerous times and daydreamed about staying), but I don't let on that I know—I continue asking questions concerning our destination.

A block away from the hotel I ask, "Are we going to Renee's to further discuss Lady's death?" Renee is an older woman, a regular at the market, who has taken a liking to me and who we visited at her apartment—right across the street from the hotel—not long ago, right after she had her dog, Lady, put down. Lillian is under the assumption that Renee is in love with me, an assumption she made after several encounters with Renee in which Renee would not address her or even so much as look at her. She may be right about this. Renee's main topic of conversation is her dog Lady, and how she had to put her down(she *was* old) so that she could get on with her own life; in turn, Renee speaks of Lillian to me as if she were *my* Lady. Of course, we are not going there.

The doorman of the hotel opens the door for us and addresses Lillian by "name"—*Mrs. Font*, to be exact. She gives me a coy smile over her shoulder as we enter.

The elevator has granite floors and a mirrored ceiling. We are the only people riding in it, and from the first to the third floor we are honeymooning—I have her pinned against one wall as I kiss her, running my hands along her warm wool dress, and her hands through my hair. The doors open up to long carpeted hallways and crown molding, backlighted pictures from old movies. This is where the movie stars stay when they come into town. (Can't help the fleeting thought of how *this* was the place little Mae the Australian actress had stayed when she was in town—but which room?)

She leads me by the hand to the end of the hallway, Room 303. From her pocket she removes the key and opens the door. She has booked us a suite. A large room with desk, couch, giant television, minibar, and bed that could fit six if we were of a different persuasion. From the minibar she removes a bottle of champagne she had taken earlier from work—and a bottle of orange juice. She makes us each a mimosa as I continue to take everything in, enamored. In the closet hang two robes, and on the floor there are two bags—one packed for each of us—and I imagine Lillian going through my belongings while I was at work, packing my toiletries with great care into the bag along with the clothes she has seen me wear most often; I imagine her coming over here by herself and checking in under our assumed married-name. She has set up everything—for me.

It is a habit of mine(as I suspect it is of many) to view my existence from a distance, as if I were watching a movie. I cannot help but view this as the exceptionally happy climax in what is actually a romantic tragedy. We go down to the hotel bar for gin and tonics and a bowl of olives. We sit together in candlelight sipping our drinks and nudging. When we return to our room, we change into the robes from the closet and drink more champagne. Lillian snaps pictures on her Polaroid camera. It has begun raining, and through the curtains the sound comes into the room like a score for a film. Why, then, this should feel like it is foreshadowing something so unhappy—I don't know. Perhaps it is in the nature of men like myself to believe we don't deserve such rare, great moments in life. And perhaps we are right to have this belief.

With the soundtrack of the rain, we stay up for hours together in bed. Exhausted, Lillian finally falls asleep. I stay awake and watch her. If this really is the top of the hill this film is soon to tumble down, the only thing I can do is try to prolong the climax—to make it last for as long as possible. As I look at Lillian's sleeping body, seemingly weightless, certainly beautiful, I resolve to tell her in the morning that I am going out for a smoke, though in reality I will be going to the front desk to reserve another night. The market opens late on Sundays, so I will go unlock the doors and make a gift basket for her: wine, champagne, cheese, crackers, juice, and other snacks. I have to work again, but she can enjoy the day in the hotel room by herself—that will be my gift to her. She can eat, drink, watch movies, do whatever she wants. Maybe she will take a long bath, and afterward sit in her robe on the bed, reading. When I return from work I will tell her to go to the bathroom; when she comes out I will be sitting in a chair, holding my illuminated Valentine that proclaims, "I love you." And I will love her. And she will love me.

28

A WELL-ESTABLISHED ROUTINE is typically easy to return to after a brief departure from its customs. Portland no longer seems foreign, as it did during those two days at The Hotel Deluxe. The rain is the same—the perpetual soft drumming sound it makes within our apartment, the leak in the bathroom; our conflicting hours at the market are the same—the loneliness caused by our shared quarters that are too often spent in alone, surrounded by the seemingly neglected belongings of our Other. Lillian, though, is not quite the same. She has undergone a strange transformation.

It happened the second day back in the apartment. I returned home late after my closing shift to find Lillian behaving distantly towards me. She was in bed, wearing my grey t-shirt as usual, but she laid facing away from me. When our feet would touch under the covers, she would pull them back onto her side of the bed. I couldn't understand it.

For five days this continued. It felt as though a shift had occurred in our relationship that drew us directly back to the beginning of everything. I was having to fight for her affection—a fight that I had long ago tired of. It wasn't until an hour or so ago that I discovered the origin of the change.

It was(and still is) Lillian's day off from work, and as usual she was sleeping in. I woke early and walked down to the nearest café. I returned with coffee for both of us. She was sitting on our bed(now a pile of coats/blankets on the floor—my side—and a small mattress), fully dressed, staring off into space. She greeted me distractedly, if at all, and accepted the coffee without thanks. I sat down in the chair at the end of our bed and watched her.

After a while, with genuine concern in my voice, I finally asked, "Is something wrong? "

It took a long time and some fidgeting with her coffee cup before she eventually answered, quietly, "I went through your things...." ("Okay," I said.) "I'm sorry I did—I know I shouldn't have...."

Tears began to well up in her eyes. She had been holding them in for days. I noticed the fat envelope containing *The Imaginaries* sitting out on the table. I began sweating. When she spoke again, her voice was trembling. "Is that really what you think about?" The tears broke the surface tension that had been holding them over her eyes and began rolling down her soft, pink cheeks. "You still think about all those girls and I'll never be enough for you...."

The patience I once had shattered inside of me—the patience I had had for her, and for myself. It all broke and went through my body in a cold wave of nausea. Inwardly, I knew that it had been too little, too late. You ruin things in private, but when you come to your senses and try to fix them, you find that the damage you have created is so far advanced that it now comes out into the open like a festering sore that has finally burst. Your attempts at resolution are useless then. Everything is ruined for good. Everything good is gone.

Outwardly, in my weariness and disappointment, I became defensive. I calmly explained, "It's just a book, Lillian—once those thoughts are put down they're dead to me."

Through tears, she mentioned names(which I never change in first drafts)—names of women who she had met over the past two years, and whose positions in my past I had understated, always telling myself it was to protect her. She said she felt foolish.

I reiterated that it was just a book. Then, switching focus, I said, "I can't believe you went through my things. I'm not mad at you—I'm not mad—but I feel like you've completely invaded my privacy. I tell you everything(a painful and blatant lie), you're always with me—so there's really *nothing* to worry about, yet you still think it's necessary to take what little privacy I *do* have. There's a reason I don't show you my writing until it's done—it's easy to misinterpret things when they're unfinished. The whole picture's not there. You know what this book is ultimately about? It's about my appreciation for you, about the realization that you're not just enough for me, but that you're the only one for me. I *know* I have a good thing here."

"But you're still thinking about all those other girls! I love you— why can't you love *just* me?"

A cold wave of nausea went through me again, and if there was any fight left in me it went out. I hung my head and stared into my coffee. Very calmly, again, I told her, "I do love you...I just don't know if I can do this anymore...."

Her tears, which had begun to slow, came streaming back down her face reinvigorated. "What—so you don't want to be with me anymore...? "

"I don't know, Lillian. I'm just sick of having to work for it. We're too young for this; it shouldn't be this much work."

She crawled over to me and put her arms around my waist, her head in my lap. She was bawling, her tears making dark splotches on my pants. She pleaded, "Please, don't do this! Don't do this—I love you! Let's just go somewhere for a few days—we just need to leave for a few days.... "

I thought about the entire course of our relationship, and how it was my own fault that I had become discontented. I thought about everything I had done wrong that she knew nothing about, and how my secrecy had done nothing but worsen the guilt I had over my actions. Ashamed, I responded, "If we go, chances are I'm going to want to keep going. Once I get moving, I won't want to stop."

She continued, lifting her head from my lap, "That's fine—you can go travel for awhile and then come back to me and everything will be fine...I promise. I'll be better...."

I ran my fingers through her hair, her beautiful golden and brown hair. Her face was glistening with tears. Her whole being was utterly innocent, earnest. I loved her wholeheartedly, and wondered how all this had happened—how had I let things get so off track? When did I go so wrong? Why had I done so much that would prevent me from allowing her to love me? I smoothed her hair be-hind her ears and became excessively sad over how tiny they were. Her nose was red from crying. Her shining green eyes hurt to look at, but I accepted the pain they caused and stared directly into them as I said, "Alright—we'll go somewhere."

29

THIS IS THE SADDEST TRAIN I'VE EVER BEEN ON. The clack of the wheels is like the chattering teeth of a sobbing giant. The constant swaying of the cars is like his shaking body. The whole train seems to be coming apart.

Outside the window the green landscape of the Northwest passes —hillsides covered with massive trees, rivers, open fields, farmland, horses milling about; it passes as though *it* were moving, rather than us, rolling dizzily across the screens of a thousand televisions from left to right. This is a dream—a sad dream that makes you want to spend the rest of the day in bed. When we wake up, we will be in Seattle.

From our seats, we quietly experience the dream. Our boss(who we told I had gotten sick—hypoglycemic shock that required a trip to the hospital—in order to get me out of work for a few days) gave us an expensive bottle of champagne last night as a gift when he was in an exceptionally good mood. With each image rolling by, propelling us further up the coast, the champagne grows exponentially in value. It is now a $3,000 bottle that I take with me into the bathroom to uncork. Two bottles of orange juice are quickly turned into two very large mimosas and the bottle is dry. I look into the mirror(a mistake I am constantly making), and my hazy features call up a quote from a short story where God speaks to the writer, telling him they are both but a dream, an invention—they are both "many, yet no one."

I am thinking of these words when I return to my seat. Lillian is staring out the window. She is dreaming too. Infinite numbers of dreams, all being had simultaneously—no wonder we all feel alone despite the closeness and interconnectedness of our "real" lives. Aside from this very lucid dream we are sharing here on the train, it is probable that Lillian is dreaming of another time we spent together on a train. We were in another country, passing through the dark, and as all the other passengers slept we laid in our bunk and silently "made love," as I'd like to call it. But that was already a year ago now. Even if this is not the thought she is having, I project it onto her. And I think about how heartbreaking it is for that memory to be so near, yet so far from the actuality of our current trip—probably the last trip we will be taking together.

I am also thinking about a woman we passed on our walk to the train station. She was a homeless woman, and she was screaming at me(they are always singing and screaming at *me*) from across the street, "Ah, you're going to hell!" These words, along with the words from God to the writer, are atrocious. It is not the Christian hell that this woman spoke of; it is the personal, living hell that Man creates for himself. Whether it was created as a consequence of my misdeeds in this shared dream, or as a consequence of the misdeeds I imagine I have done, I am still *going to hell*. It may not be permanent, but it is imminent.

Lillian continues to stare out the window, occasionally sipping from her drink. I hold her hand in the tormenting knowledge that this—Us—will all be over soon. We will be arriving at our destination—*soon*.

Seattle is like a dirtier, condensed version of Portland. Though I have spent time working here before, all I know of the actual city is one bookstore, one teahouse, and one bar; and the fact that the bums here are malicious, dangerous creatures—a banana in your hand implies that you are a rich man; they'll spit in your direction if you walk by holding one.

The train station in Seattle is in the one part of the city I am familiar with. As we get off the train, it is raining. We are walking, holding only one bag in our hands(really over my shoulder) containing a single change of clothes for each of us, and our toothbrushes. It is early in the afternoon and the bums are already at the peak of their day's first drunk. They do not notice us walking by, as they are fighting with each other. The smell of the sea and the fish is good—it covers up the stench that would otherwise be there, and it seems to open up the lungs; the lungs are in need of being opened after that stifling train ride.

A short walk lands us in Chinatown. Above a seedy bar we come across a place called The American Hotel. There is nothing deluxe about this place, yet it still costs us twenty-dollars a piece for two beds in a sixteen-bunk room.

All of the shades are drawn in the room, creating a blue haze that is lonely as hell. One person is asleep in their bunk, snoring. We claim a top and bottom bunk in the corner of the room and tiptoe out. The champagne is wearing off and we could both use another drink.

We give ourselves up to the city together. We have no idea where to go, but it doesn't matter. So long as we keep moving, none of this hurts. It is once you stop that things begin to settle in.

We don't stop. One drink in every bar we come across, then we move on. The blue haze from the bedroom creeps into the streets; it is getting later, slowly, and we still refuse to stop. In every new bar there is another story told, another memory rehashed. We are reliving all of the bright moments in our shared life, moving through the darkening haze like a single shadow of something that refuses to die; and as the night continues closing in, the shadow becomes less and less distinguishable from its surroundings. We are suspended in non-existence, just the two of us, playing out the past.

No one bar looks any different than the last. There are no actual bars—there are only the drinks that the bartender serves us, sitting in front of us in the limelight of our extended evening. In one bar, the drinks are strong; in another bar, the drinks are weak. In yet another bar, Lillian spills her drink. The liquid pours over the table and drips down onto our bag, which we have been carrying with us for lack of trust in The American Hotel's clientele and which was placed on the ground at my feet. I check the bag's contents and see that nothing is wet. Just our single change of clothes in there, dry as a bone. We laugh, but it is obvious that this marks the winding down of our night. Another drink and our thoughts would stop on that one thought that has been looming over our day like a blue haze—*everything would settle in.*

We leave the bar—they are all closing anyway. Rain is still coming down. The lights on buildings and in the streets are glowing, gleaming off everything. It was a flash, an instant. The daylight we thought to be fading slowly was actually speeding off in a hurry. Our whole two years, relived, now gone—just like that. How did it ever get this late?

We slow our walk in the night, my arm around Lillian's cold shoulders. We are quiet where others can be heard hollering outside of the bars as they close. We try to hold on where others so easily let go, continue the suspension of ourselves in the dark where we are everything here and before at once. But it will never work. No matter how slow you move, when you are moving there always comes a time when you must stop.

The hotel is dark upon our return. The hallways are barely lit by a couple of dim bulbs; we have to use that light to tiptoe back into the grey room where the sound of snoring, sighing, shifting, and heavy breathing comes from fifteen of the sixteen bunks. It appears as tho-

ugh a man has taken our bottom bunk. Lillian and I shrug, our shoulders quivering in subdued laughter(hard because we are drunk) at this
pitiful heap of a man who stole our bunk, and we climb up to the narrow top bunk. The ladder squeaks on the way up, but no one wakes.

We are forced to lay in such a way that our bodies are intertwined.
My arm is around Lillian's waist and I am holding on for dear life. I am
breathing in the smell of her hair, her warm body. With every part of
our bodies that touch, I attempt to convey the words I am thinking
over and over—"I'm sorry...I am so sorry...." She is already asleep, but
I hope it works; I hope those words come to her in her dreams and she
knows.

In the middle of the night the man who stole the bottom bunk
receives a phone call. At first he mutters, but his voice quickly rises. He
is arguing with the person on the other end of the line, whom I presume to be his wife or girlfriend, judging by the tone of his voice. He
gets up and turns the light on to dig through his belongings. Somehow
Lillian—along with everyone else in the room—sleeps through this.
He is almost screaming now, "Goddamnit—I didn't do any of that
shit! Why don't you believe me?"

Something about this man—I don't believe him either. Eventually,
he shuts off the light and leaves the room without having resolved the
issue with the person on the phone. I am unable to fall back asleep. I
continue to hold Lillian, praying that her dreams are good ones. I can't
even close my eyes. I watch as the grey room gradually begins to glow
again with that soft, blue haze of morning.

30

A WRITER IS LITTLE MORE THAN A MAN made of words. Consequently, he is often perceived to be a man *of* his word. And the
words are out: *Once I get moving, I won't want to stop.*

It is not always a positive thing to be a man of your word. It is a
mistake I am about to make, but I am already committed—I am leaving today. There is no turning back.

Lillian left on a long walk earlier to allow me the apartment to myself while I pack my things—but not before first gathering my books
in a box; I notice she has kept a select few on the shelf for herself, and
I leave them be. Around this box of books my other belongings accumulate. There's not much: a suitcase full of clothes, a bag with my
notebooks and papers(including the envelope containing *The Imaginaries*), some shoes, coats, a box full of paints and pastels, a couple of
kitchen items, a tiny wooden piano meant for children(which the tailor
gave me as a going away present), a small three-legged table we found
over a year and a half ago at the dump, and my typewriter.

I purchased a six pack of tall boys across the street to drink while I pack. My brother arrives just as I am cracking the second one. He drove up from Ashland this morning—all my things are to be stuffed into his little grey Honda Accord(which was passed down to him from our eldest brother, and which I have past experience with), which will then take me down coast until my next move.

I have left the door ajar and he comes in, stomping his feet on our wood floors. I am sitting in our green velvet recliner, staring at the wall where a dozen of my paintings hang—they are the last of my things to be packed. My brother says, "Jesus...."

The name, or word, "Jesus," does not mean to me what it did when I was a child. It is just an exclamation now, or a sigh; it is just some letters strung together to form an expression. Months from now it will come back to me. I will wake up in a basement in middle America, naked in those first hours of the day(the few to be spent partially sober), and on the wall will be three words in giant lettering —"Jesus loves me. " I will remember the implications of the name *Jesus* and I will think, 'No he doesn't love me.' I will think further, 'That thing about the Lord forgiving all our sins—that no longer applies to me.'

As for now, my brother has just made an absent comment about the sight of the boxes in the middle of the floor and of me drinking a beer in the chair, staring at the wall. I reply, "These paintings still have to come down." Then I take a big gulp of beer.

One at a time, we remove the paintings from the wall. Each one was hung using four "L" nails—sometimes more—and those are removed as well. We neatly stack them back to back, then place a sheet of cardboard, then two more paintings back to back, until the wall is barren and the paintings are wrapped in a blanket. The whole apartment looks barren with that last touch of taking down the paintings. What's worse are the holes left from the nails, and the faint smudges of color that line where the paintings had once been. I can see exactly where there used to be the man setting free the balloon that looked like his head, the man with his beard and without, the old man and his polite fish in the bowl, the tree in the diagram of an orchard, the man in a balloon vehicle he had imagined was successful, the special stationery and its folding process, the disgusting father and his poor daughter, the sobbing clown removing his make-up in the mirror, the freeing of the balloons at the memorial service, the girl letting go of her balloon which was actually a human heart nearing an attack; and down near the bottom of the wall, I can see where there was once the picture of a tiny bird perched on the tip of a man's finger, attempting to take an apple seed in through its miniature beak. All the pictures are exaggerated illustrations from a fable I once wrote—the idea came to me just after I met Lillian. I always told Lillian that she was the tiny bird in the story who was repeatedly saying that she was going on, "A-trip, atrip! A-trip, a-trip!" Only in this future it is I who am leaving.

I open another beer. My brother begins taking my things down to his car. I wash the dirty dishes in the sink. Through the kitchen door, I glance at the faint blue, red, and mustard colored splotches on the wall, again imagining their causes, which are now so neatly packed away. I imagine Lillian and I both in the apartment—I can see her sitting on the bed reading as I make her lunch. I imagine her head in my lap as I sit in the chair, and she is begging me, "Please—don't do this!" I imagine everything, from beginning to end, and know that this is not the first or the last time I will imagine these things; I know that later I will pore over them and continuously ask *why*. And knowing all this before I have even gone....

The dishes are clean, so I sweep the floors. I mop. I clean out the refrigerator and organize the cupboards. I clean the bathroom—toilet, shower, and all. I take out the trash and recycling. Next to the bed, I set an envelope that holds within it a final goodbye letter written on stationery from The Hotel Deluxe; under the envelope, I place enough cash to cover next month's rent. But there is still the wall.

I open my fourth beer as my brother comes through the door, having loaded everything for me. I fill a bucket with soap and water and go after the walls with a rag. At first I am slow, methodically moving the soapy rag in circles. Then I am more forceful, scraping so hard that sweat builds over my brow and falls down over my temples. My brother helps silently, staying in rhythm with me until we are finished because he knows that is the only thing he can do. We both take a few steps back and look. "Well," he says, "looks better than it did."

"Yeah, I suppose it does," I say. "Looks pretty lonely though...." He says nothing back, but I know that he understands. "Guess I should call Lillian now. "

My brother leaves me alone in the apartment. He goes down to his car, telling me to come out whenever I am ready. I call Lillian, who is just up the street at the park. She says she will be here in a few minutes.

The heavy feeling of absence in the apartment is too much. I go outside for a smoke while I wait for Lillian. It is only a moment before she comes around the corner. She is wearing a t-shirt, tights, and purple tennis shoes. There is mud splattered around her ankles and on her shoes. For whatever reason, this kills me. I want to take everything out of my brother's car and call the whole thing off. But I don't. Instead, I take her by the hand and walk her up to *her* apartment for the last time —to say goodbye.

When we get upstairs, I can see her taking in the surroundings, new to her because no evidence of me is in them aside from my actual, physical presence, which will only last another moment. She overlooks the envelope and cash next to her bed, and I am relieved at that. I see that she, too, has become fixated on the wall, the blank wall where for months my paintings had hung. I see that she has started to cry, and as the tears come more steadily she sits down in the green velvet recliner and hides her face. I go to her, kneeling down on the floor like those who have sinned and wish to repent, and I take her head into my hands. I lift her face into mine. Her eyes are bright red around the green and her cheeks are wet. "I promised myself I wouldn't cry," she says. "I don't want this to be the last way you remember me...."

With my jaw clenched and my teeth grinding together, I listen to her, and though I say nothing, I am thinking that this is the way I *want* to remember her. She has never been so absolutely vulnerable to me; there has never before been this lack of judgment, or suspicion, or preoccupation. She is right here, right now, and she is beautiful. I kiss her—several times I kiss her and I know that it will never be enough to fill the empty space that I am about to create by leaving her. And for a long time I just hold her—I want to take with me the memory of every curve and bend, every knot in the muscle and jut in the bone.

Finally, she pulls away and tells me she loves me. I look into her shining green eyes and I tell her I love her too. Then I kiss her one last time and leave the apartment. She doesn't even move from the chair.

Downstairs, my brother is waiting. I get into the passenger seat and put on a pair of sunglasses from the floor because I can feel my eyes burning and my jaw cannot clench hard enough. From under the seat, I pull out the last two tallboys. "Sorry," I say, "but I'm going to have to be drunk to get through this."

31

THROUGH EVERYTHING, THROUGH DARK CLOUDS of carbon dust created by sentient beings fallen—all things fallen; through the charcoal haze of mistake, and misdeed, through all things amiss, scattered about like grains of rice thrown wrongly through the shadows at a wake; through the menagerie of women that carry me down a coast I have seen but cannot say I know...I hear my grandfather's voice: "The bottle will always be there, but it will never be your friend."

And I slur, "Well, sir, I sure could use a friend, but I'll take what I can get."

Nothing fits in just so, but it all moves together nonetheless; we are moving together, all of us in these countless futures, like black scraps of lead paint that scatter further and further away...and what is the difference anyway—is this space? Between each and every thing there is another, smaller thing—I am the thing, which can be seen better when it's doubled...like that carbon dust that builds up in your nose, and up into your brain; it creates a picture like those printed in the papers—myriad dots, alone indistinguishable; together, a notable composition...just as those miniscule lives of every living creature: We cannot stand back far enough to understand, yet we tell ourselves that it must be such a beautiful creation!, because we tell ourselves things to feel better; we all take things to make ourselves feel better. Look: search between the seams—there! It is of a honey color, golden when it goes in, brown when it comes out... just give it a splash of water—it is the source of life...drop your life in and see how easy it'll go down —

The earth had a violent start...one that I cried to as I watched it—the beginning—on late night television's history channel; the digital recreation of events was startling...it made me remember how I felt when I was a kid, every time the television turned off; they make them differently now, but there used to be a last, single white flash—right in the center of the screen...as if everything had been sucked in by a vacuum, concentrated, then gone—and what about God? I would think... how many times can that white flash blink and go back until there is nothing else to go towards? Who created *you*, God? I used to say—and there was never any answer; there is never any answer...save for that One—maybe not a friend, but something certain; something that will *always be there*, which is all you need sometimes—the concrete...

The concrete, it sways under foot; it shifts because it was created by someone at sometime and anything that is created is not permanent—nothing is permanent...notice these cracks, perfectly spaced as I walk along toward...where am I...these cracks, like those in my teeth as I am standing on stage, smiling so largely that the full gleam cannot be seen—you cannot stand back far enough to see the whole smile I am wearing, or that it is not a smile at all, spouting out through my teeth the words of a well rehearsed comedy; I readjust my tie, loosening it about my neck, and with lights beating down from above the stage, I am saying, "Buy! Buy! Buy!"—because that is what salesmen do, and I may say, "Oh, well, *I am an artist!*" But I am a hooker too...it's just that a man needs to eat, and if he cannot eat then he at least must *drink*—drink to find his way, sliding in a fluid motion through everything, through dark clouds of carbon dust from everything wasted; through the menagerie of women that carry me further down this unfamiliar, well known coast—spectacular women at first glance, but set your eyes right: they've got rotten teeth, acne, and pussies full of disease...I wonder where I am again, but I can't take my gaze from the sea; behind me, there must be something—some dark cloud in the shape of violence itself, with a bright speck in the middle that gleams ever brightly in its surroundings, meaning to imply, "It's disgusting! It's disgusting!"

At the sea I call out to my grandfather, "It *is* disgusting, right?" —I only ask him questions I know the answer to...that single answer to everything; that answer that will always be there, but never be your friend, and never mean anything—

We have enough friends here—Here where these women have carried me; the chairs are full, we just need drinks on the table... forget about that problem in your stomach; anything the color of honey is incapable of causing any trouble—sure, it's a violent feeling in the gut, but did the world not begin in a similar manner? To avoid it would be to deny nature—I am not so important as to have been bestowed with that right...to deny nature...So I begin again—violently, too; first in the stomach, then out...out into this world as we know it now—no less violent, though supposedly more intelligent ...though these smiles are those of fools....

Smiles uncontrolled—unbelievable...it is the menagerie of women, they are back!, carrying me again and each and every one professes love —hear that coo in affected breath? that lie, beating out in the breast? See their bodies, curving from in then out, like a bottle—they will always be there, but they will never be my friend, and they will never mean anything—

From the forefront to the far back I scream—I scream because I see you, and I want to know: "Are you fucking him?" A call to no response; that quiet, truthful tune—*Are you fucking him?* Of course, in the same way that you are fucking her...and her...and her...etc.—

It occurs to me that those letters imply a thousand more...or more—the faces of some alcohol blur, crawling down coast on a thin-excused whirl: I have met a lot of women, but even when their backs are turned and the lights are out, they are not you...they are just the dark clouds of carbon dust; they are everything that has fallen, from nothing to nothing; they are those ashy flakes that fill the in-between as indistinguishable particles of your greater whole... They are not you. I know them well, but you—you I cannot stand back far enough to understand, though I will retreat forever, falling back to where I have come from...

...I have come from nothing, like everything; I am a dark cloud of carbon dust, a small nothing in between one something and another something; I am a charcoal haze over a giant star—that insipid, lingering thing; so many things that will not leave...and as sudden as this all began, it may end; you are fading—tell me it's just for now; tell me this dark cloud will pass, and I will see you again....

32

I AWAKE IN A COLD SWEAT ATOP THE SHEETS on a bed in a hotel room. My clothes are on except for one boot that has been kicked off. I am having a hundred miniature heart attacks; my body shakes and my breathing is uneven. There are people talking to me; they are no longer here, but I can hear their voices. The conversations are coming back. Things that have been said at one time or another, they are repeated. Things about poor kids in such and such country, about books you need to read("I really think you'd *love* it!"), about the girl they fucked last Tuesday, the girl they fucked last Wednesday, and the girl they fucked last night; they are saying things about the places they have been, about the places you need to go("I really think you'd *love* it!"), about the things they are going to do and by all probability will not. And as they are saying these things, they are standing over me, sitting next to me on the bed, crouching on the floor behind me; they are touching my arms and my legs and my face—the pressure is unbearable, what with the booze coming out of my system, through my pores in a cold sweat, and my body desperately trying to regain a sober equilibrium. There is absolutely no chance. I am going to die.

I am lying on the bed, barely able to move because of that unearthly heaviness so familiar from my youth, from those times when I stared into the mirror and felt that I might not exist, or nothing existed, or what have you(I was young); from those times when I jerked off and felt so lonely it hurt, from those (repeated) times when I decided it was a mistake as I was making it. That unearthly heaviness so familiar to me because I have felt it for years, on and off, when in the unholy night I am visited by what I think to be a demon that has come to rape me for the wrongs it is glad I have done, or I am visited by what I think is an angel that has come to cry over my wasted body for all the wrongs it is disappointed I have done. There is no difference in these things anyway. They are all horrible, and they are all real. I no longer have any friends in all of this, and no family. There is no one left to love me.

I manage to roll myself over and through one squinted eye I can make out the hotel stationery on the nightstand. The address given on the stationery is in Denver, Colorado. I have no idea what the date is; my only frame of reference as to the time is from the alarm clock next to the stationery. It says it is 12.21pm. A palindrome which represents the calendar day of the winter solstice—my birthday.

With effort, I pull myself up out of bed and go to the sink. I splash water over my face and rinse out my mouth; I leave the tap running as I relieve myself in the sink. In the mirror, I notice how swollen my face has become from too much drinking. Also, I notice one of the buttons has gone missing on my shirt, and the shirt falls open farther than it should. I can see the edge of something that has been inked into the skin on my chest. I turn the water off and zip up my pants. Slowly, I unbutton the rest of my shirt and pull it aside with my weakened left hand. Over my heart, small cursive script appears—*Ave Maria*.

Seeing the Angelic Salutation inscribed on my chest(and reciting the prayer—"Hail Mary, full of grace, the Lord is with thee; blessed art thou among women, and blessed is the fruit of thy womb, Jesus. Holy Mary, Mother of God, pray for us sinners, now and at the hour of our death. Amen"), a million jumbled images come back to me at once, and I remember everything; I remember it from an estranged distance, as though my own memories belong to someone else.

I recall leaving Lillian in Portland, deserting her under questionable pretenses; and I recall her tears as I left. I recall a few weeks in the narrow Rogue Valley, living with my brother in an old barn that had been converted into four apartments—I slept on his floor, and smoked outside at night; I would say into the dark, "I know you're out there, Mountains, closing in on the valley, even though the moon's not out." I recall leaving again, on a bus headed South; I carried a box with 75 copies of a book I had written—I said I was going on a "reading tour," reading to strangers in bars and seeing old friends. I recall train rides, walking through cities I barely knew, sleeping on couches in empty apartments, an argument with my father, and drinking cheap wine. I recall so much drinking. I recall being in Los Angeles, where I never stopped drinking; I recall meeting good people there and only being able to be partially present for them, subdued by a whiskey spell and a broken heart I had given to myself. I recall my grandmother dying— the cancer finally taking over for good. I recall winning forty dollars at a casino and blowing it, sweating in Texas and not stopping in New Mexico where it was planned that I would meet my desert pixie—I still have the blanket I bought for her; it's crumpled in the corner of the room with the rest of my things: my suitcase, my satchel, and my typewriter(the rest I left at my brother's). I recall lying to my friends who live in mountain-suburbia not far from here, telling them I would be a week late to allow myself the time to go through withdrawals, alone in this hotel room, before I made it up to their house where I am to stay for the summer helping them take care of their two year old son. I recall waking up like this every morning since I left Portland, in absolute fear for my life, terrified by all that surrounds me; I recall a hundred miniature deaths or more, caused by heart failure, caused by an aneurism, caused by that unearthly heaviness created by those creatures in my nightmares....

I am almost certain all these things happened. And I recall another thing. For months I tried contacting Lillian, with no response, until one day I received a message from her. It said: "You look like you've been drinking a lot." With technology being what it is, she must have seen pictures online. With my body wrecked and irreparable things done concerning my conscience, there was no use fighting it. I replied:

"I *have* been drinking a lot. And I am unhappy."

My brain has gotten soft. There is evidence of it all around me. From my satchel I remove the envelope that holds *The Imaginaries*—it has gotten fatter. All of its pages are laid out on the bed; the book has doubled in length.

Apparently this is not the first time I have gone over *The Imaginaries* since my departure from Portland. It appears as though I have added to it each time. This I do not remember.

As I read through the book, some of its text is incoherent to me. There are pages here that describe women whose names I do not recognize, places I have never been. I am suspicious of these events recorded in such haphazard detail; and there are several mistakes in the type, too. I am careful to avoid mistakes when I type; I have been known to switch the "e" and the "i" in "ceiling" at the bottom of an otherwise perfect page, and crumple it up to start anew.

Regardless of these discrepancies in the book that I perceive as being out of character for me, I continue reading. What I find is disturbing. It seems that what once began as one thing, became another completely. In this future as we know it, right now, I expected to find a book whose purpose was deeply personal, and set out to extinguish the dark urges within its narrator, who wished to be wholesome and free. In parts, this is the case—but not entirely. In other parts, the book is being written with the intent of its author's girlfriend finding it and breaking up with him in disgust; in other parts, the book is being written to win back the love lost from the very same girl. In other parts yet, there is no girl at all, only loneliness and despondency. And in some parts the purpose seems to be arbitrary, as though the author either could not focus his own thoughts into a central idea, or his thoughts were so utterly revealing that he chose to hide them away in the subtext of the lines.

By all appearances, there does not seem to be just one single author of *The Imaginaries*, but several authors whose purpose and plot are perpetually contradicting, or overlapping, and often just plain ludicrous, thus explaining the narrator's sparingly mentioned physical attributes, and his even more sparingly mentioned name. I wonder if this is not so much an inexplicable problem with continuity as it is a reflection of my behavior; in which case, have I lost it? With each man(they are *all* men writing the book—the most apparent common thread) I am able to identify with in a very specific way, although what I identify with in one man rarely is present in another. It is baffling.

The sight of the white pages with their cluttered black text spread out on the bed, and the floor now, the nightstand, is beginning to make me sick. There is a ringing in my ear. I have removed my typewriter from its case; it is an old Underwood Golden Touch Hideaway, which was given to me as a gift from Lillian some time ago. I am sitting at it with a blank page already inserted behind the platen and rolled through to a perfect margin. But there is nothing to write. It seems that whatever I put down in this moment is liable to be void in the next. I no longer have an understanding of *how* or *where* this book called *The Imaginaries* can or should go. Its pages and timeline are so convoluted that to attempt any amendments to the preexisting text or to attempt any additions would only create a larger mess. The blank page in front of me is actually an unusual relief, like a clean slate wherein any future can be forged; it is in a precious state of nonbeing, and my hypersensitivity to this rare state is imperative in order to attain a desirable outcome for all the events that are to follow. I refrain from moving my fingers across the keys just yet, not wanting to spoil it. I am careful not to touch anything at all. Instead, I will go out for a walk.

33

THE SUN IS OUT IN THE CITY, but the giant white clouds meandering and collecting behind the peaks in the distance mean rain later on. I decide to bring my coat; after quickly washing up and putting on my wrinkled wool suit, I sling it over my shoulder and leave the hotel—everything else stays.

There is a bite that cuts through the sunshine, a slight chill in the thin air. I am breathing deeply as I walk, my steps moving forward at a slow pace, my one hand in my pocket and the other holding my coat that is slung over my shoulder. There is no rush to get anywhere; my destination is as unclear to me now as it has always been. But the movement feels good. The blood is coming back into my brain.

Through side streets and alleyways I continue on, taking very little in by way of sights—a trashcan, a broken bottle, some gum stuck to the pavement, my own feet moving one after the other, a stop signal, a walk signal, a car that makes a wrong turn and has to turn around, etc. These are the things that make up my current reality—the immediacies of this singular environment, which I move through without much more thought than, "Here I am, here is this, here is that..."

On a quiet side street I come across a café; the noise from the busy street a few blocks away can still be heard, but it is muted in a way that makes it tolerable, even pleasant in that it drones on in one subtle and consistent rhythm like a bedside fan left on for the night. I take a seat at a table outside, resting my coat on the arm of the chair next to me.

I quit drinking coffee last year due to a combination of stomach problems and a composure that had visibly begun to tremble, but when the waiter comes over I order a coffee anyway. I used to drink quite a bit of it, all day. I figure a little in moderation won't hurt. He brings it back steaming, on a saucer. I put in one sugar, using the tiny spoon to stir it in, clinking it against each side of the cup, then sit back and light a cigarette as it cools.

At a standstill like this, sitting here so peacefully, my thoughts begin to wander vaguely back to the hotel room; in particular, they begin to wander back to *The Imaginaries*, which I left scattered about the room. Being out of its presence, I am not exactly invigorated, but I am certainly experiencing a slight feeling of liberation. I picture fondly that blank page in the typewriter, and somehow that single page seems more important than all the others combined. It is no longer about escape, or hiding, or suppressing, or fighting, like the others; it can be about anything or nothing at all. It is my decision alone to make, and the possibilities are endless. I could worry about what that decision will be, but for now I remain content in knowing that it is *mine*, because the sun is out and the air is good and my coffee is cool enough to drink.

After my first sip, the waiter approaches for what I imagine to be the standard, "How is everything?" (That is always how the question is phrased, no matter how little "everything" describes.) But he surprises me by saying, "Excuse me, sir, but this is for you—" while handing me a note written on a napkin. I tell him thanks as he half-shrugs and walks away. I read the note(written *very* neatly I might add):

> DEAR MR. FONT —
> PLEASE MEET ME AT [SUCH AND SUCH ADDRESS]
> AT [SUCH AND SUCH TIME]. IT IS A MATTER OF
> UTMOST IMPORTANCE.

When the waiter first handed me the note, I had no particular reaction to it; however, after reading it, the idea of receiving a handwritten note at a restaurant, delivered by the waiter nonetheless, strikes me as ludicrous. And with instructions to meet its anonymous sender at a specified address at a specified time! What is this, the 1930's and I'm tied in with the mob? It simply doesn't make sense.

I deliberate for awhile on how to respond to this note—its sheer absurdity is what intrigues me. I smoke a few more cigarettes, even order a second cup of coffee. I stare at the note, which I have left in plain view on the table, occasionally spinning the napkin in circles with one finger. The handwriting does not appear to be that of a woman's —the letters are too straight, rigid, too close together, and in all capitals. If it were a woman's writing on the napkin I wouldn't have a second thought about going. The fact that it is a man's handwriting is what makes me wary. Then again, he *did* address me by name.

The said meeting time is twenty minutes from now. I call the waiter over and ask him if he knows the address. He says he does, it's about a fifteen-minute walk. On the reverse side of the napkin he writes down a few simple directions. I tell him thanks, again, and ask for the check.

I wait twenty-five whole minutes before I pick up and go, with no good reason for the delay. The clouds have turned grey over the mountains and begun to press on towards the city. The sun is gone. I am glad for having decided to bring my coat as I pull the collar up around my neck and stick my hands in its warm pockets. The chill in the air has dropped a few degrees and set in motion; the wind blows down the street into my face and I avoid it by turning my head down towards the sidewalk, looking just a few paces ahead. I have already made my third and final turn and noted that the address I am looking for will be on this side of the street, just up ahead.

I arrive at the address given on the napkin and find that it does not seem to belong in the neighborhood—the architecture is completely different. The rest of the neighborhood apartment homes are in the traditional style of the modern Midwest, with that additional flair that is to be found in mountainous regions. The apartment matching the address I was supposed to be at twenty minutes ago looks more like a two story condo that belongs in an old affluent neighborhood on the east coast. The incongruity of the apartment to its surroundings reassures me that I have arrived at the right place.

I climb the half-dozen steps to the door and my heart is racing, which could possibly be attributed to those two cups of coffee. I knock on the heavy wood door, trying for four consecutives knocks but only getting to the second before the door creaks open. I call inside. "Hello?"

I poke my head in through the doorway. Everything is in shadow; within the gloom I can make out the figure of an older gentleman sitting at a desk with one of his legs crossed over the other. I direct my statement at him. "Hello. I'm Mr. Font. I was told to meet someone here twenty minutes ago—it was said to be a matter of 'utmost importance.'"

From the dark, the man responds. "Yes, I know you are Mr. Font. Please, come in. Shut the door behind you and feel free to switch on that lamp there, by the wall."

I do as I am instructed, having some difficulty finding the switch for the lamp and stumbling a bit in the process.

In the light, the man continues, "Well, Mr. Font, it was I who requested your presence and I do appreciate you coming on such short notice, though I can't say your decision to come is a surprise to me."

With everything illuminated, I am now able to get my bearings in the man's home. It is tidy and the decor is simple—the desk where the man presently sits, an armoire, a bookshelf, a few smaller items here and there. I step further into his home, quickly inspecting the bookshelf—all of my favorite authors are there, along with some I have

561

never heard of, and some whose names I know well but have never read. I approach the man at his desk, and say cordially, "It's no problem really, but do you mind telling me who you are and what this is all about? You expressed in the note that this was a matter of 'utmost importance.' "

"It certainly is a matter of *utmost importance*, as each action in all of our individual lives is a matter of such scope. "

I ignore the man's cryptic remark because the ringing in my ear has returned and on his desk I have spotted *The Imaginaries*, of which the presence is both disturbing and inexplicable. Also, it has quadrupled in size since I last left it in the hotel room just a couple of hours ago. "How did you get my manuscript—did you *break in* to my hotel room?"

"We don't have very much time together for this meeting, Mr. Font, so I will make this brief. Would you like a drink of water, or some iced tea? Perhaps you'd like hot tea instead—the weather is changing."

I am aggravated by the man's insistence on stalling and vigorously shake my head "no" to his drink offer as I pick up my manuscript off his desk. Its weight is terrifying—what has he done to it? The ringing gets louder in my ear.

"I would like to introduce myself. I, too, am Mr. Font."

I look up from the manuscript and realize why this man's appearance, ordinary as it is, struck me as eerie. His physical characteristics—even his mannerisms—oddly resemble those of my family's. "So you're my uncle that disappeared without a word—you're my dad's brother, Julien?"

"I am not Julien. But it's a fact that we are related to one another, if not in the traditional sense, then in a way that does not and will not ever make sense. I am a writer too, you know."

I am having trouble concentrating on the man's words. The ringing in my ear has grown so loud it's painful.

"Sir, just tell me how you got this manuscript and *why* there are a thousand additional pages! And *what* is that noise?! "

The pain is searing. It's like there is a tiny dentist in my head, and his drill keeps missing my teeth and getting me right between the eyes. I look rapidly about the room, attempting to find the terrible thing causing this noise—nothing.

"I'd like to consider the manuscript a collaborative effort at this point, and to be quiet honest, there is no hope for *The Imaginaries* to be finished until you and I and an infinite number of others similar to us are good and dead—even then it is likely that the project will never come to fruition as you or I image it in our minds' eye. And that noise you hear, that is the sound of the persistent flapping of an enormous fly's wings. You cannot see the fly—it is a miracle you can see me. For your own mental well being, you must imagine that this noise is coming from within your head, like a ringing in your ears that will haunt you from here on out; for even after the ringing is gone, the tone will be stuck in your memory like a song from your childhood that you cannot quite remember, and cannot quite forget."

For a split second, the pain subsides and is replaced by anger. "Listen, 'Mr. Font,' all formalities aside, you still haven't said what the point of all this is—skip all the obscure bullshit and tell me why you've called me here."

Calmly, he places his hands on his one knee; as he speaks, his voice mimics the calm in his actions, so much so that it almost sounds detached. "I understand that you're upset. I'll get down to the point: I've called you here to give you this manuscript as a gift."

"So that's it? You've called me here to give me *my own* manuscript?"

"Yes, and now that you have it I would like to ask you to leave. But not without this little bit of advice first: Read this manuscript or don't; but if you choose to read it, I want you to do so with a distanced objectivity, although some of its subject matter concerns you personally. We have sometimes lived recklessly. Sometimes we have lived with reservation. And in any case, the text of this manuscript should not guide you in your future actions; it should—again, if you choose to read it—serve as a look into a handful of possibilities, which should be considered to be infinite. You are given but one existence to live out in full, and you must continually make decisions that propel your experience along until death. These decisions need not be calculated, though they should be made with the knowledge that they are yours alone to make, and the consequences thereof are yours alone to endure—for better or for worse. It is not in your best interest to feel shame or guilt over them. Own up to the peculiarities of your own behavior and move on. If you are unhappy with the results they have on your life, then change them. If you are happy, then don't change a goddamn thing. Now please go."

Something about the man's face, and his demeanor—it is so smug and matter-of-fact, yet for whatever reason I suddenly feel immense pity; this feeling is not just for him, it is for everything. And he just sits there with his mouth straight and firm, though I can see so clearly in his eyes that he is smiling, nearly *laughing*. A surge of pain sweeps in from my eardrum to my brain and I straighten my posture to endure it with an internal wince. The anger is gone. I fold the thick manuscript in half and shove it into my coat pocket. "Well," I say, "thank you for returning my manuscript. I'll see myself out then."

Leaving the man's house, the rain has finally started dripping down over the city. I look back one last time at the ill-fitting apartment containing that strange man, then hurry off. The further away I get from that place, and that man, the more my head clears and the ringing in my ear eventually stops. I have half a mind to turn around and go back to see if the place is even there, or if it, like the voices in the hotel room, are just part of the delirium caused by my withdrawals. Even if I were to go back and find nothing, it would not erase the things I heard there. I fondle the manuscript in my pocket, and recall again the image of that single white page left untouched in the typewriter at the hotel. I mutter into the cold, "The old man was just trying to help...."

Turning the corner out of the neighborhood, the rain has turned into tiny droplets of hail. And the tiny droplets of hail now transform into wide flakes of snow, gently falling over everything and beginning to accumulate. It is dusk. The snow already blankets the streets in a half-inch of perfect white against the grey-blue forms of the evening. Behind me there is a single set of footprints in the snow; in evenly spaced indentations they trace the path I have taken to get where I am now. In another moment, fresh snow will have fallen to cover them up and it will be as if I had never been there at all. I will be no one then, and each step will be like a new beginning, sending me further along to one place and one time, wherein I will be just the one thing that I am then and there—myself.

In this particular future, as we know it right now, the bars have begun turning on their neon lights, inviting patrons to come in and get warm. Through the window of one such bar, I can see a young woman taking down the stools from their overturned positions on the counter. The way she moves about in the dim light of the bar, through the distortion of glass and snow—she might be Lillian. Or she might be some other woman that I once loved, or some woman that I could potentially fall in love with. But it doesn't matter to me who or what she is *right now*. The snow has started to seep through my coat and has already done a number on my boots—my socks are wet and my feet are cold. All that matters is that I can go inside where it's warm, and where I can sit and drink, alone.

—3 August 1988, Rocky Mts., CO

VOL
UME
IV

THE EPILOGUE

TOO SOON THE SUN SETS, OLD MAN
Or,
Subtitles For A Film
(2012)

For
my mom, of course
and for my dad,
who, though he has never admitted it,
is one of my biggest fans.

And for K.B. and A.G.,
without whom I would not still be alive.

The truth about my behavior as a child is that it was completely ordinary. Although it would please me to fool you into believing otherwise, there was nothing in it that would be considered "marked with genius." I was developing alongside my peers at an average pace. I was shy, but still managed to get along with others. I enjoyed sports, and was pretty good at all of them, but would not be called exceptional at any of them. In stature, I was shorter than most. This was compensated for by my speed, agility, and toughness. A common trait amongst short folks.

The most noteworthy detail from those formative years is that I began writing about myself at the age of ten. Perhaps younger, but the photographed document in front of me is dated, in its shaky, penciled hand, sixteen days prior to my eleventh birthday: December 5, 1997. It is the first part in a one-part story entitled, "The Legend of Ky-ky." In the first paragraph we see Ky-ky(the name my younger sister calls me by) walking along a river bank where he encounters a gardener snake. In the title and this opening sentence alone there are two spelling errors, which points to the obvious conclusion that the story itself is unremarkable. But the fact remains, although it was in third-person then, I was writing about myself.

I am now twenty-five years old and guiltier more than ever of this habit. I am the author of eight books, all either overtly, or covertly autobiographical to some extent. Undoubtedly, you have not read any of these eight books. If you have heard of them at all, it is because I was drunk and told you about them. Already I feel as though I am becoming incoherent, irrelevant. For the last year I have written nothing, aside from a few sleepy notes and a sporadic idea here or there. I no longer have access to my beloved typewriter. If I am to write now it is on a laptop with a program that allows me to use the "American Typewriter" font[*]. It seems a trivial thing, which type of font you use, but it is somehow unavoidable that I use this one, as well as it is unavoidable that I feel ridiculous while doing so.

This one year hiatus from writing I have been able to justify by working on a film, even though the film is not yet done. It would have been impossible to finish the thing in this time, being that there has been no financial backing for it, and that there are only two people work-

---

[*] The original version of this text, in fact, would have been seen in The American Typewriter font; due to economic/spatial issues, the style was changed here.

ing on it: my friend, who directed and starred, and myself, who wrote and starred. I'll give you one guess at what it's about.

Other occurrences over this past year I am unable to justify. For example, I have gained nearly thirty pounds. I knew that there had been stretches where I drank beer more consistently than water, and that perhaps I had been using butter a tad more liberally than in the past, but how in god's name nearly thirty whole pounds snuck up on me I cannot say. My aversion to mirrors is now not only due to a deep, existential dread, but also incorporates a superficial dread aimed at my rounded cheeks and belly.

Another thing is the difficulty with which I am having returning to writing. I am attempting to write a book entitled, "Subtitles For A Film," which is a sort of How-To and How-Not-To in no-budget film-making that documents the process from conception to (nearly)final product, as well as it documents the psychological/ emotional effects of acting in a film that would largely be considered "autobiographical." Even the description of this book I believe to have stolen from myself just now, unable to find new words to summarize it here. I have been in the fourth chapter for months now. How many exactly I don't know, and for how many more I will be stuck there I can't say either.

I am fat then, and washed up. At the ripe young age of twenty-five. At twenty-five, Henry Miller was working for a telegram company or some such thing, with still eight more years before he would write his first book; sure, Borges had already been publishing poems and essays for a few years, but at twenty-five he still had sixty years left in him, blindness and all!; Nabokov was about to marry Vera, who is said to be the genius behind his genius; Kerouac was still palling around on the road with Neal Cassady long before the events were fictionalized(true that fame and alcoholism would eventually get the best of him and his life was already more than half over); Steinbeck was still about a year away from giving up all else to focus on his writing in that handsome little cottage in Pacific Grove; Isaac Bashevis Singer was at that age a proofreader in Warsaw, still under his older brother's shadow; Salinger, goddam handsome bastard that he was, was still in the army and wouldn't be forced into hiding with the Glass family for another dozen or more years. And the list goes on, and on, and still I am fat, and washed up—at the ripe young age of twenty-five!

This is not meant to be in any way self-deprecating. I am not wallowing in the glory of writers come and gone in order that I might more acutely sense that my own glory has gone as well and my twilight years have arrived prematurely. No, this is simply meant to put my career into perspective: I was once something, and now I am not. I am blessed to have experienced it at all, however marginally. And all this without any sort of melodramatics, or exaggeration. I maintain that I am being straightforward, with a frankness and humor for the direness of one's own situation that can only come when you have truly reached the end of the road.

In this moment of such openness, and unrestricted honesty, I would like to take the opportunity to formally announce my retirement. This is my letter of resignation. Once the last page has been turned, I am done. I acknowledge my fate, and I accept it—with open arms and a smile on my face even.

And what freedom this has allowed me!

Earlier today I noticed an older gentleman walking across the street, wearing all black, using a sleek black cane. Only he wasn't walking so much as he was bouncing along the sidewalk, his two twisted legs being assisted by his cane, swung wildly out to the side. And now I know what it is to walk with that spring in one's step! With what lightness we can proceed when we are confident that death approaches soon. It has always been the mysteriousness of existing in the first place that has frightened me. Death is tangible, a certainty. How exactly it will come can sometimes be a surprise, sometimes not, but it remains that it will arrive, and can be watched as a spectacle as it inches nearer. Funny then that so many suppose themselves to be obsessed with death, and fear it, when what they are really concerned with is the beautiful uncertainty and inexplicability of the spectacle of life itself.

The way black holes are located is that two stars will be seen orbiting around seemingly nothing, their orbit becoming smaller and smaller until they reach that point of no return and enter the vacuum that sucks them into oblivion. That point of no return is called the event horizon. Picture it as the rim above the drain in a sink, that place where the light reflects off the water just before it disappears into the labyrinth of plumbing. That exact spot, the event horizon, is the moment of death. What follows it is incomprehensible without experiencing it personally, though a favorite pastime of humankind to speculate about. But all else is life, moving fluidly through its imagined confines, revolving about with reckless precision.

This is the freedom I am talking about! I have not given up the ghost, the ghost has given up me, and I am now at will to simply enjoy the ride, take it all in. Everything that happens henceforth is out of my hands, a product of the fates, or indeed a result of this newfound happiness in my precocious senility.

But the light is fading now and I have just caught myself yawning. It must be so that my internal clock has fallen into sync with the sun and my body receives its cues from the rising and setting thereby. Perhaps I will prepare a glass of warm milk and go to bed for the night where I will experience sleep with a peaceful joy that can only be felt by those who are obligated to do absolutely nothing at all in the world come morning.

* * *

The sun rose in this part of the world and by that fact alone so do I rise. It seems that as I slept I came down with something. My head feels as though it were twice its usual size, filled with compressed air, or perhaps helium that could potentially result in lifting me from this earth even in my current state, which adds an extra thirty pounds. If this should occur, then I will gladly float in whichever direction the wind chooses to blow.

Meanwhile I have put on my clothes from yesterday, which happens to include an oversized, gray wool sweater with barren elbows like an old grandpa would wear(proof I am really taking this whole thing to heart), strapped on my boots, grabbed a pencil and notebook, and ventured out in search of a new locale to write. If I am to continue this letter I cannot be bothered with the headache of staring at a computer screen, not to mention my lungs feel a bit tight and I require an abundance of fresh air.

I am on the move now, walking not too fast, nor too slow, but at a leisurely pace that I hope expresses to whomever is concerned, "I will get to where I am going, because my destination is wherever, and I have no specific time that I have to be there"; or, in a single word, "nonchalance." Through the filter of my sunglasses, the sunshine appears golden, the light bearing qualities of that famed 5o'clock poets' sunshine. The leaves of the trees, backlit by this alien hour, shiver in rich, otherworldly green. I usually try to avoid wearing sunglasses. They typically make me feel oddly detached from my surroundings. But today I welcome it like I welcome everything. Presently, the smoke wafting across the street from someone's cigarette. It makes me nauseous as well as it makes me want a smoke. I realize that the nausea is not caused by the smell of the smoke, but by my own negligence—I have forgotten to eat breakfast. I can afford to miss a meal or two though; there are certainly worse things that could have happened.

This makes me recall an event that when it occurred held a small amount of significance to me, but in this moment now becomes all-important. It is the moment that I should have seen all this was coming. I was riding in a car destined for the east side of downtown. We were coming up over a hill, just to the point where visibility became extremely limited, and I envisioned being blindsided by another car running a red light. I knew that if this were to happen I would not survive the accident. Before this moment I had envisioned countless other accidents of a similar nature, including more catastrophic ones involveing trains, or planes, and had always been sure that I alone would survive. To others my survival would be a miracle, but to me it would be just how things were. This time was different. I felt it in my bones with absolute certainty: I would die. Of course, we passed through the intersection unscathed, I nodded at my mortality, and we continued on down the other side of the hill. But it was there that I am able to pinpoint the shift in my existence, the subtle passing from one stage of my life into another.

In the golden years of my career as a writer, without fully admitting it, I must have considered myself a *café writer*, as I call it, of the old world type, like Hemingway or a less effeminate Fitzgerald. Many of my pages were scrawled out in public at some out of the way coffee shop amongst other handsome young men and women or at hole in the wall bars where you could always plan on seeing a bunch of Bukowski looking fellas, and where if you didn't get a couple thousand good words down you'd feel real shitty and sad, like one of those Bukowski looking fellas. There was something about the environment that added a sense of urgency to everything I wrote. It was like a constant fire under my ass, stoked always by those words of my eldest brother's as they reverberated in my ears: "You can't call yourself a writer if you don't actually write something."

It was the opportunity those places provided too. All those pages filled up for the day and a good head start on tomorrow, a reward was in order, a miniature celebration.

"I'll have a whiskey and soda, please."

The bartender was an old man whose children had long ago grown up and had children of their own. They seldom talked to him. He brought me the drink and the whiskey was bad but its effects were good. The light pouring through the stained glass had gone from golden to blue. The old drunks stopped playing their secretive dice games and their voices grew louder. The jukebox still shone its blinking neon lights advertising that it would play some music for you, only now the patrons heeded that advertisement. Crumpled dollar bills were smoothed out on jean covered thighs and swallowed by the machine. Music played but it couldn't drown out the sounds of all the voices. Everyone was talking over each other. The ruckus attracted passersby from the street, new patrons—a younger crowd. One of them was a dark haired woman who looked like she was waiting for an excuse to get out of there.

My drink was gone so I ordered another. At some point one of the men that had been there all day had moved to the stool nearest mine.

"I know I'm a convicted felon, but I gotta carry this knife with me for protection," he said. He then brandished the weapon in his hand, long enough for me to get a real good look at its dull surface and be reassured that it would hurt going in. He put it away as my drink arrived and he paid for my drink. He also paid for the dark haired girl's drink, which was a sake on the rocks. Who knew cupid was a convicted felon with terribly weathered skin? I was unaware then, but started to get the picture when the girl took her drink and brought it down to the end of the bar, sitting down right beside me. She had a look in her eye, one that rendered a mundane greeting useless. We smiled as we clinked our glasses together. The whiskey was still bad but getting better, and the effects remained good. The nearness of this girl was good. She spoke.

"You're the best looking man here and I want to kiss you."

"Then do."

She did kiss me and I kissed her back and all those old folks in the bar felt a sudden pang in their hearts because there was a time, however long ago, that this had happened to them. If not exactly this, it didn't matter because in that moment that is how they remembered it happening.

My own memory, like theirs, cannot be trusted anymore. I think that I left the bar with the dark haired girl, and that I actually went on to be very happy with her, but I will not allow this reminiscence to carry forth with even the slightest presence of doubt. It's possible I am combining a number of occasions into this one. Either way, those times and those places don't exist for me now.

Left to their own devices, my mind wandering elsewhere, my legs have delivered me to the place of their, or a higher power's, choosing: Starbucks. Another piece of evidence that my golden years are over. I go to the restroom to wipe the sweat from my brow. The AC has the little room chilled to a cool 67 degrees. Scribbled on the toilet paper dispenser are the words, "I come to Starbux just to shit." And why not? The bathroom is cool, and clean. I get out and order a small iced coffee, feeling funny about having to specifically ask for it to be *un*sweetened. I pay in quarters. The cashier's face blatantly shows pity because of this and that she does not expect a tip. She is surprised to see 75 cents go into the jar.

My coffee comes and I take it outside. The patio is separated from the busy street by some shrubbery and a low wall. The noise is mindnumbing. Everyone is always honking and the number of garbage trucks is astounding. Music plays from loudspeakers but no one seems to notice. The majority of the customers are on their cellphones—maybe texting, maybe playing games. Some appear to be on dates, first or otherwise. With my notebook I blend into the shade. Only three people have made eye contact with me. They were all women, all of a certain age. They all smiled. My dwindling career must be manifesting itself in my physical appearance. I am not yet prepared to look into the matter by way of mirror. For now I will just assume.

This gives me an idea. One that is commonplace in the minds of men who get to a certain point in their life when they wish to feel younger, and invigorated. I will take on a mistress. Someone young, beautiful. Already I have the perfect candidate in mind.

I met her a little over a year ago. We were in a bar, or a club, and without so much as a hello she said to me, "You're the best looking man here and I want to kiss you." I told her that she should, so she did kiss me and I kissed her back. She's young, beautiful, a little Italian thing with dark hair, fiery, clearly brazen. It's true that we left together that night(learned her name was Addie the following morning), and have been seeing each other ever since, but no doubt she will be open to suggestion.

I, or perhaps someone else, once sat around a fire somewhere in the midwest. It was all men gathered there—a few young, the others older. Two of the older men had gotten to talking about their marriages. In particular, the sex in those marriages. They said that as the years passed things only got weirder and weirder. One of the men related a story about how one day his wife just started pissing on him —and he loved it! The other man laughed and related a similar story with the same end result. When they noticed that the younger men were put off by their anecdotes, they remarked simply that some day the young men would understand, and that sometimes to keep from being bored you had to get pissed on.

I am not to the point in my life where I desire to have a woman piss on me, nor can I fathom ever getting there(to each their own), but a little role play wouldn't hurt. Later this evening, I will propose that Addie become my mistress.

Meanwhile though, some of you might beg the question, "How is it that she will make you feel younger, and invigorated, when we know already that you're 25 and she is 28? The whole thing is highly improbable." And to those of you uttering those words, it is clear that you have not been listening, and I hope you are prepared to feel rather silly about yourselves.

The matter in our slight difference in age—she being three years my elder—is only a concern when taking time into account in the standard, generic sense. This recent development in my career, and life in general, forces me to take time into account only in an emotional and creative sense. Where I am bloated, drained of inspiration, and lack the discipline to carry on as a writer, she is pretty as ever, determined, and hitting a stride in her career in the fashion industry. I don't know a lot about fashion, but I do know enough to see that she is good at what she does, and she enjoys doing it. She recently secured the position of senior fashion stylist at one of the fastest growing e-commerce sites in the industry. With the position came a substantial raise, a friendly, professional environment, added benefits, a sense of security, and well-being, as well as two weeks paid vacation. In the following weeks she will be moving into a new apartment in a good neighborhood(just three blocks away from my current location); it is a one bedroom with a well maintained vintage kitchen and a large living area—hardwood floors throughout, restored tile in the kitchen and bathroom, and high, exposed beam ceilings; there are windows everywhere that allow a nice breeze through the apartment and there is a nice private balcony over-looking the quiet street. In addition, the fashion blog that she keeps has garnered a considerable amount of attention, which has led to countless freelance opportunities as well as her being featured in various magazines. It has also led to her being contacted by a reputable production company who seeks to make a reality TV show about fashion bloggers. As her boyfriend, they have asked me to be a part of the show as well. I agreed. Since I am already burying my career, I may as well have the decency to settle up properly and drive the nail into the coffin.

This reminds me: tonight is to be the first night of filming; they've asked us both to come "camera ready" to a studio where our preliminary interviews are to be filmed. I can imagine perfectly how this will go.

"So what do you do?"

"I write. I'm a writer. Well, I used to be a writer. Yesterday I began my official letter of resignation from the profession. So I guess, at the moment, I don't really do anything. I'm trying to adjust to the idea of retirement."

"Okay...."

I retract the conjecture I have just made. They will not ask me what I do because they don't care. The show is not about me, it is about Addie. They will only ask me questions pertaining to her. How long have you been together? How did you meet? (I'll tell the story of the bar, most likely with variations caused by nervousness, or poor memory.) And so on and so forth. They are wise to have chosen to make the show about her, rather than me. I'd be lying if I said I hadn't googled both of our names. Her results, both web and images, are all relevant to her, and all flattering. My results provide several links to pages where different styles of fonts can be downloaded, the image results, of course, showing images of those different styles of fonts, as well as an unsettling number of goofy looking white men(only one of those being me), many old with gray beards, whose first names happen to be "Benjamin." Also, I am not in the fashion industry, and I don't have a blog.

While on this tangent, I have received word that, as it turns out, I will not be needed for filming tonight. But Addie would still like me to come along for moral support, and so I can drive while she has a few drinks to calm the nerves. The studio is located in an alley behind a bar. I imagine the alley being a fine place to wait for her. I imagine it being cool, dark, and quiet, not unlike a nice spot six feet under the earth.

* * *

When my grandpa retired from his lifelong job at the SPCA he became restless. He took up small tasks around the house, but he completed them too quickly. Everything in the house, which was already tidy, he organized then reorganized. My grandma, who was still around then and not yet aware of her cancer, grew annoyed by his puttering about. They squabbled over every little thing. She wished that he would take up a hobby to occupy his time. A short while later he went back to work.

In my chosen profession it is not so simple to come out of retirement as saying, "I would like my old job back." I'm not sure it's even possible at all. So it is that I must grant the wish that my grandma —god rest her gentle soul, whose body, even today, I can't quite believe is gone—once had for my grandpa.

A hobby is defined as "a pursuit outside one's regular occupation engaged in especially for pleasure or relaxation." There is nothing in this definition that might point an individual to any specific hobby. For this it is imperative to look inside yourself.

Rhetoric is as much a legitimate hobby as masturbation is. That being said, we must move on. But before I am capable of doing so, I am compelled, as my grandpa was, to do a little house cleaning; to sift through and organize my thoughts; to reexamine at length the unfinished work that brought me to this current station.

It began with a preface that you might recognize, which I put down here without the slightest regard for good form, or manners, and without any self-consciousness regarding my personal taste or discretion.

* * *

Subtitles For A Film

To those who think they wish to take on the endeavor of making their own independent film, let this serve as a nontraditional How-To and How-Not-To Guide in no-budget filmmaking. It documents the process from conception to final product of a film called Sex/Absurd, as well as it documents the emotional and psychological responses to acting in a film that would largely be considered "autobiographical."

It goes without saying that your own discretion should be consulted when taking

579

into account any of the following details, anecdotes, etc. for your own personal use. And of course, enjoy.

1

The fame isn't going to be a hard thing to deal with. Neither is the money. They will be handled carefully, responsibly. Their advantages will be exploited sparingly. It is the pressure which accompanies *genius* (their words, not mine) and the possibility of complacency that plagues me.

To write and star in one great film while desperate, poor, and unknown is no amazing feat in it of itself. It has been done a thousand times. But to do it a second time while well-off and -known is a wholly new and remarkable experience. There are expectations to be upheld then.

Approaching the bar in which my one-on-one interview with *The Magazine* is to be held, the great weight of a repeat-hit is upon me. The reviews are in for the first film, *Sex/Absurd*, and they are astonishingly good. The public will demand insight into my next venture.
—When will your next film come out?
—Is there anyone in mind to play the lead role? Or will you be playing it again yourself?
—Have you considered a collaboration? With Wes Anderson perhaps? Or The Cohen Brothers?
And again,
—When will your next film come out?

These are the questions I imagine will be asked. The same questions to which there are not yet any answers to, and to which I wonder if there ever will be.

After painstaking efforts, the first film has just come out. Money has begun coming in and the more urgent issues in my life—largely financial in nature—have been resolved. The little house I moved in to with my girlfriend, Addie, will soon be paid off, and with my new income she was able to quit her day job, which allows us the luxury of travel and other leisure activities. I purchased a home for my mom as well—a little place in Arizona with a yard and a pool. Or was it Washington? And all of my friends(to whom I am undyingly grateful) have been recompensed, at least monetarily, for the never-ending support they showed me during these past several years of struggling to get by, for which I still consider myself forever indebted to them.

These are the only things I consider immediately necessary to do with my newfound success, which until now had been unattainable. But fans will take little interest in such personal details, no matter the importance they hold to me. Fans will have only one interest in mind —*the next movie.*

Arriving at the bar, a strange sensation has crept through my forearms and fingertips, like that which is experienced when hanging from a high ledge and your fingers begin to slip. My body tingles with a rush of adrenaline and my palms are sweaty. I do my best to stay composed, affecting an air of confidence that could be described as an overly cool farce. I am afraid that it might be too much, that I might come off as an asshole in the interview. But there is no time to rethink my approach. This is who I will present myself as.

Outside the bar there is a patio area shaded by several large trees. The whole scene seems out of place for Los Angeles, as if it were plucked straight out of somewhere in the Midwest. But it remains there in front of me, incongruous to its surroundings, and it also remains, somehow inherently to me, *the place* I am to have my meeting.

At one of the tables there sits a man whom I presume to be the man from *The Magazine*. He looks remarkably similar to me, save for subtle differences in our facial hair and the fact that his nose is much larger than mine(big noses being a trait I have always admired). There are two bottles of beer on his table, both cold and sweating, both untouched. No one else is sitting outside.

Suddenly sitting beside the man at the table, I inquire, "Are you [such-and-such]?" I hear the words very distantly, as though someone else were saying them, and I don't quite catch the name as it comes out of my mouth.

In speech equally distant, he replies that he is not. "I am [missed the name again]," he says.

Not at all discomfited by his reply, and still not budging from my seat beside him, I find myself drinking from the beer bottle nearest me. The man speaks again. "That was actually for the young man I am supposed to be meeting—he's a filmmaker. But that's fine. You can have the beer."

"Thanks," I say plainly, taking down at least half of the beer without tasting a single drop. At this point I am positive that this indeed *is* the man from *The Magazine*, and the filmmaker who he is referring to is, in fact, me. Perhaps a bit smugly, I ask(presumably about myself), "Is he any good?"

The man gives no verbal reply. He simply tilts his head the tiniest bit to the side like a little puppy dog that is incapable of understanding the meaning of his owner's address, as if to say *'Who?'*

"The filmmaker," I say, repeating the question, "is he any good?"

The man, with infinite calm, turns to look me straight in the eye. "I no longer know what we are talking about," he says. Then he stands up, nods politely and dismisses himself.

I am alone at the table now. I note that he has left without touching his beer, and know that I will soon drink it. The encounter has not

581

alarmed me in the slightest. It seems as though it were the most natural thing in the world, except that I am no longer sitting outside of the bar. I have been miraculously transported to the door to *her* apartment.

The movie is not yet done. No money has come in and *the little house* does not exist. None of it does. This is not Addie's real apartment at all—the one she lives in in West Hollywood—but somehow I recognize it as hers. I am beating on the door, desperately attempting to get inside. She finally opens up and as I walk inside I feel sluggish, slightly paralyzed. She seems so far away from me as I tell her over and over, "I love you!" Each time the words come out they sound more deranged.

She looks at me, her eyes flat, dead. "I don't love you," she says.

And I break. Tears start coming down my face pathetically. Moving very slowly—though as fast as I can manage—I grab a pack of cigarettes from on top of her fridge(she doesn't smoke, but the cigarettes are there anyway; the notion of her cheating on me sweeps through my thoughts), and I grab one from the pack, gingerly putting it into my mouth. The window to the side of the fridge is open. Conveniently, there is a chair in front of the window. I stand on the chair and with one last look I crawl out of the window at my snail-like pace, still crying.

Laying in her comfortable bed, in her comfortable little apartment, with that warm and sweet little body of hers next to me, I realize that it was all just a dream, and that she does love me. I am relieved to have woken up and remembered this.

Then I am anxious again, panicked—we are in the middle of a scene and I can't open my eyes. This is the movie and I am playing the lead role. Addie is my character's love interest. It is a simple scene. He is supposed to be waking up from a bad dream to see this sweet little thing next to him and feeling ashamed at himself for still obsessing over every terrible detail of his past, but I just can't open my eyes to act it out. I can hear Kenneth—good friend and director of this film, *Sex/Absurd*—at the foot of the bed with camera in hand. He's ready to roll and with each second I remain still he becomes increasingly frustrated. As his frustration continues to heighten, it hits me. I never wrote this scene and it's not in the movie at all so what in god's name are you doing at the foot of the bed, Kenneth? I'm still sleeping, so get on out of here! Don't you have somewhere else to be?

Shit. The meeting. It's not too far away, but I'm already late.

I wake up startled. It's impossible to shake the feeling. Addie is already gone, probably left for work earlier. I hurry out of her place and even as I am walking towards the meeting(actually the first day of casting— 20 additional roles to fill, all female) I can't rid myself of the dream-

582

anxiety. The dreams have been going on for some time now, and I have no doubt they will continue.

A young man has fallen into step with me, keeping always eight sidewalk squares ahead. He sneezes. I want to say to him, "bless you," but I don't. And I'm glad I didn't because he stays in front of me—still those eight squares—for nearly four blocks, sneezing the entire time. It would have been too much to bless him after every one. Fuck it though—maybe he could have used it. Next time then.

Mornings have been fragmented lately. The sleepy continuity somehow altogether broken. The young man with the allergies is gone and I am in the grocery store buying cigarettes from a friendly Mexican woman with a gold tooth. I don't have quite enough(don't know how I managed to have even this much) but she lets me keep the pack anyway, telling me with a smile that I'll come back some time and repay her. This makes me love her. She's the most beautiful woman I've ever seen. I leave the store happy as hell and for a short while think about nothing in particular.

It is the casting office that brings me back. A fairly large room with a table and three chairs set up—one for me, one for Kenneth, and one for Jade, another good friend and also the producer of the movie. There is a chair in front of the table for the actresses to sit in as they read. Then there is a large black leather couch off to the side and a glass coffee table. On the door to the room there is a sign that reads, "Sex/Absurd." The girls are already sitting in the lobby, waiting to be called in.

The three of us are drinking mimosas out of little plastic cups. Aside from this detail, the whole operation appears to be incredibly professional, legitimate, especially for a production whose budget is virtually nil. Jade goes down to the lobby to retrieve the girl next on the waiting list, then escorts them up to the room where they read one of the two scenes we selected from the script. I read lines opposite the girls for the main character, Jack. Kenneth videotapes their readings on a small camcorder provided for us by the casting office (which, it should be mentioned, was given to us for next to nothing by a friend of Jade's). Then the process is repeated—roughly 40 times.

The monotony becomes painful. All of the girls begin to look alike. What began as detailed notes about each girl on the back of their headshots becomes an "N"(no), "M"(maybe), or "Y"(yes), and eventually just a flaccid penis for "No" and a hard one for "Yes." A wave of sympathy comes over me—I feel bad for them. Not for any one of them individually, but collectively for these folks who still maintain the dream of becoming an actor, making it on the big screen, etc., and who day in, day out chase after that dream only to arrive at what? Sitting in a fold-up chair in an office in Hollywood reading lines with someone who doesn't know a goddamn about the industry and who has very little, if anything at all, to offer them professionally? We have no money behind us and will not be paying anyone. We have very little help on this project and cannot promise that it will ever be completed. Even if it is completed, we cannot promise that it will be to our/your liking.

And we've told them nothing about the script. All they know is that it is a feature film with the word "Sex" in the title, that they will not be receiving money for their involvement, and the names of the two characters on the page in front of them. What's happening in the scenes themselves means nothing to them.

After this *wave of sympathy* passes, I briefly recall the actual conversation that inspired one of the scenes we are reading from. By the dozenth time reading through it the actual memory is washed away completely and becomes absolute fiction. It means nothing to me either.

This is the problem that arises when playing a character who experiences events that may or may not be partially based off of events in your own life. After you've put them down and turned them into fiction, you become detached from them. To reenact them then you must actively attempt to become that person again, to digress from your current self into who you were when those things occurred. At best, you become a caricature of yourself. And in doing so, it is possible that something bends so far in the brain that it breaks altogether. You lose sight of who's who and to whom certain things happened. You slip into the cracks between what is real and what is fiction, and wonder what that means anyway. It is a delicate affair.

That being said, I am not only reading the lines for the main character, Jack, but was actually cast as him when the film began shooting with a crew of two—Kenneth and myself. He is a character I wrote. If ever the character was based on me, in even the slightest bit, the tiniest mannerism, or slip of the tongue, then it no longer applies. I am not that person anymore and Jack, therefore, is a purely fictional character. It is true that I am vaguely familiar with his experiences, much in the same way that one recollects their actions from a previous drunken night and confuses them with a dream. I know the subject matter. I know the characters' names, and their corresponding real names. But to place myself into those vaguely familiar situations and become the character they apply to is tiring. It is a job—one that at times can be supremely uncomfortable.

The champagne is all gone and the girls have finished their readings for the day. Jade returns from the lobby with news that there is a young man there who wishes to audition for the role of Jack. A ridiculous notion, being that the role, as previously mentioned, has already been filled by none other than myself. She says he is spastic, excited—obviously crashing auditions. I am slightly drunk, and intrigued. I want to see someone else read for the role that has occasionally made me *supremely uncomfortable*. I tell her to bring him in and that she'll be reading with him. I take Kenneth's place on the video camera and press record:

He walks into the room and I pan with him. He's of average height, thin, brown hair that you can tell was once cut immaculately but has grown out a little; his beard is grown in full. Although the beard throws me off, I recognize him from somewhere. He is smiling as he excitedly shakes our hands, and when he shakes my hand(still recording all this) he seems to recognize me as well. "Do I know you from somewhere?"

I assure him that he doesn't, though I immediately recall seeing him in an after hours bar roughly a year ago. Someone fell on top of a glass table that night and it shattered—the jazz band that was playing stopped because of the commotion. He was not the man who fell on the table, but he was standing in the general vicinity of the shattered table, so when I looked over in that direction he did come into view. The reason I remember seeing him in particular is because he played the young, ambitious ad man on a television show. When the show first came out I was living in an apartment in Anaheim with two other fellas, and on the occasion of a new episode being aired we allowed ourselves to smoke indoors. It was the one tradition we had in the household.

As he finally lets go of my hand, he seems suspicious of me. The true intention of the question he directed at me was to learn whether or not I recognized him. He has given us a fake name, something commonplace, but he's been outed in my mind. I know exactly who he is, and I'm curious to know the meaning of all this. Is he playing some sort of joke on us here, or is this really just how he gets his kicks? He seems genuinely intrigued by the project as we give him the synopsis, then without delay he begins to read. It is a remarkable thing to watch a truly talented actor perform. During the rest of the day, going over these same scenes with actor after actor, it had taken all the mimosas we downed and a considerable amount of imagination to be convinced by anyone's performance. But the man standing in front of us is different, a pro. Each of the hard penises drawn on the headshots earlier seem ashamed—they go flaccid. And the further he reads the more deeply disturbed I become. It's as if the half-memory and fiction of the story has suddenly come to life before me and I am watching myself in that moment again—whether the moment actually happened before or not doesn't matter. This is it. Perhaps lending to this emotion is the fact that I'm drunk, but it seems trivial regardless. We're all drunk. Even this wiry and lively little man in front of us, by all appearances, seems to be intoxicated. And as the reading comes to an end I

585

begin to remember who he is exactly, and I begin wondering what exactly he is doing here, and how did he wind up here in the first place? And I begin turning those questions inward, asking, "What are we doing here? And how did we wind up here anyway?"

I can't be completely sure of these things, with all of their elaborate, forked paths. But it seems like forever ago.

2

It was the hottest day of the year. We had been drinking for a few days in a row already and I was vomiting hot red wine onto a newly paved parking lot. Heat was coming off the pavement and distorting the light, making the surface appear to waver. Kenneth got out of the car and I wiped my mouth. In bare feet we headed inside of the restaurant and ordered drinks—something weak to help settle our bellies and our consciences.

There was still another full day before everything would settle in. A day filled with blurry images of wandering around the streets, being stranded in hallways of apartment buildings where we weren't sure what the number was to the room where we'd been comfortably slipping into oblivion for days prior, and other randomness of which the details become so vague that they are not worth trying to mention. The only thing that can be related with any clarity is that moment the next morning when Kenneth arose, miraculously in his own bed, to find his girlfriend leaving the room.

"Where are you going?" he asked. She replied that she was going to a job interview. Even more baffled, he asked further, "Who has a job interview on a *Sunday*?" She told him that it was Monday, then left.

This exchange was recounted to me later that afternoon when I stumbled back into his downtown residence, accompanied by that abstract dread which can only be felt at the tail end of a drinking bout.

After that he purchased the camera. The money had been kept safely aside until then, being that it was procured by means that I will say nothing further about other than they were delicate, and tragic. He spent it with utmost reverence, the purchase itself, no doubt, having been sentimental, ritualistic, and difficult to carry out. He had done it alone, very quietly.

I remember meeting Kenneth for the first time. The *first time* actually constituting a period of roughly two months in early spring. I had come to Los Angeles by way of train from Portland, Oregon on a self proclaimed "reading tour," which I had donned "Reading and Drinking in Slow-Motion." Over the course of a month I had passed through a handful of cities en route, and Los Angeles was my last scheduled stop. I was only supposed to be there for three days. But when my old ho-

586

metown friend picked me up from the train station and took me back to her place, it was evident my stay would be longer.

Kenneth was one of her roommates then, in that cramped house in Echo Park where folks came and went freely at all hours, some apparently under the delusion that they were operating in some sort of cult revival of the 1970's psychadelic movement. It was a madhouse. Kenneth seemed to be the only one there that had any sort of employment, or even routine that began before one in the afternoon. He was tied to a job at a visual effects company based out of Santa Monica where he had worked for already two years. They worked him to the bone in order to produce shots for such outstanding films as "Marmadueche," and "Gallagher's Travels"(among other legitimately notable titles, these just happen to be two of which he was working on during that time). He was exhausted and fed up. He was ready to quit altogether to begin working on something of his own. I was working on a book about the infinite nature of possible realities, which involved all of the women I had ever seen, thought of, or dreamt up—especially my then-girlfriend who seemed to be actively pursuing the title of "Ex." Kenneth and I would smoke in front of the house, loosely talking about ambitions, and aspirations, not in the naive, flamboyant way that is well known to Los Angeles, but in a more candid and realistic way, like so many reveries spoken aloud to friends on front porches and in back alleys everywhere since god knows when. He shared with me an idea that he had begun working on awhile back, a work in progress, with considerable notes taken, character developments, sequences written, etc., but had since been forced to abandon due to general life and work circumstances—he couldn't find the time. I told him that if he ever decided to do something on his own, I would love to be a part of it. It was a sort of casual agreement. We both kind of nodded our heads, then went back to smoking.

The decision to begin work on the project came in late October. Kenneth had just moved into the loft downtown with two friends. One was Alan, who would later play the absurd caricature of the lead in the movie within the movie, which was a highly Fellini influenced short entitled, "Anabelle"; the other was Cat, who wound up playing the part—and indeed molding it to herself—of my character's haunting ex-girlfriend, Ana. And all of this out of necessity, both of a limited financial nature and of availability. They had no interest in acting(though Alan *had* once received an A+ in his college level acting course), but took part merely out of respect for us and belief in our work, god bless.

The two of us—Kenneth and I—drank wine and exchanged ideas. It was loose. At best, the only thing that was clearly defined that late October night was that we would make a film together, and that I

587

would write it. Once the script's skeleton had formed it would be pure collaboration.

The loft was still sparsely furnished then. I went about sleeping on an old dingy couch, stained from years of being used by a pitbull who had bad skin and whose health was failing. It was repulsive, smelled terrible. Or I slept in different corners of the loft, right there on the concrete floor using whatever bedding that was lent to me by the roommates. An air mattress was destroyed after one night's use by Kenneth's wolf hybrid, Yona—just one minute alone with it and he had gouged enough holes to render the thing useless. Once I even laid out a piece of plywood with some cardboard as a bed(when Kenneth discovered me in the morning he immediately put an end to this by purchasing a couch with a pullout bed). It was uncomfortable in a non-romantic way; in a way that said, "I'm tired of this shit and something in my life has to change." It added a sense of urgency to the project.

At once, I got to work. The book about *the infinite nature of possible realities* had been completed, but it had not been successful on my own terms. To write a book, for me, is to take experiences and sift through them, to organize them and make sense of them; to present them in a way that I am able to understand and make peace with them. There was no peace with this book. Briefly, maybe, but ultimately I couldn't shake the thoughts of the girl the book had been dedicated to— "especially L.W.," the inscription says. I still thought about her. I still got drunk and called her. I still carried pictures of her. I still had dreams about her. Silly behavior, for sure, but unarguably natural. This is where the idea came from: to write about the creative process, and how relationships integrate themselves into that process and become a part of the final work; to write about a dissolving relationship and the projections of that relationship onto several new and fleeting ones; to write a film about a character who takes those experiences, which include memories, and dreams, and writes them into a completely new film, a "drunken, 1960's, Italian type of thing." Just like Fellini said, "I could write a movie about a filet of fish, and that movie would still be about me." (Not quite what he actually said.) Except I didn't really bother with the fish part.

As I wrote, Kenneth encouraged me. "You want someone to jump out of a moving airplane? That's fine. Just write it exactly how you want it and we'll figure out a way to make it work."

Funny that later on, after the production was in full swing, he should call to my attention words of my own; words in the preface to *Sex/Absurd* the novella, the highly Fellini influenced book that gave the movie its namesake, and which was the backbone of the film within the film, *Anabelle*:

"*Sex/Absurd* is first and foremost a written undertaking, and, therefore, its mechanical specifics—such as the construction of the set, the possible hazards therein, and so on—were not given any consideration. If anyone should ever attempt to put on this multimedia performance, I wish them good luck."

3

[Scene from the film *Sex/Absurd*]

EXT. CLIFFSIDE. MORNING. DREAM.
Jack has a bed laid out on a cliff over the ocean. His set up is very tidy. His suitcase and bag, his boots; a pillow and a small red blanket. A phone and an alarm clock are plugged into a rock next to him. He is lying awake, waiting. Finally the phone rings.

JACK
Hello? Hello, Ana?
(pause)
Ana, I know it's you.... Say something.

ANA'S MOM(O/S)
This isn't Ana. This is her mother.

JACK
Oh...

ANA'S MOM(O/S)
Well, why have you called?

JACK
I want to talk to Ana.

ANA'S MOM(O/S)
She doesn't want to talk to you.

Jack begins to cry dramatically, sobbing for a few beats.

ANA'S MOM(O/S, CONT'D)
Are you crying?

JACK
(gasping)
No.... No, I'm not crying.
(after a pause)
Please hold.

He pushes the flash button on the phone, attempting to switch lines.

JACK
Ana?

589

ANA'S MOM(O/S)
No. This is still her mother.

JACK
Oh.
(pause)
Well is there a chance that I could get her
back? Somehow?

ANA'S MOM(O/S)
No. These are the decisions you've made.
Deal with them.

JACK
Okay. Sorry to have bothered you.

He hangs up the phone and lies back down, keeping his eyes open. The waves continue to crash against the shore far below.

[End Scene]

It was the first scene we shot. We were entirely unprepared, but we began regardless. Our reasoning was that we should start immediately or we would never start at all. So we packed our gear—the camera and a small sound recorder, in addition to the props, which were my suitcase and leather satchel, the bedding, the phone, and the alarm clock—into the car and took off.

We hadn't scouted any locations, but we had the perfect spot set in our minds. We weren't sure if it existed, or where it might exist if it did at all, but we set out in the direction of Malibu, hopeful. It was raining. When we pulled off onto Zuma Beach we spotted a cliffside overlooking the water. We had to hike to get to it, up a long winding staircase set in the sand and then through a narrow trail that was all mud. I was already in wardrobe, which consisted of a three-piece brown woolen suit purchased at a thrift store we stopped at on the way out. It cost thirty dollars and fit almost perfectly. We took this as a good sign.

We were hyper conscious of our surroundings, and our existence in general. It was clear that this day marked the true start of the film and everything seemed of grave importance. The rain perpetuated the notion. We were already drenched by the end of our hike, which brought us to a small, muddy clearing next to what seemed a 100ft. drop (without any protective railing) down to the shore. It was the exact spot that had been imagined. This was the second thing to strike me as odd that day; the first had occurred on the drive out there as I read over the scene. I couldn't recall whether it had been a dream that I had actually had, or if it was a piece of pure fiction that I had jotted down,

590

only afterward beginning to believe the images belonged to a dream I had had. This should have been grounds to proceed with caution; this should have caused an internal alarm to go off that said, "be careful... you don't quite know the extent of what you're getting yourself into." But the alarm didn't go off and we carried forward haphazardly.

I was still contemplating the origin of the scene as we began to shoot. I hadn't been in front of the camera in that capacity before, but it didn't matter. I was preoccupied. I laid in the mud and acted out the scene. The rain continued to come down and we continued to go through the scene over and over, getting all the angles that only one man with one camera can capture on a cliffside in the rain. Countless times we went through the actions and gradually I became less and less aware of them. It seemed a hallucination. The rain, in it's steady mist, appeared to be film grain. The waves crashed now three or four hundred feet below and the sound—of the waves, of the rain—seemed to drown out the reality of the situation completely. The fact that I was on a cliffside above the ocean, foolishly acting out something I had written, or dreamt up then written, utterly dissolved. It was fascinating. The colors were vivid. The sounds were distorted, becoming mixed-up into one single sound like a low drone, like something resonating from the bottom of the ocean.

Now five hundred, six hundred feet below I can make out the shapes of three boys in the water. They are kicking out on their backs through the surf so as to ride the waves back in. They are joking with one of the boys because he's a bad swimmer, but it's no longer funny when one of their fathers comes in on his boat and the big wave that is created ends up drowning that poor little boy who was the weak swimmer. After the tide rolls back out, and the jagged rocks and steep cliffs of the beach come poking out in the open, it not only becomes apparent that the little boy's body will never be found, but also that this is an entirely different dream altogether.

How then do I end up on top of the beach, way up on the steep cliff again, I don't know, but here I am and there is some sort of residence or school for young musical(and spiritual?) folks—mainly ladies —that had not been here before. The little dead boy seems to be forgotten now altogether, and in his place there is now some all-important amethyst. One of the girls at the school—supposedly the most gifted—is given the stone and, in fear, she gives it to the main character in what is apparently a movie(who is none other than that famous actor who auditioned for the role of "Jack"!) who then dives through two red doors deep down into the earth and disappears.

I don't actually see this diving action, though I know it is happening. I remain out in front of the school. The girl who had given the stone away is here. She swings on a very large branch up onto the neighbor's rock wall. He is standing in the window of his home, and the girl says, "You just going to stare at me or you going to ask me out," or some such thing, to which the man comes out from his window onto the balcony. He is a very handsome Japanese man wearing a fantastic suit, an expensive haircut, and drinking a can of beer. He begins to reply to the young woman, saying, "You just being coy, or—" but I can't make out the end of his statement because I am now far off, standing in a brick lined courtyard.

The rain remains a constant. It comes down over everything, making it bright with reflections. And in one of those reflections, right there in the wet bricks, I notice my ex-girlfriend with her mother, striding across the courtyard into a warm café. I get the feeling that I have just left the café myself, but I am determined to go back again. I am hanging in the alcove of a building, just out of the weather, trying to build the courage to approach this old ghost and her mother, but there is no need. Instead she is hovering over me in the alcove urging me to join them at their table inside, which I do—without moving. The entire place somehow shifts, soundlessly and effortlessly, in such a way that I end up at the table with L.W. and her mother, though I am not given a chair to sit on, merely the ground itself. I don't mind though, and go on with our tea and snacks, being as friendly and charming as possible with her mother, as I was deeply affected by that phone call we once had with each other. Quickly I become aware of the fact that my invitation was some sort of cruel joke. They thought it might be entertaining to have someone so poor sitting at their table, though still apart from them. My feelings are hurt, and I am super sensitive to the fact that I do not have any money at all, not even one cent in the world, and I begin to think, "How did this become about money? Let's talk about *us*, huh! Let's talk about this goddamn film I am making because of you and how you sit halfway across the country still cursing me for whatever reasons you've fabricated in your mind!"

I say none of this. It wouldn't have helped anything in the slightest and they're gone anyway. That first day of filming is gone too. I'm waking up on the couch and just right now seeming to open my eyes for the first time, realizing that I've written this with eyes shut on a laptop that doesn't belong to me and half dreaming still, half wishing I were capable of creating the world in front of me as I create my dreams; not because they are so much better than the reality I live in but because they are able to be experienced without any small bit of fear of the future. Today I'm worried about how and what I'm going to eat.

4

It was a mistake to start when we did, in the manner that we chose to. In hindsight, it would have been infinitely beneficial to postpone the start day of shooting to get all of our ducks in a row. The time spent in pre-production is invaluable. It would have saved us from countless false starts and burnt days had we just sat down and planned things before taking action; a strict schedule and a tighter script would have saved a lot of frustration and heartbreak. Not to mention we would have been allotted the time to ask ourselves, "Are we really ready for this? Do we know what we're getting ourselves into?" But that is how hindsight works. It remains that we did start when we did(prematurely), in the only way we knew how (disorganized, overzealous).

And it wasn't just a mistake concerning the making of the movie either, but concerning our personal well being too. We weren't really ready for it. We didn't know what we were getting ourselves into.

* * *

That's where it ends. Right there at the bottom of the first paragraph in the fourth chapter.

The humor of that accidental stopping point, which has become its permanent loose end, is not to be lost. With all of my talk of being unawares of what I had gotten myself into with the making of the movie I was then unwittingly repeating in writing the book. I was relegating myself to subject matter that had long since been dead, and was bringing me down with it, when what I actually needed to do was rid myself of it completely. But my vanity as a writer did not allow me the luxury of just shrugging it off and moving on. In taking myself a bit too seriously, I imagined it necessary to first go through the painstaking process of detailing it on paper—that was how I would kill it, as I had killed many other things before it. I pictured something of an epic success. The movie would get picked up for distribution, which would then draw attention to this behind the scenes look at the movie via my hand.

I envisioned discussing the complicated inner-world that the movie had created in me. I intended to elucidate the process that had forced me into separating from myself; the act of playing the role of my fictional self, then sitting down in front of a screen, staring at my own image, which no longer belonged to me, and editing that person into a scene coherent at least in its own context. This included becoming extremely self-conscious of my appearance, a trait that is not to be admired and until then had remained foreign to me.

It had a very Borgesian feel to it all. Nothing new, exploring the dichotomy of human nature, and furthermore the infinite nature of the internal self. I had begun referring to one version of myself as "the adventurer," and another version of myself as, "*his* biographer." What I was attempting to illustrate in the book Borges accomplished in a single page in a poem entitled, "Borges and I."

More or less, in making the movie we dived down into the rabbit hole, and emerged(after our first rough cut was completed at the tail end of 72 sleepless hours, sustained by coffee, cigarettes, and light beer) on the other side where the movie was mostly done, in a very rudimentary form, too long and full of errors, still missing vital elements(score and visual effects) that to this day remain incomplete. Much of the time between I can't remember. To write the book I would have had to create memories and experiences that I could not say truly existed. And while I am an advocate of invention, poetic license, what have you, I am not an outright liar.

I even had an ending set in my mind. It paralleled the last scene in the movie. It took place on a rooftop. I was wearing the same gray suit that Jack had worn in his final scene. But in this new scene it was raining. And the building itself—this detail being paramount—was in a symbolic location, set just below the hills, whose homes shone their dim beacons of "wealth" and "success" through the mist, yet above the distant, hazy skyline of downtown, which signified, to me, anonymity and poverty; that is to say, it was suspended there in the middle of everything, and I was still broke, and it was raining, and the rain felt good.

Essentially, the resolution was one of apparent irresolution. It was nothing. It was a farce. Had I been bestowed with that virtue called honesty, the book ultimately would have ended exactly where I am now, for this is the true result of my efforts.

And so the book is stopped in its tracks, unfinished. The subject matter is laid to rest so far as this summation of it will allow. But as Melville said, "small erections may be finished by their first architects; grand ones, true ones, ever leave the copestone to posterity. God keep me from ever completing anything."

Although he has now become more than a man, and his name carries the implications that it does, he, too, in the period of his own life, was destined for obscurity.

* * *

"Sir, please come here."

My initial instinct in hearing these words, which were whispered (feeling so close as if they came from the other side of the bed), is to think that they must have come from the mouth of my new mistress. I turn to find their origin—nothing. I am in the liquor aisle of a grocery store I don't recognize. There is a bottle in my hand, but I know I don't have money to buy it.

My secondary instinct is to believe that I must have uttered these words myself, or that they may have come from a much younger version of myself who intends to request that I buy a bottle for him. I look around further, but there is no such young man in sight.

And then the words come again, still whispered, but more sternly. "Sir, please come here." They seem to drift away from me, trailing out of the liquor aisle and through the exit of the store. I put the bottle down, without thinking about it, and follow the sound.

Outside the air is crisp, and dense. Snow covers a vast landscape much like the middle America prairie where I was raised. The light reflects off of everything, forcing you to squint. The grocery store seems to be in the middle of nowhere, yet the parking lot is obviously well traveled—it is all slush and black snow. In the middle of the otherwise empty lot there is a dark brown minivan idling. Next to it stands a tall, ancient looking Native American man, his very serious gaze intent on me, his long ponytail hanging stiffly at his back despite the wind blowing. The side door to the minivan is open. It is clear that I am supposed to walk over and get in.

This is undoubtedly a dream, and although I am aware that it is a dream, I seem to have no control over it. I am unable to call forth any images, or objects, of my desire. It is the old native man who is in charge. He wants me to get into the van. I can't deny him. Suddenly in the van, everything outside goes dark. Only from the bumping and shaking of the van can I tell that we are in motion. The old native man sits in the front seat. I cannot see who is driving. Though there was no formal, verbal challenge made, I understand that I am to duel the old man—a knife fight. We are en route to some unknown location where it is to take place.

I am not worried about the ensuing altercation. My fear is curbed by the knowledge that my own brother once found himself in this same position, with the same man—and my brother won. I see flashes of their battle. It took place in the woods. As they walked down some dark path my brother attacked him from behind, killing him in accordance with some ancient doctrine that I am unfamiliar with. How then the man has come back to life and challenged me to the same duel I don't know. It is a dream. Only I am no longer sure as to whose dream it is.

The van is stopped. It is still dark outside, though with the stars and the moon I can make out the deep blue images of my surroundings. We are in a dirt clearing encircled by trees. The old man gets out of the van and opens the side door for me. As I step out he sees the knife that I am to wield for our duel; the knife is slightly curved, about 18 inches long, with a carved wooden handle. It is poorly concealed in my jacket. The old man speaks, in the same voice as before, though for the first time I can see his lips move with the words. "So that's what kind of fight it's going to be."

In an instant the sun rises, the old man is gone, and I am floating through the hazy morning over a green countryside. I gather that this is only temporary—that the sun will go down again shortly and the man will return—and the purpose of this extraordinary flight is so that I might gain an understanding of the reasoning of the duel. The rolling green hills that I float above have traces of an extinct civilization— rock formations, building foundations in ruin, the land manipulated in places that suggest a knowledge of structure, or agriculture. Coming from the earth is a subtle energy that gives the sense that buried within it are artifacts important in understanding their culture. Inherently, I know that the land is sacred. The loser of the duel will be offered as a sacrifice to the gods who once ruled over it. But that's all that I can grasp. I don't know why these gods are in need of a sacrifice or why I have been chosen to play a part in it. In my stomach I feel a weightlessness, or mild sickness, similar to that which is felt when coming to the top of a hill then quickly beginning the descent on its opposite side. The light fades out as quickly as it came and all is dark blue again.

I am deposited back in the presence of the old man. We are walking along one of many dirt paths aligned on a grid; filling the void created between these paths are ominous looking marshes in which unnamable monsters could be harbored. I am terrified of the dark water. The old man is a few paces ahead of me, just as he was a few paces ahead of my brother in the moments before my brother killed him. I can't bring myself to raise my hand against the man. I try desperately but nothing comes of it. I check my jacket for the long knife and it's no longer there. The old man hears a noise and turns around. He stares past me into the darkness, then walks swiftly into it. This is my chance for action, whether it be to strike or to escape. Using the distraction of the noise, I slide down the small embankment into one of the marshes. The murky water is just deep enough that when I crouch it comes up to my chin. I hide myself as best as I can, attempting to avoid altogether coming face to face with the old man. But he cannot be avoided. He has already turned back around and come down into the water. He knew exactly where I was and he's coming straight at me. On the bank I see a thick branch. I grab it and swing hard in his direction as the moonlight gleams off the blade he's holding, which is no longer than a few inches. I swing again, but it does nothing and the old man keeps coming at me, just a step away now when he lunges forward and strikes with incredible precision. The tiny knife goes directly into my chest and slows down until I can feel every move of its entrance—piercing the skin first, then sliding delicately through the ribcage, avoiding grazing any bone, and straight into my heart. It is an excruciating moment that lasts a length of time that is indescribable. I can't see the old man's eyes. I have lost the duel.

Then I wake up.

* * *

It is just after eight in the morning when I arrive downtown. There are still a few more hours before the clouds burn off. There is a cool blue shade over everything. This is the first time I've returned to the loft in a couple of weeks.

Everyone is still sleeping. With all of the doors closed to the bedrooms, no natural light reaches the main living area. I turn on the blue neon light that stretches across a portion of the ceiling, and the light seems to mimic dawn. In the dim light I see that Yona, that good-natured, rambunctious wolf hybrid that lives here, has left a surprise for me. I quickly clean up the pile of shit and set the bag next to the front door to be taken out. My eyes adjusted, I scan the rest of the living area, and the kitchen—empty beer bottles, dishes here and there, a food container on the floor that Yona must have gotten into, some boxes stacked in a corner. On a table out of the way I keep a box with a few dozen copies of the last book I wrote. The copies on top have collected dust. Near this box there is a manila envelope. I go over to it and see that the envelope is addressed to me in my own handwriting, the return address belonging to a literary agency in New York. I had forgotten that I had submitted anything at all, but now that I hold the envelope in my hands I know the contents perfectly. I refrain from opening it immediately; instead I slip it into my bag and head back out the door.

Outside the building there is a TV show in production. They are still setting up, so I am allowed to pass through without a word. I see the lead actress standing off to the side, talking. I heard a rumor that a friend of mine has been seeing her on the sly, having to keep it quiet because she's still in the middle of a divorce. She has no idea that I know this about her, nor does she have any idea that I have just walked right by her. Just an old ghost in the morning fog, peaceful, serene.

On the next block is the café. It's still too early to be busy, but a few customers sit silently about. I order my coffee and take it outside. I am delighted to be here, alone, not bothered by anyone or anything as I enjoy my coffee and a smoke. I take out the envelope from the agency in New York and let it sit on the table for a moment. As I open it, the sound tears through the stillness of the morning; perhaps not to anyone else, but the sound, to me, passes with a sudden harshness that when it is gone is accompanied by a feeling of relief, similar to that which is felt after a sneeze. It feels wonderful.

I remove the letter from the envelope. It is typed on stationary with the agency's name on it, and contains a signature from the agent in blue ink. The letter itself is short, about one third of the page, and in its length alone I can surmise what it says. Regardless, I read the letter, a friendly and straightforward little thing, and with each word I am further relieved. It seems that the book in question, of which three chapters were received, indeed the very book that I have declared will never be finished, is of the most competitive type (everyone out there writing about themselves); at this time they cannot give it the attention that it deserves, etc., etc. In short, move on and best of luck.

In the whole of my life, these twenty-five glorious years, rejection has never felt so good. I breathe in deeply, put the letter back on the table, take a sip of my coffee, and a drag of my cigarette. I look around. There is no drastic change in anything. The clouds still hang in the sky, blue gray, heavy. The cool breeze still occasionally blows. The production down the street still shoots and reshoots the same scene. The tables next to me are still empty. There is no pressure coming from anywhere. No one cares when my next book will come out, or if it comes out at all. Not a single person scratches off the days on the calendar, waiting for the release of the movie. There are no expectations to be upheld whatsoever. The only requirements that are made of me are self-imposed. After the basic necessities to go on living are taken care of, I am free to do whatever. And whatever that may be, it will be done, just as in a dream, without fear of what will follow, because everything is subject to change and transformation; nothing is permanent, including retirement, as my own flesh and blood has already proved through example.

Tomorrow is the first day of spring. A detail so perfect that only nature, and not fiction, would allow me to get away with. It is a transitional season. A time where the earth, suffocated by winter, comes back to life and its inhabitants, taking their cue, renew themselves with it. The change in season here is a subtle one. It is a shift from warm to warmer. And although this shift is subtle, it is one I am looking forward to. I imagine tomorrow will be a fine day to be in the sun, getting drunk and playing bocce ball; or, rather, to sit at a café and begin a new book. Either way, it is a day that is certain to be enjoyed.

—Spring 2012, Los Angeles, CA

---

[*] Though all quotations have been altered or loosely adapted for my own purposes in this collection, it would be a shame to not point a finger in the direction of the authors who have inspired me so much, along with one or two of their books. If you haven't already, please seek them out immediately.

Miller, Henry | 26 Dec. 1891-7 June 1980, Aged 88
Tropic of Cancer | Black Spring

Nabokov, Vladimir | 22 April 1899-2 July 1977, Aged78
Lolita | Pale Fire

Neruda, Pablo | 12 July 1904-23 Sept. 1973, Aged 69
España en el Corazon("Spain in Our Hearts")

Singer, Isaac Bashevis | 21 Nov. 1902-24 July 1991, Aged 88
More Stories From My Father's Court | Gimpel The Fool and Other Stories

Steinbeck, John | 27 Feb. 1902-20 Dec. 1968, Aged 66
Cannery Row | The Short Reign of Pippin IV: A Fabrication

Thoreau, Henry David | 12 July 1817-6 May 1862, Aged 44
Walden; or, a Life In The Woods

Wolfe, Thomas | 3 Oct. 1900-15 Sept. 1938, Aged 37
Look Homeward, Angel

Font was born nine months after St. Patrick's Day under the moon of the winter solstice. He was raised in Lincoln, NE, the home of "the good life." He is now 27 years old. He currently resides in Los Angeles where he no longer writes fiction.